THE ESSENTIAL
WRITINGS OF
CHRISTIAN
MYSTICISM

THE ESSENTIAL
WRITINGS OF
CHRISTIAN
MYSTICISM

Edited and with an Introduction

by Bernard McGinn

THE MODERN LIBRARY

NEW YORK

2006 Modern Library Paperback Edition

Compilation copyright © 2006 by Random House, Inc.
Introduction copyright © 2006 by Bernard McGinn

LIBRARY OF CONGRESS CATALOGING-IN-PUBLICATION DATA

The essential writings of Christian mysticism /
edited and with an introduction by Bernard McGinn.
p.   cm.
Includes bibliographical references.
ISBN 0-8129-7421-2
1. Mysticism. I. McGinn, Bernard
BV5082.3.E87 2006
248.2'2—dc22   2006044877

www.modernlibrary.com

Printed in the United States of America

20   19

Contents

PART TWO

ASPECTS OF MYSTICAL CONSCIOUSNESS

PART THREE
IMPLICATIONS OF THE MYSTICAL LIFE

PREFACE

When I was first contacted about producing an anthology of Christian mystical literature for the Modern Library, I did not hesitate to accept. I had long been convinced that there was need for a new way of introducing interested readers to the riches of the Christian mystical tradition. Most of the anthologies dealing with Christian mysticism proceed on a chronological basis. Mysticism certainly has had a long history. For several decades I have been writing a multivolume history of Christian mysticism under the general title *The Presence of God*. In these volumes I argue that Christian mysticism has developed over time according to three broad layers or interactive stages: the monastic stage of the church Fathers and early Middle Ages; the period of the "New Mysticism" that began around 1200 CE and flourished into the seventeenth century; and the time of the crisis of mysticism begun in the mid–seventeenth century and continuing at least into the past century.

A historical presentation of mysticism is necessary for its full understanding, but mysticism also has an essence, nature, or set of fundamental characteristics that, while shaped by time, exhibits considerable consistency over the centuries. It is this essential or synchronic view of Christian mysticism that I seek to lay out in this anthology. The view of mysticism as an element in the Christian religion that underlies the structure of the book is briefly presented in the following introduction. Its fuller exposition is found in the almost one hundred selections from many Christian mystics that form the heart of the book. My hope is that the collection will both provide a resource for those who have already tasted something of the spiritual wealth of Christian mysticism, as well as invite new readers to ponder the teachings of some of the most remarkable men and women of the Christian tradition. I wish to thank Webster Younce, formerly of Random House, for first suggesting this anthology, and especially Judy Sternlight, also of Random House, who provided much sage advice in bringing it to completion. As ever, the assistance of Patricia Ferris McGinn is gratefully acknowledged.

BERNARD MCGINN
August 6, 2006

Introduction

Bernard McGinn

Attraction to mysticism, both in Christianity and in other world religions, has been on the rise in recent decades. But what is mysticism? For many the word brings to mind something strange and uncanny, even bizarre. Others see mysticism as the hidden core at the heart of all religions. Both these understandings reflect aspects of the differing ways in which the word has been used, but mysticism, at least in Christianity, presents a long tradition with a more precise meaning than these vague negative and positive senses suggest.

The roots of the current interest in mysticism defy easy characterization. Such a widespread revival across many religious traditions is a complex phenomenon. At least one factor in this upsurge is the way in which the mystics invite us to imagine and even to explore an inner transformation of the self based on a new understanding of the human relation to God. For some mystics this understanding is rooted in extraordinary forms of consciousness, such as visions and ecstasies, which most of their readers will not have shared. Other mystics, however, insist that such special experiences are only preparatory and peripheral, and perhaps even harmful if one confuses them with the core of mysticism understood as inner transformation. For believers the writings of the mystics present ideals and models for their own deepest aspirations; but even for nonbelievers, as is evident from recent concern of post-modern philosophers and cultural critics with mysticism, mystical texts have a fascination that resides in their ability to manifest important aspects of the human condition. Like great poets and great artists, the great mystics are examples of extraordinary human achievement who challenge and inspire even those who may not share their commitments. Reading the mystics puts us in touch with some of the most profound mysteries of the human spirit.

In the first volume of my ongoing history of Christian mysticism, *The Foundations of Mysticism: Origins to the Fifth Century* (New York: Crossroad, 1991), I set forth an understanding of mysticism as that part, or element, of Christian belief and practice that concerns the preparation for, the consciousness of, and the effect of what the mystics themselves have described as a direct and transformative presence of God. Although the word *mysticism* is fairly recent, created in the seventeenth century and not popular until the nineteenth century, the adjective *mystical* ("hidden" in Greek) has been widely used among Christians since at least the late second century CE. Christians used *mystical* to refer to the secret realities of their beliefs, rituals, and practices, especially to the "mystical meaning" of the Bible, that is, the inner message about attaining God that may be found beneath the literal sense of the scriptural texts and stories. They also spoke about "mystical contemplation" and, from about 500 CE on, of "mystical theology," that is, the knowledge of God gained not by human rational effort but by the soul's direct reception of a divine gift.

Some significant implications of this view of mysticism will help introduce the reader to the structure and goal of the following anthology. The first of these is the insistence that mysticism, at least until about a century and a half ago when unchurched mysticism first appeared, was always part of concrete historical religions, such as Judaism, Christianity, and Islam—not a religion in itself, nor the inner common denominator of all religions. This is why mysticism is best understood in the light of its interaction with the other aspects of the whole religious complex in which it comes to expression. Second, mysticism—or, better, the mystical life—is essentially a process, an itinerary or journey to God, not just a moment or brief state of what is often called mystical union, important as such moments may be. A proper grasp of mysticism requires an investigation of the ways by which mystics have prepared for God's intervention in their lives and the effect that divine action has had upon the mystic and those to whom he or she has communicated the message.

The third point concerns union conceived of as the goal of the mystical life. Union with God, or mystical union (*unio mystica*), has certainly been important in the history of mysticism in Christianity and its sister religions (see section 13), but to restrict mysticism to those who have spoken of their own uniting with God leaves out significant historical figures, such as Augustine of Hippo, who have avoided unitive language. There have also been many other ways in which mystics have spoken of their special contact with God, such as contemplation, vision, ecstasy, deification, birthing, endless desire and pursuit, and the like. This is why, fourth, I believe that the notion of *presence* provides a more inclusive and supple term than *union* for encompassing the variety of ways that mystics have expressed how God comes to transform their minds and lives.

God does not become present to human consciousness the way that an object in the concrete world is said to be present. Encountering God is much more like meeting a friend or loved one, and many Christian mystics have used intensely personal language in their writings, especially in their descriptions of their relation to Jesus. But God is not just another person—"person" as a limited category of the created world cannot contain or define the God who is both the source of the cosmos and infinitely beyond it. This is why speaking of God's presence is at bottom another strategy for saying the unsayable—and why many mystics have wrestled with the paradox that God is found in absence and negation more than in presence, at least as we usually conceive and experience it.

Modern authors often use the term *mystical experience* to define the object of their study. For this reason, as the fifth observation, it is helpful to comment on why in this volume the word *consciousness* is preferred to *experience*. Of course, the mystics themselves often spoke about experiencing God, though obviously not in the way we experience other things. But the term *experience*, although it seems so clear and obvious, is actually a highly complex notion when one begins to analyze it, as a survey of various philosophical epistemologies will reveal. Furthermore, *experience*, at least in the minds of many, may suggest a view of mysticism that takes it to be a particular form of feeling or sensible perception easily separable from the higher mental activities of understanding, judging, willing, and loving that form the full range of the conscious life of subjects as subjects, that is, creatures defined by their ability to know and love. Whatever epistemology or cognitional theory one may use, we can (I hope) at least agree that perceiving outer and inner data, attempting to understand and make a judgment about reality, and then loving and living on the basis of this decision are all part of an integrated series of *conscious* acts. Hence, the word *consciousness* as employed here is meant to stress that mysticism (as the mystics have insisted) is more than a matter of unusual sensations, but essentially comprises new ways of knowing and loving based on states of awareness in which God becomes present in our inner acts, not as an object to be grasped, but as the direct and transforming center of life. This perspective also suggests that simplistic understandings of the difference between what has been called mystical experience and mystical theology are misleading and unhelpful because they tend to restrict the story of mysticism to autobiographical accounts of perceptions of God, which are actually rare in the first millennium of Christian mysticism.

Two final implications of the understanding of mysticism advanced here will help guide the reader to a better grasp of the scope and intent of the book. The notion of God's presence as direct, or unmediated, is an implication of the paradoxical nature of the divine presence in absence mentioned above. In preparing for an encounter with God mystics obviously make use of many forms of mediation, such as prayer and rituals; in seeking to express their message they necessarily employ the medium of words, spoken and written. But is there a moment or aspect of immediacy and directness in the actual encounter with God? On the basis of the writings of the mystics, we can answer both yes and no. Yes, insofar as mystics emphasize that their meeting with the divine takes place on the deepest and most fundamental layer of the self and in a way that is more profound than that found through the usual religious activities. Indeed, a number of mystics, especially those who claim that God and the soul become identically one, at least on some level, explicitly insist on the absence of all mediation at that point. However, since in terms of preparation and expression mediation is always necessary, and since even those mystics who claim to have reached identity with God usually also say that on another level some distinction between Creator and creature remains, we can say that mystical consciousness involves a complex form of mediated immediacy.

My final point concerns transformation. One thing that stands out in the accounts of all the Christian mystics is that their encounter with God transforms their minds and their lives. God changes the mystics and invites, even compels, them to encourage others by their teaching to open themselves to a similar process of transformation. This is why the only test that Christianity has known for determining the authenticity of a mystic and her or his message has been that of personal transformation, both on the mystic's part and—especially—on the part of those whom the mystic has affected. The reason for putting together this anthology of Christian mystical texts is precisely to further the dissemination of this invitation.

On the basis of this understanding of mysticism, the following book is divided into three parts and fifteen sections. Part 1, "Foundations of Mystical Practice," presents five key themes concerning the preparation for the encounter with God. The longer part 2, "Aspects of Mystical Consciousness," concentrates on eight essential ways in which the mystics have spoken of their actual meetings with God. Part 3, "Implications of the Mystical Life," deals with two important effects of mystical consciousness.

These fifteen sections are not meant to be exhaustive of the nature of mysticism. (One might, for instance, conceive of adding sections on "Mystical Authority" and "Mystical Ethics" to part 3.) They do, I believe, represent the major headings or themes of mysticism as a distinctive part of Christian belief and practice. Since each of the fifteen sections has its own introduction, I need not say more about them here. Each selection within the sections also comes with a note that lays out a bit more about the author and text chosen. Naturally, mystical texts themselves were rarely composed to illustrate only one of these categories and themes. Hence the individual passages often touch on other aspects of mysticism along with those that illustrate the topic under consideration. The fact that each section is arranged chronologically will provide some sense of the historical evolution of the themes, but my intent, once again, is not so much to provide a history as to suggest something of the richness of the essential aspects of Christian mysticism considered in itself.

I am conscious of the many great mystics and mystical texts of worth that do not appear in this collection. I hope that those who miss an old favorite, or judge that I have overvalued some figures and traditions at the expense of others, will grant me the indulgence of recognizing the difficulty of presenting an adequate picture of the nature of Christian mysticism even within the generous confines of a volume of this size. As the book moved from conception to actual implementation, some texts fell by the wayside and others were added. These mutations in the development of the book helped convince me even more deeply than before that, as the mystics have taught, the pursuit of the divine mystery does not remove us from the world of space and time, but makes us ever more conscious of the intersection of time and eternity. As T. S. Eliot put it:

> But to apprehend
> The point of intersection of the timeless
> With time, is an occupation for a saint—
> No occupation either, but something given
> And taken, in a lifetime's death in love,
> Ardour and selflessness and self-surrender.

> ("THE DRY SALVAGES")

A NOTE ON THE TRANSLATIONS

Slightly more than a third of the texts in the volume are taken from translations currently under copyright. I wish to thank the publishers and those in possession of the rights for permission to use these materials. Of the remaining selections, about half are drawn from translations in the public domain. In almost all cases, however, I have updated the language to conform to present English usage, and I have tried, wherever possible, to compare these translations with recent critical editions and make any needed adjustments. Finally, in making my own translations copyright laws sometimes compelled me to make use of early editions, but I have endeavored to check these translations against more recent critical editions and make the necessary changes, usually minor.

PART ONE

FOUNDATIONS OF
MYSTICAL PRACTICE

SECTION ONE

BIBLICAL INTERPRETATION

Christian mysticism is rooted in the reading of the Bible. The mystic, however, does not seek an academic understanding of the scriptural text; nor is he or she content with viewing the Bible only as a repository of doctrine and moral regulations. The mystic wants to penetrate to the living source of the biblical message, that is, to the Divine Word who speaks in and through human words and texts. This means that the Bible has been both the origin and the norm for Christian mystics down through the ages.

The biblical basis for Christian mysticism is evident in many ways, not least in the fact that the very term *mystical* (Greek: *mystikos;* Latin: *mysticus*) entered Christianity primarily as a way to describe the inner sense of the Bible. In ancient Greek and Latin the word originally referred to anything "hidden." It was sometimes used religiously to point to the secret ceremonies of the mystery cults. From the second half of the second century CE, Christians began to employ the term to characterize the inner dimension of the realities of their religion. Although they spoke of mystical sacraments, of mystical contemplation, and, from around the year 500 on, even of mystical theology, the earliest, the most widespread, and the most continuous use of the word was in relation to the Bible—that is, the mystical meaning or mystical understanding of the scriptural text. This shows why the largest body of mystical literature until circa 1200 is directly biblical in nature, that is, mystical texts mostly occur either in commentaries on the books of the Bible or in sermons preached to bring out the inner dimension of the liturgical readings drawn from scripture. Even those mystics (mostly after circa 1200) who began to place emphasis on what Bernard of Clairvaux called the "book of experience" (*liber experientiae*) wanted to show the conformity between what they had learned through their own contact with God and the message given to the church in the biblical text.

This kind of in-depth reading delighting in multiple meanings and in illuminating one biblical text with another often seems strange to us today, in an era shaped by historical-critical readings that seek the author's original intent. Modern hermeneutical theories and studies in the history of the reception of texts, however, have begun to give us a better sense of the purpose of the mystical reading of the Bible. Mystical interpretation was not arbitrary, but was governed by two essential criteria: first, the usefulness of the reading for encouraging deeper contact with God; and second, the reading's coherence with the faith of the community.

The entire Bible was viewed as having a deeper meaning. Naturally, some books lent themselves more easily to a mystical reading, thus forming a kind of "canon within the canon" for the mystical element in the history of Christianity. Some of these books, such as the Psalms in the Old Testament, and John's Gospel and Paul's letters in the New Testament, are evident choices, but the mystical book par excellence was the Song of Songs—a surprising choice to those who feel some discomfort with the frankly erotic language of these love songs. Christian mystics, as well as Jewish mystics, found in the Song, properly read, the supreme expression of the love of God for his community and for each person within it.

Three of the six selections in this section (Origen, Bernard of Clairvaux, and Madame Guyon) illustrate varieties of mystical readings of the Song. The other three selections show how mystical interpretation was applied to other books. Gregory of Nyssa used the story of Moses from Exodus as an archetype of the soul's progression to God. Gregory's younger contemporary Augustine of Hippo preached hundreds of sermons on the Psalms. The example given here from a sermon on Psalm 41 provides insight into a mystical reading directed at the whole Christian community. Meister Eckhart expressed his teaching primarily through sermons preached on texts from the liturgy, teasing out mystical readings usually from short passages of many biblical books, such as the sentence from Luke's Gospel that is the basis for this sermon.

1.

ORIGEN

COMMENTARY ON THE SONG OF SONGS

PROLOGUE

Origen of Alexandria (circa 180–254) was the greatest exegete of the early church. His spiritual reading of the Bible continued to influence later thinkers, despite the condemnation of aspects of his teaching in the sixth century. As Hans Urs von Balthasar, one of Origen's modern interpreters, once said, "No figure is more invisibly omnipresent in the history of Christian theology." Origen can also be described as the church's first explicit mystical theologian. While the mystical element was present in Christianity from the start, it is with the Alexandrian teacher that a formal biblically based mystical theory first emerges.

Origen was not the first to interpret the Song's account of the bridegroom and bride as the story of the love between Christ and the church, but he furthered this mystical reading by applying it to the relations between Christ and each loving soul. The following four excerpts from the prologue of what survives of his commentary show how he created the elements that were to elevate the Song to the mystical text par excellence in Christian history. The first section describes his overall characterization of the Song as a dramatic account of the process of salvation. The second shows how his dual understanding of human nature (inner and outer person) allowed him to translate the sensual language of the Song into a message about the spiritual senses, the powers of inner perception lost in sin but gradually restored to the soul through the action of grace. In the third selection Origen argues that there is no essential difference between the language of passionate desire (erôs in Greek; amor in Latin) and the biblical word for God's generous love poured out upon us (agapê/caritas). Finally, in the fourth selec-

tion Origen demonstrates how the three books ascribed to Solomon (a type of Christ) form the basis for a biblical paideia, *or total education, by which we are brought back to God.*

I.

THE SONG OF SONGS AS A
MYSTICAL DRAMA

It seems to me that this little book is an epithalamium, that is to say, a marriage-song, which Solomon wrote in the form of a drama and sang under the figure of the bride, about to wed and burning with heavenly love towards her Bridegroom, who is the Word of God. And deeply indeed did she love him, whether we take her as the soul made in his image, or as the church. But this same scripture also teaches us what words this august and perfect Bridegroom used in speaking to the soul, or to the church, who has been joined to him. And in this same little book that bears the title *Song of Songs* we recognize moreover things that the bride's companions said, the maidens that go with her, and also some things spoken by the Bridegroom's friends and fellows. For the friends of the Bridegroom also, in their joy at his union with the bride, have been enabled to say some things—at any rate those that they had heard from the Bridegroom himself. In the same way we find the bride speaking not to the Bridegroom only, but also to the maidens; likewise the Bridegroom's words are addressed not to the bride alone, but also to his friends. And that is what we meant just now, when we said that the marriage-song was written in dramatic form. For we call a thing a drama, such as the enaction of a story on the stage, when different characters are introduced and the whole structure of the narrative consists in their comings and goings among themselves. And this work contains these things one by one in their own order, and also the whole body of it consists of mystical utterances.

But it behoves us primarily to understand that, just as in childhood we are not affected by the passion of love, so also to those who are at the stage of infancy and childhood in their interior life—to those, that is to say, who are being nourished with milk in Christ, not with strong meat, and are only beginning "to desire the rational milk without guile" (Heb 5:12)—it is not given to grasp the meaning of these sayings. For in the words of the *Song of Songs* there is that food, of which the Apostle says that "strong meat is for the perfect"; and that food calls for hearers "who by ability have their senses exercised to the discerning of good and evil" (Heb 5:14). And indeed, if those whom we have called children were to come on these passages, it may be that they would derive neither profit nor much harm, either from reading the text itself, or from going through the necessary explanations. But if any man who lives only after the flesh should approach it, to such a one the reading of this scripture will be the occasion of no small hazard and danger. For he, not knowing how to hear love's language in purity and with chaste ears, will twist the whole manner of his hearing of it away from the inner spiritual man and on to the outward and carnal; and he will be turned away from the spirit to the flesh and will foster carnal desires in himself, and it will seem to be the divine scriptures that are thus urging and egging him on to fleshly lust!

II.

THE INNER AND OUTER PERSON
AND THE SPIRITUAL SENSES

In the beginning of the words of Moses, where the creation of the world is described, we find reference to the making of two men, the first "in the image and likeness of God," and the second "formed of the slime of the earth" (Gen 1:26, 2:7). Paul the Apostle knew this well; and, being possessed of a very clear understanding of the matter, he wrote in his letters more plainly and with greater lucidity that there are in fact two men in every single man. He says, for instance: "For if our outward man is corrupted, yet the inward man is renewed day by day"; and again: "For I am delighted with the law of God according to the inward man" (2 Cor 4:16; Rom 7:22). And he makes some other statements of a similar kind. I think, therefore, that no one ought any longer to doubt what Moses wrote in the beginning of Genesis about the making and fashioning of two men, since he sees Paul, who understood what Moses wrote much better than we do, saying that there are two men in every one of us. Of these two men he tells us that the one, namely, the inner man, is renewed from day to day; but the other, that is, the outer, he declares to be corrupted and weakened in all the saints and in such as he was himself. If anything in regard to this matter still seems doubtful to anyone, it will be better explained in the appropriate places. But let us now follow up what we mentioned before about the inner and the outer man.

The thing we want to demonstrate about these things is that the divine scriptures make use of homonyms; that is to say, they use identical terms for describing different things. And they even go so far as to call the members of the outer man by the same names as the parts and dispositions of the inner man; and not only are the same terms employed, but the things themselves are compared with one another. For instance, a person is a child in age according to the inner man, who has in him the power to grow and to be led onward to the age of youth, and thence by successive stages of development to come to the perfect man and to be made a father. Our own intention, therefore, has been to use such terms as would be in harmony with the language of sacred scripture, and in particular with that which was written by John; for he says: "I have written to you, children, because you have known the Father; I have written to you, fathers, because you have known him who was from the beginning; I have written to you, young men, because you are strong, and the word of God abides in you, and you have overcome the wicked one" (1 Jn 2:12–14). It is perfectly clear; and I think nobody should doubt that John calls these people children or lads or young men or even fathers according to the soul's age, not the body's. Paul too says somewhere: "I could not speak to you as spiritual, but as to carnal, little ones in Christ. I gave you milk to drink, not meat" (1 Cor 3:1). A little one in Christ is undoubtedly so called after the age of his soul, not after that of his flesh. And finally the same Paul says further: "When I was a child, I spoke as a child, I understood as a child, I thought as a child; but when I became a man I destroyed childish things" (1 Cor 13:11). And again on another occasion he says: "Until we all meet . . . unto a perfect man; unto the measure of the age of the fullness of Christ" (Eph 4:13). He knows that those who believe will "all meet unto a perfect man" and "unto the measure of the age of the fullness of Christ." So, then, just as these different ages that we have mentioned are denoted by the same words both for the outer man and for the inner, so also will you find the names of the members of the body transferred to those of the soul; or rather the faculties and powers of the soul are to be called its members.

III.
AMOR AND CARITAS

In these places, therefore, and in many others you will find that divine scripture avoided the word "passion" (*erôs*) and put "charity" or "affection" (*agapê*) instead. Occasionally, however, though rarely, it calls the passion of love by its own name, and invites and urges souls to it; as when it says in Proverbs about Wisdom: "Desire her greatly and she will preserve you; encompass her, and she shall exalt you; honor her, that she may embrace you" (Prov 4:6, 8). And in the book that is called the Wisdom of Solomon it is written of Wisdom herself: "I became a passionate lover of her beauty" (Wis 8:2). I think that the word for passionate love was used only where there seemed to be no occasion of falling. For who could see anything sensuous or unseemly in the passion for Wisdom, or in a man's professing himself her passionate lover? Whereas had Isaac been spoken of as having a passion for Rebecca or Jacob for Rachel, some unseemly passion on the part of the saints of God might have been inferred from the words, especially by those who do not know how to rise up from the letter to the spirit. Most clearly, however, even in this our little book of which we are now treating, the appellation of "passionate love" has been changed into the word "charity" in the place where it says: "I have adjured you, O daughters of Jerusalem, if you find my 'Nephew,' to tell him that I have been wounded by charity" (Song 5:8). For that is as much as to say: "I have been smitten through with the dart of His passionate love." It makes no difference, therefore, whether the sacred scriptures speak of love, or of charity, or of affection; except that the word "charity" is so highly exalted that even God himself is called Charity, as John says: "Dearly beloved, let us love one another, for charity is of God; and everyone that loves is born of God and knows God. But he that loves not knows not God, for God is Charity" (1 Jn 4:7–8).

IV.
THE PLACE OF THE SONG OF SONGS
AMONG THE WORKS OF SOLOMON
(I.E., CHRIST)

Now, therefore, calling upon God the Father, who is Charity, through that same charity that is of him, let us pass on to discuss the other matters. And let us first investigate the reason why, when the churches of God have adopted three books from Solomon's pen, the Book of Proverbs has been put first, that which is called Ecclesiastes second, while the Song of Songs is found in the third place. The following are the suggestions that occur to us here.

The branches of learning by means of which men generally attain to knowledge of things are the three which the Greeks called Ethics, Physics and Epoptics; these we may call respectively moral, natural, and inspective. Some among the Greeks, of course, add a fourth branch, logic, which we may describe as rational. Others have said that logic does not stand by itself, but is connected and intertwined throughout with the three studies that we mentioned first. For this logic is, as we say, rational, in that it deals with the meanings and proper significances and their opposites, the classes and kinds of words and expressions, and gives information as to the form of each and every saying; and this branch of learning certainly requires not so much to be separated from the others as to be mingled and woven in with them. That study is called moral, on the other hand, which inculcates a seemly manner of life and gives a grounding in habits that incline to virtue. The study called natural is that in which the nature of each single thing is considered; so that nothing in life may be done which is contrary to nature, but everything is assigned to the uses for which the Creator brought it into being. The study called inspective is that by which we go beyond things seen and contemplate something of things divine and heavenly, beholding them with the mind alone, for they are beyond the range of bodily sight.

It seems to me, then, that all the sages of the Greeks borrowed these ideas from Solomon, who had learned them by the Spirit of God at an age and time long before their own, and that they then put them forward as their own inventions and, by including them in the books of their teachings, left them to be handed down also to those that came after. But, as we said, Solomon discovered and taught these things by the wisdom that he received from God before anyone; as it is written: "And God gave understanding to Solomon and wisdom exceeding great, and largeness of heart as the sand that is on the seashore. And wisdom was multiplied in him above all the sons of men that were of old, and above all the sages of Egypt" (3 Kgs 4:29–30). Wishing, therefore, to distinguish one from another of those three branches of learning, which we called general just now (that is, the moral, the natural, and the inspective), and to differentiate between them, Solomon issued them in three books, arranged in their proper order. First, in Proverbs he taught the moral science, putting rules for living into the form of short and pithy maxims, as was fitting. Secondly, he covered the science known as natural in Ecclesiastes; in this, by discussing at length the things of nature, and by distinguishing the useless and vain from the profitable and essential, he counsels us to forsake vanity and cultivate things useful and upright. The inspective science likewise he has propounded in this little book that we now have in hand—that is, the Song of Songs. In this he instills into the soul the love of things divine and heavenly, using for his purpose the figure of the bride and Bridegroom, and teaches us that communion with God must be attained by the paths of charity and love. . . .

This book comes last so that a person may come to it when his manner of life has been purified and he has learnt to know the difference between things corruptible and things incorruptible, so that nothing in the metaphors used to describe and represent the love of the bride for her celestial Bridegroom—that is, of the perfect soul for the Word of God—may cause him to stumble. For when the soul has completed these studies, by means of which it is cleansed in all its actions and habits and is led to discriminate between natural things, it is competent to proceed to doctrinal and mystical matters, and in this way advances to the contemplation of the Godhead with pure and spiritual love.

From *Origen. The Song of Songs. Commentary and Homilies,* translated and annotated by R. P. Lawson (New York: Paulist Press, 1957. Ancient Christian Writers), 21–22, 24–27, 31–32, 39–41, and 44. Used with permission of Paulist Press.

GREGORY OF NYSSA
THE LIFE OF MOSES

SELECTIONS FROM BOOK TWO

Gregory of Nyssa (circa 335–94) was the younger brother of Basil the Great. These brothers, along with their friend Gregory of Nazianzen, constitute the Cappadocian Fathers whose influence, especially in Eastern Christianity, has been immense. The bishop of Nyssa was the most speculative and mystical of the three Cappadocians, though he made signal contributions to Christian doctrine too, especially with regard to the theology of the Trinity. Like Origen, Gregory wrote a commentary on the Song of Songs in the form of fifteen homilies dedicated to a wealthy Christian named Olympias.

His other great mystical work, The Life of Moses, *is something different. It is not a formal commentary but rather a rearrangement of the story of Moses from the Old Testament, especially from Exodus, to present the patriarch as the model of mystical ascent to God. Gregory divides his work into two parts: a short part (sections 16–77) that provides the narrative of the life of Moses; and the longer second part (sections 78–318) presenting a contemplation of the meaning of the story. Gregory organizes the second part around three major theophanies, or divine manifestations, given to Moses. Each of these showings has a Christological dimension, since for Gregory the God-man is the source of all real knowledge of God. The first, the sight of the burning bush (Ex 3:1–15), was an illumination in which Moses came to understand that God is true infinite being. The second was Moses' ascent of Sinai (Ex 20:18–21) where he encountered God in cloud and darkness, the negative aspect of the mystical itinerary. The final theophany (Ex 33:7–23) was the patriarch's conversation with God in which he asked for a face-to-face vision of God's glory, but was instead granted only the vision of God's back from a location described as "a hollow in the rock." Here Gregory is able to expound his most original mystical teaching, the notion of* epektasis, *or the constant pursuit of God that is also paradoxically the enjoyment of his presence (see Phil 3:13). This teaching flows from a central theological theme of the Cappadocians: their insistence that God is absolutely infinite and therefore inexhaustible to all creatures.*

I.
THE FIRST THEOPHANY.
THE BURNING BUSH (EX 3:1–15)

As soon as we are established in this peaceable non-combative condition, the truth will shine upon us, bringing light to the eyes of the soul with its own rays. The truth that then shone on Moses through that wonderful illumination was God. And if the light which enlightens the soul of the prophet comes from a thorn bush, that too is not without its value for our search. For if the truth is God and the truth is also light—and the gospel attributes both these high and divine titles to the God who appeared in the flesh (Jn 8:12, 14:16)—it follows that a virtuous life brings us to the knowledge of that light which descends as human nature. This light comes to us not from one of the bright lights around the stars, in case anyone should suppose that the ray emanated from some underlying material. It comes instead from an earthly bush, yet exceeds the lights of heaven with its brilliance. . . .

The light instructs us what we must do if we wish to remain within the rays of the true light. If we wish to ascend to so great a height, where the light of truth is seen, we must take off our shoes. This means that the dead and earthly covering of skins must be removed from the feet of the soul; a covering we acquired in the beginning, once we had been denuded through our disobedience to the divine will (Gen 3:21). Once we have done this, the knowledge of the truth will follow us, manifesting herself to us. For knowledge of that which is (or He who is) purifies us of any unreal opinion.

In my opinion the definition of truth is "being free from error about the nature of reality." A lie is an illusion in the soul about what is unreal, which suggests that what does not exist in fact exists. Truth, on the other hand, is a firm perception of what really does exist. So anybody who has thought at leisure about such high matters will gradually perceive what "being" really is, which has being of its own nature, and what non-being is, which enjoys only apparent reality, without any substantial nature of its own. It seems to me that what the great Moses learned in the theophany is simply this, that neither those things grasped by sense, nor those that the mind can understand, have a real existence. The only reality that truly exists is the one that is above all of them, the cause of all from which everything depends.

Whatever else the intelligence finds in existence, in none of these does it discover that complete independence of all else, which enables it to exist without participation in "The Really Real." Always to exist in the same way, never to become greater and never to be diminished, to be totally beyond all change whether it be for the better or the worse, means that the Divine is doubly incapable either of deterioration or of improvement. To be totally independent of all else and, at the same time, to be the sole object of desire; to be participated in by all, yet to be in no way thereby diminished, that is to be The Really Real and knowledge thereof is the knowledge of the truth.

Once Moses then, and now those who follow in his footsteps, rid themselves of earthly encumbrances and see the light from the bush— that is the light that shines on us through the thorn bush of the flesh which is, as the gospel says, "the true light" and "the truth" (Jn 1:9, 14:6)—once, that is, they had arrived there, then they were in a position to be of service to others. They were able to destroy the evil tyranny that controlled them and to lead out into freedom all that were under the domination of an evil slavery. . . . By this it seems to me that the mystery of the appearance of the godhead of the Lord through the flesh was displayed, whereby both the destruction of the tyrant and the freedom of those under his control were indicated.

II.
THE SECOND THEOPHANY:
THE ASCENT OF MOUNT SINAI
(EX 20:18-21)

What is the meaning of Moses "being within the cloud and seeing God there" (Ex 20:21)? What is now recorded seems to be in some way the very opposite of the first theophany (Ex 3:14). Then the Deity was seen in the light, now is it seen in the cloud. We should not, however, suppose that this is out of harmony with the sequence of ideas so far considered. The sacred text teaches us that religious knowledge is a light quite distinct from the one we first encountered. In fact what is thought the opposite of piety is indeed darkness while the turning away from darkness takes place by sharing in the light. However, the further the mind advances and the greater and more perfect its attention to, and knowledge of, the realm of reality becomes, the nearer, in fact, that it draws close to contemplation, so much the more is it aware of the unavailability of the divine nature to human knowledge.

The mind leaves behind all that appears, not only what the senses grasp, but also whatever the intelligence seems to behold and ever seeks to move further inward, until it penetrates by reason of the activity of the intelligence to what is unseen and incomprehensible and there sees God. For it is precisely in this that true knowledge of what is sought consists, and precisely in this that seeing consists, that is in not seeing, because we seek what lies beyond all knowledge, shrouded by incomprehensibility in all directions, as it were by some cloud. Hence the mystical John, the same who penetrated into the shining cloud, says that "No one has ever seen God" (Jn 1:18). By this denial he insists that the knowledge of the divine nature is unavailable not only to men, but also to all rational creatures.

It is only when Moses has increased in knowledge that he confesses that he beholds God in the cloud, that is, that he knows that the divine is by nature something above all knowledge and comprehension. For Scripture says, "Moses entered the darkness where God was" (Ex 20:21). Who is God? "He who," as David says, "made the darkness his hiding place" (Ps 18:12). For David also had been initiated into the secret mysteries in that very same shrine.

Once arrived there he is once again taught by reason what he had already learnt through the cloud. The reason for this is, I think, that our conviction on this matter might be more firmly grounded once it had been assured by the divine voice. What the divine word above all inhibits is human assimilation of the divine to anything that we know. Every thought and every defining conception which aims to encompass and grasp the divine nature is only forming an idol of God, without declaring him as he truly is. Religious virtue may be distinguished in the following way. Part deals with the divine; part deals with moral behavior, for part of religion is purity of life. To begin with we must know how we are to think of God, and that knowledge entails entertaining none of the ideas which are derived from human understanding. The second part of virtue is taught by learning by what practices the life of virtue is realized.

III.
THE THIRD THEOPHANY:
FACE-TO-FACE VISION (EX 33:7-23)

When the soul is moved towards what is naturally lovely, it seems to me that this is the sort of passionate desire with which it is moved. Beginning with the loveliness it sees, it is drawn upwards to what is transcendent. The soul is forever inflaming its desire for what is hidden, by means of what it has already grasped. For this reason, the ardent lover of beauty understands what is seen as an image of what he desires, and yearns to be filled with the actual substance of the archetype. This is what underlies the bold and excessive desire of him who desires to see no longer "through mirrors and reflections, but instead to enjoy beauty face to face" (1 Cor 13:12). The divine voice concedes what is demanded by actually refusing it, and in a few words displays the immeasurable depths of its ideas. On the one hand, the divine generosity grants the fulfillment of his desire; on the other hand, it promises no end to desire nor satiety of it. In fact, he would never have shown himself to his servant if what was seen were enough to still the desire of the beholder. For, he declares, "My face you shall not see; for no one shall see my face and live" (Ex 33:20).

Scripture makes it plain that it is not the vision [of God] that is the cause of death. For how should the face of life be the cause of death to those who draw near it? But since the Divine is naturally life giving and, further, that it is the special character of the divine nature to lie above all definition, whoever supposes that God is one of the things he knows, is himself without life, having turned aside from The Really Real to what is supposed to be grasped by a concept. For The Really Real is the true life and is inaccessible to our understanding. If, then, the life giving lies beyond our knowledge, what we have grasped cannot be the life. And what is itself not life is powerless of itself to communicate it. Moses' desire, therefore, is satisfied precisely in so far as his desire remains unsatisfied.

Moses is instructed through what has been said that the Divine is of itself infinite, circumscribed by no limit. For if the Divine could be thought of as in some way limited, it would be absolutely necessary to consider what comes after it along with it. Whatever has a limit has a boundary, even as air is a limit for winged creatures and water for what lives in the water. And even as fish are surrounded in all their parts by water, so, too, are birds by the air; so, too, the limit of the water for the fish, and of the air for the birds, is the extreme surface of either which serves as a boundary for the fish of the sea or the birds of the sky, respectively. The same operates in the case of the Divine. If it were thought to have a boundary, this would imply the existence of a limit distinct in character from itself. And our argument has shown that whatever limits is greater than that which it encloses. . . .

And the true vision of God consists in this, in never reaching satiety of the desire. We ought always to look through the things that we can see and still be on fire with the desire to see more. So let there be no limit to curtail our growth in our journey upwards to God. This is because no limit to the beautiful has been found nor can any satiety cut short the progress of the soul in its desire for the beautiful.

What is the place referred to by God? What is the rock? And again what is the space within the rock? What is the hand of God, which covers the mouth of the hollow in the rock? What is the passage of God? What is the back part of God, which God promised to give Moses who had asked him for a face-to-face vision of himself? [All references to Ex 33:22–23.]

It should be the case that each of these things is great and worthy of the munificence of the giver. Once his great servant had received this wonderful revelation, what followed must be believed to be both grander and more lofty still. How might anyone grasp the nature of this loftiness from what has been said? For it is there that after all his previous ascents Moses himself desires to ascend, as does He who "works in all things for good to those who love God" (Rom 8:28), and so through his leadership facilitates each ascent. For, "behold," he says, "there is a place beside me" (Ex 33:21).

This idea is in close agreement with our previous discoveries. For when it speaks of "place" it does not mean by that something circumscribed by quantity (for where there is no size there can be no measure either), but by using the image of a measured surface it conducts the listener to what is unlimited and infinite. The sense of the utterance seems to be something like this. Your desire is always strained forwards and your forward motion knows no weariness; further, you know no limit to the good and your desire is always intent on something more. This all means that the "place" is ever near you, so that whoever runs therein never comes to an end of his running.

Yet from another point of view this running is also a standing still for, he says, "I will station you upon the rock" (Ex 33:22). And this is the greatest paradox of all, that the same thing is both standing still and on the move. For normally he who ascends never stays still, while he who stands still does not ascend. Yet, in this case, it is precisely through being still that the ascent occurs. The meaning of this is that the more firm and immoveable a person is in the good, so much the more does he accomplish the race of virtue. For whoever is uncertain and unstable in his convictions, has an unsure grasp on the noble; he is "storm-tossed and carried around," as the Apostle says (Eph 4:14), and in doubt and shaken in one's conceptions about reality and, as a result, incapable of ascending to the height of virtue.

It is like people who endeavor to make their way upward through sand, who despite their taking great strides, labor fruitlessly. Their footing always slips on the sand as they go down with the result that, despite their perpetual motion, they fail to make any advance. But if anyone, in the words of the psalmist (Ps 40:2), "extracts his feet from the miry bog" and sets them instead firmly on the rock, that is, on Christ (1 Cor 10:5), who is perfect virtue, he will be firm and immoveable in virtue. So, as the Apostle exhorts us (1 Cor 15:58), so much the more speedily will he accomplish his course. He uses his stability as a sort of wing and makes his way upward, his heart winged as it were by his firmness in the good. In showing Moses the place God encourages him in his course, and by promising him stability on the rock, he shows him how he is to run this divine course.

Reprinted from *Gregory of Nyssa,* translated by Anthony Meredith (Routledge, 1999), 102–9.

3.

AUGUSTINE OF HIPPO
SERMON ON PSALM 41 (VULGATE)

Augustine of Hippo (354–430) was the dominant theological figure in Western Christianity for more than a millennium, and still remains one of the essential voices in Christian history. This North African convert contributed to every area of Christian belief and practice, not least that of mysticism. Augustine's accounts of his experiences of contact with God, as recounted in his Confessions, *will be treated in section 10.2. Bishop Augustine's most detailed teaching on mysticism, however, comes in the sermons on the Psalms that he preached to his flock in Hippo in North Africa during a period of almost thirty years (circa 392–420).*

Two things should be noted about this mystical preaching. First, Augustine's teaching was presented not to any spiritual elite of clerics or monastics, but to the whole Christian community of his small diocese. Second, this teaching is presented not in any formal treatise, but as a commentary on the meaning of the Psalms, the "prayer book of the Church." Augustine's spiritual interpretation of the "deer longing for water-brooks" of Psalm 41 (42 in the Hebrew Bible) as the soul thirsting for God is typical of the way in which most Christian mystics have read the Bible—not in terms of a modern historical-critical view of trying to find out what the text meant when it was written, but as exploring what it says to the soul questing for God, both in the fifth century and in the twenty-first.

—

"As the deer longs for the water-brooks, so my soul longs for You, O God" (Ps 41:1).

2. Let then our "understanding" be roused: and if the psalm be sung to us, let us follow it with our "understanding." . . . Run to the brooks; long for the water-brooks. "With God is the fountain of life" (Ps 35:10), a fountain that shall never be dried up: in his light is a light that shall never be darkened. Long for this light, for a certain fountain, for a certain light, such as your bodily eyes know not; a light to see which the inward eye must be prepared; a fountain to drink of which the inward thirst must be kindled. Run to the fountain, long for the fountain; but do not run anyhow, be not satisfied with running like any ordinary animal; run only "like a deer." What is meant by "like a deer"? Let there be no sloth in your running. Run with all your might. Long with all your might for the fountain. For we find in the deer an emblem of swiftness.

3. But perhaps Scripture meant us to consider in the deer not this point only, but also another. Hear what else there is in the deer. It destroys serpents, and after the killing of serpents, it is inflamed yet more violently with thirst. Having destroyed serpents, it runs to the water-brooks with a thirst more keen than before. The serpents are your vices. Destroy the serpents of iniquity, then you will long yet more for the Fountain of Truth. . . .

5. "My soul is thirsty for the living God" (Ps 41:2). What I am saying, that "as the deer longs after the water-brooks, so longs my soul after You, O God," means this—"My soul is thirsty for the living God." For what was it thirsty? "When shall I come and appear before the face of the Lord?" (Ps 41:3). This is what I am thirsty for, "to come and appear before him." I am thirsty in my pilgrimage, in my running; I shall be filled on my arrival. But "when shall I come?" What is soon in the sight of God is late for our longing. "When shall I come and appear before the face of God?" This too proceeds from that longing that in another Psalm text evokes the cry: "One thing have I desired of the Lord and that I will seek after: that I may dwell in the house of the Lord all the days of my life" (Ps. 26:4). Why so? "That I may behold the beauty of the Lord" (ibid.). "When shall I come and appear before the face of the Lord." . . .

8. Seeking my God in visible and corporeal things, I did not find him. Seeking his substance in myself, as if he were something like

me, I also did not find him. I am aware that my God is something above my soul, and therefore, so that I might touch him, "I thought on these things and poured out my soul above myself" (Ps 41:5). When would my soul attain to that object of its search, which is above my soul, if it were not poured out above itself? For were it to rest in itself, it would not see anything else beyond itself; and in seeing only itself it would certainly not see its God. Let then my insulting enemies now say, "Where is your God?" (Ps 41:4). Yes, let them say it! As long as I do not see him, as long as I am put off, I will eat my tears days and night. Let them still say, "Where is your God?" I seek my God in every corporeal nature, terrestrial or celestial, and find him not. I seek his substance in my own soul, and I find it not. Yet still I have pondered on this search for my God, and wishing to "behold the invisible things of my God by understanding them through the things that were made" (Rom 1:20), I have poured forth my soul above myself, and there remains nothing left for me to attain, save my God. For there, above my soul, is the house of my God. There he dwells; from there he beholds me; from there he created me; from there he directs me and provides for me; from there he arouses me, calls me, directs me, leads me on; from there he will lead me to the goal.

9. He who has his highest home in a secret place also has his tabernacle on earth. His tabernacle on earth is his church, which is still a pilgrim. But he is to be sought there, because in his tabernacle is found the way that leads to his house. For when I was pouring out my soul above myself in order to reach my God, why did I do so? "For I will go into the place of your tabernacle" (Ps 41:5). For I should be in error if I should seek my God without the place of his tabernacle. "For I will go into the place of your wonderful tabernacle, even unto the house of God." I will enter the place of the tabernacle, the wonderful tabernacle, even unto the house of God. For there are already many things that I admire in the tabernacle. See how great are the wonders I admire in the tabernacle! The faithful are God's tabernacle on earth. I admire in them the obedience even of their bodily members, for "sin does not reign in them so that they should obey its bodily lusts, nor do they yield their members as instruments of unrighteousness unto sin, but unto the living God in good works" (Rom 6:12–13). I admire the sight of bodily members warring in the service of the soul that serves

God. I also gaze upon the soul obeying God, putting its works in order, restraining its desires, casting out ignorance, stretching itself out to bear all that is harsh and difficult, and exercising justice and love toward others.

I admire these virtues in the soul, but I am still walking in the place of the tabernacle. I will pass beyond all this, and although the tabernacle is wonderful, I will be struck with awe when I come unto the house of God. Concerning that house the psalmist says in another verse when he had put a hard and difficult question to himself: "I tried to know this, but it is too hard for me until I go into the sanctuary of God, and understand the last things" (Ps 72:16–17). For there, in the sanctuary of God, in the house of God, is the fountain of understanding. . . . And it was in the sanctuary of God that the psalmist understood this, and "understood the last things." Ascending to the tabernacle, he came unto the house of God. It was thus that while admiring the members of the tabernacle, he was led unto the house of God—by following a certain delight, an inward mysterious and hidden pleasure, as if some instrument sounded sweetly from the house of God. While he was walking in the tabernacle, he heard this inward sound; he was led on by its sweetness, and following the guidance of the sound and withdrawing himself from all noise of flesh and blood, he made his way even to the house of God. For he tells us of his progress and of his guidance to it, as if we had been saying, "You are admiring the tabernacle here on earth; how did you come to the sanctuary of the house of God?" He says, "In the voice of joy and praise, the sound of keeping holiday" (Ps 41:5). . . . In the house of God there is a never-ending festival: For there it is not an occasion celebrated once, and then to pass away. The angelic choir makes an eternal holiday: the presence of God's face, joy that never fails. This is a holiday of such a kind as neither to be opened by any dawn, nor terminated by any evening. From that everlasting, perpetual festivity a certain sweet and melodious strain strikes on the ears of the heart, provided only that the world does not drown out the sounds. As he walks in this tabernacle and contemplates God's wonderful works for the redemption of the faithful, the sound of that festivity charms his ears and bears the deer away to the waterbrooks.

10. But seeing, brethren, so long as "we are at home in this body, we

are absent from the Lord" (2 Cor 5:6), and that "the corruptible body presses down the soul, and the earthly tabernacle weighs down the mind that muses on many things" (Wis 9:15), even though we have in some way or other dispersed the clouds by walking as longing leads us on, and for a brief while have come within reach of that sound, so that by an effort we may catch something from that house of God, yet through the burden, so to speak, of our infirmity, we sink back to our usual level and relapse to our ordinary state. And just as there we found cause for rejoicing, so here there will not be lacking an occasion for sorrow. For that deer that "made its tears its bread day and night," carried along "by longing for the water-brooks" (that is, to the spiritual delights of God), "pouring forth his soul above himself" that he might attain to what is above his own soul, walking toward "the place of the wonderful tabernacle, even unto the house of God," and led on by the sweetness of that inward spiritual sound to feel contempt for outward things and be ravished by interior things, is still just a mortal man. He is still groaning here, still bearing about the frailty of the flesh, still in danger in the midst of the offenses of this world. He therefore looks back at himself, as if he were coming from that other world, and says to himself, now placed in the midst of these sorrows, comparing these with the things to see which he had entered in there, and after seeing which he had come out of there, says, "Why are you cast down, O my soul, and why do you disturb me?" (Ps 41:6). See, we have just now been gladdened by certain inward delights; with the mind's eye we have been able to behold, even though with only a momentary glance, something not susceptible to change. Why do you still disturb me, why are you still cast down? For you do not doubt your God. For now you are not without something to say to yourself in answer to those who say, "Where is your God?" I have now had the perception of something that is unchangeable, so why do you still disturb me? "Hope in God" (ibid.). Just as if his soul was silently replying to him, "I disturb you because I am not yet there where that delight is to which I was rapt as it were in passing. Am I already drinking from this fountain with nothing to fear? Do I no longer have anything to be anxious about, as if all my passions were conquered and thoroughly subdued? Is not my foe, the devil, on the watch against me? Would you have me not disturb you, placed as I am still in the world, and on pilgrimage from the house of God?" Still, "Hope in God" is his answer to the soul that disturbs him.

Translation adapted and emended from *Expositions on the Book of Psalms by Saint Augustine*, by A. Cleveland Coxe, in *A Select Library of the Nicene and Post-Nicene Fathers of the Christian Church*, edited by Philip Schaff. First Series. Volume VIII (New York: The Christian Literature Company, 1886–90), 132–35.

4.

BERNARD OF CLAIRVAUX
SERMONS ON THE SONG OF SONGS 23

Bernard of Clairvaux (1090–1153) was not a theorist of the interpretation of scripture, but his biblical sermons are among the most famous and influential of the Middle Ages. His premier mystical work, the eighty-six sermons on the Song of Songs composed between about 1135 and 1153, is one of the greatest works of mystical exegesis of the medieval period. Bernard's exegesis proceeds with contemplative leisure, reaching only to verse 4 of chapter 3 of the Song.

*The rhetorical richness and theological subtlety of these sermons are difficult to convey in English, but sermon 23 shows how the Cistercian abbot used the text of the Song to present an overview of the soul's journey to loving union with Christ the Incarnate Word. Bernard's comment begins with Song 1:3, "The King [i.e., Christ] has brought me [i.e., the soul as bride] into his rooms [cellars, or storerooms, in the Latin]." This in turn reminds him of two other locations mentioned in the Song, the garden of Song 5:1 and the bedroom of Song 3:4. Bernard changes the order of the biblical text, using these three places to sketch an itinerary of the soul that is also the gradual progression through three levels of reading the biblical text. The garden is the historical meaning (*historia*), that is, the Bible's presentation of salvation history. The storerooms are the moral teachings (*moralis sensus*), i.e., the three classes of virtues by which humans correct their faults and prepare for encountering God. Finally, the bedroom where the lovers meet represents divine contemplation (*theorica contemplatio*), the place of the various forms of mystical union. Bernard mentions three types of union in the sermon.*

———

"The King has brought me into his rooms" (Song 1:3). This is where the fragrance comes from, his is the goal of our running. She [i.e., the bride] had said that we must run, drawn by that fragrance, but did not specify our destination. So it is to these rooms that we run, drawn by the fragrance that issues from them. The bride's keen senses have been quick to detect it, so eager is she to experience it in all its fullness. But first of all we ought to give thought to the meaning of these rooms. To begin with, let us imagine them to be perfume-laden places within the Bridegroom's quarters, where varied spices breathe their scents (Rev 5:8), where delights are manifold. The more valuable products of garden and field are consigned for preservation to storerooms like these. To these therefore people run, at least those who are aglow with the Spirit (Rom 12:11). The bride runs, so do the maidens; but the one to arrive first is the one whose love is most ardent, because she runs more quickly (Jn 20:4). On arrival she brooks no refusal, not even delay. The door is promptly opened to her as to one of the family, one highly esteemed, loved with a special love, uniquely favored....

Since the implications of the text are clear from what I have said, let us now try to discover the spiritual meaning of the storerooms. Further on there is mention of a "garden" (Song 5:1) and a "bedroom" (Song 3:4), both of which I join to these rooms for the purpose of this present discussion. When examined together the meaning of each becomes clearer. By your leave then, we shall search the Sacred Scriptures for these three things: the garden, the storeroom, the bedroom. The person who thirsts for God eagerly studies and meditates on the inspired word, knowing that there he is certain to find the one for whom he thirsts. Let the garden, then, represent the plain, unadorned historical sense of Scripture, the storeroom its moral sense, and the bedroom the mystery of divine contemplation.

For a start I feel that my comparison of scriptural history to a garden is not unwarranted, for in it we find people of many virtues, like fruitful trees in the garden of the Bridegroom, in the Paradise of God (Ezek 31:9). You may gather samples of their good deeds and good habits as you would apples from trees. Who can doubt that a good person is a tree of God's planting? Listen to what St. David says of such a one: "He is like a tree that is planted by a stream of water, yielding its fruit in season, and its leaves never fade" (Ps 1:3). Listen to Jeremiah, speaking to the same effect and almost in similar words: "He is like a tree that is planted by a stream of water that thrusts its roots to the stream: when the heat comes it fears not" (Jer 17:8). . . . History therefore is a garden in which we may recognize three divisions. Within its ambit we find the creation, the reconciliation, and the renewal of heaven and earth. Creation is symbolized in the sowing or planting of the garden; reconciliation by the germination of what is sown or planted. For in due course, while the heavens showered from above and the skies rained down the Just one (Is 45:8), the earth opened for a Savior to spring up, and heaven and earth were reconciled. "For he is the peace between us, and has made the two into one" (Col 1:20), making peace by his blood between all things in heaven and on earth. Renewal however is to take place at the end of the world. Then there will be "a new heaven and a new earth" (Rev 21:1), and the good will be gathered from the midst of the wicked like fruit from a garden, to be set at rest in the storehouse of God. As Scripture says: "In that day the branch of the Lord shall be beautiful and glorious, and the fruit of the land raised on high" (Is 4:2). Here you have the three aspects of time represented by the garden in the historical sense.

In its moral teaching too, three things are to be taken into account, three apartments as it were in the one storeroom. It was for this reason perhaps that she used the plural, rooms, instead of room, since she must have been thinking about these apartments. Later on she glories in being admitted to the wine-room (Song 2:4). We therefore, in accord with the advice: "Give occasion to a wise man and he will be still wiser" (Prov 9:9), take occasion from the name given by the Holy Spirit to this room, and give names to the other two: the room of spices and the room of the ointments. Afterwards we shall see the reason for these names. For the moment take note that all these possessions of the Bridegroom are wholesome and sweet: wine, ointments, and spices. . . . Rightly then the bride's happiness abounds on being admitted to a place filled to overflowing with such rich graces!

But I can give them other names, whose application seems more obvious. Taking them in due order, I name the first room discipline, the second nature, and the third grace. In the first, guided by moral principles, you discover how you are inferior to others, in the second you find the basis for equality, in the third what makes you greater; that is:

the grounds for submission, for co-operation, for authority; or if you will: to be subject, to co-exist, to preside. In the first you bear the status of learner, in the second that of companion, in the third that of master. For nature has made men equal. But since this natural moral gift was corrupted by pride, men became impatient of equal status. Driven by the urge to surpass their fellows, they spared no efforts to achieve this superiority; with an itch for vainglory and prompted by envy, they lived in mutual rivalry (Gal 5:26). Our primary task is to tame this wilfulness of character by submission to discipline in the first room, where the stubborn will, worn down by the hard and prolonged schooling of experienced mentors, is humbled and healed. The natural goodness lost by pride is recovered by obedience, and they learn, as far as in them lies, to live peacefully and sociably with all who share their nature, with all men, no longer through fear of discipline but by the impulse of love. When they pass from here into the room of nature, they discover what is written: "How good, how delightful it is to live together as one like brothers: fine as oil on the head" (Ps 132:1–2). For when morals are disciplined there comes, as to spices pounded together, the oil of gladness (Ps 44:8), the good of nature; the resulting ointment is good and sweet. The man who is anointed with it becomes pleasant and temperate, a man without a grudge, who neither swindles nor attacks nor offends another; who never exalts himself nor promotes himself at their expense (2 Cor 7:2; Lk 3:14), but offers his services as generously as he willingly accepts theirs (Phil 4:15). If you have adequately grasped the characteristics of these two rooms, I think you will admit that I have appropriately named them the spice room and the ointment room. . . .

With regard to the wine room, I do not think there is any other reason for its name than that the wine of an earnest zeal for the works of love is found there. One who has not been admitted to this room should never take charge of others. This wine should be the inspiring influence in the lives of those who bear authority, such as we find in the Teacher of the Nations, when he said: "Who is weak and I am not weak? Who is made to fall and I am not indignant?" (2 Cor 11:29). . . . I have also named this the room of grace; not because a man may enter the other two without the aid of grace but because grace is especially found here in its fullness. For "love is the fullness of the law" (Rom

13:10), and "if you love your brother you have fulfilled the law" (Rom 13:8).

The person whose character I most admire, who has attained supreme success in the way of life I have portrayed, is the one to whom it is given to sprint through or ramble round all these rooms without stumbling, who never contends with his superiors nor envies his equals, who does not fail in concern for his subjects nor use his authority arrogantly. To be obedient to superiors, obliging to one's companions, to attend with kindness to the needs of one's subjects—these sure marks of perfection I unhesitatingly attribute to the bride. We infer this from the words she speaks: "The king has brought me into his rooms" (Song 1:3), which show that she was introduced, not to any room in particular but to the whole complex of rooms.

Let us at last enter the bedroom. What can be said of it? May I presume that I know all about it? Far from me the pretension that I have experienced so sublime a grace, nor shall I boast of a privilege reserved solely to the fortunate bride. I am more concerned to know myself, as the Greek motto advises, that with the Prophet, "I may know what is wanting to me" (Ps 38:5). However, if I knew nothing at all, there is nothing I could say. What I do know I do not begrudge you or withhold from you; what I do not know may "he who teaches men knowledge" (Ps 93:10) supply to you.

You remember that I said the bedroom of the King is to be sought in the mystery of divine contemplation. In speaking of the ointments I mentioned that many varieties of them are to be found in the Bridegroom's presence, that all of them are not for everybody's use, but that each one's share differs according to his merits. So too, I feel that the King has not one bedroom only, but several. For he has more than one queen; his concubines are many, his maids beyond counting (Song 6:7). And each has her own secret rendezvous with the Bridegroom and says: "My secret to myself, my secret to myself" (Is 24:16). All do not experience the delight of the Bridegroom's private visit in the same room, the Father has different arrangements for each (Mt 20:23). For we did not choose him but he chose us and appointed places for us (Jn 15:16); and in the place of each one's appointment there he is too. Thus one repentant woman was allotted a place at the feet of the Lord Jesus (Lk 10:39); another—if she really is another—found fulfillment for her devotion at his head (Mt 26:7). Thomas attained to this mystery of grace in the Savior's side (Jn 20:27); John on his breast (Jn 13:25); Peter in the Father's bosom (Mt 16:17); Paul in the third heaven (2 Cor 12:2).

Who among us can see the difference between these various merits, or rather rewards? But in order to draw attention to what is known to us all, I suggest that the first woman took her rest on the secure ground of humility, the second on the seat of hope, Thomas in firm faith, John in the breadth of charity, Paul in the insights of wisdom, Peter in the light of truth. There are many rooms therefore in the Bridegroom's house (Jn 14:2); and each, be she queen, or concubine, or one of the bevy of maidens (Song 6:7), finds there the place and destination suited to her merits until the grace of contemplation allows her to advance further and share in the happiness of her Lord (Mt 25:21), to explore her Bridegroom's secret charms. Relying on the light it may please him to give me, I shall try to demonstrate this more clearly in its proper place. For the moment it suffices to know that no maiden, or concubine, or even queen, may gain access to the mystery of that bedroom which the Bridegroom reserves solely for her who is his dove, beautiful, perfect, and unique (Song 6:8). Hence it is not for me to take umbrage if I am not admitted there, especially since I can see that even the bride herself is at times unable to find fulfillment of her desire to know certain secrets. . . .

But I shall tell you how far I have advanced, or imagine I have advanced; and you should not accuse me of boasting, because I reveal it solely in the hope of helping you. The Bridegroom who exercises control over the whole universe has a special place from which he decrees his laws and formulates plans as guidelines in weight, measure, and number for all things created (Wis 11:20). This is a remote and secret place, but not a place of repose. For although as far as in him lies he arranges all things sweetly (Wis 8:1)—the emphasis is on arranging—the contemplative who perchance reaches that place is not allowed to rest and be quiet. In a way that is wondrous yet delightful he teases the awe-struck seeker till he reduces him to restlessness. Further on the bride beautifully describes both the delight and the restlessness of this stage of contemplation when she says that though she sleeps her heart is awake (Song 5:2). . . . This place then, where complete repose is not attainable, is not the bedroom.

There is another place from which God, the just Judge, "so much to be feared for his deeds among mankind" (Ps 65:5), watches ceaselessly with an attention that is rigorous yet hidden, over the world of fallen humanity. The awe-struck contemplative sees how, in this place, God's just but hidden judgment neither washes away the evil deeds of the wicked nor is placated by their good deeds....Who will want to rest in such a place when he sees that he, whose judgments are like the mighty deep (Ps 35:7), only spares and shows mercy to these sinners in this life that he may not do so in eternity? This kind of vision inspires a terror of judgment, not the secure confidence of the bedroom. That place is awe-inspiring (Gen 28:17), and totally devoid of quiet. I am horror-stricken when suddenly pitched into it, and over and over I think on the words: "What man knows whether he deserves love or hate?" (Eccles 9:1). . . . Do not be surprised that I have assigned the beginning of wisdom to this place and not to the first. For there we listen to Wisdom as a teacher in a lecture-hall, delivering an all-embracing discourse (1 Jn 2:27); here we receive it within us; there our minds are enlightened, here our wills are moved to decision. Instruction makes us learned, experience makes us wise. . . . And so with God: to know him is one thing, to fear him is another. . . . How truly is the fear of the Lord the beginning of wisdom (Ps 110:10), because the soul begins to experience God for the first time when fear of him takes hold of it, not when knowledge enlightens it. . . . Hence you must not look for the bedroom in these places, one of which resembles a teacher's auditorium, the other a bar of justice.

But there is a place where God is seen in tranquil rest, where he is neither Judge nor Teacher but Bridegroom. To me—for I do not speak for others—this is truly the bedroom to which I have sometimes gained happy entrance. Alas! How rare the time, and how short the stay! There one clearly realizes that "the Lord's love for those who fear him lasts forever and forever" (Ps 102:17)....

O place so truly quiet, so aptly called a bedroom where God is not encountered in angry guise nor distracted as it were by cares, but where his will is proved good and desirable and perfect (Rom 12:2). This is a vision that charms rather than terrifies; that does not arouse an inquisitive restlessness, but restrains it; that calms rather than wearies the senses. Here one may indeed be at rest. The God of peace pacifies all things, and to gaze on this stillness is to find repose. It is to catch sight of the King who, when the crowds have gone after the day-long hearing of cases in his law-courts, lays aside the burden of responsibility, goes at night to his place, and enters his bedroom with a few companions whom he welcomes to the intimacy of his private suite. . . . If it should ever happen to one of you to be enraptured and hidden away in this secret place, this sanctuary of God, safe from the call and concern of the greedy senses, from the pangs of care, the guilt of sin and the obsessive fancies of the imagination so much more difficult to hold at bay—such a person, when he returns to us again, may well boast and tell us: "The King has brought me into his bedroom." Whether this be the same room that makes the bride so jubilant I do not dare to affirm. But it is a bedroom, the bedroom of the King, and of the three that I have described in the three visions, it is the only place where peace reigns (Ps 75:3). . . .

From Bernard of Clairvaux, *The Works of Bernard of Clairvaux. On the Song of Songs II*, translated by Kilian Walsh. Copyright 1976 by Cistercian Publications, Inc., Kalamazoo, Michigan. All rights reserved.

MEISTER ECKHART

SERMON 2

Meister Eckhart (circa 1260–1328), the noted Dominican preacher, was also a scriptural mystic. Almost all of Eckhart's technical scholastic writings that provide the foundation for his mysticism are biblical commentaries. His vernacular mystical teaching, aside from a few treatises, is given in the approximately 120 surviving sermons preached on Bible texts found in the liturgy. Eckhart's exegesis, however, is unusual even by medieval standards, since he believed that the "excessive" or "saturated" nature of God's overflowing and inexhaustible word invited the interpreter and listener not only to read the hidden message within, but even to "break through" all images in the text to reach the divine source and then re-create the text from the perspective of the unity of God and human. This explains Eckhart's exegetical boldness in interpreting the biblical passages he preached upon.

A good example of this procedure can be found in the following sermon in which the Dominican reinterprets the opening verse of Luke's Gospel text for the Feast of the Assumption to show how it reveals fundamental themes of his mystical teaching. Eckhart plays with three aspects of Luke 10:38. First, the Latin text says that Jesus was received by a "woman," but Eckhart changes this into the paradoxical expression "a virgin who was a wife," thus enabling him in the first part of the sermon to present his teaching that it is only by becoming a "virgin," that is, empty of all images and perfectly detached from created things, that we can pass to the higher stage of being a "wife"—a soul constantly bearing God in fruitfulness. Eckhart reinforces this point by employing the German verb enpfangen—*which can mean both "received" and "conceived"—to translate the Latin* excepit *(received). Therefore, the soul that "receives" God correctly (i.e., as a virgin) actually "conceives" God through becoming one with the eternal birth of the Word from the Father. Finally, Eckhart interprets the town, or citadel, into which the virgin mother receives Jesus as the hidden inner power that he elsewhere calls the "ground" (*grunt*), the mysterious inner reality, beyond both intellect and will, where we become one with God without distinction. For Eckhart the one ground lies beyond even the three persons in the Trinity.*

———

"Intravit Jesus in quoddam castellum et mulier quaedam excepit illum" (Lk 10:38). I have first quoted this saying in Latin, it is written in the Gospel and in German it means: "Our Lord Jesus Christ went up into a citadel and was received/conceived by a virgin who was a wife."

Now mark this word carefully. It must of necessity be a virgin, the person by whom Jesus was received. "Virgin" is as much as to say a person who is void of alien images, as empty as he was when he did not exist. Now the question may be asked, how a man who has been born and has reached the age of rational understanding can be as empty of all images as he was when he was not; for he knows many things, all of which are images: so how can he be empty of them? Note the explanation which I shall give you. If I were possessed of sufficient understanding so as to comprehend within my own mind all the images ever conceived by all men, as well as those that exist in God Himself—if I had these without attachment, whether in doing or in leaving undone, without before and after but rather standing free in this present now ready to receive God's most beloved will and to do it continually, then in truth I would be a virgin, untrammeled by any images, just as I was when I was not.

And yet I say that being a virgin by no means deprives a man of works that he has done: he yet remains virgin-free, offering no hindrance to the highest Truth, even as Jesus is empty and free and virginal in himself. Since according to the masters union comes only by the joining of like to like, therefore that man must be a maiden, a virgin, who would receive the virgin Jesus.

Now attend, and follow me closely. If a man were to be ever virginal, he would bear no fruit. If he is to be fruitful, he must needs be a wife. "Wife" is the noblest title one can bestow on the soul—far nobler than "virgin." For a man to receive God within him is good, and in receiving he is virgin. But for God to be fruitful in him is better, for only the fruitfulness of the gift is the thanks rendered for that gift, and herein the spirit is a wife, whose gratitude is fecundity, bearing Jesus again in God's paternal Heart.

Many good gifts, received in virginity, are not reborn back into God in wifely fruitfulness and with praise and thanks. Such gifts perish and all comes to naught, and a man is no more blessed or the better for them. In this case his virginity is useless because to that virginity he does not add the perfect fruitfulness of a wife. Therein lies the mischief. Hence I have said, "Jesus went up into a citadel and was received by a virgin who was a wife." It must be thus, as I have shown you.

Married folk bring forth little more than one fruit in a year. But it is other wedded folk that I have in mind now: all those who are bound with attachment to prayer, fasting, vigils and all kinds of outward discipline and mortification. All attachment to any work that involves the loss of freedom to wait on God in the here and now, and to follow him alone in the light wherein he would show you what to do and what not to do, every moment freely and anew, as if you had nothing else and neither would nor could do otherwise—any such attachment or set practice which repeatedly denies you this freedom, I call a year; for your soul will bear no fruit till it has done this work to which you are possessively attached, and you too will have no trust in God or in yourself before you have done the work you embraced with attachment, for otherwise you will have no peace. Thus you will bring forth no fruit till your work is done. That is what I call "a year," and the fruit of it is paltry because it springs from attachment to the task and not from freedom. These, then, I call "wedded folk," for they are bound by attachment. They bring forth little fruit, and paltry at that, as I have said.

A virgin who is a wife, is free and unfettered by attachment; she is always as near to God as to herself. She brings forth many and big fruits, for they are neither more nor less than God Himself. This fruit and this birth that virgin bears who is a wife, bringing forth daily a hundred and a thousandfold! Numberless indeed are her labors begotten of the most noble ground or, to speak more truly, of the very ground where the Father ever begets His eternal Word: it is thence she becomes fruitful and shares in the procreation. For Jesus, the light and splendor of the eternal heart, as St. Paul says (Heb 1:3), that he is the glory and splendor of the Father's heart and illumines the Father's heart with power, this same Jesus is made one with her and she with him; she is radiant and shining with him in one single unity, as one pure brilliant light in the paternal heart.

Elsewhere I have declared that there is a power in the soul [i.e., intellect] which touches neither time nor flesh, flowing from the spirit, remaining in the spirit, altogether spiritual. In this power, God is ever verdant and flowering in all the joy and all the glory that He is in Himself. There is such heartfelt delight, such inconceivably deep joy as none can fully tell of, for in this power the eternal Father is ever begetting his eternal Son without pause, in such wise that this power jointly begets the Father's Son and itself, this self-same Son, in the sole power of the Father. Suppose a man owned a whole kingdom or all the goods of this world; then suppose he gave it up purely for God's sake, and became one of the poorest of the poor who ever lived on earth, and that God then gave him as much suffering as he ever imposed on any man, and that he bore all this to his dying day, and that God then gave him one fleeting glimpse of how he is in this power—that man's joy would be so great that all this suffering and poverty would still be insignificant. Yea, though God were never to vouchsafe him any further taste of heaven than this, he would yet be all too richly rewarded for all that he had ever endured, for God is in this power as in the eternal now. If a man's spirit were always united with God in this power, he would not age. For the now in which God made the first man and the now in which the last man shall cease to be, and the now I speak in, all are the same in God and there is but one now. Observe, this man dwells in one light with God, having no suffering and no sequence of time, but one equal eternity. This man is bereft of wonderment and all things are in him in their essence. Therefore nothing new comes to him from future things nor any accident, for he dwells in the now, ever new and without intermission. Such is the divine sovereignty dwelling in this power.

There is another power [i.e., will], immaterial too, flowing from the spirit, remaining in the spirit, altogether spiritual. In this power God is fiery, aglow with all his riches, with all his sweetness and all his bliss. Truly, in this power there is such great joy, such vast unmeasured bliss that none can tell of it or reveal it fully. Yet I declare that if ever there were a single person who in intellectual vision and in truth should glimpse for a moment the bliss and the joy therein, all his sufferings and all God intended that he should suffer would be a trifle, a mere nothing to him—in fact I declare it would be pure joy and comfort to him.

If you would know for certain whether your suffering is your own or God's, then you can know by this: If you suffer for yourself, in whatever way, that suffering hurts and is hard to bear. But if you suffer for God and God alone, your suffering does not hurt and is not hard to bear, for God bears the load. In very truth, if there were a person willing to suffer purely for God's sake and for God alone, then although he were suddenly called upon to bear all the suffering that all men have ever endured, the collective sufferings of all the world, it would not hurt him or bear him down, for God would bear the burden. If they put a hundredweight burden on my neck and another were to bear it on my neck, I would as willingly bear a hundred pounds as one, for it would not burden me or cause me pain. In brief, whatever a man suffers for God and God alone, God makes light and pleasant. As I said in the beginning, in the opening words of this sermon: "Jesus went up into a citadel and was received by a virgin who was a wife." Why? It had to be so, that she was a virgin and a wife. Now I have told you that Jesus was received, but I have not yet told you what the citadel is, as I shall now proceed to do.

I have sometimes said that there is a power in the soul which alone is free. Sometimes I have called it the guardian of the spirit, sometimes I have called it a light of the spirit, sometimes I have said that it is a little spark. But now I say that it is neither this nor that; and yet it is a something that is more exalted over "this" and "that" than are the heavens above the earth. So now I shall name it in nobler fashion than I ever did before, and yet it disowns the nobler name and mode, for it transcends them. It is free of all names and void of all forms, entirely exempt and free, as God is exempt and free in himself. It is as completely one and simple as God is one and simple, so that no man can in any way glimpse it. This same power of which I have spoken, wherein God ever blooms and is verdant in all his Godhead, and the spirit in God, in this same power God ever bears his only-begotten Son as truly as in himself, for truly he dwells in this power, and the spirit gives birth with the Father to the same only-begotten Son, and to itself as the self-same Son, and is itself the self-same Son in this light, and is the Truth. If you could know with my heart, you would understand, for it is true, and Truth itself declares it.

Now pay attention! So one and simple is this citadel in the soul, elevated above all modes, of which I speak and which I mean, that that noble power I mentioned [i.e., intellect] is not worthy even for an instant to cast a single glance into this citadel; nor is that other power I spoke of [i.e., will], in which God burns and glows with all his riches and all his joy, able to cast a single glance inside; so truly one and simple is this citadel, so mode- and power-transcending is this solitary One, that neither power nor mode can gaze into it, nor even God himself! In very truth and as God lives! God himself never looks in there for one instant, in so far as he exists in modes and in the properties of his persons. This should be well noted: this Single One [German: *einic ein*] lacks all mode and property. And therefore, for God to see inside it would cost him all His divine names and personal properties: all these he must leave outside, should he ever look in there. But only in so far as he is one and indivisible, without mode or properties (can he do this): in that sense he is neither Father, Son, nor Holy Spirit, and yet is a something which is neither this nor that.

See, as he is thus one and simple, so he can enter that One that I here call the citadel of the soul, but in no other mode can he get in: only thus does he enter and dwell therein. In this part the soul is the same as God and not otherwise. What I tell you is true: I call the Truth as a witness and offer my soul as pledge.

That we may be such a citadel to which Jesus may ascend and be received to abide eternally in us in such wise as I have said, may God help us to this! Amen.

From *Meister Eckhart. Sermons and Treatises. Vol. I*, 71–78, translated by M. O'C. Walshe. Copyright 1979. Reprinted by permission of The English Sangha Trust, Amaravati Buddhist Monastery. Walshe, following the edition of Franz Pfeiffer, numbers this as sermon 8, but in the German critical edition it is sermon 2.

MADAME GUYON
COMMENTARY ON THE SONG OF SONGS

*Madame Guyon (Jeanne Bouvier de la Motte Guyon, 1648–1717) is a contro-
versial figure due to her condemnation as a Quietist (i.e., someone who teaches
complete passivity to God's action, even to the point of not wishing to be saved).
Even for those who view the Quietist condemnations (see section 14.4) as an unfortunate repression of mystical piety, Guyon's excessive claims for her own status
as a totally annihilated mystic have continued to raise questions.*

*Despite the debates about Guyon, her writings reflect the continuing impor-
tance of the Bible among later figures in Christian mysticism. Women by definition could not be professional exegetes, because academic theological training was
closed to them. Nevertheless, many female mystics knew the Bible well, cited it
often, and, without composing formal commentaries, included much commmen-
tarial material in their writings. A few women mystics even wrote commentaries
on the Song of Songs, the text that was so central to the mystical tradition. About
1566 Teresa of Avila composed a series of meditations on the Song, but her confessor commanded her to destroy them; they survive only in part. The Ursuline
nun Marie of the Incarnation speaks of interpreting the Song of Songs for her
fellow sisters in 1633.*

*Madame Guyon, after experiencing a conversion to the mystical life in 1680,
spent time in 1682–83 at the convent of Thonon near Lake Geneva. Here she
embarked on an exposition of the whole Bible—an astonishing undertaking for
a woman. Guyon claimed that she wrote her commentary on the Song of Songs,
the first full exposition by a woman, in a day and a half. The book gave her the*

opportunity to set forth many of the central themes of her mysticism, such as the modes of union with God, the mystic's annihilation, the way that full union provides access to the "apostolic life," and the indifference to hope for any reward from God that was seen as one of the dangers of Quietism.

I.

CHAPTER 1:1: "LET HIM KISS ME WITH THE KISS OF THE MOUTH."

The kiss which the soul desires of its God is essential union, or a real, permanent and lasting possession of its divine object. It is the spiritual marriage. That this may be understood, it is necessary to explain the difference between a union of the powers and essential union. Either of them may be transitory, and for a few moments only, or permanent and lasting.

The union of the powers is that by which God unites the soul to himself, but very superficially; it is more properly a touch than a union. It is nevertheless united to the Trinity of persons according to the different effects proper to the individual persons.... This union is accomplished in order, in all the powers of the soul, and is sometimes perceived in one or two of them according to the designs of God, and at other times in all three together. This constitutes the application of the soul to the Holy Trinity according to the distinct persons. When the union is in the understanding alone, it is a union of pure intellect and is attributed to the Word as a distinct person. When the union is in the memory, which is effected by an absorption of the soul into God and a profound forgetfulness of the creature, it is attributed to the Father as a distinct person. And when it takes place in the will alone by a loving joy without sight or knowledge of anything distinct, it is a union of love and is attributed to the Holy Spirit as a distinct person. This last is the most perfect of all, because it approaches nearer than any other to essential union, and is generally the road by which the soul arrives at it. All these unions are divine embraces—but they are not the kiss of his mouth.

These unions are of two sorts: one transitory and very short lived, the other permanent and sustained by the perpetual presence of God, and a sweet and tranquil love which continues in the midst of everything. Such, in a few words, is the union of the powers which is a union of betrothal. It implies the affection of the heart, caresses and mutual presents, as is the case with the betrothed, but not the full enjoyment of its object.

Essential union and the kiss of his mouth is the spiritual marriage, where there is a union of essence with essence and a communication of substance—where God takes the soul for a spouse and unites himself to it, no longer by way of the persons of the Trinity, nor by any act or means, but immediately by reducing all into unity and by possessing it in his own unity. Then it is the kiss of his mouth, and real and perfect possession. It is an enjoyment which is neither barren nor unfruitful, since it extends to nothing less than the communication of the Word of God to the soul.

We must remember that God is all mouth, as he is all word, and that the application of this divine mouth to the soul is the perfect enjoyment and consummation of the marriage by which the communication of God himself and of his Word is made to the soul. This is what may be called the apostolic state, in which the soul is not only espoused but also fruitful, for God as mouth is some time united to the soul before rendering it fruitful by his own fecundity. There are some who maintain that this union cannot take place until the next life; but I am confident that it may be attained in this life, with the reservation that here we possess without seeing, there we shall behold what we possess.

II.
CHAPTER 6:4: "TURN AWAY YOUR EYES FROM ME, BECAUSE THEY HAVE MADE ME TO FLEE AWAY; YOUR HAIR IS AS A FLOCK OF GOATS THAT APPEAR FROM GILEAD"

It is impossible to conceive the delicacy of the love of God and the extremity of purity which he requires of souls that are to be his brides; the perfection of one state is the imperfection of another. Heretofore the Bridegroom rejoiced infinitely that his spouse never turned her eyes away from him; now he desires her not to look at him. He tells her that her eyes have made him to flee away. When once the soul has begun to flow into her God, like a river into its original source, she must be wholly submerged and lost in him. She must then lose the perceptible vision of God and every distinct knowledge, however small it may be. Sight and knowledge exist no longer where there is neither division nor distinction, but a perfect fusion. The creature in this state cannot look at God without beholding herself and perceiving at the same time the working of his love. Now, the whole of this must be concealed and hidden away from her sight, so that like the Seraphim she may have her eyes veiled (Is 6:2), and may never see anything more in this life. That is, she is not to will to see anything or to make any discoveries of herself, which she cannot do without infidelity [to God]. But this is no hindrance to God's causing her to discover and understand whatever he pleases. Nothing remains uncovered but the heart, for it is impossible to love too much.

When I speak of distinction, I do not mean the distinction of some divine perfection in God himself, for that is gone long since; for since the first absorption the soul has had but a single view of God in herself by a confused and general faith with no distinction of attributes or perfections. And though she has often spoken of the greatness and sovereign qualities of her Well-beloved, it was only done for the purpose of winning souls, and not for any need in herself of these distinct views which are given her according to necessity, either in speaking or writing. The distinction I now refer to is that between God and the soul. Here the soul cannot and ought not any longer to make such a distinction; God is she and she is God, since by the consummation of the marriage she is absorbed into God and lost in him without power to distinguish or find herself again. The true consummation of the marriage causes an admixture of the soul with God so great and so intimate that she can distinguish and see herself no longer; and it is this fusion that divinizes, so to speak, the actions of the creature arrived at this lofty and sublime position, for they emanate from a principle which is wholly divine in consequence of the unity which has been effected between God and the soul melted and absorbed in him, God becoming the principle of her actions and words, though they are spoken and manifested externally through her.

The marriage of the body whereby two persons are rendered one flesh (Gen 2:24) is but a faint image of this, by which, in the words of St. Paul, God and the soul become one spirit (1 Cor 6:17). Many are exceedingly anxious to know when the spiritual marriage takes place. It is easy to ascertain this from what has been said. The betrothal, or the mutual engagement, is made in the union of the powers when the soul surrenders herself wholly to God and God gives himself wholly to the soul with the intention of admitting her to union. This is an agreement and mutual promise. But ah!, what a distance is yet to be traveled and what sufferings to be undergone before this eagerly desired union can be granted or consummated! The marriage takes place when the soul falls dead and senseless into the arms of the Bridegroom, who, beholding her more fitted for it, receives her into union. But the consummation of the marriage does not come to pass until the soul is so melted, annihilated, and freed from self that it can unreservedly flow into God. Then is accomplished that admirable fusion of the creature and the Creator which brings them into unity, so to speak, though with such an infinite disproportion as exists between a single drop of water and the ocean. The drop has become ocean, but it forever remains a little drop, though it has become assimilated in character with the waters of the ocean and thus fit to be mingled with it and to make but one ocean with it.

III.
CHAPTER 8:14: "FLEE AWAY, MY BELOVED, AND BE LIKE TO THE ROE OR TO THE YOUNG HART UPON THE MOUNTAINS OF SPICES"

. . .The soul, arrived at this point, enters so fully into the interests of Divine Righteousness, both in respect to herself and others, that she can desire no other fate for herself, nor for any other, than that which the Divine Righteousness would allot, both for time and eternity. She has at the same time a more perfect charity than ever before for her neighbor, serving him now for God only and in the will of God. But though she is always ready to be cursed for her brethren, like St. Paul (Rom 9:3), and is incessantly laboring for no other end than their salvation, she is nevertheless indifferent as to her success. She would not be afflicted either at her own damnation or at that of any other creature, regarded from the point of view of God's Righteousness. What she cannot bear is that God should be dishonored, because he has set love in order in her (Song 2:4). Since then she has entered into the purest affections of perfect charity.

... She has no more to do with sighing for seasons of distinct and conscious enjoyment; and, besides, she is in such an absolute state of abandonment as to everything that she could not fasten a desire of any kind upon anything whatever, not even upon the delights of Paradise. This state is the evidence that she is possessed at the center [of the soul]. This is why she here testifies to the Bridegroom that she is satisfied he should go where he pleases, visit other hearts, gain them, purify them, and perfect them in all the mountains and hills of the church. He should take his delight in the "souls of spices" embalmed in grace and virtue. But, for herself, she has nothing to ask or desire of him except he himself be the author of the emotion. Does she therefore despise or reject the divine visits and consolations? Not at all; she has too much respect and submission for the work of God to do that. It is just that such graces are no longer adapted to her state, annihilated as she is and established in the enjoyment of the center. Having lost all her will in the will of God, she can no longer will anything. This is beautifully expressed in this pleasant figure: "Flee away, my beloved, and be like to the roe and to the young hart upon the mountains of spices."

So great is the indifference of this soul that she cannot lean either to the side of enjoyment or deprivation. Death and life are equally acceptable. Although her love is incomparably stronger than it ever was before, she cannot, nevertheless, desire Paradise because she remains in the hands of her Bridegroom, as among the things that do not exist. Such is the effect of the deepest annihilation.

Translation by James W. Metcalf in *The Song of Songs of Solomon with Explanations and Reflections Having Reference to the Interior Life by Madame Guyon* (New York: A. W. Dennett, 1879), 23–25, 100–2, 128–31.

ASCETICISM AND PURGATION

The term *asceticism* is derived from the Greek word *askêsis,* which originally meant any kind of serious physical training, such as that practiced by athletes. Beginning in the patristic period, Christians began to use the word in relation to the practices of self-denial and preparation for a more intense religious life. Various forms of self-denial of bodily pleasure, especially of food, sex, sleep, and possessions, seen as ways of training and preparation for contact with the divine, are common to many religious traditions. The broad diffusion of such practices argues that they play an essential role in the religious dimension of humanity, but this role is largely an instrumental one in the sense that asceticism is usually a means to an end rather than the goal itself.

Although not all forms of Christian asceticism are related to the search for more direct contact with God, within the Christian mystical tradition asceticism does play an important role. Asceticism is seen as a necessary, if not sufficient, preparation for mystical grace. The need for asceticism is rooted in two aspects of Christian belief. The first is the fact of sin, both the sin inherited from Adam and Eve (original sin) as well as the actual sins committed by each person during his or her life. Exterior and interior "training" was seen as necessary to restore the balance and harmony that God had intended, insofar as this is possible in the lapsed condition. The second and deeper root of ascetical practice is perhaps better expressed by the word *purgation.* The divine nature in its majesty, goodness, and purity is so far removed from the imperfect world that for any created being to dare to approach God implies a purification that goes beyond just overcoming the effects of sin. In this sense purgation of the exterior and interior person is not just preparation, but becomes something like an essential condition for anyone who seeks God in this life.

The most detailed programs of asceticism are connected with the rise of specialized forms of religious life, beginning with the desert monastics in the fourth century. Monastic asceticism was the foundation for much that came later, but subsequent types of religious life, such as those practiced by the friars and beguines of the thirteenth century, added complexity to the story of asceticism. Many of these forms of asceticism continue in contemporary Christianity. Others were too culture-bound to have much meaning today. Some were considered questionable, even bizarre, in their own time. The feats of asceticism ascribed to some saints are often examples of hagiographical exaggeration that were not meant to be taken literally. Nevertheless, asceticism, real and imagined, is integral to understanding mysticism.

The five selections given here present some highlights of the relation between asceticism and mysticism. The first two texts, one by Athanasius of Alexandria dating from about the middle of the fourth century, the other by Evagrius Ponticus written toward the end of the century, represent the monastic foundation of asceticism. The third selection is a classic account of the at times extreme asceticism of one of the early beguines. Finally, two selections from famous early-modern mystics, Catherine of Genoa and John of the Cross, develop the motif of purgation, the ontological root of ascetical effort.

1.

ATHANASIUS OF ALEXANDRIA
THE LIFE OF ST. ANTONY

Hagiography, or the writing of lives of the saints, was among the earliest and most important ways of communicating models for the pursuit of God. Accounts of the Christian martyrs, beginning as early as the second half of the second century, witness to how these holy men and women found God in their ultimate devotion to Jesus as Lord and Savior. By the time of the peace of the church under the emperor Constantine in 313 CE, the age of the martyrs was over and a new model of sanctity began to emerge—the monachos, *solitary one. The roots of monasticism go back to the desert experience of biblical figures such as Moses, Elijah, and John the Baptist. From as early as the second century CE there were loosely organized groups of ascetics in the Christian East. The ascetical practices and virginal lifestyle of these "proto-monastics" were transformed toward the end of the third century when some ascetics began the practice of* anachôrêsis, *that is, withdrawal from society into the desert. This separation was not only geographical but also spiritual in the sense that the desert was both the abode of the demons who must be overcome for the soul to make progress, as well as the place where God can be found by the purified soul.*

The most significant of the early monks was Antony of Egypt (circa 250–356), whose life, written by Athanasius of Alexandria, became an international best seller and remains one of the most influential of all hagiographies. The Life of Antony presents an itinerary of conversion, withdrawal, ascetic purgation, and spiritual transformation. The first fourteen chapters excerpted here tell the story of Antony's transformation into "the father of monks." The longer second part (chapters 15–94) illustrates Antony's wisdom and miraculous powers. Athanasius' achievement was the masterful way in which he showed the relation of ascetic preparation and mystical fulfillment.

I.
ANTONY'S CALL AND HIS FIRST STEPS
IN ASCETICISM (CHAPTERS 2-4)

Upon his parents' death he was left alone with an only sister who was very young. He was about eighteen or twenty years old at the time and took care of the house and his sister. Less than six months had passed since his parents' death when, as usual, he chanced to be on his way to church. As he was walking along, he collected his thoughts and reflected how the Apostles left everything and followed the Savior (Mt 4:20, 19:27); also how the people in Acts sold what they had and laid it [the money] at the feet of the Apostles for distribution among the needy (Acts 4:35–37); and what great hope is laid up in heaven for such as these (Eph 1:18; Col 1:5). With these thoughts in his mind he entered the church. And it so happened that the gospel was being read at that moment and he heard the passage in which the Lord says to the rich man: "If you will be perfect, go sell all that you have, and give it to the poor; and come, follow me and you shall have treasure in heaven" (Mt 19:21). As though God had put him in mind of the saints and as though the reading had been directed especially to him, Antony immediately left the church and gave to the townspeople the property he had from his forebears—two hundred and seven acres, very fertile and beautiful to see. He did not want it to encumber him or his sister in any way whatever. He sold all the rest, the chattels they had, and gave the tidy sum he received to the poor, keeping back only a little for his sister.

But once again as he entered the church, he heard the Lord saying in the Gospel: "Do not be solicitous about tomorrow" (Mt 6:34). He could not bear to wait longer, but went out and distributed those things also to the poor. His sister he placed with known and trusted virgins, giving her to the nuns to be brought up. Then he himself devoted all his time to ascetic living, intent on himself and living a life of self-denial, near his own house. For there were not yet so many monasteries in Egypt, and no monk even knew of the faraway desert. Whoever wished to concern himself with his own destiny practiced asceticism by himself not far from his own village.

Now, at that time there was in the next village an old man who had lived the ascetic life in solitude from his youth. When Antony saw him, he was "zealous for that which is good" (Gal 4:18), and he promptly began to stay in the vicinity of the town. Then, if he heard of a zealous soul anywhere, like a wise bee he left to search him out, nor did he return home before he had seen him; and only when he had received from him, as it were, provisions for his journey to virtue, did he go back.

There, then, he spent the time of his initiation and made good his determination not to return to the house of his fathers nor to think about his relatives, but to devote all his affections and all his energy to the continued practice of the ascetic life. He did manual labor, for he had heard that "he that is lazy, neither let him eat" (2 Thess 3:10). Some of his earnings he spent for bread and some he gave to the poor. He prayed constantly, having learned that we must pray in private (Mt 6:6) and without cease (Lk 18:1). Again, he was so attentive at the reading of the scripture lessons that nothing escaped him: he retained everything and so his memory served him in place of books.

Thus lived Antony and he was loved by all. He, in turn, subjected himself in all sincerity to the pious men whom he visited and made it his endeavor to learn for his own benefit just how each was superior to him in zeal and ascetic practice. He observed the graciousness of one, the earnestness at prayer in another; studied the even temper of one and the kindheartedness of another; fixed his attention on the vigils kept by one and on the studies pursued by another; admired one for his patient endurance, another for his fasting and sleeping on the ground; watched closely this man's meekness and the forbearance shown by another; and in one and all alike he marked especially devotion to Christ and the love they had one for another.

II.
ANTONY'S GROWING ASCETICISM
(CHAPTER 7)

... He resolved, therefore, to accustom himself to a more austere way of life. And many marveled at him, but he bore the life easily. The zeal that had pervaded his soul over a long time had effected a good frame of mind in him, with the result that even a slight inspiration received from others caused him to respond with great enthusiasm. For instance, he kept nocturnal vigil with such determination that he often spent the entire night sleepless, and this not only once, but many times to their admiration. Again, he ate but once a day, after sunset; indeed, sometimes only every other day, and frequently only every fourth day did he partake of food. His food was bread and salt; his drink, water only. Meat and wine we need not even mention, for no such thing could be found with the other ascetics either. He was content to sleep on a rush mat, though as a rule he lay down on the bare ground. He deprecated the use of oil for the skin, saying that young men should practice asceticism in real earnest and not go for the things that enervate the body; rather they should accustom it to hard work, bearing in mind the words of the Apostle: "When I am weak, then I am powerful" (2 Cor 12:10). It was a dictum of his that the soul's energy thrives when the body's desires are feeblest.

III.
ANTONY'S WITHDRAWAL INTO
THE DESERT AND TWENTY YEARS
IN THE FORT (CHAPTERS 11-14)

On the next day he went out, inspired with an even greater zeal for the service of God. He met the old man referred to above [the ascetic who helped train him] and begged him to live with him in the desert. The other declined because of his age and because such a mode of life was not yet the custom. So he at once set out for the mountain by himself [Pispir, on the eastern bank of the Nile]....

So, having grown stronger and stronger in his purpose, he hurried to the mountain. On the far side of the river he found a deserted fort which in the course of time had become infested with creeping things. There he settled down to live. The reptiles, as though someone were chasing them, left at once. He blocked up the entrance, having laid in bread for six months—this the Thebans do and often loaves keep fresh for a whole year—and with water in the place, he disappeared as in a shrine. He remained there alone, never going forth and never seeing anyone pass by. For a long time he persisted in this practice of asceticism; only twice a year he received bread from the house above.

His acquaintances who came to see him often spent days and nights outside, since he would not let them come in. They heard what sounded like riotous crowds inside making noises, raising a tumult, wailing piteously and shrieking: "Get out of our domain! What business have you in the desert? You cannot hold out against our persecution." At first those outside thought there were men fighting with him and that they had entered in by means of ladders, but as they peered through a hole and saw no one, they realized that demons were involved; and filled with fear, they called out to Antony. But he was more concerned over hearing them than to pay any attention to the demons. Going close to the door he suggested to them to leave and to have no fear. "It is only against the timid," he said, "that the demons conjure up spectres. You, now, sign yourselves and go home unafraid, and leave them to make fools of themselves."

So they departed, fortified by the sign of the cross, while he remained without suffering any harm whatsoever from them. Nor did he grow weary of the contest, for the assistance given him through visions coming to him from on high, and the weakness of his enemies brought him great relief in his hardships and gave him the stamina for greater zeal. His friends would come again and again, expecting, of course, to find him dead; but they heard him singing: "Let God arise and let his enemies be scattered; and let them that hate him flee from before his face. As smoke vanishes, so let them vanish away; as wax melts before the fire, so let the sinners perish before the face of God" (Ps 67:2). And again: "All nations compassed me about; and in the name of the Lord I drove them off" (Ps 117:10).

So he spent nearly twenty years practicing the ascetic life by himself, never going out and seldom seen by others. After this, as there were many who longed and sought to imitate his holy life and some of his friends came and forcefully broke down the door and removed it, Antony came forth as out of a shrine, as one initiated into sacred mysteries and filled with the spirit of God. It was the first time that he showed himself outside the fort to those who came to him. When they saw him, they were astonished to see that his body had kept its former appearance, that it was neither obese from want of exercise, nor emaciated from his fastings and struggles with the demons: he was the same man they had known before his retirement. Again, the state of his soul was pure, for it was neither contracted by grief, nor dissipated by pleasure nor pervaded by jollity or dejection. He was not embarrassed when he saw the crowd, nor was he elated at seeing so many there to receive him. No, he had himself completely under control—a man guided by reason and stable in his character. Through him the Lord cured many of those present who were afflicted with bodily ills, and freed others from impure spirits. He also gave Antony charm in speaking; and so he comforted many in sorrow, and others who were quarreling he made friends. He exhorted all to prefer nothing in the world to the love of Christ. And when in his discourse he exhorted them to be mindful of the good things to come and of the goodness shown us by God, "who spared not his only Son, but delivered him up for us all" (Rom 8:32), he induced many to take up the monastic life. And so now monasteries also sprang up in the mountains and the desert was populated with monks who left their own people and registered themselves for citizenship in Heaven.

Translated by Robert T. Meyer, *St. Athanasius. The Life of St. Antony* (New York: Paulist Press, 1950. Ancient Christian Writers), 19–21, 25, 30–33. Used with permission.

2.

EVAGRIUS PONTICUS
PRAKTIKOS

Christian asceticism is rooted in Gospel texts, such as Christ's statement, "If you wish to be perfect, go and sell your possessions and give the money to the poor, and you will have treasure in heaven; then come, follow me" (Mt 19:21). Voluntary poverty and chastity, forms of self-denial like restriction of food and drink, and other ascetical practices were inculcated by Christian texts from the beginning. Ascetical practice of a more rigorous and formal character, however, was connected with the rise of the monastic movement. Early monastic leaders were depicted as great ascetics, and their sayings about practices of self-denial were passed on by their followers.

Toward the end of the fourth century Evagrius Ponticus, a learned courtier and deacon who became a monk, organized the ascetical and contemplative teaching of the Desert Fathers into a systematic theology based on Origen. Evagrius saw progress in theology (i.e., in the life of prayer) as consisting of three interdependent stages. First comes the ascetical life (praktikê) in which the soul struggles against vices and acquires the virtues that lead it to the state of spiritual and emotional tranquility that Evagrius called apatheia *(freedom from disturbing passion). Evagrius was the first to specify eight evil or passionate thoughts or tendencies that block the way to God—gluttony, impurity, avarice, sadness, anger, akêdia (spiritual restlessness), vainglory, and pride. (These are the ancestors of the later seven deadly sins.) As these evil tendencies and the demons who foster them are gradually overcome through asceticism, the three parts of the soul—the concupiscible (power of desire), the irascible (power of rejection), and the rational—are cleansed of the effects of sin and the person attains* apatheia, *which in turn gives birth to love (*agapê*). Then the monk is prepared for the two stages of the contemplative life of* theôria: *first the contemplation of the created universe, and then the higher and endless contemplation of the mystery of the Trinity.*

Evagrius conveyed his teaching not in formal treatises, but by means of collections of longer or shorter "chapters," or aphorisms, meant to be studied in the meditative exercise so beloved of the monks. His Praktikos *consists of a hundred chapters on the ascetical life and was meant to form the first part of the trilogy that also contained the* Gnostikos *(fifty chapters on contemplation and spiritual knowledge) and the long* Kephalaia Gnostica *(six collections of ninety chapters each dealing with the contemplation of the Trinity).*

THE HUNDRED CHAPTERS

1. Christianity is the dogma of Christ our Savior. It is composed of *praktikê* [i.e., the ascetical life], of the contemplation [*theôria*] of the physical world, and of the contemplation of God.

2. The Kingdom of Heaven is *apatheia* of the soul along with true knowledge of existing things.

3. The Kingdom of Heaven is knowledge of the Holy Trinity coextensive with the capacity of the intelligence and giving it a surpassing incorruptibility.

[Nos. 6–14 introduce the eight kinds of passionate thoughts.]

[Nos. 15–39 give advice about how to overcome the eight passionate thoughts.]

15. Reading, vigils and prayer—these are the things that lend stability to the wandering mind. Hunger, toil and solitude are the means of extinguishing the flames of desire. Turbid anger is calmed by the singing of Psalms, by patience, and almsgiving. But all these practices are to be engaged in according to due measure and at the appropriate times. What is untimely done, or done without measure, endures but a short time. And what is short lived is more harmful than profitable.

[Nos. 40–56 are instructions about the monastic life.]

52. To separate the body from the soul is the privilege only of the One who has joined them together. But to separate the soul from the body lies as well in the power of the person who pursues virtue. For our Fathers gave to the meditation on death and to the flight from the body a special name: *anachôrêsis.*

[Nos. 57–90 deal with the state bordering on *apatheia* and with the signs of *apatheia* itself.]

60. Perfect purity of heart develops in the soul after the victory over all the demons whose function it is to offer opposition to the ascetic life. But there is designated an imperfect purity of heart in consideration of the power of the demon that meantime fights against it.

63. When the spirit begins to be free from all distractions as it makes its prayer then there commences an all-out battle day and night against the irascible part.

64. The proof of *apatheia* is had when the spirit begins to see its own light, when it remains in a state of tranquility in the presence of the images it has during sleep, and when it maintains its calm as it beholds the affairs of life.

65. The spirit that possesses health is the one which has no images of the things of this world at the time of prayer.

78. The ascetic life is the spiritual method for cleansing the affective part of the soul.

79. The effects of keeping the commandments do not suffice to heal the powers of the soul completely. They must be complemented by a contemplative activity appropriate to these faculties and they must penetrate the spirit.

81. *Agapê* [i.e., love] is the progeny of *apatheia. Apatheia* is the very flower of *askêsis. Askêsis* consists in keeping the commandments. The custodian of these commandments is the fear of God which is in turn the offspring of true faith. . . .

83. The spirit that is engaged in the war against the passions does not see clearly the basic meaning of the war for it is something like

a man fighting in the darkness of night. Once it has attained to purity of heart though, it distinctly makes out the designs of the enemy.

84. The goal of the ascetic life is charity; the goal of contemplative knowledge is theology. The beginnings of each are faith and contemplation of nature respectively. Such of the demons that fall upon the affective part of the soul are said to be the opponents of the ascetic life. Those again who disturb the rational part are the enemies of all truth and the adversaries of contemplation.

86. The rational soul operates according to nature when the following conditions are realized: the concupiscible part desires virtue; the irascible part fights to obtain it; the rational part, finally, applies itself to the contemplation of created things.

87. The person who is progressing in the ascetic life diminishes the force of passion. The person progressing in contemplation diminishes his ignorance. As regards the passions, the time will come when they will be entirely destroyed. In the matter of ignorance, however, one type will have an end [i.e., ignorance of the world], but another type will not [i.e., ignorance of God].

[Nos. 91–100 are sayings of holy monks, a genre typical of the literature of the desert.]

94. I went over to see the holy Father Macarius at the very hottest time of the day and since I was burning with thirst I asked him for a drink of water. He answered me: "Be content with the shade, for many there are who are making a journey on land or on sea who are deprived of this." Then as I struggled about temperance with him, wrestling with my thoughts, he said: "Take courage, my son. For twenty full years I have not taken my fill of bread or water or sleep. I have eaten my bread by scant weight, and drunk my water by measure, and snatched a few winks of sleep while leaning against a wall."

97. One of the brethren owned only a book of the Gospels. He sold this and gave the money for the support of the poor. He made a statement that deserves remembrance: "I have sold the very word

that speaks to me saying: 'Sell your possessions and give to the poor' (Mt 19:21)."

From *Evagrius Ponticus. The Praktikos. Chapters on Prayer,* 15–40, translated by John Eudes Bamberger, OCSO. Copyright 1970 by Cistercian Publications, Inc., Kalamazoo, Michigan. All rights reserved.

3.

JAMES OF VITRY
THE LIFE OF MARY OF OIGNIES

The new mysticism that burst upon Western Europe around 1200 involved innovative forms of asceticism, as well as new kinds of mystical contact with God. Although heroic feats of asceticism had been ascribed to the Fathers and Mothers of the desert, the late-medieval asceticism that was seen as preparation for ecstatic union was more directly centered on the imitation of Christ's passion (imitatio passionis) than had been common in antiquity. In this period women emerged as the primary exponents of extreme forms of self-discipline in the following of the Crucified Lord.

One of the main figures was the first beguine, Mary of Oignies. Mary was born in 1176 at Nivelle in the diocese of Liège. Married at fourteen, she convinced her husband to live a chaste marriage with her in service to poor lepers. Mary soon began to acquire a reputation as a new kind of holy woman. She did not live a cloistered life following an approved rule, but rather adopted a free form of devout life marked by strenuous asceticism and manual labor, as well as by mystical gifts of a new kind (such as the thirty-five-day Eucharistic rapture described below). Mary eventually retired to live near a community of Augustinian canons in the town of Oignies, where she died in 1213. Here she became the center of "flocks of beguines" (i.e., women desiring to live according to her apostolic model), as well as their clerical supporters.

One of these supporters was James of Vitry, a theology student from Paris who met Mary about 1208. He became a model of the learned and sometimes powerful clerics who saw in holy women such as Mary living mediators of God's

grace to the world. Under Mary's influence, James became a famous preacher,
later archbishop, and defender of the beguines at the papal court. Soon after
Mary's death he began writing her life as a manifesto for the beguine life and its
new style of asceticism and mysticism. The excerpts that follow from the first book
of The Life *illustrate the close connection between ascetical practices (compunc-*
tion and the gift of tears, frequent confession, fasting, night vigils, etc.) and the
ecstasies that characterized beguine mysticism. Some of Mary's more unusual
ascetical practices, such as the cutting off of a piece of her flesh rather discreetly
recounted here, made even James uncomfortable, since at one point in The Life
he says, "I do not say this to commend her excessive practice, but rather to show
her fervor."

I.
BOOK I, CHAPTER I, 16–18

The beginning of her conversion to you, the first fruits of her love, was
your cross and your passion. She "heard your hearing and was afraid;
she considered your works and was frightened" (Hab 3:2; Eccles 7:14).
One day you came ahead and visted her so that she might think upon
the good things you mercifully showed to the human race when you
were in the flesh. She discovered in your passion so much grace of
compunction, such a flood of tears pressed out in the winepress of
your cross (Is 62:2–3), that her tears flowing copiously on the pave-
ment marked out her footsteps through the church. For a long time
after this visitation she was not able to look at an image of the cross, or
to speak about it, or even hear others speaking about Christ's passion
without falling into ecstasy from the weakness of her heart. In order to
assuage the pain a bit and to restrain the flood of tears, she left Christ's
humanity behind and lifted up her soul to his divinity and majesty so
that she could take consolation in his freedom from suffering. But
whenever she tried to restrain the flowing river, a greater flood of tears
would miraculously arise, for when she considered how great he was
who suffered such indignities for us, her pain was renewed again and
her soul broke out with new tears in sweet compunction. . . .

Once I was moved with compassion for her and asked her if after
long fasting and many vigils, and after such great floods of tears, she
was aware of any injury or pain when her head was so drained (as is

usually the case). She said: "These tears are my food; they are my bread day and night. They do not afflict my head, but nourish my mind; they torture me with no pain, but refresh my soul with deep peacefulness. They don't empty my head, but fill my soul with plenty, relaxing it with a sweet kind of anointing, as long as they are not compelled to come forth through violence but are freely given by the Lord as a healing potion."

II.
CHAPTER II, 19–25

After her compunction, let us briefly look at her manner of confessing. With God as my witness, I was never able to perceive a single mortal sin in her whole life and manner of acting. If ever by chance it seemed to her that she had committed a small venial sin, she presented herself to the priest with such sorrow of heart, such great shame and blushing, and such contrition that often, from the powerful anxiety of her heart, she was compelled to cry out like a woman giving birth, though it was often the case that she guarded herself so carefully from small venial sins that she couldn't discover a single disorderly thought in her heart over a fifteen-day period. . . .

After she had freed herself from childish things, she was careful to guard her soul with such great fear, and her senses with such great diligence, and her heart with such great purity that she always had before her eyes the text: "He who neglects small things falls away little by little" (Ecclus 19:1). I rarely or never could see a useless word, a disordered appearance, an unfitting garb, an immoderate look, or an unworthy or disordered bodily gesture, though often due to the immense joy in her heart she was scarcely able to contain herself while she was compelled to express the rejoicing of her heart by letting go a bit with a beaming face and some external gesture. This happened with a small smile issuing from the peacefulness of her heart, or with a modest and chaste embrace from overflowing goodness when she met one of her friends, or with a very devout kiss to the hands or feet of some priest. When she returned to herself after a kind of mental intoxication, while she called to mind and strictly surveyed all her deeds every evening, if she thought that she had gone too far in the slightest way she made confession and punished herself with admirable contrition of heart. In doing this she often was fearful where there was no reason to fear. I sometimes reprimanded her for one thing alone (seeking some consolation for my own sloth)—she confessed these little sins more frequently than I wanted ...

She had tasted of the Spirit to such an extent that all fleshly delight paled to her. One day she recalled that after a certain very grave illness she had been compelled to eat meat and take a bit of watered wine. She punished herself out of disgust at this former pleasure and had no rest of spirit until she had made recompense for former delights of any kind whatever by torturing her flesh in a marvelous way. As if she were drunk in fervor of spirit, she scorned her own flesh for the sake of the sweetness of the Paschal Lamb. With impunity she cut off a not insignificant piece [of flesh] and hid it in the ground out of a sense of modesty. Since while afire with such a great fervor of love she had conquered the flesh's pain, in her ecstasy of mind she beheld one of the Seraphim standing next to her. When her dead corpse was being washed the women discovered the place of the wounds and were amazed. Those who knew of it from her own confession understood what it was. Why are those who show reverent amazement at the worms that swarmed from St. Symeon's wounds, or at the fire with which St. Antony burned his feet, not also in awe at such strength in a woman of the frail sex, when she, wounded with charity (Song 2:4) and nourished by Christ's own wounds, took no notice of the wounds of her own body?

This handmaid of Christ was so preeminent for her fasting that on the days when she did come to dinner to restore her little body she came as if she were taking medicine. She ate only once a day and only a little bit, in the summer in the evening and in winter at the first hour of the night. She did not drink wine, or eat meat. She rarely or never ate fish, and then only the smallest. She survived on fruits, herbs, and beans. For a long time she ate only the blackest and hardest bread that dogs could scarcely eat. Due to its exceeding hardness and staleness her mouth was torn up inside and blood flowed from the wounds, reminding her of Christ's sweet blood. Her wounds were soothed by Christ's wounds and the harshness of that hard bread was made soft by the sweetness of the heavenly bread. ...

At times she would rest sweetly with the Lord in a pleasant and blessed silence for thirty-five days, during this time taking no bodily food and being unable to say anything but: "I want the Body of Our Lord Jesus Christ." When she received it, she remained in silence with the Lord for whole days. In these days she felt as if her spirit was separated from her body, or as if it were in the body as though it were lying in a clay pot—her body was like a clay garment surrounding and clothing her spirit. In this way she was drawn forth out of the senses and rapt above herself in an ecstasy. Finally, after five weeks she returned to herself and opened her mouth and spoke to the amazement of those standing around her and she took some food. For a long time after this she could not stand the smell of meat or any kind of cooking or wine, except when she took wine as an ablution after receiving the Body of Christ. Then she could bear its odor and taste without any harm. When she journeyed through some towns on the way to a bishop to receive the sacrament for gaining strength the odors she couldn't stand before caused her no trouble.

III.
CHAPTER IV, 33–39

. . . She took the greatest care never to let pass an idle hour, day or night, insofar as she could. She rarely slept at night, conscious that the Lord in his mercy gave us sleep not to gain merit, but for the recreation of human weakness. (We gain no merit when we sleep because we don't have the use of free choice.) Hence, as far as she was able, she abstained from sleep, serving the Lord in nocturnal watchings that were as devout as they were freely given, without any disturbance from other people being around her. The power of her abstinence dried out her body and made it thin, and the fire of love burning within drove all sleepiness out of her. The sweet songs of the angelic spirits with whom she often spent nights without sleep withheld all slumber from her eyes without any bodily harm. Far from human crowds, she was the companion of the hosts of heavenly spirits through her nightly vigils. Their sound soothed her ears in a wondrous way by a sweet harmony as though of a multitude of armies. It drove away all sleepiness, refreshed her head, sprinkled her with wondrous sweetness, aroused her mind with devotion, and enflamed her desire for praise and thanksgiving. Frequently repeating, "Holy, holy, holy," she invited others by her example. . . .

This prudent woman knew that after the sin of our first parents the Lord enjoined a penance through them to their children, that is, "You shall earn your bread in the sweat of your brow" (Gen 3:19). For this reason she worked with her hands as much as she could, in order to afflict her body through penance, and also to furnish life's necessities for those in need, and finally to gain her own food and clothing, even though she had left all things to follow Christ. The Lord gave her such strength for working that she far surpassed all her companions. From the fruit of her hands she was able to provide for herself and her female companion, paying careful attention to the Apostle's statement: "Whoever will not work, will not eat" (2 Thess 3:10). . . .

Her external bearing and the disposition of her exterior expression showed the interior disposition of her mind. Her face's cheerful tranquility could not hide the joy of her heart. Her grave face tempered her heart's gaiety with a marvelous moderation, and the simple expression of her modest face hid her mind's delight to some degree. Because the Apostle said, "Women should pray with veiled head" (1 Cor 11:15), the white veil with which she covered her head hung down over her eyes. She walked with her head down looking at the ground, with a humble, slow, and mature step. The grace of the Holy Spirit shone out in her face from the fullness of her heart to such a degree that many people were spiritually refreshed by her appearance and moved to devotion and tears. In her face, reading the anointing of the Holy Spirit as though in a book, they recognized the power that came out of her. . . .

Translated by Bernard McGinn from James of Vitry, *Vita Beatae Mariae Oigniacensis,* as found in the *Acta Sanctorum* (various publishers, 1643–1940), Junius, Vol. 6:640–46.

4.

CATHERINE OF GENOA
PURGATION AND PURGATORY

Catherine of Genoa (1447–1510) is the third of the great Italian female mystics of that name. Born of a noble Genoese family, she was married at an early age. In Lent of 1473 she underwent a conversion experience through a vision of Christ on the cross. After a period of withdrawal, she began serving the poor of her city, convincing her dissolute husband to reform his ways, adopt a life of mutual continence, and assist her work. Her Life, written by her follower Ettore Vernazza, describes her as exercising prolonged fasting (like Catherine of Siena), enjoying frequent ecstasies, and living with a great desire for the Eucharist, which she was allowed to receive every day, a rare privilege at that time. In 1479 she and her husband moved into the Pammatone Hospital to make themselves more available to assist the sick and the poor. She was especially active when the plague struck Genoa in 1493, wiping out much of the population. Catherine cooperated with Vernazza, a wealthy businessman, to form the Oratory of Divine Love, a group of clergy and laity devoted to achieving a deeper spiritual life through both contemplative prayer and active charity.

Catherine wrote nothing during her life. Her "writings" are actually from the pens of her followers, especially Vernazza and the priest Cattaneo Marabotta (her confessor). Though there has been debate about the degree to which they represent Catherine's own views, and also about which versions are more authentic, there is good reason to believe that the distinctive views found in this corpus of texts reflect the teaching of this married mystic who was able to combine action and contemplation so effectively. Along with The Life, *there are two treatises:* Purgation and Purgatory *and the* Spiritual Dialogue, *a three-part conversation among personifications representing Soul, Body, and Self Love, or Human Frailty.*

Two themes dominate Catherine's thought. The first is the conception of God as the overwhelming force of Pure Love. The second is a strong sense of human sinfulness and imperfection as demanding, both in this life and the next, willing submission to the purifying fire that wipes away every stain until the soul is ready for perfect union with God. Catherine's emphasis on the importance of purgation locates traditional practices of asceticism in their widest and most proper context. Purgation becomes the condition of human existence until the soul reaches the divine goal for which it was created.

The following translation is based upon the first printed edition of Catherine's works in 1551, the form in which they were most widely read, though not necessarily the most authentic form of the original collection of her writings made in the 1520s.

I.
THE ROLE OF PURGATORY

Chapter 1. The State of Souls in Purgatory

While still in the flesh, this holy soul [i.e., Catherine] found herself placed in the purgatory of God's burning love, a love that consumed and purified her from whatever she had to be purified, in order that passing out of this life she might enter at once into the immediate presence of God her Beloved. By means of this furnace of love she understood how the souls of the faithful are placed in purgatory to get rid of all the rust and stain of sin that in this life was left unpurged. As she, plunged in the divine furnace of purifying love, was united to the object of her love and satisfied with all that he wrought in her, she also understood that the same was the case with the souls in purgatory. . . .

Chapter 8. The Necessity of Purgatory and how Terrible it is

Again I say that on God's part, I see paradise has no gate, but that whoever wants to may enter in because God is all mercy and stands with open arms to admit us to his glory. But I also see that the essence of

God is so pure (far more than one can imagine) that should a soul see in itself even the least mote of imperfection, it would rather cast itself into a thousand hells than go with that spot into the presence of the divine majesty. Therefore, seeing that purgatory is ordained to take away such blemishes, it plunges into it and deems it a great mercy that it can thus remove them.

No tongue can express, no mind can understand, how dreadful purgatory is. Its pain is like that of hell, and yet (as I have said) I see any soul with the least stain of imperfection accept it as a mercy, not thinking it of any moment when compared with being kept from its Love. It appears to me that the greatest pain the souls in purgatory endure proceeds from their being sensible of something in themselves displeasing to God, and that it has been done voluntarily against so much goodness, for, being in the state of grace, they know the truth and they know how grievous is any obstacle that does not let them approach God.

Chapter 9. How God and the Souls regard one another in Purgatory

All the things of which I have spoken, when compared with that which I am assured of in my intelligence (so far as I am able to comprehend it in this life), are of such intensity that in comparison with them all things seen, all things felt, all things imagined, all things just and true, seem to me lies and things of naught. I am confounded at my inability to find stronger words. I see that God is in such perfect conformity with the soul that when he beholds it in the purity wherein it was created by his divine majesty, he imparts it a certain attractive impulse of his burning love sufficient to annihilate it, although it is immortal. In this way God so transforms the soul into himself, its God, that it sees in itself nothing but God, who goes on thus attracting it and inflaming it until he has brought it to that state of existence whence it came forth, that is, the spotless purity wherein it was created.

When the soul by interior illumination perceives that God is drawing it up to himself by such loving ardor there immediately springs up within it a corresponding fire of love for its most sweet Lord and God that causes it wholly to melt away. In the divine light it sees how considerately and with what unfailing providence God is always leading it up to its full perfection, and that he does it all through pure love. It finds itself stopped by sin and unable to follow the heavenly attraction—I mean that look that God casts on it to bring it into union with him. This sense of the grievousness of being kept from the divine light, coupled with that instinctive longing that wants to be without hindrance to follow the enticing look, these two things, I say, make up the pains of souls in purgatory. Not that they think anything of their pains, however great they may be. They think far more of the opposition they are making to the will of God, which they see clearly is burning intensely with pure love for them. Meanwhile, God goes on drawing the soul mightily to himself by his looks of love, and, as it were, with undivided energy. This the soul knows well; and could it find another purgatory greater than this by which it could sooner remove so great an obstacle, it would immediately plunge into it, impelled by that conforming love that is between God and the soul.

Chapter 10. How God makes use of Purgatory to Render the Soul perfectly Pure

Again, I see that the love of God directs toward the soul certain burning rays and shafts of light that seem penetrating and powerful enough to annihilate not merely the body, but, were it possible, the soul itself. These work in two ways: They purify, and they annihilate. Look at gold: The more it is melted, the better it becomes; and it is possible to be so melted as to destroy every single defect. Such is the action of fire on material things. Now, the soul cannot be annihilated as far as it is in God, but only as far as it is in itself. The more it is purified, so much the more it annihilates self till at last it becomes quite pure and rests in God. Gold that has been purified to a certain point ceases to suffer any diminution from the action of fire, however great it be, for fire does not destroy gold, but only the dross that it may happen to have. In like manner the divine fire acts on souls: God holds them in the furnace until every defect has been burned away, and he has brought them, each in its own degree, to a certain standard of perfection. Thus purified, they rest in God without any alloy of self; their very being is God. They become impassible because there is nothing left to be consumed. If in this state of purity they were kept in the fire, they would feel no pain; rather, it would be to them a fire of divine love, burning on without opposition like the fire of life eternal. . . .

II.
CATHERINE'S OWN EXPERIENCE
OF PURGATION

Chapter 17. The Saint applies what she has said of the Souls in Purgatory to what she Feels and Experiences in her own Mind

... I am sensible of all the things I have described as it were by sight and touch, but I cannot find fitting words to express myself as I could wish. I have said what I have because I was conscious of its going on spiritually within me. The prison in which I fancy myself shut up is the world; the chain by which I am held is the body; the enlightened soul is she who, knowing well the grievousness of being detained and kept back by any hindrance from reaching her end, therefore suffers great pains due to her great tenderness. By his grace God bestows upon her a dignity that makes her like God, and not only like God, but even one with him through participating in his goodness. And since it is impossible that God should suffer pain, so it is with the souls that approach him. The nearer they approach him, the more they share in that which belongs to him. The hindrance, then, that the soul meets with causes it to feel an intolerable pain, and the pain together with the hindrance obstruct the properties that it has by nature and which by grace are revealed to it. The soul remains in a suffering as great as is its appreciation of God, because although it is capable of these properties it is not able to attain them.

This appreciation of God grows with the soul's knowledge of God, and its knowledge is greater the more it is free from sin. The delay becomes more and more terrible because the soul, wholly immersed in God, knows him without error, there being nothing in the way to prevent such knowledge. The person who would sooner die than offend God feels death and the pain of dying, but the sight of God supplies him with a zeal that makes him think more of the divine honor than bodily death. In like manner, a soul who knows what God has appointed for it thinks more of the appointment than of any outward or inward pain, no matter how dreadful. This is because God, the author of it, surpasses everything that can be thought or imagined. The participation of himself that God grants the soul, however slight it be, keeps it so wholly taken up with his majesty that it can think of nothing else. Everything to do with self passes away. It neither sees, speaks, nor knows loss or pain of its own. But all this, as has been already clearly said, it perceives at the instant of passing from this life. Finally, in conclusion, I mean that God, who is good and great, destroys all that belongs to humanity, and purgatory purifies it.

Adapted from the translation found in *The Treatise on Purgatory by St. Catherine of Genoa* (London: Burns & Oates, 1880), 7, 16–20, 27–28.

5.

JOHN OF THE CROSS
THE ASCENT OF MOUNT CARMEL

BOOK 1, CHAPTERS 1–3

John of the Cross (1542–91) stands out not only as a profound mystical poet, but also as a great systematician of mystical theology. Born Juan de Yepes, he entered the Carmelite order in 1563 and studied theology at Salamanca. In 1567 he met Teresa of Avila and joined her reform movement. Between 1572 and 1577 he served as confessor and spiritual director at the Convent of the Incarnation in Avila, where Teresa was prioress. In December 1577 he was kidnapped and subjected to harsh imprisonment by Carmelites opposed to the reform. After his escape in August 1578, he served in various official positions in the reformed group for a decade. It was during this time that most of his writing was done.

John's poems were outpourings from his ecstatic states. His four commentaries on these lyrics form a carefully orchestrated synthesis of mystical theology. Despite the complex structure of the collection, even the driest sections and chapters display something of the inner fire of the Carmelite's love for God. The eight stanzas of the poem beginning "En una noche oscura" ("Upon a dark night") were written shortly after his escape from prison. Between 1579 and 1583 John composed a commentary on the first two stanzas and the beginning of the third. This work, The Dark Night of the Ascent of Mount Carmel, *treats the first, or purgative, stage of the mystical path and is customarily divided into two parts.* The Ascent of Mount Carmel *contains three books describing the active purgation of the senses and the spirit, a purging in which the soul cooperates with God by asceticism and practice of the virtues. The second part is the treatise called* The Dark Night of the Soul, *divided into two smaller books dealing with the soul's passive purgation, that is, the more painful process in which God alone acts to purify the soul from within (see section 11.4). John did not write a commentary on the final stanzas of this poem in which he was to have treated the illuminative and unitive stages of the mystical path. However, two other works commenting on other poems take up this task—*The Spiritual Canticle *(see section 13.6) and* The Living Flame of Love *(see section 6.5). In the following selection from the beginning of* The Ascent, *John explains its structure and emphasizes the necessity of purgation as the foundation of the mystical life.*

BOOK I. CHAPTER 1.
SPEAKS ABOUT THE TWO DIFFERENT
NIGHTS THROUGH WHICH SPIRITUAL
PERSONS PASS IN THE LOWER AND
HIGHER PERSON, AND EXPLAINS
THE FOLLOWING STANZA

STANZA I

Upon a dark night,
With anxious love inflamed,
O happy lot!
Forth unobserved I went,
My house being now at rest.

This stanza describes the happy state of the soul at its departure from all things, from the desires and imperfections to which our sensual nature is subject because it is not ordered by reason. The meaning of it is this: In order to reach perfection, the soul ordinarily has to pass through two kinds of night, which spiritual writers call purgations, or purifications, of the soul, and which I have called nights, because in the one as well as in the other the soul travels, as it were, by night, in darkness.

The first night is the night, or purgation, of the sensual part of the soul, treated in this first stanza and in the first part of this work [*Ascent,* book 1]. The second night, of which the second and following stanza speaks, is the night of the spiritual part. I shall discuss this night in the second part of my work, insofar as it relates to the soul's activity in the second and third parts [*Ascent*, books 2–3], and insofar as it relates to its passive condition in the fourth part [*Dark Night*, books 1–2].

This first night pertains to the beginners at the time when God begins to put them into the state of contemplation in which the spirit also has a part, as we shall say later on. The second night or purification pertains to the advanced at the time when God wants to lead them into a state of union with him. This state is a more obscure, dark, and terrible purgation, as will be said below.

The meaning of the stanza then is that the soul went forth, led by God, through love of him only, and with that love inflamed, in the dark night. This is the privation and purgation of all sensual desires for the outward things of this world, the pleasures of the flesh, and the satisfactions of the will. This is accomplished in this purgation of sense, and for this reason it is said that the soul went forth, its house (i.e., the sensual part) being at rest—all its desires being at rest and asleep, and the soul asleep to them. One has not departed from the pains and vexations of these desires until they are mortified and put to sleep. The happy lot of the soul, then, lies in this unobserved departure, which no carnal desire or anything else was able to hinder. It was also happy that this departure took place by night, which signifies that the privation was done in it by God, a condition that is night to the soul.

This was the "happy lot," then, that God should lead it into this night from which so great a blessing results, but into which it could not have entered of itself, because no one is able in his own strength to empty his heart of all desires in order to draw near to God....

CHAPTER 2.1–4.
EXPLAINS THE NATURE OF THE DARK NIGHT THROUGH WHICH THE SOUL HAS PASSED ON ITS WAY TO UNION

"Upon a dark night." The journey of the soul to the divine union is called night for three reasons. The first is derived from the point from which the soul sets out, the privation of the desire of all pleasure in all the things of this world, by detachment. This is night for every desire and sense of a person. The second, from the road by which it travels; that is, faith, for faith is obscure, like night, to the understanding. The third is from the goal to which it tends, God, incomprehensible and infinite, who in this life is as night to the soul. We must pass through these three nights if we are to attain to divine union with God.

They are foreshadowed in holy scripture by the three nights that were to elapse, according to the command of the angel, between the betrothal and the marriage of the young Tobias (Tb 6:18–22). On the first night he was "to burn the heart of the fish" in the fire, which signifies that the heart's affections are set on the things of this world. In order to enter on the road that leads to God, these must be burned up and purified of all created things in the fire of his love. This purgation drives away the evil spirit who has dominion over our soul, because of our attachment to those pleasures that flow from temporal and corporeal things.

On the second night the angel told him that he would be admitted into the society of the holy patriarchs, the fathers of the faith. The soul having passed the first night, which is the privation of all sensible things, enters immediately into the second night, being alone in pure faith, not to the exclusion of love, but in a faith that excludes other forms of knowledge (as we will explain later), for this does not pertain to the senses.

The third night the angel said he would "obtain a blessing"—that is, God, who, in the second night of faith communicates himself so secretly and so intimately to the soul. This is another night, since this communication is more obscure than the others, as I shall presently explain. When this night is over, which is the accomplishment of the communication of God in the spirit (ordinarily effected when the soul is in great darkness), the union with the bride, which is the Wisdom of God, immediately ensues. The angel also adds to Tobias that after the third night has passed he would be "joined to his bride with the fear of our Lord." This fear and the love of God become perfect together, and are then perfect when the soul is transformed by love. . . .

CHAPTER 3.1–4.
THE FIRST CAUSE OF THE NIGHT,
THE PRIVATION OF THE APPETITE IN
ALL THINGS, WHICH IS THE REASON
FOR THE USE OF THE TERM NIGHT

We here call "night" the deprivation of pleasure in the desire for all things. For just as night is nothing else but the absence of light, and consequently of visible objects, in which state the faculty of vision remains in darkness and emptiness, so too the mortification of the desires is night to the soul. For when the soul denies itself those pleasures that outward things furnish to the desire, it is as it were in darkness, without occupation. As the faculty of vision is nourished by light and fed by visible objects, and ceases to be so fed when the light is withdrawn, so the soul by means of desire feeds on those things that correspond with its powers and give it pleasure. But when the desire is mortified, it derives no more pleasure from them, and thus, so far as the desire is concerned, the soul abides in darkness, without occupation.

This may be illustrated in the case of all the faculties of the soul. When the soul denies itself the pleasure arising from what gratifies the ear, it remains, so far as the faculty of hearing is concerned, in darkness, without occupation. When it denies itself in all that is pleasing to the eye, it remains in darkness, so far as it relates to the faculty of sight.... Hence, the soul that has denied and rejected the gratifications that come from all things by mortifying its desire for them may be said to live in the darkness of night, and this is nothing else but an emptiness within itself of all things.

The reason for this, as the philosophers say, is that the soul is like a clean slate when God first infuses it into the body, without knowledge of any kind whatever and incapable of receiving knowledge, in the course of nature, in any other way than through the senses. Thus, while in the body, the soul is like a person in a dark prison who has no knowledge of what passes on the outside beyond what he can learn by looking through the window of his cell, and who, if he did not look outside, could in no other way learn anything at all. Thus, the soul cannot naturally know anything but through the senses, the windows of its cell.

If the impressions and communications of the senses be rejected and denied, we may well say that the soul is in darkness and empty, because according to this view there is no other natural way for light to enter in. It is true, indeed, that we cannot help hearing, seeing, smelling, tasting, and touching; but this is of no moment, and does not trouble the soul, when the objects of sense are repelled, any more than if we neither heard nor saw, for he who shuts his eyes is as much in darkness as a blind man who cannot see. This is the meaning of David when he said, "I am poor and in labors from my youth" (Ps 87:16). Though he was certainly rich, he says that he is poor, because he had not set his mind upon riches; he was really like a poor man. But if he had been really poor, yet not in spirit, he would not have been truly poor, for his soul would have been rich and full of desires.

For this reason we call this detachment the night of the soul, for we are not speaking here of the absence of things—for absence is not detachment, if the desire remains—but of that detachment which consists in suppressing desire and avoiding pleasure. It is this that sets the soul free, even though possessions may be still retained. It is not things of this world that occupy or injure the soul, for they do not enter into it; it is rather the wish and desire for them that abide within it.

Adapted and corrected from the translation of David Lewis, *The Ascent of Mount Carmel by St. John of the Cross* (London: Thomas Baker, 1906), 9–15.

PRAYER, LITURGY, AND SACRAMENTS

Prayer is as essential to Christianity as it is to other religions. The early Christians took over the Jewish Psalms as an important component of their devotion, but there were also distinctive forms of prayer created by the new religion. The apostles asked Jesus how to pray, and he responded by teaching them the "Our Father," the cornerstone of all Christian prayer (Mt 6:9–13; Lk 11:2–4). Another significant text was Paul's command in 1 Thessalonians 5:17 to "Pray constantly." Prayer, most simply defined as "the lifting of the heart and mind to God," has taken myriad forms over the centuries—vocal and mental, private and public, liturgical and nonliturgical. One customary division of prayer (based on 1 Tim 2:1) speaks of four forms: praise, thanksgiving, penance, and petition. Prayer is both an instrument in the preparation for mystical consciousness, as well as an aspect of the goal in the case of what is called contemplative prayer (see section 10). Further, the Christian always prays in and with the church as the Body of Christ, so private prayer and the public prayer of the liturgy are not two separate things, but differing manifestations of the one prayer offered by Christ the High Priest to God the Father in the power of the Holy Spirit. A proper view of the role of prayer in the mystical life needs to keep both modalities in mind.

The central component of liturgical prayer for Christians is the celebration of the sacraments, the ritual acts that Christians believe were established by Christ and that transmit his saving grace to subsequent believers. The sacrament of baptism, which begins the new life of the Christian, is the foundation for all that follows and hence may be described as the basis of mysticism, but among later Christians, for whom infant baptism became the rule, it was the Eucharist, the reception of Christ's Body and Blood, that was the center of heightened consciousness of God. Given the variety of ways in which prayer, liturgy, and sacrament have functioned in Christian mysticism, the following selections can only begin to suggest the richness of this dimension of the mystical life.

1.

ORIGEN

PRAYER

Around 200 CE Tertullian wrote the first Christian treatise on prayer, a practical discussion about styles and practices of praying. About a generation later (circa 233) Origen composed a more penetrating theological tract. Origen divides his work into three parts: general issues about prayer, especially its usefulness; a commentary on the Lord's Prayer; and issues relating to the person who prays. The following selections from the introduction and first part of the work feature some of the Alexandrian's comments about the importance of prayer in the life of the Christian, as well as excerpts from his discussion of the advantages of prayer. For Origen prayer is not really about trying to influence God by petition, but is intended to enable us to come into union with the spirit of the Lord. Especially noteworthy is the insistence on the necessity of praying in and with Christ, as well as Origen's understanding of formal prayer (three times a day) as being part and parcel of an entire "prayerful life."

I.

INTRODUCTION

The grace of God, immense and beyond measure, showered by him on men through Jesus Christ, the minister to us of this superabundant grace, and through the co-operation of the Spirit, makes possible through his will things which are to our rational and mortal nature impossible. For they are very great, and beyond man's compass, and far transcend our mortal condition. It is impossible, for example, for human nature to acquire wisdom by which all things were made, for according to David, God "has made all things in wisdom" (Ps 104:24); yet from being impossible it becomes possible through Our Lord Jesus Christ, "who of God is made for us wisdom and justice and sanctification and redemption" (1 Cor 1:30).... And who will deny that it is impossible for men to search out the things that are in heaven? Yet this impossibility becomes possible through the overflowing grace of God. For he that was "caught up to third heaven" probably did search out the things that are in the three heavens, since he heard "secret words which it was not granted to man to utter" (2 Cor 12:2–4). And who can say that it is possible for man "to know the mind of the Lord" (Rom 11:34)? Yet even this is granted by God through Christ....

But probably you, my most pious and industrious Ambrose, and you, Tatiana, most modest and valiant lady, ... are puzzled why, when we are speaking of prayer, mention has been made in the introduction about things impossible for men becoming possible through God's grace. The reason is that I feel that to give any accurate and reverent explanation of prayer—of what it is to be about, of how one should pray, how one should speak to God in prayer, and what times are most suitable for prayer—this is one of the things that, considering our infirmity, is impossible. ... Since then to treat of prayer is such a great task that one needs for it the illumination of the Father, the instruction of the first-born Word himself, and the operation of the Spirit, in order to understand and speak as one ought of such a problem, I beseech the Spirit—imploring him as a man (for I myself make no claim whatever of being able to pray) before I begin to speak of prayer—that we may be given to speak fully and spiritually and may explain the prayers recorded in the Gospels. So let us now begin our discussion on prayer.

II.

PART I. PRAYER IN GENERAL, VIII–XII

I think that he profits in many ways from his prayer who prays in the proper way or as well as he can. In the first place he certainly benefits somewhat who disposes his mind to pray, because by the very attitude with which he prays he shows that he is placing himself before God and speaking to him as present, convinced that he is present and looking at him. For as certain mental images and remembrances of things which are recalled defile the minds occupied by these same images, we must hold in the same way that we profit by the recollection of the God in whom we believe and who sees the most secret movements of the soul. The soul is disposing itself to please him as being present and looking on and anticipating every thought, "the searcher of hearts and reins" (Ps 7:10). Even if we suppose that no other advantage comes to the man who prepares his mind to pray, we must not think that he who thus carefully disposes himself in the time of prayer receives a benefit that is negligible. Those who give themselves continually to prayer know by experience that through this frequent practice they avoid innumerable sins and are led to perform many good deeds. For if the remembrance and recollection of some illustrious man confirmed in wisdom induces us to emulate him and often restrains our impulses towards what is evil, how much more does the remembrance of God, the Father of all, and prayer to him benefit those who are convinced that they are present with and speaking to God who is there and listens to them! . . .

And the prophet David says that the saint who prays enjoys many other benefits. It will be quite expedient to mention them now so that we may see clearly the very great advantages which, even if considered by themselves, the disposition and preparation for prayer confer upon him who has dedicated himself to God. He says: "To you have I lifted up my eyes, who dwells in heaven" (Ps 123:1); and "To you, O God, have I lifted up my soul" (Ps 25:1). The eyes of the spirit are lifted up when they cease to truck with things of the earth and to be filled with the images of things material, and are so elevated that they condemn the things that are made and think only of God who listens to them and with whom they converse respectfully and in a fitting manner. Truly do those eyes already profit in the greatest measure, "beholding" as they do "the glory of the Lord with open face and being transformed into the same image from glory to glory" (2 Cor 3:18). Then do they partake of the effect of some intellectual principle that is divine, as is made clear from the text: "The light of your countenance, O Lord, is signed upon us" (Ps 4:6). And the soul which is lifted up and follows the Spirit, which is separated from the body and not only follows the Spirit but lives in him—as is made clear from the text: "To you have I lifted up my soul"—surely it has ceased to be soul and becomes spiritual. . . .

The person who prays in this way and who has already received such benefits, becomes more fitted to be united with the Spirit of the Lord who fills the whole world and with him who fills the whole earth and heavens and who speaks thus by the mouth of the prophet: "Do I not fill heaven and earth? Says the Lord" (Jer 23:24). Moreover, because of the purification already mentioned, he shares in the prayer of the Word of God, who stands in the midst even of those who are not aware of it, who is not wanting to the prayer of anyone and prays to the Father with him whose mediator he is. For the Son of God is the High Priest of our offerings and our advocate with the Father, praying for those who pray and pleading with those who plead. He will not pray for us as his friends if we do not pray constantly through his intercession. Nor will he be an advocate with God for his followers if we do not obey his teaching that we ought always to pray and not to faint. . . .

Moreover, I believe that the words of saints when praying are charged with great power, especially when they "pray with the spirit and understanding" (1 Cor 14:15). This is like a light issuing from the mind of him who is praying (Ps 96:11); and, proceeding from his mouth, it frees him through the power of God from the intellectual venom injected by the adverse powers in the minds of those who neglect prayer and ignore the "pray without ceasing" (1 Thess 5:17) which Paul prescribes following the exhortations of Jesus. For it issues from the soul of the holy man who prays, like an arrow shot from the saint by knowledge and reason and faith, wounding to subjugation and destruction the spirits that are hostile to God and wish to ensnare us in the toils of sin.

He "prays without ceasing" who joins prayer to works that are of obligation, and good works to his prayer. For virtuous works, or the carrying out of what is enjoined, form part of prayer. It is only in this way that we can understand the injunction, "pray without ceasing," as something that we can carry out; that is to say, if we regard the whole life of the saint as one great continuous prayer. What is usually termed "prayer" is but a part of this prayer, and it should be performed not less than three times each day. This is clear from what we hear of Daniel, who prayed three times each day as long as great danger threatened him (Dan 6:13). And Peter—"going up to the housetop to pray about the sixth hour" (Acts 10:9, 11), . . . when "he saw . . . a vessel descending" from heaven, "let down by the four corners"—indicates the second of the three prayers, that which is spoken of also by David before him: "In the morning you shall hear my prayer; in the morning I will stand before you and will see" (Ps 5:3). And the third is indicated by: "The lifting up of my hands as an evening sacrifice" (Ps 141:2). Nor can we without this prayer spend the nighttime as we ought, as David says: "I rose at midnight to give praise to you for the judgments of your justice" (Ps 119:62). And Paul, as is told in the Acts of the Apostles, at Philippi "at midnight praying with Silas praised God" so that "they that were in prison heard them" (Acts 16:25).

From *Origen. Prayer. Exhortation to Martyrdom,* translated and annotated by John J. O'Meara (New York: Paulist Press, 1954. Ancient Christian Writers), 15–17, 21, 37–40, 41–42, 46–47. Used with permission.

EPHREM THE SYRIAN
ARMENIAN HYMN NO. 1

Ephrem was born in Nisibis in northern Mesopotamia about 309 CE and spent much of his early life there as the head of the Christian school under Bishop Jacob, who built the first church in that city. After the Persians captured Nisibis, Ephrem fled to Edessa where he spent the last decade of his life, dying in 373. Theodoret of Cyrrhus, the last Antiochene theologian, referred to him as "the lyre of the Spirit, who daily waters the Syrian nation with streams of grace" (Letter 146). Ephrem is said to have written commentaries on all the books of the Bible, though only a few survive. His major contribution is in his numerous hymns, of which hundreds are known in Syriac, as well as in translation into other languages.

Ephrem's symbolic mode of presenting Christian faith avoids the philosophical language of the Greek Fathers, but is remarkably effective in conveying the fundamental message of salvation through divinization. As he once put it, "The Deity imprinted itself on humanity, so that humanity might also be cut into the seal of the Deity" (Hymn on the Nativity, No. 1). Ephrem is a strong witness to the essential role of prayer in the path to God. The following hymn, surviving only in Armenian, uses many Old Testament figures and types to emphasize the role of prayer in opening up "the door of heaven" and allowing us to converse directly with God.

———

Open up the treasury door for us Lord, at the prayers of our supplications; let our prayers serve as our ambassador, reconciling us with your divinity. Listen, all who are wise (Prov 4:5), pay attention, all who are learned, acquire understanding and knowledge, seeing that you are instructed and wise, I will relate before you the accomplishments of holy prayer.

Prayer divided the Red Sea (Ex 14:22), allowing the people to cross through its midst; by the same prayer the sea was reunited once more, swallowing up Pharaoh, the rebellious and impious (Ex 14:28). Prayer brought down manna from heaven, prayer brought the quails from the sea (Ex 16), prayer struck the rock in the desert, causing water to gush forth for the thirsty (Ex 17:1–7).

Blessed is the person who has consented to become the close friend of faith and of prayer: he lives in single mindedness and makes prayer and faith stop by with him. Prayer that rises up in someone's heart serves to open up for us the door of heaven: that person stands in converse with the divinity and gives pleasure to the Son of God. Prayer makes peace with the Lord's anger and with the vehemence of his wrath. In this way too, tears that well up in the eyes can open the door of compassion.

Come, let us look at those warriors who conquered, who excelled in both faith and prayer. Prayer caused the sun to stop in its course at Gibeon and the moon at the field of Ayyalon (Josh 10:12–13); it overturned the sevenfold walls of Jericho that mighty city (Josh 6); it brought devastation to Amalek with its king (Ex 17:8–13), it slew Sisera along with Madon, Sihon, Og and all their princes (Josh 11:1), giving their land as an inheritance to Israel, the People of God (Num 21:21–35).

I will show you, my brethren, what faith and prayer have effected: the prayer which held back the sun at Gibeon can hold back evil from us: He who held back the moon at the field of Ayyalon, who overthrew the sevenfold walls of Jericho that mighty city, who drove off Amalek along with its king, will drive off and break into pieces the might of Satan.

Prayer gave manna to the people, and by the same prayer the just are nourished. The prayer that bound the heavens (1 Kgs 17:1) released them too, just as it had first bound them (1 Kgs 18:41–45). Prayer brought down from heaven the fire (1 Kgs 18:38) that devoured the sacrifice and licked up the water; prayer seized and finished off the four hundred and fifty priests of Baal (1 Kgs 18:40).

For forty days prayer accompanied the prophet in the recesses of his cave on Horeb (1 Kgs 19:3–8); he openly conversed with the deity (1 Kgs 19:9–13). Fiery chariots were harnessed and descended (2 Kgs 2:11); they took him up, ascending with him to the God whom he loved. The Watchers on high rejoiced at the ascent of the prophet to heaven in his body.

Prayer shut up and fettered the mouths of lions inside the pit, so that the just Daniel was not harmed (Dan 6). Prayer preserved the three children in the furnace of fire (Dan 3). Prayer opened up the wombs of barren women (1 Sam 1), providing them with heirs. Such are the wonders that prayer and faith have continuously brought about—and there are others even greater than these!

From *The Syriac Fathers on Prayer and the Spiritual Life*, translated by Sebastian Brock, 36–38. Copyright 1987 by Cistercian Publications, Inc., Kalamazoo, Michigan. All rights reserved.

3.

JOHN CASSIAN
CONFERENCES 9 AND 10

John Cassian (circa 360–435) was a link between Eastern monasticism and early Western monasticism. A Latin speaker, though born in the East, he spent time in Palestine and Egypt as a young monk visiting the famous Fathers (abbas) of the desert. His thought was influenced by the writings of Evagrius Ponticus (see section 2.2). Cassian wandered to Constantinople and Rome before settling down around 415 in southern Gaul, where he established several monasteries. His two major writings were of great influence in the West for more than a millennium. The first was The Conferences *(circa 426–29), twenty-four recollections of conversations with noted abbas about the interior spiritual practices of the monastic life. The second was* The Institutes *(circa 430), which describes the exterior practices of cenobitical monks (i.e., monastics living in community).*

While the theological content of Cassian's thought was based on Evagrius, he brought many refinements and original elements to Evagrius's Origenist perspective. Especially important was his emphasis on "purity of heart" (puritas cordis: Mt 5:8) as the aim, or direction, the monk uses to attain the goal of the kingdom of heaven. Cassian wrote for fellow monastics, but important parts of his teaching are applicable to all devout Christians. This is especially true of his teaching on prayer, summarized in Conferences 9 and 10 by Abba Isaac. Building on Origen and Evagrius, these conferences lay out the meaning of perfect unceasing prayer and the method by which it may be attained. Conference 9 is a general treatise, structured around the four kinds of prayer mentioned in 1 Timothy 2:1 and a treatment of the "Our Father." Conference 10 emphasizes the constant repetition of a single verse ("O God, come to my aid; Lord, make haste to help me": Ps 69:2) as a preparation for the highest form of prayer, which Cassian speaks of as "fiery prayer" (oratio ignita).

I.
SELECTIONS FROM CONFERENCE 9

(A) Preparation for Prayer (Sections II–III)

The Blessed Isaac finally spoke these words:

"The end of every monk and the perfection of his heart incline him to constant and uninterrupted perseverance in prayer; and, as much as human frailty allows, it strives after an unchanging and continual tranquility of mind and perpetual purity. On its account we tirelessly pursue and ceaselessly apply ourselves to every bodily labor as well as to contrition of spirit. Between the two there is a kind of reciprocal and inseparable link. For, as the structure of all the virtues tends to the perfection of prayer, so, unless all things have been joined together and cemented under this capstone, in no way will they be able to remain firm and stable. For just as the perpetual and constant tranquility of prayer about which we are speaking cannot be acquired and perfected without those virtues, neither can these latter, which lay the foundation for it, achieve completion unless it be persevered in.

"Therefore we shall be unable to deal properly with the effect of prayer or by an abrupt discourse to arrive at its principal end, which is achieved as a result of the work of all the virtues, if everything that should be either rejected or acquired in order to obtain it has not first been set out and discussed in an orderly way, and unless the things that pertain to the construction of that spiritual and sublime tower, following the directives of the gospel parable, have been carefully reckoned and prepared beforehand. Yet the things that have been prepared will be of no benefit nor will they let the highest capstones of perfection be placed properly upon them unless a complete purging of vice has been carried out first. And once the tottering and dead rubbish of the passions has been dug out, the firm foundations of simplicity and humility can be placed in what may be called the living and solid ground of our heart, on the gospel rock. When they have been constructed, this tower of spiritual virtues which is to be built can be immovably fixed and can be raised to the utmost heights of the heavens in full assurance of its solidity. For if it rests upon such foundations, even though the heaviest rains of the passions should come down and violent torrents of persecutions should beat against it like a battering ram and a savage tempest of adversary spirits should rush upon it and press upon it, not only will it not fall into ruin but no force of any kind will ever disturb it.

"Therefore, so that prayer may be made with the fervor and purity that it deserves, the following things should be observed in every respect. First, anxiety about fleshly matters should be completely cut off. Then, not only the concern for but in fact even the memory of affairs and business should be refused all entry whatsoever; detraction, idle speech, talkativeness, and buffoonery should also be done away with; the disturbance of anger, in particular, and of sadness should be entirely torn out; and the harmful shoot of fleshly lust and of avarice should be uprooted. And thus, when these and similar vices that could also make their appearance among men have been completely thrust out and cut off and there has taken place a cleansing purgation such as we have spoken of, which is perfected in the purity of simplicity and innocence, the unshakable foundations of deep humility should be laid, which can support a tower that will penetrate the heavens. Then the spiritual structure of the virtues must be raised above it, and the mind must be restrained from all dangerous wandering and straying, so that thus it might gradually begin to be elevated to the contemplation of God and to spiritual vision.

"For whatever our soul was thinking about before the time of prayer inevitably occurs to us when we pray as a result of the operation of the memory. Hence we must prepare ourselves before the time of prayer to be the prayerful persons that we wish to be. For the mind in prayer is shaped by the state that it was previously in, and, when we sink into prayer, the image of the same deeds, words, and thoughts plays itself out before our eyes. This makes us angry or sad, depending on our previous condition, or it recalls past lusts or business, or it strikes us with foolish laughter—I am ashamed even to say it—at the suggestion of something ludicrous that was said or done, or it makes us fly back to previous conversations. Therefore, before we pray we should make an effort to cast out from the innermost parts of our heart whatever we do not wish to steal upon us as we pray, so that in this way we can fulfill the apostolic words: 'Pray without ceasing' (1 Thess 5:17). And: 'In every place lifting up pure hands without anger and dissension' (1 Tim 2:8). For we shall be unable to accomplish this command unless our mind, purified of every contagion of vice and given over to virtue alone as to a natural good, is fed upon the continual contemplation of almighty God."

(B) The Four Kinds of Prayer (Sections IX–XV)

"Therefore, once these aspects of the character of prayer have been analyzed—although not as much as the breadth of the material demands but as much as a brief space of time permits and our feeble intelligence and dull heart can grasp hold of—there remains to us a still greater difficulty: We must explain one by one the different kinds of prayer that the Apostle divided in fourfold fashion when he said: 'I urge first of all that supplications, prayers, intercessions, and thanksgivings be made' (1 Tim 2:1). There is not the least doubt that the Apostle established these distinctions in this way for a good reason.

"First we must find out what is meant by supplication, what is meant by prayer, what is meant by intercession, and what is meant by thanksgiving. Then we must investigate whether these four kinds are to be used simultaneously by the person praying—that is, whether they should all be joined together in a single act of prayer—or whether they should be offered one after the other and individually, so that, for example, at one time supplications should be made, at another prayers, at another intercessions or thanksgivings; and whether one person should offer God supplications, another prayers, another intercessions, and another thanksgivings, depending on the maturity to which each mind is progressing according to the intensity of its effort.

"First, therefore, the very properties of the names and words should be dealt with and the difference between prayer, supplication, and intercession analyzed. Then, in similar fashion, an investigation must be made as to whether they are to be offered separately or together. Third, we must look into whether the very order that was laid down on the authority of the Apostle has deeper implications for the hearer or whether these distinctions should simply be accepted and be considered to have been drawn up by him in an inconsequential manner. This last suggestion seems quite absurd to me. For it ought not to be believed that the Holy Spirit would have said something through the Apostle in passing and for no reason. And therefore let us treat of them again individually in the same order in which we began, as the Lord permits.

" 'I urge first of all that supplications be made.' A supplication is an imploring or a petition concerning sins, by which a person who has been struck by compunction begs for pardon for his present or past misdeeds.

"Prayers are those acts by which we offer or vow something to God, which is called 'vow' in Greek. Where the Greek text has, 'I shall offer my vows to the Lord,' the Latin has it: 'I will pay my vows to the Lord' (Ps 117:14). According to the nature of the word this can be expressed as follows: I will make my prayers to the Lord. . . .

"This will be fulfilled by each one of us in this way. We pray when we renounce this world and pledge that, dead to every earthly deed and to an earthly way of life, we will serve the Lord with utter earnestness of heart. We pray when we promise that, disdaining worldly honor and spurning earthly riches, we will cling to the Lord in complete contrition of heart and poverty of spirit. We pray when we promise that we will always keep the most pure chastity of body and unwavering patience, and when we vow that we will utterly eliminate from our heart the roots of death-dealing anger and sadness. When we have been weakened by sloth and are returning to our former vices and are not doing these things, we shall bear guilt for our prayers and vows and it will be said of us: 'It is better not to vow than to vow and not to pay' (Eccles 5:4). . . .

"In the third place there are intercessions, which we are also accustomed to make for others when our spirits are fervent, beseeching on behalf of our dear ones and for the peace of the whole world, praying (as I would say in the words of the Apostle himself) 'for kings and for all who are in authority' (1 Tim 2:1–2).

"Finally, in the fourth place there are thanksgivings which the mind, whether recalling God's past benefits, contemplating his present ones, or foreseeing what great things God has prepared for those who love him, offers to the Lord in unspeakable ecstasies. And with this intensity, too, more copious prayers are sometimes made, when our spirit gazes with most pure eyes upon the rewards of the holy ones that are stored up for the future and is moved to pour out wordless thanks to God with a boundless joy.

"These four kinds sometimes offer opportunities for richer prayers, for from the class of supplication which is born of compunction for sin, and from the state of prayer which flows from faithfulness in our offerings and the keeping of our vows because of a pure conscience, and from intercession which proceeds from fervent charity, and from thanksgiving which is begotten from considering God's benefits and his greatness and loving kindness, we know that frequently very fervent and fiery prayers arise. Thus it is clear that all these kinds which we have spoken about appear helpful and necessary to everyone, so that in one and the same man a changing disposition will send forth pure and fervent prayers of supplication at one time, prayer at another, and intercession at another.

"Nonetheless the first kind seems to pertain more especially to beginners who are still being harassed by the stings and by the memory of their vices; the second to those who already occupy a certain elevated position of mind with regard to spiritual progress and virtuous disposition; the third to those who, fulfilling their vows completely by their deeds, are moved to intercede for others also in consideration of their frailty and out of zeal for charity; the fourth to those who, having already torn from their hearts the penal thorn of conscience, now, free from care, consider with a most pure mind the kindnesses and mercies of the Lord that he has bestowed in the past, gives in the present, and prepares for the future, and are rapt by their fervent heart to that fiery prayer which can be neither seized nor expressed by the mouth of man."

(C) The Lord's Prayer as the Model (Sections XVIII and XXV)

"And so a still more sublime and exalted condition follows upon these kinds of prayer. It is fashioned by the contemplation of God alone and by fervent charity, by which the mind, having been dissolved and flung into love of him, speaks most familiarly and with particular devotion to God as to its own father. The schema of the Lord's Prayer has taught us that we must tirelessly seek this condition when it says: 'Our Father' (Mt 6:9). When, therefore, we confess with our own voice that the God and Lord of the universe is our Father, we profess that we have in fact been admitted from our servile condition into an adopted sonship. . . .

"This prayer, then, although it seems to contain the utter fullness of perfection inasmuch as it was instituted and established on the authority of the Lord himself, nonetheless raises his familiars to that condition which we characterized previously as more sublime. It leads them by a higher stage to that fiery and, indeed, more properly speaking, wordless prayer which is known and experienced by very few. This transcends all human understanding and is distinguished not, I would say, by a sound of the voice or a movement of the tongue or a pronunciation of words. Rather, the mind is aware of it when it is illuminated by an infusion of heavenly light from it, and not by narrow human words, and once the understanding has been suspended it gushes forth as from a most abundant fountain and speaks ineffably to God, producing more in that very brief moment than the self-conscious mind is able to articulate easily or to reflect upon. Our Lord himself represented this condition in similar fashion in the form of those prayers that he is described as having poured out alone on the mountain and silently (Lk 5:16), and when he prayed in his agony he even shed drops of blood as an inimitable example of his intense purpose" (Lk 22:44).

II.
SELECTIONS FROM CONFERENCE 10

(A) Prayer Unites us with God (Section VII)

"For then will be brought to fruition in us that prayer of our Savior which he prayed to his Father on his disciples' behalf when he said: 'That the love with which you have loved me may be in them, and they in us' (Jn 17:26). And again: 'That all may be one, as you Father in me and I in you, that they also may be one in us' (Jn 17:21). Then that perfect love of God, by which 'he loved us first' (1 Jn 4:10), will have also passed into our heart's disposition upon the fulfillment of this prayer of the Lord, which we believe can in no way be rendered void. This will be the case when every love, every desire, every effort, every undertaking, every thought of ours, everything that we live, that we speak, that we breathe, will be God, and when that unity which the Father now has with the Son and which the Son has with the Father will be carried over into our understanding and our mind, so that, just as he loves us with a sincere and pure and indissoluble love, we too may be joined to him with a perpetual and inseparable love and so united with him that whatever we breathe, whatever we understand, whatever we speak, may be God. In him we shall attain, I say, to that end of which we spoke before, which the Lord longed to be fulfilled in us when he prayed: 'That all may be one as we are one, I in them and you in me, that they themselves may also be made perfect in unity' (Jn 17:22–23). And again: 'Father, I wish that those whom you have given me may also be with me where I am' (Jn 17:24).

"This, then, is the goal of the solitary, and this must be his whole intention—to deserve to possess the image of future blessedness in this body and as it were to begin to taste the pledge of that heavenly way of life and glory in this vessel. This, I say, is the end of all perfection— that the mind purged of every carnal desire may daily be elevated to spiritual things, until one's whole way of life and all the yearnings of one's heart become a single and continuous prayer."

From *John Cassian. The Conferences,* translated and annotated by Boniface Ramsey, OP (New York: Paulist Press, 1997. Ancient Christian Writers), 329–31, 336–38, 340–41, 345–46, 375–76. Used with permission.

SYMEON THE NEW THEOLOGIAN
THE THIRD ETHICAL DISCOURSE

Symeon, called "the New Theologian," was born in Asia Minor about 949 and died in 1022. His life spanned the greatest period of the Byzantine empire under the rule of Basil II (960–1025). Raised at the imperial court, as a young man he came under the direction of a monk named Symeon the Pious of the Stoudion monastery in Constantinople. About 970 he began to receive the experiences of divine light that he describes throughout his writings (see section 10.4). Symeon eventually entered Stoudion, but soon transferred to the monastery of St. Mamas. In 980 he became abbot, a post he held until 1005. In 1009 he was forced into exile. Though later rehabilitated, Symeon lived a life of solitude with a few disciples until his death.

Symeon was well educated in the riches of the spirituality of the Christian East, but his writings strike a new note, especially in the way in which he drew upon his own experience of divine light. His works include fifty-eight "Hymns of Divine Love" and several series of discourses. There are thirty-four Catechetical Discourses *given while he was abbot of St. Mamas, as well as a group of* Practical and Theological Chapters *and three* Theological Discourses. *The fifteen* Ethical Discourses, *his most mature work, seem to come from the decade after he gave up his abbatial office.*

This selection from the third of The Ethical Discourses *illustrates one of the essential themes of Orthodox mysticism, and, indeed, all Christian mysticism—its root in the sacramental presence of Christ in the Eucharist. The discourse begins with a discussion of the rapture and hearing of "ineffable speech" that Paul describes in 2 Corinthians 12:2–4. Symeon argues that Paul had a direct experience of the divine light. The purpose of the discourse, however, is not just to admire Paul, but also to teach that we can enjoy the same experience if we realize that what Paul once enjoyed is present for us today in the Eucharist. Through the action of the Holy Spirit, who effects the change of bread and wine into Christ's Body and Blood, we can enjoy the vision of the glory of the Incarnate Word.*

I.
THE VISION OF GOD
AND THE EUCHARIST

I say that the ineffable speech which Paul heard spoken in Paradise (2 Cor 12:2–4) was the eternal good things which eye has not seen, nor ear heard, nor the heart of man conceived (1 Cor 2:9). These things, which God has prepared for those who love him, are not protected by heights, nor enclosed in some secret place, nor hidden in the depths, nor kept at the ends of the earth or sea. They are right in front of you, before your very eyes. So, what are they? Together with the good things stored up in heaven, these are the Body and Blood of our Lord Jesus Christ which we see every day, and eat, and drink. These, we avow, are those good things. Outside of these, you will not be able to find one of the things spoken of, even if you were to traverse the whole of creation. If you do want to know the truth of my words, become holy by practicing God's commandments and then partake of the holy things, and you will know precisely the force of what I am telling you. But, for further confirmation, listen to the words of the Lord himself when he speaks thus to the Jews and to his own disciples:

"Truly, truly, I say to you, it was not Moses who gave you the bread from heaven; my Father gives you the true bread from heaven. For the bread of God is that which comes down from heaven and gives life to the world." They said to him: "Lord, give us this bread always." Jesus said to them: "I am the bread of life; he who comes to me shall not hunger, and he who believes in me shall never thirst." ... The Jews then murmured at this, because he said I am the bread which came down from heaven. They said: "Is this not the son of Joseph whose father and mother we know? How does he now say, I have come down from heaven?" (Jn 6:32–35, 41–42).

So then, you must not be like the Jews as well, muttering and saying: "Is not this the bread on the diskos and the wine in the chalice which we see every day, and which we eat and drink? How does this man say that these are those good things which eye has not seen, nor ear heard, nor the heart of man conceived?" Listen instead to what the Lord said in reply to them: "Do not murmur among yourselves. No one can come to me unless the Father who sent me draws him; and I will raise him up at the last day" (Jn 6:44). He says, as it were: "Why do you disbelieve and doubt this? No one can know my divinity—for this is the same as to come to me—unless my Father draws him." In speaking of attraction, he makes it clear that there is no compulsion, but rather that he has invited through revelation those whom he foreknew and predestined, it being evident that he attracts them by virtue of their love for the One who is thus revealed to them. This is indicated still more clearly in the following: "It is written in the prophets, 'And they shall be taught by God'" (Jn 6:45). He who is taught by God is thus able to believe in the Son of God and, having learned from the Father, comes to me. "Not that anyone has seen the Father except him who is from God; he has seen the Father" (Jn 6:46). Again he says: "Truly, truly I say to you, he who believes has eternal life. I am the bread of life. Your fathers ate the manna in the wilderness, and they died. This is the bread which comes down from heaven, that a man may eat of it and not die. I am the living bread which came down from heaven; if anyone eats of this bread he will live forever; and the bread which I shall give for the life of the world is my flesh" (Jn 6:47–51). . . .

You have heard that the communion in the divine and immaculate mysteries is everlasting life, and that the Lord says he will raise up at the last day those who have everlasting life. This is not, certainly, that anyone else will be left in the tombs, but that those who have life will be raised by the Life to life everlasting while the rest are raised to the eternal death of damnation. And, that this is the truth, listen to what follows: "He who eats my flesh and drinks my blood abides in me, and I in him. As the living Father sent me, and I live because of the Father, so he who eats me will live because of me" (Jn 6:54–55). Do you see what he is saying? The Son of God cries out plainly that our union with him through communion is such as the unity and life which he has with the Father. Thus, just as he is united by nature to his own Father and God, so are we united by grace to him, and live in him, by eating his flesh and drinking his blood. And, in order that we not think that everything is reduced to the visible bread, he says several times on this account: "I am the bread which comes down from heaven." Now, he did not say "Who came down," because this would indicate that the "coming down" was a one-time event. What then? He says, "Who comes down," clearly because he is always and forever descending on those who are worthy, and that this occurs both now and at every hour. And more: detaching our minds from visible things, or better, leading us up through them to the invisible glory of the divinity in his Person, he says: "I am the bread of life" (Jn 6:48). And again: "My Father gives you bread not from the earth, but the true bread from heaven" (Jn 6:32). When he said "the true bread from heaven," he indicated that the bread of earth is false, that it profits nothing.

II.
SPIRITUAL SENSES ALONE PERCEIVE THE REALITY OF THE EUCHARIST

Now, in order to make this still more clear, he says: "The bread of God is that which comes down from heaven and gives life to the world" (Jn 6:33). Once more he says "comes down," and "gives life." Why this? So that you should suspect nothing physical, nor conceive anything earthly, but instead see this bread with spiritual eyes, and see that this little particle is made divine, and has become altogether like the bread which came down from heaven, which is true God, both the bread and drink of immortal life; so that you should not be content with unbelief and with just the visible bread which is perceived by the senses, and so not eat the heavenly, but only the earthly bread, and thus be deprived of life for not having eaten the heavenly bread in spirit. So Christ himself says: "It is the Spirit which gives life; the flesh is of no avail" (Jn 6:63). Whom, then, does it not profit? Those, he says, who say he is merely a man, and not God. Therefore, if you, yourself a believer, partake of mere bread and not of a deified body when receiving him, the whole Christ himself, how do you hope to take life from him and with full awareness possess within yourself him, the same Lord who says: "He who eats the bread which comes down from heaven will live forever" (Jn 6:58); and again: "The flesh avails nothing; it is the Spirit who gives life"? It is the Spirit who is really the true food and drink. It is the Spirit who changes the bread into the Lord's body. It is the Spirit who really purifies us and makes us partake worthily of the Body of the Lord. Those, on the other hand, who partake unworthily of the same, as the Apostle says, "eat and drink judgment upon themselves" as not discerning the Lord's body (1 Cor 11:29).

Come therefore, as many as believe, as many of you as understand the power of the mysteries as we have explained it, as many as have eaten the heavenly bread, as many as from it and through it and in it and with it possess everlasting life, and, in this true life, let us all be caught up in the Spirit to the third heaven, or better, in spirit to the heaven itself of the Holy Trinity, so that, at once seeing and hearing, tasting and smelling and assuredly touching with the hands of our soul everything which has been said—and all that which remains ineffable—we may send up a hymn of thanksgiving to God and say: "Glory to you, who have appeared and deigned to be revealed to and seen by us." Let us also say publicly to all our brothers: "O fathers and brothers, monks and lay, rich, poor, slaves and free, young and old, and all of every age and race, listen to us!"

St. Symeon The New Theologian. On the Mystical Life: The Ethical Discourses. Vol. 1: *The Church and the Last Things,* translated by Alexander Golitzin, 130–35. By permission of St. Vladimir's Press, 575 Scarsdale Road, Crestwood, New York 10757.

5.

HADEWIJCH OF ANTWERP
VISION VII

The beguine known to history as Hadewijch of Antwerp is still a mystery. Her literary skills equal, if not surpass, those of any other medieval woman mystic. Her corpus of writings involves highly accomplished poetry in two genres: forty-five "Poems in Stanzas," modeled on the songs of the northern French troubadors; and sixteen "Poems in Couplets" of a more didactic nature. In addition, we have two different collections of prose works: thirty letters, which are works of spiritual counsel for other beguines; and her Book of Visions, *which is one of the earliest collections of visionary narratives. It is not easy to assign a date to Hadewijch. A few sparse internal references suggest that she was active circa 1250; but since her works did not begin to circulate until the middle of the fourteenth century, some think that she lived in the first part of that century.*

Hadewijch's mystical writings display an intensity of devotion to divine love (minne) *that is remarkable, even excessive. As she put it in one poem: "O powerful, wonderful minne, / You who can conquer all with wonder! / Conquer me, so that I may conquer you, / In your unconquered power" ("Poems in Stanzas" 19.50–53). For all her extreme language, however, it is clear that Hadewijch had received a sound theological education and had an original perspective on many of the doctrinal foundations of mysticism, such as the Trinity and the nature of redemption. The mystical piety of beguines and other women mystics of the thirteenth century fixed on the Eucharist, especially on the physical reception of Christ, the Bridegroom of the soul. Eucharistic visions and ecstasies experienced during the reception of the sacrament were staples of late-medieval female mysticism. Few of these accounts are more intriguing than Hadewijch's "Vision VII." As in many such narratives, the liturgical and sacramental setting introduces a highly personal and deeply erotic encounter with Jesus. For the Dutch beguine, however, the erotic encounter begun with sacramental communion is the prelude to an even deeper form of union "without distinction."*

———

One Pentecost at dawn I had a vision. Matins were being sung in the church and I was there. And my heart and my veins and all my limbs trembled and shuddered with desire. And I was in such a state as I had been so many times before, so passionate and so terribly unnerved that I thought I should not satisfy my Lover and my Lover not fully gratify me; then I would have to desire while dying and die while desiring. At that time I was so terribly unnerved with passionate love and in such pain that I imagined all my limbs breaking one by one and all my veins were separately in tortuous pain. The state of desire in which I then was cannot be expressed by any words or any person that I know. And even that which I could say of it would be incomprehensible to all who hadn't confessed this love by means of acts of passion and who were not known by Love. This much I can say about it: I desired to consummate my Lover completely and to confess and to savor to the fullest extent—to fulfill his humanity blissfully with mine and to experience mine therein, and to be strong and perfect so that I in turn would satisfy him perfectly: to be purely and exclusively and completely virtuous in every virtue. And to that end I wished, inside me, that he would satisfy me with his Godhead in one spirit (1 Cor 6:17) and he be all he is without restraint. For above all gifts I could choose, I choose that I may give satisfaction in all great sufferings. For that is what it means to satisfy completely: to grow to being god with God. For it is suffering and pain, sorrow and being in great new grieving, and letting this all come and go without grief, and to taste nothing of it but sweet love and embraces and kisses. Thus I desired that God should be with me so that I should be fulfilled together with him.

When at that time I was in a state of terrible weariness, I saw a great eagle, flying towards me from the altar. And he said to me: "If you wish to become one, then prepare yourself." And I fell to my knees and my heart longed terribly to worship that One Thing in accordance with its true dignity, which is impossible—I know that, God knows that, to my great sadness and burden. And the eagle turned, saying, "Righteous and most powerful Lord, show now the powerful force of your Unity for the consummation with the Oneness of yourself." And he turned back and said to me, "He who has come, comes again, and wherever he never came, there he will not come."

Then he came from the altar, showing himself as a child. And that child had the very same appearance that he had in his first three years. And he turned to me and from the ciborium he took his body in his right hand and in his left hand he took a chalice that seemed to come from the altar, but I know not where it came from. Thereupon he came in the appearance and in the clothing of the man he was on that day when he first gave us his body, that appearance of a human being and a man, showing his sweet and beautiful and sorrowful face, and approaching me with the humility of one who belongs entirely to another. Then he gave himself to me in the form of the sacrament, in the manner to which people are accustomed. Then he gave me to drink from the chalice in the manner and taste to which people are accustomed. Then he came to me himself and took me completely in his arms and pressed me to him. And all my limbs felt his limbs in the full satisfaction that my heart and my humanity desired. Then I was externally completely satisfied to the utmost satiation.

At that time I also had, for a short while, the strength to bear it. But all too soon I lost external sight of the shape of that beautiful man, and I saw him disappear to nothing, so quickly melting away and fusing together that I could not see or observe him outside of me, nor discern him within me. It was to me at that moment as if we were one without distinction. All of this was external, in sight, in taste, in touch, just as people may taste and see and touch receiving the external sacrament, just as a beloved may receive her lover in the full pleasure of seeing and hearing, with the one becoming one with the other. After this I remained in a state of oneness with my Beloved so that I melted into him and ceased to be myself. And I was transformed and absorbed in the spirit, and I had a vision about the following hours.

Translated by Theodor W. Dunkelgrün and Emily Kadens from *Hadewijch. Visioenen*, edited by Frank Willaert, 78–82. © Prometheus/Bert Bakker/Ooievaar. Poastbus 1662. 1000 Br Amsterdam.

6.

JOHN TAULER

SERMON 39

PART 1

The Dominican John Tauler (circa 1300–61) was born in Strasbourg and as a young friar lived in the same convent with Meister Eckhart. Although he received a good theological education, unlike Eckhart he was never a university man. Indeed, Eckhart's condemnation in 1329 (see section 14.3) led many of his followers to become suspicious of the theology of the schools. Tauler's career was that of a preacher and spiritual director, a lebemeister *(master of life) in medieval German parlance. Although a number of mystical treatises came to be ascribed to Tauler, his only authentic writings are the eighty or more sermons that survive. Tauler was much influenced by Eckhart, but he was an original mystic who corrected and developed aspects of Eckhart's teaching in his own way. Much of Tauler's preaching was made to religious women, especially Dominican nuns, but his teaching was meant for all devoted to living a deeper spiritual life, those people Tauler and his contemporaries referred to as "friends of God" (gotes-*
frúnt).

Tauler's mysticism is deeply ecclesial. He often preached about the Eucharist and the other sacraments, especially penance. Like Eckhart, he did not deprecate the role of external and verbal prayer, but he did insist that the essence of prayer is the "ascent of the mind to God," a definition first made by John of Damascus. Tauler's sermon for the fifth Sunday after Pentecost, preached on the text of the epistle of the Mass, is an excellent summary of prayer as the conversion of the interior ground of the soul to God. Tauler says that in the highest form of prayer, "enjoyment" (gebruchlicheit) and "work" (wúrklicheit) become one when our *interior joy in God is not disturbed by any exterior action. He suggests that this represents a sharing in the life of the Trinity where there is no distinction between the enjoyment of God's being as "one simple One" (*ein einig ein*) and the inner "work," or activity, by which the three Persons of the Trinity relate to one another. True prayer, then, reflects God as one and three. The sermon concludes with Tauler's teaching on the three stages of the path to God, which can be found in section 5.5.*

———

Carissimi, estote unanimes in oratione ("Beloved, have unity of spirit in prayer, etc." [1 Pet 3:8]).

Today one reads in this Sunday's epistle that my lord St. Peter said: "Dearest ones, be of one spirit in prayer." Children, here St. Peter touches on the most useful, enjoyable, and noble work. It is the most productive, desirable work that one can do on this earth.

Now, hear what prayer is, the essence of prayer, what the manner of prayer is, how one should pray and where, and what the place is where one should pray. What, then, is prayer? The essence of prayer is an ascent of the mind to God, as the saints and learned teachers say. The place where one should pray is in the spirit, as our Lord himself said (Jn 4:23–24).

How, then, should one pray? How should one dispose oneself and act? That is what I now intend to discuss a bit. Every good person, when he intends to pray, should gather together to himself his external senses and look into his heart and mind to see that they are well focused on God. A person can do this in the highest, lowest, or intermediate manner. And to this end it is good for a person to examine very carefully what is most suitable and what most moves him to proper, true devotion; and let him then make use of this manner or work. But you should realize that whatever good person wants to engage in true, proper prayer, so that his prayer will truly be heard, must have already turned his back on all temporal and external things and on whatever is not divine, whether it be friend or foe, and on all vanity, whether it be clothes or jewels or anything of which God is not the true source. And he must separate his words and actions from all disorder, internal or external.

This is how a person should prepare himself for true prayer. This is what St. Peter calls being of one spirit—that the heart and mind are attached completely to God alone, and that a person have the focus of his ground and spirit completely turned to God as present, and have a tender, benevolent attachment to God.

Children, everything we have, after all, we have from God. And how could it ever be otherwise than that we offer back completely everything that we have ever received from him with our interior focus and spirit, undivided and simple, turned toward him. And then one should engage all one's faculties, interior and exterior, and should carry them up entirely into God.

This is the proper manner of true prayer. And do not imagine that true prayer is when one babbles away outwardly with the mouth, reads the Psalter a lot, keeps vigils often, and fingers a rosary while one's heart is running hither and yon. You should realize truly: all prayers or actions that hinder your spirit from praying should simply be let go, whatever they might be or be called, or however great or good they might seem, with the sole exception of prayers prescribed for those obliged by order of holy church. Except for that, simply let go whatever else keeps you from true, essential prayer.

Now it sometimes happens that a lot of serious external prayer for some cause or other is imposed on a community. How should an interior person react to this, whom prayer spoken aloud hinders in his interior prayer because of its exteriority? He should perform and omit both. But how? He should recollect himself and turn to his interior ground with upraised heart and mind and with his faculties ready, with an interior gaze focused on God present, and with an interior desire, especially for the dearest will of God, in a sinking away of one's own self from people and all creatures and a sinking deeper and deeper into the transfigured will of God. And then a person should with devotion draw in all things that were entrusted to him and should desire that God bring about his own honor and praise for the advantage and consolation of those people that are entrusted to him. Child, then you have prayed much better than if you had prayed with a thousand mouths. This prayer, which takes place in the spirit, surpasses immeasurably all external prayer. For the Father desires that one pray to him in this way, and all other kinds of prayer serve this kind; and if they don't, simply let them go. Everything should serve this kind of prayer. Just as when there is building going on in a cathedral, there are many kinds of jobs and work. There might well be more than a hundred persons at work inside with many kinds of skills. Some carry the stones, others the mortar—all the many skills. All this is directed to serving one accomplishment—that the construction of the cathedral be done thoroughly and be completed. All this is so that it may become a house of prayer. And this marvel is only for the sake of prayer: that all these kinds of work and skills serve this purpose. And when this interior, true prayer of the spirit is achieved, everything that served this purpose is preserved and brought to completion. This goes far beyond external prayer, unless a person is so well versed that his external prayer can exist as one with the interior without any obstacles. In this case, the enjoyment and work would be one, since the one would be unobstructed by the other. It is indeed essential for a rightly directed and solidly transformed person that work and enjoyment become one and that the one remain unobstructed by the other, as is the case with God. In him there is the greatest of all work and the purest of all enjoyment—one simple One without obstacles—and each in the highest degree and each does not obstruct the other. The work is in the Persons, the enjoyment is attributed to the simple Being.

The heavenly Father, insofar as he is Father, is pure work. Everything that is in him is work where, in the knowing of himself, he gives birth to the Son; and both of them spiritually create outside themselves the Holy Spirit in an inexpressible embrace. The love of them both is an eternal, essential work of their Persons and accordingly of the essence and simplicity of their being. There one finds a calm, simple enjoyment and a simple pleasure in his Divine Being, and work and enjoyment are one.

In this sense God made all creatures working like himself—the heavens, the sun, the stars, and then far above all things, the angels and men, each according to its kind. Nowhere is there a flower so small, or a leaf, or a sprout of grass, the expanse of the heavens, the stars, the sun and moon—in these things there is continuously work, and especially God working with himself. Should not man, then, noble and formed with dignity according to God's image, should he not work, formed in his faculties like God and in God and like him in his being?

A noble creature will be far superior in its work to nonrational creatures like the heavens. These should be subject to the noble creature in work and contemplation in proportion to their similarity. In whatever direction a person is directed with all his faculties, both the highest and the lowest, he is working and each of his faculties, in acting upon its object, whether its object be divine or created, works on it according to what is put before it.

The person who has made all the objects of his work divine and heavenly, and turns his back completely on all temporal things—such a person's work becomes divine. That noble dear soul of our Lord Jesus Christ in its highest powers was directed unceasingly toward the Godhead as its object. From the very beginning of its existence it was turned toward its object, and it was as blessed and enjoying as it now is. And according to its lower faculties it was working, moving, and suffering, and it had enjoyment, work, and suffering all together. When he was suffering on the cross and died, he had, in his highest powers, the same enjoyment that he now has. Those who are now following him most closely in being turned toward divine objects, where work and enjoyment become one, shall in the hereafter be most like him in the essential enjoyment eternally. . . .

Translated for this volume by Frank Tobin from *Die Predigten Taulers,* edited by Ferdinand Vetter (Berlin: Weidmann, 1910), 154–57.

TERESA OF AVILA

ON THE FOUR STAGES OF PRAYER

SELECTIONS FROM THE *LIFE*, CHAPTERS 11–22

*Teresa of Avila (1515–82) is one of the premier Christian mystics and the first woman to be declared a "doctor of the church." Born to a family of Jewish origins, she entered the Carmelite order about 1535, but it was not until almost twenty years later that she experienced a conversion to the higher states of contemplative prayer. In 1559 the Grand Inquisitor of Spain published an Index, or list of forbidden books, barring access to the devotional and mystical literature that had nourished Teresa and her nuns. At that stage (*Life*, chapter 26.6) Christ appeared to Teresa and told her: "Do not be distressed, for I will give you a living book." He then began to grant her the visions and experiences of union that moved her to write the account of her inner life known as the* Vida, *or* Life.

The first version was completed about 1562, the same year that Teresa began the reform of the Carmelite nuns. Teresa's confessors asked for revisions of the original, a task she completed about 1565. Part of this revision was the insertion of a treatise on the four degrees of prayer found in chapters 11–22. For Teresa, progress in prayer is identical with the advance to deepening union with God. Several times in her later writings she presented other analyses of the stages of prayer and union, qualifying or altering the picture presented in the Life. *Nevertheless, this account, with its attractive symbolizing of prayer as ways of watering the garden of the soul, remains one of the most detailed and subtle presentations in Christian mystical literature.*

CHAPTER 11.
SHE BEGINS, BY MEANS OF A
COMPARISON, A DESCRIPTION OF
FOUR DEGREES OF PRAYER;
PROCEEDS TO DEAL WITH THE FIRST
DEGREE, WHICH IS MOST PROFITABLE
FOR BEGINNERS AND FOR THOSE
WHO FIND NO TASTE IN PRAYER

I speak now of those who begin to be servants of love; that seems to me to be nothing else but to resolve to follow him who has so greatly loved us in the way of prayer. It is a dignity so great that I have a strange joy in thinking of it, for servile fear vanishes at once if in this first state we act as we should. O Lord of my soul and my Good, how is it that when a soul is determined to love you—doing all it can by forsaking all things in order that it may the better occupy itself with the love of God—it is not your will that it should have the joy of ascending at once to the possession of perfect love? I spoke wrongly. I ought to have said and complained why we ourselves do not, for the fault is wholly our own that we do not rejoice at once in a dignity so great, seeing that attaining to the perfect possession of this true love brings all blessings with it. We are so niggardly and slow in giving ourselves wholly to God that since his Majesty does not let us have the enjoyment of something so precious save at a fitting cost, we do not perfectly prepare ourselves for it.

I see plainly that there is nothing by which so great a good can be procured in this world. But if we did what we could, not clinging to anything on earth, but having all our thoughts and conversation in heaven, I believe that this blessing would quickly be given to us, provided we perfectly prepared ourselves for it at once, as some of the saints have done. . . .

Speaking, then, of their beginnings who are determined to follow after this good and to succeed in this enterprise—I shall proceed hereafter with what I began to say about mystical theology, as I believe they call it [*Life* 10.1]—I have to say that the labor is the greatest at first, for it is they themselves who labor and the Lord who gives the increase.

In the other degrees of prayer there is more enjoyment, although those who are in the beginning, the middle, and the end all have their crosses, however different. Those who follow Christ, if they do not wish to be lost, must walk in the way he walked. Blessed labors that even here in this life are so abundantly rewarded!

. . . The beginner must look upon himself as making a garden in which the Lord is to take his delight, but in a soil unfruitful and abounding in weeds. His Majesty roots up the weeds and plants good seed. Let us then take for granted that this is already done when the soul is determined to give itself to prayer and has actually begun the practice of it. With the help of God we, as good gardeners, have to see that the plants grow, and to water them carefully so that they do not die but produce blossoms that shall send forth much fragrance, refreshing to our Lord, so that he may come often for his pleasure into this garden and take delight in the midst of these virtues.

Let us now see how this garden is to be watered, so that we may understand what we have to do: how much trouble it will cost us, whether the gain be greater than the trouble, and how long a time it will take us. It seems to me that the garden can be watered in four ways: by water taken from a well, which is very laborious; or by a waterwheel and buckets, drawn by a windlass (I have drawn it this way sometimes; it is less troublesome than the first and gives more water); or by a stream or brook (this waters the garden much better; the ground absorbs more water that way and needs to be watered less, and the labor of the gardener is much less); or by heavy rain, when our Lord himself waters it without labor on our part—this way is incomparably better than all the others mentioned.

Now for the application of these four ways of irrigation by which the garden is to be maintained (for without water it must fail). The comparison is to my purpose, and it seems to me that with its help I shall be able to explain in some measure the four degrees of prayer to which our Lord in his goodness has sometimes raised my soul. . . .

We may say that beginners in prayer are those who draw the water up out of the well. This process is very laborious, as I have said. They must tire themselves out in keeping the senses recollected, and this is a great labor because the senses are accustomed to distractions. It is necessary for beginners to accustom themselves to disregard what they hear or see, and they must practice this during the hours of prayer.

They must be alone and in solitude think over their past life. Although the beginners as well as the more advanced must all do this many times, they do not all do so equally, as I will show later [chapter 13.14–15].... They must strive to meditate on the life of Christ, and this wearies the mind.

Thus far we can advance of ourselves—that is, by the grace of God, for without that, as everyone knows, we can never have one good thought. This is beginning to draw water up out of the well, and God grant that there may be water in it! At least we are doing our part, for we are already drawing it and doing what we can to water the flowers. God is so good that when for reasons known to his Majesty (perhaps for our greater good), the well is dry and we, like good gardeners, do what lies within our power, he preserves the flowers without water and makes our virtues grow. By "water" here I mean tears, and when there are no tears, tenderness and interior feelings of devotion....

[The first kind of water takes up the rest of chapters 11–13.]

CHAPTER 14.
BEGINS TO EXPLAIN THE SECOND DEGREE OF PRAYER, IN WHICH GOD ALREADY GIVES THE SOUL SPECIAL CONSOLATIONS

Having spoken of the toilsome efforts and of the strength required for watering the garden when we have to draw the water out of the well, let us now speak of the second manner of drawing the water, which the Lord of the garden has ordained. By using a device of wheel and buckets the gardener may be able to draw more water with less labor and is able to take some rest without being continually at work. This is what I am now going to describe, and I apply it to the prayer called the prayer of quiet.

Here the soul begins to recollect itself and comes to touch on the supernatural, to which it could never attain by its own efforts. True, it seems at times to have been wearied by its work at the wheel, laboring with the understanding and filling the buckets, but in this second degree the water is higher, and accordingly much less labor is needed than when the water had to be drawn up out of the well. I mean that the water is nearer to it, for grace reveals itself more distinctly to the soul. This state is a recollecting of the faculties of the soul within itself, so that its fruition of that contentment may be greater sweetness. But the faculties are not lost; nor are they asleep. The will alone is occupied in such a way that, without knowing how it has become captive, it gives simple consent to become a prisoner of God, for it knows well what it is to be the captive of him it loves. O Jesus and my Lord, how valuable is your love to us here! It binds our own love so closely that it is not in its power at this moment to love anything else but you.

The other two faculties [i.e., memory and intellect] help the will so that it can be capable of the enjoyment of so much good. Nevertheless, it sometimes happens that even while the will is in union, they hinder it very much. But then it should not heed them at all, simply abiding in its enjoyment and quiet. . . .

Everything that now takes place in this state brings the very greatest consolation, and the labor is so slight that the prayer is never wearisome, even if persevered in for some time. The reason is that the understanding is now working very gradually and it is drawing much more water than it drew out of the well. The tears that God now sends flow with joy; though we feel them, they are not the result of any efforts of our own. . . .

[The second kind of water, the prayer of quiet, occupies the rest of chapters 14–15.]

CHAPTER 16.
TREATS THE THIRD DEGREE OF PRAYER. TREATS ELEVATED MATTERS AND WHAT THE SOUL THAT HAS COME THUS FAR CAN DO, AND THE EFFECTS PRODUCED BY THE GREAT FAVORS OF GOD

Let us now speak of the third water with which the garden is watered, that is, of running water coming from a river or brook. By this means the garden is watered with very much less trouble, though some is required to direct the water. In this state our Lord desires to help the gardener in such a way that he may almost be said to be the gardener himself, since he does all the work. The prayer is a sleep of the faculties of the soul, which are not wholly lost, nor able to understand how they are at work. The pleasure, sweetness, and delight are incomparably greater than in the former state of prayer because the waters of grace have risen up to the neck of the soul so that it can neither advance nor retreat; it does not know how to; it seeks only the enjoyment of exceeding bliss. It is like a dying man with a candle in his hand on the point of dying the death he desired—he is rejoicing in this agony with unutterable joy. This seems to me to be nothing else but an almost complete death to all the things of this world and an enjoyment of God. I don't know other words to describe it or explain it. Neither does the soul then know what to do, for it doesn't know whether to speak or to be silent, whether to laugh or to weep. This prayer is a glorious folly, a heavenly madness, in which true wisdom is acquired, and to the soul a kind of fruition most full of delight.

It is now some five or six years, I believe, since the Lord raised me to this state of prayer in abundance, and that more than once. I have never understood it, and never could explain it. My intention at this point was to say very little or nothing about it. I knew well enough that it was not a complete union of all the faculties, and yet most certainly it was higher than the previous state of prayer, but I confess that I could not determine or understand the difference....

[The account of the third water, involving the sleep of the faculties and the beginnings of ecstasy, continues through to the end of chapter 17. Teresa says that in this prayer the soul is able to combine the Mary representing contemplation with the Martha of activity.]

CHAPTER 18.
TREATS OF THE FOURTH DEGREE
OF PRAYER. BEGINS TO DESCRIBE IN
AN EXCELLENT MANNER THE GREAT
DIGNITY CONFERRED BY THE LORD
ON THE SOUL IN THIS STATE . . .

May the Lord teach me the words in which to say something to describe the fourth water. I have great need of his help, even more than when describing the last water, for in that state the soul still feels that it is not dead altogether. (We may speak this way, seeing that it is really dead to the world.) But, as I said [chapter 16.1], it retains the sense to know that it is in the world and to feel its own loneliness, and it makes use of exterior things for the purpose of manifesting its feelings, at least by signs. In the whole of the prayer already spoken of and in each of its stages the gardener does some work, although in the later stages the work is accompanied with so much bliss and consolation for the soul that it would never willingly pass out of it—the work is not felt as work but as bliss. In this fourth state there is no feeling, only enjoyment without any understanding of the thing in which the soul is rejoicing. It understands that it is enjoying some good in which all good is gathered together, but this good is incomprehensible. The senses are all occupied in this enjoyment in such a way that not one of them is at liberty to be able to attend to anything else, either outward or inward. . . .

How this prayer they call union happens and what it is, I cannot explain. Mystical theology explains it, and I am unable to use the proper terms. I cannot understand what the mind is and how it differs from the soul and spirit. All three seem to me to be one, although I do know that the soul sometimes leaps forth out of itself like a fire that is burning and has become a flame, and at times this fire becomes a forceful blaze. The flame ascends high above the fire, but it is not therefore a different thing: It is still the same flame of the same fire. . . .

What I'm trying to explain is what the soul feels when it is in this divine union. It is plain enough what union is: two distinct things become one. O my Lord, how good you are! May you be blessed forever! Let all creatures praise you, my God, for you have so loved us that we can truly speak of this communication that you engage in with souls even in this exile. . . . [Teresa goes on to speak about the differences between union and elevation on the basis of her own experience: "I shall say nothing about what I myself have not had abundant experience." Finally, she turns to the following account of what happens in the depths of the soul.]

Now let us come to what the soul feels interiorly. Let him describe it who knows it, for just as it is impossible to understand it, so much the more is it to describe it! As I was getting ready to write this (I had just received communion and had been experiencing this very prayer I'm speaking of), I was thinking of what the soul was doing at that time. The Lord said these words to me: "It dies wholly to itself, my daughter, in order that it may give itself more and more to me. It is not itself that lives, but I. As it cannot comprehend what it understands, it understands by not understanding."

One who has had experience of this will understand it in some measure, for it cannot be clearly described, because what then takes place is so obscure. All I am able to say is that the soul appears to be joined to God and that there abides within it a conviction so strong and certain that it cannot help believing it. All the faculties now fail and are suspended in such a way that, as I have said [chapters 18.10 and 13], one cannot think they are working. If the soul is making a meditation on any subject, the memory of it is lost at once as if it had never been thought of. If it has been reading, there is no memory of what has been read. The same is true with regard to vocal prayer. Thus this restless little butterfly of the memory has its wings burned now and it cannot fly. The will must be fully occupied in loving, but it cannot understand how it loves; the intellect, if it understands, does not understand how it understands, or at least it can comprehend nothing of what it understands. It does not seem to me to be understanding, because, as I say, it doesn't understand—I really don't understand this!

[The description of the fourth degree of water, or prayer, continues through chapter 22.]

Adapted, corrected, and modernized from the translation of David Lewis, *The Life of St. Teresa of Jesus* (London: Thomas Baker, 5th ed., 1916), 77–147.

8.

THE WAY OF THE PILGRIM

The invocation of the name of Jesus according to the formula "Lord Jesus Christ have mercy on me a sinner" (often known as "the Jesus Prayer") has played a central role in the spiritual life of the Christian East. The practice of the prayer and the effects that this had upon believers have been described in many texts and treatises over the centuries, notably in The Philokalia *(see section 4.1). Nevertheless, the power of the prayer to effect inner (and even outer) transformation is best known through the popular collection of stories about an anonymous pilgrim of nineteenth-century Russia called* The Pilgrim's Tale, *or* The Way of the Pilgrim.*

Recent research has clarified the history of this text, which has been well known in Russia since the 1880s and was translated into many other European languages in the twentieth century. The core of the original four stories about the pilgrim was composed about 1859 by Fr. Mikhail Kozlov (circa 1826–84), at one time a monk of Athos and later a missionary in Siberia. The first edition was published in 1881 by Paisii Fedorov. Later editions added three further stories and many layers to the text, in the manner typical of Russian spiritual literature. The leisurely narrative character of the work makes it difficult to give a sense of its attraction and power through brief excerpts. The selections here are restricted to the opening paragraphs and a later description of the technique and somatic effect of the Jesus Prayer.

I.

CHAPTER 1

By the grace of God I am a Christian, by my deeds a great sinner, and by my calling a homeless wanderer of humblest origin, roaming from place to place. My possessions consist of a knapsack with dry crusts of bread on my back and in my bosom the Holy Bible. This is all!

On the twenty-fourth Sunday after Pentecost I came to church to attend the liturgy and entered just as the epistle was being read. The reading was from Paul's First Letter to the Thessalonians, which says in part, "Pray constantly." These words made a deep impression on me and I started thinking of how it could be possible for a man to pray without ceasing when the practical necessities of life demand so much attention. I checked my Bible and saw with my own eyes exactly what I had heard, that it is necessary to pray continuously (1 Thess 5:17); to pray in the Spirit on every possible occasion (Eph 6:18); in every place to lift your hands reverently in prayer (1 Tim 2:8). I thought and thought about these words, but no understanding came to me. . . .

What shall I do? I thought. Where can I find a person who will explain this mystery to me? I will go to the various churches where there are good preachers and perhaps I will obtain an explanation from them. And so I went. . . . I heard many very good homilies on prayer, but they were all instructions about prayer in general: what is prayer, the necessity of prayer, and the fruits of prayer, but no one spoke of the way to succeed in prayer. I did hear a sermon on interior prayer and ceaseless prayer but nothing about attaining that form of prayer. Inasmuch as listening to public sermons had not given me any satisfaction, I stopped attending them and decided, with the grace of God, to look for an experienced and learned person who would satisfy my ardent desire and explain ceaseless prayer to me.

II.
CHAPTER 4. [IN THE FOURTH MEETING, OR TALE, THE PILGRIM ENCOUNTERS A BLIND MAN, WHO IS ALSO A PRACTITIONER OF THE JESUS PRAYER. THEY JOURNEY TOGETHER AND DISCUSS THE PRAYER]

... So my blind friend and I walked slowly and only a little bit at a time, covering ten to fifteen kilometers a day, and all the remaining time we sat in quiet places and read *The Philokalia*. I read to him about the prayer of the heart in the order which my late elder had shown to me, that is, beginning with the writings of Nicephorus the Solitary, Gregory of Sinai, etc. How avidly and attentively he listened and what great joy and comfort he found in it! But then he began to ask me questions about prayer which were beyond my ability to answer.

After I had read the appropriate sections from *The Philokalia* to him, he earnestly asked me to show him a practical method of locating the heart with the mind, introducing the name of Jesus Christ to it, and thus experiencing the joy of praying with the heart. So I began to explain it to him: "Well, even though you are blind and cannot see anything with your eyes, with your mind you can imagine and represent to yourself that which you saw before, a man, some object, or a part of your body like the hand or the foot. You can imagine any object as vividly as though you were looking at it, can't you?" "Yes, I can," he responded. So I continued, "Then in exactly the same way imagine your heart; direct your eyes as though you were looking at it through your breast, see the heart as vividly as you can, and listen attentively to its rhythmic beat. And when you have become accustomed to this, then begin to say the words of the Prayer, while looking into your heart, to the rhythm of your heartbeat. With the first beat say 'Lord,' with the second 'Jesus,' with the third 'Christ,' with the fourth 'have mercy,' and with the fifth 'on me.' And repeat this very frequently. This should be fairly easy for you, because you have practiced the preliminary part of the prayer of the heart. The next step, according to the writings of the Fathers, is to direct the flow of the Jesus Prayer in the heart in harmony with your breathing; that is, while inhaling say, 'Lord Jesus

Christ,' and while exhaling say, 'have mercy on me.' Practice this as often as possible, gradually increasing the time, and before too long you will experience a kind of pleasant pain in the heart, a warmth, and a sense of burning. Thus, with the help of God you will attain self-activating prayer of the heart. However, you must be extremely careful in all this to guard your imagination against any kind of visions; the holy Fathers strictly warn against this so as not to fall into deception."

My blind friend listened to all this with great attention and began fervently to do what I had suggested, especially when we stopped for the night. After five days he experienced warmth and unspeakable joy in the heart as well as a great desire ceaselessly to say the Prayer, which led him to greater love of Jesus Christ. Sometimes he would see a light without any objects, and at other times it seemed to him that when he entered his heart a bright flame, as from a lighted candle, illumined his heart and his whole being and by this he could see faraway objects.

INNER AND OUTER PRACTICES

Along with prayer and the sacraments, there are many other inner and outer practices, as well as forms of personal relationship, that have been seen as helpful, even necessary, for advancing in the mystical life. These exercises are part of a life commitment to the pursuit of God. Many of these spiritual activities, rooted in the Bible, found their earliest institutional form in monasticism, as can be seen in selection 1. Among the most important are solitude and silence. The role of voluntary separation from human contact in order to be more fully devoted to God is found in many religions. In the Sermon on the Mount, Jesus says: "But when you pray, go into a room by yourself, shut the door, and pray to your Father who is in secret; and your Father who sees what is done in secret will reward you" (Mt 6:6). Solitude was a primary value for the eremitical, or hermit, tradition among the monks (see selection 2), but Jesus' command shows that it was a practice that all could to some extent employ. So too, both outer and inner silence have been seen as ways of stilling and emptying the mind to prepare for divine visitation. The negative, or apophatic, dimension of Christian mysticism (see section 9.1) emphasizes that since God is beyond all human knowing and speaking, he is encountered primarily in verbal and mental silence. The importance of silence will be evident from other selections throughout this collection; in this section it is represented especially by selection 5, a passage from a popular, if controversial, treatise, *The Spiritual Guide* of Miguel de Molinos. Solitude and silence are intimately connected to a range of other mystical practices, such as detachment, releasement, and abandonment, touched on in some of the passages given here and also evident in other sections of this collection.

Other practices integral to the mystical life involve the relations among believers as they aid each other on the path to God. Christian theology teaches that the primary guide of the spiritual life is the Holy Spirit given to each believer at baptism, but the primacy of the Spirit does not negate the role of secondary guides, skilled and wise persons more advanced in the mystical life who share their wisdom to help others. Spiritual guidance was most often conducted in private conversations and sacramental confessions that have left no written record, but one type of literature, namely letters of spiritual direction, provides us with insight into this dimension of mysticism (see selection 4). Among the Celtic monks spiritual advisers were known as "soul friends," a reminder that at least some of this advice was based not just on the formal relationship of priest and penitent, but upon a deep inner affection and true "spiritual friendship" between two persons who saw their love for each other as grounded in their love for God (selection 3).

1.

THE PHILOKALIA

"DISCOURSE ON ABBA PHILIMON"

The Philokalia *(i.e., Love of the Beautiful), the treasury of the spirituality and mysticism of Eastern Christianity, is a collection of ascetical and mystical texts dating from the fourth through the fifteenth centuries, centering on the practice of the recitation of the Jesus Prayer. The anthology was put together by Nicodemus the Hagiorite (1749–1809), a monk of Mount Athos, and Makarios of Corinth.* The authorities cited in The Philokalia *are the major teachers of Eastern Orthodoxy: Antony the Great, Evagrius, Mark the Ascetic, Maximus the Confessor, John of Damascus, Symeon the New Theologian, Gregory of Sinai, and Gregory Palamas, to name only some. The three volumes of the work, first published in Greek in 1782, were translated in an abridged form into Slavonic by Paisii Velichkovsky in 1793, and into Russian in an enlarged version by Bishop Theophane the Recluse between 1876 and 1890.*

Among the texts in volume 2 is the "Discourse on Abba Philimon," which is a gem of the life and teachings of the desert monks, the foundation for so much later spirituality and mysticism. We are not sure when Philimon lived, but it seems to have been around 600 CE. The narrative about him provides a picture of the inner and outer practices of monastic mysticism: asceticism, poverty, humility, constant prayer, solitude and stillness, repetitive reading of scripture, the gift of tears, remembrance of death, and much more—all in the service of attaining deep contemplation. These activities constitute Philimon's personal monastic "rule." The discourse also gives us a picture of the spiritual direction practiced by the Desert Fathers, as well as containing what may be the earliest reference to what became the standard form of the Jesus Prayer, though the practice under various guises was certainly older.

It is said that Abba Philimon, the anchorite, lived for a long time enclosed in a certain cave not far from the Lavra of the Romans. There he engaged in the life of ascetic struggle, always asking himself the question which, it is reported, the great Arsenios used to put to himself: "Philimon, why did you come here?" [*Sayings of the Desert Fathers*, Arsenios no. 40]. He used to plait ropes and make baskets, giving them to the steward of the Lavra in exchange for a small ration of bread. He ate only bread and salt, and even that not every day. In this way he took no thought for the flesh (Rom 13:14), but, initiated into ineffable mysteries through the pursuit of contemplation, he was enveloped by divine light and established in a state of joyfulness. When he went to church on Saturdays and Sundays he walked alone in deep thought, allowing no one to approach him lest his concentration should be interrupted. In church he stood in a corner, keeping his face turned to the ground and shedding streams of tears. For, like the holy fathers, and especially like his great model Arsenios, he was always full of contrition and kept the thought of death continually in his mind.

When a heresy arose in Alexandria and the surrounding area, Philimon left his cave and went to the Lavra near that of Nikanor. There he was welcomed by the blessed Paulinos, who gave him his own retreat and enabled him to follow a life of complete stillness. For a whole year Paulinos allowed absolutely no one to approach him, and he himself disturbed him only when he had to give him bread.

On the feast of the holy resurrection of Christ, Philimon and Paulinos were talking when the subject of the eremitical state came up. Philimon knew that Paulinos, too, aspired to this state, and with this in mind he implanted in him teachings taken from scripture and the fathers that emphasized, as Moses had done, how impossible it is to conform to God without complete stillness; how stillness gives birth to ascetic effort, ascetic effort to tears, tears to awe, awe to humility, humility to foresight, foresight to love; and how love restores the soul to health and makes it dispassionate, so that one then knows that one is not far from God.

He used to say to Paulinos: "You must purify your intellect completely through stillness and engage it ceaselessly in spiritual work. For just as the eye is attentive to sensible things and is fascinated by what it sees, so the purified intellect is attentive to intelligible realities and becomes so rapt by spiritual contemplation that it is hard to tear it away. And the more the intellect is stripped of the passions and purified through stillness, the greater the spiritual knowledge it is found worthy to receive. The intellect is perfect when it transcends knowledge of created things and is united with God: having then attained a royal dignity it no longer allows itself to be pauperized or aroused by lower desires, even if offered all the kingdoms of the world. If, therefore, you want to acquire all these virtues, be detached from every man, flee the world, and sedulously follow the path of the saints. Dress shabbily, behave simply, speak unaffectedly, do not be haughty in the way you walk, live in poverty and let yourself be despised by everyone. Above all, guard the intellect and be watchful, patiently enduring indigence and hardship, and keeping intact and undisturbed the spiritual blessings that you have been granted. Pay strict attention to yourself, not allowing any sensual pleasure to infiltrate. For the soul's passions are allayed by stillness; but when they are stimulated and aroused they grow more savage and force us into greater sin; and they become hard to cure, like the body's wounds when they are scratched and chafed. Even an idle word can make the intellect forget God, the demons enforcing this with the compliance of the senses.

"Great struggle and awe are needed to guard the soul. You have to divorce yourself from the whole world and sunder your soul's affection for the body. You have to become cityless, homeless, possessionless, free from avarice, from worldly concerns and society, humble, compassionate, good, gentle, still, ready to receive in your heart the stamp of divine knowledge. You cannot write on wax unless you have first expunged the letters written on it. Basil the Great teaches us these things [Basil, *Letters* 2.2].

"The saints were people of this kind. They were totally severed from the ways of the world, and by keeping the vision of heaven unsullied in themselves they made its light shine by observing the divine laws. And having mortified their earthly aspects (Col 3:5) through self-control and through awe and love for God, they were radiant with holy words and actions. For through unceasing prayer and the study of the divine scriptures the soul's noetic eyes are opened, and they see the

King of the celestial powers, and great joy and fierce longing burn intensely in the soul; and as the flesh, too, is taken up by the Spirit, man becomes wholly spiritual. These are the things which those who in solitude practice blessed stillness and the strictest way of life, and who have separated themselves from all human solace, confess openly to the Lord in heaven alone."

When the good brother heard this, his soul was wounded by divine longing; and he and Abba Philimon went to live in Sketis where the greatest of the holy fathers had pursued the path of sanctity. They settled in the Lavra of St. John the Small, and asked the steward of the Lavra to see to their needs, as they wished to lead a life of stillness. And by the grace of God they lived in complete stillness, unfailingly attending church on Saturdays and Sundays but on other days of the week staying in their cells, praying and fulfilling their rule.

The rule of the holy Elder was as follows. During the night he quietly chanted the entire psalter and the biblical canticles, and recited part of the gospels. Then he sat down and intently repeated "Lord have mercy" for as long as he could. After that he slept, rising towards dawn to chant the First Hour. Then he again sat down, facing eastward, and alternately chanted psalms and recited by heart sections of the epistles and gospels. He spent the whole day in this manner, chanting and praying unceasingly, and being nourished by the contemplation of heavenly things. His intellect was often lifted up to contemplation, and he did not know if he was still on earth.

His brother, seeing him devoted so unremittingly to this rule and completely transformed by divine thoughts, said to him: "Why, father, do you exhaust yourself so much at your age, disciplining your body and bringing it into subjection?" (1 Cor 9:27). And he replied: "Believe me, my son, God has placed such love for my rule in my soul that I lack the strength to satisfy the longing within me. Yet longing for God and hope of the blessings held in store triumph over bodily weakness." Thus at all times, even when he was eating, he raised his intellect up to the heavens on the wings of his longing.

Once a certain brother who lived with him asked him: "What is the mystery of contemplation?" Realizing that he was intent on learning, the Elder replied: "I tell you, my son, that when one's intellect is completely pure, God reveals to him the visions that are granted to the ministering powers and angelic hosts." The same brother also asked:

"Why, father, do you find more joy in the psalms than in any other part of divine scripture? And why, when quietly chanting them, do you say the words as though you were speaking with someone?" And Abba Philimon replied: "My son, God has impressed the power of the psalms on my poor soul as he did on the soul of the prophet David. I cannot be separated from the sweetness of the visions about which they speak: they embrace all scripture." He confessed these things with great humility, after being much pressed, and then only for the benefit of the questioner.

A brother named John came from the coast to Father Philimon and, clasping his feet, said to him: "What shall I do to be saved? For my intellect vacillates to and fro and strays after all the wrong things." After a pause, the father replied: "This is one of the outer passions and it stays with you because you still have not acquired a perfect longing for God. The warmth of this longing and of the knowledge of God has not yet come to you." The brother said to him: "What shall I do, father?" Abba Philimon replied: "Meditate inwardly for a while, deep in your heart; for this can cleanse your intellect of these things." The brother, not understanding what was said, asked the Elder: "What is inward meditation, father?" The Elder replied: "Keep watch in your heart; and with watchfulness say in your mind with awe and trembling: 'Lord Jesus Christ, have mercy upon me.' For this is the advice which the blessed Diadochos gave to beginners" [Diadochus of Photiki, *On Spiritual Knowledge*, nos. 59, 61].

The brother departed; and with the help of God and the Elder's prayers he found stillness and for a while was filled with sweetness by this meditation. But then it suddenly left him and he could not practice it or pray watchfully. So he went again to the Elder and told him what had happened. And the Elder said to him: "You have had a brief taste of stillness and inner work, and have experienced the sweetness that comes from them. This is what you should always be doing in your heart: whether eating or drinking, in company or outside your cell, or on a journey, repeat that prayer with a watchful mind and an undeflected intellect; also chant, and meditate on prayers and psalms. Even when carrying out needful tasks, do not let your intellect be idle but keep it meditating inwardly and praying. For in this way you can grasp the depths of divine scripture and the power hidden in it, and give unceasing work to the intellect, thus fulfilling the apostolic command:

'Pray without ceasing' (1 Thess 5:17). Pay strict attention to your heart and watch over it, so that it does not give admittance to thoughts that are evil or in any way vain and useless. Without interruption, whether asleep or awake, eating, drinking, or in company, let your heart inwardly and mentally at times be meditating on the psalms, at other times be repeating the prayer, 'Lord Jesus Christ, Son of God, have mercy upon me.' And when you chant, make sure that your mouth is not saying one thing while your mind is thinking about another."

Excerpt from *The Philokalia: The Complete Text, Volume II*, compiled by St. Nikodimos of the Holy Mountain and St. Makarios of Corinth, translated by G.E.H. Palmer, Philip Sherrad, and Kallistos Ware. Translation copyright © by the Eling Trust. Reprinted by permission of Faber and Faber, Inc., an affiliate of Farrar, Straus and Giroux, LLC.

2.

GUIGO I

CARTHUSIAN CUSTOMS

CHAPTER 80

The Carthusian order has played a special role in the history of monasticism and mysticism. The Carthusians are the most successful attempt to combine the ideal of the eremitical life of the hermit based on solitude and silence with elements of the communal, or cenobitical, life of corporate monasticism that helps ensure stability and continuity. The slow growth of the order due to its insistence on fidelity to the ideals of its founders meant that the Carthusians alone among the religious orders of the Catholic Church have never experienced a movement of reform. The Carthusian contribution to mysticism comes not only from the mystical works written by members of the order, but also from the fact that these hermits were dedicated to the copying of manuscripts, so that in the late Middle Ages, Carthusian monasteries often served as mystical "publishing houses." The order takes its name from the monastery of the Grande Chartreuse founded by Bruno of Cologne in the French Alps in 1084. The new house and its daughters became famous for their devotion to silence, solitude, and simplicity.

A good deal of the success of the Carthusians is owed to Guigo I, the fifth prior of the order (1109–36), who wrote the first Customs *(set of monastic rules and observances) for the new hermits, as well as a series of theological* Meditations. *Guigo's* Customs *deals mostly with traditional monastic virtues and practices, but the final chapter is a short and powerful presentation of the role of solitude in attaining God through mental ecstasy (*excessus mentis*).*

CHAPTER 80.
THE PRAISE OF THE SOLITARY LIFE

Dearly beloved, as you requested, you have our monastic customs, such as they are, described in some manner. Among them there are many rather common and unimportant ones; perhaps they should not have been written down, had we not been compelled by your love, which judges nothing, but is rather ready to embrace everything. Still, we do not think that in this way everything can be put down in this one text so that nothing further remains. But if anything has escaped us, it can be easily pointed out through a personal communication.

We have been almost totally silent in praise of this solitary life, conscious that it has been so abundantly recommended by many holy and wise men of such authority that we are not worthy to follow in their footsteps, and that you judge it superfluous that we show you something that you know as well or better than we do. You are aware that in the Old Testament, and especially in the New, almost all the greater and more profound secrets were revealed to God's friends when they were alone and not in the midst of milling crowds. These same friends of God almost always avoided the hindrance of crowds and sought out the convenience of solitude when they wanted to meditate more deeply on something, or to pray with greater freedom, or when they wished to be removed from earthly concerns through mental ecstasy.

This is why (to touch on only a bit of this line of thought) Isaac went forth by himself into the field to meditate (Gen 24:63), something that we can believe was his custom and not just an accident. Jacob, having sent ahead everything over the ford of Jaboc, remained alone and saw God face-to-face (Gen 32:23–30). He was rewarded both by a blessing and by a change of name for the better [i.e., to Israel]. He gained more in one moment alone than a whole lifetime in the company of others. Scripture is the witness to how much Moses, Elias, and Eliseus loved solitude and to how much by means of solitude they increased in revelations of divine secrets.

As we noted above, Jeremiah also sat alone because he had been filled with divine threats (Jer 15:17). When he asked that water be given for his head and a flood of tears for his eyes so that he might weep over the slain of his people (Jer 9:1), he also asked for a place where he might more freely exercise himself in so holy a work, saying,

"Who will give me a lodging place of wayfarers in solitude" (Jer 9:2), in this manner indicating that he was not able to do this in the city because the presence of companions impedes the gift of tears. He also said, "It is good to await the salvation of God in silence" (Lam 3:26)—and solitude gives great assistance to this work. He added: "It is good for a man to have borne the yoke from his youth" (Lam 3:27), something that is a great consolation for us, since almost all of us have taken up this vocation from our youth. He added these words, "The solitary one will sit down and keep silent, because he will lift himself above himself" (Lam 3:28), thus signifying almost all the things that are best in our way of life: quiet and solitude, silence and the desire for heavenly things (Heb 11:16). Afterward he shows what these efforts do to those who have devoted themselves to this school, when he says, "He will give his cheek to the one who strikes him and will be filled with reproaches" (Lam 3:30). Such people in one way are in the highest patience and in another show forth perfect humility.

John the Baptist, who, according to the Savior's praise, "of those born of women no greater has arisen" (Mt 11:11), clearly showed the security and usefulness that solitude brings. He did not put faith in himself despite the divine messages that foretold he would be filled by the Holy Spirit from the womb so that he could go before Christ in the spirit and power of Elias (Lk 1:13–17), and despite his miraculous birth and the holiness of his parents. He fled human company as something dangerous and chose desert solitude as something safe (Lk 1:80), and he was ignorant of danger and death as long as he lived alone in the desert. His baptizing of Christ and the death he accepted for justice show what kind of virtue and merit he gained there. In solitude he was made the kind of person who alone was worthy to wash the Christ who washes all things (Mt 3:13–17). For the sake of truth he refused neither prison nor death (Mt 14:3–12).

Jesus himself, Lord and God, whose virtue could neither receive increase in the secret of the desert, nor be impeded in a public place, nevertheless, so that he might instruct us by an example, was proved by fasting and temptation in solitude before he preached and performed miracles (Mt 4:1–11). Scripture also says of him that leaving behind the crowds of his disciples he went up the mountain alone to pray (Mt 14:23). As the time of the passion already grew near, he left the apostles and went alone to pray (Mt 26:39–44), showing us especially by this example how much solitude aids prayer, since even though the apostles were his companions, he did not wish to pray along with them.

In the case of those holy and venerable monastic fathers, Paul, Antony, Hilarion, Benedict, and so many more we can't count, you should take into account how much they advanced in mind through solitude, and you should agree that solitude is the greatest support for sweet psalmody, pious reading, fervent prayer, deep meditation, ecstatic contemplation, and the baptism of tears.

These few things that we have said to you do not provide sufficient examples for the praise of this vocation you have taken up, but rather you should gather together a larger number, either from your present mode of life, or from the pages of the holy scriptures, even though this vocation does not need such approval, since it sufficiently commends itself by its rarity and by the small number of its adherents. If, according to the Lord's words, "Narrow is the path that leads to life and few that find it, but broad is that which leads to death and many follow it" (Mt 7:13–14), then, within the forms of life of the Christian religion, the fewer the members the more one form shows itself to be of better and higher merit, and the more the members the more a form is lower and inferior. We hope that you are always well and mindful of us.

Translated by Bernard McGinn from Guigo, *Consuetudines,* as found in *Patrologiae cursus completus. Series Latina,* edited by J.-P. Migne (Paris, 1844–64), Vol. 153, columns 755–58. Hereafter this collection will be abbreviated as PL with appropriate volume and column numbers.

3.

AELRED OF RIEVAULX
SPIRITUAL FRIENDSHIP

Aelred of Rievaulx (1110–67) was born in the northern border country of England. Writing of his youth, Aelred reveals much about his character: "When I was just a boy at school and the charm of my companions was a great delight, amidst the habits and vices that usually threaten that age, I gave my whole mind to affection and vowed myself to love, so that nothing seemed more pleasant to me, more delightful, more useful, than to love and be loved." He entered the Cistercian house of Rievaulx in 1134. In 1142 he met Bernard of Clairvaux, a meeting that had a profound effect on him personally and intellectually. In 1147 Aelred became abbot of Rievaulx, where he died twenty years later.

With Bernard's sponsorship, Aelred wrote a mystical treatise titled The Mirror of Charity, *but he is best known for his analysis of the form of charity that he felt was both the model for the most direct experience of God and the way to attain the goal—the love he called spiritual friendship* (spiritualis amicitia). *In his work of that title, written in dialogue form, Aelred took many ideas from the classical ideal of friendship set forth in Cicero's treatise on the subject, but he transformed these notions on the basis of his understanding of God as offering us the highest of friendships and his insistence that all true friendship is a gift from above given through Christ. The English Cistercian's conviction that deep spiritual friendship is not in any way a hindrance, but rather a sure way to experience Christ, is a reminder of how important the role of friendship has been in the mystical path. Aelred's friendships were between male monks; other examples of spiritual friendship have been between men and women, as we find in the case of Teresa of Avila and John of the Cross. In these relationships the male was often both confessor and guide, on the one hand, and also pupil and admirer of the female mystic, on the other.*

I.
BOOK I. THE ORIGIN OF FRIENDSHIP, SECTIONS 1–10, 69–70

AELRED. Here we are, you and I, and I hope that Christ may be the third between us. Now there is nothing to disturb us; there is no one who interrupts our friendly discussion; nobody's voice or shout creeps into this thankful solitude. Now then, my beloved, open your heart and pour forth whatever you want into these friendly ears. Let us be thankful for this place, time, and leisure. . . .

IVO. That is how it is, and I am very thankful, knowing that you care about your son whose mind and intention have been revealed to you by the Spirit of Charity himself. I hope that your esteem would grant me this at least, that as often as you visit your sons who are in this place, you will at least once let me have your full attention when the others have gone away so that I can pour out my burning heart without any worry.

AELRED. Of course, and freely! I am very delighted to see that you are not ready for vain and useless matters, but always ready to talk about something useful and even necessary for your progress. Speak with confidence and share all your concerns and thoughts with your friend so that you may both learn and teach something, both give and receive, both pour out and draw in.

IVO. I'm ready to learn, not to teach; to accept, not to give; to draw in, not to pour out. This is how my youth orders, my inexperience compels, and my monastic profession commands. But so that I don't foolishly waste the time needed for other things on these matters, I want you to teach me something about spiritual friendship, namely, what it is; what usefulness it brings; what its beginning and end are; whether it can exist among all people (and if not, among whom); how it may be preserved unharmed and brought to a holy conclusion without any harmful dissension. . . .

AELRED. I confess that you have won me over, but since I do not know myself and don't want to lie about my abilities, on these matters I will not teach you, but rather talk with you about them. You yourself have opened up the way for both of us, and enkindled that most splendid light at the very threshold of our search, a light that will not allow us to wander away on bypaths, but that will lead us on the right path to the sure goal of the question under review. What can be said about friendship that is higher, or truer, or more useful, than that it ought and is proven to begin in Christ, advance according to Christ, and be brought to perfection by Christ? . . .

[There follows a discussion on the relation of charity and friendship and the three kinds of friendship: carnal, based on harmony in vice; worldly, based on hope of gain; and spiritual, based on similarity of life, morals, and pursuits among just persons.]

IVO. What is this? Are we to say of friendship what John, the friend of Jesus, said about charity (1 Jn 4:16), "God is friendship"?

AELRED. It is unusual for sure and has no scriptural authority, but what follows concerning charity [in John's epistle] I do not hesitate to apply to friendship, that is, "he who abides" in friendship, "abides in God and God in him" (1 Jn 4:16). . . .

II.

BOOK II. THE FRUIT AND EXCELLENCE OF FRIENDSHIP, SECTIONS 18-21

AELRED. . . . Pay heed to a few things about how friendship is a step toward the love and knowledge of God. There is nothing dishonorable in friendship, "nothing feigned, nothing of pretense, and whatever it is, is holy, and voluntary, and true" (Cicero, *On Friendship* 26). This all belongs also to charity. Friendship shines forth beyond other things with the special prerogative that those who are joined together with the glue of friendship feel that everything is delightful, everything is safe, everything is charming, everything is sweet. Therefore, on the basis of the perfection of charity we love many people who are a burden and pain to us. We are concerned about them in an honest, not a feigned or pretended way, but truly and voluntarily. But we do not admit them to the secrets of our friendship. So in friendship honesty and sweetness are joined, truth and delight, charm and will, attraction and action. All these things are begun by Christ, are advanced through Christ, and are brought to perfection in Christ. Therefore, it does not seem to be too steep or unnatural an ascent from the Christ who inspires us to love our friend to the Christ who offers himself as a friend to be loved, so that sweetness will follow upon sweetness, and charm upon charm, and attraction upon attraction. And so the friend who cleaves to his friend in the spirit of Christ is made one heart and one soul with him (Acts 4:32). Ascending to the friendship of Christ through the stages of love, he is made one spirit with him (1 Cor 6:17) in a single kiss. The holy soul sighs for that kiss, saying, "Let him kiss me with the kiss of his mouth" (Song 1:1).

III.

BOOK III. HOW AND WITH WHOM FRIENDSHIP MAY BE PRESERVED UNBROKEN, SECTIONS 128–33

AELRED. So that we can finally close our discussion as the sun is setting, I take it you do not doubt that friendship comes from love. How can a person love another person who does not love himself, since he ought to order the love he has for his neighbor from a likeness of the love by which he is dear to himself? But someone who demands from himself or requests for himself something shameful and dishonorable does not love himself. The first thing therefore is that each person chastise himself, not allowing himself anything that is indecent, and not taking away from himself anything useful. Loving himself in this way, let him also love his neighbor according to the same rule. But because this love gathers many together, let him choose from them those he may admit to the secrets of friendship by an intimate bond, in whom he may pour out his affection with abundance, baring his breast even as far as his vitals and marrow, that is, the inner thoughts and intentions of the heart. He ought to choose him not according to frivolous attraction, but according to reasonable observance, and according to similarity of manners and contemplation of the virtues. After that, let him depend on his friend in such a way that all foolish levity is banished and delight is present; and let the duties and services of goodwill and love not be lacking. And then let his faithfulness, honesty, and patience be tested. Little by little then add the sharing of advice, the dedication to common pursuits, and even a certain similarity in expression. . . .

Prayer for one another is added to this, which, in memory of a friend, is more efficacious the more lovingly it is sent forth to God, with flowing tears that either fear excites, or loves brings out, or sorrow evokes. Praying to Christ for a friend in this way, and wishing to be heard by Christ for a friend, directs the attention to Christ lovingly and longingly. Suddenly and insensibly, when at times one attraction passes over into the other, touching Christ's sweetness from near at hand, as it were, the person begins "to taste how sweet he is," and "to feel how delicious he is" (Ps 33:9, 99:5). In this way he ascends from the holy love by which he embraces a friend to the love in which he embraces Christ. He will joyfully feed upon the spiritual fruit of friendship with an open mouth, awaiting the fullness of all the things to come in the future. That will be the time when the fear we now have for each other, and which causes us concern, will be taken away, and all the trouble that we now have to bear for each other will be removed. Then death's sting will have been destroyed, along with death itself (1 Cor 15:54), whose pangs now often burden us so that it is necessary that we grieve for each other. Then we will rejoice in the eternity of the Highest Good with full assurance, when this friendship to which we now admit only a few will be poured out upon all, and from all poured back into God, and "God will be all in all" (1 Cor 15:28). The End.

Translated by Bernard McGinn from Aelred of Rievaulx, *Liber de spirituali amicitia*, in PL 195:661–62, 669–70, 672, 700–2.

4.

LETTERS OF SPIRITUAL DIRECTION

Letters of spiritual direction have played a role in the history of mysticism. Such missives have dealt with many topics, from questions of ascetical practices, forms of prayer, and the inner attitudes necessary to begin the mystical path, through to profound teaching about the nature of union with God. These letters have been penned by both men and women. In the thirteenth century, for example, both Clare of Assisi and Hadewijch (see section 3.5) wrote letters of spiritual guidance, and Teresa of Avila in the sixteenth century was a noted letter writer. The following two selections give some sense of this wealth of literature.

The first example, an anonymous letter from fourteenth-century Germany sometimes called "The Silent Outcry," is a gem of apophatic mysticism. The piece seems to be from a confessor to a person who has undertaken to live a life of detachment and releasement characteristic of the "friends of God." Although the negative theology of the letter goes back to Dionysius (see section 9.1), the language reflects the teaching of Meister Eckhart and his followers, especially Henry Suso. In rhythmic prose the letter begins with a series of axioms summarizing the mental attitudes and inner practices designed to lead from the God concealed beneath the veils of revelation and all human speech toward the even more secret mystery of the naked God beyond all thought. The essential message appears at the beginning and the end: It is only by letting go of God that God can be found.

The second example is from one of the most noted letter writers of Christian mysticism, Francis de Sales (see section 13.7). More than two thousand of Fran-

cis' letters of spiritual direction survive. Especially noteworthy are the letters he sent to his close spiritual friend Jane Frances de Chantal, a widowed French aristocrat whom he first met in 1604. In 1610 the two collaborated in founding a new religious order for women, the Visitandines. Francis was Jane's spiritual guide, but it is clear that her own mystical graces were important for his life and teaching. Francis wrote about four hundred letters to Jane.

I.

THE SILENT OUTCRY

Learn how to let go of God through God, the hidden God through the naked God. Be willing to lose a penny in order to find a guilder. Get rid of the water, so that you can make wine. The creature is not strong enough to take God away from you, not even the least grace, as long as you yourself want him.

If you want to avoid things, learn to suffer; if you want to eat of the honey, you should not be put off by the bee's sting. If you want to catch fish, learn to get wet; if you want to see Jesus on the shore (Jn 21:4), learn to sink down into the sea first (Mt 14:30).

Were it the case that you should see the heavens torn open and the stars falling, you should not let it make you lose your composure; God will not take himself from you unless you will it; how much less can a creature remove him.

Listen. Look. Suffer and be still. Release yourself into the light. See with intellect. Learn with discretion. Suffer with joy. Rejoice with longing. Have desire with forbearance. Complain to no one. My child, be patient and release yourself, because no one can dig God out from the ground of your heart.

O deep treasure, how will you be dug up? O high perfection, who may attain you? O flowing fountain, who can exhaust you? O burning Brilliance; outbursting Power; simple Return; naked Hiddenness; hidden Security; secure Confidence; simple silent One in all things; manifold Good in a single silence; You silent Outcry, no one can find you who does not know how to let you go.

Release yourself, my child, and thank God that he has given you such a way of life.

Translation by Bernard McGinn from Karl Bihlmeyer, "Kleine Beiträge zur Geschichte der deutschen Mystik," in *Beiträge zur Geschichte der Renaissance und Reformation. Festgabe für Josef Schlecht,* edited by L. Fischer (1917), 58–59.

II.
FRANCIS DE SALES, LETTER TO MOTHER DE CHANTAL (MARCH 1618)

My dear daughter. This night during my wakeful times I have had a thousand good thoughts for my sermons; but strength has failed me to bring them forth. God knows all, and I direct all to his greater glory, and adoring his Providence I remain at peace. There is no help for it: I must do what I will not, "and the good which I will, I do not" (Rom 7:19). I am here in the midst of preachings and of a large audience, larger than I thought; but if I do nothing here it will be little consolation to me.

Believe that meantime I think at every moment of you and of your soul, for which I incessantly express my desires before God and his angels that it may be more filled with the abundance of his graces. My dearest daughter, what ardor do I seem to have for your advancement in most celestial holy love, to which, while celebrating Mass this morning, I have again dedicated and offered you, mentally lifting you up in my arms as one does little children, and big ones too, when one is strong enough to lift them. Behold something of what imaginations our hearts make on these occasions! Truly I am pleased with it, that it should thus employ all things for the sweetness of its incomparable affection, referring them to holy things.

I have not failed to make a special memento of your dear deceased husband. Ah, what a happy exchange you made that day, embracing the state of perfect resignation, in which with such consolation I found you! And your soul, taking a Spouse of so high a condition, has reason indeed to find an extreme joy in the commemoration of the hour of your betrothal to him. And so it is true, my dear daughter, that our unity is wholly consecrated to the sovereign Unity; and I feel with ever increasing force the reality of the union of our hearts, which will truly keep me from ever forgetting you until after, and long after, I have forgotten myself to fasten myself so much the better to the cross. I am going to try to keep you ever exalted permanently on the throne which God has given you in my heart, a throne based upon the cross.

For the rest, my daughter, go on establishing ever more and more your good purposes, your holy resolutions; deepen more and more your consideration of the wounds of Our Lord, where you will find an abyss of reasons which will confirm you in your generous undertaking, and will make you feel how vain and low is the heart which makes its dwelling or which builds on other tree than that of the cross. O my God, how happy shall we be if we live and die in this holy tabernacle! No, nothing, nothing of this world is worthy of our love: it is all due to this Savior who has given us all his own.

In truth, I have had great sentiments these last days of the infinite obligations which I have to God; and with a thousand emotions of sweetness I have again resolved to serve him with the greatest fidelity I can and to keep my soul more continually in his divine presence. And with all this I find in myself a certain joyfulness, not impetuous, but I think efficacious at undertaking my amendment. Shall you not be very glad, my dear daughter, if one day you will see me well fitted for the service of our Lord? Yes, my dear daughter, because our interior goods are inseparably and wholly united. You wish me perpetually many graces; and as for me, with incomparable ardor I pray God to make you absolutely his own.

God knows, most dear daughter of my soul, how gladly I would wish to die for the love of my Savior! But at least if I cannot die for it, may I live for it alone. My daughter, I am greatly pressed. What more can I say to you save—may this same God bless you with his great benediction. Adieu, my dear daughter; press closely this dear Crucified One to your bosom. I beseech him to clasp and unite you more and more to himself. . . .

Letter XXXIII in the *Library of St. Francis de Sales,* 7 vols., *Volume IV. Letters to Persons in Religion,* 158–60, translated by Henry Benedict Mackey (London: Burns & Oates, 1873–1910).

MIGUEL DE MOLINOS

THE SPIRITUAL GUIDE

BOOK I, CHAPTERS 13 AND 17

The central figure in the Quietist controversy was the Spanish priest Miguel de Molinos, who was born in Aragon in 1628 and ordained in 1652. Little is known of his life until he came to Rome in 1663. In Rome he became a noted confessor and spiritual director, as well as a friend of many high ecclesiastics. His international fame began in 1675 with the publication of The Spiritual Guide *(Guia espiritual), three books on "mystical science" directed to advanced souls and emphasizing the importance of "interior recollection" (recogimiento interior).* The Spiritual Guide *was an overnight sensation, being translated into six languages and going through twenty editions in five years.*

Molinos's work is not very original. He had studied many mystical authors and cites them often, especially Teresa, John of the Cross, Francis de Sales, and Jane de Chantal. Molinos's writings and work as a spiritual guide, however, aroused opposition, especially among the Italian Jesuits and some of the French clerics resident in Rome. A war of books and pamphlets erupted between his attackers and defenders, culminating in his arrest by the Inquisition on July 18, 1685. The details of his imprisonment and the subsequent investigation are still murky. During the course of the next two years many of Molinos's supporters abandoned him, as some witnesses testified to his unorthodox methods of spiritual direction and others even accused him of taking sexual liberties with his penitents. Pope Innocent XI, once a supporter, is said to have exclaimed, "We were really made fools of!" In May 1687 Molinos confessed his errors and immoral conduct, and on September 13, after having made a solemn abjuration of sixty-eight erroneous articles, he was condemned to perpetual imprisonment (for more on these errors, see section 14.4). He died in 1697.

Judgments about Molinos's life and teaching have varied. His writings, and those of other condemned Quietists such as Madame Guyon (see section 1.6), became popular with some English Protestants, as the translation used here demonstrates. Until recent times he was generally viewed as a dangerous heretic by Roman Catholics. Nevertheless, there is little in The Guide *that cannot be found in orthodox mystics, though Molinos's language is not always clear. It is quite possible that he confessed to immorality to spare himself torture and public execution. One of his most recent students wisely says, "Perhaps it is better to leave judgment to the Last Judge." Molinos's teaching on interior recollection, which he argued could be brought down to a single continuous act within the soul (one of the views for which he was condemned), picked up on some of the traditional practices of former mystics. He also stressed the necessity for interior silence, a theme that has been central to mysticism. These two chapters from the first book of* The Guide *show how Molinos understood the relation between recollection and the practice of silence.*

I.

CHAPTER 13. WHAT THE SOUL OUGHT TO DO IN INTERIOR RECOLLECTION

When you go to prayer, you should deliver yourself wholly up into the hands of God with perfect resignation, making an act of faith, believing that you are in the divine presence, afterwards remaining in that holy repose with quietness, silence, and tranquility, and endeavoring for a whole day, a whole year, and your whole life to continue that first act of contemplation by faith and love. . . .

By this you will be undeceived and know what is the perfect and spiritual manner of prayer, and be advised what is to be done in internal recollection. You will know that to the end that love may be made perfect and pure, it is expedient to curtail the multiplication of sensible and fervent acts, the soul continuing quiet and resting in that inward silence. Because tenderness, delight, and sweet sentiments, which the soul experiences in the will, are not purely spiritual, but are acts blended with the sensibility of nature. Nor is it perfect love, but sensible pleasure, which distracts and hurts the soul, as the Lord revealed to the venerable Madame de Chantal.

How happy and how well disposed will your soul be, if retreating within itself, she there abide in her own nothingness, both in her center and superior part, without minding what she does: whether she recollects or not; whether she carries herself well or ill; whether she operates or not, without heeding, thinking, or minding any sensible thing. At that time the intellect believes with a pure act, and the will loves with perfect love, without any kind of impediment, imitating that pure and continued act of intuition and love which the saints say the blessed in heaven have, with no other difference than that they see God himself there face to face, and the soul here sees only through the veil of an obscure faith.

O how few are the souls that attain to this perfect way of praying because they do not penetrate enough into this internal recollection and mystical silence, and because they do not strip themselves of imperfect reflection and sensible pleasure! O that your soul without thoughtful attention even to herself might give herself in prayer to that holy and spiritual tranquility and say with St. Augustine, "Let my soul be silent, and pass beyond herself, not thinking of herself" (*Confessions* 9.10). Let her be silent, and desire neither to act nor to think; let her forget herself and plunge into that obscure faith. How secure and safe would she be, though it might seem to her that abiding thus in nothingness she would be lost. . . .

II.
CHAPTER 17. INTERNAL AND MYSTICAL SILENCE

There are three kinds of silence; the first is of words, the second of desires, and the third of thoughts. The first is perfect; the second more perfect; and the third most perfect. In the first, that is, of words, virtue is acquired; in the second, to wit of desires, quietness is attained; in the third, that of thoughts, internal recollection is gained. By not speaking, not desiring, and not thinking, one arrives at the true and perfect mystical silence, wherein God speaks with the soul, communicates himself to her, and in the abyss of her own depth, teaches her the most perfect and exalted wisdom.

He calls and guides her to this inward solitude and mystical silence, when he says that he will speak to her alone, in the most secret and hidden part of the heart (Hos 2:14). You are to keep yourself in this mystical silence, if you want to hear the sweet and divine voice. For gaining this treasure it is not enough to forsake the world, nor to renounce your own desires and all created things, if you do not wean yourself from all desires and thoughts. Rest in this mystical silence, and open the door, so that God may communicate himself with you and unite you and transform you into himself.

The perfection of the soul consists not in speaking nor in thinking a great deal about God but in loving him sufficiently. This love is attained to by means of perfect resignation and internal silence; it all consists in works: The love of God has but few words. Thus St. John the Evangelist confirms and inculcates it: "My little children, let us not love in word, nor in tongue, but in deed and in truth" (1 Jn 3:18).

You are clearly convinced now that perfect love consists not in loving acts nor tender ejaculations, nor yet in the internal acts in which you tell God that you have an infinite love for him and you love him more than yourself. It may be that at the time you seek yourself more, and the love of yourself, than the true love of God, because love consists in works and not in fair speeches.

In order for a rational creature to understand the secret desire and intention of your heart, it is necessary for you to express it to him in words. But God, who searches the heart, does not need you to profess and assure him of it; nor is he satisfied, as the evangelist says, with love in word or in tongue, but with that which is true and active. What good does it do to tell him with great zeal and fervor that you love him tenderly and perfectly above all things, if at one bitter word or slight injury you fail to resign yourself, not being mortified for the love of him? A manifest proof that your love was a love in tongue and not in deed.

Strive to be resigned in all things with silence, and in so doing, without saying that you love him, you will attain to the most perfect, quiet, effectual, and true love. St. Peter most affectionately told the Lord that for his sake he was ready and willing to lay down his life, but at the word of a young woman he denied him and there was an end to his zeal (Mt 27:69–72). Mary Magdalen said not a word, and yet the Lord himself, taken with her perfect love, became her panegyrist, saying that she had loved much (Lk 7:47). It is internally then, with dumb silence, that the most perfect virtues of faith, hope, and charity are practiced, without any necessity of telling God that you love him, hope and believe in him, because the Lord knows better than you do what the internal motions of your heart are.

How well was that pure act of love understood and practiced by that profound and great mystic, the Venerable Gregory Lopez [a Mexican hermit who died in 1596], whose whole life was a continual prayer and a continued act of contemplation, and of so pure and spiritual a love of God that it never gave way to affections and sensible emotions. Having for the space of three years continued the ejaculation, "Your will be done in time and in eternity," repeating it as often as he breathed, God Almighty revealed to him the infinite treasure of the pure and continued act of faith and love with silence and resignation, so that he came to say that during the thirty-six years he lived after that, he always continued, in his inward self, that pure act of love, without ever uttering the least petition, ejaculation, or any thing that was from the senses or sprung from nature. O incarnate seraphim and deified man! How well you knew how to enter into that internal and mystical silence and to distinguish between the outward and inward self.

Adapted from the translation first published in London in 1688 under the title *The Spiritual Guide Which Disentangles the Soul and Brings It by the Inward Way to the Getting of Perfect Contemplation.* This version, based on the 1685 Italian edition, has been often reprinted.

MYSTICAL ITINERARIES

The journey motif, the conception of life as a passage through a series of stages on the way to an intended goal, is deeply rooted in the human mind. The notion of being on an itinerary not only corresponds to everyday experience but also allows us to give structure and meaning to the confusion we often find in life. It is scarcely surprising that many mystics, both in Christianity and in other religious traditions, have used itineraries to describe what they experienced and what they wish to hand on to their followers.

Each person's journey to God, of course, is unique, even if it takes place within the context of the beliefs and rituals of a religious community. To that extent, the construction of standard mystical itineraries such as those found in this section is to some degree artificial—like reading a map, not actually walking through the terrain. These itineraries are intended to be guidebooks to help people, usually with the advice of a spiritual director, to gain some sense of where they are and what lies ahead. Due to this quasi-artificial character, some mystics, such as Meister Eckhart, have refrained from constructing itineraries, but many mystical writers have left us descriptions of stages on the path to God in their writings, always with the understanding that there are many such roads, and that one type of itinerary does not rule out others.

1.

THE THREEFOLD WAY

Progression in terms of three stages—a beginning, an intermediary, and a concluding one—is perhaps the most natural form of itinerary. Hence, it is not surprising that attempts to describe the path to God adopted a threefold pattern from at least as early as Origen. As we have seen (see section 1.1), the Alexandrian exegete interpreted Solomon's three books of Proverbs, Ecclesiastes, and the Song of Songs as teaching the three stages of the new Christian version of the Greek philosophical education (paideia): *moral, natural, and inspective or contemplative science. Origen's pupil Evagrius Ponticus adapted the threefold schema to describe the ascetical and contemplative life of the desert monastics (see section 2.2). As he put it in his* Gnostikos, *chapter 49: "The goal of* praktikê *[the ascetic life] is to purify the intellect and render it impassible; that of* physikê *[contemplation of the created universe] is to reveal the truth hidden in all beings; but to remove the intellect from all material things and to turn it toward the first Cause is the gift of* theologikê*"—the contemplation of God that attains what Evagrius called "essential knowledge of the Holy Trinity."*

The classic formulation of the threefold way was created around 500 CE by the writer who adopted the disguise of Dionysius the Areopagite (Acts 17:34; see section 9.1). In his twin treatises The Ecclesiastical Hierarchy *and* The Celestial Hierarchy, Dionysius *defines* hierarchia *as "a sacred order, a state of understanding, and an activity approximating as closely as possible to the divine." The created universe consists of ordered hierarchies, or manifestations* *of God, designed to bring the soul back to union with the hidden divinity. In the Dionysian ascension process (*anagogia*) each hierarchy has three levels and three modes of anagogic activity—purifying, illuminating, and perfecting—hence the triple pattern of purgation–illumination–perfection/union.*

This understanding of the threefold way reappears in Dionysius's ninth-century pupil John Scotus Eriugena. It was widely used, if often under different names, by the Cistercian mystics of the twelfth century, such as Bernard of Clairvaux (see section 1.4) and William of Saint-Thierry. In his Golden Letter, *William's division of the three stages and three groups of monks into animal, rational, and spiritual is based on Paul's view of the human person as composed of body, soul, and spirit (1 Thess 5:23). Perhaps the most famous exposition of this threefold itinerary is in Bonaventure's popular treatise of 1259,* The Threefold Way. *In this work the Franciscan creates an intricate picture of how the three essential practices of meditation, prayer, and contemplation are integrated to lead the soul through hierarchical stages to the point where she is lifted up to the incomprehensible mystery of the Trinity.*

I.

DIONYSIUS: CELESTIAL HIERARCHY 3.2

If one talks then of hierarchy, what is meant is a certain perfect arrangement, an image of the beauty of God which sacredly works out the mysteries of its own enlightenment in the orders and levels of understanding of the hierarchy, and which is likened to its own source as much as is permitted. Indeed for every member of the hierarchy perfection consists in this, that it is uplifted to imitate God as far as possible and, more wonderful still, that it becomes what scripture calls a "fellow workman for God" (1 Cor 3:9) and a reflection of the workings of God. Therefore when the hierarchic order lays it on some to be purified and others to do the purifying, on some to receive illumination and others to cause illumination, on some to be perfected and others to bring about perfection, each will actually imitate God in the way suitable to whatever role it has.

Translated by Colm Luibhead, *Pseudo-Dionysius. The Complete Works* (New York: Paulist Press, 1987), 154.

II.
WILLIAM OF SAINT-THIERRY: THE
GOLDEN LETTER I.41–45

Just as star differs from star in brightness (1 Cor 15:41), so does cell from cell in the way of life of beginners, of advanced, and of perfect. The state of beginners is called animal, the state of the advanced rational, the state of the perfect spiritual. In the case of those who are still animal sometimes something may be allowed that would not be in those who have already attained the rational state. Certain things are allowed in the rational state that are not allowed in the spiritual state, whose members should be perfect in all things and worthy of imitation and praise rather than blame.

Every religious form of life is made up of these three kinds of persons. Just as each is distinguished by its own name, so too are they recognized by their distinctive activities. All who are sons of the daylight (1 Thess 5:5) ought always to investigate in the light of the present day what is lacking to them, where they have come from, how far they have progressed, and the degree of progress that they estimate they have gained in each day and hour.

The animal types are those who on their own are not led by reason or drawn by attraction, but they are nevertheless pushed by authority, or inspired by teaching, or moved by example to approve the good where they find it. Like blind men, led by the hand, they follow along, that is, they imitate. The rational types are those who through the judgment of reason and the discernment of natural knowledge have both knowledge and desire for the good. But they do not yet have loving attraction. The perfect are those who are led by the spirit, who are more fully illuminated by the Holy Spirit, and they are called wise [literally: tasters] because they taste the good that draws them on. The Holy Spirit puts them on like clothes, just as he once put on Gideon (Judg 6:34), and as the vesture of the Holy Spirit they are called spirituals.

The first state is concerned with the body; the second with the intellectual soul, and the third has its rest only in God. Each of them has its own mode of advance, just as each has a measure of perfection in its own class. The beginning of good in the animal life is perfect obedience; its advance is subjugating the body and reducing it to servitude; its perfection is when habitual doing good has become a pleasure. The beginning of the rational life is to understand what is presented to it in the teaching of faith; its advance is to prepare things that fit that teaching; its perfection is when reason's judgment passes over into loving affection of mind. The perfection of the rational life is the beginning of the spiritual life; its advance is "to behold God's glory with unveiled face"; its perfection is "to be transformed into the same image, from glory to glory, as by the Spirit of the Lord" (2 Cor 3:18).

Translated by Bernard McGinn from William of Saint-Thierry, *Epistola ad Fratres de Monte Dei,* in PL 184:315–16.

III.
BONAVENTURE: THE THREEFOLD WAY, PROLOGUE AND CHAPTER 3.1

(A) Prologue

"Behold I have described it to you in a threefold way" (Prov 22:20). Because every kind of knowledge bears a token of the Trinity, especially the knowledge taught in sacred scripture, each ought to represent a vestige of the Trinity in itself. This is why Solomon says that he has described this sacred teaching in a threefold way because of its threefold spiritual understanding, namely, the moral, the allegorical, and the anagogical. This triple understanding corresponds to the triple hierarchical activity, that is, purgation, illumination, and perfection. Purgation leads to peace, illumination to truth, perfection to charity. When these three have been obtained in perfection, the soul is made blessed, and according to the manner in which it busies itself with them, the soul receives an increase in merit. The knowledge of the whole of sacred scripture depends on knowing these three things, just as does the merit of eternal life. Therefore, you should also recognize that there is a threefold way of exerting oneself in this threefold path, namely, by reading and meditating, by praying, and by contemplating. . . .

(B) Chapter 3.1

After speaking of how we ought to work toward wisdom through meditation and prayer, now let us briefly touch on how by contemplating we come to true wisdom. Through contemplation our mind journeys into the heavenly Jerusalem, according to whose model the church has been formed, as in the text in Exodus: "Look and make it according to the model that was shown you on the mountain" (Ex 25:40). As far as possible, it is necessary that the church militant be conformed to the church triumphant, and our merits to our rewards, and those still in this life to the blessed in heaven. In glory there is a threefold gift that is the perfection of the reward: an eternal grasp of the highest peace, an open vision of the highest truth, and the full enjoyment of the highest goodness and charity. According to this there is a triple order in the supreme celestial hierarchy of Thrones, Cherubim, and Seraphim. For someone who wishes by merit to come to that state of blessedness it is necessary to gain for oneself in this life a likeness to those three orders, as far as possible. That is, the person should have the sleep of peace, the splendor of truth, and the sweetness of charity. God himself rests in these three things, dwelling in them as in his proper throne. Therefore, it is also necessary to ascend to each of these three through three steps according to the threefold way—through the purgative, which consists in getting rid of sin; through the illuminative, which consists in the imitation of Christ; and through the unitive, which consists in receiving the Bridegroom. And thus each way has its different steps through which we begin from the bottom and move toward the top.

Translated by Bernard McGinn from *S. Bonaventurae Opera Omnia* (Quaracchi: Collegium S. Bonaventurae, 1898), Vol. 8:3, 11–12.

2.

RICHARD OF ST. VICTOR
THE FOUR DEGREES OF VIOLENT CHARITY

Richard of St. Victor was born in Scotland, traveled to Paris, and joined the community of canons at Saint Victor, where he died in 1173. Whether he was a direct student of Hugh of St. Victor (see section 10.6) or not, he was deeply influenced by Hugh's desire to present an ordered account of the mystical ascent to God. Richard wrote two influential treatments of the soul's preparation for and enjoyment of contemplation, the treatises often called the Benjamin minor *and the* Benjamin major, *but better named* The Twelve Patriarchs *and* The Mystical Ark *after the scriptural passages that form the basis for their exposition.*

A shorter tract had even greater influence. The Four Degrees of Violent Charity *sketches an itinerary of the soul's progress to God according to four forms of violent love. In this work Richard turns to the "book of experience," specifically an analysis of love that owes much to courtly love motifs. Richard's psychology of the madness of love insists that four stages of insanity are present in all love, but that they have a different valence depending upon whether the beloved is a human and finite spirit, or the infinite Divine Lover. Only the first level of violent love can be legitimately and safely directed to a human subject. If we try to love a human with the violence and insanity due only to God, we will wind up deifying the person and eventually destroying ourselves and the beloved. Richard's itinerary of love was often cited by later mystics, particularly the erotic mystics of the later Middle Ages.*

"I have been wounded by charity" (Song 2:5). Charity compels us to speak about charity. I give myself freely to charity's service, and it is sweet and completely delightful to speak about charity. It is a joyful subject and quite large, and in no way can it cause either fatigue to the writer or boredom to the reader, for what savors of charity tastes superior to the heart's palate. "If a person were to give up the whole substance of his house for love, he shall despise it as nothing" (Song 8:7).

Great is the strength of love, wonderful the power of charity. There are many degrees in it and a great difference among them. Who can worthily sort them out or even number them? Certainly there is in charity affection for humanity in general, affection for intimate comrades, affection for kindred, affection for blood relations, affection for brethren, and in like manner many more. But above all these kinds of love is that ardent and burning love that penetrates the heart and inflames the affection, and pierces the soul itself to the very marrow so that she can truly say: "I have been wounded with charity."

Let us consider then what is "that surpassing charity of Christ" (Eph 3:19) that conquers love of parents, love of offspring, transcends and even extinguishes affection for a wife, and finally moves the soul to despise itself. O vehemence of love! O violence of charity! O excellent and surpassing charity of Christ! This, brethren, is what we are considering, this is what we are speaking about—the vehemence of charity and the surpassing status of perfect zeal. You well know that it is one thing to talk about charity and another to talk about its consummation; one thing to talk about it, another to talk about its vehemence.

I turn to the works of violent charity and I discover what the vehemence of perfect zeal may be. Behold, I see some people wounded, some bound, some languishing, some fading away—and all from charity. Charity wounds, charity binds, charity makes ill, and charity brings about cessation. Which of these is not powerful? Which is not violent? These are the four degrees of burning charity that we are totally intent upon investigating in what follows. Hold steadfast in soul, brethren, and pay heed to her whom you desire so much; hear and pay attention to her whom you so greatly desire. Do you want to hear about wounding charity?—"You have wounded my heart, my sister, spouse, with one of your eyes and one hair of your neck" (Song 4:9). Do you want to hear about binding charity?—"I will draw them with the cords of Adam, with the bonds of charity" (Hos 11:4). Do you want to hear about languishing charity?—"Daughters of Jerusalem, if you find my Beloved, tell him I am languishing with love" (Song 5:8). Do you want to hear about charity fading away and bringing cessation?—He says, "My soul faded away in your salvation and I have hoped beyond hope in your word" (Ps 118:81). Charity has its chains; charity makes its wounds. . . .

But now let us return to the degree of love that we placed first and already called wounding love. Does not your heart sometimes seem shot through when that fiery dart of love penetrates the human mind to its interior and pierces the affection through and through to such an extent that it cannot in any way restrain or hide the heat of its desire? He burns with desire, he is aflame in affection, he is feverish, he gasps, deeply groans and sighs at length. These are your sure signs of a wounded soul: groans and sighs, and a pale and haggard face. . . .

We called the first degree of love that which wounds, the second that which binds. Surely a soul is truly and certainly bound when it cannot forget or think about anything save this one thing. Whatever it does, whatever it says, it always turns this thing over in its mind and constantly thinks about it. When the soul sleeps, she dreams of it; when she is awake, she thinks about it at every hour. I think it is easy to understand how this degree, which does not allow a person's mind any peace, even for an hour, surpasses the first, for the former is rightly said to be that which wounds, the second that which binds. It is often less to be wounded than to be bound. [Richard gives the example of a wounded knight escaping a battle contrasted with a knight who is wounded and captured.] . . .

Love now ascends to the third degree of violence when it excludes every other attraction and when it loves nothing but that one thing and for the sake of that one thing. In this third stage of violent charity nothing is able to satisfy the soul save the one thing, just as it has no taste for anything save for the sake of that one thing. The soul loves that one, desires it, thirsts for it, yearns after it. The soul gasps for it, sighs after it, is on fire from it, and finds its rest in it. The soul takes its refreshment in it and finds its satisfaction in it alone. Nothing is sweet or tasty that is not flavored with it. Anything else that comes along, or that happens by chance, is quickly rejected and trodden underfoot because it does not serve that attraction and pay homage to its desire. But who can fittingly describe the tyranny of that attraction—how it excludes every pastime, how it violently represses every activity that it sees does not cater to its desires? [A comparison of the evil effects of the first three degrees follows.] . . .

The fourth degree of violent charity is when nothing at all is able to satisfy the desire of the burning soul. This stage, because it goes beyond the bounds of human capability once and for all, unlike the others, knows no limit to its growth because it always finds something more to long after. Whatever the soul may do, or whatever may happen to it, does not satisfy the desire of the burning soul. It thirsts and drinks, but its drinking does not assuage its thirst; rather, the more it drinks, the more it thirsts. [A description of the evil effects of the fourth degree of the insanity of love follows.] . . .

So, we now have the four degrees of violence in burning love that I have set forth above. The first degree of violence is when the mind cannot resist its desire; the second degree is when the mind cannot forget it; the third degree is when it cannot taste anything else; the fourth and last degree is when even that desire cannot satisfy it. Therefore, in the first degree love is insuperable, in the second inseparable, in the third singular, and in the fourth insatiable. Insuperable love is what does not allow other attractions; inseparable love is what cannot be forgotten; singular love is what admits no companion; insatiable love is what cannot be satisfied. Although different points were noted about each degree, in a more special way the first degree illustrates love's excellence, the second degree its vehemence, the third degree its violence, the fourth degree its surpassing greatness. How great the excellence of love that surpasses every other attraction! How great, I say, the vehemence of desire that does not allow the mind any rest! How great, I beseech, the violence of charity that violently expels every other attraction! How great the surpassing greatness of yearning fervor that can in no way be satisfied! O excellence of love; O vehemence of desire; O violence of charity; O surpassing greatness of yearning fervor!

These four degrees of love are related in one way in divine attractions, and in another way in human attractions; they are totally different in the case of spiritual desires and in carnal desires. In spiritual desires, the greater, the better; in carnal desires, the greater, the worse. In divine attractions the highest is also the best. In human attractions the highest is the worst. Surely in human attractions the first degree can be good, the second without doubt is bad, while the third is worse and the fourth the worst of all. [Richard identifies the first degree of love in human attractions with marriage, which, in his words, "makes an indissoluble and perpetual companionship, pleasant and happy." He notes that to apply the other three forms to any finite person is in effect to make the person divine, a process that can only lead to sin and destruction. He then proceeds with an analysis of the four degrees when applied to love of God.] . . .

In the first degree the betrothal takes place, in the second the wedding, in the third sexual union, in the fourth childbirth. In the first degree the Lord says to the beloved soul: "I will espouse you to me forever, and I will espouse you to me in justice and in judgment and in mercy and in commiserations, and I will espouse you in faith" (Hos 2:19–20). In the second degree the marriage in Cana of Galilee takes place and he says to her: "Lo, I am your husband and you will not cease to follow after me" (Jer 3:14, 19). In the third degree is said, "He who adheres to the Lord becomes one spirit with him" (1 Cor 6:17). In the fourth is said, "We have conceived, and we have been as it were in labor, and we have brought forth the spirit" (Is 26:18). Therefore, in the first degree the beloved soul is visited frequently; in the second she is led to marriage; in the third she is joined with her Lover; in the fourth she is made fruitful. . . .

Let us penetrate still deeper and speak more openly. In the first degree the soul thirsts for God, in the second she thirsts to go to God, in the third she thirsts to go into God, and in the fourth she thirsts to live as God lives. That soul thirsts for God who says: "My soul has thirsted for you in the night, and in my spirit in my inmost depths I will watch for you in the morning" (Is 26:9). The soul thirsts to go to God who says: "My soul has thirsted for God the living fountain, when will I come and appear before the Lord's face?" (Ps 41:3). The soul thirsts to go into God who says, "My soul has thirsted in you; how many ways has my flesh sought you" (Ps 62:2). That soul thirsts to live as God does who says, "O Lord, my soul has desired your precepts at all times" (Ps 118:20). The soul thirsts for God when she desires to experience what that internal sweetness is that is meant to inebriate a person's mind when he begins to taste and see "how sweet is the Lord" (Ps 33:3). The soul thirsts to God when she desires to be lifted up above herself through the grace of contemplation and to see "the King in his beauty" (Is 33:17), so that she may truly say, "I have seen the Lord face to face and my soul has been saved" (Gen 32:30). Then the soul thirsts into God when through mental ecstasy she desires to pass totally into God so that she is wholly oblivious of herself and can truly say: "Whether in the body, or out of the body, I do not know, God knows" (2 Cor 12:2). The soul thirsts to live as God lives when the intellectual soul, by its own choice not so much in carnal affairs as even in spiritual ones, leaves nothing to its own free choice, but commits herself wholly to the Lord, never thinking of "what is hers, but only of what is Jesus Christ's" (Phil 2:21). Then she can say, "I do not come to do my will but the will of my Father who is in heaven" (Jn 5:30).

Therefore, in the first degree God enters into the intellectual soul and the intellectual soul comes back into herself. In the second degree she ascends above herself and is lifted up to God. In the third degree, lifted up to God, the soul passes into him. In the fourth degree the soul goes forth on God's behalf and descends below herself. In the first degree the intellectual soul enters into herself; in the second she passes beyond herself. In the first she proceeds into herself; in the third she proceeds into her God. In the first she enters for her own sake; in the fourth she goes out for her neighbor's sake. In the first she enters by meditation; in the second she ascends by contemplation; in the third she is brought in by jubilation; in the fourth she goes forth from compassion. [The following paragraphs describe the first and second degrees in detail.] . . .

Therefore, the third degree of love is when a person's mind is so raptured into that abyss of divine light that the human intellectual soul in this state, having forgotten all exterior things, does not even know itself and completely passes over into its God. Then what is written is fulfilled: "Even those not believing dwell in the Lord God" (Ps 67:19). In this state the host of carnal desires are fully subdued and put into a deep sleep, and "there is silence in heaven for about a half-hour" (Rev 8:1). Any disturbance in the soul is absorbed by glory. In this state, for as long as the mind is abstracted from itself while rapt into the hiding place of the divine secret and while surrounded on all sides by the fire of divine love, it is intimately penetrated and inflamed to such a degree that it totally puts itself off and puts on a kind of divine desire. Wholly conformed to the beauty it looks upon, it passes over into that form of glory. [The following passage develops an analogy of the liquefaction of the soul to molten iron to illustrate the third degree.] . . .

Those who can lay down their souls for their friends have already reached the very height of charity and are in its fourth degree. They already fulfill the apostolic command: "As beloved children, be imitators of God, and walk in love just as Christ loved you and gave himself up for you as an offering and victim to God in the odor of sweetness" (Eph 5:1–2). In the third degree the soul is glorified into God; in the fourth it is humbled for God's sake. In the third degree she is conformed to the divine splendor; in the fourth she is conformed to Christian humility. While in the third degree she is, as it were, "in form of God," in the fourth degree nevertheless she begins to "empty herself, taking on the form of a slave and again being found in her vesture as a human being" (Phil 2:6–7). In the third degree she is in a way put to death in God; in the fourth she is resurrected with Christ, and therefore those in the fourth degree can truly say, "I live, now not I, but Christ lives in me" (Gal 2:20). [The conclusion gives a further discussion of the fourth degree and provides a summary of the treatise.]

Translated by Bernard McGinn from Richard of St. Victor, *De quatuor gradibus violentae charitatis,* in PL 196:1207–10, 1212, 1213–14, 1216–17, 1220–21, 1222–23.

3.

BONAVENTURE
THE MIND'S JOURNEY INTO GOD

PROLOGUE AND CHAPTERS 1 AND 7

Bonaventure wrote this treatise in 1259 while on retreat at Mount Alverna, the place where St. Francis received the stigmata (see section 7.2). In this brief and powerful work the Seraphic Doctor fused a rich range of mystical themes taken from Augustinian, Dionysian, Cistercian, and Victorine sources into a synthesis of seven stages of the mind's journey into God. Bonaventure's itinerary is structured around six levels of progressive contemplation, symbolized by the six wings of the crucified Christ-Seraph figure that appeared to Francis. The contemplative person looks toward God through and in creation as the various powers of the soul are drawn upward. On the first two levels (chapters 1–2) sense-knowledge contemplates God first through his vestiges—that is, exterior created things— and then imagination gazes at God in the vestiges. Then the soul turns inward, contemplating God by means of reason through itself as the created image (chapter 3), and then, by the higher power of intellect, in the image insofar as it is reformed by the action of grace (chapter 4).

In chapters 5 and 6 the highest knowing power (intelligentia) is lifted up to contemplate the divine light, first through the light by considering the divine unity under the name of existence (esse), and then in the light through the revelation of the proper name of the Trinity, bonum, the overflowing goodness of the three persons. The contemplative soul is then symbolically identified with the two Cherubim of Exodus 25:16–20, gazing in amazement alternatively at the essential and proper attributes of God. The Cherubim also look at the Mercy Seat over

the Ark, which Bonaventure identifies with Jesus Christ, who unites God and
man. Wondering amazement at God-made man provokes the ecstasy by means of
which the mind in the seventh stage described in chapter 7 transcends itself to
attain union with God through the burning love for the Crucified that Francis
exemplified.

I.
PROLOGUE

At the outset I invoke the Eternal Father, the First Principle from whom all illuminations flow down as "from the Father of Lights," from whom "is every good present and every perfect gift" (James 1:17). I invoke him through his Son, our Lord Jesus Christ, so that by the intercession of the most holy Virgin Mary, bearer of the same God and our Lord Jesus Christ, and of St. Francis our leader and father, he may "illumine the mind's eyes to direct our feet on the way of his peace" (Eph 1:17–18; Lk 1:79), which "surpasses all understanding" (Phil 4:7). This is the peace that Our Lord Jesus Christ gave and preached in the gospel. Our father Francis repeated his preaching. At the beginning and end of every sermon he announced peace, in every greeting he wished for peace, in every contemplation he sighed for ecstatic peace, as a citizen of that Jerusalem about which that man of peace spoke when he said, "with those who hated peace, he was peaceable: pray for the things which are for the peace of Jerusalem" (Ps 119:7, 121:6). For he knew that the throne of Solomon exists only in peace, since it is written: "His place has been made in peace, and his dwelling in Sion" (Ps 75:3).

Therefore, following the example of the most holy father Francis, I was seeking this peace with a gasping spirit, I, the sinner who, though totally unworthy in all things, succeed to that most holy father's place as the seventh Minister General of the brethren since his death. It happened by God's plan that around the thirty-third year after the saint's death I turned aside to Mount Alverna as a quiet place with the desire of seeking peace of spirit. While I was there, my mind was occupied with some forms of mental ascent to God, among them that miracle that happened to St. Francis himself in that same place, namely, the vision of the winged Seraph in the form of the Crucified. As I was thinking it over, it immediately occurred to me that the vision set forth our father's elevation in contemplation and the path by which he got there.

The six wings can be rightly understood as six illuminative elevations by which the soul is disposed by certain steps or paths to pass over to peace through the ecstatic raptures of Christian wisdom. The only way there is through the most ardent love of the Crucified that so transformed Paul into Christ when he was "rapt to the third heaven" (2 Cor 12:2) that he said, "I am fixed to the cross with Christ; I live, now not I, Christ lives in me" (Gal 2:19–20). It also so absorbed the mind of Francis that his mind was openly visible in his flesh while he bore the most holy marks of the passion in his body for two years before his death. Therefore, the image of the six wings of the Seraph hint at six illuminative stages, which begin from creatures and lead up to God. No one can enter upon them save through the Crucified, because "one who does not enter through the door, but goes up some other way, is a thief and robber" (Jn 10:1). But if "a person shall have entered through the door, he will go in and go out and find pasture" (Jn 10:9). Therefore John says in the Apocalypse: "Blessed are those who have washed their garments in the blood of the Lamb so that they may have the right to the Tree of Life and they may enter the city through the gates" (Rev 22:14). That is to say that only through the blood of the Lamb as if through a door is it possible to enter the heavenly Jerusalem through contemplation. No one can be made ready in any way for the divine contemplations leading to mental raptures unless, like Daniel, he be "a man of desires" (Dan 9:23). These desires are enkindled in us in two ways: either through the "outcry of prayer," which causes us to cry out "with the heart's groan" (Ps 37:9); or through "a blaze of insight" by which the mind turns itself to rays of light in the most intense and direct way.

Therefore, first of all I invite the reader to groaning prayer through Christ crucified whose blood purges us from the stains of vices. I do so lest the reader might think that reading is sufficient without heavenly anointing, or thinking without devotion, or investigation without admiration, or mere observation without rejoicing, or effort without piety, or knowledge without charity, intelligence without humility, endeavor without divine grace, [the soul as] mirror without divinely inspired wisdom. Therefore I am setting forth the following insights to those who have been prepared by divine grace, to the humble and faithful, to those with compunction and devotion, to those anointed "with the oil of gladness" (Ps 44:8), to the lovers of divine wisdom who are enflamed with its desire, to those wanting to be free to magnify the Lord, to be in awe of him, and even to taste him. I am suggesting the mirror [of the world] set forth outside counts for little or nothing unless the mirror of our mind has been cleansed and polished. Rouse yourself up, then, man of God, first to the biting goad of conscience before you lift your eyes up to the rays of Wisdom reflected in its mirrors, lest by looking at these rays you perhaps fall into a deeper pit of darkness.

It helps to divide the treatise into seven chapters, first setting forth titles to facilitate the understanding of what will be said. I therefore beg that you give more weight to the writer's good intention than to the work itself, to the sense of the words than to the uncultivated style, to the truth than to the decoration, to the exercising of the affection than to the instruction of the intellect. So that this may be the case, you should not run through the course of these insights in an inattentive way, but you should chew them over most assiduously. [Here Bonaventure lists the titles of the seven chapters of the treatise.]

II.
THE CONTEMPLATION OF THE POOR MAN IN THE DESERT BEGINS

Chapter 1. The steps of ascension to God and contemplating him through his vestiges in the universe.

"Blessed the man whose help is from you! In his heart he has decided to ascend by steps, in the valley of tears, in the place which he has set" (Ps 83:6–7). Since happiness is nothing else than the enjoyment of the Supreme Good, and the Supreme Good is above us, then no one can be made happy unless he ascends above himself, not by a bodily ascent, but by one of the heart. But we cannot be lifted up above ourselves unless a higher power elevates us. However many interior steps are set out, nothing will happen unless divine aid comes to our assistance. Divine aid will come to the assistance of those who ask for it with a humble and devout heart: that is what it is to sigh for it "in the valley of tears," which takes place through fervent prayer. Therefore prayer is the mother and source of all lifting up. And so Dionysius, wishing to instruct us about mental rapture in his *Mystical Theology*, begins with a prayer. Hence, let us pray and say to the Lord our God: "Lead me, Lord, on your path, so that I may enter your truth; let my heart rejoice so that I may fear your name" (Ps 85:11).

By praying with this kind of prayer we are illuminated to knowledge of the stages of ascent to God. In accord with our created state, the universe itself is a ladder for ascending to God. Among things we find some that are *vestiges* and some that are *images;* some that are *corporeal,* some *spiritual;* some that are *temporal,* some *everlasting;* and hence some that are *outside us,* others *within us.* In order to come to thoughtful consideration of the First Principle, which is totally spiritual and eternal and above us, we must *pass through* the vestiges that are corporeal and temporal and outside us; this is "to be led along God's path"; then we must *enter into* our own mind, which is God's image, everlasting, spiritual, and within us: this is "to go into God's truth"; finally, we must *pass beyond* to what is eternal, totally spiritual, and above us, by gazing toward the First Principle; this is "to rejoice in knowledge of God and reverence for his majesty" (Ps 85:11).

This is the path of the three-day journey into the desert (Ex 3:18). This is the threefold illumination of a single day, in which the first is like the evening, the second like the morning, and the third like midday. This reflects the three forms of the existence of things, that is, in matter, in the intelligence, and in the Eternal Art, according to which it was said, "Let it be made, he made it, and it was made" (Gen 1:3ff). This also reflects the threefold substance in Christ, our ladder, namely the corporeal, the spiritual, and the divine. Our mind has three chief ways of perceiving in accord with this threefold advance. The first is toward external corporeal things, and accordingly is called animal or sensual nature. The second is within and in the self, and is hence called spirit. The third is above the self and is called mind. On the basis of all these a person ought to set himself in order so that he can ascend to God so that he can love him "with all his mind and all his heart and all his soul" (Mk 12:30). The perfect observance of the Law, along with Christian wisdom, is found in this.

Each of these modes can be doubled, insofar as God can be considered as Alpha and as Omega (Rev 1:8), and insofar as one can see God in each of the modes both "through a mirror" and "in a mirror," or insofar as any single one of these considerations can be mixed with another or can be treated in its purity. Therefore, it is necessary that these three main steps advance to six, so that just as God perfected "the whole world" in six days and rested on the seventh, so too the microcosm [of man] can be led in a very well-ordered way to the repose of contemplation by six stages of illumination succeeding one another. There is a figure of this in the six steps that led up to Solomon's throne (3 Kgs 10:19). Also, the Seraph that Isaiah saw had six wings (Is 6:2); after six days the Lord "called to Moses from the midst of the cloud" (Ex 24:16); and, as it says in Matthew, "after six days Christ led the disciples up the mountain and was transfigured before them" (Mt 17:1).

Just as there are six steps of ascent to God, there are also six levels of the soul's powers by means of which we ascend from the depths to the heights, from exterior things to those within, from temporal things to those eternal. They are sensation, imagination, reason, intelligence, understanding, and the high point of the mind, or the spark of *synderesis* [i.e., conscience]. These levels are implanted in us by nature, deformed through sin, reformed through grace, purged through justifying grace, exercised through knowledge, and made perfect through wisdom.

According to nature's first state, humanity was created fit for the repose of contemplation, which is why "God planted him in the paradise of pleasure" (Gen 2:15). But when he turned away from the true light to an unstable good, he was bent crooked through his own sin and infected the whole human race by means of original sin in a twofold way: mental ignorance and carnal concupiscence. This is why humans, blinded and bent down, sit in darkness and cannot see the light without the aid of the graceful justice that acts against concupiscence and the wise knowledge that counteracts ignorance. This all happens through Jesus Christ, "whom God makes for us Wisdom and Justice and Sanctification and Redemption" (1 Cor 1:30). Since he is God's Power and Wisdom, the Incarnate Word "full of grace and truth" (Jn 1:14), he created grace and truth. He pours out the grace of charity that, since it comes "from a pure heart and good conscience and unfeigned faith" (1 Tim 1:5), justifies the whole soul following the three ways of perceiving mentioned above. He has taught the "science of truth" according to the threefold modes of theology—symbolic, proper, and mystical. Through the symbolic we make correct use of sensible objects; through theology proper we correctly use intelligible objects; through mystical theology we are swept up to raptures above the mind.

For someone who wants to ascend to God it is necessary that after he has gotten rid of the sin that deforms nature, he must work with his natural powers in [four ways]: by prayer in the service of reforming grace; by his manner of life for purifying justice; by meditation for illuminating knowledge; and by contemplation for perfect wisdom. Just as nobody comes to wisdom without grace, justice, and knowledge, so too no one comes to contemplation without lucid meditation, a holy way of life, and devout prayer. Just as grace is the basis for an upright will and an incisive light of reason, so too we have first to pray, then lead a holy life, and third direct our attention to truth's manifestations and, so intending, climb up, little by little, even unto "the high mountain where the God of gods is seen in Sion" (Ps 83:8).

Chapter 7. The Mental and Mystical Rapture in which Repose is Granted to the Intellect when the Affection Passes Over Totally into God in Rapture.

Therefore, we have passed through these six considerations like "the six steps of the true Solomon's throne" (3 Kgs 10:19) by means of which a truly peaceful person comes to rest in the Jerusalem within with the mind at rest. They are like the six wings of the Seraph by means of which the mind of the true contemplative filled with the enlightenment of heavenly wisdom can be carried above. They are like the first six days in which the mind is at work so that it may finally arrive at the Sabbath rest. After our mind has gazed upon God outside itself through his vestiges and in his vestiges, and within itself through and in his image, and also above itself through a likeness of the divine light shining down over us, and in the light itself insofar as this is possible according to our station in life and our mind's effort, then, at last, in the sixth step it comes to the point where, in the First and Highest Principle and in the Mediator of God and men, Jesus Christ, it may look upon things that are unlike anything to be found in creatures and which surpass every perception of the human intellect. It now remains that this contemplation transcends and passes beyond not only this world of sense, but also itself. In this passing, over Christ is the "way and the door" (Jn 14:6), Christ is the ladder and the vehicle insofar as he is "mercy seat placed over the Ark of God" (Ex 25:21), as well as the "mystery hidden from eternity" (Eph 3:9).

The person who looks toward the Mercy Seat with full attention—in faith, hope, and charity, devotion, awe, rejoicing, appreciation, praise, and jubilation—beholding him hanging on the cross, makes a "Pasch," that is, a passing over, along with him, in that he passes over the Red Sea through the rod of the cross, going out of Egypt into the desert where he feeds on the "hidden manna" (Rev 2:17) and rests in the tomb with Christ, dead on the outside, but perceiving how it is still possible in this life to hear what was said on the cross to the thief who joined with Christ: "Today you shall be with me in paradise" (Lk 23:43).

This was also shown in St. Francis, when in contemplative rapture on the high mountain (where I thought out the things I have written down) there appeared to him the six-winged Seraph fastened to the cross, as I and many others heard there from the companion who was with him at that time. In that place he passed over into God through contemplative rapture and was established as an example of perfect contemplation just as he had previously been of action, like another Jacob [who also became] Israel, so that through him, more by example than by word, God might invite all truly spiritual people to this form of passing over and mental rapture.

If this kind of passing over is to be perfect, it is necessary that all mental activities be left behind, and that the high point of affectivity [*apex affectus*] be wholly transferred and transformed into God. This is mystical and most secret. "No one knows it who has not received it" (Rev 2:17), and no one receives it who has not desired it, and no one desires it who is not set aflame within by the fire of the Holy Spirit that Christ sent upon the earth. This is why the Apostle says that this mystical wisdom is revealed through the Holy Spirit (1 Cor 2:10).

Nature is able to do nothing in this regard, and effort but little. Little belongs to investigation and much to unction; little to speaking and much to interior rejoicing; little to word and text, but everything to God's gift, that is, the Holy Spirit. Little or nothing belongs to the creature, and everything to the creative essence, that is, to the Father, Son, and Holy Spirit, as Dionysius says in speaking of God the Trinity: "Trinity, Essence above essence and God above God, and more than best Guardian of the wisdom of Christians, direct us into the more than unknown and more than illuminating and most sublime height of mystical forms of speaking. There new, absolute, and unchangeable mysteries of theology are hidden according to the superluminous darkness of the silence that teaches in hidden fashion and in the deepest dark what is beyond manifestation, beyond all light, and in which all things shine forth—a darkness that more than fills the unseen intellects [of the angels] by the splendors of the invisible realities beyond goodness" [*Mystical Theology* 1.1]. This is addressed to God. To the friend to whom he writes, let us say with him: "You, O friend, in the question of mystical visions should renew your journey and leave behind all senses and intellectual operations, things sensible and invisible, and all that is not and all that is, so that, if possible, you may unknowingly be restored to unity with him who is above all essence and knowledge. Leaving behind all things and becoming free of all things, lift yourself up to the superessential ray of divine darkness by means of an immeasurable and absolute rapture of a pure mind" [ibid.].

If you ask how this all comes to be, ask grace not teaching, desire not understanding, the groan of prayer not the effort of reading, the Bridegroom not the teacher, God not man, darkness not brightness, not light but rather the fire that wholly enflames and transforms into God by its extreme anointments and most ardent affections. This fire is God and "its furnace is in Jerusalem" (Is 31:9). Christ enkindles it in the heat of his most ardent passion; he alone perceives it who says, "My soul chooses hanging and my bones death" (Jb 7:15). Whoever loves this death can see God because it is unquestionably true that "No one can see me and live" (Ex 33:20). Therefore let us die and enter into this darkness, putting silence to cares, false desires, and imaginings. Let us pass with Christ crucified "from this world to the Father" (Jn 13:1), so that when the Father has been shown to us we can say with Philip, "It is enough for us" (Jn 14:8). Let us hear along with Paul, "My grace is enough for you" (2 Cor 12:9). Let us rejoice with David and say: "My flesh and my heart have fainted away; you are the God of my heart and my lot, God forever. Blessed be the Lord forever, and let all the people say, 'So be it, So be it'" (Ps 72:26, 105:48). Amen. The End of the *Journey into God.*

Translated by Bernard McGinn from *S. Bonaventurae Opera Omnia* (Quaracchi: Collegium S. Bonaventurae, 1891), Vol. 5:295–98, 312–13.

4.

MARGUERITE PORETE
THE MIRROR OF SIMPLE ANNIHILATED SOULS
CHAPTER 118

Marguerite Porete was executed as a relapsed heretic in Paris in 1310 after refusing to stop disseminating her book The Mirror of Simple Annihilated Souls. *We know little about her, save that she came from northern France and lived as an unenclosed beguine, a lifestyle that had come under increasing suspicion by ecclesiastical authorities in the second half of the thirteenth century. Around 1296 she had been ordered by the bishop of Cambrai to cease teaching her book, presumably through a form of itinerant preaching. But Marguerite revised the work and received the approbation of three learned theologians. (The extent to which Porete's work is or is not heretical has continued to divide interpreters in the twentieth century as much as in the fourteenth.)*

The structure and message of the book, written in the form of a courtly dialogue, defy easy generalization. The Mirror *centers on a deeply apophatic form of mysticism involving the annihilation of the created will through the power of totally disinterested love. The text is a mixture of prose and poetry in 140 chapters, the longest of which contains a seven-stage itinerary that summarizes the challenging teachings of the beguine. Six stages of the journey can be realized in this life; the seventh, only after death. It is noteworthy that the ordinary summit of mystical experience for monastic mystics, loving union with God, for Porete is only the fourth stage—and she typically criticizes those who can see no farther. Although the thirteen condemned articles extracted from her work have mostly been lost, we know that they were influential at the Council of Vienne (1311–12) that issued the decree "Ad Nostrum," the source for subsequent pronouncements against what was seen as dangerous forms of mysticism (see section 14.2). Despite the condemnation, Porete's* Mirror *was fairly popular, surviving in six versions in four languages and thirteen manuscripts.*

CHAPTER 118.
OF THE SEVEN STATES OF THE DEVOUT SOUL, WHICH ARE OTHERWISE CALLED STATES OF BEING

THE SOUL. I have promised, says this Soul, to say something of the seven states which we call states of being, after Love has come and taken hold; and states of being they are. And they are the steps by which one climbs from the valley to the summit of the mountain, which is so isolated that one sees nothing there but God; and at each step is found the corresponding state of being.

THE FIRST STATE. The first state, or step, is when the Soul which is touched by God's grace and stripped bare of sin, so far as is in its power, has the intention of keeping for life, that is, until death, the commandments of God, which he commands in the Law. And so this Soul considers and ponders with great fear that God has commanded her to love him with all her heart, and her neighbor also as herself (Mt 22:37). This seems to this Soul to be labor enough for her and for all that she is capable of doing; and it seems to her that if she were to live a thousand years, that it would take her all her might to keep and observe the commandments.

THE SOUL THAT IS FREE. I was for a time at this stage and in this state, and this was long ago, says the Soul that is Free. Now let no one be dismayed at mounting higher; he shall not be dismayed if he has a great heart and is filled within with noble courage; but a little heart lacks the courage to undertake a great matter or to climb up higher, for lack of love. Such folk are cowards indeed; but that is no wonder, for they dwell in an apathy that does not allow them to seek God, and they will never find him if they do not seek him diligently.

THE SECOND STATE. The second state or step is when the Soul considers what God recommends to his special loved ones over and above what he commands; and he is no true lover who can abstain from doing all that he knows will please his love. And so the creature abandons self, and strains to act beyond the counsels of men in mortifying nature, in despising riches, delights and honors, to achieve the perfection of the evangelical counsels of which Jesus Christ is the exemplar. So she does not fear loss of possessions, nor people's words, nor feebleness of body, for her Beloved did not fear them, nor can any Soul who has been overwhelmed by him.

THE THIRD STATE. The third state is when the Soul considers herself filled with love for the work of perfection, where her spirit is spurred by a burning longing of that love to multiply in herself such works; and this is brought about by the knowing subtlety of her love's understanding which can make no offering to its beloved that could comfort him except of what he loves. For no other gift is esteemed in loving except to give the loved one that which the lover most loves.

Now it is the case that the will of this creature loves nothing except works of goodness, through her, through the inflexibility with which she undertakes every labor with which she can restore her spirit. Therefore it seems right to her, from what she sees, that she should love only works of goodness, and so she does not know what to give to Love, unless she sacrifices this to him; for there is no death which would be martyrdom to her except to abstain from the work which she loves, which is to delight in pleasing him, and the life of the will which takes nourishment from this. And so she renounces those works in which she has this delight, and puts to death the will which had its life from this, and, to become a martyr, obliges herself to obey the will of another, to abstain from doing works, and willing to fulfill the other's will, so as to destroy her will. And this is harder, indeed much harder than the two states described before; for it is harder to conquer the works which the spirit wills than it is to conquer the body's will and to do the will of the spirit. So one must crush oneself, hacking and hewing away at oneself to widen the place in which Love will want to be, burdening oneself down with several states of being, so as to unburden oneself and to attain to one's being.

THE FOURTH STATE. The fourth state is when the Soul is drawn up by the exaltation of love into delight in the thoughts that come in meditation, and she is freed from all outward labors and from obedience to another, through the exaltation of contemplation, whereby the Soul becomes so vulnerable, so noble and so delicate that she cannot endure anything to touch her, except only the touch of Love's pure delight, which makes her full of joy and lighthearted, and overweening in her abundance of love, in which she is the mistress of the luster—that is, of the brightness—of her soul, which fills her wonderfully full of a love of great fidelity, through that harmony of union which has given her the possession of its delights.

Then the Soul holds that there is no higher life than to have this of which she is made mistress, for Love has so generously filled her with his delights that she does not believe that God has any greater gift to bestow on any soul here below than this love which Love for love has poured forth within her.

Ah, it is no wonder if such a Soul is overwhelmed, for Gracious Love makes her wholly drunken, and so drunken that she does not let her pay heed to anything but to herself, because of the intensity with which Love delights her. And therefore the Soul can esteem no other state of being, for Love's great brightness has so dazzled her sight that she does not let her see anything except her love. And in this she is deceived, for there are two other states of being, here below, which God bestows, which are greater and nobler than is this; but Love deceived many a soul by the sweetness of the pleasure of its love, which overwhelms the Soul as soon as it draws near to her. No one can resist such insistence, and this the Soul knows, whom Love has exalted by Perfect Love beyond herself.

THE FIFTH STATE. The fifth state is when the Soul considers that God is "He Who Is" (Ex 3:14), of whom all things are, and that she is not, and that it is not from her that all things are. And these two considerations give her a wondrous sense of dismay, and she sees that he is all goodness who has put free will into her, who is not, except in all evil.

Now divine goodness has put free will into her, out of pure divine goodness, so within that which is not, except in evil, which therefore is all evil, is enclosed free will of the being of God, who is being, and who wishes that that which has no being should have being through this gift from him. And so the coming of Divine Goodness is preceded by a rapturous outpouring in the movement of Divine Light. And this movement of Divine Light which is spread by light within the Soul shows to the spirit's will that He Who Is deals justly, so that she who is not, the Soul, may wish her will to move from the place where it is, and where it must not be, so that it can be returned to where it is not, whence it came, and where it must be.

Now the Soul's Will sees, by the light of the spreading of Divine Light—which light is given to this Will to return it to God, to where it cannot return without this light—that it cannot progress by itself if it does not separate itself from her own willing, for her nature is evil by that inclination towards nothingness to which nature tends, and her willing has reduced her to less than nothing. Now the Soul sees this inclination and this perdition in nothingness of her nature and of her own willing and by the light she sees that one's Will must will only the Divine Will and not any other, and that it was for this that this Will was given her. And so the Soul abandons this Will and the Will abandons this Soul, and then returns and surrenders and submits to God, there whence it was first derived, without keeping back anything of its own, in order to fulfill the perfect Divine Will which, unless such a gift is made, cannot be fulfilled in the Soul without the Soul's experiencing conflict or deprivation. This gift brings about this perfection in her, and changes her into Love's nature, which delights her with consummate peace, and gives her her fill of divine food. And so she is no longer concerned about the strife of nature, for her will has been completely restored to the place from where it was taken and where, by right, it must be; and this Soul was always in conflict for as long as she retained in her a will which was not in its own being.

Now such a Soul is nothing, for through her abundance of Divine Knowledge she sees her nothingness, which makes her nothing and reduces her to nothingness. And yet she is everything, for she sees herself through the depth of her knowledge of her own evil, which is so profound and so great that she cannot find there any beginning, compass or end, but only an abyss, deep beyond all depths, and there she finds herself in a depth in which she cannot be found. No one can find himself who cannot attain to himself; the more that one sees himself when he has such knowledge of his own evil, the more he knows in truth that he cannot know his evil, not the least fraction of it; and so this Soul is an abyss of such evil, and a gulf which can shelter and protect in it as much as can that flood of what is sin, which contains within it all perdition. This Soul sees herself to be so, and does not see it. And who makes her see herself? It is the depth of humility, which seats her on the throne, where she rules without pride. No pride can enter by force there, because she sees herself, and yet she does not see herself; and this not seeing makes her to see herself perfectly.

Now this Soul is seated in the lowest depths, there deep beyond all depths, and so it is lower than low; and these lowest depths make her see very clearly the true Sun of most exalted goodness, for there is no one to prevent her seeing this. And this Divine Goodness shows himself to her through goodness, which draws her and changes her and joins her through union with goodness into that pure Divine Goodness of which goodness is mistress. And the knowledge of these two natures of which we have spoken, of Divine Goodness and of her evil, is the instrument which has endowed her with such goodness. And because she wishes only for one, for the Spouse of her youth, and only one is he, Mercy has made peace for her with inflexible Justice, which has changed this Soul into its goodness. Now she is everything, and yet she is also nothing, for her beloved makes her one.

Now this Soul has fallen from love into nothingness, without which nothingness she cannot be everything. And this fall has been so low, if she falls as she should, that the Soul is not able to raise herself up again from such an abyss; nor must she do this, but rather remain where she is. And there the Soul loses her pride and her girlishness, for her spirit has grown old, and no longer lets her be lighthearted and glad, because her will has left her, which often, when she felt the stirrings of love, made her proud and overweening and fastidious, when she was exalted in contemplation in the fourth state. But the fifth state has subdued her in showing to the Soul her own self. Now she sees by herself, and she knows the Divine Goodness, and this knowing of the Divine Goodness makes her look again at herself, and these two things that she sees take away from her will and longing and works of goodness, and so she is wholly at rest, and put in possession of her own state of free being, the high excellence of which gives her repose from every thing.

THE SIXTH STATE. The sixth state is when the Soul does not see herself at all, whatever the abyss of humility she has within herself, nor does she see God, whatever the exalted goodness he has. But God of his divine majesty sees himself in her, and by him this Soul is so illumined that she cannot see that anyone exists, except only God himself, from whom all things are; and so she sees nothing except herself, for whoever sees that which is sees nothing except God himself, who sees himself in this very Soul by his Divine Majesty. And so this Soul in the sixth state is made free of all things and pure and illumined, yet not glorified, for glorification is of the seventh state, and that we shall have in glory, of which no one is able to speak. But this Soul, thus pure and illumined, sees neither God nor herself, but God sees himself of himself in her, for her, without her, who—that is, God—shows to her that there is nothing except him. And therefore this Soul knows nothing except him, and loves nothing except him, and praises nothing except him, for there is nothing but he. For whatever is has its being of God's Goodness; and God loves his goodness, wherever he has given it in goodness, and his given goodness is God himself, and God cannot so separate his goodness that it does not remain in him; and therefore he is what goodness is, and goodness is what God is. And therefore goodness, of his goodness, sees itself by divine light in the sixth state, in which the Soul is illumined. And so there is no one except Him Who Is, and who sees himself of his Divine Majesty in this state of being through the transformation of love of that goodness which has been poured forth and has been restored to him. And so of himself he sees himself in such a creature, without appropriating anything from the creature; all is his own, but his very own. This is the sixth state which we promised to tell to listeners, when Love takes hold, Love who of herself by her exalted greatness has paid this debt.

THE SEVENTH STATE. And the seventh state Love keeps within herself, to give to us in everlasting glory, of which we shall have no knowledge until our souls shall have left our bodies.

From *The Mirror of Simple Souls. Margaret Porette,* translated by Edmund Colledge, J. C. Marler, and Judith Grant, 140–46. Copyright 1999 by the University of Notre Dame Press. Notre Dame, Indiana 46556.

JOHN TAULER

SERMON 39

PART 2

Like many mystics, Tauler viewed the path to union with God as a process, or journey, that could be presented in terms of stages. In a number of his sermons he makes use of a threefold pattern, but not the familiar itinerary of the purgative, illuminative, and unitive ways described in section 5.1. Rather, the Dominican describes a journey that begins with a stage that he calls jubilatio, *or rejoicing— an enjoyment of spiritual delights sent from God to encourage the person on the journey. (The term* jubilus, *found in Psalm texts such as Psalms 46:6 and 99:1, was used by contemporary female mystics to describe wordless mystical singing and delight in God.) The next stage, however, negates this delight. In this step God withdraws his presence and the person experiences bitter interior suffering and distress* (getrenge), *even a feeling of being abandoned by God (see section 11.3). The third and final stage is one of true and lasting union, a state of divinization (see section 12) that Tauler speaks of in language close to that of Meister Eckhart.*

———

. . . Now we intend to talk about the three stages that a person can be at—the lowest, the middle, or the highest. The first stage of an interior virtuous life that leads one directly to the closest proximity to God happens when a person turns to the marvelous works and signs of inexpressible gifts and effusions of the hidden goodness of God. Out of this is born a state of soul called *jubilatio*. The second stage is poverty of spirit (Mt 5:8) and a strange abandonment by God that leaves the spirit tortured and naked. The third stage is the transformation to a divine-like existence, into a unity of the created spirit with the very being of the spirit of God. This one can call a conversion to an essentially higher plane. And one cannot imagine that those who rightly reach this stage could ever fall away from God.

In the first stage, that of *jubilatio,* a person becomes intensely aware of the dear signs of his love that God has marvelously given us in the heavens and on earth, how marvelously much good he has done for us and all creatures, how everything blossoms, sprouts forth, and is filled with God, and how the unimaginable generosity of God has inundated all creatures with his great gifts and how God has gone searching for him, led him, showered him with gifts, carried him, advised him, waited for him, cared for him, and for his sake became human and suffered, how he offered up his life, his soul, and himself for us, and to what inexpressible nearness to him he has invited him, and how the most Holy Trinity has expectantly awaited him eternally so that he might be filled with joy forever. And when a person experiences this fully through loving insight, there is born in him great genuine joy. The person who perceives these things with genuine love is so flooded with an interior joy that his frail body cannot contain this joy and erupts in its own strange way. If it did not do so, blood would perhaps burst forth from his mouth, as has often been observed, or the person might feel a great pressure weighing on him. And in this way our Lord showers him with great sweetness and gives him inwardly an embrace of palpable union. Thus does God lure, pull, and yank a person, first of all out of himself, and then out of all dissimilarity to himself. Let it be forbidden to everyone to cause such people any trouble or to hinder them or to distract them through base external practices or activities. You would then cause your own ruin. A prior has no business asking where a fellow religious is going after choir, once the singing is ended, unless it is a shallow person whose comings and goings, as well as his activities, have to be watched.

It happened to a special friend of our Lord that our Lord offered him a divine kiss. His spirit said, "Truly, dear Lord, I really don't want it, for from its bliss I would so lose myself that I could be of no further use to you. How would I then pray for your poor souls and help them get out of purgatory, and pray for poor sinners?" Sinners and the poor souls cannot help themselves unless we, who still live in time, want to help them. Without our help God cannot do anything for them because his justice must be given its due. Hence his friends must act while they are still living. What great love that was that this person was willing to give up great consolation for such a reason!

The second stage is like this: When God has drawn a person so far away from all things, and he is no longer a child and he has been strengthened with the comfort of sweetness. Then indeed one gives him good coarse rye bread. He has become a man and has reached maturity. Solid, strong food is what is good and useful for a grown man. He shouldn't be given milk and soft bread any longer, and such is withheld from him. He is then led onto a terribly wild path, very gloomy and forsaken. And on this path God takes back from him everything that he had ever given him. Then and there the person is left so completely to himself that he loses all notion of God and gets into such a distressful state that he cannot remember whether things had ever gone right for him, whether he has a God or not, and whether he is the same person; and he suffers such incredible pain that this whole wide world is too confining for him. He has neither any feeling for nor knowledge of God, and he has no liking for any other things. It seems to him that he is suspended between two walls with a sword in back of him and a sharp spear in front. What does he do then? He can go neither forward nor back. He can only sit down and say, "Hail, bitterer bitterness, full of grace!" If there could be hell in this life, this would seem to be more than hell—to be bereft of loving and the good thing loved. Anything that one might then say to such a person would console him about as much as a stone. And he could stand even less hearing about creatures. The more the sense of and feel for God stood formerly in the foreground, the greater and more unendurable are the bitterness and misery of this abandonment.

Even then take heart! The Lord is certainly nearby. Hold fast to the support of the true living faith. Things will be fine. But it is unbelievable to the poor soul in its tortured state that this unbearable darkness could ever turn into light.

When our Lord has thus prepared a person in this unbearable state of misery—for this prepares him much better than all the spiritual practices that all people might be able to accomplish—then our Lord comes and leads him to the third stage. In this stage the Lord removes the cloak from his eyes and reveals the truth to him. Bright sunshine appears and lifts him right out of all his misery. It seems to this person just as though the Lord had raised him from the dead. In this stage the Lord leads a person out of himself into himself. He makes him forget all his former loneliness and heals all his wounds. God thus draws the person out of his human mode into a divine mode, out of all misery into divine security. Here a person becomes so divinized that everything he is and does God does and is in him. And he is lifted up so far above his natural state that he becomes through grace what God in his essence is by nature. In this state a person feels and is aware that he has lost himself and does not at all feel himself or is he aware of himself. He is aware of nothing but one simple Being.

Children, to be truly in this stage is the deepest ground of genuine humility and annihilation. This, in truth, cannot be grasped by the senses. For here he receives the most profound insight possible into his nothingness. Here he sinks as deep as it is possible into the ground of humility; the deeper, the higher, because here high and deep are one and the same. And if it happened that a person were, in selfishness, to fall back onto himself or in arrogance back onto what belonged just to him, it would be like Lucifer's fall. In this state one achieves true unity of prayer spoken of in the epistle that truly brings it about that a person becomes one with God. May God help us all experience this. Amen.

Translated for this volume by Frank Tobin from *Die Predigten Taulers*, edited by Ferdinand Vetter (Berlin: Weidmann, 1910), 159–62.

WALTER HILTON
THE LADDER OF PERFECTION

BOOK II, CHAPTERS 13 AND 30

The fourteenth century saw a revival of the study of Paul, not only in academic theology but also in mysticism. The message of the Apostle of the Gentiles about salvation through solidarity in the Body of Christ was especially important for the great English mystics of this era. Not least among these was the Augustinian canon Walter Hilton, who died in 1396. Hilton was a trained theologian, but he chose to write mostly in English for the growing lay interest in spirituality. His writings include translations of mystical classics, such as The Goad of Love, *a free adaptation of a treatise of the fourteenth-century Franciscan James of Milan. The canon's major contribution to mysticism is his* Ladder of Perfection, *two books on the path to contemplation. Hilton was deeply versed in the writings of Augustine, as well as those of the major mystics of the twelfth century and Bonaventure. Unlike many of the handbooks of mysticism that became popular in the late Middle Ages, however, Hilton's work was more than a compilation of materials for clerical confessors and spiritual directors.*

The two books of The Ladder *were written for an anonymous anchoress. In the first Hilton adopts a traditional threefold division of stages of contemplation: knowledge of God through reason; love of God that does not depend on intellectual light; and finally, "the third degree of contemplation, which is the highest attainable in this life, of both knowledge and love"* (Ladder I.4–8). *The second book shifts to an original analysis of the soul's progress to God. Using Augustine's distinction between upper and lower reason, Hilton bases his teaching on the restoration of the image of God in humans, distinguishing reformation in faith, given in the sacraments and sufficient to salvation, from reformation in faith and feeling, which is the gradual destruction of the image of sin and growth in the contemplative life. These two forms of reformation underlie three progressive degrees of loving God: (1) loving God in faith alone; (2) loving God in faith accompanied by an imaginative love of Christ's humanity; and finally (3) loving contemplation of the Godhead united to the manhood in Christ.*

I.
BOOK II. CHAPTER 13.
ON THE THREE TYPES OF PEOPLE; THOSE WHO ARE REFORMED, THOSE WHO ARE UNREFORMED, AND THOSE WHO ARE REFORMED BOTH IN FAITH AND FEELING

You will realize from what I have already said that people are of various types according to the varying states of their souls. Some are not reformed to the likeness of God, and some are reformed only in faith, while some are reformed both in faith and feeling.

For you must understand that the soul has two faculties. One is called sensibility, that is, the faculty of perception through the senses, which man shares with the animals. When this sensibility is not rightly directed and controlled, the image of sin arises; for if the senses are not ruled by the reason, the result is sin. The other faculty is called reason, and this itself has two powers, the higher and the lower reason. The higher may be termed male since it should exercise control, and it is in this faculty that God's likeness exists, for it is only through this faculty that the soul knows and loves him. The lower faculty may be termed female, and should obey the higher reason as woman obeys man. Its function is to understand and control mundane things, to employ them with discretion as necessary, and to reject whatever is not essential. It must always watch, respect, and follow the higher rational faculty. Now a man who lives only to gratify his bodily desires like an unreasoning animal, and who has neither knowledge of God nor desire for virtue and holy living, but is blinded by pride, gnawed by envy, dominated by greed, and corrupted by lust and other grave sins, is not reformed to the likeness of God. For such a man is entirely satisfied with and subject to the image of sin. But one who fears God and refuses to obey the dangerous impulses of the senses keeps control over worldly things, and makes it his aim to please God in all that he does. In this way the soul is reformed to the likeness of God in faith, and although it experiences the same temptations as the other soul, they cannot harm it since it does not surrender to them. But a soul which receives grace to resist all sensual temptations, both mortal and venial, and is not even disturbed by them, is reformed in feeling. For it follows the higher powers of reason, and is enabled to see God and spiritual things, as I shall explain later.

II.
BOOK II. CHAPTER 30.
HOW TO ATTAIN SELF-KNOWLEDGE

. . . Understand, then, that the love of God has three degrees, all of which are good, but each succeeding degree is better than the other. The first degree is reached by faith alone, when no knowledge of God is conveyed by grace through the imagination or understanding. This love is common to every soul that is reformed in faith, however small a degree of charity it has attained; and it is good, for it is sufficient for salvation. The second degree of love is attained when the soul knows God by faith and Jesus in his manhood through the imagination. This love, where imagination is stimulated by grace, is better than the first, because the spiritual perceptions are awakened to contemplate our Lord's human nature. In the third degree the soul, as far as it may in this life, contemplates the Godhead united to manhood in Christ. This is the best, highest, and most perfect degree of love, and it is not attained by the soul until it is reformed in feeling. Those at the beginning and early stages of the spiritual life do not possess this degree of love, for they cannot think of Jesus or love him as God, but always think of him as a man living under earthly conditions. All their thoughts and affections are shaped by this limitation. They honor him as man, and they worship and love him principally in his human aspect, and go no further. For instance, if they have done wrong and offended against God, they think that God is angry with them as a man would be had they offended him. So they fall down as it were at the feet of our Lord with heartfelt sorrow and ask for mercy, trusting that our Lord will mercifully pardon their offense. And although this practice is commendable, it is not as spiritual as it might be. Similarly, when they wish to worship God they imagine our Lord in a bodily form aglow with wondrous light; then they proceed to honor, worship, and revere him, throwing themselves on his mercy and begging him to do with them what he wills. In the same way, when they wish to love God, they think of him, worship him, and reverence him as man, recalling the passion of Christ or some other event in his earthly life. Nevertheless, when they do this they are deeply stirred to the love of God.

Such devotion is good and inspired by grace, but it is much inferior to the exercise of the understanding, when grace moves the soul to contemplate God in man. For there are two natures in our Lord, that of God and that of man. And as the divine nature is higher and nobler than the human, so the soul's contemplation of the Godhead in the manhood of Jesus is more exalted, more spiritual, and more valuable than the contemplation of his manhood alone, whether the soul is thinking of his manhood as passable or glorified. For the same reason the love felt by a soul when grace enables it to contemplate God in man is more exalted, more spiritual, and more valuable than the fervor of devotion aroused by the contemplation of Jesus' manhood alone, however strong the outward signs of this love. For this latter love is a natural love, and the former a spiritual love; and our Lord does not reveal himself to the imagination as he is, for the frailty of man's nature is such that the soul could not endure his glory. . . .

PART TWO

ASPECTS OF MYSTICAL CONSCIOUSNESS

SECTION SIX

LIVING THE TRINITY

Belief in three persons in one God is fundamental to Christianity. At the end of the Gospel of Matthew, Christ commands the apostles: "Go, therefore, make disciples of all nations, baptizing them in the name of the Father, of the Son, and of the Holy Spirit" (Mt 28:19). Although the trinitarian view of God has been present in Christianity from the outset, what it means to confess belief in God as three in one was the subject of controversy and theological development, especially between circa 200 and 400 when the creedal formulations of trinitarian belief were hammered out.

The basic issues were two. The first involved the Word, or second person of the Trinity (and by extension the Holy Spirit, the third person). Was the Word of God who had taken on human nature in Jesus fully equal to God the Father, or only a lesser being adopted into divine sonship for the salvation of humans? The question was difficult because texts in the New Testament seemed to support either view. The second issue concerned the unity of God. Some Christians argued that if God is really one, then the Son and Holy Spirit should be understood as manifestations of the single Father, not as distinct persons. This latter view was condemned in the late third century. The former view of a subordination of Son to Father, expressed in different ways in the second and third centuries, was put to the test in the fourth century by the extreme formulations of the Alexandrian priest Arius, who denied the co-eternity and equality of the Son with the Father. His views were condemned at the Council of Nicaea in 325, but it took two generations before the dogmatic formula won out that God was one in nature, essence, or being, and three in persons, or hypostases.

The dogmatic agreement prompted an explicit consideration of how believers could deepen their participation in the life of the Trinity. The cornerstone of Christian anthropology was taken from Genesis 1:26 where God says (in the plural!), "Let us make man in our image and after our likeness." Christians read this as a declaration that humans were created not just in the image of God (*imago dei*), but also specifically as the image of the Trinity (*imago trinitatis*). In this sense all Christian mysticism is trinitarian, at least by implication. Many Christian mystics, however, have been explicitly trinitarian in the sense that they have made the inner relations of the three persons a focus of their teaching about how we attain consciousness of God. Even though no created intellect can ever understand how three distinct persons are one God, the mystics have insisted that what cannot be understood can nevertheless in some way become present in the depths of consciousness.

These selections begin with passages from the final book of Augustine's *On the Trinity,* the most influential Western account of the mystery. William of Saint-Thierry in the twelfth century and John of the Cross in the sixteenth show how Augustine's theology helped mystics express their inner sense of sharing in the life of the Trinity. A selection from Gregory Palamas represents the rich tradition of trinitarian mysticism of Eastern Orthodoxy, and passages from the beguine mystic Mechthild of Magdeburg illustrate the originality that many women brought to this aspect of Christian mystical teaching.

1.

AUGUSTINE

ON THE TRINITY

EXCERPTS FROM BOOK 15

Augustine's greatest work of speculation is the treatise On the Trinity, *composed between about 399 and 420. Written in the wake of the Arian controversy, Augustine pursued two aims in the book. First, he wished to provide an exposition of the biblical sources and doctrinal "grammar" of orthodox trinitarian belief. The first part, therefore, presents the faith of the church through an analysis of the scriptural texts on the Trinity (books 1–4) and a discussion of the proper language for talking about the three persons in one God (books 5–7).*

Augustine says that the unity of God is best spoken of in terms of one essence or substance, while the three persons are constituted by their relations to one another (i.e., the Son proceeds from the Father, while the Holy Spirit proceeds from both Father and Son). Although the Trinity is a mystery beyond human understanding, the bishop nevertheless sought for some "understanding of faith" (intellectus fidei) in the second part of the work. Books 8 and 9 explore the possibility of finding an analogy for how three can be one in God through an analysis of love of self. Augustine seems to have become dissatisfied with this approach, however, because books 9–15 move on to explore how the human mind in its activities of remembering, knowing, and loving provides a distant analogy of the Trinity of persons. Augustine summarizes this analogy in one passage as follows: "The image [of the Trinity] is to be recognized in these three things, that is, memory, understanding, and will" (14.7).

For Augustine, the mental operations of self-consciousness in the memory, of understanding in the act of the intellect that proceeds from this consciousness, and of love that proceeds from both, do not grant real knowledge of the Trinity it-self, but do reveal the mind's participation in the divine life. Hence, especially in book 15, Augustine emphasizes the personal and mystical dimension of his the-ology of the Trinity. It is only by turning toward the Trinity with all the re-sources of our inner life that the reformation of the trinitarian image can lead us forward on the road to the vision of the triune God to come in heaven. These selections from books 15.22–24 and 28 express the mystical goal of the bishop's trinitarian theology.

———

22.... In brief, in all these three things it is I that remember, I that un-derstand, I that love—I who am neither memory, understanding, nor love, but who have them. These things, then, can be said by a single person who has all three, but is not these three. But in the sim-plicity of that highest nature which is God, although there is one God, there are three persons, the Father, the Son, and the Holy Spirit.

23.... What is certainly wonderfully ineffable, or ineffably wonder-ful, is that while this image of the Trinity is one person, but the high-est Trinity itself is three persons, yet that Trinity of three persons is more indivisible than this of one. For that [Trinity], in the nature of the divinity (or perhaps better, deity), is that which it is, and is mutu-ally and always unchangeably equal: And there was no time when it was not, or when it was otherwise; and there will be no time when it will not be, or when it will be otherwise. But these three that are in the in-adequate image, although they are not separate in place, for they are not bodies, yet are now in this life mutually separate in magnitude. Just because there is no bulk present there does not hinder our seeing that memory is greater than understanding in one person, but the contrary in another; and that in yet another these two are overpassed by the greatness of love; and this whether the two themselves are or are not equal to each other. And so each two by each one, and each one by each two, and each one by each one: The less are surpassed by the greater. And when they have been healed of all infirmity and are mu-tually equal, not even then will that thing that by grace will not be changed [i.e., the mind] be made equal to that which by nature cannot change, because the creature cannot be made equal to the Creator; and when it shall be healed from all infirmity, it will be changed.

But when the sight shall have come that is promised anew to us face-to-face (1 Cor 13:12), we shall see this not only incorporeal but also absolutely indivisible and truly unchangeable Trinity far more clearly and certainly than we now see its image, which we ourselves are. And yet they who see through this mirror and in this enigma, as it is permitted in this life to see, are not those who behold in their own mind the things that we have set in order and pressed upon them; but those who see this precisely as an image, so as to be able to refer what they see, in some way be it what it may, to him whose image it is, and to see that other reality by conjecturing through the image that they see by beholding, since they cannot yet see the reality face-to-face. For the apostle does not say, "Now we see a mirror," but "We see now through a mirror" (1 Cor 13:12).

24. ... They, then, who see their own mind, in whatever way that is possible, and in it that trinity of which I have treated as I could in many ways, and yet do not believe or understand it to be an image of God, see indeed a mirror, but do not so far see through the mirror him who is now to be seen through the mirror alone that they do not even know the mirror that they see is a mirror, that is, an image. And if they knew this, perhaps they would feel that he too whose mirror this is should be sought by it, and somehow provisionally seen, with unfeigned faith purging their hearts (1 Tim 1:5), so that he who is now seen through a mirror may be able to be seen face-to-face. And if they despise this faith that purifies the heart, what do they accomplish by understanding the most subtle disputes concerning the nature of the human mind, except that they are condemned by the witness of their own understanding? And they would certainly not so fail in understanding, and hardly arrive at anything certain, if they were not involved in penal darkness and burdened with the corruptible body that presses down the soul (Wis 9:15). And for what evil save that of sin is this evil inflicted on them? Wherefore, being warned by the magnitude of so great an evil, they ought to follow the Lamb that takes away the sins of the world (Jn 1:29). ...

28. O Lord our God, we believe in you, the Father and the Son and the Holy Spirit. For the Truth would not say, "Go, baptize all nations in the name of the Father and of the Son and of the Holy Spirit" (Mt 28:19), unless you were a Trinity. Nor would you, O Lord God, bid us to be baptized in the name of him who is not the Lord God. Nor would the divine voice have said, "Hear, O Israel, the Lord your God is one

God" (Dt 6:4), unless you were a Trinity in such a way as to be one Lord God. And if you, O God, were yourself the Father, and were yourself the Son, your Word Jesus Christ, and the Holy Spirit your gift, we should not read in the book of truth, "God sent his Son" (Gal 4:5), nor would you, O Only-Begotten, say of the Holy Spirit, "Whom the Father will send in my name" (Jn 14:26), and "Whom I will send to you from the Father" (Jn 15:26). Directing my purpose by this rule of faith, so far as I have been able (so far as you have made me to be able), I have sought you and have desired to see with my understanding what I believed, and I have argued and labored a great deal. O Lord my God, my one hope, listen to me, lest through weariness I be unwilling to seek you, "but let me always ardently seek your face" (Ps 105:4). Give me strength to seek, you who have made me find you and given me the hope of finding you more and more. My strength and my infirmity are in your sight: preserve the one, and heal the other. My knowledge and my ignorance are in your sight; where you have opened to me, receive me as I enter; where you have closed, open to me as I knock. May I remember you, understand you, love you. Increase these things in me, until you fully refashion me.

From *Basic Writings of Saint Augustine,* translated by A. W. Haddon and revised by W.G.T. Stead (New York: Random House, 1948), Vol. 2:868–70, 877. I have modernized and corrected the translation.

WILLIAM OF SAINT-THIERRY
THE MIRROR OF FAITH

SECTIONS 105–121

William of Saint-Thierry (circa 1080–1148) received scholastic training before entering the Benedictine abbey of St. Nicaise in Rheims. About 1120 he became abbot of Saint-Thierry and began his writing career. Around this time he also became friendly with the younger Cistercian abbot Bernard of Clairvaux. The close relation of these two giants of monastic theology over almost three decades was a major factor in the development of twelfth-century mysticism. In 1135 William was allowed to fulfill his dream of joining the more rigorous Cistercian order as a simple monk at the abbey of Signy. Although he began the first Life *of his friend Bernard, he died before him, leaving a rich range of mystical writings, including a famous letter on the monastic life (*The Golden Letter; *see section 5.1), a commentary on the Song of Songs, a number of short treatises, some powerful* Meditations, *and two tracts on the Trinity that reveal his profound theological vision.* The Enigma of the Trinity *is primarily an exercise in "faith seeking understanding," while* The Mirror of Faith *deals more with the mystical aspect of entering into the life of the Trinity.*

*William's teaching builds on that of Augustine, but goes beyond that of the bishop of Hippo in its detailed exploration of how the soul, created as the image of the Trinity (*imago trinitatis*), regains its lost likeness to the Trinity (*similitudo trinitatis*) through the life of prayer and contemplation. William's mysticism can be described as "Spirit-centered" in that he sees the action of the Holy Spirit—the very oneness of the Father and the Son—as essential in the process by which we come to share in the inner life of the three persons. William's mysti-*

*cal message reveals how through the action of the Holy Spirit our love is lifted up and transformed into an experimental knowledge of God (*intelligentia amoris*) that conveys a real, though nondiscursive, knowledge of the Trinity.*

———

There is one recognition of God that comes from faith, another from love or charity. That of faith belongs to this life, but that of charity to eternal life, or rather, as the Lord says: "This is eternal life" (Jn 17:3). It is one thing to recognize God as a man recognizes his friend, another to recognize him as he recognizes himself (1 Cor 13:12). General recognition is to have within oneself in one's memory the image of the person recognized or of a thing recognized, conceived from having somehow seen it; by this image the reality, when it is absent, can still be reflected on or, when it is present, be recognized. This recognition in respect to God is one of faith, not that it has some resemblance to an image, but rather that it has the definite *affectus* [i.e., tendency] of piety. Derived from faith and confided to the memory this *affectus*, as often as it turns again to the experience of the person who remembers, gently influences the conscience of the person who reflects.

But the recognition which is mutual to the Father and Son is the very unity of both, which is the Holy Spirit. The recognition by which they recognize one another is nothing other than the substance by which they are what they are. Yet in this recognition no one learns to know the Father except the Son, and no one learns to know the Son except the Father and him to whom he chooses to reveal him (Mt 11:27). These are the Lord's words. The Father and the Son reveal this to certain persons then, to those to whom they will, to those to whom they make it known, that is, to whom they impart the Holy Spirit, who is the common knowing or the common will of both. Those therefore to whom the Father and the Son reveal themselves recognize them as the Father and the Son recognize themselves, because they have within themselves their mutual knowing, because they have within themselves the unity of both, and their will or love: all that the Holy Spirit is.

Yet this is so in one way in the divine substance wherein the Spirit himself is consubstantially one with the Father and Son, but in another way in inferior matter. One way in the Creator, another way in creatures; one way in his own nature, another way in grace; one way in him

who gives, another way in him who receives; one way in the unchange-
ableness of eternity, another way into the changes of time. There, in
the first way, the Holy Spirit, naturally and consubstantially, is mutual
charity, unity, likeness, recognition, and whatever else is common to
both. Here, however, he accomplishes this in the person in whom he
comes to be and by accomplishing this through grace is integrated in
him. There the mutual recognition of the Father and Son is unity.
Here it is a likeness of a human to God; of it the Apostle John says in
his epistle: "We will be like to him because we will see him as he is"
(1 Jn 3:2). There, to be like God will be either to see or to recognize
him. One will see or recognize him, will see or recognize to the extent
that he will be like him. He will be like him to the extent that he will
see and recognize him. For to see or to recognize God there is to be
like God and to be like God is to see or to recognize him.

This perfect recognition will be eternal life: the joy which no one
takes from the person who has it (Jn 16:22). Here, this joy can never be
full; it can only be made full in the full recognition of God, because
those things about God of which one has knowledge or recognizes
here can never be known or recognized as they shall be in that life
when he will be seen face to face (1 Cor 13:12), as he is (1 Jn 3:2). This
way of recognizing cannot be expected here from the mouth of any
man, for it could not be learned from the mouth of Truth himself (Jn
16:12). It is not that the Lord could not have taught it, but that human
weakness could not bear it. Yet even here he does not entirely withdraw it from those who love him and whom he has loved, to the end
that they may know what they are missing (Ps 38:5).

Over the impoverished and needy love of those poor in spirit and
over what they love anxiously hovers the Holy Spirit, the Love of God.
That is: He performs his works in them, not through the compulsion of
any need, but through the abundance of his grace and generosity. This
was signified when he hovered over the waters (Gen 1:2), whatever
those waters may have been. As the sun hovers over the waters, warm-
ing and lighting them and drawing them to itself by its heat, by some
natural force, that it may thereby furnish rains to a thirsty earth in the
time and place of God's mercy, so the love of God hovers over the love
of his faithful person by breathing upon and by doing him good, seiz-
ing to himself the person who follows him by some natural hunger and
who has the natural ability of rising upwards like fire. He unites him to

himself so that the spirit of the person who believes, having trusted in God (Ps 77:8), may be made one with him (1 Cor 6:17).

The Father and the Son are equally addressed by the same word: for God is spirit (Jn 3:24). It is also proper for the Holy Spirit to be particularly addressed by the same word: he who seems not so much to be the spirit proper to each of them as in fact their communality. The Holy Spirit himself communicates to man this word "spirit," to the end that, according to the Apostle, the man of God may be made one spirit with God (1 Cor 6:17), both by the grace of the name and by the effect of its power. It is not one person only but many persons who have one heart and one soul in him, as a result of the sharing in this supreme charity at the source of which is the unity of the Trinity.

And such is the astounding generosity of the Creator to the creature; the great grace, the unknowable goodness, the devout confidence of the creature for the Creator, the tender approach, the tenderness of a good conscience, that a person somehow finds himself in their midst, in the embrace and kiss of the Father and Son, that is, in the Holy Spirit. And he is united to God by that charity whereby the Father and Son are one. He is made holy in him who is the holiness of both.

The sense of this good and the tenderness of this experience, as great as it can be in this miserable and deceptive life, although it is not now full, is yet a true and truly blessed life! In the future it will be the fully blessed and full life, unchangeably eternal; that means, when Paul recognizes as he is recognized (1 Cor 13:12), when what is in part will have been done away with and what is perfect will have come (1 Cor 13:10), when God will be seen as he is (1 Jn 3:2)! It is a dangerous presumption to look for the fullness of his knowledge in this life. In the same way, just as unbelief concerning what should be believed is to be avoided, so is rashness concerning what is to be understood. For the time being, authority governs faith and truth governs intelligence....

Both the words of the Lord and this our explanation we have by use and reason taught our mouth to speak and our hearts to reflect as many times as we wanted to. Yet, however much we want to, we do not always understand them except through the experience of *affectus* and an inner sense of enlightened love. Therefore just as the Lord himself, appearing in the flesh to people, took away from the world the vanity of idols, so too he proposed to those pondering God the unity of the Trinity and the Trinity in unity. The glistening radiance of his divinity took away from any reflections of faith about God all vanity of the imagination. When he taught that the understanding of divinity is beyond humans, he was teaching humans to think in his own way.

All the acts or words of the Word of God are for us therefore one word. Everything about him which we read, we hear, we see, we speak, we meditate on, call us, either by provoking love or inculcating fear, to the One, sends us to the One of whom many things are said and nothing is said, because a person does not come to that which is unless he who is sought runs to him and shines his face upon us. May he shine his face upon us (Ps 66:2) so that in the light of his face (Ps 88:16) we may know how we are progressing. . . .

William of Saint Thierry. The Mirror of Faith, 75–81, 85, translated by Thomas X. Davis. Copyright 1979 by Cistercian Publications, Inc., Kalamazoo, Michigan. All rights reserved.

3.

MECHTHILD OF MAGDEBURG
THE FLOWING LIGHT OF THE GODHEAD

Mechthild of Magdeburg (circa 1208–circa 1282) was one of four remarkable thirteenth-century figures whose vernacular writings mark a new stage in the role of women in Christian mysticism (the others are Hadewijch of Antwerp, Angela of Foligno, and Marguerite Porete). Women had certainly had a place in earlier mystical traditions, but they were rarely writers, so the outpouring of texts from these four mystics and those who succeeded them was unusual. Mechthild was a beguine in Magdeburg for most her life. Under the guidance of Dominican friars, she recorded her revelations and gradually collected them into the seven books that make up the compendium she called The Flowing Light of the Godhead. *Mechthild's book is a mixture of prose and poetry whose complexity still has not been fully explored. She is noted for the erotic nature of her encounters with Christ, but* The Flowing Light *demonstrates theological originality on many fronts, not least in its teaching on the Trinity.*

Mechthild's mysticism was based upon the activity of the Trinity flowing forth into all things. In one chapter (book V, ch. 26) the three persons sing about their individual roles before concluding as one voice. The voice of the Father sings: "I am an overflowing spring that no one can block," and the Son continues, "I am constantly recurring richness that no one can ever contain except the boundlessness that always flowed out and shall ever flow from God." The Holy Spirit hymns, "I am an insuperable power of truth," before the whole Trinity concludes: "I am so strong in my undividedness that no one can ever divide me or shatter me in all my eternity." Among the most remarkable passages in Mechthild's presentation of the Trinity are the three chapters where she describes being rapt into the inner life of the three persons to overhear their "counsel, or deliberation" concerning the creation of the universe and the Incarnation of the Word from the Virgin Mary, foreordained from all eternity.

Mechthild's original text, written in the Low German of northern Germany, does not survive. The work exists in two translations. The earliest is a partial Latin version made by the Dominican community in Halle in the last decade of the thirteenth century; the second is the Middle High German version made by the priest Henry of Nördlingen about 1343–45. Since several English versions of the German text exist, the following translation of one of the counsels of the Trinity chapters is from the Latin (book I, chapter 5 equates to book III, chapter 9 in Middle High German).

THE COUNSEL OF THE DIVINE PERSONS AND THE CREATION OF ALL THINGS BEGUN BY THE HOLY SPIRIT

God, Father of mercies, I your unworthy one give thanks to your faithfulness by which you have led me outside myself into your wonders, because in your truth I have seen and heard the deliberation that was foreordained to be made before the ages. This was when you alone existed and none shared in your delights; you shone forth in the Son and Holy Spirit, and they likewise in you. The undivided unity of this Trinity existed as omnipotence in the Father, wisdom in the Son, and goodness in the Holy Spirit: and these things are adored in equal fashion in the three.

The free generosity of the Holy Spirit at play in the delights of Trinity said to the Father: "I offer the counsel of charity from you and to you, venerable Father. To be without fruit is not fitting for us; we wish to have a created realm. You will form the angelic spirits to be like me, but as created spirits; their profuse number is called a true joy." The Father answered: "You are one spirit with me, and therefore your advice and will are pleasing to me." Therefore the uncreated Holy Spirit gave loving-kindness to created spirits so that they would minister to human beings and rejoice with them over their salvation. Even if all the angels had remained in heavenly blessedness, man would still have to have been created.

THE SON'S AGREEMENT WITH THE FATHER AND HOLY SPIRIT ABOUT THIS ADVICE

The Son who is co-eternal with the Father and the Holy Spirit spoke in this manner in good order: "O Father, I do not want to be devoid of the glory of fruitfulness. Since we have agreed to begin to do wondrous things, let us make man to our image and likeness (Gen 1:26). Even though I foresee the great miseries to come, I will still love man with everlasting love." The Father answered: "The internal sweetness of your love, O Son, touches me; I will not hold back my feelings from you for the sake of love. Therefore, we will become fruitful by creating so that we can be loved in return and so that the greatness of our majesty may be acknowledged in some small way. I will prepare for myself a bride who will greet me with her mouth and overcome me with her beautiful face. These are the first stages of love." The Holy Spirit said: "For you I will deliver this bride to the bed in your bridal chamber." And the Son added: "Father, you know that I finally will die for love, but still joyfully we wish to make this creature in great holiness."

THE CREATION OF MAN TO GOD'S IMAGE

When they had made this deliberation, the whole Trinity agreed to create the entire universe, making man composed of rational soul and body with surpassing love. The Son of God is the Father's Image (Col 1:15) by means of which Adam and Eve were created as glorious beings endowed with wisdom and power through him so that they might love and cherish him in a perfect way and steadfast in sanctity rule over all created things, something now of great worth to us. Adam received from God a wife filled with every virtue and endowed with beauty of body. She was lovable and perfectly ordered, being conformed to the Son in all these things. Their bodies were created without lustful heat, clothed with an angelic garment; they were able to bear their children in holy love, just as the sun in its brightness shines through pure water. But when they ate the forbidden fruit, their bodies were deformed, just as we now, alas, experience. If the Holy Trinity had created us with such deformity, we would not have been able to be ashamed on that basis.

THE SUBLIMITY OF THE SOUL THAT GOD GAVE IT IN CREATION

The Father, God of gods, gave the soul divine love, saying: "I am the God of gods and you are the goddess of creation. Behold, I make an agreement with you that I shall never desert you unless you lose yourself through neglect. My angels will serve you, and I give my Holy Spirit as your assistant, and I grant you free choice so that you do not fall unaware into some reprehensible misdeed. Now then, O much beloved, look to your future with great care, 'and let your eyelids go before your steps' (Prov 4:25). Guard my little commandment so that you may remember your God." The pure food that was lawfully given them in paradise was to strengthen their hearts in great holiness and constancy. But when they ate of the forbidden tree in disobedience, the deadly poison spread through their members and took away their angelic purity and virginal chastity. Then the soul was troubled and, covered with great darkness, cried out in a tearful voice from exile: "O my dearly Beloved, where has your surpassingly sweet love gone? You have strongly cast aside the queen who was lawfully joined to you. O great God, how long will you bear such lengthy miseries and not take away our sins! I know that you will be born for us upon the earth. All your works are perfect; bring your wrath to perfection so that it may come to an end."

THE DESIRE OF THE HOLY FATHERS FOR THE LIBERATION OF THE HUMAN RACE

This cry pierced the clouds and came to the ears of the Lord of Hosts. The Eternal Father said: "I regret my work. I made a bride so praiseworthy that I destined her for my high majesty. I assigned the supreme powers for her service; even Lucifer himself, had he remained in glory, would have been her servant. For her alone was the bed in the marriage chamber made ready, but she rejected the divine beauty and was made ugly and very contemptible, 'going your same ways over again' (Jer 2:36). And who will stoop to take such filthiness upon himself?" The Only-Begotten Son of God, recognizing his image in man, bowing his majesty low in a fitting fashion before the Father, said: "With your blessing Father, I will freely take on human nature despite its pollution, and I will wash its wounds through my innocent blood, and I will heal its broken places with the bindings of the scorn of my exile, even unto death. I will lay down my soul for sin, and through the death I have not merited I will then settle the debt that I have not snatched away by force. 'I will return to you, with life accompanying me' (Gen 18:14), having taken the kingdom with the two squadrons of Jews and Gentiles, leading all back to you with the victory of all Israel."

When he heard these things, the sweet Spirit of both of them said: "Almighty God, our procession into the world will be beautiful and totally marvelous. Let us then go forth from here with great glory, but without leaving behind this majesty by withdrawing our present high station from those beings that exist here. Even unto the present I have served as the faithful guardian and attendant of the Virgin Mary in this same place." [The reference here is to Mary's pre-existence in God's plan.] Then the Father, bowed down in love by the appeal of both, said to the Holy Spirit: "You will be the one who bears my light before the Son into the hearts of all who will be devoutly moved to his fiery speech in a strong fashion. And you, Son, will take up your cross, 'and go forth into Egypt and free my people' (Ex 4:14). I will be with you more than I was with Moses, and I will walk with you in all your paths, 'I will hold your right hand, I will lead you forth with my will and will lead you back to me with eternal glory' (Ps 72:24). For you I have prepared the immaculate unimpaired Mother of unsullied virginity so that you may be able to bear the deadly nature of the base crowd of humans more honorably and more purely than all others and to exalt the nature united to you in an ineffable manner." Then the procession set forth with joy from the height of heaven down to the mystical temple of Solomon [i.e., Mary], in which through nine months the Almighty Son of God deigned to remain and to be adored, "until the days for the Virgin Mother Mary to bring forth were completed" (Lk 2:6).

Translated by Bernard McGinn from *Sororis Mechtildis Lux Divinitatis Fluens in Corda Veritatis,* Vol. 2 of *Revelationes Gertrudianae et Mechtildianae,* edited by the Monks of Solesmes (Paris/Poitiers: Oudin, 1875–77), 450–54.

4.

GREGORY PALAMAS
THE ONE HUNDRED AND FIFTY CHAPTERS

Gregory Palamas (1296–1359) stands out as one of the foremost proponents of Hesychasm, the tradition of mystical practice centered on the Jesus Prayer and directed to the interior "quiet" (Greek: hêsychia*) that prepares for the gift of the uncreated divine light, the radiance that emanated from Jesus at the Transfiguration. The roots of Hesychasm go deep in the Orthodox tradition, but it was primarily at the monasteries on Mount Athos in Gregory's time that this form of prayer was given its classical formulation. Gregory lived as a monk on Athos under the tutelage of several of the Athonite masters, among them Gregory of Sinai. In the 1330s he was drawn into the controversies that marked the rest of his life, defending the Hesychasts against a series of opponents, such as Barlaam of Calabria and Gregory Akindynos, who accused them of destroying the divine unity by their distinction between the unknowable divine substance and the manifested divine energies. Gregory Palamas's defense of Hesychasm was approved in two councils held at Constantinople in 1341, an approval subsequently ratified by several other councils. In 1347 Gregory was made archbishop of Thessalonica, where he died in 1359. Many of Gregory's writings are polemical. His earliest major work is* The Triads in Defense of the Holy Hesychasts, *a series of nine treatises divided into three groups composed between 1338 and 1341. In this treatise Gregory provides the theological justification for Hesychast teaching about the deification of humans in Christ, insisting that this goal is open to all the baptized.*

Gregory's most mature theological work, written about 1350, is titled The One Hundred and Fifty Chapters. *The book is divided into two parts. The first sixty-three chapters, much like the first of the triads, show the superiority of Christian wisdom based on scripture over the errors of natural science and philosophy. Chapters 64–150 constitute a refutation of Gregory's opponents and a defense of the Hesychast view of union with God. A brief consideration of the doctrine of the Trinity (chapters 34–36) introduces Gregory's treatment of how humans bear the image of the Trinity within their souls in an even more powerful way than do the angels. Although it is customary to identify such trinitarian analogies with Augustine and Western theology, Gregory shows that there is a distinctive Eastern form of this theology—one that provides the basis for the Hesychast doctrine of union, as several other chapters from the second part of the work show.*

CHAPTER 37. Our mind too, since it is created in the image of God, possesses the image of this highest love in the relation of the mind to the knowledge which exists perpetually from it and in it, in that this love is from it and in it and proceeds from it together with the innermost word. The insatiable desire of men for knowledge is a very clear indication of this even for those who are unable to perceive their own innermost being. But in that archetype, in that absolutely and supremely perfect goodness wherein there is no imperfection, leaving aside the being derived from it, the divine love is indistinguishably identical in every way with that goodness. Therefore, this love is the Holy Spirit and another name for the Paraclete and is so called by us, since he accompanies the Word, in order that we may recognize him as perfect in a perfect and proper hypostasis, in no way inferior to the substance of the Father but being indistinguishably identical with both the Son and the Father, though not in hypostasis—a fact which indicates to us that he is derived from the Father by way of procession in a divinely fitting manner—and in order that we may revere one true and perfect God in three true and perfect hypostases, certainly not threefold, but simple. For goodness is not something threefold nor a triad of goodnesses; rather, the supreme goodness is a holy, august and venerable Trinity flowing forth from itself into itself without change and abiding with itself before the ages in divinely fitting manner, being both unbounded and bounded by itself alone, while setting bounds for all things, transcending all things and allowing no beings independent of itself. . . .

CHAPTER 39. The intellectual and rational nature of the soul, alone possessing mind and word and life-giving spirit, has alone been created more in the image of God than the incorporeal angels. It possesses this indefectibly even though it may not recognize its own dignity nor think or act in a manner worthy of the one who created him in his own image. Therefore, we did not destroy the image even though after our ancestor's transgression through a tree in paradise we underwent the death of the soul which is prior to bodily death, that is, separation of the soul from God, and we rejected the divine likeness. Thus, on the one hand, if the soul rejects attachment to inferior things and cleaves in love to one who is superior by submitting to him through the works and the ways of virtue, it receives from him illumination, adornment and betterment, and it obeys his counsels and exhortations from which it receives true and eternal life. Through this life it receives also immortality for the body joined to it, for at the proper time the body attains to the promised resurrection and participates in eternal glory. But, on the other hand, if it does not reject attachment and submission to inferior things whereby it inflicts shameful dishonor upon the image of God, it becomes alienated and estranged from the true and truly blessed life of God, since if it has first abandoned the one who is superior, it is justly abandoned by him.

CHAPTER 40. The triadic nature posterior to the supreme Trinity, since, more so than others, it has been made by it in its image, endowed with mind, word and spirit (namely, the human soul), ought to preserve its proper rank and take its place after God alone and be subject, subordinate and obedient to him alone and look to him alone and adorn itself with perpetual remembrance and contemplation of him and with most fervent and ardent love for him. By these it is marvelously drawn to itself, or rather, it would eventually attract to itself the mysterious and ineffable radiance of that nature. Then, it truly possesses the image and likeness of God, since through this it has been made gracious, wise and divine. Either when the radiance is visibly present or when it approaches unnoticed, the soul learns from this now more and more to love God beyond itself and its neighbor as itself (Dt 6:4–5), and from then on to know and preserve its own dignity and rank and truly to love itself. For he who loves wrongdoing hates his own soul and, in tearing apart and disabling the image of God, he experiences suffering similar to that of madmen who pitilessly cut their own flesh to pieces without feeling it. For he unwittingly inflicts the most miserable sort of harm and rending upon his own innate beauty, and mindlessly breaks apart the triadic and supercosmic world of his own soul which was filled interiorly with love. What could be more wrong, what more ruinous than to refuse to remember, to look upon and to love perpetually the one who created and adorned in his own image and thereby granted the power of knowledge and love and also lavishly endowed those who use this power well with ineffable gifts and with eternal life? . . .

CHAPTER 66. Now that our nature has been stripped of this divine illumination and radiance as a result of the transgression [of Adam], the Word of God has taken pity on our disgrace and in his compassion has assumed our nature and has manifested it again to his chosen disciples, clothed more remarkably on Tabor (Mt 17:1–13). He indicated what we once were and what we shall become through him in the future age if we choose here below to live according to his ways as much as possible, as John Chrysostom says [*Homily 56 on Matthew*]. . . .

CHAPTER 75. There are three realities in God, namely substance, energy, and a Trinity of divine hypostases. Since it has been shown above that those deemed worthy of union with God so as to become one spirit with him (even as the great Paul has said, "He who clings to the Lord is one spirit with him" [1 Cor 6:17]) are not united to God in substance, and since all theologians bear witness in their statements to the fact that God is imparticipable in substance and the hypostatic union happens to be predicated of the Word and God-man alone, it follows that those deemed worthy of union with God are united to God in energy and that the spirit whereby he who clings to God is one with God is called and is indeed the uncreated energy of the Spirit and not the substance of God, even though Barlaam and Akindynos may disagree. For God foretold through the prophet not "My Spirit," but rather, "Of my Spirit I will pour out upon those who believe" (Joel 3:1). . . .

CHAPTER 105. Those who have pleased God and attained that for which they came into being, namely, divinization—for they say it was for this purpose that God made us, in order to make us partakers of his own divinity (2 Pet 1:4)—these then are in God since they are divinized in him and he is in them since he divinizes them. Therefore, these too participate in the divine energy, though in another way, but not in the substance of God. And so the theologians maintain that "divinity" is a name for the divine energy.

From *Saint Gregory Palamas. The One Hundred and Fifty Chapters,* edited by Robert E. Sinkewicz, 122–29, 161, 171, 201, by permission of the publisher. Copyright 1988 by the Pontifical Institute of Mediaeval Studies, Toronto.

5.

JOHN OF THE CROSS
THE LIVING FLAME OF LOVE

STANZA 2

The Living Flame of Love *is the last of the four works that constitute John of the Cross's "summa" of the mystical life. Like the other works, the treatise is in the form of a commentary on the four stanzas of the poem of the same name that John wrote in 1585 while in a state of ecstasy. John produced the commentary at the request of one of his penitents, Dona Ana de Penalosa. The work was composed quickly over a two-week period in 1586. Toward the end of his life in 1591, John completed an expanded version, but there is no great difference between the A and B forms of the text (the A version is used here).*

Each of John's works has a controlling image. The Spiritual Canticle *uses the erotic images of the Song of Songs, while* The Ascent of Mount Carmel *employs the mountain and* The Dark Night of the Soul *centers on the cloud and darkness of Moses' ascent of Sinai.* The Living Flame of Love *employs the image of fire, specifically the divine fire that gradually heats the inert log of the human soul until it becomes totally enflamed and united to God. The first stanza concentrates on the action of the Holy Spirit as the fire of divine love. In the second stanza, which is excerpted here, John lays out the trinitarian dimension of loving union with God. The third stanza continues the analysis of the work of the three persons in the depths of the soul. The fourth stanza begins with the communion of the Word in the soul and the knowledge that this provides. It concludes with a return to the action of the Holy Spirit.*

STANZA II

O sweet burn!
O delicious wound!
O tender hand! O gentle touch
That savors of eternal life,
And pays every debt!
In slaying you have changed death into life.

EXPOSITION

We learn here that it is the three persons of the Most Holy Trinity, Father, Son, and Holy Spirit, who accomplish the divine work of union in the soul. The "hand," the "burn," and the "touch" are in substance one and the same; and the three terms are employed because they express effects peculiar to each. The "burn" is the Holy Spirit; the "hand" is the Father; and the "touch" is the Son. Thus the soul magnifies the Father, the Son, and the Holy Spirit, extolling those three grand gifts and graces that they perfect within it, in that they have changed death into life, transforming it in themselves.

The first of these gifts is the delicious wound, attributed to the Holy Spirit, and so the soul calls it the "burn." The second is the "taste of everlasting life," attributed to the Son, and the soul calls it the "gentle touch." The third is the "gift" that is the perfect recompense of the soul, attributed to the Father, and is therefore called the "tender hand." Though the three persons of the Most Holy Trinity are referred to severally because of the operations peculiar to each, the soul is addressing itself to but one essence, saying, "You have changed it into life," for the three persons work together and the whole is attributed to each and to all. There follows the verse:

O sweet burn!

In the book of Deuteronomy, Moses says, "Our Lord God is a consuming fire" (Dt 4:24), that is, a fire of love. And as his power is infinite, he consumes infinitely, burning with great vehemence, and transforming into himself all he touches. But he burns everything according to the measure of its preparation, some more, others less; and also according to his own good pleasure, as, and when, and how, he will. And as this is an infinite fire of love, so when he touches the soul somewhat sharply, the burning heat within it becomes so extreme as to surpass all the fires of the world. This is the reason why this touch of God is said to be a "burn": for the fire there is more intense, and more concentrated, and the effect of it surpasses that of all other fires. When the divine fire shall have transformed the soul into itself, the soul not only feels the burn, but itself is become wholly and entirely burned up in this vehement fire.

It is wonderful and worthy of telling that though this fire is so vehement and so consuming, though it can destroy a thousand worlds with more ease than the material fire can destroy a single straw, it consumes not the spirit wherein it burns, but rather, in proportion to its strength and heat, delights and deifies it, burning sweetly within according to the purity and perfection of their spirits. Thus, on the day of Pentecost the fire descended with great vehemence upon the Apostles, who, according to St. Gregory [*Homilies on the Gospels* 30], sweetly burned interiorly. The church also says, when celebrating that event: "The divine fire came down, not consuming but enlightening" [Responsory for Matins at Pentecost]. For as the object of these communications is to elevate the soul, the burning of the fire does not distress it but gladdens it; does not weary it but delights it, and renders it glorious and rich. This is the reason why it is said to be sweet.

Thus then the blessed soul, which by the mercy of God has been burned, knows all things, tastes all things, "whatsoever it shall do shall prosper" (Ps 1:3), against it nothing shall prevail, nothing shall touch it. It is of that soul that the Apostle said: "The spiritual man judges all things, and he himself is judged of no man" (1 Cor 2:15). And again, "The Spirit searches all things, even the deep things of God" (1 Cor 2:10), because it belongs to love to search into all that the Beloved has.

O, the great glory of the souls who are worthy of this supreme fire that, having infinite power to consume and annihilate you, consumes you not, but makes you infinitely perfect in glory! Wonder not that God should elevate some souls to so high a degree, for he alone is wonderful in his marvelous works. As the Holy Spirit says, it burns the mountains of the just in three ways (Ecclus 43:4). As this burn then is so sweet—as it is here said to be—how happy must that soul be which this fire has touched! The soul would speak of it, but cannot, so it says only, "O delicious wound."

O delicious wound!

He who inflicts the wound relieves and heals while he inflicts it. It bears some resemblance to the caustic usage of natural fire, which when applied to a wound increases it, and renders a wound, which iron or other instruments occasioned, a wound of fire. The longer the caustic is applied, the more grievous the wound, until the whole matter be destroyed.

Thus the divine burn of love heals the wound that love has caused, and by each application renders it greater. The healing that love brings is to wound again what was wounded before, until the soul melts away in the fire of love. So when the soul shall become wholly one wound of love it will then be transformed in love, wounded with love. For herein he who is most wounded is the most healthy, and he who is all wound is all health.

And yet even if the whole soul be one wound, and consequently sound, the divine burning is not interrupted; it continues its work, which is to wound the soul with love. But then, too, its work is to soothe the healed wound, and the soul therefore cries out, "O delicious wound," and so much the more delicious the more penetrating the fire of love. The Holy Spirit inflicted the wound that he might soothe it, and as his will and desire to soothe it are great, great will be the wound that he will inflict, in order that the soul he has wounded may be greatly comforted.

O blessed wound inflicted by him who cannot but heal it! O happy and most blessed wound! For you are inflicted only for the joy and comfort of the soul. Great is the wound, because he is great who has wrought it; and great is the delight of it: for the fire of love is infinite. O delicious wound then, and the more delicious the more the burn of love penetrates the inmost substance of the soul, burning all it can burn that it may supply all the delight it can give. This burning and wound, in my opinion, are the highest condition attainable in this life. There are many other forms of this burning, but they do not reach so far, neither are they like this: for this is the touch of the divinity without form or figure, either natural, formal, or imaginary.

But the soul is burned in another and most excellent way, which is this: When a soul is on fire with love, but not in the degree of which I am now speaking—though it should be so, that it may be the subject of this—it will feel as if a Seraph with a burning brand of love had struck it, and penetrated it already on fire as glowing coal, or rather as a flame, and burns it utterly [a reference to Teresa of Avila, *Life*, chapter 29; see section 10.10]. And then in that burn the flame rushes forth and surges vehemently as in a glowing furnace or forge; the fire revives and the flame ascends when the burning fuel is disturbed. Then when the burning brand touches it, the soul feels that the wound it has thus received is delicious beyond all imagination. For beside being altogether moved or stirred, at the time of this stirring of the fire, by the vehement movement of the Seraph, wherein the ardor and the melting of love is great, it feels that its wound is perfect, and that the herbs that serve to temper the steel are efficacious; it feels the very depths of the spirit transpierced, and its delight to be exquisite beyond the power of language to express.

The soul feels, as it were, a most minute grain of mustard seed, most pungent and burning in the inmost heart of the spirit, in the spot of the wound, where the substance and the power of the herb reside, diffuse itself most subtly through all the spiritual veins of the soul in proportion to the strength and power of the heat. It feels its love to grow, strengthen, and refine itself to such a degree as to seem to itself as if seas of fire were in it filling it with love.

The fruition of the soul now cannot be described otherwise than by saying that it understands why the kingdom of heaven is compared in the gospel to a mustard seed, which by reason of its great natural heat grows into a lofty tree. "The kingdom of heaven is like a grain of mustard seed, which a man took and sowed in his field. Which is surely the least of all seeds; but when it is grown up, it is greater than all herbs, and is made a tree, so that the birds of the air come and dwell in its branches" (Mt 13:31–32). The soul beholds itself now as one immense sea of fire. Few souls, however, attain to this state, but some have done so, especially those whose spirit and power is to be transmitted to their spiritual children; since God bestows on the founder gifts and graces, according to the succession of the order in the first fruits of the Spirit.

To return to the work of the Seraph, which in truth is to strike and wound. If the effect of the wound is permitted to flow exteriorly into the bodily senses, an effect corresponding to the interior wound itself will manifest itself without. Thus it was with St. Francis, for when the Seraph wounded his soul with love, the effects of that wound became outwardly visible [see section 7.2]. God confers no favors on the body that he does not confer in the first place chiefly on the soul. In that case, the greater the joy and violence of the love that is the cause of the interior wound, the greater will be the pain of the visible wound, and as the former grows so does the latter. The reason is this: Such souls as these, being already purified and strong in God, their spirit, strong and sound, delights in the strong and sweet Spirit of God; who, however, causes pain and suffering in their weak and corruptible flesh. It is thus a most marvelous thing to feel pain and sweetness together. Job felt it when he said, "Returning, you torment me wonderfully" (Jb 10:16). This is marvelous, worthy of the "multitude of the sweetness of God, which he has hidden for them that fear him" (Ps 30:20). The greater the sweetness and delight, the greater the pain and suffering.

O infinite greatness, in all things showing yourself omnipotent. Who, O Lord, can cause sweetness in the midst of bitterness, and pleasure in the midst of pain? O delicious wound, the greater the delight the deeper the wound. But when the wound is within the soul, and not communicated to the body without, it is then much more intense and keen. As the flesh is bridle to the spirit, so, when the graces of the latter overflow into the former, the flesh draws in and restrains the swift steed of the spirit and checks its course; "For the corruptible body is a load upon the soul, and the earthly habitation presses down the mind that muses upon many things" (Wis 9:15).

He, therefore, who shall trust much to the bodily senses will never become a very spiritual man. This I say for the sake of those who think they can ascend to the heights and power of the spirit by the mere energy and action of the senses, which are mean and vile. We cannot become spiritual unless the bodily senses are restrained. It is a state of things wholly different from this when the spirit overflows into the senses, for there may be great spirituality in this; as in the case of St. Paul, whose deep sense of the sufferings of Christ overflowed into his body, so that he said in Galatians: "I bear the marks of our Lord Jesus in my body" (Gal 6:17).

Thus, as the wound and the burn are such as this, what will be the hand that inflicted it; and what will be the touch that causes it? This the soul shows in the following verse, extolling more than explaining, saying:

O tender hand! O gentle touch

O hand, as generous as you are powerful and rich, giving me gifts with power. O gentle hand! laid so gently upon me, and yet, if you were to press at all, the whole world would perish; for only at the sight of you the earth trembles (Ps 103:32), the nations melt, and the mountains are crushed in pieces (Hab 3:6). O gentle hand, I say it again, for him you touched so sharply. Upon me you are laid so softly, so lovingly, and so tenderly. You are the more gentle and sweet for me than you were hard for him (Jb 19:21); the loving sweetness with which you are laid upon me is greater than the severity with which he was touched. You kill and you give life and there is no one who shall escape out of your hand.

But you, O divine life, never kill but to give life, as you never wound but to heal (Dt 32:39). You have wounded me, O divine hand, so that you may heal me. You have slain in me that which made me dead and without the life of God which I now live. This you have done in the liberality of your gracious generosity through that touch with which you touch me, by the brightness of your glory and the figure of your substance (Heb 1:3), that is, your only-begotten Son in whom, since he is your Wisdom, you reach "from end to end mightily" (Wis 8:1).

O gentle, subtle touch, the Word, the Son of God, who, because of the pureness of your divine nature, penetrates subtly the very substance of my soul, and, touching it gently, absorbs it wholly in divine ways of sweetness not "heard of in the land of Canaan," nor "seen in Teman" (Bar 3:22). O touch of the Word, so gentle, so wonderfully gentle to me; and yet you were "overthrowing mountains, and breaking rocks in Horeb," by the shadow of your power going before, when you announced your presence to the prophet in "the whisper of a gentle air" (3 Kgs 19:11–12). O soft air, how is it that you touch so softly when you are so terrible and so strong? O blessed soul, most blessed, which you, who are so terrible and so strong, touch so gently. Proclaim it to the world, O my soul—no, proclaim it not, for the world does not know the "gentle air," nor will it listen to it, because it cannot comprehend matters so deep.

O my God and my life, they shall know you (Jn 14:17), and behold you when you touch them, who, making themselves strangers upon earth, shall purify themselves, because purity corresponds with purity. The more gently you touch, the more you are hidden in the purified soul of those who have made themselves strangers here, hidden from the face of all creatures, and whom "You shall hide in the secret of your face from the disturbance of men" (Ps 30:21).

O, again and again, gentle touch, which by the power of its tenderness undoes the soul, removes it far away from every touch whatever, and makes it your own. You who leave behind you effects and impressions so pure that the touch of everything else seems vile and low, the very sight offensive, and all relations with them a deep affliction.

The more subtle any matter is, the more it spreads and fills, and the more it diffuses itself, the more subtle it is. O gentle touch, the more subtle you are, the more infused. And now the vessel of my soul, because you have touched it, is pure and clean and able to receive you. O gentle touch! as in you there is nothing material, so your touch is the more penetrating, changing what in me is human into divine, for your divine essence, with which you touch me, is wholly unaffected by modes and manner, free from the husks of form and figure. Finally then, O gentle touch, and most gentle, for you touch me with your most simple and pure essence, which being infinite is infinitely gentle; therefore it is that this touch is so subtle, so loving, so deep, and so delicious, that it

Savors of eternal life

From *The Living Flame of Love by St. John of the Cross*, translated by David Lewis (London: Thomas Baker, 1912), 32–43. The language has been updated and some adjustments and corrections made.

ENCOUNTERING CHRIST

Christian mysticism by definition is Christological—that is to say, it is only in, through, and by Christ, the God-man, that access to God is possible. As Jesus says in the Gospel of John, "I am the way, the truth, and the life" (Jn 14:6). Almost all the texts found in this anthology illustrate in one way or another Christ's role as both the way and the goal of the mystical life. The selections in this section highlight some of the more specific ways in which mystics have presented Christ's action in their lives.

BERNARD OF CLAIRVAUX
SERMONS ON THE SONG OF SONGS 74

In his Sermon 74 on the Song of Songs, *Bernard comments on the bride's cry to the Bridegroom: "Return, my Beloved, like a roe or a fawn" (Song 2:17). How, Bernard wonders, can the Word of God be said to return, when as God he is everywhere at all times? The answer, says the abbot, rests "in the soul's perception, not in any movement of the Word." To illustrate how the Word comes and goes to heighten our desire for him, Bernard introduces a rare autobiographical account of his own experience. (The abbot of Clairvaux, like most Christian mystics up to the thirteenth century, rarely spoke about himself, but concentrated on expounding the scriptural message about how to attain direct contact with God.) Bernard is imitating Paul, who was also willing to speak of his own experiences when he thought this was helpful for his audience (e.g., 2 Cor 12). The abbot's subtle and rhetorically superb presentation, difficult to render adequately in translation, is among the most famous first-person accounts of experiencing Christ's presence.*

———

Now bear with my foolishness for a bit (2 Cor 11:1). I want to tell you, as I agreed, how it was with me in this matter. There's no need, to be sure (2 Cor 12:1), but I want to reveal it for my own sake. If it helps you, I will be consoled over being a fool, and if not, I make my foolishness plain. I have to confess that the Word has come to me, and come often—I'm talking as a fool (2 Cor 11:17). As often as he would enter into me, I didn't perceive the different times when he came. I perceived he was present; I remembered that he had been there. Now and then I would be able to get a premonition of his coming, but never perceive it, nor sense when he left (Ps 120:8). Where he came from when he entered my soul, or where he went to when he left it again, and whatever the means were of his entry and exit, I must confess I'm still quite ignorant of, for, as it says, "You do not know whence he comes or goes" (Jn 3:8). You need not wonder at this, because he is the one of whom it is said, "Your footsteps are not to be known" (Ps 76:20). Surely he did not enter through the eyes, because he is not something colored; nor through the ears, since he does not make a sound. He does not enter by the nose, because he who created air does not mix with it, or mix it up, but mixes with the mind. Nor does he enter through the mouth, being neither eaten nor drunk; nor explored by touch since he is not of that nature. How then does he enter? But perhaps he does not have to enter because he is already within? He is not something on the outside (1 Cor 5:12). But it may be that because he is good and I know that I am not, he does not come from within me. I ascended beyond what was highest in me, and look, the Word was still above that! As an avid investigator, I descended to my lowest depths, and nevertheless discovered him still farther down! If I looked to the outside, I found him to be far beyond everything that was mine; if I looked within, he was more interior than I was! Then I knew the truth of what I had read, that "In him we live, and move, and have our being" (Acts 17:28). Someone in whom that Word exists who gives the person life and movement is blessed.

Since his ways are beyond all investigation (Rom 11:33), you may want to ask how I could know that he was present? He is life and power, and as soon as he came within he roused my sleeping soul to instant wakefulness. He moved and mollified and wounded my heart (Song 4:9), since it was hard as a rock and desperately ill. And then he began to root up and to destroy, to build up and to plant, to water what was parched, to enlighten what was dark (Jer 1:10), to set free what was chained up, to set on fire what was cold, as well as to set the crooked ways straight and the rough ways plain (Is 40:4), so that my soul might bless the Lord, and all that is in me might bless his holy name (Ps 102:1). Therefore, when the Word and Bridegroom entered into me from time to time, his coming was never made known by any signs—

by word, or appearance, or footstep. I was never made aware by any action on his part, nor by any kinds of motions sent down to my most inward parts. As I have said, it was only from the motion of my heart that I understood he was present. And I recognized the power of his might from the way vices were banished and how carnal desires were repressed. I was in awe at his profound wisdom by the way he uncovered and refuted my hidden sins, and I experienced the goodness of his mercy by even the very slight ways he improved my way of life. I perceived his beauty from the recasting and renewal of the mind's spirit (Eph 4:23), that is, the interior self; and from the sight of all these things at one time I was in great fear of his manifold greatness (Ps 150:2).

This is all true, because when the Word has departed, just as if a boiling pot had been removed from the fire, all these things began to become frigid and cold by a kind of torpor. This was the sign of his going away—my soul would necessarily be sad until he returned once more. When my heart was re-enkindled in the usual way within me, I knew that it was the sign of his return. Having had such an experience of the Word, why wonder if I usurp the voice of the bride, calling him back when he has gone away—I who burn with a desire that is partly like that of the bride, though not equal? As long as I shall live that word of recall by which the Word is called back will be dear to me: the very words "Come back!" (Song 2:17). As often as he slips away, I will repeat it; and I will not cease to cry out with burning heart's desire behind his back as he departs so that he might return and give back to me the joy of his salvation, that is, to give himself to me.

Translated by Bernard McGinn from *Sancti Bernardi Sermones in Cantica,* Sermo LXXIV, in PL 183:1141–42.

2.

FRANCIS OF ASSISI AND THE STIGMATA

*The imitation of Christ is a central theme of Christian spirituality and mysticism. In the later Middle Ages to imitate Christ often meant imitating the Savior's passion (*imitatio passionis*). No event served more to focus attention on becoming one with Christ than the reception of the stigmata, the wounds of the passion, by Francis of Assisi in 1224. Although there have been many later stigmatics, Francis's case is unique, not only because he was the first, but also due to the way Francis's followers seized on the event to put the seal on their claims for his unique status—the "Little Poor Man" (*poverello*) of Assisi was not just another follower of Christ, but the exemplar of all who set out to follow Jesus in life and in death.*

Francis himself does not talk about the event in his sparse writings, and much about it still remains mysterious. The earliest mention, in the encyclical letter that Francis's successor, Brother Elias, issued announcing his death in 1226, does not refer to the Seraph figure. "I announce a great joy to you (Lk 2:10) and a new miracle. Such a sign has been unheard of from the beginning (Jn 9:2), save only in the Son of God, who is Christ our Lord. Not long before his death, our brother and father appeared crucified, bearing in his body the five wounds which are truly the stigmata of Christ." The first extended account, that of Thomas of Celano in his First Life of Francis *(1229), includes the appearance of the Seraph and Francis's reaction. The Seraph (Is 6), a traditional image for divine love, may well be connected with Francis's theology of the Father's love in send-*

ing his Son to redeem the world. Celano does not explicitly identify the Seraph with Christ, a development that first appears in the theological presentation given by Bonaventure in his official Large Life of Saint Francis, *written 1260–63.*

I.

THOMAS OF CELANO, *FIRST LIFE*, BOOK 2, CHAPTER 3, NOS. 94–95

While he was staying in the hermitage that is named Alverna after its location, two years before he returned his soul to heaven, he saw in a vision of God a man "like a six-winged Seraphim," standing above him with hands outstretched and feet together, fixed to a cross. "Two wings were lifted up over his head, two were stretched out to fly, and two covered the whole body" (Is 6:2). When the blessed servant of the Most High saw these things he was filled with the greatest wonder, but he did not know what this vision was supposed to mean to him. He rejoiced greatly and was really delighted in the kind and gracious look with which the Seraph gazed upon him. The Seraph's beauty was far beyond all estimation, but the nailing to the cross and the bitterness of that passion really frightened him. And so he rose up, sad and happy so to say, and joy and sorrow took alternate turns in him. He was carefully considering what this vision might signify, and his spirit was very anxious to draw some understanding from it—he certainly had perceived nothing about it in his intellect, though the vision's novelty had lodged itself deep in his heart—when the signs of the nails began to appear in his hands and feet, just as he had seen them a short while before in the crucified figure above him.

His hands and feet seemed to be pierced in the middle by nails, with the nail heads showing on the inner side of the hands and the tops of the feet and their points coming out on the other side. The marks were round on the inner side of the hands and oblong on the outer side. There was a kind of fleshy growth, pushed out and bent back, that appeared at the tops of the nails, extending beyond the rest of the flesh. So too the signs of the nails were impressed on his feet and lifted up above the remaining flesh. His right side was pierced as though by a lance, with a scar covering the surface. It frequently dripped blood, so that his tunic and his undergarments were often sprinkled with the sacred blood.

Alas, while the crucified servant of the crucified Lord was still alive, how few merited to see the sacred wound in his side! Happy was Brother Elias who was worthy to see it in some way while the saint was alive; no less fortunate was Rufinus who "touched it with his own hands" (1 Jn 1:1). The same Brother Rufinus one time put his hand into the holy man's bosom to relieve his irritation and the hand slipped down to his right side, as often happened, and it chanced to touch that most precious scar. The holy man of God had considerable pain at the touch and pushing the hand away cried out, "May the Lord spare you" (Gen 19:16). He very carefully hid all this from strangers; he even cautiously concealed it from those near him, so that his closest brothers and most devout followers had no knowledge of it for a long time. Although the servant and friend of the Most High saw himself adorned with such great pearls of this kind, like very precious gems—wonderfully decorated "above the glory and honor of all others" (Ps 8:6)—he did not falter in his heart, nor did he seek to satisfy anyone about it through any appetite for vainglory. Rather, lest human respect rob him of the grace bestowed on him, he took efforts to conceal the matter in every way.

Translated by Bernard McGinn from *Fontes Franciscani,* edited by Enrico Menestò and Stefano Brufani (Assisi: Edizioni Porziuncola, 1995), 370–72.

II.

BONAVENTURE, *THE LARGE LIFE OF SAINT FRANCIS,* CHAPTER 13.1–4

Two years before he returned his spirit to heaven, under the leadership of divine providence and after many different labors, he was led "apart to a high place" (Mt 17:1), which is called Alverna. When, as was his custom, he began to fast there for forty days in honor of St. Michael the Archangel, filled from above more fully than usual by the sweetness of supernal contemplation and set afire by a more ardent flame of celestial desires, he began to experience the gifts of supernal influxes in a more abundant way. He was borne aloft, not as a "meddlesome searcher to be overwhelmed by glory" (Prov 25:27), but as a "faithful and prudent servant" (Mt 24:25), searching out God's good pleasure to which he desired to conform himself in every way and with the greatest ardor.

Through a divine message it entered his mind that in the act of opening the book of the gospels Christ would reveal to him what would be most acceptable to God in him and for him. Therefore, first having prayed with great devotion, he took the sacred gospel book from the altar and had his companion, a holy man devoted to God, open it three times in the name of the Holy Trinity. When the threefold opening of the book always met with the Lord's passion, the God-filled man understood that just as he had imitated Christ in the active life, so too he should be conformed to him in the afflictions and pains of the passion, before "he would pass from this world" (Jn 13:1). Even though he was already weakened in body due to the great austerity of his past life and his constant carrying of the Lord's cross, he was in no way afraid, but was emboldened to receive martyrdom even more vigorously. The unconquerable fire of the love of the good Jesus grew great in him even unto "lamps of fire and flames," so that "many waters were not able to quench his charity" (Song 8:6–7), so strong it was.

Therefore, he was lifted up into God by seraphic burning desire and transformed by compassionate sweetness into him who willed to be crucified out of "excessive love" (Eph 2:4). One morning around the time of the Feast of the Holy Cross [September 14], while he prayed on the mountainside, he saw descending from heaven's height a Seraph having six wings, both burning and shining. When in swift flight he had come to a place in the air near the man of God, the figure of a crucified man appeared in the midst of the wings, having his hands and feet stretched out in the manner of a cross and also fastened to a cross. "Two wings were raised above his head," two "were stretched out to fly," and "two covered the whole body" (Is 6:2). When he saw this, he wondered greatly, his heart experiencing joy mixed with sorrow. He rejoiced in the kindly gaze with which Christ under the form of a Seraph looked upon him, but the fact that he was fastened to a cross "pierced his soul with the very sword" (Lk 2:35) of compassionate sorrow. He was in exceedingly great awe at the sight of such an unfathomable vision, knowing that the weakness of Christ's passion was scarcely compatible with the immortality of a seraphic spirit. Finally, he understood by a revelation from the Lord that this kind of vision was presented to his sight by divine providence so that Christ's friend should know beforehand that he would be transformed into the likeness of Christ crucified not through bodily martyrdom but through complete conflagration of mind. Therefore, as the vision disappeared it left a marvelous burning in his heart, but in his flesh it impressed a no less marvelous copy of the marks. Immediately the marks of the nails began to appear in his hands and feet just as he had beheld them shortly before in the image of the crucified man. His hands and feet seemed to be pierced in the middle by the nails, with the nail heads showing on the inner side of the hands and on the tops of the feet, and their points coming out on the other side. The nail heads in the hands and feet were black and round; their points were oblong, pushed and bent back as it were, and they emerged from the flesh and extended beyond the rest of the skin. His right side was pierced as though by a lance and a red scar covered the surface, which often poured out sacred blood, sprinkling his tunic and undergarments.

When Christ's servant saw that the stigmata so splendidly impressed in his flesh could not be hidden from his close associates, still fearing to publicize the Lord's mystery, he found himself in a great agony of doubt whether he should talk about what he saw or keep silent. He called together some of the brothers and speaking in a general way he placed his doubt before them and asked their advice. One of the brethren, by grace and by name called Brother Illuminato, understanding that Francis had seen something marvelous because he seemed still quite in awe, said to the holy man: "Brother, you know that you have at times been shown divine mysteries not only for yourself, but also for the sake of others. Therefore, you have good reason to fear that you could be judged guilty 'of burying the talent' (Mt 25:25) if in the future you were to hide what you have received for the sake of many." At these words the holy man was moved. Although at other times he used to say, "My secret is mine" (Is 24:16), at that time he gave a full account of the vision with great trepidation, adding that the one who had appeared to him said some things that he would never reveal to anyone as long as he lived. We can surely believe that the words of the holy Seraph who miraculously appeared on the cross were so secret that perhaps "it was not permitted to people to speak them" (2 Cor 12:2).

Translated by Bernard McGinn from *S. Bonaventurae Opera Omnia* (Quaracchi: Collegium S. Bonaventurae, 1898), Vol. 8:542–43.

HENRY SUSO

THE CLOCK OF WISDOM

SELECTIONS FROM THE PROLOGUE,
BOOK I, CHAPTERS 1 AND 4

Henry Suso (circa 1295–1366) was the third great male mystic produced by the German Dominicans in the fourteenth century. Born in Constance, Suso joined the order at an early age and was influenced by Meister Eckhart. He aspired to an academic career, but in the wake of Eckhart's condemnation and his own defense of the Meister in a treatise called The Little Book of Truth *(circa 1329), he was attacked by some of his confrères and gave up teaching to concentrate on preaching and spiritual advising of Dominican nuns and other "friends of God."*

Suso was the most conscious literary stylist among the Dominican mystics. Toward the end of his life he edited his four German treatises into what he called The Exemplar. *Besides* The Little Book of Truth, *this contained* The Little Book of Wisdom, The Little Book of Letters, *and* The Life of the Servant. *This last is the work for which Suso is best known today. It has been read as a quasi-autobiographical account of Suso's spiritual path from severe practices of literal imitation of Christ's passion to a more Eckhartian state of mystical detachment and union with the Trinity. The book's complexity, however, militates against a simple autobiographical reading.*

In Suso's own time his most read work was The Little Book of Wisdom *and its Latin recasting as* The Clock of Wisdom. *The German version of the work was very popular; the Latin version, which appears to date to about 1335, was even more widely known, being translated into eight languages and surviving in more than six hundred manuscripts (second only to* The Imitation of Christ,* *by Thomas à Kempis, among medieval spiritual writings). The Clock's Christological mysticism features a series of parables or allegories involving conversations between Divine Wisdom (a female figure) and her servant the male friar Amandus ("the Lovable One"). Part of the fascination of the book is the way it portrays the gender malleability of their relationship. In speaking of his love for Wisdom, the disciple keeps his male persona, but in relating to Divine Wisdom made flesh in Jesus Christ, it is the friar's soul (anima, a feminine word) that seeks loving union with the Divine Bridegroom who suffered for us on the cross.*

I.
PROLOGUE

You should know that this conversation between Wisdom and the disciple had its beginning and favorable occasion in this way. One time after Matins when the disciple had completed his imitation of that most bitter procession in which Christ was condemned and led to the place of the passion, he stood at the lectern before the crucifix, lamenting to the crucified Lord with a sorrowful soul, because he did not have, nor had he had up until then, the burning attraction worthy of his passion. Then at once he was put into a kind of ecstasy and a type of heavenly light shone out and showed his mental eyes a hundred meditations or considerations of the passion. He was told that every day in devout meditation he ought to go through these hundred points with a hundred prostrations and adding the same number of petitions in order to conform himself in a spiritual way to the suffering Christ as far as possible. (For brevity's sake I omit putting these down openly here, but I have faithfully communicated them in our German vernacular to devout people, learned and unlearned.) Therefore the disciple, who prior to this had been unmoved by the affection of compassion, through continuous use of this meditation began to be receptive to the remembrance of such suffering and to receive different forms of enlightenment as will appear in what follows. When he had begun to write these things down, just as he had been taught, the adversity that tests good folk tried to pull him back from what he had begun. Christ appeared to him in a vision in the form in which he was at the pillar when he was scourged. Coming down, he allowed him to touch his fresh and bloody wounds. He healed adversity's wounds and encouraged him to complete what he had started.

II.
PASSAGES FROM BOOK I

The content of this first book is Christ's most precious passion, which itself is the motive for much fervent love, as well as how the true disciple of Wisdom ought to conform himself to her in all his actions. . . .

Chapter 1. How Some Elect People, Favored Beforehand by Divine Grace, are Drawn to God in a Marvelous Way, and especially how a Certain Youth was Drawn. The First Section.

"I have loved her and sought her from my youth and I have desired to make her my Bride" (Wis 8:2). Once there was a certain young man known to God who while he was in youth's early flower began to get involved in worldly vanities. Dragged down by the world's passing delights, he wanted to wander away from the right road of salvation into "the region of unlikeness" [Augustine, *Confessions* 7.10]. But divine mercy took pity on him, enlightened him in an ineffable way, and through paths both pleasant and difficult drew him along and finally brought him back to the path of truth through love of Wisdom. . . . [A description of the young friar, his love for Divine Wisdom, and his trials follows.]

In the face of these and similar mental temptations an internal taste of Wisdom answered in the following manner: "O youthful Amandus, with loving heart regard the fact that it is proper for all lovers to undergo hardships for love's sake, because 'there are as many sorrows in love as there are seashells on the shore' [Ovid, *Art of Love* 2.519]. If this is the case, isn't it totally justified that the lover who has chosen by special right a Bride so sublime and so beautiful and richly adorned in an incomparable way with every grace should bear some adversities? Indeed, he surely ought to bear incomparably more in his soul, the more desirable the object he has as the reward of his labor. Just think about the countless and marvelous things you have read and heard that the lovers of this world (alas!) have borne for their completely worthless love!"

When the youth heard this he cried aloud out of an interior outburst of excessive love: "It is true! It is true! Nothing could be more true! It is now fixed—I have decided! I will surely give myself over to death in order to have her as my Beloved and Bride. She is the Bride and I will be her little servant. She the Mistress, and I her disciple. Oh, if this most beloved Bride would allow herself to speak to me, would that she might only once allow me to see her! O Eternal God, who is she and what is she of whom I hear such wonderful things?"

While ardently desiring to know these things and burning up in desire, lo, some kind of indescribable interior recognition became present to him in which the Bride was manifested to him in the following way. [What follows is partly based on Boethius's vision of Lady Philosophy in *The Consolation of Philosophy*.] An "ivory throne in the pillar of a cloud" (Ecclus 24:7), one of exceedingly great beauty, appeared, and on it shone forth the Bride in all her superb beauty, "clad in golden garments and fringed with embroidery" (Ps 44:10). Her crown was eternity and her dress was joyful felicity, her words were sweetness itself, her embrace was the perfect fullness of all joy. When the disciple wanted to talk with her in a familiar way, she seemed to be quite near; but a little later he saw her at a great distance. Her height at one time stretched above the dome of the height of heaven; at another time she appeared quite tiny, and, although not moving in herself, she seemed "to be more agile than all that moves" (Wis 7:24). She was present, but she still could not be seen; she allowed herself to take hold of things, but she herself was still not comprehended. She "stretched from one end to the other mightily and disposed all things sweetly" (Wis 8:1). When he thought of her as a tender young girl, he at once found her to be a very beautiful young man. Sometimes she put on a very revered face as if she were the Mistress of all the arts, and then she appeared with blooming beauty and rosy cheek. Meanwhile, as the disciple looked intently at her and clung to her suspended in desirous love, she bent down to him in a friendly way, and, with a pleasant face and tenderly smiling eyes, but still with a most divine and to all minds awesome light coming from her most revered countenance, she spoke to him and said: "My son, give me your heart" (Prov 23:26). When he heard this, he melted from the overpowering sweetness of love, and, in a kind of ecstasy, he fell at her feet, thanked her, and delighted beyond measure at her presence. . . .

Chapter 4. How the Soul, which Lost the Bridegroom through Sin, with the Aid of Christ's Passion Found Him under the Cross through Fervent Penance.

[The chapter begins with the soul, speaking in the feminine voice, bewailing its sins and coming near to despair. There follows this section commencing with the male disciple conversing with the female Divine Wisdom, but soon switching back to the female soul's love of the Divine Bridegroom.]

WISDOM: Don't you know how dangerous despair is? You should not in any way despair of your salvation, because "I have come into this world to seek and to save what was lost" (Jn 11:27).

DISCIPLE: What is this that I hear, that resounds so sweetly in my ears, in me, a miserable wretch and cast-away dog?

WISDOM: What has happened that you don't know me? How have you fallen apart, "collapsing on the ground" (Jb 1:20)? Have you gone crazy from so much grief? O my beloved son, look, I am that same Eternal Wisdom, the Son of the Heavenly Father, the bearer of mercy, the chief of forgiveness and legislator of loving-kindness, who has opened up the abyss of mercy that is incomprehensible to every created spirit by reason of its infinity. I will receive you, as well as all who want to return to me, into my most loving bosom. Recognize my face—I am the one who endured poverty to make you rich, who bore a most bitter death to give you life. Here I stand, "Mediator of God and humans" (1 Tim 2:5), bearing still the marks of the cross, holding them up between the strict judgment of the Eternal Father and all your sins. So now don't be afraid. Look, I am your Brother, your Bridegroom, prepared to have mercy and to cover over "your sins and cast them into the depths of the sea" (Micah 7:19) and to forgive them as if they never were, as long as you want to be converted and from here on be careful. Wash in my blood, I say, in the blood of the Lamb without stain, totally filled with love and glowing with a "rosy hue" (Esth 15:10). Raise your head from the earth; open your eyes, and be strong of heart. Look how "the best garment is offered to you," and "the ring and shoes are given" to your understanding; "the fatted calf is slaughtered" (Lk 15:22–23), a loving name is restored so that you may be and may be called the bride of the Eternal King. "I have redeemed you not with corruptible things, such as gold and silver, but with my precious blood" (1 Pet 1:18–19), and I have purchased you with such great labor that I may fittingly rejoice over your salvation and be ready to pardon. . . .

DISCIPLE: O unheard-of devotion of the Father's bosom! O awe-inspiring love of brotherly fidelity! O one joy of my heart, is it possible that you are ready to take back this abject son of perdition? Do you still want to bestow grace on someone guilty of death and detestable in every kind of iniquity? O unique grace, O inexpressible kindness, O infinite sea of divine mercy beyond the understanding of all humans, surpassing all thoughts, going beyond our prayers, and finally exceeding all forms of merit. Therefore, "for this reason I now bend the knee" of my heart to you, "Father of mercies" (Eph 3:14), and falling down upon the ground I prostrate myself at your most merciful feet, giving thanks from the depths of my heart, and I ask that you look upon your Only-Begotten Son, whom you have handed over to death from the surpassing greatness of your love for us, and that for the sake of the multitude of his sufferings you forget all my iniquities. . . .

Therefore, I flee to you, Father of Mercies; I ask for the protection of your grace. Even more, with very ardent desire and a heartfelt embrace, O Son of the Eternal King, I press myself within your naked, stretched-out, blood-bedewed arms, unwilling to be separated from you in life or in death. O sweet and loving Father, for this reason forgive me, forgive me, for love of your Only-Begotten Son, the sins by which I have deserved wrath "and done evil before you" (Ps 50:6). . . .

I address you, "O my Lord and my God" (Jn 20:28), my Redeemer and one Joy of my heart, because I have saddened you and have shown some irreverence to you. Hence, were I now able to fill all the heavens with uncontrollable cries and to bring such pressure to bear on my heart that it broke in a thousand pieces, I would prefer this to any form of solace that I have had "in all my days" (Ps 26:4). The more mercifully I am dealt with, the more tearfully I afflict my soul, because I have been ungrateful to so devoted a Beloved and so faithful a Father.

Now, Eternal Wisdom, "you teacher of the knowledge of God" (Wis 8:4), teach me, I beg, how I may bear in my body your most sweet and dear wounds, and how I ought always to keep them in my memory so that at least in this way I can show those dwelling in heaven and on earth what thanks I give back for so many unnumbered good things freely given to my miserable self from the superabundance of your love.

WISDOM: Offer me yourself and everything that is yours and do not take back what you offer. You should abstain from unnecessary things, and sometimes even from necessary ones. And so you will have displayed the hands fixed to my cross. Do what is good and bear the ills inflicted on you calmly. Gather together your distracted soul and scattered thoughts and make them secure in me, the Highest Good. And you have fixed your feet to the cross. Do not allow the power of your body and soul to grow weak with sloth, but strive to stretch them out with total effort in my service after the manner of my arms. When you are tired and worn out from any kind of work, give thanks and bear it with patience, and in a manful way restrain any movements of sensuality. And so you will answer to the violence and weariness that my legs suffered. And so "my flesh will flourish again" (Ps 27:7) through the devout and reasonable mortification of your flesh, and you will make for my back tortured by the affliction of the cross a sweet resting place through your voluntary bearing of these different hardships. Always have the soul that is weighed down by the body lifted up to the Lord—"Present your members to justice and sanctification, just as you formerly used to present them to injustice" (Rom 6:19). Let your heart always be ready to bear all adversity for my name's sake. Thus, as a faithful disciple, spiritually crucified with his Lord, and in a way sprinkled with the blood of compassion, you will be made like me and lovable.

Translated by Bernard McGinn from *Heinrich Seuses Horologium Sapientiae,* edited by Pius Künzle (Freiburg, Switzerland: Universitätsverlag, 1977), 369–70, 371, 373, 376, 379–80, 400–3.

4.

JULIAN OF NORWICH
REVELATIONS OF DIVINE LOVE

The two selections given here provide only a taste of one of the most accessible of all Christian mystical accounts, Revelations of Divine Love, *written by the English anchoress Julian of Norwich. Little is known of her life. In the night of May 13, 1373, at the point of death Julian received fifteen "showings," or revelations, which restored her to health. These visions comprised graphic images of Christ's crucifixion, but since the cross is the ultimate proof of divine love for humanity, much else was revealed in and through the bodily appearances of Jesus' sufferings. Julian's revelations, as she insists, involved a mixing of forms of mystical insight—"All this blessed teaching of our Lord was shown to me in three parts, that is by bodily vision and by words formed in my understanding and by spiritual vision." The young woman became an anchoress, that is, a female hermit enclosed in a cell attached to a church in her native Norwich. There she wrote down an account of her revelations and their meaning, the* Short Text *in twenty-five chapters. But the anchoress continued pondering the showings God had given her, contemplatively drawing out further riches of the mystery of love.*

About 1393 she finished the Long Text *of the revelations in eighty-six chapters. The last chapter of this version summarizes the essence of her teaching: "And from the time that it was revealed, I desired many times to know in what was our Lord's meaning. And fifteen years after and more, I was answered in spiritual understanding, and it was said: 'What, do you wish to know your Lord's meaning in this thing? Know it well, love was his meaning. Who reveals it to you? Love. What did he reveal to you? Love. Why does he reveal it to you? For love.'"*

Julian's mystical message is rooted in the Pauline theology of sin, grace, and redemption in Jesus, especially in the notion of the solidarity of humanity in Christ. But she goes beyond the typically Pauline perspective in many ways, not least in her teaching about the motherhood of Jesus, both in his role as the second person in the Trinity and in his salvific action bringing humans to new birth on the cross. Julian did not invent the notion of the motherhood of Jesus, but she developed it with a sophistication beyond anything previously known.

I.

CHAPTERS 3-5

Chapter 3. Of the sickness obtained from God by petition.

And when I was thirty and a half years old, God sent me a bodily sickness in which I lay for three days and three nights; and on the fourth night I received all the rites of Holy Church and did not believe that I would live until morning. And after this I lingered on for two days and two nights. And on the third night I often thought that I was dying, and so did those who were with me. And I thought it was a great pity to die while still young; but this was not because there was anything on earth that I wanted to live for, nor because I feared any suffering, for I trusted God's mercy. I wanted to live so as to love God better and for longer, and therefore know and love him better in the bliss of heaven. For it seemed to me that all the short time I had lived here was as nothing compared with that heavenly bliss. So I thought, "Good Lord, may my ceasing to live be to your glory!" And I understood, both with my reason and by the bodily pains I felt, that I was dying. And I fully accepted the will of God with all the will of my heart. Thus I endured till day, and by then my body was dead to all sensation from the waist down. Then I felt I wanted to be supported in a sitting position, so that my heart could be more freely at God's disposition, and so that I could think of God while I was still alive.

My parish priest was sent for to be present at my death, and by the time he came my eyes were fixed and I could not speak. He set the cross before my face and said, "I have brought you the image of your Maker and Savior. Look upon it and be comforted." It seemed to me that I was well as I was, for my eyes were looking fixedly upwards into heaven, where I trusted that I was going with God's mercy. But nevertheless I consented to fix my eyes on the face of the crucifix if I could, and so I did, because I thought that I might be able to bear looking straight ahead for longer than I could manage to look upwards. After this my sight began to fail and the room was dark all around me as though it had been night, except for the image of the cross, in which I saw an ordinary, household light—I could not understand how. Everything except the cross was ugly to me, as if crowded with fiends. After this the upper part of my body began to die to such an extent that I had almost no feeling and was short of breath. And then I truly believed that I had died. And at this moment, all my suffering was suddenly taken from me, and I seemed to be as well, especially in the upper part of my body, as ever I was before. I marveled at this sudden change, for it seemed to me a mysterious work of God, not a natural one. And yet, although I felt comfortable, I still did not expect to live, nor did feeling more comfortable comfort me entirely, for I felt that I would rather have been released from this world.

Then it suddenly occurred to me that I should entreat our Lord graciously to give me the second wound [of three wounds mentioned in chapter 2], so that my whole body should be filled with remembrance and feeling of his blessed passion; for I wanted his pains to be my pains, with compassion, and then longing for God. Yet in this I never asked for a bodily sight or showing of God, but for fellow-suffering, such as a naturally kind soul might feel for our Lord Jesus; he was willing to become a mortal man for love, so I wanted to suffer with him.

Chapter 4. Here begins the first revelation of the precious crowning of Christ, as listed in the first chapter; and how God fills the heart with the greatest joy; and of his great meekness; and how the sight of Christ's passion gives sufficient strength against all the temptations of the fiends; and of the great excellency and meekness of the blessed Virgin Mary.

Then I suddenly saw the red blood trickling down from under the crown of thorns, hot and fresh and very plentiful, as though it were the moment of his passion when the crown of thorns was thrust on to his blessed head, he who was both God and man, the same who suffered for me like that. I believed truly and strongly that it was he himself who showed me this, without any intermediary. And as part of the same showing the Trinity suddenly filled my heart with the greatest joy. And I understood that in heaven it will be like that for ever for those who come there. For the Trinity is God, God is the Trinity; the Trinity is our maker and protector, the Trinity is dear friend for ever, our everlasting joy and bliss, through our Lord Jesus Christ. And this was shown in the first revelation, and in all of them; for it seems to me that where Jesus is spoken of, the Holy Trinity is to be understood. And I said, "Benedicite domine!" [i.e., Blessed be you, O Lord]. Because I meant this with such deep veneration, I said it in a very loud voice; and I was astounded with wonder and admiration that he who is so holy and awe-inspiring was willing to be so familiar with a sinful being living in wretched flesh. I supposed that the time of my temptation had now come, for I thought that God would allow me to be tempted by fiends before I died. With this sight of the blessed passion, along with the Godhead that I saw in my mind, I knew that I, yes, and every creature living, could have strength to resist all the fiends of hell and all spiritual temptation.

Then he brought our blessed Lady into my mind. I saw her spiritually in bodily likeness, a meek and simple maid, young—little more than a child, of the same bodily form as when she conceived. God also showed me part of the wisdom and truth of her soul, so that I understood with what reverence she beheld her God and Maker, and how reverently she marveled that he chose to be born of her, a simple creature of his own making. And this wisdom and faithfulness, knowing as she did the greatness of her Maker and the littleness of her who was made, moved her to say very humbly to Gabriel, "Behold the handmaid of the Lord" (Lk 1:38). With this sight I really understood that she is greater in worthiness and grace than all that God made below her; for, as I see it, nothing that is made is above her, except the blessed manhood of Christ.

Chapter 5. How God is everything that is good to us, tenderly enfolding us; and everything that is made is as nothing compared to almighty God; and how there is no rest for man until he sets himself and everything else at nothing for the love of God.

At the same time, our Lord showed me a spiritual vision of his familiar love. I saw that for us he is everything that we find good and comforting. He is our clothing, wrapping us for love, embracing and enclosing us for tender love, so that he can never leave us, being himself everything that is good for us, as I understand it.

In this vision he also showed a little thing, the size of a hazel-nut in the palm of my hand, and it was as round as a ball. I looked at it with my mind's eye and thought, "What can this be?" And the answer came to me, "It is all that is made." I wondered how it could last, for it was so small I thought it might suddenly disappear. And the answer in my mind was, "It lasts and will last for ever because God loves it; and everything exists in the same way by the love of God." In this little thing I saw three properties: the first is that God made it, the second is that God loves it, the third is that God cares for it. But what the maker, the carer and the lover really is to me, I cannot tell; for until I become one substance with him, I can never have complete rest or true happiness; that is to say, until I am so bound to him that there is no created thing between my God and me.

We need to know the littleness of all created beings and to set at nothing everything that is made in order to love and possess God who is unmade. This is the reason why we do not feel complete ease in our hearts and souls: we look here for satisfaction in things which are so trivial, where there is no rest to be found, and do not know our God who is almighty, all wise, all good; he is rest itself. God wishes to be known, and is pleased that we should rest in him; for all that is below him does nothing to satisfy us; and this is why, until all that is made seems as nothing, no soul can be at rest. When a soul sets all at nothing for love, to have him who is everything, then he is able to receive spiritual rest.

Our Lord God also showed that it gives him very great pleasure when a simple soul comes to him in a bare, plain and familiar way. For, as I understand this showing, it is the natural yearning of the soul touched by the Holy Spirit to say, "God, of your goodness, give me yourself; you are enough for me, and anything less that I could ask for would not do you full honor. And if I ask anything that is less I shall always lack something, but in you alone I have everything." And such words are very dear to the soul and come very close to the will of God and his goodness; for his goodness includes all his creatures and all his blessed works, and surpasses everything endlessly, for he is what has no end. And he has made us only for himself and restored us by his blessed passion and cares for us with his blessed love. And all this is out of his goodness.

II.
CHAPTERS 59-60. JESUS AS MOTHER

Chapter 59. In the chosen, wickedness is turned into blessedness through mercy and grace, for the nature of God is to do good for evil, through Jesus, our mother in kind grace; and the soul which is highest in virtue is the meekest, that being the ground from which we gain other virtues.

. . . Our great father, God almighty, who is Being, knew and loved us from before the beginning of time. And from his knowledge, in his marvelously deep love and through the eternal foreseeing counsel of the whole blessed Trinity, he wanted the second person to become our mother, our brother, our savior. From this it follows that God is our mother as truly as God is our father. Our Father wills, our Mother works, our good lord the Holy Spirit confirms. And therefore we should love our God in whom we have our being, reverently thanking and praising him for our creation, praying hard to our Mother for mercy and pity, and to our lord the Holy Spirit for help and grace; for our whole life is in these three—nature, mercy and grace; from them we have humility, gentleness, patience and pity, and hatred of sin and wickedness; for it is a natural attribute of virtues to hate sin and wickedness. And so Jesus is our true mother by nature, at our first creation, and he is our true mother in grace by taking on our created nature. All the fair work and all the sweet, kind service of beloved motherhood is made proper to the second person; for in him this godly will is kept safe and whole everlastingly, both in nature and in grace, out of his very own goodness.

I understood three ways of seeing motherhood in God: the first is that he is the ground of our natural creation, the second is the taking on of our nature (and there the motherhood of grace begins), the third is the motherhood of works, and in this there is, by the same grace, an enlargement of length and breadth and of height and deepness without end, and all is his own love.

Chapter 60. How we are redeemed and enlarged by the mercy and grace of our sweet, kind and ever-loving mother Jesus; and of the properties of motherhood; but Jesus is our true mother, feeding us not with milk, but with himself, opening his side for us and claiming all our love.

But now it is necessary to say a little more about this enlargement, as I understand it in our Lord's meaning, how we are redeemed by the motherhood of mercy and grace and brought back into our natural dwelling where we were made by the motherhood of natural love; a natural love which never leaves us. Our natural Mother, our gracious Mother (for he wanted to become our mother completely in every way), undertook to begin his work very humbly and very gently in the Virgin's womb. And he showed this in the first revelation, where he brought that humble maiden before my mind's eye in the girlish form she had when she conceived; that is to say, our great God, the most sovereign Wisdom of all, was raised in this humble place and dressed himself in our poor flesh to do the service and duties of motherhood in every way. The mother's service is the closest, the most helpful and the most sure, for it is the most faithful. No one ever might, nor could, nor has performed this service fully but he alone. We know that our mothers only bring us into the world to suffer and die, but our true mother, Jesus, he who is all love, bears us into joy and eternal life; blessed may he be! So he sustains us within himself in love and was in labor for the full time until he suffered the sharpest pangs and the most grievous sufferings that ever were or shall be, and at the last he died. And when it was finished and he had borne us to bliss, even this could not fully satisfy his marvelous love; and that he showed in these high surpassing words of love, "If I could suffer more, I would suffer more."

He could not die any more, but he would not stop working. So next he had to feed us, for a mother's dear love has made him our debtor. The mother can give her child her milk to suck, but our dear mother Jesus can feed us with himself, and he does so most generously and most tenderly with the holy sacrament which is the precious food of life itself. And with all the sweet sacraments he sustains us most mercifully and most graciously. And this is what he meant in those blessed words when he said, "It is I that Holy Church preaches and teaches to you," that is to say, "All the health and life of the sacraments, all the power and grace of my word, all the goodness which is ordained in Holy Church for you, it is I."

The mother can lay the child tenderly to her breast, but our tender mother Jesus, he can familiarly lead us into his blessed breast through his sweet open side, and show within part of the Godhead and the joys of heaven, with spiritual certainty of endless bliss; and that was shown in the tenth revelation, giving the same understanding in the sweet words where he says, "Look how I love you," looking into his side and rejoicing. This fair, lovely word "mother," it is so sweet and so tender in itself that it cannot truly be said of any but of him, and of her who is the true mother of him and of everyone. To the nature of motherhood belong tender love, wisdom and knowledge, and it is good, for although the birth of our body is only low, humble and modest compared with the birth of our soul, yet it is he who does it in the beings by whom it is done. The kind, loving mother who knows and recognizes the need of her child, she watches over it most tenderly, as the nature and condition of motherhood demands. And as it grows in age her actions change, although her love does not. And as it grows older still, she allows it to be beaten to break down vices so that the child may gain in virtue and grace. These actions, with all that is fair and good, our Lord performs them through those by whom they are done. Thus he is our natural mother through the work of grace in the lower part, for love of the higher part. And he wants us to know it; for he wants all our love to be bound to him. And in this I saw that all the debt we owe, at God's bidding, for his fatherhood and motherhood, is fulfilled by loving God truly; a blessed love which Christ arouses in us. And this was shown in everything, and especially in the great, generous words where he says, "It is I that you love."

From *Revelations of Divine Love* by Julian of Norwich, translated by Elizabeth Spearing, introduction and notes by A. C. Spearing, 1998, New York, 44–48, 139–42. Translation copyright © Elizabeth Spearing, 1998. Introduction and notes © A. C. Spearing, 1998. Reproduced by permission of Penguin Books Ltd.

5.

SIMONE WEIL

ENCOUNTERS WITH CHRIST

The French philosopher and social critic Simone Weil (1909–43) is numbered among the most influential thinkers and spiritual writers of the twentieth century. Born into an intellectually distinguished Jewish family, she rejected her background. While working on her degree in philosophy, she became identified with radical social causes. In the late 1930s she became fascinated with Catholicism and spent Easter of 1938 at the Benedictine monastery of Solesmes, famous for its Gregorian chant. After the fall of France to the Germans, Weil moved to Marseilles in 1940. Here she became close to several Catholics, including the writer Gustave Thibon and the Dominican priest Fr. Perrin. As she wrestled to understand her mystical experiences and to work out her attitude toward Catholicism (she decided not to be baptized), Fr. Perrin convinced her to write a letter in the form of a Spiritual Autobiography *(May 1942). Later that year she sailed to the safety of America with her parents, but Weil was not satisfied with so easy an escape from the fate of millions of others. She returned to London to work for the French government in exile. At this time she deliberately reduced her consumption of food for reasons that are still debated. In this weakened state she contracted pneumonia, and died on August 29, 1943 (the coroner's verdict was one of suicide).*

Weil published almost nothing in her lifetime, but left a large mass of materials whose publication has had an impact in many fields, not least on the role of religion in modern secularized and technological society. What has endeared her to so many is not only her penetrating mind, but also the authenticity and direct-

ness of her witness to the truth. The following texts provide a window on the intense sense of the presence of Christ that this unbaptized woman experienced in her last years. The contact described in the first passage from Spiritual Autobiography *has been dated to November 1938; the second passage talks about subsequent more frequent meetings found through the recitation of the Our Father. Finally, the last part of her* Notebooks, *composed in the months before her death, contains the mysterious text on the unnamed visitor who feeds her with bread and wine.*

I.

FROM *SPIRITUAL AUTOBIOGRAPHY*

(A). In 1938 I spent ten days at Solesmes, from Palm Sunday to Easter Tuesday, following all the liturgical services. I was suffering from splitting headaches; each sound hurt me like a blow; by an extreme effort of concentration I was able to rise above this wretched flesh, to leave it to suffer by itself, heaped up in a corner, and to find a perfect and pure joy in the unimaginable beauty of the chanting and the words. This experience by analogy enabled me to get a better understanding of the possibility of divine love in the midst of affliction. It goes without saying that in the course of these services the thought of the passion of Christ entered into my being once and for all.

There was a young English Catholic there from whom I gained my first idea of the supernatural power of the sacraments because of the truly angelic radiance with which he seemed to be clothed after going to communion. Chance—for I always prefer saying chance rather than Providence—made him a messenger to me. For he told me of the existence of those English poets of the seventeenth century who are named metaphysical. In reading them later on, I discovered a poem of which I read you what is unfortunately a very inadequate translation. It is called "Love" [a poem of George Herbert], I learned it by heart. Often, at the culminating point of a violent headache, I make myself say it over, concentrating all my attention upon it and clinging with all my soul to the tenderness it enshrines. I used to think I was merely reciting it as a beautiful poem, but without my knowing it the recitation had the virtue of a prayer. It was during one of these recitations that, as I told you, Christ himself came down and took possession of me.

In my arguments about the insolubility of the problem of God I had never foreseen the possibility of that, of a real contact, person to person, here below, between a human being and God. I had vaguely heard of things of this kind, but I had never believed them. In the *Fioretti* [stories about St. Francis] the accounts of the apparitions rather put me off if anything, like the miracles in the Gospels. Moreover, in this sudden possession of me by Christ, neither my senses nor my imagination had any part; I only felt in the midst of my suffering the presence of love, like that which one can read in the smile on a beloved face.

I had never read any mystical works because I had never felt any call to read them. In reading as in other things I have always striven to practice obedience. There is nothing more favorable to intellectual progress, for as far as possible I only read what I am hungry for at the moment when I have an appetite for it, and then I do not read, I *eat*. God in his mercy had prevented me from reading the mystics, so that it should be evident to me that I had not invented this absolutely unexpected contact.

Yet I still half refused, not my love but my intelligence. For it seemed to me certain, and I still think so today, that one can never wrestle enough with God if one does so out of pure regard for the truth. Christ likes us to prefer truth to him because, before being Christ, he is truth. If one turns aside from him to go toward the truth, one will not go far before falling into his arms. . . .

(B). Last summer [1941], doing Greek with T____, I went through the Our Father word for word in Greek. We promised each other to learn it by heart. I do not think he ever did so, but some weeks later, as I was turning over the pages of the Gospel, I said to myself that since I had promised to do this thing and it was good, I ought to do it. I did it. The infinite sweetness of this Greek text so took hold of me that for several days I could not stop myself from saying it over all the time. A week afterward I began the vine harvest. I recited Our Father in Greek every day before work, and I repeated it very often in the vineyard.

Since that time I have made a practice of saying it through once each morning with absolute attention. If during the recitation my attention wanders or goes to sleep, in the minutest degree, I begin again until I have once again succeeded in going through it with absolutely pure attention. Sometimes it comes about that I say it again out of sheer pleasure, but I only do it if I really feel the impulse.

The effect of this practice is extraordinary and surprises me every time, for, although I experience it each day, it exceeds my expectation at each repetition.

At times the very first words tear my thoughts from my body and transport it to a place outside space where there is neither perspective nor point of view. The infinity of the ordinary expanses of perception is replaced by an infinity of the second or sometimes the third degree. At the same time, filling every part of this infinity of infinity, there is silence, a silence which is not an absence of sound but which is the object of a positive sensation, more positive than that of sound. Noises, if there are any, only reach me after crossing this silence.

Sometimes, also, during this recitation or at other moments, Christ is present with me in person, but his presence is infinitely more real, more moving, more clear, than on that first occasion when he took possession of me.

II.

FROM *THE NOTEBOOKS OF SIMONE WEIL*

He entered my room and said: "Poor creature, you who understand nothing, who know nothing. Come with me and I will teach you things which you do not suspect." I followed him.

He took me into a church. It was new and ugly. He led me up to the altar and said: "Kneel down." I said "I have not been baptized." He said "Fall on your knees before this place, in love, as before the place where lies the truth." I obeyed.

He brought me out and made me climb up to a garret. Through the open window one could see the whole city spread out, some wooden scaffoldings, and the river on which the boats were being unloaded. The garret was empty, except for a table and two chairs. He bade me be seated.

We were alone. He spoke. From time to time, someone would enter, mingle in the conversation, then leave again.

Winter had gone; spring had not yet come. The branches of the trees lay bare, without buds, in the cold air full of sunshine.

The light of day would arise, shine forth in splendor, and fade away; then the moon and the stars would enter through the window. And then once more the dawn would come up.

At times he would fall silent, take some bread from a cupboard, and we would share it. This bread really had the taste of bread. I have never found that taste again.

He would pour out some wine for me, and some for himself—wine which tasted of the sun and of the soil upon which this city was built.

At other times we would stretch ourselves out on the floor of the garret, and sweet sleep would enfold me. Then I would wake and drink in the light of the sun.

He had promised to teach me, but he did not teach me anything. We talked about all kinds of things, in a desultory way, as do old friends.

One day he said to me: "Now go." I fell down before him, I clasped his knees, I implored him not to drive me away. But he threw me out on the stairs. I went down unconscious of anything, my heart as it were in shreds. I wandered along the streets. Then I realized that I had no idea where this house lay.

I have never tried to find it again. I understood that he had come for me by mistake. My place is not in that garret. It can be anywhere—in a prison cell, in one of those middle-class drawing-rooms full of knick-knacks and red plush, in the waiting-room of a station—anywhere, except in that garret.

Sometimes I cannot help trying, fearfully and remorsefully, to repeat to myself a part of what he said to me. How am I to know if I remember it rightly? He is not there to tell me.

I know well that he does not love me. How could he love me? And yet deep down within me something, a particle of myself, cannot help thinking, with fear and trembling, that perhaps, in spite of all, he loves me.

From *The Notebooks of Simone Weil*, translated from the French by Arthur Wills, 2 vols., Vol. 2:638–39. Copyright 1976, Routledge.

LOVE AND KNOWLEDGE

Almost all mystics insist that on the path to God it is necessary to employ both love and knowledge, the two forms of spiritual activity essential to the human subject. Since the New Testament identifies God as love (1 Jn 4:8), Christian mystics have generally given loving a higher role than knowing in attaining God. Although God is Truth, the divine nature remains incomprehensible to every finite intellect, so knowledge always reaches a limit in its search for God. God, however, is always lovable, at least to the extent that a finite spirit can continue to love the Infinite Spirit. Human experience of loving another, nevertheless, can grant a new kind of awareness that is not conceptual but interpersonal, the knowledge that the lover has of the beloved. Many mystics have insisted that the height of loving God grants a similar form of interpersonal and connatural (i.e., a knowing by sympathetic contact) knowledge of God.

The ways in which knowing and loving have been related in the history of mysticism have varied. Augustine observed that we cannot love what we are totally ignorant of, identifying the beginning knowledge of God with what we are given in the darkness of faith. But is faith alone sufficient for the God-loving person? Is there an increment in knowing that comes from contemplative love for God? Further, what kinds of human experience of love provide us with models or analogues for the love between God and creature? How are these different forms of loving and knowing related? Many Christian mystics, represented in the following selections from William, Bernard, and Nicholas of Cusa, strove to present a coordinated picture of what might be called a "subsuming" relationship between knowing and loving, one in which contemplative love of God raises preliminary forms of knowledge into the higher stage in which "love itself becomes understanding" (i.e., a supra-rational, connatural perception). Some late-medieval mystics (represented here by *The Cloud of Unknowing*) expressed a more negative view about the place of knowledge, questioning how far knowing can enter into the supreme affectivity that seeks God. Other mystics, such as the Lutheran Johann Arndt, affirmed the continuing need for both knowing and loving, as well as the higher role of love, while avoiding any theoretical attempts to describe their exact relationship.

WILLIAM OF SAINT-THIERRY
THE GOLDEN LETTER

*One important way of understanding the relation of knowing and loving origi-
nated with a remark made by Gregory the Great that "love itself is a form of
knowledge" (*Homilies on the Gospels *27.4). The notion of the "understanding of love" (*intelligentia amoris*) was richly developed by twelfth-century
mystics, especially the Cistercians and Victorines. William of Saint-Thierry's
considerations stand out as the most profound. His notion of the* intelligentia
amoris *emphasizes an interpenetration of knowing and loving that takes place
at the height of mystical consciousness, involving a supra-rational and nondiscursive knowledge best described as connatural.*

Although he does not use the term intelligentia amoris *in the following passage from his* Golden Letter, *this text is one of his most detailed expositions of
how the knowing and loving given in mystical contact with God differs from ordinary knowing. William explains how both natural and mystical knowing are
realized through the activation of the three mental powers specified by Augustine:
memory, intellect, and will. Ordinary thinking requires the cooperation of the
three powers in two stages and has two sources of activity: the will that compels
the memory and intellect, and the intention of the thinker (*acies cogitantis*) that
guides the operation. The higher mystical form of knowing utilizes the same three
powers of the soul, but it has a new primary agent, the Holy Spirit, and takes place
in four stages. First, as the soul thinks upon God, the Holy Spirit becomes more and
more active until finally "memory becomes wisdom"—that is, the good things of
God are actually present and "tasted" by the soul. Second, under the action of the*

Holy Spirit the memory brings to the intellect what is to be understood so that it can be given form as a desire or tendency in the soul (affectus). Then, third, the intellect receives loving contemplation in a totally passive way; and finally, the intellect cooperates with the action of the Holy Spirit by forming this loving contemplation "into certain experiences of spiritual and divine sweetness" that bring indescribable joy.

There are three powers that create thought: the will itself, memory, and intellect. The will compels the memory to bring forth the material. It compels the intellect to give form to what has been brought forth by applying intellect to memory so that it may be given form and by applying the intention of the thinker to the intellect so that a thought may be created. Because the will collects all these operations into a unity and binds them together by an easy command, thinking [*cogitatio*] receives its name from the verb "to compel" [*cogere*].

This is the origin of all forms of thought: some are good and holy and worthy of God; others are evil and perverse, separating us from God; others are senseless, that is, empty and vain, from which God removes himself. This is why it is said, "Evil thoughts separate from God" (Wis 1:3), and "The Holy Spirit keeps far away from thoughts that are senseless" (Wis 1:5). These words inform us that it is impossible to think without making some sense; there is no thinking without some kind of understanding. Still, one form of understanding arises from natural reason, while another comes from the power of the rational mind. Understanding itself is the same. Whether it is applied to the good or to the bad it has a natural vigor, but it exists in one way when it is left to itself and in another when it is enlightened by grace. [A passage follows that further expounds upon the normal modes of thinking.]

When we think about God or the things that belong to God, and the will advances to the stage of becoming love, immediately the Holy Spirit, the Spirit of Life, infuses himself by means of love and makes everything alive, assisting the weakness of the thinker whether in prayer, or in meditation, or in consideration of some action. At once memory becomes wisdom since it tastes with sweetness the good things of the Lord. Memory brings the thoughts that arise from these good things to the intellect so that they can be given form as an *affectus* [i.e., a state of being drawn to God]. Thus the thinker's understanding becomes the lover's contemplation. The intellect shapes its object into certain experiences of spiritual and divine sweetness and by means of them arouses the thinker's intention so that it becomes the joy of a person who has found delight.

At that moment God is conceived of correctly, at least according to the human mode of thinking. It might not even be called thinking since there is no compelling or being compelled, but only the outpouring of God's sweetness in the memory (Ps 144:7). There is then exaltation and jubilation and true perception of the Lord in goodness by the person who has sought him in this simplicity of heart (Wis 1:1).

This mode of thinking about God does not lie at the disposal of the thinker, but rests in the grace of him who gives, that is, the Holy Spirit who breathes where he wills (Jn 3:8), when he wills, and how he wills, and in this matter breathes upon whom he wills. Our part is always to prepare the heart by ridding the will of foreign attachments, keeping the reason and understanding free from cares, and the memory clear of useless things, of forms of business, and sometimes even of necessary concerns. It does this so that on the Lord's good day, and in the hour of his good pleasure, when the voice of the Spirit breathing shall have been heard, the powers that create thinking may be free at once to come together and to cooperate for the good, making a kind of single form for the thinker's joy, with the will demonstrating pure affection for the joy of the Lord, the memory presenting faithful material, and the intellect the sweetness of experience.

Translated by Bernard McGinn from William of Saint-Thierry, *Epistola ad Fratres de Monte Dei*, in PL 184:346–47.

2.

BERNARD OF CLAIRVAUX
SERMONS ON THE SONG OF SONGS 83

As Bernard approached death (August 20, 1153), he continued to work on his
Sermons on the Song of Songs. *The last seven sermons form a summary of
his teaching about the original nature of humanity, the effects of Adam's fall, and
the restoration brought to us through Christ. In these homilies the abbot does not
directly comment on the Song of Songs, but rather steps back to consider the nature of the soul as the bride of Christ revealed in Solomon's love poem. Following
Genesis 1:26, Bernard, along with other patristic and medieval theologians, held
that the essence of humanity was its nature as the image and likeness of God. In
sermons 80–81 Bernard treats the meaning of being created in God's image and
likeness. In sermon 82 he treats the effects of sin on the soul's likeness to God. Sermons 83–86 consider how the likeness is recovered through the love between the
Divine Bridegroom and the loving soul as bride. This mini treatise begins with
the following sermon, which may be described as Bernard's most profound presentation of the mutuality of the love between God and human figured in the spousal
relation.*

———

Insofar as the regular hour set aside for speaking permits, we have devoted three days to showing the relationship of the Word and the soul.
What use is all this effort? Just this: We have taught that every soul—
despite being burdened with sins, ensnared by vices, captured by en-
ticements, caught in exile, imprisoned in the body, embedded in mud,

fixed in slime, bound by its limbs, assailed by cares, distracted by troubles, bothered by fears, afflicted by pains, caught in errors, made anxious by worries, disturbed by suspicions, and even a stranger in the land of its enemies, as the prophet says (Ex 2:22), "defiled with the dead, and counted among those who go down to hell" (Bar 3:11)— even though, as I say, it is damned and filled with despair in this fashion, nevertheless we have taught that such a soul can find in itself not only a source for expectation of pardon so that it may seek after hope, but even something by which it may dare to aspire to be married to the Word, and not fear to enter into a pact with God, nor shrink from contracting a sweet yoke of love with the King of the angels. For what ought she not safely dare in the case of the one whose image she sees that she bears and by whose likeness she knows she is distinguished? What, I say, ought she to fear of majesty who has been given confidence by her very origin? It is sufficient that she is concerned to preserve her freeborn nature by honesty of life, or rather that she makes the effort to embellish and decorate the celestial dignity in her from her origin by means of some worthy adornments of virtuous customs and desires.

Why, then, does she keep sleeping? Surely, the gift of nature in us is something great, and if it does not strive after its effects sufficiently, won't the remainder of our nature fall into ruin with the whole being covered over with a kind of rust of old decay? Such a state is an affront to the Creator. This is why God the Creator wished the mark of his divine goodness to be always preserved in the soul so that she would forever have within her from the Word a constant source of warning so that she should either remain there with the Word, or, if she has moved away, return to him. She does not move away by changing location, or by walking, but she moves in the manner that spiritual substances do, that is, with her acts of affection, and even of defection, when she departs from herself for something worse and makes herself unlike him by wicked life and deeds, rendering herself inferior. This unlikeness, however, is a vice, not a destruction of nature; it removes the good of nature only insofar as it sullies itself by association with evil. The soul's return is its conversion to the Word, its reformation through him, its conformation to him. How? In charity, for he says: "Be imitators of God, like beloved children, and walk in love, just as Christ has loved you" (Eph 5:1).

Such a conformity marries the soul to the Word. Although it is similar to him through nature, the soul can also show it is like him through will when it loves as it has been loved. Therefore, if she loves perfectly, she marries. What is more delightful than this conformity? What is more desirable than the charity by which it comes to pass that through yourself, O soul, not being content with human teaching, you approach the Word in trust, join with the Word in constancy, and question and consult the Word in a familiar way about everything, as much as intellect can understand and desire can dare? Truly, this is the contract of a spiritual and holy marriage. But "contract" says too little; it is an embrace, for that is surely an embrace where willing the same and not willing the same make one spirit of two persons (1 Cor 6:17). Do not fear that disparity of persons will in any way weaken the agreement of the wills, because love knows no reverence. Love receives its name from loving, not from giving honor. Someone who is afraid, who is in awe, who is scared, who is amazed, pays honor—but these are all absent with lovers. Love overflows in itself; love, where it comes, hands over and takes captive all other forms of affection. That is why someone who loves, loves—and knows nothing else. The God who deserves honor, who deserves admiration and marveling, nonetheless loves much more to be loved. Thus they are bride and Groom. What other need or connection is there between spouses than to be loved and to love?

This bond overcomes even the one that nature joins so strongly between parents and children. Hence, it says, "For this reason, a man shall leave his father and mother and join to his spouse" (Mt 19:5). So you see that this form of affection between spouses is not only more powerful than other forms of attraction, but is also stronger than itself.

Now this Spouse is not only loving, but is Love itself. Is he then honor? I haven't read this. I have, however, read that "God is Love" (1 Jn 4:16), and not that he is honor. This is not because God does not want honor, for he says: "If then I am the Father, where is my honor?" (Mal 1:6). That is the true Father. But if he were to present himself as a spouse, I think he would have to change the word and say: "If I am a Spouse, where is my love?" Previously, he had spoken this way: "If I am the Lord, where is my fear?" (Mal 1:6). Therefore, it is necessary that God be feared as Lord, honored as Father, so that he may be loved as Spouse. Which of these is the foremost, which stands out? It is love.

Without love fear deserves punishment and honor has no grace. Fear is slavish as long as it is not given its freedom by love, and the honor that does not come from love is not true honor but is flattery. Truly, "To God alone be honor and glory" (1 Tim 1:17), but God will accept neither of these if they are not sweetened by love's honey. Love suffices in itself; it pleases in itself and for its own sake. It is its own merit and reward. Love does not need any cause beyond itself, nor any fruit—its fruit is its use. I love because I love; I love so that I may love. Love is a great thing. If it reverts to its own principle, if it returns to its origin, if it flows back into its source, it always draws from it the power to flow forth continuously. It is love alone of all the motions, perceptions, and affections of the soul by which the creature, though not in equal measure, can repay something to the Creator, weigh back from the same measure. For example, if God is angry with me, am I also going to get angry with him? Surely not; but I will fear, tremble, and beg pardon. So also if he accuses me, he will not be accused by me in turn, but he will rather be justified in accusing me. If he judges me, I will not judge him but rather adore him. When he saves me he does not seek to be saved by me; nor likewise does he who frees all need to be freed by anyone. If he exercises rule over me I must serve him; if he commands I must obey. I do not respond in turn by requiring service or obedience from him. Now you can see how different it stands with love. When God loves, he wants only to be loved; he loves for no other reason than to be loved, knowing that those who have loved him are made blessed by that love.

Love is a great thing, but there are degrees in it. The bride stands at the summit. Sons love, but they are thinking about their inheritance, and as long as they fear they might in some way lose it they give more reverence than love to the one from whom they await it. I am suspicious of a love in which there seems to be anything of a hope for gaining something. It is a weak love, for if the hope were to be taken away perhaps it would be snuffed out or lessened. Love which desires anything else is impure. Pure love is not mercenary. Pure love does not take its force from hope and does not feel the weight of lack of confidence. This is the nature of a bride, because she is a bride, whatever else she is. Love is the bride's single reality and hope. The bride is rich in this; this is what contents the Bridegroom. He seeks nothing else; she has nothing else: this is what it is to be a groom and this is what it is to be a bride. This is proper to the spouses, and no one else attains it, not even a son.

Thus he calls out to sons, "Where is my honor?" (Mal 1:6), and not "Where is my love?"—preserving the Bride's prerogative. A person is commanded to honor father and mother (Dt 5:16), with nothing said about love. This is not because parents are not to be loved by their children, but because many children are drawn to honor their parents more than to love them. So too, "The king's honor loves judgment" (Ps 98:4), but the Bridegroom's love (or rather the Bridegroom who is Love) asks only mutual love and faithfulness. Let him then love her in return. How can the bride, and the bride of Love, not love? How can Love not be loved?

Correctly renouncing all other forms of affection, she rests totally and solely on the love which answers his love by giving back love. Although she pours herself totally out in love, how does that measure up to his inexhaustible flood? The human lover and Love, the soul and the Word, the bride and the Bridegroom, the creature and Creator, do not flow with like richness, any more than do a thirsty person and a welling fountain. But what of it? Should the bride's promise, her sigh of desire, her loving ardor, her confident trust, be nullified because of the fact that she cannot run as fast as the giant, or cannot contend in sweetness with honey itself, or with the Lamb in mildness, or with the lily in whiteness, or with the sun in brightness, or in charity with him who is Charity itself? No. Even though the creature loves less because it is less, nevertheless, if it loves totally, there is nothing lacking where all is present. Furthermore, as I said, to love like this is to be married, since one cannot love in this manner (and be no less beloved) other than in the consent of two persons that is the whole and perfect state of marriage. Otherwise, a person might doubt that the Word loved the soul both beforehand and also more powerfully. Hence, the soul is both anticipated and surpassed in loving. Happy is she who merits to be anticipated in such a blessed sweetness! Happy is she who receives the experience of an embrace of such great delight! This is nothing else than holy and chaste love, sweet and delightful love, a love of such calm and serenity, a mutual love, deep and strong, that joins two persons and makes the two no longer two but one, not in one flesh, but in one spirit, as Paul says, "The person who is joined to God is one spirit with him" (1 Cor 6:17). But on these matters let us now listen to her [i.e., the bride] whose teaching charism and frequent experience have made her the master of all these things.

Translated by Bernard McGinn from *Sancti Bernardi Sermones super Cantica*, Sermo LXXXIII, in PL 183:1181–84.

3.

THE CLOUD OF UNKNOWING

CHAPTERS 4–6

The late-fourteenth-century Middle English text called The Cloud of Unknowing *is the most famous work of an anonymous priest, perhaps a Carthusian, who was one of the most creative figures in the history of Dionysian mysticism (see section 9.1). The decades between 1230 and 1250 saw an explosion of interest in the Dionysian writings. Thomas Gallus (d. 1246), a Victorine canon resident in Italy, produced a series of translations and commentaries that reinterpreted the Dionysian language about the limitations of all knowledge of God in an affective manner, that is, on the basis of the supremacy of love over knowing. This reading fused the tradition of commentary on the Song of Songs (the textbook of affective, or positive, mysticism, according to Gallus) with the Dionysian corpus as the basis for negative mysticism. Gallus's views were taken up by Franciscans, such as Bonaventure (see selection 5.3), and among the late-medieval Carthusians, especially Hugh of Balma, who wrote an important mystical handbook called* The Roads to Zion Mourn *about 1290. This tradition reached a culmination in* The Cloud.

The work was written for a young contemplative as an advanced "how-to-do-it" book. The Cloud's most original contribution is its distinction between "the cloud of unknowing"—the darkness and ignorance that persists between us and the hidden God—and the "cloud of forgetting," which the contemplative must place between herself or himself and all created things. The Cloud also has instructions on how to seek the unknowable God through love, specifically by means of "the sharp dart of longing love" expressed in ejaculatory prayer (see chapters 6, 12, 39–40). The Cloud *'s author did not lack all appreciation of the role of reason in the preparatory stages to mystical ascent, but he weighted the balance strongly in favor of love.*

CHAPTER 4.
OF THE SIMPLICITY OF CONTEMPLATION; THAT IT MAY NOT BE ACQUIRED THROUGH KNOWLEDGE OR IMAGINATION

I have described a little of what is involved in the contemplative work but now I shall discuss it further, insofar as I understand it, so that you may proceed securely and without misconceptions.

This work is not time-consuming even though some people believe otherwise. Actually it is the shortest you can imagine; as brief as an atom, which, as the philosophers say, is the smallest division of time. The atom is a moment so short and integral that the mind can scarcely conceive it. Nevertheless it is vastly important, for of this minute measure of time it is written: "You will be held responsible for all the time given you" [Anselm, *Meditation 2*]. This is entirely just because your principal spiritual faculty, the will, needs only this brief fraction of a moment to move toward the object of its desire.

If you were now restored by grace to the integrity man possessed before sin you would be complete master of these impulses. None would ever go astray, but would fly to the one sole good, the goal of all desire, God himself. For God created us in his image and likeness, making us like himself, and in the Incarnation he emptied himself of his divinity becoming a man like us. It is God, and he alone, who can fully satisfy the hunger and longing of our spirit which transformed by his redeeming grace is enabled to embrace him by love. He whom neither men nor angels can grasp by knowledge can be embraced by love. For the intellect of both men and angels is too small to comprehend God as he is in himself.

Try to understand this point. Rational creatures such as men and angels possess two principal faculties, a knowing power and a loving power. No one can fully comprehend the uncreated God with his knowledge; but each one, in a different way, can grasp him fully through love. Truly this is the unending miracle of love: that one loving person, through his love, can embrace God, whose being fills and transcends the entire creation. And this marvelous work of love goes on forever, for he whom we love is eternal. Whoever has the grace to appreciate the truth of what I am saying, let him take my words to heart, for to experience this love is the joy of eternal life while to lose it is eternal torment.

He who with the help of God's grace becomes aware of the will's constant movements and learns to direct them toward God will never fail to taste something of heaven's joy even in this life and, certainly in the next, he will savor it fully. Now do you see why I rouse you to this spiritual work? You would have taken to it naturally had man not sinned, for man was created to love and everything else was created to make love possible. Nevertheless, by the work of contemplative love man will be healed. Failing in this work he sinks deeper into sin further and further from God, but by persevering in it he gradually rises from sin and grows in divine intimacy.

Therefore, be attentive to time and the way you spend it. Nothing is more precious. This is evident when you recall that in one tiny moment heaven may be gained or lost. God, the master of time, never gives the future. He gives only the present, moment by moment, for this is the law of the created order, and God will not contradict himself in his creation. Time is for man, not man for time. God, the Lord of nature, will never anticipate man's choices which follow one after another in time. Man will not be able to excuse himself at the last judgment, saying to God: "You overwhelmed me with the future when I was only capable of living in the present."

But now I see that you are discouraged and are saying to yourself: "What am I to do? If all he says is true, how shall I justify my past? I am twenty-four years old and until this moment I have scarcely noticed time at all. What is worse, I could not repair the past even if I wanted to, for according to his teaching such a task is impossible to me by nature even with the help of ordinary grace. Besides I know very well that in the future, either through frailty or laziness, I will probably not be any more attentive to the present moment than I have been in the past. I am completely discouraged. Please help me for the love of Jesus."

Well have you said "for the love of Jesus." For it is in his love that you will find help. In love all things are shared and so if you love Jesus, everything of his is yours. As God he is the creator and dispenser of time; as man he consciously mastered time; as God and man he is the rightful judge of men and their use of time. Bind yourself to Jesus, therefore, in faith and love, so that belonging to him you may share all he has and enter the fellowship of those who love him. This is the communion of the blessed and these will be your friends: our Lady, St. Mary, who was full of grace at every moment; the angels, who are unable to waste time; and all the blessed in heaven and on earth, who through the grace of Jesus employ every moment in love. See, here is your strength. Understand what I am saying and be heartened. But remember, I warn you of one thing above all. No one can claim true fellowship with Jesus, his Mother, the angels, and the saints, unless he does all in his power with the help of grace to be mindful of time. For he must do his share however slight to strengthen the fellowship as it strengthens him.

And so do not neglect this contemplative work. Try also to appreciate its wonderful effects in your own spirit. When it is genuine it is simply a spontaneous desire springing suddenly toward God like spark from fire. It is amazing how many loving desires arise from the spirit of a person who is accustomed to this work. And yet, perhaps only one of these will be completely free from attachment to some created thing. Or again, no sooner has a man turned toward God in love when through human frailty he finds himself distracted by the remembrance of some created thing or some daily care. But no matter. No harm is done; for such a person quickly returns to deep recollection.

And now we come to the difference between the contemplative work and its counterfeits such as daydreaming, fantasizing, or subtle reasoning. These originate in a conceited, curious, or romantic mind whereas the blind stirring of love springs from a sincere and humble heart. Pride, curiosity, and daydreaming must be sternly checked if the contemplative work is to be authentically conceived in singleness of heart. Some will probably hear about this work and suppose that by their own ingenious efforts they can achieve it. They are likely to strain their mind and imagination unnaturally only to produce a false work which is neither human nor divine. Truly, such a person is dangerously deceived. And I fear that unless God intervenes with a miracle inspiring him to abandon these practices and humbly seek reliable counsel he will most certainly fall into mental aberrations or some great spiritual evil of the devil's devising. Then he risks losing both body and soul eternally. For the love of God, therefore, be careful in this work and never strain your mind or imagination, for truly you will not succeed this way. Leave these faculties at peace.

Do not suppose that because I have spoken of darkness and of a cloud I have in mind the clouds you see in an overcast sky or the darkness of your house when your candle fails. If I had, you could with a little imagination picture the summer skies breaking through the clouds or a clear light brightening the dark winter. But this isn't what I mean at all so forget this sort of nonsense. When I speak of darkness, I mean the absence of knowledge. If you are unable to understand something or if you have forgotten it, are you not in the dark as regards this thing? You cannot see it with your mind's eye. Well, in the same way, I have not said "cloud," but *cloud of unknowing*. For it is a darkness of unknowing that lies between you and your God.

CHAPTER 5.
THAT DURING CONTEMPLATIVE PRAYER ALL CREATED THINGS AND THEIR WORKS MUST BE BURIED BENEATH THE CLOUD OF FORGETTING

If you wish to enter into this cloud, to be at home in it, and to take up the contemplative work of love as I urge you to, there is something else you must do. Just as the *cloud of unknowing* lies above you, between you and your God, so you must fashion a *cloud of forgetting* beneath you, between you and every created thing. The *cloud of unknowing* will perhaps leave you with the feeling that you are far from God. But no, if it is authentic, only the absence of a *cloud of forgetting* keeps you from him now. Every time I say "all creatures," I refer not only to every created thing but also to all their circumstances and activities. I make no exception. You are to concern yourself with no creature whether material or spiritual nor with their situation and doings whether good or ill. To put it briefly, during this work you must abandon them all beneath the *cloud of forgetting*. For although at certain times and in certain circumstances it is necessary and useful to dwell on the particular situation and activity of people and things, during this work it is almost useless. Thinking and remembering are forms of spiritual understanding in which the eye of the spirit is opened and closed upon things as the eye of a marksman is on his target. But I tell you that everything you dwell upon during this work becomes an obstacle to union with God. For if your mind is cluttered with these concerns there is no room for him.

Yes, and with all due reverence, I go so far as to say that it is equally useless to think you can nourish your contemplative work by considering God's attributes, his kindness or his dignity; or by thinking about our Lady, the angels, or the saints; or about the joys of heaven, wonderful as these will be. I believe that this kind of activity is no longer of any use to you. Of course, it is laudable to reflect upon God's kindness and to love and praise him for it; yet it is far better to let your mind rest in the awareness of him in his naked existence and to love and praise him for what he is in himself.

CHAPTER 6.
A SHORT EXPLANATION OF CONTEMPLATION IN THE FORM OF A DIALOGUE

Now you say, "How shall I proceed to think of God as he is in himself?" To this I can only reply, "I do not know."

With this question you bring me into the very darkness and *cloud of unknowing* that I want you to enter. Through grace a man may know completely and ponder thoroughly every created thing and its works, yes, and God's works, too, but not God himself. Thought cannot comprehend God. And so, I prefer to abandon all I can know, choosing rather to love him whom I cannot know. Though we cannot know him we can love him. By love he may be touched and embraced, never by thought. Of course, we do well at times to ponder God's majesty or kindness for the insight these meditations may bring. But in the real contemplative work you must set all this aside and cover it over with a *cloud of forgetting.* Then let your loving desire, gracious and devout, step bravely and joyfully beyond it and reach out to pierce the darkness above. Yes, beat upon that thick *cloud of unknowing* with the dart of your loving desire and do not cease come what may.

NICHOLAS OF CUSA
TWO LETTERS ON MYSTICAL THEOLOGY

Nicholas of Cusa (1401–64) ranks among the extraordinary figures in the history of Christianity. This Renaissance cardinal made outstanding contributions to philosophy, theology, science, and church reform. He also had an interest in mystical theology, as is shown both in the following letters and in his treatise On the Vision of God *(see section 10.8).* Pope Nicholas V sent Cusa on a reforming legation through Germany between 1450 and 1452, during which the cardinal visited the Benedictine monastery of Tegernsee in Bavaria and became acquainted with its abbot, Kaspar Ayndorffer, and the community. The monks were interested in Cusa's theology and also in contemporary debates over the nature of Dionysian mystical theology. One interpretation of mystical theology, namely that found in The Cloud of Unknowing, *was basically "affective,"* insisting that God could be attained only by the height of the affective power beyond all knowing. Some who followed this interpretation seemed to claim that intellect and knowledge of any sort were hindrances in the ascent to God. The more "intellective" view of mystical theology read Dionysius in terms of the importance of both love and knowledge in the path toward a supra-intellective union.

In the summer of 1452 Abbot Ayndorffer wrote Cusa asking for his view on the relation of love and knowledge in mystical theology, especially in light of the attacks on the cardinal and Jean Gerson by the Carthusian Vincent of Aggsbach (circa 1389–1464), an adherent of affective Dionysianism. The debates sparked a decade-long flood of letters and pamphlets. Cusa first responded with the letter *of September 22, 1452, translated below, briefly stating his overall position. In June 1453 Vincent of Aggsbach wrote another treatise, giving his interpretation of what Dionysius meant in* Mystical Theology 1 *(see section 9.1) when he told Timothy "to rise up unknowingly" (*ignote consurge*). Cusa responded with the second letter given here, a summary of his position that mystical union involves both loving and knowing, aiming toward the coincident theology that combines the positive and the negative approaches to God on a higher level.*

I.
LETTER OF NICHOLAS OF CUSA TO KASPAR AYNDORFFER (SEPTEMBER 22, 1452)

Nicholas the Cardinal in his own hand with haste to the Reverend Father Kaspar, Abbot of Tegernsee, our very special friend. Reverend Father with many greetings. I have received the Martyrology and very quickly send it back. The secretary I am awaiting has not yet brought the books you asked for. I will send them when I have them. I have become accustomed to your special intimacy and the trust of true friendship so that I've sent you writings that are rough and unpolished. Read them with care. To those who find them unclear they can be explained so that they will bear fruit. The inexpressible fruitfulness of the divine scriptures is expounded differently to different people so that its infinity shines forth in such great variety—there is but one divine word that gleams in all things.

This is not a fitting time for responding to the question you present due to my obligations regarding the celebration of holy orders. Nevertheless, in my first sermon on the Holy Spirit, on the text "Sit until you are filled" (Lk 24:49), you will find in the first major point there something on the first of the issues you asked of me: how knowing coincides with loving.

It is impossible for the power of desire to be moved except by love, and whatever is loved can only be loved under the aspect of the good. No one is good but God alone, as the Truth says (Lk 18:19). Everything that is loved or chosen by reason of goodness is not loved without any knowledge of goodness at all, because it is loved insofar as it is good. Therefore, in every such love by which a person is carried into God knowledge enters in, although it does not know the essence that it loves. There is, then, a coincidence of knowledge and ignorance, or a learned ignorance. For if it did not know some good, it would not love the good, and yet the one who loves does not know the essence of the good. Love of the good presents the good as not yet grasped, for the spirit's motion that is love would cease if it attained its goal. It is always moved to attain more, and because the good is infinite, the spirit will never cease being moved forward. Therefore, the loving spirit can never stop, because the lovableness of the one loved cannot be attained. The loving person is swept up, but not without any knowledge. Knowledge is perceived from adhering to God—"My soul," says the prophet, "has adhered to you; your right hand has received me" (Ps 62:9). Because this is the gospel, that is, attaining by means of faith while in the world, there is no love of God that sweeps the lover up into God apart from belief in Christ who has revealed what he saw when he was with the Father, namely, there is an immortal life which we can attain through the joining of the divine life to pure human nature in the Son of God and of Man.

This faith, namely that a person can attain divinity in this way, is the highest form of knowledge in this world, which also surpasses every knowledge of the world. The world is overcome by this faith: "This is the victory, your faith" (1 Jn 5:4). Since even the uneducated can be led to faith by the word, they are swept up into God's friendship—"For the untaught arise and are swept up." This is the revelation that is made to very many and is hidden from the wise of this world who only love what they attain with their own wisdom and who spurn the divine wisdom, which is to believe in God. Therefore, let believers come to the experience of faith, as St. John the Baptist says: "Whoever accepts the testimony of Christ will seal that God is true" (Jn 3:33). John the Evangelist says: "To as many as received him he gave the power of becoming children of God" (Jn 1:12). Therefore, the wise of this world will not attain the God who is life, as the Baptist says: "He who believes in the Son of God will have life; who does not believe in the Son will not see life" (Jn 3:36). So see how necessary faith is to every form of vision, and we experience faith from observing the commandments. Therefore, if we find a simple and zealous observer of God's commandments and know him to be a faithful Christian, we believe that such a one is capable of being swept up to vision just like Paul (2 Cor 12:1–4). But in rapture many people are deceived who get stuck in images and think that an imaginary vision is real. Truth is the object of the intellect and can only be seen in an invisible way. A lot more could be said about this, but not now. It perhaps may never be fully explained.

I ask you to forgive me this time. At a later time a better attempt may be made, if God grants it. Someone can show others the way he knows to be true from hearing, even if he himself has not walked the path; but the person who advances by sight is more secure. Whatever I have written or said will remain less certain, for I have yet to taste how sweet is the Lord (Ps 33:9). Farewell and pray for me, my most dear Father.

From Brixen on the 22nd of September, 1452.

II.
LETTER OF NICHOLAS OF CUSA TO
THE MONKS OF TEGERNSEE
(SEPTEMBER 14, 1453)

Nicholas, Cardinal of St. Peter in Chains, to the Abbot of Tegernsee and his brethren concerning the term *mystical theology.* A thousand salutations to the reverend fathers and justly much-beloved brothers in Christ.

I see from the always welcome letters you sent me that you want me to say what I think about the great Areopagite Dionysius's command to Timothy "ascend unknowingly to mystical theology" (*Mystical Theology* 1). Although the Carthusian [Vincent of Aggsbach], a man zealous for God, has carefully read the writings of Chancellor Gerson and judged him to be wrong, especially because he called mystical theology contemplation, nonetheless, for my part, and on the basis of the recently translated text [Ambrogio Traversari's version of the Dionysian corpus], this is my view. Dionysius intended nothing else than to reveal to Timothy how the contemplative gaze concerned with the ascent of our rational spirit to union with God and the unveiled vision will not be completed as long as there is any understanding of what is thought to be God. In Letter 1 to the monk Gaius he clearly says the same thing. Hence he says that it is necessary that such a person ascend above everything intelligible, even beyond himself, on which basis he may enter into cloud and darkness. If the mind no longer understands, it is placed in the cloud of ignorance. When it perceives the darkness, this is a sign that the God it seeks is there. This is like someone who tries to look at the sun; if he really sees it, he finds in his weak mode of seeing a darkness that comes from the surpassing brightness of the sun. This darkness is a sign that the one seeking to see the sun has gone the right way; if the darkness does not appear, he has not correctly arrived at the most excellent form of physical light.

Even though almost all the most learned commentators say that the darkness is found when all attributes are removed from God so that nothing further meets the one seeking, it is not my view that those who concern themselves only with negative theology have entered the darkness in the correct way. Since negative theology removes but does not posit, God will not be seen in an open way through it. It discovers not what God is, but what he is not. And if God is sought by affirmative theology, he will not be found save by imitation and in a veiled manner, never in an open way.

In many places Dionysius hands down to us a theology by disjunction, that is, we approach God either affirmatively or negatively. But in this little book [i.e., *Mystical Theology*], where he wants to show mystical and secret theology in a likely way, he leaps beyond the disjunction up to combination and coincidence, that is, to the most simple union that is not one-sided, but directly above all remotion and positing. Here remotion coincides with positing and negation with affirmation. This is the most secret theology to which no philosopher had access nor could have, as long as the principle common to all philosophy is in force, that is, that two contradictories do not coincide. And so it is necessary that someone doing theology in the mystical manner place himself in the darkness beyond all reason and intellect, even leaving self behind. He will discover how what reason judges impossible, i.e., that being and not-being are one and the same, is actually necessary. Indeed, unless such a great darkness and obscurity are seen, the highest form of necessity that does not contradict what is impossible to reason would not be found. Impossibility is the very necessity itself.

If a person reads the Greek and Latin text, he will see how Dionysius is to be understood in my view. This is why he says that when all intelligible realities have been trodden down Timothy ought to direct his mind "unknowingly," since he will then find that the confusion into which he rises up unknowingly is really certitude, the darkness is light, and the ignorance is knowledge. The mode that the Carthusian speaks about can be neither known nor handed on. He himself says he has not experienced it. It is necessary that some kind of knowledge be permitted to every lover seeking to rise up unknowingly to union with the Beloved. What is totally unknown can neither be loved, nor found; even if it is found, it is not apprehended as found. This is why the road by which a person strives to ascend unknowingly is neither without trouble nor capable of being handed on in writing. The "angel of Satan who changes himself into an angel of light" (2 Cor 11:14) could easily lead the overconfident person astray. It would be necessary for the lover to have an idea of the Beloved. For such an idea to exist, it would have to be formed in an intelligible way. If he did not enter the darkness, he might think that he found God when he only found something like what he had imagined.

I don't want to condemn anyone, but I do not think that Dionysius wanted Timothy to ascend unknowingly save in the way I've spoken about, not in the manner the Carthusian desires, that is, through an affectivity that leaves understanding behind. The verb *rise up* expresses what I said. *Rising up* does not express drawing near to God unless the person moves upward. This motion, even though it may be above the self so that the self is unknown, is also nonetheless a movement to union with what is sought in an unknown way. To rise up "unknowingly" can only be said in relation to the intellectual power. The affective power cannot rise up unknowingly because it is not "knowing" without receiving knowledge from the intellect. Knowledge and ignorance concern the intellect, not the will, just as good and evil concern the will and not the intellect. It is true that it is difficult to hand on how we are able to carry ourselves over to mystical theology in order to taste necessity in the impossible and affirmation in negation. This taste, which involves supreme sweetness and love, cannot be perfectly possessed in this world. It has seemed to me that the whole of mystical theology is to enter Absolute Infinity itself, for infinity expresses the coincidence of contradictories, that is, the end without end, and no one can see God mystically save in the darkness of coincidence that is infinity. You will see more about this, if with God's help he gives me more to say. . . .

From Branzoll on the Feast of the Exaltation of the Cross, 1453. Your Nicholas, Cardinal of St. Peter, in his own hand.

Translation by Bernard McGinn from Edmond Vansteenberghe, *Autour de la Docte Ignorance. Une controverse sur la théologie mystique au XVe siècle* (Münster: Aschendorff, 1915), 111–17.

5.

JOHANN ARNDT
TRUE CHRISTIANITY

BOOK 3

Among the most influential Protestant mystics was the Lutheran pastor Johann Arndt (1555–1621). Luther himself, while not a mystic, used mystical themes in his writings, such as the notion of union with Christ, the sacred marriage exchange, and even deification. Luther also praised some mystical authors, such as Bernard of Clairvaux, John Tauler, and the Theologia Deutsch, *over the dry scholastic theology that he felt had undermined the true understanding of the Gospel. In the generations after Luther's death, however, many Lutheran and Reformed theologians adopted the methods of the scholastics in their disputes with Catholics and with each other. Arndt was a leader of the opposing group, which argued that merely intellectual knowledge of Christ was not sufficient. Rather, loving desire for Christ and total conformity to his will were necessary for Christian perfection and union with God. As he put it in the foreword to* True Christianity, *his most famous work: "It is not enough to know God's word; one must also practice it in a living, active manner. Many think that theology is a mere science or rhetoric, whereas it is living experience and practice."*

Arndt published the first four books of this work between 1606 and 1610. In advancing his case, he made use of the ancient threefold itinerary of progress to God (see section 5.1) and also took up the perennial issue of the relation of love and knowledge. The first three books, as explained in the following prologue, deal in a broad way with the three stages of the standard itinerary, while book 4 treats of God's work in the macrocosm of the world and the microcosm of man. The work was instantly popular, with twenty editions prior to Arndt's death and no fewer than 125 before 1800. In later editions two more books were often added—book 5 collected some of Arndt's mystical treatises, and book 6 was an answer to his critics. Pastor Arndt also wrote a popular prayer book called The Paradise Garden Full of Christian Virtues *(1612). Arndt's treatises and his editions of the* Theologia Deutsch *(see section 12.5) had great impact on the rise of the Pietist movement of spiritual and theological reform in the seventeenth and eighteenth centuries.*

PROLOGUE

Just as our natural life has its stages, its childhood, manhood, and old age, so too our spiritual and Christian life is set up. It has its beginning in repentance, through which a person does penance every day. A greater enlightenment follows after this like middle age, through the contemplation of divine things, through prayer, through the cross, through which all God's gifts are increased. Finally comes the perfection of old age, being established in complete union through love, which St. Paul calls "the perfect age of Christ" and being "a perfect man in Christ" (Eph 4:13).

I have taken up this order in these three books in so far as I could, and I think that the whole of Christianity is necessarily described in them, though the prayer book is to be added. Even though not all the description is perfect, nothing could be desired in carrying it out. I want to add a fourth book so that someone can see how scripture, Christ, humanity, and the whole of nature agree, and how all these things flow back again and lead into the one, eternal, living Source who is God himself.

In order to understand me rightly in this third book, know that it is directed toward how you must seek and find the kingdom of God in yourself (Lk 17:21). In order for this to happen, you must give God your whole heart and soul, not just your understanding, but also your will and your sincere love. Many people think that it is quite enough and even excessive for their Christianity if they grasp Christ with the understanding, through reading and disputation. This is the general "study of theology," which consists in pure "theoria" and in science. They do not realize that the other chief power of the soul, namely the will and the dear love, also belong there. Both must be given to God and to Christ if you wish to give him your whole soul. For there is a great distinction between the understanding by which one knows Christ and the will by which you love him. We understand Christ as far as we are able; we love him as he is. It is of no use to know Christ through pure understanding and not to love him. It is a thousand times better "to love Christ than to be able to say and dispute much about him" (Eph 3:19). Therefore, we should seek Christ with our understanding so that we can love him with our sincere will and pleasure. The love of Christ comes from true knowledge of Christ. If we do not perform this, we shall surely find him, but to our great shame, for this is what we read where the Lord says in Matthew 7:21: "Not everyone who says to me, 'Lord, Lord,' shall come into the kingdom of heaven." There are then two ways to gain wisdom and understanding: the first is to read and dispute much, and this is what is called being "learned"; the second is through prayer and through love, and this is called being "holy." There is a great difference between the two. Those who are learned and have no love are proud and filled with themselves; the others are lowly and humble. Through the first way you will not find your inner treasure; through the second you will find it in yourself. This is the subject matter of the whole third book.

How wonderful, and precious and lovely it is that our highest and best treasure, the kingdom of God, is not something exterior, but is an indwelling good that we always have with us, hidden from the whole world and from the devil himself so that neither the world nor the devil can take it from us. For it, we need no great skill, speech, or many books, but rather a heart released and surrendered to God. For this purpose let us diligently turn within to this inner, hidden, heavenly, and eternal goodness and kingdom. What should we seek for externally in the world, we who have everything within us, the whole kingdom of God and all its goods? In our hearts and souls is the true school of the Holy Spirit, the true workshop of the Holy Trinity, the true temple of God, "the true house of prayer in spirit and in truth" (Jn 4:23). Although God is in all things through his general presence, not contained within them, but in an incomprehensible way filling heaven and earth, he is still in a special and singular sense in the enlightened souls of those people in whom he dwells and has his resting place (1 Cor 6:19; Is 66:2), as in his own image and likeness. There he performs the works that he himself is. There in our heart he always answers our sighs. How is it possible for him to deny those in whom he has his dwelling, whom he himself moves and draws? Nothing is more delightful and pleasant to him than to give himself to all those who seek him.

All this belongs to a refined, quiet, and peaceful soul. The soul becomes quiet and peaceful when she turns herself away from the world. Even the pagans have said of this: "Our soul will finally become wise when she is quiet and peaceful." St. Cyprian rightly says of it, "This is," he says, "constant rest and security, if a person is freed from the continual storms and winds of this world and lifts up his eyes and heart from the earth to God, and draws near to God with his mind (*mente DEO fit proximus*), understanding also that everything among worldly things that is held high and costly lies hidden in his heart and mind. . . ."

There is great wisdom in these words and herein is a summary of this third book. Often the hidden treasure in our hearts is aroused as in an instant, and this instant is better than heaven and earth and all the charm of creatures. As St. Bernard says: "A soul that has once rightly learned how to turn herself within and to seek God's face and to taste God's presence in her interior, I do not know if for such a soul it would be more painful and terrible to suffer in hell for a time than, having known and experienced the sweetness of this holy exercise, to have to return again to the pleasure, or rather to the displeasure and trouble, of the world and the flesh and to the unsatisfied desire and unrest of the senses." For such a soul not only finds the highest good in herself if she turns to God, but also the highest wretchedness in herself if she loses God. She well knows that she lives in God as in the source of her life if she dies to the world; and on the other side, the more she lives to the world, the more she dies to God. Such a soul who has died to the world truly lives in God, and is God's delight and joy, a sweet and ripe grape in Christ's vineyard, as the Song of Solomon says (Song 5:10). The other hearts that seek the world are bitter unripe grapes. . . .

See, here is the true perfection of the Christian life. For perfection is not as some think a high, great, spiritual, heavenly joy and meditation, but it is the denial of your own will, love, honor, a knowledge of your own nothingness, a lasting completion of God's will, a burning love for neighbor, a sincere compassion, and in sum a love that desires, thinks, and seeks for God alone as far as possible in the weakness of this life. This is also true Christian virtue, true freedom and peace, in overcoming the flesh and fleshly affections. You will read more about this in the third book and find its exercise. To that end I desire both for you and for me the grace of the Holy Spirit, which begins, carries on, and perfects everything in us to God's honor, homage, and praise. Amen.

Translated by Bernard McGinn from *Johann Arndts Vier Bücher vom Wahren Christenthum* (Halle: Im Waissenhause, 1779. 14th ed.), 489–93.

POSITIVE AND NEGATIVE WAYS TO GOD

In Christian belief all things are manifestations, or *theophaniae*, of God their Creator. But God also is infinitely beyond his creatures since they are defined by their limited nature. The first truth founds the way of *cataphasis*, or positive speaking about God based on creation, while God's infinite otherness founds the way of *apophasis*, or the negative speaking in which all statements must be unsaid in deference to God's hidden reality. Although Christian mystics affirm the superiority of the apophatic way—lest God be thought to be just another reality—they have insisted that both the positive and the negative approaches to speaking about God are necessary, though in different measures depending upon one's spiritual progress. This is true even of the premier representative of apophatic mysticism, the mysterious monk of the Eastern Church who wrote under the name Dionysius and who first used the term *mystical theology*.

Many mystics have concentrated on the intricacies and paradoxes of negation, the ever-challenging task of unsaying God. This is evident from a number of selections scattered throughout this anthology, such as those from Gregory of Nyssa (see section 1.2), Marguerite Porete (see section 5.4), Meister Eckhart (see section 13.3), *The Cloud of Unknowing* (see section 8.3), Nicholas of Cusa (section 10.8), and John of the Cross (section 2.5), to name just some. But other mystics have presented messages that dwell more on the positive language of finding God in erotic love and sense experience, such as Bernard of Clairvaux (see section 7.1), Hadewijch (see section 3.5), Mechthild (see section 6.3), Richard Rolle (see section 10.7), and Henry Suso (see section 7.3). Another positive form of mysticism is nature mysticism, which is found in Christianity not in the sense of the identification of nature with the divine, but as discerning God's presence in, with, and through his beautiful creation. In this section two selections, those from Dionysius and from the Eckhartian poem and commentary called "Granum Sinapis," emphasize the apophatic way. Three other selections, two of them poetic, highlight how the universe gives us positive access to God.

1.

DIONYSIUS
THE MYSTICAL THEOLOGY

The collection of texts known as the Dionysian corpus dates from circa 500 CE. Five works constitute the collection (others referred to are either lost or fictitious). Two treatises deal with different kinds of hierarchies, that is, ordered manifestations of God that lead the soul back by anagogy (upward movement) to the divine source. The Ecclesiastical Hierarchy *explains how the liturgy and the ecclesiastical offices contribute to this process, while* The Celestial Hierarchy *investigates how the biblical descriptions of the angels reveal their role in our uplifting. Along with ten letters, we also find the treatise known as* The Divine Names *containing thirteen chapters dealing with the positive names or attributes of God as Creator. This work introduces aspects of the higher negative theology in which all symbols and names of God are denied in a process of "stripping away" (aphairesis) leading toward the darkness of "unknowing" (agnôsia) in which union (henôsis) is attained. The positive and negative paths aim toward what Dionysius called mystical theology, to which he devoted the following short summary work of five chapters. Mystical theology, as Dionysius conceives it, goes beyond both affirmation and negation.*

The author of these writings presents himself as Dionysius of the Areopagus, Paul's convert mentioned in Acts 17:34. This pious fiction gave the writings a quasi-apostolic reputation that made them the *authority in matters mystical for most writers of East and West down to modern times, although some Reformation figures, such as Luther, found Dionysius more Platonic than Christian. When modern scholarship showed that the Dionysian corpus used pagan Neoplatonic thinkers of the fifth century the debate heated up. Was "Dionysius" (I prefer this title to the often-used "Pseudo-Dionysius") a Neoplatonist masquerading as a Christian, or was he a devout monastic mystic, possibly from Syria, who transposed pagan mystical philosophy in a way that would both give theological depth to Christian mystical traditions and also perhaps attract pagan thinkers to Christ? The discussion is by no means ended, but recent study has tended to support the second view.*

Dionysius's difficult thought had great impact on the history of Christian theology and mysticism, not only with regard to the positive and negative ways to God and the nature of mystical theology, but also on such matters as the role of the angels, the use of symbols, liturgical theology, and the nature of union. Translating Dionysius's idiosyncratic Greek is always a difficult exercise. In the medieval period no fewer than five different Latin versions were made. There are a number of modern English translations. The translation I have used here gives something of the flavor of Dionysius's unusual language.

CHAPTER I.
THE NATURE OF THE DIVINE DARKNESS

1. Trinity beyond all essence, all divinity, all goodness! Guide of Christians to divine wisdom, direct our path to the ultimate summit of your mystical lore, most incomprehensible, most luminous, and most exalted, where the pure, absolute, and immutable mysteries of theology are veiled in the dazzling obscurity of the secret silence, outshining all brilliance with the intensity of their darkness, and surcharging our blinded intellects with the utterly impalpable and invisible fairness of glories surpassing all beauty.

Let this be my prayer; but do you, dear Timothy, in the diligent exercise of mystical contemplation, leave behind the senses and the operations of the intellect, and all things sensible and intellectual, and all things in the world of being and nonbeing, that you might rise up unknowingly toward the union [*henôsis*], as far as is attainable, with him who transcends all being and all knowledge. For by the unceasing and absolute renunciation of yourself and of all things, you may be borne on high, through pure and entire self-abnegation, into the superessential radiance of the divine darkness.

2. But these things are not to be disclosed to the uninitiated, by whom I mean those attached to the objects of human thought, and who believe there is no superessential reality beyond, and who imagine that by their own understanding they know him who has made darkness his secret place. And if the principles of the divine mysteries are beyond the understanding of these people, what is to be said of others still more incapable of it, who describe the transcendental First Cause of all by characteristics drawn from the lowest order of beings, while they deny that he is in any way above the images which they fashion after various designs; whereas they should affirm that while he possesses all the positive attributes of the universe (being the universal Cause), yet, in a more strict sense, he does not possess them, since he transcends them all; wherefore there is no contradiction between the affirmations and the negations, inasmuch as he infinitely precedes all conceptions of privation, being beyond all positive and negative distinctions.

3. Thus the blessed Bartholomew asserts that the divine science is both vast and minute, and that the gospel is great and broad, yet concise and short; signifying by this that the beneficent Cause of all is most eloquent, yet utters few words, or rather is altogether silent, as having neither speech nor understanding, because he is superessentially exalted above created things, and reveals himself in his naked truth only to those who pass beyond all that is pure or impure, and ascend above the topmost altitudes of holy things, and who, leaving behind them all divine light and sound and heavenly utterances, plunge into the darkness where truly dwells, as the biblical oracles declare, that One who is beyond all things (Ex 20:21).

It was not without reason that the blessed Moses was commanded first to undergo purification himself, and then to separate himself from those who had not undergone it; and after the entire purification heard many-voiced trumpets and saw many lights streaming forth with pure and manifold rays; and that he was thereafter separated from the multitude, with the elect priests, and pressed forward to the summit of the divine ascent (Ex 19–20). Nevertheless, he did not attain to the presence of God himself; he saw not him (for he cannot be looked upon), but the place where he dwells. And this I take to signify that the divinest and highest things seen by the eyes or contemplated by the mind are but the symbolical expressions of those that are immediately beneath him who is above all. Through these his incomprehensible presence is manifested upon those heights of his holy places. But then Moses breaks forth, even from that which is seen and that which sees, and he plunges into the truly mystical darkness of unknowing from which all perfection of understanding is excluded; and he is wrapped up in that which is altogether intangible and intelligible, being wholly absorbed in him who is beyond all. Here, being neither oneself nor another, one is supremely united to the Wholly Unknown by the inactivity of all his reasoning powers, and thus, by knowing nothing, knows beyond the mind.

CHAPTER 2.
THE NECESSITY OF BEING UNITED
WITH AND OF RENDERING PRAISE
TO HIM WHO IS THE CAUSE OF
ALL AND ABOVE ALL

We pray that we may come into this darkness that is beyond light, and, without seeing and without knowing, see and know that which is above vision and knowledge through the realization that by not-seeing and by not-knowing we attain to true vision and knowledge, and thus praise, superessentially, him who is superessential, by the abstraction [*aphairesis*] of the essence of all things. This is like those who, carving a statue out of marble, abstract or remove all the surrounding material that hinders the vision which the marble conceals and by that abstraction bring to light the hidden beauty.

It is necessary to praise this negative method of abstraction differently from the positive method of affirmation. For with the latter we begin with the universal and primary, and pass through the intermediate and secondary to the particular and ultimate attributes. But now we ascend from the particular to the universal conceptions, abstracting all attributes in order that, without veil, we may know that unknowing [*agnôsia*] that is shrouded under all that is known and all that can be known, and that we may begin to contemplate the superessential darkness that is hidden by all the light that is in existing things.

CHAPTER 3.
WHAT ARE THE AFFIRMATIVE
THEOLOGIES AND WHAT THE NEGATIVE?

In the *Theological Outlines* [a lost work] we have set forth the principal affirmative expressions concerning God, and have shown in what sense God's holy nature is one, and in what sense three; what is within it which is called Paternity, what Filiation, and what is signified by the name Spirit; how from the uncreated and indivisible good, the blessed and perfect rays of its goodness proceed, and yet abide immutably, one both within their origin and within themselves and each other, co-eternal with the act by which they spring from it; how the super-essential Jesus enters an essential state in which the truth of human nature meets it; and other matters made known by the oracles [i.e., scripture] are expounded in the same place.

Again, in the treatise on *Divine Names*, we have considered the meaning, as concerning God, of the titles of Good, of Being, of Life, of Wisdom, of Power, and of such other names as are applied to him [*Divine Names*, chapters 4–8]. Further, in the *Symbolic Theology* [another lost work] we have considered what are the metaphorical titles drawn from the world of sense and applied to the nature of God; what is meant by the material and intellectual images we form of him, or the functions and instruments of activity attributed to him; what are the places where he dwells and the raiment in which he is adorned; what is meant by God's anger, grief, and indignation, or the divine inebriation; what is meant by God's oaths and threats, by his slumber and waking; and all sacred and symbolical representations. And it will be observed how far more copious and diffused are the last terms than the first, for the *Theological Outlines* and the discussion of the divine names are necessarily more brief than the *Symbolic Theology*.

For the higher we soar, the more limited become our expressions of that which is purely intelligible; even as now, when plunging into the darkness which is above the intellect, we pass not merely into brevity of speech, but even into absolute silence, of thoughts as well as of words. Thus, in the former discourse, our thoughts descended from the highest to the lowest, embracing an ever-widening number of conceptions, which increased at each stage of the descent; but in the present discourse we mount upward from below to that which is the highest, and, according to the degree of transcendence, so our speech is restrained until, the entire ascent being accomplished, we become wholly voiceless, inasmuch as we are absorbed in him who is totally ineffable. But why, you may ask, does the affirmative method begin from the highest attributions, and the negative method with the lowest abstractions? The reason is that, when affirming the subsistence of that which transcends all affirmation, we necessarily start from the attributes most closely related to it and upon which the remaining affirmations depend; but when pursuing the negative method to reach that which is beyond all abstraction, we must begin by applying our negations to things which are most remote from it. For is it not more true to affirm that God is life and goodness than that he is air or stone; and must we not deny to him more emphatically the attributes of inebriation and wrath than the applications of human speech and thought?

CHAPTER 4.
THE PREEMINENT CAUSE OF ALL THAT IS SENSIBLE IS NOT HIMSELF SENSIBLE

We therefore maintain that the universal and transcendent Cause of all things is neither without being nor without life, nor without reason or intelligence; nor is he a body, nor has he form or shape, quality, quantity, or weight; nor has he any localized, visible, or tangible existence; he is not sensible or perceptible; nor is he subject to any disorder or disturbance, nor influenced by any earthly passion; neither is he rendered impotent through the effects of material causes and events; he needs no light; he suffers no change, corruption, division, privation, or flux; none of these things can either be identified with or attributed to him.

CHAPTER 5.
THE PREEMINENT CAUSE OF
ALL THINGS INTELLIGIBLE IS NOT
HIMSELF INTELLIGIBLE

Again, ascending yet higher, we maintain that he is neither soul nor intellect; nor has he imagination, opinion, speech, or understanding; nor can he be expressed or conceived, since he is neither number nor order; nor greatness nor smallness; nor equality nor inequality; nor similarity nor dissimilarity; neither is he immovable, nor moving, nor at rest; neither has he power nor is power, nor is he light; neither does he live nor is he life; neither is he essence, nor eternity nor time; nor is he subject to intelligible contact; nor is he knowledge nor truth, nor kingship, nor wisdom; neither one nor oneness, nor divinity nor goodness; nor is he Spirit according to our understanding, nor Filiation nor Paternity; nor anything else known to us or to any other beings of the things that are or the things that are not; neither does anything that is know him as he is; nor does he know existing things according to existing knowledge; neither can the reason attain to him, nor name him, nor know him; neither is he darkness nor light, nor the false nor the true; nor can any affirmation or negation be applied to him, for although we may affirm or deny the things below him, we can neither affirm nor deny him, inasmuch as the all-perfect and unique Cause of all things transcends all affirmation, and the simple preeminence of his absolute nature is outside of every negation—free from every limitation and beyond them all.

Adapted and corrected from the anonymous translation found in *The Mystical Theology and the Celestial Hierarchies of Dionysius the Areopagite,* translated from the Greek with commentaries by the editors of The Shrine of Wisdom and Poem by St. John of the Cross (Nr. Godlaming, Surrey: The Shrine of Wisdom, 1923), 9–16.

2.

FRANCIS OF ASSISI
TWO SONGS OF PRAISE

Francis of Assisi (circa 1181–1226) ranks among the most famous Christian mystics, at least on the strength of his reception of the stigmata, or wounds of Jesus (see section 7.2). But to what extent do Francis's own writings support viewing him as a mystic? Francis was not a literary person, though he could read and with help express himself in a form of Latin close to his Italian vernacular. His works are deceptively simple. Modern study, however, has shown that Francis had a deep (it has been called "archaic") theology, rooted in the Bible, and the liturgy, as well as in his attempt to live the Gospel without compromise.

Among Francis' writings, some of his songs provide the best access to his sense of God's presence in the world and in his own life. "The Canticle of Brother Sun" (his only vernacular work), written about 1225, is the best example. This hymn to God's presence "with" and "in" the different elements of creation has deep biblical roots, but also expresses an original perspective on finding God in creation (an "enfraternization" of the cosmos, as it has been called). Less well known is the Latin poem "The Praises of God Most High." Tradition has it that Francis composed this hymn on the occasion of his reception of the stigmata in 1224. The hymn is a pastiche of biblical texts, but for that reason it is all the more revelatory of how Francis discovered that the God of the Bible was the God who had come into his own soul.

I.

THE CANTICLE OF BROTHER SUN

Most High Omnipotent Good Lord,
   yours are the praises, the glory, the honor, and all blessing.
To you alone, Most High, do they belong,
   and no one is worthy to mention your name.
Praise be to you, my Lord, with all your creatures,
   especially Lord Brother Sun,
   who is the day and through whom you enlighten us,
And he is most beautiful and shining with great splendor;
   And bears likeness of you, Most High.
Praise be to you, my Lord, through Sister Moon and the stars,
   in heaven you formed them, shining and precious and beautiful.
Praise be to you, my Lord, through Brother Wind,
   and through air, both cloudy and clear, and all weather,
   through which you give sustenance to your creatures.
Praise be to you, my Lord, through Sister Water;
   she is very useful and humble and precious and chaste.
Praise be to you, my Lord, though Brother Fire,
   through whom you enlighten the night,
   and he is beautiful and joyful and robust and strong.
Praise be to you, my Lord, through our Sister Mother Earth,
   who sustains and rules us,
   and produces different fruits with colored flowers and herbs.
Praise be to you, my Lord, through those who give pardon for your love,
   and who bear infirmity and tribulation.
Blessed are those who endure in peace,
   they will be crowned by you, Most High.
Praise be to you, my Lord, through our Sister Bodily Death,
   from whom no living person escapes.
   Woe to those who die in mortal sin;
   blessed are those who find themselves in your most holy will,
   for the second death will not do them evil.
Praise and blessing to you, my Lord,
   and thanks and service with great humility.

II.
THE PRAISES OF GOD MOST HIGH

You are the Holy Lord God who alone does wonders;
You are strong, you are great, you are most high.
You are powerful, you, Holy Father, King of heaven and earth,
You are three and one, the Lord God of gods.
You are the good, the whole good, the highest good.
Lord God, living and true.
You are Charity; you are Wisdom, you are Humility;
You are Patience, you are Security;
You are Repose, you are Joy and Gladness;
You are Justice and Temperance.
You are overflowing Richness;
You are Beauty, you are Meekness;
You are the Protector, the Guardian, the Defender,
You are the Strength, you are the Refuge;
You are the Hope; you are the Faith; you are the Love.
You are our entire Delight.

Translated by Bernard McGinn from *Fontes Franciscani,* edited by Enrico Menestò and Stefano Brufani (Assisi: Edizioni Porziuncola, 1995), 39–40, 45–48.

3.

THE GRANUM SINAPIS: POEM AND COMMENTARY

"The Granum Sinapis" ("mustard seed"; see Mt 13:31) is a Middle High German poem in the form of a Latin liturgical sequence. The poem's eight strophes are of a deeply Eckhartian nature. The first three summarize Eckhart's teaching on the Trinity: the procession of the Son from the Father; the flowing forth of the Holy Spirit from both; and the divine mystery. The next three strophes present intellect as the power that leads up the divine mountain and out in the depths of the divine desert, or wasteland, where opposites coincide. The final two strophes invite the reader to appropriate the meaning of the mystery through detachment and annihilation, first in the second person and then in a self-address. Could Eckhart himself have been the author? Scholars are divided on this issue, but no one questions that the poem is a masterpiece.

"The Granum Sinapis" is also unusual in that in a number of manuscripts it is accompanied by a Latin commentary explaining the dense images through the citation of mystical authorities. The commentary is certainly not by Eckhart, but was probably written by a follower of the Dominican who was interested in explaining and defending him, probably after his condemnation in 1329 (see section 14.3). The comment makes use of the usual authorities, such as Dionysius and Thomas Aquinas, and also some unexpected ones, like John Scotus Eriugena and Thomas Gallus, the Dionysian commentator whose affective interpretation of the writings of Dionysius was quite different from Eckhart's. What follows is a version of the poem, as well as two selections from the commentary, the longer dealing with the divine desert, a mystical symbol used by both Eckhart and Gal-

lus. *(The letters in the first strophe of the translation indicate the rhyming structure, which I have not tried to imitate in English.)*

I.

THE SEQUENCE "THE GRANUM SINAPIS"

1. In the Beginning (a)   High over understanding (a)
The Word always is. (b)   O rich treasure, (b)
Where the Beginning always gave birth to the Beginning! (c)
O Father's heart, (d)   From whose delight (d)
The Word always flows! (e)   Yet the breast (e)
Holds on to the Word within—truly. (c)
2. One flood from both,   A glowing Love,
The bond of both,   Known to both,
Flows the all-sweet Spirit,
Equal in all things,   Undivided.
The three are one.   Do you grasp it? No!
It alone understands what it is.
3. The threefold clasp   Is deep and fearful,
The circle's span   Cannot be comprehended:
Here is a bottomless depth.
Check and mate   To time, forms, place!
The wondrous ring   Is gushing forth,
Its central point is immovable.
4. The mountain of this point   Ascend without activity,
Intellect!   The way leads you out
Into a wondrous wasteland,
So deep, so wide,   It extends without limit.
The wasteland possesses   Neither time nor place,
Its mode of being is unique.
5. The wasteland that is Goodness   No foot has trod.
Created understanding   Never enters there.
It exists and no one knows how.
It is here, it is there;   It is far, it is near;
It is deep, it is high;   It exists in such a way
That it is neither this nor that.
6. It is light, it is bright;   It is completely dark;
It is unnamed;   It is unknown,
Without beginning and also free of ending.

It goes forth out of silence,   Empty, unclothed.
Who knows its dwelling?   Let him come forth
And tell us what its form may be.
7. Become like a child,   Become deaf, become blind!
Your own something   Must become nothing.
Drive away all something, all nothing!
Leave place, leave time,   Avoid images too!
Go out without any path   On the narrow way,
And then you will find the wasteland's hint.
8. O soul of mine   Come out, God in!
Sink all my something   Into God's Nothing,
Sink down in the bottomless flood!
If I flee from you,   Then you will come to me.
If I lose myself,   Then I will find you,
O Superessential Goodness!

II.
THE LATIN COMMENTARY

[The first selection is a brief part from the prologue on the name and content of the poem; the second is the commentary on strophe 4.]

(1) The Content Begins. Just as "the mustard seed, small in substance, great in power" is a healthy antidote for many ills, so too the content of this small book, although it does not have a great quantity of words, is endowed by the power of supercelestial things to provide devout souls with remedies against vices. . . .

The first strophe sets down the inseparable procession of the Only-Begotten from the Unbegotten; the second strophe the emanation of Divine Love and the union of the three persons. The third strophe declares that this union surpasses created perception and understanding, comparing it to a sphere whose center is immobile. The fourth strophe says how this center may be known and that knowledge of it leads into the wondrous solitude. The fifth says that this solitude is incomprehensible and does not belong to what exists. The sixth sets down that the solitude is both bright and dark, unmoved and without disposition. The seventh strophe commands that cognitive perception and intellect be left behind, as well as all that exists. In the eighth the author bids his soul lose itself so that it may go forth into God.

(2) ... In the above strophe 3 there was a discussion of the mystical circle and its superunknown point. Here he teaches how we come to know it, dividing the treatment into two parts: In the first, he says how the point's height is to be climbed when everything that perception or intellect understands has been removed; in the second, he shows where this height leads, when he says "The way leads you out." This also is in two parts: In the first he says that the height leads into a kind of mystical desert; in the second he describes the desert, when he says, "So deep, so wide."

He says, "the mountain of this point," just as if he were agreeing with St. Dionysius, who says in *Mystical Theology*, chapter 1.1: "Concerning the mystical sight" of this point, "leave behind with a strong effort senses and intellectual operations, and all sensibles and intelligibles, and all existing and nonexisting things, and, insofar as possible, rise up unknowingly to union with him who is above every substance and knowledge." Whoever sets his heart on these ascensions necessarily must "take up eagle's wings" (Is 40:31), and "make perfect his feet like those of the deer" (Ps 17:34), and firmly fix his footsteps "above the heights" of this mountain, "establishing" himself in the sublime and unitive contemplations of the divine mind. It is necessary that those ascending to divine uniting with the superlucent and unknown darkness, where he truly dwells who is over all things, surpass the truly superexcelling eminence of this point and its high places.

There follows: "The way leads you out." Here he shows where the point's height leads, declaring that it leads into a wondrous and solitary desert, to the solitude of the wholly supersubstantial and inscrutable divine majesty of the Trinity, which is truly abandoned and impenetrable in that it is unique and totally hidden from every creature. No one is allowed to have knowledge of it as it is in itself, because "No one ever saw or will see God" (Jn 1:18). A journey is made unto the Trinity "through the paths of the three eternal days" (Jon 3:3), by the intellectible footsteps of knowing and loving, until, when all impediments have been removed, the contemplative mind is lifted up to the superunitive simplicity and supersimple unitivity of this point.

Then follows the third part of this strophe, which describes the mystical desert as "So deep, so wide, etc." This declares that the breadth and size of this desert is immense, lacking time and place. This was also spoken about in the former strophe. It is true, however, that here the treatment concerns the breadth and extension of the mystical desert, because it is like the crossroad where the threefold path of the divine persons reaches out into the simplicity of the unity and the unity of the simplicity of the divine existence. There is also an exposition of how the divine existence itself, although abandoned and forsaken by every act of understanding and knowing insofar as it is inaccessible to all, "enlarges" itself and extends itself out to all things. "All existing things participate in this existence," because "the existence of all things," according to Dionysius, "is the superexistence of divinity" [*Celestial Hierarchy* 4]. Therefore, Hugh of St. Victor says: "The very one and the same self-existing divine nature, insofar as its effect, and power, and operation are concerned, is the principle for all the subsisting beings and essences and natures created by it; they receive existence from it, and it is the essence of all the things that subsist in it" [*Commentary on the Celestial Hierarchy,* chapter 5]. According to Dionysius, "It belongs to the cause of all things to call to communion with it all that exists, so that each of them may be defined by its proper analogy [to God]" [*Celestial Hierarchy* 4].

But it may be asked how God or the divine existence can be "the existence of all things," so that it diffuses itself so far and wide that it touches all things, whether causally, or formally, or in both modes at the same time. . . . Because every form of existence, when compared with the divine existence, comes out as derivative and lacking, one can say that the divine existence names all things. All things came to be through the divine existence, which nonetheless does not inhere in things since it is totally unmixed with things. Therefore, with regard to the solitude and singularity of this desert which is the superintelligibility of the divine existence, it is truly said that "Its mode of being is unique," insofar as it is the superexistence that gives all things existence.

Translated by Bernard McGinn from the edition of Maria Bindschedler, *Der lateinische Kommentar zum Granum Sinapis* (Basel: Benno Schwabe, 1949), 38–40 for the poem, 34–36 and 86–90 for the commentary. © Schwabe AG Verlag, Steinentorstrasse 13, CH-4010 Basel.

4.

ENGLISH POETS ON GOD IN NATURE

The relation between mysticism and poetry is not as strong in the Christian tradition as it is in Islam, though a number of mystics have turned to poetry as a way of trying to convey what is beyond description but can be suggested, or pointed to, in human words. In the thirteenth and fourteenth centuries several mystics used poetry along with prose to express their love for God. Examples can be found in Hadewijch, Mechthild, Marguerite Porete, and Richard Rolle. In the case of the Franciscan Jacopone da Todi (circa 1236–1306), we have a mystic whose message was put forth solely through the medium of his moving vernacular poems "The Lauds." Among the sixteenth-century Spanish mystics, we find perhaps the premier mystical poet of the Christian tradition in John of the Cross, as well as other distinguished poet-mystics, such as Luis de León (1527–91). In seventeenth-century France the blind Carmelite John of St. Samson (1571–1636) stands out as a mystical poet (Madame Guyon and François Fénelon also wrote poetry, but not of a distinguished character).

Some mystical poems, such as "The Granum Sinapis" sequence presented in the last selection, use poetry to convey the stripping away of images and language of the apophatic way to God, but it has been more customary to employ poetry to present a sense of the cataphatic, or positive, presence of God in and through the created universe, and also through humans created in God's image and likeness. English religious poets have been particularly insightful, as William Blake once put it, for their ability to see "a World in a grain of sand, And a Heaven in a wild flower" ("Auguries of Innocence"). The following five lyrics come from five different poets over three centuries—two Anglican, two Catholic, and one (Blake) a great independent. Some of these poems are simple and direct; others, more complex. They are not of equal poetic merit, though they address the same goal.

I.
GEORGE HERBERT (1593–1632)

THE ELIXER

Teach me, my God and King,
In all things Thee to see,
And what I do in any thing
To do it as for Thee.

Not rudely, as a beast,
To runne into an action;
But still to make Thee prepossest,
And give it his perfection.

A man that looks on glasse,
On it may stay his eye;
Or if he pleaseth, through it passe,
And then the heav'n espie.

All may of Thee partake:
Nothing can be so mean
Which with his tincture, "for Thy sake,"
Will not grow bright and clean.

A servant with this clause
Makes drudgerie divine;
Who sweeps a room as for Thy laws
Makes that and th' action fine.

This is the famous stone
That turneth all to gold;
For that which God doth touch and own
Cannot for lesse be told.

II.
THOMAS TRAHERNE (1636–74)

THE RAPTURE

Sweet Infancy!
O fire of heaven! O sacred Light
How fair and bright,
How great am I,
Whom all the world doth magnify!

O Heavenly Joy!
O great and sacred blessedness
Which I possess!
So great a joy
Who did into my arms convey?

From God above
Being sent, the Heavens me enflame:
To praise his Name
The stars do move!
The burning sun doth shew His love.

O how divine
Am I! To all this sacred wealth,
This life and health,
Who raised? Who mine
Did make the same? What hand divine?

III.
WILLIAM BLAKE (1757–1827)

THE DIVINE IMAGE

To Mercy, Pity, Peace, and Love
All pray in their distress;
And to these virtues of delight
Return their thankfulness.

For Mercy, Pity, Peace, and Love
Is God, our Father dear,
And Mercy, Pity, Peace, and Love
Is man, His child and care.

For Mercy has a human heart,
Pity a human face,
And Love, the human form divine,
And Peace, the human dress.

Then every man, of every clime,
That prays in his distress,
Prays to the human form divine,
Love, Mercy, Pity, Peace.
And all must love the human form,
In heathen, Turk, or Jew;
Where Mercy, Love, and Pity dwell
There God is dwelling too.

IV.

GERARD MANLEY HOPKINS (1844–89)

GOD'S GRANDEUR

The world is charged with the grandeur of God.
It will flame out, like shining from shook foil,
It gathers to a greatness like the ooze of oil
Crushed. Why do men then now not reck His rod?
Generations have trod, have trod, have trod;
And all is seared with trade; bleared, smeared with toil;
And bears man's smudge, and shares man's smell; the soil
Is bare now, nor can foot feel being shod.
And for all this, nature is never spent;
There lives the dearest freshness deep down things;
And though the last lights from the black west went,
Oh, morning at the brown brink eastwards springs—
Because the Holy Ghost over the bent
World broods with warm breast, and with, ah, bright wings.

V.

JOSEPH MARY PLUNKETT (1887–1916)

I SEE HIS BLOOD UPON THE ROSE

I see his blood upon the rose
And in the stars the glory of his eyes,
His body gleams amid eternal snows,
His tears fall from the skies.

I see his face in every flower;
The thunder and the singing of the birds
Are but his voice—and carven by his power
Rocks are his written words.

All pathways by his feet are worn,
His strong heart stirs the ever-beating sea,
His crown of thorns is twined with every thorn,
His cross is every tree.

From *The Oxford Book of English Mystical Verse,* chosen by D.H.S. Nicholson and
A.H.E. Lee (Oxford: At the Clarendon Press, 1st ed., 1917).

PIERRE TEILHARD DE CHARDIN
HYMN OF THE UNIVERSE

The Jesuit scientist and writer Pierre Teilhard de Chardin was born in France in 1881 and died in New York, fittingly on Easter Sunday, 1955. After his theological studies, he was trained in geology and paleontology. Teilhard made his first trip to China in 1923–24; he returned several times for extended periods, teaching and excavating. He spent World War II in Beijing, and then returned to France for a time (1946–51) before ending his days in the United States. Teilhard achieved fame as a paleontologist due to his role in the discovery of the early hominid known as Peking man (1928–29). His reputation as a thinker and writer came later, as he worked over his major texts for several decades. Teilhard's desire to show the harmony between evolution and Christian faith was set forth in The Phenomenon of Man. *The work was finished in 1940, but Teilhard's challenging views aroused suspicion among some Jesuits and in the Roman curia. He was denied permission to publish this and other works. It was only after his death that his writings began to appear.*

Teilhard was many things—not least a mystic. Indeed, the inner vision that unifies his many endeavors was a mystical sense of God's presence in the created cosmos and the role of divine energy in the evolutionary process aimed toward what he called the "Omega point," or "the Prime Mover ahead." Teilhard's conviction about the divine presence in matter marks him as one of the most original Christian cosmic mystics, but, as the following excerpts show, his mysticism is also deeply trinitarian, Christological, and eucharistic. For the French Jesuit the meaning of the universe is found in the taking on of flesh by the Word of God so that, as he once put it: "Jesus on the Cross is both the symbol and the reality of the immense labor of the centuries which has, little by little, raised up the created spirit and brought it back to the depths of the divine milieu." Other aspects of his mystical vision are illustrated in the excerpts given here, such as the need to integrate the positive forces of nature (what he elsewhere called the divinization of activities, in this text equated with the eucharistic Body of Christ) with the negative, or deathly forces (the divinization of passivities, symbolized by Christ's Blood). The origin of the following meditation goes back to an incident in 1923 when, on the Feast of the Transfiguration (August 6), Teilhard found himself on an expedition in the Ordos desert without the bread and wine necessary to celebrate the Eucharist (the work was not published until 1961).

THE MASS ON THE WORLD

The Offering

Since once again, Lord—though this time not in the forests of the Aisne but in the steppes of Asia—I have neither bread, nor wine, nor altar, I will raise myself beyond these symbols, up to the pure majesty of the real itself; I, your priest, will make the whole earth my altar and on it will offer you all the strivings and sufferings of the world.

Over there, on the horizon, the sun has just touched with light the outermost fringe of the eastern sky. Once again, beneath this moving sheet of fire, the living surface of the earth wakes and trembles, and once again begins its fearful travail. I will place on my paten, O God, the harvest to be won by this renewal of labor. Into my chalice I shall pour all the sap which is to be pressed out this day from the earth's fruits.

My paten and my chalice are the depths of a soul laid widely open to all the forces which in a moment will rise up from every corner of the earth and converge upon the Spirit. Grant me the remembrance and the mystic presence of all those whom the light is now awakening to the new day.

One by one, Lord, I see and I love all those whom you have given me to sustain and charm my life. One by one also I number all those who make up that other beloved family which has gradually surrounded me, its unity fashioned out of the most disparate elements, with affinities of the heart, of scientific research and of thought. And again one by one—more vaguely it is true, yet all-inclusively—I call before me the whole vast anonymous army of living humanity; those who surround me and support me though I do not know them; those who come, and those who go; above all, those who in office, laboratory and factory, through their vision of truth or despite their error, truly believe in the progress of earthly reality and who today will take up again their impassioned pursuit of the light.

This restless multitude, confused or orderly, the immensity of which terrifies us; this ocean of humanity whose slow, monotonous wave-flows trouble the hearts even of those whose faith is most firm: it is to this deep that I thus desire all the fibers of my being should respond. All the things in the world to which this day will bring increase; all those that will diminish; all those too that will die: all of them, Lord, I try to gather into my arms, so as to hold them out to you in offering. This is the material of my sacrifice; the only material you desire.

Once upon a time men took into your temple the first fruits of their harvests, the flower of their flocks. But the offering you really want, the offering you mysteriously need every day to appease your hunger, to slake your thirst is nothing less than the growth of the world borne ever onwards in the stream of universal becoming.

Receive, O Lord, this all-embracing host which your whole creation, moved by your magnetism, offers you at this dawn of a new day.

This bread, our toil, is of itself, I know, but an immense fragmentation; this wine, our pain, is no more, I know, than a draught that dissolves. Yet in the very depths of this formless mass you have implanted—and this I am sure of, for I sense it—a desire, irresistible, hallowing, which makes us cry out, believer and unbeliever alike: "Lord, make us *one*."

Because, my God, though I lack the soul-zeal and the sublime integrity of your saints, I yet have received from you an overwhelming sympathy for all that stirs within the dark mass of matter; because I know myself to be irremediably less a child of heaven than a son of earth; therefore I will this morning climb up in spirit to the high places, bearing with me the hopes and the miseries of my mother; and there—empowered by that priesthood which you alone (as I firmly believe) have bestowed on me—upon all that in the world of human flesh is now about to be born or to die beneath the rising sun I will call down the Fire.

Fire over the Earth

Fire, the source of being: we cling so tenaciously to the illusion that fire comes forth from the depths of the earth and that its flames grow progressively brighter as it pours along the radiant furrows of life's tillage. Lord, in your mercy you gave me to see that this idea is false, and that I must overthrow it if I were ever to have sight of you.

In the beginning was *Power*, intelligent, loving, energizing. In the beginning was the *Word,* supremely capable of mastering and molding whatever might come into being in the world of matter. In the beginning there were not coldness and darkness: there was the *Fire.* This is the truth.

So, far from light emerging gradually out of the womb of our darkness, it is the Light, existing before all else was made which, patiently, surely, eliminates our darkness. As for us creatures, of ourselves we are but emptiness and obscurity. But you, my God, are the inmost depths, the stability of that eternal *milieu,* without duration or space, in which our cosmos emerges gradually into being and grows gradually to its final completeness, as it loses those boundaries which to our eyes seem so immense. Everything is being; everywhere there is being and nothing but being, save in the fragmentation of creatures and the clash of their atoms.

Blazing Spirit, Fire, personal, super-substantial, the consummation of a union so immeasurably more lovely and more desirable than that destructive fusion of which all the pantheists dream: be pleased yet once again to come down and breathe a soul into the newly formed, fragile film of matter with which this day the world is to be freshly clothed.

I know we cannot forestall, still less dictate to you, even the smallest of your actions; from you alone comes all initiative—and this applies in the first place to my prayer.

Radiant Word, blazing Power, you who mould the manifold so as to breathe your life into it; I pray you, lay on us those your hands—powerful, considerate, omnipresent, those hands which do not (like our human hands) touch now here, now there, but which plunge into the depths and the totality, present and past, of things so as to reach us simultaneously through all that is most immense and most inward within us and around us.

May the might of those invincible hands direct and transfigure for the great world you have in mind that earthly travail which I have gathered into my heart and now offer you in its entirety. Remould it, rectify it, recast it down to the depths from whence it springs. You know how your creatures can come into being only, like shoot from stem, as part of an endlessly renewed process of evolution.

Do you now therefore, speaking through my lips, pronounce over this earthly travail your twofold efficacious word: the word without which all that our wisdom and our experience have built up must totter and crumble—the word through which all our most far-reaching speculations and our encounter with the universe are come together into a unity. Over every living thing which is to spring up, to grow, to flower, to ripen during this day say again the words: This is my Body. And over every death-force which waits in readiness to corrode, to wither, to cut down, speak again your commanding words which express the supreme mystery of faith: This is my Blood.

Fire in the Earth

... At this moment when your life has just poured with superabundant vigor into the sacrament of the world, I shall savor with heightened consciousness the intense yet tranquil rapture of a vision whose coherence and harmonies I can never exhaust.

What I experience as I stand in face of—and in the very depths of—this world which your flesh has assimilated, this world which has become your flesh, my God, is not the absorption of the monist who yearns to be dissolved into the unity of things, nor the emotion felt by the pagan as he lies prostrate before a tangible divinity, nor yet the passive self-abandonment of the quietist tossed hither and thither at the mercy of mystical impulses. From each of these modes of thought I take something of their motive force while avoiding their pitfalls: the approach determined for me by your omnipresence is a wonderful synthesis wherein three of the most formidable passions that can unlock the human heart rectify each other as they mingle: like the monist I plunge into the all-inclusive One; but the One is so perfect that as it receives me and I lose myself in it I can find in it the ultimate perfection of my own individuality;

—like the pagan I worship a God who can be touched; and I do indeed touch him—this God—over the whole surface and in the depths of that world of matter which confines me: but to take hold of him as I would wish (simply in order not to stop touching him), I must go always on and on through and beyond each undertaking, unable to rest in anything, borne onwards at each moment by creatures and at each moment going beyond them, in a continuing welcoming of them and a continuing detachment from them;

—like the quietist I allow myself with delight to be cradled in the divine fantasy: but at the same time I know that the divine will, will only be revealed to me at each moment if I exert myself to the utmost: I shall only touch God in the world of matter, when, like Jacob, I have been vanquished by him.

Thus, because the ultimate objective, the totality to which my nature is attuned has been made manifest to me, the powers of my being begin spontaneously to vibrate in accord with a single note of incredible richness wherein I can distinguish the most discordant tendencies effortlessly resolved: the excitement of action and the delight of passivity: the joy of possessing and the thrill of reaching out beyond what one possesses; the pride in growing and the happiness of being lost in what is greater than oneself.

Rich with the sap of the world, I rise up towards the Spirit whose vesture is the magnificence of the material universe but who smiles at me from far beyond all victories; and, lost in the mystery of the flesh of God, I cannot tell which is the more radiant bliss: to have found the Word and so be able to achieve the mastery of matter, or to have mastered matter and so be able to attain and submit to the light of God.

Pierre Teilhard de Chardin, *Hymn of the Universe,* translated by Simon Bartholomew (New York and Evanston: Harper & Row, 1965), 19–23, 26–27. From *Hymne de l'universe* by Pierre Teilhard de Chardin. Éditions du Seuil, 1961.

VISION, CONTEMPLATION, AND RAPTURE

What can it mean to see God? In many ancient religions this was not a problem, because the gods were conceived of as taking animal or human forms and as being present in cult images. But in the centuries before Christ the possibility of seeing the real God had been attacked both by Jewish prophets and Greek philosophers. Nevertheless different layers in the Hebrew Bible and the New Testament present contradictory views on seeing God, at least in this life. God tells Moses (Ex 33:20), "You cannot see my face, for no one will see my face and live"; but in Genesis 32:30, Jacob who becomes Israel ("he who sees God") announces, "I have seen God face to face and my soul has been saved." In the beatitudes Jesus says, "Blessed are the pure of heart for they shall see God" (Mt 5:8), but the prologue of John's Gospel declares, "No one has ever seen God; the Only Begotten Son of God, who is in the Father's bosom, has revealed him" (Jn 1:18). Texts from the Pauline and Johannine letters stress the difference between vision here and now and the eschatological vision to come in heaven. Foremost among these is 1 Corinthians 13:12: "We see now mysteriously through a mirror, but then face to face; now I know in part; then I will know as I am known" (see 1 Jn 3:2).

Despite these divergent views, early Christian texts are replete with visionary narratives. From the second century on, we also find increasing emphasis on the contemplative vision of God (*theôria theou*) as the ultimate goal of the devout Christian. The Greek contemplative ideal behind such accounts goes back at least to Plato (circa 429–347 BCE), who taught that the soul's fulfillment was in the beatifying sight of the Absolute Good. In his *Symposium,* Plato has the seer Diotima describe how the true lover begins from love engendered by the sight of a beautiful body to gradually ascend to a momentary glimpse of the very Form of Beauty: "Turning towards the main ocean of the Beautiful, he may by contemplation of this bring forth in all their splendor many fair fruits of discourse and meditation in a plenteous crop of philosophy." In the second century CE Justin Martyr, describing his philosophical journey that ended in Christianity, says of his time as a Platonist, "I expected quite soon to look upon God, for this is the goal of Plato's philosophy." Justin became convinced, however, that while Plato was right about the goal, he was wrong about how to get there: Seeing God depends on the grace given by Christ.

Although visionary narratives have been part of Christianity from the outset, not all visions need be thought of as mystical. Stories of appearances of God and other celestial beings have served many purposes in Christian history, such as admonition, encouragement, instruction, as well as the direct and transformative contact with God that is properly mystical. Many Christian mystics have expressed their teaching through visionary accounts, as will be evident from selections 2, 3, 4, 5, 9, 10, and 11 in this section. Some mystics, Augustine prominent among them, sought to describe and classify the types of visions (selection 2); others analyzed the nature and forms of contemplative vision and explored how contemplation is related to the beatific vision of heaven (selection 6). Seeing or contemplating God has often been associated with extraordinary states of consciousness, periods of being "snatched away, or raptured" (Latin: *raptus*), or "standing outside oneself" (*ecstasis*), or being "outside or beyond the mind" (*excessus mentis*). These terms, all found in the Latin Bible, helped nourish belief that God could be experienced and/or seen and known in special modes of consciousness during this life (see selections 2, 3, 9, 10, 11, and especially 7). Despite the variety of uses of vision, contemplation, and ecstasy in the mystical tradition, there is an inner connection among these themes that the following selections are designed to reveal.

CONTEMPLATION IN THE FATHERS

Among the most powerful contributions of the Classical tradition to Christian mysticism was the introduction of the term contemplation *(theôria) as a favored way of expressing the vision of God promised in scripture. The word had already enjoyed a long development in Greek thought; in Christianity it was to have an even more lengthy and intricate history. Clement of Alexandria, a late-second-century convert, was among the most learned of the Fathers in Hellenic philosophy and culture; he was also the pioneer in introducing* contemplation *into Christian thought. Clement was not a systematic thinker, but he did explore some of the key issues involved in trying to understand what it means to gaze at, or contemplate, God. For Clement, "contemplation of God" was connected to two other essential themes: the saving knowledge* (gnôsis) *made available in Christ; and the state of perfect harmony* (apatheia) *that ascetic practice and contemplative vision are meant to grant in this life.*

Texts in John's Gospel (e.g., 1:18 and 14:8–9) insist that the only way to "see" the hidden divine Father is through his eternal Son, the Word, who became flesh in Jesus Christ. This element distinguishing Christian contemplation from purely philosophical forms came more and more to the fore among the Fathers, as seen in the passage from Origen's Commentary on John *given here. The patristic writers also wrestled with the paradox of how the invisible God allows himself to be in some way seen without ever being comprehended, or exhausted, by human gaze. A passage from Gregory of Nyssa's* Homilies on the Song of

Songs *shows how this issue was dealt with by one Eastern mystic (selection 8 below illustrates a later Western view).*

I.

CLEMENT OF ALEXANDRIA, STROMATEIS (MISCELLANIES)

(1) Stromateis 4.6.39

And since there are two paths of reaching the perfection of salvation, works and knowledge [*gnôsis*], he called the "pure in heart blessed, for they shall see God" (Mt 5:8). And if we really look to the truth of the matter, knowledge is the purification of the leading faculty of the soul and is a good activity. Some things accordingly are good in themselves, and others by participation in what is good, as we say good actions are good. But without things intermediate which hold the place of the material element, neither good nor bad actions are constituted, I mean such things as life, health, and other necessary things or circumstances. Therefore, he means those people are pure as respects corporeal lusts, and pure in respect to holy thoughts, who attain to the knowledge of God when the chief faculty of the soul has nothing adulterated to stand in the way of its power. When, therefore, he who partakes gnostically of this holy quality devotes himself to contemplation, communing in purity with the divine, he enters more closely into the state of impassable identity [*apatheia*], so as to no longer have science and possess knowledge, but to be science and knowledge.

From the *Ante-Nicene Fathers. Translations of the Writings of the Fathers Down to* A.D. *325,* edited by Alexander Roberts, DD, and James Donaldson, LLD (Buffalo: The Christian Literature Publishing Company, 1885–96), Vol. 1:416. Hereafter abbreviated as ANF.

(2) Stromateis 7.3.13

... I want to speak of the gnostic souls that surpass in the grandeur of contemplation the mode of life of each of the holy ranks among whom the blessed abodes of the gods are allotted by distribution, holy souls reckoned among the holy, transferred from the entire to the entire, reaching places better than the better places, embracing the divine contemplation not in mirrors or by means of mirrors (1 Cor 13:12), but in a transcendentally clear and absolutely pure insatiable vision that is the privilege of intensely loving souls, holding festival through endless ages, who are judged worthy to remain in the identity of their excellence through all ages. Such is the contemplation attainable by the pure of heart (Mt 5:8). This is the function of the gnostic who has been perfected, to have converse with God through the great High Priest (Heb 4:14), being made like the Lord to the measure of his capacity, in the whole service of God, which tends to the salvation of humanity through the care of the beneficence which has us as its object, on the one hand, and, on the other, through worship, through teaching, and through beneficence in deeds.

Adapted and corrected from the translation in ANF 1:526.

(3) Stromateis 7.10.56–57

This takes place whenever one hangs on to the Lord by faith, by knowledge, by love, and ascends along with him to where the God and guardian of our faith and love is. And so at last, because of the necessity for very great preparation and previous training in order to hear what is said, and for the composure of life, and for advancing intelligently to a point beyond the Law, knowledge is committed to those fit and selected for it. This leads us to the endless and perfect end, teaching us beforehand the kind of life that we shall lead according to God and with the gods [i.e., angels], after which we are free from all the punishment and penalty we undergo in consequence for our sins for salutary discipline. After this deliverance, the reward and honors are assigned to those who have become perfect, when they are done with purification and are free from all service, though it be holy service among the saints. Then, become pure of heart and near the Lord, there awaits them restoration and everlasting contemplation. They are called by the name "gods" (Ps 81:6), being destined to sit on the thrones of the other gods that have been first put in their places by the Savior. Knowledge is therefore quick in purifying and fit for that acceptable transformation to the better.

Hence it easily takes the soul to that which is akin to it, the divine and the holy, and by its own light it conveys humans through the mystical stages of advancement until it restores the pure of heart to the crowning place of rest, teaching them to gaze upon God face-to-face (1 Cor 13:12), with comprehensive knowledge. For in this consists the perfection of the gnostic soul, in its being with the Lord, where it is in immediate subjection to him, having risen above all purification and all service. . . .

Adapted and corrected from the translation in ANF 1:539.

II.
ORIGEN, *COMMENTARY ON JOHN*, BOOK 19.35–38

. . . The one who knows the Father ascends from the knowledge of the Son to knowledge of the Father, and the Father is not seen otherwise than by seeing the Son. "For," he says, "he who has seen me has seen the one who sent me" (Jn 14:9). . . .

And he who beholds Wisdom, which God created before the ages for his works (Prov 8:22), ascends from knowing Wisdom to Wisdom's Father. It is impossible, however, for the God of Wisdom to be apprehended apart from the leading of Wisdom. And you will say the same thing also about the truth. For one does not apprehend God or contemplate him, and afterwards apprehend the truth. First one apprehends the truth, so that in this way he may come to behold the essence, or the power and nature of God beyond essence.

And perhaps, just as in the temple there were certain steps by which one might enter the Holy of Holies, so the Only-Begotten of God is the whole of our steps. And, just as the first step is the lowest, and the next higher, and so on in order up to the highest, so our Savior is the whole of our steps. His humanity is the first lower step, as it were. When we set foot on it we proceed the whole way on the steps in accordance with those aspects that follow after his humanity. . . .

Translated by Ronald Heine, *Origen. Commentary on the Gospel According to John. Books 13–32* (Washington, DC: Catholic University Press, 1993), 175–76.

III.

GREGORY OF NYSSA, *HOMILIES ON THE SONG OF SONGS* 12

But as great and exalted as he was with such experiences, Moses still had an insatiable desire for more. He implored God to see him face to face, despite the fact that scripture already says that he had been allowed to speak with God face to face. But neither did his act of intimately speaking with God as a friend make him cease to desire more; rather, "If I have found favor before you, show me your face clearly" (Ex 33:11). And he who promised to grant this request said, "I have known you above all others" (Ex 33:17). God passed Moses by at the divine place in the rock shadowed over by his hand. Moses could hardly see God's back even after he had passed by (Ex 33:22–23). I believe that we are taught that the person desiring to see God can behold the desired one by always following him. The contemplation of God's face is a never ending journey toward him accomplished by following right behind the Word. Once the soul has risen through death and has been filled with myrrh, she places her hands on the door bolts by means of good works and hopes that the desired One will enter within (Song 5:5–6). The Bridegroom passes by and the bride exits; she no longer remains in the place where she had been, but touches the Word who leads her on.

Translated by Casimir McCambley, OCSO, *Saint Gregory of Nyssa. Commentary on the Song of Songs* (Brookline, Massachusetts: Hellenic College Press, 1987), 219.

2.

AUGUSTINE ON VISION AND RAPTURE

Augustine's Confessions *ranks among the masterworks of Christian literature. Composed circa 397–400, the book is a prayerful meditation on human nature in light of Augustine's life story (books 1–9), as remembered in the present (book 10) and illuminated through an interpretation of the Genesis account of creation (books 11–13). Augustine portrays one man as everyman, using his own story of sinful fall away from God and gradual conversion through the action of grace as a model for the meaning of human existence. The* Confessions *is a conversation that we are invited to overhear, as Augustine addresses his prayerful witness to God, who responds to him in the words of scripture (constituting about a third of the work).*

As a part of the ongoing conversion process, Augustine recounts several experiences of contact with God granted him during his time at Milan (386) and in Ostia (388). These narratives owe much to Augustine's reading of the pagan philosopher-mystic Plotinus, but they also reflect his own deepening awareness of God's action in his life. Book 7 recounts several brief visions of Divine Truth. Augustine emphasizes that these contemplations were imperfect because they were not rooted in Christ. More famous is the account from book 9 of the ascent to a "touching" of Divine Wisdom that he shared with his mother, Monica. The joint nature of this rapture, more an auditory and tactile experience than a visionary one, underlines Augustine's message that finding God is not a solipsistic affair, but is essentially ecclesiological, something given to believers as members of the church.

Later in life, in book 12 of his Literal Commentary on Genesis *(circa 415), Augustine took up vision and rapture more systematically, exploring the meaning of the paradise to which Paul was raptured in 2 Corinthians 12:2–4, and seeking to reconcile biblical prohibitions against seeing God in this life with the accounts of the visions ascribed to Moses and Paul. At this point the bishop advances a distinction of three forms of vision that was to have great influence on subsequent mysticism.*

I.

VISIONS OF GOD AT MILAN
(CONFESSIONS 7.10 AND 17–18)

(A) And so, admonished to return to myself, I entered into my inmost parts with you leading me on. I was able to do so because you had become my helper. I entered and saw with my soul's eye (such as it was) an unchanging Light above that same soul's eye, above my mind. It was not this common light that can be seen by all flesh, nor was it like a greater one of the same kind, as if this light should gleam forth more and more brightly and fill up everything with its greatness. It was not like this, but was different, very different from all these. It was not above my mind as oil floats above water, nor as heaven is above earth; but it was higher because it created me, and I was lower because I was something made. He who knows the truth knows that light, and he who knows it knows eternity. Love knows it. O Eternal Truth and True Love and Beloved Eternity! You are my God, to you I sigh day and night. When I first came to know you, "You lifted me up" (Ps 26:10) so that I might see that there was something to be seen but that I was not yet the one to see it. And you beat back the weakness of my gaze, powerfully blazing into me; and I trembled with love and dread. And I found myself to be far from you in the land of unlikeness, as I heard your voice from on high: "I am the food of the strong. Grow and you will eat of me. And you will not change me into yourself, like the food of your flesh; but you will be changed into me." . . .

(B) And I marveled that I now loved you, and no phantasm instead of you. And yet I did not merit to enjoy my God, but was transported to you by your beauty, and presently torn away from you by my own weight, sinking with grief into these inferior things. This weight was carnal custom. Yet was there a remembrance of you with me; nor did I any way doubt that there was one to whom I might cleave, but that I was not yet one who could cleave to you; for the body that is corrupted presses down the soul, and the earthly dwelling weighs down the mind that thinks upon many things (Wis 9:15). And I was most certain that your invisible things are clearly seen from the creation of the world, being understood by the things that are made, even your eternal power and Godhead (Rom 1:20). For, inquiring whence it was that I admired the beauty of bodies, whether celestial or terrestrial, and what supported me in judging correctly about mutable things and pronouncing, "This should be thus, this not"—inquiring, then, whence I so judged, seeing I did so judge, I had found the unchangeable and true eternity of Truth, above my changeable mind. And thus, by degrees, I passed from bodies to the soul, which makes use of the senses of the body to perceive; and thence to its inward faculty, to which the bodily senses represent outward things, and up to which reach the capabilities of beasts; and thence, again, I passed on to the reasoning faculty, to which whatever is received from the senses of the body is referred to be judged, which also, finding itself to be variable in me, raised itself up to its own intelligence, and from habit drew away my thoughts, withdrawing itself from the crowds of contradictory phantasms; that so it might find out that light by which it was besprinkled, when, without all doubting, it cried out that the unchangeable was to be preferred before the changeable; whence also it knew that unchangeable, which, unless it had in some way known, it could have had no sure ground for preferring it to the changeable. And thus, with the flash of a trembling glance, it arrived at That Which Is. And then I saw your invisible things understood by the things that are made (Rom 1:20). But I was not able to fix my gaze on it; and, my infirmity being beaten back, I was thrown again on my accustomed habits, carrying along with me nothing but a loving memory of it, and an appetite for what I had, as it were, smelled the odor of, but was not yet able to eat.

And I sought a way of acquiring strength sufficient to enjoy you; but I did not find it until I embraced that Mediator between God and man, the man Christ Jesus (1 Tim 2:5), who is over all, God blessed for ever (Rom 9:5), calling me, and saying, "I am the way, the truth, and the life" (Jn 14:6), and mingling that food which I was unable to receive with our flesh. For the Word was made flesh (Jn 1:14), so that your wisdom, by which you created all things, might provide milk for our infancy. For I did not grasp my Lord Jesus—I, though humbled, grasped not the humble One; nor did I know what lesson that infirmity of his would teach us. For your Word, the Eternal Truth, preeminent above the higher parts of your creation, raises up those that are subject to itself; but in this lower world built for itself a humble habitation of our clay, whereby he intended to abase from themselves such as would be subjected and bring them over unto himself, allaying their swelling, and fostering their love; to the end that they might go on no further in self-confidence, but rather should become weak, seeing before their feet the divinity weak by taking our coats of skins (Gen. 3:1), and wearied, might cast themselves down upon it, and it rising, might lift them up.

II.
THE RAPTURE AT OSTIA
(CONFESSIONS 9.10)

As the day now approached on which she [Monica] was to depart this life (which day you knew, we did not), it happened—you, as I believe, by your secret ways arranging it—that she and I stood alone, leaning in a certain window, from which the garden of the house we occupied at Ostia could be seen. At this place, removed from the crowd, we were resting ourselves for the voyage, after the fatigues of a long journey. We then were conversing alone very pleasantly; and, forgetting those things that are behind, and reaching forth to those things that are before (Phil 3:13), we were seeking between ourselves in the presence of the Truth, which you are, of what nature the eternal life of the saints would be, which eye has not seen, nor ear heard, neither has it entered into the heart of man (1 Cor 2:9). But yet we opened wide the mouth of our heart, after those supernal streams of your fountain, the fountain of life, which is with you (Ps 35:10); that being sprinkled with it according to our capacity, we might in some measure weigh so high a mystery.

And when our conversation had arrived at that point, that the very highest pleasure of the carnal senses, and that in the very brightest material light, seemed by reason of the sweetness of that life not only not worthy of comparison, but not even of mention, we, raising our-selves up with a more ardent affection toward the Selfsame (Ps 4:9), did gradually pass through all corporeal things, and even the heaven itself, whence sun, and moon, and stars shine upon the earth. Yes, we soared higher yet by inward musing, and discoursing, and admiring your works; and we came to our own minds, and went beyond them, that we might advance as high as that region of unfailing plenty, where you feed Israel forever with the food of truth (Ezek 34:14). There life is that Wisdom by whom all these things are made, both which have been, and which are to come. Wisdom is not made, but is as she has been, and so shall ever be. Rather, to have been and to be hereafter are not in her, but only to be, seeing she is eternal—for to have been and to be hereafter are not eternal. And while we were speaking like this, and straining after Wisdom, we slightly touched her with the whole ef-fort of our heart. And we sighed and there left bound the first fruits of the Spirit (Rom 8:23), and we returned to the noise of our own mouths where the word uttered has both beginning and end. And what is like your Word, our Lord, who remains in himself without becoming old and makes all things new? (Wis 7:27).

We continued to talk, saying: If to any person the tumult of the flesh were silenced—silenced the images of earth, waters, and air—silenced, too, the poles of heaven; yes, the very soul be silenced to her-self and go beyond herself by not thinking of herself—silenced be dreams and imaginary revelations, every tongue, and every sign, and whatsoever exists by passing away, since, if any could listen, all these say, "We did not create ourselves, but were created by him who lives forever." If, having uttered this, they now should be silenced, having only awakened our ears to him who created them, and he alone speak not by them, but by himself, that we may hear his word, not by fleshly tongue, nor angelic voice, nor sound of thunder, nor the obscurity of a similitude, but might hear him whom in these we love without them, it would be just as we now strained forward and with rapid thought touched on that Eternal Wisdom that remains over all. If this could be sustained, and other visions of a far different kind be withdrawn, and this one ravish, and absorb, and envelop its beholder amid these in-ward joys, so that his life might be eternally like that one moment of knowledge that we now sighed after, were not this to "Enter thou into the joy of Thy Lord"? (Mt 25:21). And when shall that be? When we shall all rise again; but all shall not be changed (1 Cor 15:51).

Such things was I saying, and if not after this manner and in these words, yet, Lord, you know that on that day when we were talking like this, this world with all its delights grew contemptible to us, even while we spoke. . . .

III.
THE THREE FORMS OF VISION
(*LITERAL COMMENTARY ON GENESIS* 12).

[Augustine's theory of the three forms of vision and the nature of rapture is presented in a detailed and digressive way in book 12. The following selections provide the gist of his thought.]

(A) Book 12.6.15

To see something not in an imaginative way, but properly, and not to see by means of a body, is to see by a form of seeing that surpasses all others. I will try to explain these kinds of seeing and their differences, insofar as God gives me aid. The three kinds of visions come together in the one precept that reads, "You shall love your neighbor as yourself" (Mt 22:39). One way is through the eyes by which the letters are seen; the second is through the human spirit by which we think about our neighbor, even when absent; the third is through a mental gaze by means of which love itself is beheld in an intellectual way. [These three modes of seeing—corporeal, spiritual, intellectual—are realized on both a natural and a supernatural register. The supernatural mode is when God directly provides new bodily forms, images, or truths to the visionary.]

(B) Book 12.12.25

When we are awake and not mentally separated from our bodily senses, we are in a state of corporeal vision and we distinguish it from the spiritual vision by means of which we think in an imaginative way of absent bodies, whether by remembering those we knew, or by somehow mentally forming in the spirit others that we have not known, even by arbitrary fancy ones that do not exist. We distinguish the bodies that we actually see and are present to our corporeal senses from all these images, so that we do not doubt that these are bodies and those are images of bodies. But it sometimes happens that by too much mental concentration, or due to some illness (as happens to those delirious with fever), or by the action of some spirit, good or bad, images of corporeal things are produced in the spirit in such a way that they are presented to the corporeal senses as if they were bodies, although we still remain attentive in our senses. In this way we see what are images of bodies in the spirit, just as we see real bodies by means of the body, so that at the same time we behold a present person with our eyes and an absent person with the eyes of the spirit. . . . But when the soul's intention is completely turned away or snatched away from the body's senses, then it is more usually called ecstasy. Then whatsoever kind of bodies are present are not seen, even with open eyes, nor are any voices heard. The soul's entire gaze is directed to images of bodies in its spiritual power, or through its intellectual power toward incorporeal things without any bodily form. . . .

(C) Book 12.26.53–54

For this reason there are times when the soul is raptured into things seen that are similar to bodies, but are beheld in the spirit in such a way that the soul is totally removed from the bodily senses, more than in sleep but less than in death. By divine warning and assistance the soul knows that she does not behold bodies, but things like bodies seen in a spiritual way, just as people sometimes know they are dreaming even before they awake. Even future things seen there in present images are recognized as future, either because the person's mind is assisted by God, or because there is someone present in the vision to explain the meaning, as in the case of John in the Apocalypse (Rev 1:10). This is a major revelation, even if the person to whom it is shown does not know whether he is out of the body, or is still in the body with his spirit seeing while removed from the senses (2 Cor 12:2). A person raptured in this way may not know this, if it is not manifested to him.

Furthermore, it is possible that a person may be raptured from the corporeal senses to be present amid the likenesses of bodies seen by the spirit in such a way that he is also raptured above them in order to be lifted up into the region of intellectual and intelligible realities where the plain truth is beheld without any bodily likeness. There no clouds of false opinions darken the scene, nor are the soul's virtues difficult and laborious. . . . There the one and total virtue is to love what you see and the greatest happiness is to have what you love. There the blessed life is imbibed at its source, and from that source something of it is sprinkled on this human life so that one can live with temperance, fortitude, justice, and prudence in the midst of the world's temptations.

For the sake of attaining this goal, where there will be secure rest and the ineffable vision of truth, we take on the work of restraining ourselves from pleasure, of bearing hardships, of helping those in need, and of resisting deceivers. There the brightness of the Lord will be seen, not through a vision signifying something else, either a bodily one like that seen on Mount Sinai (Ex 19:18), or a spiritual one such as that Isaiah saw (Is 6:1), or John in the Apocalypse; but through direct appearance, not through enigmatic vision, insofar as the human mind can grasp it with the aid of God's elevating grace, so that God speaks mouth-to-mouth to him who has been made worthy of such conversation—by the mouth of the mind, not of the body.

Translations: *Confessions* 7.10 is translated by Bernard McGinn from the text in PL 32:742; the other passages from *Confessions* 7 and 9 are adapted from the version of J. G. Pilkington in Whitney J. Oates, *Basic Writings of Saint Augustine* (New York: Random House, 1948), Vol. 1:104–6, 140–41. The translations from book 12 of *Literal Commentary on Genesis* are by Bernard McGinn from the text in PL 34:458–80.

GREGORY THE GREAT
DIALOGUES 2.35

The four books of Gregory the Great's Dialogues, *probably composed in the 590s, recount the lives and miracles of the holy men of sixth-century Italy. Their popular style and delight in the miraculous have led some critics to condemn them as an example of the new "vulgar Catholicism" of the Middle Ages, but they were popular both in the West and in translation in the Greek East. The second book of the work is devoted to Benedict of Nursia, the author of the* Rule for Monks *that became standard in the West in the ninth century. (Gregory mentions it briefly but tellingly: "He wrote a rule for monks that is remarkable for its discretion and its clearness of language.") Gregory gives a portrait of Benedict as archetypal holy man and monastic founder. As the only source for the life of the saint, Gregory's account became one of the most influential hagiographical works of the Latin tradition.*

*Toward the end of Benedict's life, Gregory recounts a number of visions granted to the saint. The one given here, which would have taken place in 541, is the most famous nonbiblical vision of the early Middle Ages. Gregory's account of Benedict's sight of the soul of Bishop Germanus of Capua ascending to heaven falls into two parts: a historical narration perhaps based on an oral tradition; and the pope's explanation of the deeper meaning of the event to his dialogue partner, Deacon Peter. The vision is the culminating point of the three stages of Benedict's life: separating himself from the world; living within himself as an anchorite; and his final years as a spiritual leader whom God raptures above himself (*rapitur super se*). The text fuses language taken from Stoic and Pla-*

tonic sources with a deep biblical teaching about contemplation. The interplay of inner and outer light, the notion of the expansion of the soul due to divine action, and the insistence on the limitation of all vision here below are hallmarks of Gregory's teaching on contemplation.

———

GREGORY. Before the night office began, when the man of God Benedict was standing at the window in prayer to Almighty God while the brethren were asleep, in the dead of night he suddenly gazed and saw light poured down from on high that cast away all the night's gloom and blazed forth with such splendor that this light illuminating the darkness would have surpassed daylight. A very marvelous thing followed that sight, because, as he himself later said, the whole world was brought before his eyes, gathered together, as it were, in one ray of light. As the venerable father fixed his gaze on this brilliant gleam of light, he saw the soul of Germanus the bishop of Capua carried into heaven in a fiery sphere by angels. Then, wanting to have a witness of so great a miracle, he called out for Deacon Servandus, two or three times repeating his name with a loud voice. When Servandus was aroused by the unaccustomed shout of the great man, he went up, looked, and just in time saw a small bit of the light. The man of God told him what had happened in detail as he stood in wonder at so great a miracle. And Benedict immediately ordered the devout Theoprobus to go to Cassino and to send a messenger the same night to the city of Capua to find out what had happened to Bishop Germanus and let us know. It was done, and the one who was sent discovered that the most reverend bishop was already dead, and, after asking more closely, he learned that he had died at the very same moment that the man of God had seen his ascent.

PETER. This is certainly a wonderful event; quite marvelous! But what was said about the whole world being brought before his eyes, as though gathered into one ray of light, I don't know how to take since I've never had such an experience. How is it possible that the whole world can be seen by one person?

GREGORY. Pay attention to what I say, Peter. To the soul that sees the Creator every creature is limited. To anyone who sees even a little of the light of the Creator everything created will become small, because in the very light of the inner vision the mind's core is opened up.

It is so expanded in God that it stands above the world. The soul of someone who sees in this way is even above itself. When the soul is raptured above itself in God's light, it is enlarged in its interior parts, and while it gazes upon what is beneath it, in its elevated state it comprehends how small something is that it could not grasp when it was in its lowly state. Therefore, the person who gazed upon the fiery sphere and also saw the angels returning to heaven without doubt could only do so in God's light. What wonder is it then if he also saw the world gathered together before him, since he was lifted up outside the world in the light of the mind? That the world is said to have been gathered together before his eyes is not because heaven and earth were made small, but because the intellectual soul of the person seeing was enlarged. A person who is raptured up in God can see everything that is beneath God without difficulty. In the light that shone upon his external eyes there was an interior light in the mind that showed the intellectual soul or the person seeing, because he had been rapt to higher things, just how limited everything beneath it really is.

Translated by Bernard McGinn from Gregory's *Vita Sancti Benedicti* (*Dialogi* II.35), in PL 66:198–200.

SYMEON THE NEW THEOLOGIAN
HYMN 18

Symeon the "New Theologian" (thus equated with John the Evangelist and John Chrysostom) was a monastic leader in Constantinople at the turn of the first millennium (see section 3.4). Symeon was famous for descriptions of his reception of the divine light. Although it was unusual for early mystics to speak of their own experiences, it is important to remember that Symeon grounded his personal accounts in a solid grasp of the patristic theology of divinization—"God became man, so that man might become God" (see section 12). Nevertheless, Symeon was a controversial figure in his day, not least due to his insistence that receiving the divine light was the mark of the true Christian and that such experiences provided mystics with authority in the church.

Symeon's theology of divine illumination made him a key figure in the development of Hesychast tradition in the Christian East—that is, the teaching that special forms of prayer, physical and mental, can lead to the vision of divine light. While Symeon's prose works are often polemical, his fifty-eight surviving hymns, written in the last decades of the tenth century, present the light experience in an evocative, personal way. The following excerpts from hymn 18 give some sense of a message that, though often repeated, never seems to become repetitious due to the power of Symeon's personal testimony.

TITLE: INSTRUCTION MINGLED WITH THEOLOGY ON THE OPERATIONS OF LOVE, WHICH IS NONE OTHER THAN THE LIGHT OF THE HOLY SPIRIT

Who will be able, O Master, to speak of you? Those who ignore you fail, for they know nothing at all and those who in their faith acknowledge your divinity are seized with great fear and remain stunned with fright and they do not know what to say because you are beyond our mind. Entirely incomprehensible, entirely imperceptible are your works, both your glory and the knowledge we have of you. That you are, we can know it, and your light, we see it, but what you are and of what kind, we are all ignorant of it. Nevertheless, we have the hope, we possess the faith, and we know the love that you gave us—boundless, indestructible, which nothing can contain—which is light, inaccessible light, light which operates everything. This light we name your hand, we call it your eye, your most holy mouth, your power, your glory. We recognize your face in it, more beautiful than everything. It is a sun inaccessible even to the most advanced in divine things. It is a star that always shines for those who cannot receive more of it.

[The next lines consider the effects of the divine light on those who receive it. Symeon then begins to speak in the first person.]

Possessing it, I do not see it, but I contemplate it when it goes away; I quickly dash to seize it and it completely flies away. I do not know what to do. I am enflamed and I learn to ask and in tears to seek with great humility and not to regard what goes beyond my nature as possible, or as an effect of my strength or of human zeal, but as the fruit of God's compassion and his infinite mercy. This light appears a short moment and withdraws, it banishes one passion from the heart, but only one. For a man cannot overcome his passions if the latter does not come to our assistance, and, moreover, it does not banish them all at once.

Psychically man indeed cannot suddenly receive the Spirit fully and become passionless, but when he will have achieved all that is in his power: the stripping, the indifference, the separation from one's family, the pruning of his will, the renunciation of the world, the endurance of trials, prayer, compunction, poverty, humility, with all the fortitude he can, then, dimly, like a delicate ray, minute, having enveloped his mind suddenly, it enraptures him in ecstasy, rapidly forsaking him so that he might not die. Therefore, in consequence of this great rapidity, the one who has seen acknowledges that he has not understood and does not remember its beauty. That is so that he, the child, may not eat the food of perfect men and that he may not burst or have pain or vomit.

From that time onwards therefore it leads us by the hand, strengthens us, teaches us, appearing and fleeing when we need it, not when we desire it—this is the attribute of the perfect. But when we are in trouble or totally worn out, it comes to our aid; it appears from afar and it causes me to be aware of it in my heart. I call out, I choke in my desire to seize it and all is night, and my poor hands are empty. I forget everything, I sit down and weep, despairing of seeing it in this manner once again.

But when I've wept a lot and consented to stop, then, mystically arrived, it takes possession of my head—and I burst into tears being unaware of who is there—and it enlightens my mind with a very sweet light. But when I discerned what it was, it rapidly took flight after having left me the fire of its divine desire which prevents me from laughing, or from looking at man, or from welcoming the desire of anything visible. Gradually this light is kindled, stirred up by waiting, and it becomes a big flame which reaches to heaven. Relaxation extinguishes it, both the troubles of one's own concerns and the solicitude for life (for that happens in the beginning).

It invites silence and hatred of all glory, to be beaten and trampled underfoot like dirt. It is in these things that it rejoices and desires to be, for it teaches the all-powerful humility. When, therefore, I will have acquired it and will have become humble, then it also remains inseparably with me; it converses with me, enlightens me, looks at me and I also look at it. It is in my heart; it exists in heaven. It reveals the scriptures to me and increases my knowledge; it teaches me mysteries that I cannot express. It shows me how it tore me away from the world and commands me to have mercy on all those who are in this world.

[There follows a section describing more of the effects of the light on Symeon himself. Then he narrates how his master, Symeon the Pious, became his spiritual guide and inspiration, using the typology of Moses rescuing the Egyptians from Pharaoh, i.e., the devil.]

Who has shown me the path of repentance and compunction from which I discovered the day which has no end? It was an angel, not a man; nevertheless he is a man, and the world is ridiculed by him and the dragon is trampled under foot and the demons tremble in his presence. How shall I tell you, brothers, what I've seen in Egypt, the marvels and the wonders he accomplished? I will only tell you what is here, for I cannot say everything. The fact is that he came down and found me a slave and stranger and said, "Come, my child, I will lead you to God!" I told him from the depth of my unbelief: "And what sign will you show me to ensure me that you, you, can tear me away from Egypt and snatch me from the hands of the crafty Pharaoh, so that, after having followed you, I do not risk greater dangers?" "Light a fire," he said, "so that I may penetrate to the center, and if I do not remain untouched, do not follow me!" This remark struck me with amazement and I did what he had commanded. And the flame burned and he stood in the middle, intact, uninjured, and he called me to him. "Master," I said, "I am afraid, I am a sinner." He stepped out, he came towards me and he embraced me: "Why were you afraid, tell me, why fear and tremble? The marvel is great and redoubtable, but you will see greater ones yet." Struck with amazement, I said to him: "Lord, I dare not approach you and do not wish to appear bolder than the fire, for I see that you are a man who is more than a man. I dare not even look at you, you whom the fire has spared." He made me come close, he clasped me in his arms and he kissed me again with a holy kiss and he himself gave out a scent of immortality.

Translated by George A. Maloney, SJ, *Hymns of Divine Love by St. Symeon the New Theologian* (Denville, New Jersey: Dimension Books, n.d.), 79–82.

HILDEGARD OF BINGEN AS VISIONARY AND THEORIST OF VISIONS

In recent decades Hildegard of Bingen has emerged as one of the most remarkable women in the history of Christianity. Born in 1098 to a noble family, she joined the convent at an early age and was trained under a female recluse named Jutta. Around 1141 she began to record the visions she had been receiving from childhood, at the same time embarking on a campaign of public dissemination of her message through letters sent to the major clerical and lay leaders of Europe. In the course of this campaign, Hildegard moved her community of nuns from Disibodenberg to the Rupertsberg near Bingen at the confluence of the Rhine and Nahe rivers. The acceptance of Hildegard's claims to have received messages directly from God about the state of the church, the need for reform, and the impending end of time gave her an authority perhaps never before accorded to a woman in Christian history, as shown by the four preaching missions she conducted in Germany in the years between 1158 and her death in 1179.

Hildegard's three major works, Scivias *(i.e., Know the Lord's Ways),* The Book of the Life of Merits, *and* The Book of Divine Works, *were based on the interpretation of her visions and auditions. In these books Hildegard speaks primarily as an original monastic theologian with a strong interest in cosmology and eschatology (her later reputation was largely as an apocalyptic reformer), but she was also a poet, a playwright, a composer, an artist, a physician, and more. Hildegard's reputation was founded on her visionary claims. The extent to which her visions can be described as mystical is still under discussion.*

While many of her showings are primarily didactic, others are unitive and trans-
formative in a mystical sense. Hildegard was not only a visionary but also a "vi-
sionologist," in the sense of someone who reflected on the mode in which her
showings were received and the effect that they had upon her consciousness.

I.
LETTER 103R. TO GUIBERT
OF GEMBLOUX (1175)

HILDEGARD TO GUIBERT THE MONK. I speak these words not on
my own or from another person, but I set them forth as I received them
in a vision from on high. O servant of God, you look into the mirror
of faith in which God is known, and, O son of God, this is possible
through the formation of humanity in whom God established and
sealed his miracles. Just as in the case of a mirror whatever is seen in it
is fixed in its container, so too the rational soul is placed into the body
as in an earthen vessel, so that it may rule it by giving it life and the
soul may contemplate things celestial through faith. Listen to what the
never-failing Light declares....

O faithful servant, I, a poor little person in female form, speak these
words to you again in a true vision. If God were pleased to lift up
my body in this vision, just as he has my soul, I would still have fear
in mind and heart, because I know that I am a human being, though
from infancy I have been a cloistered nun. Many wise men were so
filled with miracles that they revealed a great number of secrets, but
they fell because in their vanity they ascribed these miracles to themselves....

From my infancy, when my bones and nerves and veins were not yet
full grown, even unto the present time, I have always enjoyed the gift
of this vision in my soul—I who am already over seventy! In this vision, as God wills, my spirit ascends into the height of the firmament
and the shifting air, and it spreads itself abroad among different peo-
ples though they are in distant regions and places far from me. And
because I see these things in such a manner, I therefore also behold
them in changing forms of clouds and other created elements. But I do
not hear them with my bodily ears, nor with my heart's thoughts, nor

do I perceive them by the use of any of my five senses, but only in my soul, with my outer eyes open, so that I never experience their failure in ecstasy. Rather, I see these things wide awake, day and night. But I am inhibited by constant illness and so wrapped in terrible pain that the threat of death is near. But God has sustained me up to the present.

The light that I see is not spatial, yet it is far brighter than a cloud surrounding the sun. I cannot discern height or length or breadth in it, and I call it "the shadow of the Living Light." As the sun, moon, and stars appear reflected in water, so too writings, speeches, virtues, and deeds of people are given form and shine out to me in this light.

Whatever I see or learn in this vision, I retain for a long time in my memory, so that I remember what I heard and saw at any time. At one and the same time I see and I hear and I know, and in an instant I learn what I know. I have no knowledge of what I don't see there, because I am not learned. What I see and hear in the vision I write down, and I put down only the words I hear there. In unpolished Latin words I put forth what I hear in the vision, since I have not learned to write down the vision as philosophers write. The words I see and hear in the vision are not like the words that sound from a human mouth, but they are like shooting flame and a cloud moved in clear air. I am in no way able to understand the form of this light, just as I can't gaze fully upon the sphere of the sun.

In the same light I sometimes, not often, see another light, which I call "the Living Light." I can say much less about how I see it than in the case of the other light, and while I am gazing at it all sadness and all pain are taken from me, so that I am like an innocent girl and not an old woman. But due to the constant illness I suffer, I sometimes am exhausted in putting forth the words and visions that are shown me there. Still, when my soul sees and tastes them, I am so changed into a different mode of being that, as I said above, I consign all pain and suffering to forgetfulness. My soul drinks in as from a fountain what I see and hear at that time in the vision, and that fountain remains always full and inexhaustible.

My soul never lacks the first kind of light, what I called the shadow of the Living Light. I see it like the dome of heaven in a bright cloud and I behold it without stars. In this light I see what I often speak about, and from the flash of the Living Light I give answer to those who ask questions of me. . . .

Translated by Bernard McGinn from "Sanctae Hildegardis Epistola II," in *Analecta Sanctae Hildegardis Opera* [*Analecta Sacra, Vol. VIII*], edited by J.-B. Pitra (Monte Cassino: Abbey Press, 1882), 331–33.

II.
LIFE OF SAINT HILDEGARD, BOOK 2, CHAPTER 16

[Book 2 of the monk Theodore's *Life of Saint Hildegard* is based upon a lost spiritual diary in which the seer recounted the different kinds of visions given her over the years. The following is the last and highest form.]

THE SEVENTH VISION. Finally, at a later time [circa 1167] I saw a mystical and wondrous vision, such that my insides were disturbed and my body's power of sensation was extinguished, because my knowing was transmuted to another mode as if I did not know myself. And from God's inspiration, as it were, drops of sweet rain splashed into my soul's knowing, just as the Holy Spirit filled John the Evangelist when he sucked supremely deep revelation from the breast of Jesus, when his understanding was so touched by holy divinity that he revealed hidden mysteries and works, saying, "In the beginning was the Word" (Jn 1:1).

The Word, who existed without beginning before all creatures and who will exist without end after them, commanded all creatures to come forth, and he produced his work in the likeness of a smith who causes his work to blaze out, because what he had kept in his predestination before the ages, now appeared in a visible way. And so humanity and every creature is God's work. But humanity is also the workman of divinity and the reflection of his mysteries, and he ought to reveal the Trinity in all things, because God made him "in his image and likeness" (Gen 1:26). Just as Lucifer in his ill will was not able to break God apart, so too he is not capable of destroying humanity's state of being, although he attempted it in the case of the first man. Therefore, this vision taught and made clear to me the message and the words of this gospel, which are about the beginning of God's work. And I saw that the same explanation ought to be given to the beginning of the other writing that was not yet made manifest. In this writing are to be sought many inquiries of creatures about the divine mystery.

Translated by Bernard McGinn from *Vita Sanctae Hildegardis*, in PL 197:116.

6.

Hugh of St. Victor
Contemplation and Its Forms

Hugh of St. Victor (circa 1090–1141) was the first systematician of Western mysticism. He was a member of the community of regular canons (priests living according to a monastic rule) founded in 1108 at St. Victor just outside the walls of Paris. For a century this community was at the forefront of those who sought to combine traditional monastic theology with its strong emphasis on mysticism and the new procedures and scholarly techniques of scholasticism, i.e., the scientific mode of theology born in the French schools around 1100. Hugh was among the great schoolmasters of the Middle Ages; his extensive writings touch on almost every area of theology. Deeply influenced by Augustine, he also was interested in the Dionysian writings, as his Commentary on the Celestial Hierarchies *shows.*

Hugh's biblical expositions include a trilogy devoted to the exegesis of the Genesis account of Noah's ark in which he explored the ark as a master symbol of salvation history, as well as of the soul's ascent to God. His interest in the stages of contemplative ascent appears in many works, an impetus that was to bear fruit in the next great Victorine thinker, Richard (see section 5.2). The treatise Contemplation and Its Forms *may not be by Hugh himself, but seems to have been put together from his lectures and notes by his students. As one of the earliest works specifically devoted to a systematic presentation of contemplation, it is not as clear as later summaries, such as those of Richard. Nevertheless, the tract witnesses to an important stage in the study of contemplation. Two defini-*

tions are given at the start of the treatise: "Contemplation is the journey of the intellectual soul through the various roads of salvation; or contemplation is the illumination of the mind that draws the intellectual soul to the invisible things of God in a saving way." The work proceeds by analyzing four forms of this broad view of contemplation: meditation, self-conversation (soliloquium), *observation of the world* (circumspectio), *and ascension. The last of these comprises properly mystical contemplation, which the work presents in a typically scholastic threefold manner: ascension in action; ascension in affection; and ascension in understanding. The intellectual ascent is in turn subdivided in rather complex ways, concluding with five forms of divine knowing that identify the highest type of contemplation as knowledge by means of a preliminary taste of the beatific vision.*

SECTION 5. THE FIFTH AND SUPREME MODE OF DIVINE KNOWING FROM THE JOY OF BEATIFYING VISION.

The fifth mode of divine knowing is the supreme kind of contemplation called the joy of beatifying vision. Beatifying vision, enjoyed by very few blessed folk in this life, is that in which, raptured in the abounding sweetness of the divine taste, they contemplate God alone. This mode differs from the fourth mode, for in that one the intellectual soul is enlightened by the ray of contemplation so that it can make an expedition into the world and into itself and thus experience a return of greater awareness to things invisible. But in this mode the intellectual soul is totally enlightened by the splendor of the eternal light, constantly and perfectly hates sin, disregards the world, rejects the self, and—entire, apart, naked, and pure—moves on into God. Never departing totally from him, but uniting itself totally to the one God, it is free from matter, stripped of form, and clear of limitation.

There are three kinds of this supreme contemplation, described by three theologians under three names: by Job it is described as a suspension; by John as a silence; by Solomon as a sleep. Job says: "My soul chooses suspension and my bones death" (Jb 7:15); John says: "There was silence in heaven for the space of a half hour" (Rev 8:1); and through Solomon the bride in the Song of Songs says: "I sleep and my heart wakes" (Song 5:2). The first kind belongs to purity, the second to charity, the third to beatitude.

Three steps lead up to the first kind of contemplation [i.e., suspension]. The first step is for the soul to collect itself within; the second is for the soul to see what kind of soul it is when it has been collected; the third is for the pure soul to submit itself purely to this form of contemplation so that it may rise above itself to invisible things, and, purified and enlightened in this manner, it may move on into God in a total way. The soul will be completely unable to collect itself in so great a perfection of purity unless it has learned to restrain the images of earthly things from the mind's eye during the course of the prior kinds of contemplation. She must put an end to whatever comes from the senses so that she may inwardly find herself as she was when she was created, that is, without external things. Then, when the soul has been lifted up to itself and understands its capacity, it knows that it surpasses all corporeal things and it moves on from its intellect to the intellect of its Maker. What is it doing then, but that already purified through the excellence of suspension, the soul is now moving on to heavenly tranquility and heavenly silence?

Silence is threefold—first of the mouth, second of the mind, and third of reason. The mouth does not speak at all because the whole soul is raptured within. The mind is also silent because it can in no way comprehend the ineffable joy it feels. And reason is oppressed with silence because this business has nothing to do with human reason since the mind is flooded from within by divine anointing. Sweet heavenly sleep snatches the soul that has been anointed in this way, and then it dissolves and rests in the embrace of the Highest Light.

The soul's sleep is said to be threefold because it is raptured to things ineffable according to its own triple power. As long as the blessed soul is at rest, she then undergoes a kind of blessed sleep; forgetful of world and of self, she is placed before and even upon God's seat. The soul's reason sleeps because, since it does not know the cause of such great happiness, it is not able to grasp its origin, progress, and goal. The memory sleeps because what is totally lulled by ineffable rejoicing and sweetness can remember nothing of the past. The will sleeps because it is not aware of the sweetness of ineffable joy that it perceives. This is why the Apostle says, "He who adheres to God becomes one spirit with him" (1 Cor 6:17).

Therefore, the soul happily sleeps on, dead to self and world. While her senses are fully asleep, wholly open to the gaze of her Spouse and taken up in his blessed embrace, she is led through the first step to the house of the handmaids, through the second step to the bridal chamber of the young girls, and through the third step to the heavenly banquet. In the first she is washed by the handmaids; in the second she is adorned by the young girls; and in the third she is fed by the Spouse himself in splendid fashion. The handmaids are the inspirations that touch the mind in various ways and that impel it to tread worldly things underfoot and to seek ardently after heavenly things—fear of hell, dread of notoriety, fear of present punishment, consideration of our own weakness, the pain and misfortune of this exile, hope of heavenly reward which does not disappoint (Rom 5:5), brotherly compassion, remembrance of the sweet homeland, and the sweetly torturing love of the blessed life. These are the handmaids that carry the spiritual waters, light the fire, make ready the bath, wash and purify the bride, and prepare her so that without spot or stain (Eph 5:27) she is ready for the embraces of the Bridegroom.

She is first washed with the waters of wisdom; second she is clothed with the garments of justice; and third she is fed with the food of life and made merry with celestial banqueting. The first place is that of compunction; the second of love; the third of refreshment. Compunction washes; charity adorns; the banquet brings rest. This is why the Bridegroom in the Song of Songs speaks to her, commanding her to hasten to him, saying: "Come from Lebanon, my bride, come from Lebanon, come!" (Song 4:8). Lebanon is interpreted as "cleansing." Therefore, he bids her to come as she has been cleansed so that she may appear as beautiful to the most chaste eyes of the beautiful Bridegroom. May she present herself without a spot of feigned friendship and without a stain of impurity. And so she responds to the Bridegroom in the same Song of Songs: "I turn to my Beloved and his turning is to me" (Song 7:10). She also says, "My Beloved to me, and I to him who feeds among the lilies" (Song 2:16). Therefore, let her come to the house of compunction in order to be cleansed; let her ascend to the bridal chamber of prayer to be adorned; let her go up to the banquet of Solomon to be satiated. In the first place she receives the mirror of beauty; in the second the kiss of peace; in the third the food of eternal happiness.

Translated by Bernard McGinn from *Hugues de Saint-Victor. La contemplation et ses espèces,* introduction, text, and notes by Roger Baron (Desclée: Tournai, 1955), 86–90.

RICHARD ROLLE

THE FIRE OF LOVE

SELECTIONS FROM CHAPTERS 14 AND 37

Richard Rolle (circa 1300–1349) was the first of the four mystics whose writings have led to the fourteenth century being described as the Golden Age of English Mysticism. These figures were quite different. Rolle was a freelance hermit and something of an outsider who wrote in both Latin and English. Walter Hilton (see section 5.6) was an Augustinian priest who wrote in the vernacular. The anonymous author of The Cloud of Unknowing *(see sections 8.3 and 15.4) was also a priest writing in Middle English, as well as an original interpreter of Dionysian mysticism. The anchoress Julian of Norwich (see section 7.4), less well known in the Middle Ages, has emerged in the past century as one of the most read of Christian mystics.*

*Rolle was a prolific author who used his works to establish himself as guide to souls and a legitimate authority on mystical teaching despite his lay status. The hermit's concentration on the physical manifestations of mystical graces, especially the triad of "heat, song, and sweetness" (*fervor-canor-dulcor*), have led some to doubt that he was really a mystic in the most exact sense. But mystics come in many varieties, and Rolle's highly somatic mysticism has many parallels in both the East and the West, such as in his contemporary Henry Suso (see section 7.3). Rolle's most popular work was the Latin treatise called* The Mending of Life, *which treats the essential ascetical practices leading to contemplation in its first ten chapters before turning to a consideration of mystical love of God based on the teaching of Richard of St. Victor (see section 5.2). His most power-*

ful work, however, is the lyrical Fire of Love, *in which he provides accounts of his mystical experiences as well as his teaching on the nature of rapture.*

I.

CHAPTER 14. PRAISE OF THE SOLITARY LIFE AND ITS FIRST LOVERS, AND THAT THE LOVE OF GOD CONSISTS IN HEAT, SONG, AND SWEETNESS AND THAT REPOSE IS NECESSARY

... Insofar as I have been able to study the scriptures, I have discovered and recognized that the highest love of Christ consists in three things: in heat, in song, and in sweetness. I have experienced that these three cannot last long in the mind without great repose. If I wanted to contemplate while standing, or walking about, or prostrating on the ground, I used to see that I would sink far away from them and found myself almost empty of them. Under the pressure of this necessity, I have chosen to sit in order to attain and continue in the highest devotion. This is why I know that if a person stands or walks a lot his body becomes tired and so his soul is obstructed and somewhat irritated due to the burden. He is not in his highest repose, and consequently not in perfection, because, as the Philosopher says, the soul becomes prudent in sitting and resting [Aristotle, *Physics* 1.7.3]. Therefore, a person who still delights in matters divine more by standing than by sitting should know that he is far from the height of contemplation. Since the highest perfection of the Christian religion without any doubt is found in these three things that are the signs of the most perfect love, with the grace of Jesus and to the measure of my ability I have accepted them, without daring to put myself on the same level as the saints who were eminent in them and who perhaps knew them more perfectly. I still pursue them with whatever power I have so that I can love more ardently, sing more purely, and feel love's sweetness more fully. For you are mistaken, brethren, if you think that there are no saints now like the prophets and apostles.

I call it "heat" when the mind is truly set afire by eternal love, and the heart in the same manner feels itself now burning with love, not by a guess but in reality. A heart that is transformed in fire will have a feeling of fiery love. I call it "song" when, as the fire grows great, the soul now receives the sweetness of eternal praise and thinking is turned into singing and the mind lingers in its honeyed melody. These two gifts are not received in idleness, but in the height of devotion. From them comes the third, that is, priceless sweetness. Heat and song cause marvelous sweetness in the soul, and they too can be caused by surpassing sweetness.

There is no deception in their abundance, but rather the most realized perfection of all activities, although people ignorant of the contemplative life can be deceived by the "midday devil" (Ps 90:6) in false and feigned devotion, because they think they are at the top when they are really at the bottom. But the soul in which these three things come together remains completely armored against the enemy's arrows, as long as it thinks about the Beloved with steadfast intention and lifts itself up to higher things and rouses itself to loving. Don't be surprised that melody is given to a soul that is ordered in love in such a way (Song 2:4), and the soul takes a constant poetic and consoling song from her Lover. She lives as though she were not subject to the world's vanity (Rom 8:20), with heavenly support so that she may blaze eternally in the uncreated warmth, so that she never fall away. Therefore, when she loves ceaselessly and ardently, as mentioned above, she feels a most blessed heat within her and she knows that she is entirely consumed by the fire of eternal love in a subtle way. Thoroughly conscious of her Most Beloved in the desirable sweetness, meditation mutates into the song of glory, and renewed nature is wrapped round in sweet-sounding pleasantness. This is why the Creator gives her what the whole heart desires—to pass from the corruptible body without fear or sadness, so that without death's sorrow she leaves the world. She who is the friend of light and the enemy of darkness loves only life.

People like this, who are taken up to such a lofty love, should not be chosen for offices or public prelacies; nor are they called to any secular business. They are like the gem topaz, which is rare and hence precious and held in high regard. There are two colors in it: one very pure and like gold, the other shining like the heaven in good weather. It surpasses the brightness of all other gems, and there is nothing more beautiful to see. If someone tries to polish it, it grows dull; if left by itself, it retains its beauty. So too, the holy contemplatives we spoke about are very rare and very beloved. They are like gold because of their outstanding heat of charity, and like heaven because of the brilliance of their heavenly way of life which surpasses that of all other saints, and therefore they are the more beautiful and gleaming among the gems, that is, among the elect. Those who love and possess only this kind of life are more shining than all other persons, present or past. Someone who wished to polish such people, that is, to honor them with various dignities, is trying to lessen their ardor and to dull their beauty and brilliance in a certain manner. If these people were to agree to accept a princely honor, they would surely become more ordinary and of less worth. They should be left to their pursuits so that their brilliance may increase.

II.

CHAPTER 37. THAT THE TRUE LOVER LOVES THE BELOVED ALONE; AND ABOUT THE TWOFOLD RAPTURE, OUTSIDE THE BODY, AND THE ELEVATION OF THE MIND INTO GOD, AND THE EXCELLENCE OF THE SECOND

... It is clear that rapture can be understood in two ways. The first way is when a person is so carried outside fleshly sensation that during the time of the rapture he does not feel anything in the flesh or what is done by the flesh. Nevertheless, he is not dead, but alive, because the soul still gives life to the body. In this manner sometimes saints and chosen people are raptured for their own instruction and for the instruction of others, as Paul was raptured to the third heaven (2 Cor 12:2). This kind of rapture sometimes even happens to sinners, so that in a vision they see either the joys of the good in heaven or the punishments of the evil for their correction and that of others, as we read in many cases.

In the second way rapture is said to be an elevation of the mind to God through contemplation. This way is in all perfect lovers of God and in none save those who love God. It is rightly called rapture, just as the other one was, because it happens by means of a kind of violence and it is contrary to nature in a way. It is truly supernatural that from being a vile sinner a person becomes a son of God, filled with spiritual joy and carried into God. This kind is very desirable and beloved, for Christ always had divine contemplation, but never experienced the removal of the body's control. It is one thing to be raptured in the midst of fleshly sensation; it is another to be raptured out of sensation into some vision, either terrifying or pleasing. I think that love's rapture, in which a person gains great merit, is better. To be granted to see celestial things that belong to the reward of heaven does not pertain to merit.

People are described as raptured who are totally and perfectly given over to desires for their Savior and who ascend in strength to the height of contemplation. They are enlightened by uncreated Wisdom and they deserve to feel the heat of that uncircumscribed light by whose beauty they are raptured. This happens to the devout souls when all their thoughts are ordered to divine love and all the wanderings of their minds become stable, and the mind itself no longer wavers or hesitates, but led on and fixed in one thing by a total act of love, it pants for Christ with great ardor, stretched out and intent on him as if there were no one else but these two people, Christ and the loving soul herself. Hence she is glued to him with an inseparable bond of love, and through mental ecstasy she flies beyond the cloister of the body and drinks down an absolutely marvelous draft from the heavens. This is something she could never attain if God's grace had not snatched her away from lower attractions and set her upon the height of the spirit in which without doubt she receives the healing gifts of grace.

Since she consciously thinks only upon divine and celestial matters, with an unshakable and free heart, she sees her mind beyond everything corporeal and visible, transferred and raptured to supernal things. Then, without doubt, she is near to receiving and feeling the heat of love in herself in a real way, and then to melting into song in honeyed sweetness. This follows from rapture for one so chosen. This is the reason why rapture of this sort is marvelous, excelling, I believe, all other actions and paths, because it is judged to be a kind of foretaste of eternal sweetness. Unless I am mistaken, it surpasses all other gifts given by God to the saints for their merit in this pilgrimage. In this state they merit a higher place in heaven, because through it they loved God in life more ardently and more peacefully. In this manner the highest restfulness is demanded for seeking and retaining this state, because it can never be gained or retained in too much bodily motion or in inconstancy or mental wandering. Therefore, where a person has been chosen to be elevated to this, he lives in great joy and full of virtue, and he dies in a sweet peacefulness. After this life he will be placed among the higher choirs of angels and nearer to God....

Translated by Bernard McGinn from *The Incendium Amoris of Richard Rolle of Hampole,* edited by Margaret Deansley (Manchester: At the University Press, 1915), 184–87, 254–56.

8.

NICHOLAS OF CUSA
ON THE VISION OF GOD

EXCERPTS FROM CHAPTERS 5, 6, AND 13

Nicholas of Cusa's major contribution to the history of mysticism is the treatise
On the Vision of God, *which he sent to the monks of Tegernsee in the fall of*
1453. In this work the cardinal rethought the basic issues found in previous at-
tempts to bring together the opposing scriptural texts that on the one hand pre-
sented the vision of God as the goal of existence (e.g., Mt 5:8) and on the other
hand denied that God could ever be seen (e.g., 1 Tim 6:16). Cusa's solution used
aspects of the thought of Neoplatonic mystics, such as Dionysius, John Scotus
Eriugena, and Meister Eckhart, but it was also very much a new creation.
Like Dionysius, he insisted that seeing God always remains a paradoxical "not-
seeing seeing." Along with Eriugena, he identified God's seeing with his creative
activity; finally, he took over from Eckhart the idea of the mutuality of the gaze
that the Dominican expressed in the famous statement: "The eye in which I see
God is the same eye in which God sees me."

Cusa's treatise begins with a practical exercise designed to provide "ready ac-
cess to mystical theology." He sent the monks an all-seeing picture of Christ and
suggested a para-liturgy in which the community would process around the icon
to induce wonder in the "change of the unchangeable gaze" directed to each and
all. This experiment was accompanied by a treatise in the form of a prayer di-
vided into three parts. Chapters 4–16 are an extended analysis of the meaning
*of "seeing God" (*visio dei*), understood both as God's own seeing and our vision*
of him. Central to this section are the notions of the biblical "face-to-face vision"
*(1 Cor 13:12); the "wall of paradise" (*murus paradisi*), or limit of all rational*

*thought; and finally naming God as "absolute infinity" (*infinitas absoluta). *The core message of this presentation of the dynamics of the gaze is that God is never the object of seeing but is always its subject. The brief second section (chapters 17–18) shows why the proper understanding of seeing God reveals that God is a loving Trinity of persons. Finally, chapters 19–25 demonstrate that the only way we can attain to the vision of the triune God is through the filiation, or adoptive sonship, made available to us through the union of the divine and human natures in Jesus. The selections given here illustrate the three essential themes of the first section.*

I.

CHAPTER 5.13–15. GOD'S SEEING IS
TASTING, SEEKING, SHOWING
MERCY, AND WORKING

"How great is the multitude of your sweetness which you have hidden from those who fear you" (Ps 30:20). This is the inexpressible treasury of the greatest joy. To taste your sweetness is to apprehend by experiential contact the sweetness of all delights in its principle; it is to attain the source of all that is desired in your wisdom. To see the absolute source, which is the source of all things, is nothing else but to taste you mentally, God, since you are the very sweetness of existence, life, and understanding. Lord, what else is your seeing than for you to be seen by me when you look upon me with the eye of your mercy? In seeing me, you, who are the hidden God (Is 45:15), give yourself to be seen by me. No one can see you unless you grant that you may be seen. To see you is nothing else than for you to see the one who sees you.

I see in this icon of you how ready you are, Lord, to show your face to all who seek you, for you never close your eyes and you never turn them somewhere else. And although I turn myself away from you when I look completely toward something else, you nonetheless do not change your eyes or your gaze because of this. If you do not look upon me with the eye of grace, it's my fault because I have separated from you through turning away and turning toward something else that I prefer to you. You still do not turn totally from me, but follow after me with your mercy so that I might at some time want to return to you in order to be open to your grace. Your not looking upon me is because I do not look toward you, but reject and spurn you.

O infinite mercy, how unhappy is every sinner who has deserted you, the source of life, and who seeks you not in yourself but in what is nothing in itself and would remain nothing did you not call it forth from nothingness. How foolish is the one who seeks you, Goodness itself, and while he seeks you departs from you and turns his eyes away. All seekers seek only the good, and everyone who seeks the good and departs from you departs from what he seeks. Therefore, every sinner wanders away from you and goes off a long way. But when he returns to you, you meet him without delay, and before he looks upon you, you cast your eyes of mercy upon him with fatherly love (Lk 15:20).

For you to have mercy is the same thing as for you to see. Your mercy follows after each person as long as he lives, and wherever he goes, just as your seeing never abandons anyone. As long as a person lives, you do not cease to follow after him and to urge him on with a sweet and interior warning to leave error and to be converted to you in order to live happily. Lord, you are the companion of my pilgrimage. Wherever I go, your eyes are always upon me. Your seeing is also your moving. Therefore, you move with me and never cease moving as long as I move. If I am at rest, you are with me; if I ascend or descend, so do you; wherever I go, you are there (Ps 138:8). You do not forsake me in time of tribulation. As often as I call on you, you are there, for to call on you is for me to turn myself to you. You cannot fail a person who turns toward you, nor can anyone turn toward you unless you are there first. You are present before I turn myself to you, for unless you were present and invited me, I would be wholly ignorant of you. And how could I be converted to you if I did not know you? . . .

II.

CHAPTER 6.17. FACIAL VISION

Lord my God, the longer I behold your face the more it appears to me that you cast the gaze of your eyes more acutely upon me. Your gaze now moves me to consider how this icon of your face is painted in a perceptible way in such a manner that the face cannot exist without color, just as the color cannot exist without quantity. I behold the truth of your invisible face signified in this contracted shadow here not by the fleshly eyes that look upon it but by mental and intellectual eyes. But your true face is free from every form of limitation: it has no quantity, quality, time, or place. It is the absolute form, the face of faces. I am astounded when I consider how this face is the truth and most exact measure of all faces. There is no quantity in this face that is the truth of all faces; it is not smaller or greater than any other face. Because it is not more nor less, it is equal to any and every face, but it is not equal to any single face because it is not quantified but is unlimited and high above all: It is therefore the truth that is equality itself free from every form of quantity. Thus, Lord, I grasp that your face precedes every face capable of taking a form and is the exemplar and truth of all faces. All faces are images of your face, which is incapable of contraction and of participation. Therefore, every face that can gaze upon your face sees nothing different or other than itself, because it sees its truth. Exemplary truth cannot be different or strange, but these aspects occur in an image because it is not the Exemplar. . . .

III.
CHAPTER 13.51–54. GOD IS SEEN TO BE ABSOLUTE INFINITY BEYOND THE WALL OF PARADISE

Lord God, the helper of all who seek you, I see you in the garden of paradise and I do not know what I see because I see nothing of what is visible. I know this alone, that I know I do not know what I see and that I can never know it. I do not know how to name you because I do not know what you might be. If anyone were to ask me to use one or another name, by the very fact that the name would be used I know that it is not your name. The limit of every mode of signifying by names is the wall beyond which I see you. If anyone were to make use of some concept in order to conceive of you, I know that that concept is not yours, because every concept reaches its limit at the wall of paradise. And if someone were to make use of some likeness and to say that you are conceivable according to it, I also know that that likeness is not yours. If someone were to proclaim some understanding of you, desiring to provide a mode for understanding you, this would still be far from you, for you are separated from all such things by the most lofty wall. The wall separates you from everything that can be said or thought, because you are free from all that can fall under any kind of concept whatever.

Hence, when I am lifted up on high, I see you as infinity. It is because of this that you are inaccessible, incomprehensible, unnameable, unmultiplied, and invisible. Therefore, it is necessary that someone approaching you ascend above every limit and every end and everything finite. But how can someone come to you who are the end toward which he aims if he ought ascend above that end? Doesn't someone who ascends above the end enter into what is undetermined and confused and thus into the ignorance and darkness of intellectual confusion as far as the intellect is concerned? Therefore, if someone wants to see you, his intellect must become ignorant and set in shadow. O my God, what is an intellect in ignorance? Isn't it learned ignorance? No one can draw near you who are infinity, God, save through one whose intellect is ignorance itself, that is, who knows that he is ignorant of you. How can any intellect grasp you who are infinity? To understand infinity is to comprehend the incomprehensible. The intellect knows that it is ignorant of you because it knows that you cannot be known save by knowing what is not knowable and seeing what is not visible and drawing near to what is not accessible.

My God, you are absolute infinity itself, which I see as the infinite end. But I do not know how to grasp how an end without end can be an end. God, you are your own end, because you are whatever you have. If you have an end you are that end. Therefore, you are the infinite end because you are your own end and because your end is your essence. The essence of the end is not limited or ended in something other than the end but in itself. Therefore, the end that is its own end is infinite, and every end that is not its own end is a finite end. Lord, because you are the end that puts an end to all things, therefore you are the end that is not an end, and thus an end without end, or infinite. What surpasses all reason involves a contradiction. Hence when I assert the existence of the infinite, I admit a light that is dark, a knowledge that is ignorant, and something necessary that is impossible. Because we admit to an end of what is finite, we necessarily admit to the infinite, or the final end, or the end without end. Just as we must admit that finite things exist, we must also admit that the infinite exists. Therefore, we admit a coincidence of contradictories above which is the infinite. That kind of coincidence is the contradiction without contradiction, just as it is the end without end.

You tell me, Lord, that just as in unity otherness exists without otherness because it is unity, so too in infinity contradiction exists without contradiction because it is infinite. Infinity is simplicity itself. Contradiction cannot exist without otherness, but in simplicity otherness exists without otherness because it is simplicity itself. Everything that is predicated about absolute simplicity coincides with it because there is where it exists. The opposite of opposites is an opposite without opposite just as the end of things finite is the end without end. Therefore, you, God, are the opposite of opposites because you are infinite. And because you are infinite you are infinity itself—in infinity the opposite of opposites exists without an opposite. . . .

Translated by Bernard McGinn from *Nicolai de Cusa Opera Omnia*, Vol. VI:17–19, 20, 44–46. © Felix Meiner Verlag, Hamburg.

IGNATIUS OF LOYOLA

AUTOBIOGRAPHY

Ignatius of Loyola (1491–1556) is best known as the founder of the Jesuits, the new religious order that helped revitalize Roman Catholicism in the wake of the Reformation. Ignatius was a superb organizer and a skilled spiritual director; he was also a mystic. One of his followers spoke of him as "contemplative in action" (in actione contemplativus). Born of minor nobility in the Basque area of Spain, Ignatius became a soldier. Badly wounded in 1521, he experienced a conversion during his convalescence and took up the life of a wandering holy man. He spent almost a year (1522–23) at Manresa near Montserrat, deepening his prayer life, undergoing temptations, and experiencing visions. During this time he began writing down the notes on spiritual direction that eventually grew into his most famous work, the Spiritual Exercises *(first published in 1548). The* Exercises *are a set of guidelines for spiritual directors to use in giving retreats.*

Ignatius made pilgrimages to Rome and Jerusalem before deciding that God wanted him to become a priest, so he spent the years 1524 to 1535 studying in Spain and Paris. During this time the force of his personality and the depth of his spiritual vision began to attract followers, and in 1534 he and six others founded what was to become the Society of Jesus, officially sanctioned by Paul III in 1540. Ignatius moved on to Rome in 1537 and spent the rest of his life there, organizing the order, preaching and guiding souls, and conducting a large correspondence. During this time he continued to experience visions and other mystical gifts, often while saying Mass. Fragments of a Spiritual Diary *that he kept*

*(only the notes for 1544–45 survive) provide some insight into his frequent ec-
static experiences. In 1552 Ignatius's associates in Rome convinced him to tell
them the story of his life, "so that his explanation could serve us as a testament
and paternal instruction."* The Autobiography, *as it came to be known, covers only the years 1521 to 1538. What follows here is the account of some of the
visions that Ignatius received during his time at Manresa—both the divine
showings, and also the vision of the devil as a shining serpent-like figure.*

AUTOBIOGRAPHY, SECTIONS 27-31

... At that period God dealt with him as a teacher instructing a pupil.
Was this on account of his ignorance or dullness, or because he had no
one else to teach him? Or on account of the fixed resolve he had of
serving God with which God himself had inspired him? He was firmly
convinced, both then and afterward, that God had treated him thus. If
he were to have a doubt in this matter, he would consider that he had
offended the Divine Majesty. The five following points will prove what
he says.

First. He had a great devotion to the Most Holy Trinity. Every day
he prayed to each of the three Persons separately and also to the whole
Trinity. While thus praying, the thought came to him: Why did he
offer fourfold prayers to the Trinity? This thought, however, caused
him little or no trouble. Once, while reciting the little hours in honor
of the Blessed Virgin on the steps of the monastery [of St. Dominic],
his understanding began to be lifted up so that he seemed to behold
the Most Holy Trinity in the form of three musical keys. This vision
affected him so much that he could not refrain from tears and sighs.
On the same day he accompanied the procession from the church, and
even up to the time of dinner he could not withhold his tears, and after
dinner he could speak of no subject except the Most Holy Trinity,
making use of many different comparisons to illustrate his thoughts
with much joy and consolation. Such an impression was made on him
on that occasion that during his later life, whenever he prayed to the
Most Holy Trinity, he experienced great devotion.

Second. Once, to his great joy, God permitted him to understand
how he had created this world. He seemed to see a white object with
rays emanating from it. From this object God sent forth light. How-

ever, he could not clearly explain this vision, nor could he recall the illuminations given to him by God on that occasion.

Third. During his stay of about a year at Manresa [March 1522–February 1523], after he had begun to receive consolations from God and saw the fruits he had for the direction of others, he gave up his former rigorous penances. At that time he trimmed his nails and hair. During the time of his residence at Manresa, while assisting at Mass in the monastery church, he had another vision. At the elevation of the body of the Lord he beheld, with the eyes of his soul, white rays descending from above. Although he cannot, after so long an interval, explain the details of this vision, still, he saw clearly with his understanding the manner in which Our Lord Jesus Christ is present in the Most Blessed Sacrament.

Fourth. Often in prayer, and even during a long space of time, he saw the humanity of Christ with the eyes of the soul. The form under which this vision appeared was that of a white body, neither large nor small; but there seemed to be no distinction of members. This vision appeared to him often at Manresa, perhaps twenty or even forty times, without telling a lie. He saw it once at Jerusalem, and once when he was journeying to Padua. He saw Our Lady under the same form, without any distinction of members. These visions gave him such strength, then and always, that he often thought within himself that even though scripture did not bear witness to these mysteries of faith, still, from what he had seen, it would be his duty to lay down his life for them.

Fifth. One day out of devotion he went to a church situated about a mile from Manresa—I think it is called St. Paul and the road goes by the river. Going along occupied with his devotions, he sat down for a while looking at the river that was flowing by. While seated there, the eyes of his understanding were opened. He did not have any special vision, but his mind was enlightened on many subjects, spiritual as well as matters of faith and learning. So clear was this knowledge that from that day on everything appeared to him in a new light. The particular things he understood then, although they were many, he was not able to declare, but only that he had received a great clarification in his understanding. Such was the abundance of this light in his mind that all the divine helps he received, and all the knowledge acquired up to his sixty-second year, even adding them all together, were not equal to it. [Here the scribe adds: This left his understanding so enlightened that from that day on he seemed to be quite another man, and possessed of a new intellect.]

This illumination lasted a long time. While kneeling before a nearby cross to give thanks to God, there appeared to him that object he had often seen before, but had never understood. It seemed to be something most beautiful, and, as it were, gleaming with many eyes. This is how it always appeared. While before the cross, he clearly noticed that the object did not have its former beautiful color. He understood clearly with strong agreement of his will that it was the devil. Later, whenever the vision appeared to him for a long time, as it did often, with contempt he dispelled it with the staff he used to carry in his hand.

Adapted and corrected from the translation of J.F.X. O'Connor, SJ, *The Autobiography of St. Ignatius* (New York: Benziger Brothers, 1900), 52–58.

10.

TERESA OF AVILA

LIFE

CHAPTER 29.10–14

Among the most noted descriptions of an ecstatic vision in Christian mysticism is the account given by Teresa of Avila in her Life *of the piercing, or "trans-verberation," of her heart. The event appears to have taken place about 1560. The theme of the "wound of love, or charity" often invoked the text of Song of Songs 2:5, which in the Old Latin version reads, "because I have been wounded by charity." In commenting on this verse, Origen gave a rare personal reference: "If there is anyone who at some time has received the sweet wound of him who is the chosen dart, as the prophet says [Is 49:2]; if there is anyone who has been pierced by the loveworthy spear of his knowledge, so that he yearns and longs for him by day and night, . . . if such there be, that soul then says in truth, 'I have been wounded by charity' " (*Commentary on the Song of Songs, book 3).*

During the late-medieval period, many mystics, especially women, provide us with descriptions of the wound of love. Teresa's account is among the most potent and erotic. The experience became emblematic of her status as the premier Catholic mystic of the Counter-Reformation period. Editions of her works often included a picture of the scene, and Gian Lorenzo Bernini's sculptural version (1647–51) in the Cornaro chapel of the church of Santa Maria della Vittoria in Rome is the most famous depiction of ecstasy in the history of Christian art. The trans-verberation was accorded its own feast day by Benedict XIII in 1726.

—

These other impulses are very different. It is not we who apply the fuel; the fire is already kindled and we are thrown into it in a moment to be consumed. It is by no efforts of the soul that it sorrows over the wound caused by the Lord's absence. Rather, an arrow is driven into the entrails to the very quick, and into the heart at times, so that the soul knows not what is the matter with it, nor what it wishes for. It understands clearly enough that it wishes for God, and that the arrow seems tempered with some herb that makes the soul hate itself for the love of our Lord, and willingly lose its life for him. It is impossible to describe or explain the way in which God wounds the soul, or the very grievous pain inflicted, which deprives it of all self-consciousness; yet this pain is so sweet that there is no joy in the world that gives greater delight. As I have just said, the soul would wish to be always dying of this wound.

This pain and this bliss carried me out of myself, and I could never understand how it was. Oh, what a sight a wounded soul is—a soul, I mean, so conscious of it as to be able to say of itself that it is wounded for so good a cause! It sees distinctly that it never did anything whereby this love should come to it, and it sees that it does come from that exceeding love our Lord bears it. A spark seems to have fallen suddenly upon it that has set it all on fire. Oh, how often I remember, when in this state, those words of David: "As the hart longs for the fountains of waters, so is my soul longing for you, O my God" (Ps 41:2). They seem to me to be literally true of myself. . . .

Our Lord was pleased that I should have at times a vision of this kind: I saw an angel close by me, on my left side, in bodily form. This I am not accustomed to see, except very rarely. Though I have visions of angels frequently, yet I see them only by an intellectual vision, such as I have spoken of before [chapter 27.2]. It was our Lord's will that in this vision I should see the angel in this way. He was not large, but small of stature, and most beautiful—his face burning, as if he were one of the highest angels, who seem to be all of fire: They must be those whom we call Cherubim. Their names they never tell me; but I see very well that there is in heaven so great a difference between one angel and another, and between these and the others, that I cannot explain it. I saw in his hand a long spear of gold, and at the iron's point there seemed to be a little fire. He appeared to me to be thrusting it at times into my heart, and to pierce my very entrails; when he drew it out, he seemed to draw them out also, and to leave me all on fire with a great love of God. The pain was so great that it made me moan; and yet so surpassing was the sweetness of this excessive pain that I could not wish to be rid of it. The soul is satisfied now with nothing less than God. The pain is not bodily, but spiritual; though the body has its share in it, even a large one. It is a caressing of love so sweet that now takes place between the soul and God that I pray God of his goodness to make him experience it who may think that I am lying.

During the days that this lasted I went about as if beside myself. I wished to see or speak with no one, but only to cherish my pain, which was to me a greater bliss than all created things could give me. I was in this state from time to time, whenever it was our Lord's pleasure to throw me into those deep raptures that I could not prevent even when I was in the company of others, and which, to my deep vexation, came to be publicly known. Since then I do not feel that pain so much, but only that which I spoke of before—I do not remember the chapter [chapter 20.9]—which is in many ways very different from it and of greater worth. On the other hand, when this pain of which I am now speaking begins, our Lord seems to lay hold of the soul and to throw it into an ecstasy, so that there is no time for me to have any sense of pain or suffering, because fruition ensues at once. May He be blessed for ever, who has bestowed such great graces on one who has responded so ill to blessings so great!

Adapted from the translation of David Lewis in *The Life of St. Teresa of Jesus* (London: Thomas Baker, 5th ed., 1916), 264–68.

GEORGE FOX

EXCERPTS FROM *THE JOURNAL*

In 1643 George Fox (1624–91), apprentice to a shoemaker, felt compelled to leave his friends and family and begin wandering in search of enlightenment. In 1646, as recounted below, he started to receive illuminations from the inner light of Christ, an event that moved him to give up regular church attendance and preach the message of reliance on the inner light rather than the external trappings of religion. The success of Fox's preaching and its reception by like-minded souls soon led to the formation of the Friends of the Truth, which later became known as the Society of Friends, or the Quakers (according to Fox, the name was first used in 1650 by a Justice Bennett of Derby "because we bid him tremble at the word of God").

Fox's preaching was troubling to the English authorities; he and other early Quakers were often persecuted and imprisoned. Fox, however, proved to be an able organizer and an effective missionary. The Quakers spread throughout the British Isles, to the Continent, and to the British colonies in North America, especially Pennsylvania, founded by the Quaker William Penn in 1682. The Toleration Act of 1687 ended overt persecution of the group, but they remained suspect in establishment circles for a long time.

While he was imprisoned in Worcester in 1673–75, Fox dictated an account of his spiritual itinerary that was published after his death as The Journal *(1694). Although digressive in style and structure,* The Journal *contains striking accounts of visionary illumination. Fox was a contemporary of the Catholic*

Quietist mystics, such as Miguel de Molinos (see section 4.5) and Madame Guyon (see section 1.6). His emphasis on the supremacy of interior illumination has analogues in their writings, and it is no accident that later Quakers did much to spread Quietist texts in the English-speaking world.

I.
1646–1647

But as I had forsaken the priests, so I left the separate preachers also, and those esteemed the most experienced people, for I saw that there was none among them who could speak to my condition. When all my hopes in them and in all men were gone, so that I had nothing outwardly to help me, nor could I tell what to do, then, oh, then, I heard a voice which said: "There is one, even Christ Jesus, that can speak to thy condition"; and when I heard it, my heart did leap for joy.

Then the Lord let me see why there was none on earth who could speak to my condition, namely, that I might give him all the glory. For all are concluded under sin, and shut up in unbelief, as I had been, that Jesus might have the preeminence, who enlightens, and gives grace, and faith, and power. Thus when God doth work, who shall hinder it? And this I knew experimentally.

My desire after the Lord grew stronger, and zeal in the pure knowledge of God, and of Christ alone, without the help of any man, book, or writing. For though I read the Scriptures that spoke of Christ and of God, yet I knew him not, but by revelation, as he who hath the key did open (Rev 3:7), and as the Father of Life drew me to his Son by his Spirit. Then the Lord gently led me along, and let me see his love, which was endless and eternal, surpassing all the knowledge that men have in the natural state, or can obtain from history or books, and that love let me see myself as I was without him.

I was afraid of all company, for I saw them perfectly where they were through the love of God which let me see myself. I had not fellowship with any people, priests or professors, or any sort of separated people, but with Christ who hath the key and opened the door of Light and Life unto me. I was afraid of all carnal talk and talkers, for I could see nothing but corruption and the life lay under the burden of corruption.

When I myself was in the deep, shut up under all, I could not believe that I should ever overcome. My troubles, my sorrows, and my temptations were so great that I thought many times that I should have despaired, I was so tempted. But when Christ opened to me how he was tempted by the same devil and overcame him and bruised his head (Gen 3:15), and that through him and his power, light, grace, and Spirit I should overcome, I had confidence in him, so that he it was that opened to me when I was shut up and had no hope nor faith. Christ who had enlightened me gave me his light to believe in. He gave me hope, which he himself revealed in me, and he gave me his Spirit and grace which I found sufficient in the deeps and in weakness. Thus in the deepest miseries and in the greatest sorrows and temptations that many times beset me the Lord in his mercy did keep me.

I found that there were two thirsts in me—the one after the creatures to get help and strength there, and the other after the Lord, the Creator, and his Son Jesus Christ. I saw all the world could do me no good. If I had had a king's diet, palace, and attendance, all would have been as nothing, for nothing gave me comfort but the Lord by his power. At another time I saw the great love of God and was filled with admiration at the infiniteness of it.

One day when I had been walking solitary abroad and was come home, I was taken up in the love of God, so that I could not but admire the greatness of his love. And while I was in that condition, it was opened up to me by the eternal light and power, and I therein clearly saw that all was done and was to be done in and by Christ, and how he conquers and destroys this tempter the devil and all his works, and is atop of him; and that all these troubles were good for me and temptations for the trial of my faith which Christ had given me.

The Lord opened me so that I saw all through these troubles and temptations. My living faith was raised so that I saw all was done by Christ the life, and my belief was in him. When at any time my condition was veiled, my secret belief was kept firm, and hope underneath held me as an anchor in the bottom of the sea and anchored my immortal soul to its Bishop, causing it to swim above the sea, the world, where all the raging waves, foul weather, tempests, and tribulations are. But O! Then did I see my troubles, trials, and temptations more clearly than ever I had done. As the light appeared, all appeared that is out of the light: darkness, death, temptations, the unrighteous, the ungodly. All was manifest and seen in the light.

II.
1648

(A) Soon after there was another great meeting of professors and a captain whose name was Amor Stoddard came in. They were discoursing of the blood of Christ, and as they were discoursing of it, I saw, through the immediate opening of the invisible Spirit, the blood of Christ. And I cried out among them and said, "Do you not see the blood of Christ: See it in your hearts to sprinkle your hearts and consciences from dead works to serve the living God," for I saw the blood of the New Covenant, how it came into the heart. This startled the professors who would have the blood only outside them and not in them. But Captain Stoddard was reached and said, "Let the youth speak; hear the youth speak," when he saw that they endeavored to bear me down with many words....

(B) Now I was come up in spirit through the flaming sword into the paradise of God (Gen 3:24). All things were new and all creation gave unto me another smell than before, beyond what words can utter. I knew nothing but pureness and innocency and righteousness, being renewed into the image of God by Christ Jesus to the state of Adam which he was in before he fell. The creation was opened to me, and it was showed to me how all things had their names given them according to their nature and virtue.

I was at a stand in my mind whether I should practice physic [i.e., medicine] for the good of mankind, seeing the nature and virtues of things were so opened to me by the Lord. But I was immediately taken up in the spirit to see into another and more steadfast state than Adam's innocency, even into a state in Christ Jesus that should never fail. And the Lord showed me that such as were faithful to him in the power and light of Christ should come up into that state in which Adam was before he fell, in which the admirable works of the creation and of the virtues thereof may be known through the openings of that divine Word of wisdom and power by which they were made.

Great things did the Lord lead me into and wonderful depths were opened up unto me beyond what can by words be declared; but as people come into subjection to the Spirit of God and grow up in the image and power of the Almighty, they may receive the Word of wisdom that opens all things and come to know the hidden unity in the Eternal Being.

From *George Fox. An Autobiography,* edited with an introduction and notes by Rufus M. Jones (Philadelphia: Friends' Book Store, 1903), 82–85, 90–91, 97–98.

DISTRESS AND DERELICTION

The delights of rapture and contemplative vision by no means exhaust the variety of ways in which mystics have described their consciousness of God. Rudolf Otto in his classic work *The Holy* (1917) analyzed the religious sense of the divine in terms of what he called the *mysterium tremendum*, the mystery that induces both awe that attracts, as well as fear and trembling. This basic religious attitude is heightened in many mystical accounts exploring the fear and distress that the overwhelming majesty of God brings to those humans who draw near to him. (The sense of unworthiness in the face of God is the root of the need for continuing purgation explored in section 2.) Christian mystics noted that certain biblical figures who had direct contact with God, such as Abraham, Job, and Elijah, had experienced a similar sense of deep dread.

Closely allied to these accounts of distress is the even more frightening experience of dereliction, the feeling of being abandoned by God. It may seem paradoxical that those who dedicate their lives to the pursuit of God have so often been visited with periods of abandonment and dereliction, involving temptations to despair, loss of faith, and even the conviction that they have been damned. (Teresa of Avila once said to God: "Lord, if this is the way you treat your friends, no wonder you have so few of them.") In confronting this most painful of all aspects of mystical consciousness devout souls once again looked to the Bible, especially to Christ's wrenching cry on the cross, "My God, my God, why have you abandoned me?" (Mt 27:46, citing Ps 21:2), to gain some understanding of the meaning of this test. Some mystics taught that a willingness to be consigned to hell, if that be God's will, was a necessary aspect of the mystical path. (Scriptural backing for this was found in Paul's statement in Romans 9:2–3 that he would be willing to be accursed and separated from Christ if only his fellow Jews could be saved.) Expressions of this "resignation to hell" (*resignatio ad infernum*) were condemned during the Quietist controversies at the end of the seventeenth century (see section 14.4), but the theme had a long history and was capable of orthodox expression.

The five selections given here cover thirteen centuries. Gregory the Great's commentary on Job and his trials is one of the earliest explicit explorations of the importance of fear and distress in Christian mysticism. A sense of dereliction was especially pronounced among the late-medieval female mystics. Many texts might be presented from such figures as Hadewijch, Margaret the Cripple, and Mechthild of Magdeburg in the thirteenth century, or Catherine of Bologna in the fifteenth. I have chosen a passage from the Franciscan tertiary Angela of Foligno as representative of medieval women's experience of dereliction. The witness of the fourteenth-century Dominican John Tauler shows that such states (Tauler once called them "night work") were not restricted to women. Tauler's sermons were appreciated by Martin Luther, who had a powerful, if not exactly mystical, sense of the importance of the anguish caused by the God who hides himself. John of the Cross, so opposed to Luther in many ways, agreed with him in emphasizing utter dependence on faith in what he called the dark night of the spirit. Mystical dereliction, however, is not just a thing of the past. The doubts, darkness, and loss of hope experienced by Thérèse of Lisieux in the last year of her short life provide a modern example of this theme.

GREGORY THE GREAT
MORAL INTERPRETATION OF JOB

BOOK V.29(51)–31(55)

*Gregory the Great, pope from 590 to 604, is among the most influential figures in the history of Christianity. His role in the development of mysticism, especially in the Middle Ages, is just one aspect of his impact. Gregory's longest work is the moral commentary on Job (*Moralia in Iob*) that he wrote between about 586 and 591. Gregory considers Job as the primary type, or prophetic figure, of the total Christ, that is, both the God-man whose death brings redemption, as well as the members of the church, his body, who are meant to share in Christ's suffering. Over the course of the thirty-five books of this work Gregory touches upon the main themes of his mystical spirituality, especially the twin centers of his message, compunction and contemplation.*

For Gregory fallen humans need to be "pierced" by compunction (Acts 2:37) in order to begin the path back to God. As explained in the passage here commenting on Job 4:12–13, compunction comes in two forms. The first is the compunction of fear when God strikes us with a sense of our sinfulness and the need to repent; the second is the compunction of love by which God draws us to heaven. The compunction of love is another term for contemplation, the attentive interior gaze toward God that according to Gregory is the purpose of human life. Adam's fall left us trapped in exteriority and forgetfulness of God; Christ, the rock upon whom we must rest our head, restores the possibility of brief moments of the contemplation of divine light in this life. (This is what Gregory sometimes calls "the chinks, or flashes, of contemplation.") Gregory insists that contemplative ex-

perience, at least in this life, is always partial and subject to "relapse," or being beaten back by our own weakness and finiteness. His sense of the overwhelming majesty of the divine nature and his reading of the contemplative experiences of biblical figures such as Job, Jacob, Elijah, and Paul led him to believe that contemplative contact with God involves as much terror and dread as joy and delight.

NOW THERE WAS A WORD SPOKEN TO ME IN PRIVATE, AND MY EARS, AS IT WERE STEALTHILY, RECEIVED THE VEINS OF ITS WHISPERS (JOB 4:12)

The ear of the heart "received stealthily the veins of heavenly whispering" in that both in a moment and in secret the inspired soul is made to know the subtle quality of the inward utterance. For unless it hides itself from external objects of desire, it fails to enter into the internal things. It is both hidden that it may hear, and it hears that it may be hidden; in that at one and the same time being withdrawn from the visible world its eyes are on the invisible, and being replenished with the unseen, it entertains a perfect contempt for what is visible. Note that he does not say, "My ear received as it were by stealth its whispering," but "the veins of its whispering." This is because "the whispering of the hidden word" is the very utterance of inward inspiration itself; but "the veins of whispering" is the name for the sources of the occasions whereby that inspiration itself is conveyed to the mind. For it is as if it opened "the veins of its whispering" when God secretly communicates to us in what ways he enters into the ear of our understanding. Thus at one time he pierces us with love; at another time with terror. Sometimes he shows us how little present reality is and lifts up our hearts to desire the eternal world; sometimes he first points to the things of eternity so that temporal things may grow worthless in our eyes. Sometimes he discloses to us our own evil deeds and from there draws us on to the point of feeling sorrow for the evil deeds of others; sometimes he presents to our eyes the evil deeds of others and reforms us from our own wickedness, pierced with a wonderful feeling of compunction. And so to "hear the veins of divine whispering by stealth" is to be made to know the secret methods of divine inspiration, at once gently and secretly.

Yet we may interpret "the whispering," or "the veins of whispering," in another way. For he that "whispers" is speaking in secret, and he does not give out a voice, but imitates one. Therefore, so long as we are beset by the corruptions of the flesh, we in no way behold the brightness of the divine power as it abides unchangeable in itself. This is because in the eye of our weakness we cannot endure that which shines above us with intolerable luster from the ray of his eternal being. And so when the Almighty shows himself to us by the chinks of contemplation, he does not speak to us, but whispers, in that though he does not fully make himself known, yet he reveals something of himself to the human mind. But then he no longer whispers at all, but speaks, when his appearance is manifested to us in certainty. It is for this that the Truth says in the Gospel, "I shall show you plainly of the Father" (Jn 16:25). Hence John says, "For we shall see him as he is" (1 Jn 3:2). And so Paul says, "Then shall I know even as I am known" (1 Cor 13:12). Now in this present time the divine whispering has as many veins for our ears as the works of creation over which the divinity rules. While we view all created things, we are lifted up in admiration of the Creator. . . . But we must bear in mind that in proportion as the soul being lifted up contemplates his power, so, being held back, it fears his omnipotence. Hence it rightly says:

IN THE HORROR OF A VISION OF THE NIGHT (JOB 4:13)

"The horror of a vision of the night" is the shuddering of secret contemplation. For the higher the elevation, where the mind of man contemplates the things that are eternal, so much the more, terror-struck at her temporal deeds, she shrinks with dread in that she thoroughly discovers herself guilty, in proportion as she sees herself to have been out of harmony with that light that shines in the midst of darkness above her. Then it happens that the enlightened mind entertains the greater fear, as it more clearly sees by how much it is at variance with the rule of truth. And she that before seemed as it were more secure in seeing nothing, trembles with grave fear at her very own success. Yet whatever her progress in virtue, she does not as yet understand anything of eternity in a clear way, but still sees under a kind of dark imagining. And hence this is called a "vision of the night." For as we have said above, in the night we see doubtfully, but in the day we see steadily. Therefore, because in contemplating the ray of the interior Sun the cloud of our corruption interposes itself and the unchangeable Light does not burst forth such as it is to the weak eyes of our mind, we still behold God as it were "in a vision of the night," since we most surely walk the way under shadowy contemplation. Though the mind may have conceived but a distant idea about God, nonetheless, in considering his greatness she recoils with dread and is filled with greater awe because she feels herself unequal even to the traces of contemplation of him. And falling back upon herself, she is drawn with closer bonds of love to him whose marvelous sweetness she is unable to bear, but of which she has barely tasted in her shadowy vision. But, because she never attains to such a height of elevation unless the troublesome and clamorous throng of carnal desires be first brought under governance, it is rightly added:

WHEN DEEP SLEEP FALLS UPON MEN (JOB 4:13B)

Whoever desires to do things that belong to the world, is, as it were, awake; whoever seeks inward rest eschews the riot of this world and is as it were asleep. But first we must know that in holy scripture, sleep, when put figuratively, is understood in three senses. For sometimes sleep expresses the death of the flesh, sometimes the lethargy of neglect, and sometimes the tranquility of life when earthly desires have been trodden underfoot. Thus by the designation of sleep or slumbering the death of the flesh is implied; as when Paul says, "And I would not have you ignorant, brethren, concerning those who are asleep" (1 Thess 4:13). And shortly after, "Even so those also who sleep in Jesus will God bring with him" (1 Thess 4:14). Again, by sleep is designated the lethargy of neglect, as where the same Paul says, "Now it is high time to awake out of sleep" (Rom 13:11). And again, "Awake, you righteous ones, and sin not" (1 Cor 15:34). By sleep too is represented tranquility of life when carnal desires are trodden down, as where these words are uttered by the voice of the bride in the Song of Songs, "I sleep, but my heart is awake" (Song 5:2). For in truth, in proportion as the holy mind withholds itself from the turmoil of temporal desire, the more truly it knows interior matters, and the more it hides itself from exterior disturbance, the more quickly it wakes to inward concerns. And this is well represented by Jacob sleeping on his journey (Gen 28:11–13). He put a stone to his head and slept. He beheld a ladder from the earth stretching up to heaven and the Lord resting upon the ladder, and angels also ascending and descending. For to "sleep on a journey" is, in the passage of this present life, to rest from the love of temporal things. To sleep on a journey in the course of our passing days is to close the eyes of the mind to the desire for those visible things that the seducer opened up to the first humans when he said, "For God knows that in the day you eat from it, then your eyes shall be opened" (Gen 3:5). Hence it soon adds, "She took from the fruit, and ate, and gave it also to her husband with her, and he ate. And the eyes of them both were opened" (Gen 3:6–7). For sin opened the eyes of concupiscence, which innocence kept shut. But to "see angels ascending and descending" is to behold the citizens of the land above, either with what love they cleave to their Creator above them, or with what fellow feeling in charity they condescend to aid our infirmities.

It is very deserving of observation that he who "lays his head upon a stone" sees the angels in his sleep, because that same person, by resting from external works, penetrates internal truths when with intent mind (the governing principle of man) he looks to imitating his Redeemer. For to "lay the head upon a stone" is to cleave to Christ in mind. Those who are withdrawn from this life's sphere of action yet are not drawn by love to heavenly things may have sleep, but they can never see the angels because they despise keeping their head upon the stone. For there are some who do flee the business of the world, but exercise themselves in no virtues. These certainly sleep from lethargy, not from serious design, and therefore they never behold interior things because they have laid their head upon the earth not upon the stone. It is most frequently their lot that the more surely they rest from outward actions, the more amply they gather within themselves from their idleness an uproar of unclean thoughts. And thus under the likeness of Judea the prophet bewails the soul stupefied by indolence where he says, "The adversaries saw her, and did mock at her Sabbaths" (Lam 1:7). According to the precept of the law, there is a cessation from outward work upon the Sabbath. Thus, her "enemies looking on mock at her Sabbaths" when evil spirits forcefully drag the waste hours of such folk to unlawful thoughts. Hence every such soul, in proportion as it is supposed to be devoted to the service of God by being removed from external action, will be the more subject to their tyranny by entertaining unlawful thoughts. But holy people, who sleep to the works of the world not from lethargy but from virtue, are more laborious in their sleep than they would be awake. For insofar as they are made superior to this world's doings by abandoning them, they daily fight against themselves in brave conflict in order that the mind not be rendered dull by neglect, nor subdued by indolence, nor cool down to the harboring of impure desires, nor be more fervent in good desires than is right, nor by sparing the mind under the pretext of discretion slacken its endeavor after perfection. These are the things the mind does: she both wholly withdraws herself from the restless appetite of this world, and she also gives up the turmoil of earthly actions. And, in pursuit of tranquility, while bent on virtuous attainments, she sleeps waking. She is never led on to contemplate internal things unless she be earnestly withdrawn from those things that entwine themselves about her from without. And it is hence that Truth declares by his own mouth, "No one can serve two masters" (Mt 6:20). Hence Paul says, "No soldier entangles himself with the affairs of this life, that he may please him who has chosen him to be a soldier" (2 Tim 2:4). Hence the Lord charges us by the Prophet, saying "Be still, and know that I am the Lord" (Ps 46:10). Therefore, because inward knowledge is not recognizable unless there is a cessation of exterior entanglement, the time of the hidden word and of the divine whisper is rightly set forth here when it says, "In the horror of a vision of the night, when deep sleep falls upon men" (Jb 4:13). This is the case because our mind is never truly snatched up to the power of inward contemplation unless it be first carefully lulled to rest from all agitation of earthly desires. But the human mind, lifted on high by the engine of its contemplation as it were, in proportion as it sees things higher above itself, trembles more terribly within itself.

Translation based upon that of "C. M." in *Morals on the Book of Job* (Oxford: John Henry Parker, 1844), Vol. I:279–84. My thanks to David C. Albertson for assistance in modernizing the translation.

ANGELA OF FOLIGNO
THE MEMORIAL

*Angela of Foligno (circa 1250–1309) is one of the female mystics whose emergence in the thirteenth century helped initiate the "New Mysticism" of the late-medieval and early-modern periods. Though details of the two texts that recount her life and teaching (*The Memorial *and* The Instructions*) contain elements introduced to foster the cause of the Spiritual Franciscans, there is no reason to doubt that these materials reflect the life and teachings of a historical woman with a special message and personality.*

"Angela" (we are not sure if this was her real name) was born in Umbria into a middle-class family. Married and with children, she experienced a conversion about 1285 through the intervention of St. Francis. Soon after, her husband and children died, and she began to live the life of a penitent woman, being accepted into the third order of Franciscans about 1291. In the same year, she experienced a public ecstasy while on pilgrimage to Assisi, an event that brought her to the attention of the Franciscan friar who became her scribe. Angela related her mystical path to the friar, who tried to put it in some order in the work called The Memorial.

Angela's itinerary is complex. "Brother scribe" tells us that she had completed twenty stages by the time he began writing it down in 1292. The further ten stages that led to final union with God were completed in 1296, but the friar had trouble understanding these, so he condensed them into seven "supplementary steps" appended to the first twenty. Angela's early mystical stages contain many visionary and erotic manifestations of Jesus, but the final steps pass beyond the visionary dimension. The account of the sixth step given here is a searing description of mystical dereliction. The scribe tells us that it coexisted with the seventh supplementary step, which is described as a deeply apophatic form of union "in and with darkness."

CHAPTER EIGHT.
THE SIXTH SUPPLEMENTARY STEP

The sixth step is a martyrdom of multiple and intolerable suffering and martyring, both through bodily ills and through countless torments of soul and body stirred up by many demons in a horrible way.

The words of brother scribe introduce the theme of "Angela's Torments of Body and Soul."

I, friar scribe, did not take much trouble to write about the sixth step of the multiple sufferings, both through bodily ills and unnumbered torments of soul and body stirred up by many demons in a horrible way. I was not able to note down the many stories in writing that I understood would have been worthwhile and useful. But I have tried to write, just as I heard from her mouth, some little bit of the words of Christ's faithful lover about what she suffered and the testimony she bore. I do this as a hasty sketch, because I cannot understand enough to write down a full account.

Christ's faithful one told me, brother scribe, that she did not believe that the illnesses of her body, as well as the illnesses and sufferings of her soul, could be written down, many of which she said were beyond comparison. In brief, concerning the sufferings of her body, I heard from her that there was not a single part of her body that did not suffer in a horrible way.

Concerning the torments of soul that she suffered from the demons, she was able to come with no better comparison than that of a person hung by the neck, with his hands bound behind his back and blindfolded, who is hung by a rope on the gallows and yet lives, who remains without any aid, any kind of support or help. And she added that she was even more desperately and cruelly tortured by the demons.

I, brother scribe, also heard said and learned the following. A certain Franciscan friar, and one I believe worthy of faith, was in great awe and compassion when he heard from the faithful of Christ how she had been most horribly tormented. This trustworthy friar saw in a revelation made to him by God how whatever the faithful lover of Christ said she had suffered from the martyrdom of those horrible torments was true, and more than true. This is the reason why from that time on this friar was always attached to her with great and wondrous compassion and devotion. These were the words that I, brother scribe, hastily and briefly was able to sketch.

The narration of Angela's terrible torments of body and soul, especially those relating to concupiscence.

First, the description of how she was enticed by the devil in such a way that her vices came to life again and her virtues grew weak.

Christ's faithful one spoke as follows. I behold the demons hold my soul up in suspension in such a way that, just as a hanged person has no support, so too there seems to be no support left for my soul. All its virtues are overthrown while the soul sees, knows, and looks on. Then, when the soul sees that all the virtues have been overthrown and departed, and that she can do nothing about it, there is such great pain—such desperate pain as well as anger of the soul—that I am scarcely able at any time to weep over this desperate sorrow and anger. There are times that I cry without being able to stop. There are times when such great anger ensues that I am scarcely able to stop from totally tearing myself apart. There are also times when I can't hold myself back from striking myself in a horrible way, and sometimes my head and limbs are swollen. When the soul begins to see all the virtues fall down and fall away, then there is fear and lament, and I speak to God, calling out again and again to God without letup, saying to him, "My Son, my Son, do not leave me, my Son!" (Mt 27:46).

Christ's faithful said that there was not a single part of her body that was not struck and punished by the demons. And hence she said that she did not believe that the infirmities of her body were any more capable of being written down than those of her soul. She said that all her vices revived, not in order to last for life, but to provide and cause great punishment. Even great vices that had never existed in her before, came into the body and caused great punishment, though they did not have a continuing life. When they died once again, [she said] that they gave me this consolation at least: I see that I have been handed over to demons who revive and bring back to life vices long dead and add those that never were. And then, remembering that God was afflicted, despised, and poor, I wish that all my evils and afflictions were doubled.

Second, the description of how the vices, especially those opposed to chastity, that had once died in the soul, now rise up again in the body through diabolical temptation.

Christ's faithful one said: While I am in the most horrible darkness of the demons it seems that any kind of hope of the good is lacking— it is a terrible darkness. The vices that I know were dead in my soul are brought back to life, and the demons rouse them up in the soul from the outside—and they even raise to life vices that were never there. They did the same in the body (where I suffer less) in three places, that is, in the sexual places. There was so great a fire there that I used to use material flame to extinguish the other fire, until you [i.e., her confessor and scribe] forbade it. For the time during which I am in that darkness, I believe that I would rather be burned than to suffer those pains; indeed, I would then call out and shout for any kind of death that God would give me. Then I tell God that if he has to send me to hell, not to delay it, but do it at once. And I say: "Because you have abandoned me, finish it and drown me." Then I understand that this is the work of demons and that these vices do not live on in the soul because the soul never consents to them, but they are given to the body in a violent manner. The sorrow and fatigue that affect the body come from its own action in not being able to bear this state of affairs. But the soul also sees that all power is taken away from her and although she does not agree to it, she has no power in any way of resisting the vices. She sees that this is contrary to God; and yet she falls into these things.

Third, the description of how God permits that as she labors with a vice that was unknown to her previously, she learns to fight against it with a special virtue for this task.

Christ's faithful said: There was a certain vice God clearly permitted to be given to me that was never in me before, but I know that God openly permitted it to come into me. The vice was so great that it surpassed all other vices. And there was a certain virtue openly given to me by God against this vice that immediately overcame it in so powerful a way that even if I had no secure confidence in God regarding any other virtue, I would still have sure and secure faith in him about this one and would not be able to doubt it. The virtue remains forever; the vice then faded away. The virtue took hold of me and did not permit me to fall into vice. The virtue was so strong that it not only took hold of me, but it also gave me so much strength of its power that I truly recognize God in it, because nothing visible, or nothing audible, or nothing sinful could move me by a sinful motion away from this virtue. If all the people in the world made the attempt, and in every way, and if all the demons of hell made an attempt against me, they would not be able to move me to the slightest sin. This is why I have absolute faith in God. The reason is that the vice is so great that I am ashamed to name it. It is so great that when this virtue was hidden from me and seemed to have left me, there was nothing that could hold me up, neither for shame, nor for any punishment, so that I would not fall at once into that sin. Nevertheless, when that virtue came upon me, it freed me in so powerful a way that it seemed that I could not sin for all the good things or the bad things in this world.

I, brother scribe, saw Christ's faithful one suffer more horribly in this sixth step than I can recount. But the sixth step lasted only a brief time, about two years [circa 1294–96]. It ran together with the seventh step, which began a little while before the sixth step, and what followed was more marvelous than all the rest. I saw that the sixth step grew weak and ceased in a brief time, but it did not fade totally and in every way, especially with regard to the many bodily ills that always filled her. ...

Translated by Bernard McGinn from *Il Libro della Beata Angela da Foligno (Edizione critica)*, edited by Ludger Thier, OFM, and Abela Calufetti, OFM (Gottaferrata: Collegii S. Bonaventurae, 1985), 336–46.

3.

JOHN TAULER

SERMON 3

John Tauler (see section 5.5) lived through some of the most difficult years of the fourteenth century, being witness to climate changes, natural disasters, endemic warfare, persecutions of the Jews, and the Black Death that killed almost half the population in large parts of Europe. Tauler's sense of the necessity for suffering on the path to God, however, does not appear to be a reaction to these external ills, terrible as they were. Rather, it was his experience as a preacher and spiritual guide among both religious women and other devout seekers after God that moved him to explore the role of inner dereliction and suffering with such penetration. The preacher makes clear that the purpose of these trials is to cleanse a person of all self-reliance and pride in his or her accomplishments and to teach pure and disinterested reliance on God. In this sermon for the Feast of the Epiphany, Tauler puts inner affliction into the wider framework of the meaning of suffering in the Christian life and the proper attitude to profit from it. Tauler, like Eckhart, was convinced that detachment was essential for finding God, and that suffering was the best way to realize detachment.

The sermon, taken from the Gospel of St. Matthew (2:1–12) for the twelfth day of Christmas about the three kinds of myrrh, tells how God out of great love has foreseen and ordained all sufferings for the eternal advantage of each and every person, however one may encounter them, great or small.

The kings offered myrrh, incense, and gold. Take, first of all, myrrh, which is bitter and indicates the bitterness that is involved in a person's finding God—when a person first turns away from the world to God, but before he drives out all desires and pleasures. For it is necessary that everything a person possessed with desire must be driven out. This is at first very bitter and very hard. All things must become bitter for you to the degree that you found pleasure in them. This must always be the case and requires much discernment and well-directed zeal. To the degree that the pleasure was great, the myrrh becomes bitter, and it is a great bitterness indeed.

Now one might say: How can one live without being satisfied while living on this earth? I get hungry and I eat; I get thirsty and I drink; I get sleepy and I sleep; I get cold and I warm myself. Indeed, it cannot happen that this be bitter for me or without natural pleasure. I can't make it happen as long as nature is nature. But this satisfaction should not enter into or have any place in one's inner self. It should flow along with one's actions and not remain a lasting presence. It should not deposit pleasure but rather flow on, not as one's own possession where one takes one's rest satisfied and with pleasure; rather, let go of all the satisfaction in the world and in creatures that you find within yourself. Here you must kill and conquer nature with nature. Even the enjoyment you find with the friends of God and good persons and everything else to which you feel an inclination you must overcome completely until Herod and all his court, who seek the child's soul, are truly and certainly dead in you. And so do not deceive yourself. Constantly take note of how things stand with you, and don't be too free.

There is another kind of myrrh that by far transcends the first kind. This is the myrrh that God gives, whatever kind of suffering it might be, interior or external. The person who accepts this myrrh in love and out of the ground from which God gives it—what a blissful life might be born in such a person! Also, what joy, what peace, what a noble thing that would be! Indeed, the least and the greatest suffering that God lets befall you issues forth from the ground of his inexpressible love, a love so great that it is the loftiest and best gift that he could give you or ever did give. If you only know how to accept it, it would be of very great advantage to you. Indeed, all suffering, the smallest bit of hair that ever fell from your head that you didn't even notice—our Lord says, "A single hair shall not go uncounted" (Mt 10:30)—never can suffering, be it ever so small, befall you that God has not noticed from eternity, loved, and intended it; and so it comes to you.

If your finger hurts or you have a headache, if your feet are cold, if you are hungry or thirsty, if someone saddens you by word or deed, or whatever might happen to cause you distress—all this molds you and serves to make you a noble and joyful person. It has been completely ordained by God that this should happen to you. It has been measured, weighed, and counted; and it cannot be less or otherwise. That my eye is placed in my head has been foreseen from eternity by God, the heavenly Father. If I now lose it and become blind or deaf, the heavenly Father foresaw from eternity that that would happen, and he planned for it from eternity, and in this plan it was lost from eternity. Should I not, therefore, open my inner eyes or ears and thank my God that his eternal plan for me has been accomplished? Should it make me sad? It should make me extremely grateful. If you lose friends, property, honor, consolation, or whatever it is that God gives you, all this molds you and serves to bring you true peace, if only you can accept it. Some people say, "Father, things are really going badly for me and I'm suffering terribly." I tell them that is the way things should be. Then they say, "No, Father, I deserved this; I entertained an evil thought." Dear child, it doesn't matter whether it was deserved or not. As long as the suffering is from God, submit and surrender.

All the myrrh that God gives us is rightly ordered, so that he might lead a person to great things through suffering. He has arranged it that all things vex humankind. God could just as well and just as easily have made bread grow instead of grain. But men must toil in all things. He has ordained and predetermined each and every thing in the eternal order. A painter, as he applies the blue and red colors, considers carefully how he should apply each brushstroke to the picture, how short, long, or broad—that it be just so and not otherwise if the painting is to take on the form from the master. But God is a thousand times more careful about how he might apply the strokes of suffering and colors to create in a person the form that pleases him the best. One has only to give these gifts and myrrh their proper due.

Some people, however, are not satisfied with the myrrh God gives them. They want to pile more onto themselves, racking their brain and indulging in unsound thoughts. They have suffered a long time and plenty but don't manage things rightly, and little grace results from their persistence. For they are carrying out their own designs, be it penances, fasting, prayer, or devotions. God always has to wait until they finish doing what they want before they come to rest. Nothing comes of this. God has decided that he only rewards his own works. In heaven, he only crowns his work, not yours. Whatever in you is not his work has no value for him.

Now, there is one kind of very bitter myrrh that God gives: interior affliction and darkness. If a person becomes aware of this and accepts it, it eats away at his flesh, blood, and nature, and this internal struggle changes his appearance much more than external penitential practices do. For God visits upon him horrible trials in strange and unusual ways that no one notices except the person going through it. Such people have such astounding sufferings, strange myrrh, and hardly anyone knows what to make of it; but God knows what he has in mind with it. But if a person is not aware of the great love with which he gives this myrrh, it causes such incredible harm that no one's laments can do it justice. And if a person lets it be out of laziness and neglects it and nothing comes of it, some then say, "Lord, I am experiencing such inner aridity and darkness." Dear child, be content; you are much better off than if you were feeling deep emotions.

Myrrh is resisted in two ways: with the senses and with the faculty of reason. External myrrh is resisted through the senses in the following way. Some people think themselves so wise and imagine they are deflecting it with their wisdom and attribute these external reversals to good or bad luck, and they think they might have better preserved themselves against suffering. If this or that had been done, they imagine, things would have turned out well and suffering would have been avoided. They consider themselves wiser than God and want to teach him a thing or two as his schoolmaster, and they don't know how just to accept things from him. They have great sufferings and their myrrh is very bitter for them.

Others resist interior myrrh with their natural good skill; they break out of their distressful state by applying rational ideas. Simple people often do this more quickly than those with high-sounding intellectual concerns because simple people obey God simply. They don't know any different. But, truly, if the thinkers would obey and surrender themselves to God alone, they would succeed much more nobly and happily because their reason serves them nicely in all matters. Ah, those who really surrender themselves to him, no drop of blood would be too small to serve especially well this purpose.

From this grows a precious wisp of smoke, a sprout from a kernel of precious incense. Incense has a fragrant smell. When fire envelops this kernel, it lies in wait and searches out the fragrance in the kernel. It releases the fragrance that was imprisoned in the kernel, so that it escapes and turns into a fine fragrance. The fire is nothing other than one's burning love of God contained in prayer. The incense releases the really fine fragrance of holy devotion, for it is written: Prayer is nothing other than the ascent of the mind to God. Just as straw exists only for the sake of grain, unless one wants to make a bed out of it to rest on or make dung out of it, so too external prayer is only useful insofar as it impels a person to this noble devotion. It is from here that the precious fragrance issues forth. When this emerges, just forget about oral prayer. But I exclude those who are bound to such prayers by the commands of holy church.

Translated for this volume by Frank Tobin from *Die Predigten Taulers,* edited by Ferdinand Vetter (Berlin: Weidmann, 1910), 16–20.

4.

JOHN OF THE CROSS
THE DARK NIGHT OF THE SOUL

BOOKS I.8 AND II.5

The work now known as The Dark Night of the Soul *is really part of the treatise commenting on the poem "En una noche oscura" (see section 2.5). In the popular mind John of the Cross is the mystic most associated with the notion that mystical purification demands extreme suffering and inner dereliction, though, as the previous selections have demonstrated, this was an ancient theme in Christian mysticism. What John brought to this strand of mysticism was his deep theological penetration and systematic organization.* The Dark Night *falls into two books. The first begins with an introduction (chapters 1–7) and proceeds with an analysis of the passive night of the senses (chapters 8–14). The second book takes up the deeper and more painful passive night of the spirit. Chapters 1–3 form an introduction, while chapters 4–8 provide a basic description of the effect of this night on the soul. Chapters 9–25 describe the characteristics of the night in detail, highlighting the relation of the night to the intellect and will, as well as the role of the three theological virtues.*

BOOK I, CHAPTER 8.
EXPLANATION OF THE FIRST LINE OF
THE STANZA, AND A BEGINNING OF THE
EXPLANATION OF THE "DARK NIGHT"

This night, which as we say is contemplation, produces in spiritual persons two sorts of darkness or purgations corresponding to the two divisions of man's nature into sensual and spiritual. Thus the first night or purgation will be sensual, in which the soul is purified according to the senses, subjecting them to the spirit. The other is that night or purgation that is spiritual, in which the soul is purified and stripped in the spirit, and which subdues and disposes it for union with God in love. The night of sense is common and happens to many: These are the beginners, of whom I shall first speak. The spiritual night is the portion of very few; and they are those who have made some progress, who are proficient, of whom I shall speak later.

The first night or purgation is bitter and terrible to sense. The second is not to be compared with it, for it is horrible and frightful to the spirit, as I shall soon show. But as the night of sense is the first in order and the first to be entered, I shall speak of it briefly—for being of ordinary occurrence, it is the matter of many treatises—so that I may pass on to treat more at large of the spiritual night; for of that very little has been said, either by speech or in writing, and little is known of it even by experience....

BOOK II, CHAPTER 5.
SETS DOWN THE FIRST LINE ["UPON A
DARK NIGHT"] AND BEGINS TO EXPLAIN
HOW THIS DARK CONTEMPLATION
IS NOT ONLY NIGHT FOR THE SOUL,
BUT IS ALSO PAIN AND TORMENT

The dark night is an inflowing of God into the soul, which cleanses it of its ignorances and imperfections, habitual, natural, and spiritual. Contemplatives call it infused contemplation, or mystical theology, by which God secretly teaches the soul and instructs it in the perfection of love, without effort on its own part or understanding how this happens. Insofar as infused contemplation is the loving wisdom of God, it produces two special effects in the soul, for by both purifying and enlightening it, this contemplation prepares the soul for union with God in love. It is the same loving wisdom that by enlightening purifies the blessed spirits that here purifies and enlightens the soul.

But it may be asked: Why does the soul call the divine light that enlightens the soul and purges it of its ignorances a dark night? The answer to this is that for two reasons this divine wisdom is not only night and darkness, but also pain and torment. The first is because the divine wisdom is so high that it transcends the capacity of the soul, and therefore in that respect is darkness. The second reason is based on the meanness and impurity of the soul, and in that respect the divine wisdom is painful to it, afflictive, and also dark.

To prove the truth of the first reason, we take for granted a principle of the Philosopher, namely, the more clear and evident divine things are, the more dark and hidden they are to the soul naturally [Aristotle, *Metaphysics* 2.2]. Thus the more clear the light the more it blinds the eyes of the owl, and the stronger the sun's rays the more it blinds the visual organs, overcoming and overwhelming them in their weakness. So too the divine light of contemplation, when it strikes on a soul not yet perfectly enlightened, causes spiritual darkness, because it not only surpasses its natural strength, but also blinds it and deprives the soul of its natural perception. It is for this reason that St. Dionysius and other mystical theologians call infused contemplation a ray of darkness, that is, for the unenlightened and unpurified soul [*Mystical Theology* 1.1]. For this great supernatural light masters the natural power of the intellect and deprives it of its vigor. Therefore, David also said: "Clouds and darkness are round about him" (Ps 46:2); not that this is so in reality, but in reference to our weak understanding, which, in light so great, becomes dimmed and blind, unable to ascend so high. Hence he explained, saying: "Clouds passed before the splendor of his presence" (Ps 47:13), that is, between God and our understanding. This is the reason why when God sends the illuminating ray of hidden wisdom from himself into the soul that is not yet transformed, it produces thick darkness in the understanding.

It is evident that this dark contemplation in its beginnings is also painful to the soul. For as the infused divine contemplation contains many excellences in the highest degree, and as the soul that receives them, not yet purified, has many extreme miseries, and because two contraries cannot coexist in the same subject, the soul must suffer and be in pain. Due to the purgation of the imperfections of the soul produced by this contemplation, the soul becomes the subject in which the two contraries meet and resist each other. I shall show it to be so by the following induction.

In the first place, because the light and wisdom of contemplation is most pure and bright, and because the soul on which it beats is in darkness and impure, the soul that receives it must suffer greatly. As eyes weakened and clouded by humors suffer pain when the clear light beats upon them, so the soul, by reason of its impurity, suffers exceedingly when the divine light really shines upon it. And when the rays of this pure light strike upon the soul in order to expel its impurities, the soul perceives itself to be so unclean and miserable that it seems as if God had set himself against it and that itself were set against God. So grievous and painful is this feeling—for it thinks now that God has abandoned it—that this was one of the heaviest afflictions of Job during his trial, when he said: "Why have you set me against you, and I become burdensome to myself?" (Jb 7:20). The soul, seeing its own impurity distinctly in this bright and pure light, though dimly, acknowledges its own unworthiness before God and all creatures. That which pains it the most is the fear that it never will be worthy, and that all its goodness is gone. This is caused by the deep immersion of the mind in the knowledge and sense of its own wickedness and misery. For now the divine and dark light reveals to it all its wretchedness, and it sees clearly that of itself it can never be other than it is. In this sense we can understand the words of David: "For iniquities you have chastised man, and you have made his soul to be undone and consumed: he wastes away as a spider" (Ps 38:12).

The second way in which the soul suffers pain comes from its natural, moral, and spiritual weakness, for when this divine contemplation strikes it with a certain vehemence in order to strengthen it and subdue it, it is then so pained in its weakness that it almost faints away. This is especially so at times when the divine contemplation strikes it with greater force, for sense and spirit, as if under an immense and dark burden, suffer and groan in agony so great that death itself would be a desired relief. This was the experience of Job, when he said, "I desire not that he commune with me with much strength, lest he oppress me with the weight of his greatness" (Jb 23:6).

The soul under the burden of this oppression and weight feels itself so removed from God's favor that it thinks—and correctly so—that all the things that consoled it formerly have utterly failed it, and that no one is left to pity it. In this sense Job also cried out: "Have pity on me, have pity on me, at the least you my friends, because the hand of our Lord has touched me" (Jb 19:21). It is amazing and pitiful that the soul's weakness and impurity is so great that the hand of God, so soft and so gentle, should now be felt to be so heavy and oppressive. For God's hand neither presses nor rests on it, but merely touches it, and that mercifully; for he touches the soul not to chastise it, but to grant it favors.

Adapted from the translation of David Lewis, *The Dark Night of the Soul, a Spiritual Canticle, and the Living Flame of Love of Saint John of the Cross* (London: Thomas Baker, 2nd ed., 1891), 27–28, 68–72.

THÉRÈSE OF LISIEUX

STORY OF A SOUL

SELECTION

The importance of suffering, especially spiritual dereliction and abandonment by God, also appears among modern mystics. A classic example of dereliction as temptation against faith can be found in St. Thérèse of Lisieux (1873–97), the Carmelite nun who became the third female doctor of the church by the declaration of John Paul II in 1997. Thérèse was born into a pious French family and entered the Carmelite convent in Lisieux in 1888. Her time there was to be short. Thérèse adapted to the life of austerity and contemplative prayer of the enclosed Carmelites with total dedication to the love of God, but she also wished, if possible, to take on a more apostolic life. She once wrote, "Ah! In spite of my littleness, I would like to enlighten souls as did the Prophets *and* Doctors. *I have the* vo- cation *of the* apostle" *(she often italicized important words in her writings). Thérèse contracted tuberculosis and suffered greatly before her death on September 30, 1897.*

During her time in the convent she was encouraged by the prioress, Mother Agnes (her own older sister Pauline), to write down reminiscences of her early years and life as a sister. These memoirs, consisting of three different manuscripts, grew into what came to be known after her death as Story of a Soul. *First published in 1898, it did much to spread the young nun's fame (she was canonized in 1925).*

Controversy continues to surround the book, as well as the other writings of Thérèse, mostly letters, poems, and plays. It is evident that Mother Agnes, anxious to foster the cause of Thérèse's canonization, altered the texts to conform to nineteenth-century ideals of piety. The rediscovery of the original versions of the manuscripts has revealed a far stronger and sometimes stranger figure than the traditional simple nun popularly known among Catholics as "the Little Flower." Her temptations against faith and loss of hope for heaven, downplayed in the early editions, are a case in point.

CHAPTER TEN. THE TRIAL OF FAITH (1896–1897)

... At this time I was enjoying such a living faith, such a clear *faith*, that the thought of heaven made up all my happiness, and I was unable to believe there were really impious people who had no faith. I believed they were actually speaking against their own inner convictions when they denied the existence of heaven, that beautiful heaven where God himself wanted to be their eternal reward. During those very joyful days of the Easter season, Jesus made me feel that there were really souls who have no faith, and who, through the abuse of grace, lost this precious treasure, the source of the only real and pure joys. He permitted my soul to be invaded by the thickest darkness, and that the thought of heaven, up until then so sweet to me, be no longer anything but the cause of struggle and torment. This trial was to last not a few days or a few weeks, it was not to be extinguished until the hour set by God himself and this hour has not yet come. I would like to be able to express what I feel, but alas! I believe this is impossible. One would have to travel through this dark tunnel to understand its darkness. I will try to explain it by a comparison.

I imagine I was born in a country that is covered in thick fog. I never had the experience of contemplating the joyful appearance of nature flooded and transformed by the brilliance of the sun. It is true that from childhood I heard people speak of these marvels, and I know the country I am living in is not really my true fatherland, and there is another I must long for without ceasing. This is not simply a story invented by someone living in the sad country where I am, but it is a reality, for the King of the fatherland of the bright sun actually came and lived for thirty-three years in the land of darkness. Alas! the darkness did not understand that this Divine King was the Light of the world (Jn 1:5, 9).

Your child, however, O Lord, has understood your divine light, and she begs pardon for her brothers. She is resigned to eat the bread of sorrow as long as you desire it; she does not wish to rise up from this table filled with bitterness at which poor sinners are eating until the day set by you. Can she not say in her name and in the name of her brothers, "Have pity on us, O Lord, for we are poor sinners!" (Lk 18:13). Oh! Lord, send us away justified. May all those who were not enlightened by the bright flame of faith one day see it shine. O Jesus! if it is needful that the table soiled by them be purified by a soul who loves you, then I desire to eat this bread of trial at this table until it pleases you to bring me into your bright kingdom. The only grace I ask of you is that I never offend you! . . .

I was saying that the certainty of going away one day far from the sad and dark country had been given me from the day of my childhood. I did not believe this only because I heard it from persons much more knowledgeable than I, but I felt in the bottom of my heart real longings for this most beautiful country. Just as the genius of Christopher Columbus gave him a presentiment of a new world when nobody had even thought of such a thing, so also I felt that another land would one day serve me as a permanent dwelling place. Then suddenly the fog that surrounds me becomes more dense; it penetrates my soul and envelops it in such a way that it is impossible to discover within it the sweet image of my fatherland; everything has disappeared! When I want to rest my heart fatigued by the darkness that surrounds it by the memory of the luminous country after which I aspire, my torment redoubles; it seems to me that the darkness, borrowing the voice of sinners, says mockingly to me: "You are dreaming about the light, about a fatherland embalmed in the sweetest perfumes; you are dreaming about the *eternal* possession of the Creator of all these marvels; you believe that one day you will walk out of this fog that surrounds you! Advance, advance; rejoice in death which will give you not what you hope for but a night still more profound, the night of nothingness."

Dear Mother, the image I wanted to give you of the darkness that obscures my soul is as imperfect as a sketch is to the model; however, I don't want to write any longer about it; I fear I might blaspheme; I fear even that I have already said too much.

Ah! may Jesus pardon me if I have caused him any pain, but he knows very well that while I do not have *the joy of faith*, I am trying to carry out its works at least. I believe I have made more acts of faith in this past year than all through my whole life. At each new occasion of combat, when my enemies provoke me, I conduct myself bravely. Knowing it is cowardly to enter into a duel, I turn my back on my adversaries without deigning to look them in the face; but I run toward my Jesus. I tell him I am ready to shed my blood to the last drop to profess my faith in the existence of *heaven*. I tell him, too, I am happy not to enjoy this beautiful heaven on this earth so that he will open it for all eternity to poor unbelievers. Also, in spite of this trial which has taken away *all my joy*, I can nevertheless cry out, "You have given me DELIGHT, O Lord, in ALL your doings" (Ps 91:5). For is there a *joy* greater than that of suffering out of love for you? The more interior the suffering is and the less apparent to the eyes of creatures, the more it rejoices you, O my God! But if my suffering was really unknown to you, which is impossible, I would still be happy to have it, if through it I could prevent or make reparation for one single sin against *faith*.

My dear Mother, I may perhaps appear to you to be exaggerating my trial. In fact, if you are judging according to the sentiments I express in my little poems composed this year, I must appear to you as a soul filled with consolations and one for whom the veil of faith is almost torn aside; and yet it is no longer a veil for me, it is a wall which reaches right up to the heavens and covers the starry firmament. When I sing of the happiness of heaven and of the eternal possession of God, I feel no joy in this, for I sing simply what I WANT TO BELIEVE. It is true that at times a very small ray of the sun comes to illumine my darkness, and then the trial ceases for *an instant*, but afterward the memory of this ray, instead of causing me joy, makes my darkness even more dense.

Never have I felt before this, dear Mother, how sweet and merciful the Lord really is, for he did not send me this trial until the moment I was capable of bearing it. A little earlier I believe it would have plunged me into a state of discouragement. Now it is taking away everything that could be a natural satisfaction in my desire for heaven. Dear Mother, it seems to me now that nothing could prevent me from flying away, for I no longer have any great desires except that of loving to the point of dying of love. June 9 [1897].

DEIFICATION AND BIRTHING

Over the centuries mystics have made use of the language of deification, or divinization, as a central way of expressing the conformity with God that is the essence of the mystical path. This language and tradition is rooted in scripture, especially in the Genesis account of humans being created in "God's image and likeness" (Gen 1:26). In exploring what it means to bear "likeness to God," Christians sometimes used Greek philosophical language about the soul's assimilation to God; nevertheless, the fundamentals of the doctrine of deification are rooted in the New Testament's teaching about redemption achieved for humanity through the saving action of God become man. Paul wrote to the Galatians: "For through faith you are all children of God in Christ Jesus" (Gal 3:26), and 1 John says: "Beloved we are God's children now; what we shall be has not yet been revealed. We do know that when it is revealed we shall be like him, for we shall see him as he is" (1 Jn 3:2). One late New Testament text expresses divinization more explicitly when it speaks of God bestowing on us "the precious and very great promises, so that through them you may come to share in the divine nature, after escaping from the corruption that is in the world because of evil desire" (2 Pet 1:4). Later authors also appealed to a Psalm text that in the Christian Bible features God addressing the "assembly of gods" as follows: "I have said: you are gods and all of you the sons of the Most High" (Ps 81:6).

Deification is related to the notion of rebirth as "children of God." In John's Gospel, Jesus tells Nicodemus, "Unless you be born again of water and the spirit you cannot enter the kingdom of God" (Jn 3:5), and Paul speaks of being baptized in the death of Jesus so that "as Christ was raised from the dead by the Father's glory, we too might have a new life" (Rom 6:4). Early Christians held that in baptism believers receive a new divinized form of life. The birthing motif, however, had wider implications in Christian mysticism. One could not only be reborn, but the believer might even come to participate in the birthing process whereby God is born in us and in others—that is, a person could in some sense bring God to birth. This notion also had a scriptural root. Paul describes himself as giving birth to his converts in Galatians 4:19: "You are my own children and I am in labor with you all over again until you come to have the form of Christ."

The daring idea of giving birth to God is founded on the mystery of Christ. Since Christians hold that the Word, the second person of the Trinity, had actually been born of a human mother, they soon came to the conviction that it was possible to share in Mary's privilege, spiritually if not physically. Beginning with Origen, many writers adopted the formula that Mary was worthy to conceive and bear the Lord in her body because she had already brought him forth in her soul. Another foundation for the birthing motif is found in the doctrine of the Trinity, according to which the Son is eternally begotten of the Father. If grace grants believers a share in the life of the Trinity, that is, a form of deification, is there a sense in which the soul also shares in bringing the Word to birth? Aspects of this doctrine, which was developed especially by Meister Eckhart and his followers, are found in the patristic period and among some early-medieval mystics.

1.

DEIFICATION AMONG THE FATHERS

Among the Apostolic Fathers and their successors, deification was conceived in an eschatological way: It was to be realized at the end of time in the immortality and bodily incorruptibility to come after the resurrection of the body. But Christian thinkers soon realized that the process of becoming like God begins in this life with baptism, and increases with the growth of the "saving knowledge" (gnôsis) brought by Christ. The following texts from the Fathers on the nature of deification provide the foundation for understanding this aspect of Christian mysticism.

I.

IRENAEUS OF LYONS
(CIRCA 130–CIRCA 200)

[Irenaeus is a primary witness to early orthodoxy in the struggle over the meaning of salvation, combating Gnostic interpretations of Jesus' activity as redeemer. His great work, the five books *Against Heresies* (circa 180), advances a physical understanding of deification through our union with the incarnate Logos.]

But again, those who assert that he was simply a mere man, begotten by Joseph, remaining in the bondage of the old disobedience, are in a state of death, having not yet been joined to the Word of God the Father. . . . To such the Word says, mentioning his own gift of grace: "I said, you are all the sons of the Most High and gods, but you shall die like men" (Ps 81:6–7). He undoubtedly speaks these words to those who have not received the gift of adoption, but who despise the incarnation of the pure generation of the Word, defraud human nature of promotion into God, and prove themselves ungrateful to the Word of God who became flesh for them. For it was for this end that the Word of God was made man, and he who was the Son of God became the Son of man, that man, having been taken into the Word, and by receiving adoption, might become the son of God. For by no other means could we have attained to incorruptibility and immortality, unless we had been united to incorruptibility and immortality.

Against Heresies 3.19.1, as translated in ANF 1:448.

II.
CLEMENT OF ALEXANDRIA
(CIRCA 150–CIRCA 215)

[This learned convert presents a rather different view of deification, tying it more closely to the growth in *gnôsis* based on faith and manifesting itself in love. Clement is the first Christian author to use the verb *to divinize* (*theopoiein*).]

. . . It is possible for the Gnostic already to have become God. "I said, you are gods and sons of the Most High" (Ps 81:6). And Empedocles says that the souls of the wise become gods, writing as follows: "At last prophets, minstrels, and physicians, and the foremost among mortal men, approach; whence spring gods supreme in honors. . . ." Accordingly, the Pythagorean saying was mystically uttered respecting us, "That man ought to become one," for the High Priest himself is one, God being one in the immutable state of the perpetual flow of good things. Now the Savior has taken away wrath in and with lust, wrath being lust of vengeance. For universally liability to feeling belongs to every kind of desire; and man, when deified purely into a passionless state, becomes a unit. As, then, those who at sea and held by an anchor pull at the anchor, but do not drag it to them, but rather drag themselves to the anchor, so too those who according to the Gnostic life draw God towards them, imperceptibly bring themselves to God: for he who reverences God, reverences himself. In the contemplative life, then, in worshiping God one attends to himself, and through his own spotless purification beholds the holy God holily, for self-control, when present, surveying and contemplating itself uninterruptedly, is as far as possible assimilated to God.

Stromateis 4.23, as translated in ANF 2:437.

III.
ORIGEN OF ALEXANDRIA
(CIRCA 185–254)

[The significance of deification is illustrated by the fact that Origen did not shrink from appealing to the doctrine in his major polemical work, the treatise *Against Celsus*, written to counter a second-century critic of Christianity. This passage provides a summary of the pre-Nicene understanding of divinization.]

Both Jesus himself and his disciples did not want people who came to them to believe only in his divine nature and miracles, as though he did not share in human nature and had not assumed the human flesh which lusts against the spirit (Gal 5:17); but as a result of their faith they also saw the power that descended into human nature and human limitations, and which assumed a human soul and body, combined with divine characteristics, to bring salvation to believers. For Christians see that with Jesus human and divine nature began to be woven together, so that by fellowship with divinity human nature might become divine, not only in Jesus, but also in all those who believe and go on to undertake the life which Jesus taught, the life which leads everyone who lives according to Jesus' commandments to friendship with God and fellowship with Jesus.

Against Celsus 3.29, as translated by Henry Chadwick, *Origen: Contra Celsum* (Cambridge: Cambridge University Press, 1980), 146.

IV.
ATHANASIUS OF ALEXANDRIA
(CIRCA 300–373)

[With Athanasius the doctrine of divinization attained a central place in the developing orthodox theology of the full and perfect divinity of Christ. The patriarch often repeats the phrase "God became man, so that man might become God." Athanasius was among the first to begin to discuss how all three persons of the Trinity play a role in the process of deification. In his *Letter to Serapion* he says: "What the Spirit distributes to each comes from the Father through the Son. This is why what is given through the Son in the Spirit is a grace of the Father."]

And so the truth shows us that the Word is not of things created, but rather himself their Framer. Therefore, he assumed a body created and human, that having renewed it as Framer, he might deify it in himself, and thus might introduce us all into the kingdom of heaven after his likeness. For man had not been deified if joined to a creature, or unless the Son were very God; nor had man been brought into God's presence, unless he had been his natural and true Word who had put on the body. And as we had not been delivered from sin and the curse, unless what the Word put on had been by nature human flesh (for we should have had nothing common with what was foreign), so also, man had not been deified, unless the Word who became flesh had been by nature from the Father and true and proper to him. Therefore the union was of this kind, that he might unite what is man by nature to him who is in the nature of the Godhead, and his salvation and deification [*theopoiêsis*] might be sure.

Discourses Against the Arians 2.70, in *The Nicene and Post-Nicene Fathers,* Series 2, Vol. 4:386.

V.
AUGUSTINE (354-430)

[Deification is sometimes thought of as an exclusively Eastern Christian teaching, but the witness of the following text from Augustine shows that it was also used by Western Fathers.]

"You have been called not that you may be a man, but that you may be a son of God." This is not a cause for someone to bring false accusations against me and say to me: "I would be lying, because I am a man." I myself would say and most assuredly: "Do not wish to be a man in order that you do not lie." "So," he says, "I will not be a man." Not at all. You are called by the one who for your sake made you man not to be a man. Don't get angry. I'm not telling you not to be a man so that you might become an animal, but rather that you might be numbered among those to whom he gave the power to be made children of God (Jn 1:12). God wants to make you god—not by nature, as in the case of the One he gave birth to, but by his gift and by adoption. Just as Christ was made a sharer in your mortality through his humanity, so he makes you a sharer in his immortality by way of exaltation. Give thanks then, and embrace what has been given you so that you may be worthy to enjoy where you are called to. Do not want to be Adam, and you will not be a man. If you are not a man, you will not be a liar, for "Every man is a liar" (Ps 115:11). When you begin not to lie, don't attribute it to yourself and get puffed up as if it were something of your own, lest you extinguish a lantern lit from another source with the wind of pride and remain stuck in your lying. Do not lie, brethren, for you were "old men," but having drawn near God's grace, you have been made "new men." The lie belongs to Adam, the truth to Christ. Therefore, "laying aside the lie, speak the truth" (Eph 4:25), so that this mortal flesh that you still have from Adam, with the newness of the Spirit leading it on, may itself merit renewal and change at the time of its resurrection. Thus the whole deified man [*homo deificatus*] will be firmly fixed in the perpetual and unchangeable truth.

Augustine, *Sermon* 166.4, translated by Bernard McGinn from PL 38:909.

BIRTHING IN PATRISTIC
AND MEDIEVAL TEXTS

The birth of the Word in the soul, usually associated with Eckhart and his fol-
lowers, had roots in patristic and medieval thought, which often spoke of Christ
as being born within the heart of the church. The mysticism of the Song of Songs
developed by Origen (see section 1.1) incorporated a procreative motif early on.
The Alexandrian exegete declared that every devout soul was both bride and
mother. In a fragment from his Commentary on Matthew *he says: "And every*
soul, virgin and uncorrupted, which conceives by the Holy Spirit so as to give
birth to the Will [i.e., Word] of the Father, is the mother of Jesus." In his Homily
on Jeremiah *9.4 he speaks of God giving birth to the righteous person continu-*
ously, just as he always begets the Son. Eckhart was to take this motif a step far-
ther in his teaching about the just man himself giving birth to the Word within
the Trinity.

Among the Fathers the birthing motif was mostly used in a doctrinal sense,
that is, as emphasizing the relation between Christ and the church. A more per-
sonal and mystical understanding, both of our being born from God and our giv-
ing birth to Christ, is found in some early-medieval thinkers, such as Maximus
the Confessor. Maximus's Latin translator, John Scotus Eriugena, also developed
a mystical sense of birthing. In his Commentary on the Gospel of John,
speaking of the verse "You do not know where the spirit comes from nor where it
goes" (Jn 3:8), he says, speaking in the voice of Christ: "Although you hear my
voice when I speak about my Spirit, you do not know where that Spirit comes

from, that is, by what means he wishes a person to be born from him in the spirit and to what perfection he leads the person that is born from him. For someone who is born from him is made one with him, and in the same way that he is the Holy Spirit through nature, the person born from him becomes the Holy Spirit through grace."

In the twelfth century we find explicit treatments of the birthing motif. Two examples are included here. The first is from the visionary narrative that the Benedictine abbot Rupert of Deutz (circa 1070–1129) included in the twelfth book of his commentary on Matthew. The seventh of Rupert's visions is an account of a form of spiritual pregnancy in which the monk, like a new Mary, gives birth to the golden object, the Christological meaning of the biblical text. The second passage, from a sermon for the Annunciation of the Cistercian abbot Guerric of Igny (circa 1087–1157), discusses how monks should aspire to bring Christ to birth in their souls in this life, and, at the time of resurrection, also in their bodies.

I.
RUPERT OF DEUTZ, THE GLORY AND HONOR OF THE SON OF MAN, BOOK 12

Therefore I rejoice, Lord God, Holy Spirit, because I have wrestled in this fashion, that is, by prayer and tears. This was the way Jacob wrestled (Gen 32:23–26), that is, by prayer and tears, according to the truth of the scriptural prophecy, because the prophet Hosea said, "And in his strength Jacob had success with an angel; he prevailed over the angel and was strengthened"; and the prophet immediately added the manner of this strength, by saying, "he wept and made supplication to him" (Hos 12:3–4). I rejoice because I would not let you go until you had blessed me (Gen 32:26), and you blessed me in the following way.

It was the night preceding the day that the Christian religion calls Ash Wednesday, when heads are solemnly sprinkled with ashes in healing correction of the sin of our first parents who wanted to be like God, although they were only "dust and ashes" (Gen 18:27). While I was sleeping lightly, I seemed to be speaking to a friend, who was asking me what I should do, with how much effort I ought to renew my search for finding death. In response I said (as is true) that it was a weighty matter and that I really did desire it because of the many dangers from the sins that occur in this life. Nevertheless, I should recognize that considerable outlay is needed to prepare, even a little bit, to depart from this life. While I was saying such things, suddenly I was taken away from the person I was speaking with and I saw, as it were, heaven above open slightly and from there a golden glowing mass of ineffable substance from the Living Substance quickly and rapidly descend. Heavier than gold and sweeter than honey, it fell into my breast and by its size and weight woke me up right away. The place where it had fallen at first was quiet for a little space of time and kept itself from any movement; and I also was quiet, lying flat and awaiting what would happen. But soon it began to move and to circulate in the womb of my interior person (the soul's womb), to what extent of its capacity I do not know. This living thing and true life moved around in a wondrous way, and each circuit was always greater and much larger than the one preceding it. There were many circuits, but I did not stop to count them. In a wonderful and unspeakable way these floods moved around, one after the other, and poured into each other, until finally the last flood, like some vast overflowing river, led me to understand and perceive that the whole capacity of the heart and the soul was full and could hold no more.

When that happened, it again was still for a little while, not flowing inward as it had before, nor flowing outward as it was to do later. In the meantime my interior person, as it were, wished to see the appearance of the living substance more clearly, but it hid itself in some way so that its appearance could not be seen, since it could only be borne as a very great weight and felt as a great sweetness. Later it began to turn back, and on the other side, under the gaze of the eyes of the inner person, the active circling poured forth from the left side like a river. When the final circuit had flowed out, it stopped for a bit, and I looked and saw that the substance was extremely beautiful, like liquid gold. When it was over and my sensation of it gone, I did not know what ought to be done in the future. I was only sorry that it had said nothing about my intention. I would have received it as a very great grace if it had said: "This year, as you hoped, you will depart from the body!"

Translated by Bernard McGinn from Rupert of Deutz, *De Gloria et Honore Filii Hominis super Matthaeum,* in PL 168:1597–99.

II.
GUERRIC OF IGNY, *SERMON 2*
ON THE ANNUNCIATION

... I do not know if there is any more effective and pleasing form of moral training than the faithful and devout consideration of this mystery, that is, of the Word made flesh. For what could so arouse someone to the love of God more than the fact that God's love anticipates human love and is so ardent for humanity that it desires to become man for man's sake? What could nourish love of neighbor in the same way as the likeness and the nature of the neighbor in God's humanity? I think that no greater example of humility can be conceived than God's emptying out of himself into the form of a slave and a servitude that is more than slavery (Phil 2:7). What could recommend chastity as well as the chastity that gives birth to the Savior? What shows the power and merit of faith more than that the Virgin conceived God by means of faith and by faith merited to have all the divine promises made to her fulfilled? It is said, "Blessed is she who has believed because what the Lord has said to her will be brought to fulfillment" (Lk 1:45).

So that you may more fully recognize that the Virgin's conception is not only mystical [i.e., a hidden dogmatic truth] but also moral [a truth for emulation], what is a mystery for redemption is also an example for your imitation, so that you will certainly cancel out the grace of the mystery in you if you do not imitate the virtue given in the example. For she who conceived God by faith promises you the same if you have faith. Hence, if you want to receive the Word from the mouth of the heavenly messenger in faithful fashion, you too will be able to conceive the God whom the whole world cannot contain, but in your heart and not your body. Yet more, even in your body, although not by bodily work or manner, but still certainly in your body, since the Apostle commands us "to glorify and bear God in our body" (1 Cor 6:20).

Therefore, as it is written, "Pay careful attention to your hearing" (Sir 13:16), because "faith is from hearing, and hearing is through God's word" (Rom 10:17). Without doubt God's angel is giving you an evangelical message when a faithful preacher, who you cannot deny is an angel of the Lord of Hosts, treats with you about the love and fear of God. How blessed are those who can say, "O Lord, out of fear of you we have conceived and given birth to the spirit of salvation" (Is 26:17–18). Surely, the spirit of salvation is none other than the truth of Jesus Christ. Behold the ineffable condescension of God together with the power of the unfathomable mystery! The one who created you is created in you, and as if it were too little that you should have him as a Father, he also wants you to be his mother. He says, "Whoever does the will of my Father is my brother and sister and mother" (Mt 12:50). O faithful soul, open wide your breast, enlarge your desire so that you do not become too narrow within; conceive him whom no creature is able to contain! Open the ear of your hearing to the Word of God. This is the way of the Spirit conceiving in the womb of the heart; for "this reason the bones of Christ" (that is, the virtues) "are knit together in the womb of the pregnant woman" (Eccles 11:5).

Thanks be to you, O Spirit, who breathes where you will (Jn 3:8). I behold that by your gift you make pregnant not just one, but unnumbered souls of the faithful with such a noble offspring. Protect your work, so that not one of them may abort the divine child they have conceived and expel it dead or disfigured.

You too, O blessed mothers of so glorious a child, pay close attention until "Christ be formed in you" (Gal 4:19). Take care lest any violent shock from without injure the tender fetus, lest you take something into the womb (that is, the mind) that might snuff out the spirit you have conceived. Spare, if not yourselves, at least the Son of God who is in you. Spare him, I say, not only from evil words and works, but also from the deadly thoughts and death-dealing delights that easily choke God's seed (Mt 13:22). Therefore, "Keep your hearts under every guard, because life will come forth from it" (Prov 4:23), namely, that the mature birth may take place and that the life of Christ that is now hidden in your hearts will be manifested in your mortal flesh (Col 3:3; 2 Cor 4:11). You have conceived the spirit of salvation, but you are still in labor, having not yet given birth. If there is effort in this labor, there is great consolation in the hope of a child. "A woman about to give birth has sorrow, but when she has brought forth a son she no longer remembers the anguish because of her joy that the man Christ has been born into the world" (Jn 16:21), that is, the exterior world of our body, which is customarily called the "microcosm." The one who is now conceived in our spirits as God configures them to the spirit of his charity, and then, when he is born as man in our bodies, he configures them to his glorified body in which he lives and is glorified as God forever and ever.

Translated by Bernard McGinn from Guerric of Igny, *Sermones per Annum, In Annuntiatione Dominica II,* in PL 185:122–24.

3.

MAXIMUS THE CONFESSOR
QUESTIONS TO THALASSIUS

QUESTION 22

Maximus the Confessor (580–662) was the last common Father of both East and West. Not only did he live in Rome for many years and collaborate with the popes and other Western leaders to overcome the heresy of Monothelitism (the teaching that Christ had only one will), but some of his Greek writings were translated by John Scotus Eriugena in the ninth century and thus became available to Latin thinkers. Maximus's position in Orthodox Christianity is that of the great synthesizer of the patristic heritage and a major source of later Greek theology and mystical teaching. His Mystagogy *(circa 625) is a liturgical contemplation of the mystery of Christ and the church. In it and in his more speculative writings the monk transformed the mystical teaching of Evagrius and Dionysius through a pan-Christic ontology centered on his insight that "on account of Christ, that is the mystery of Christ, all the ages, and all the things in the ages, take in Christ their beginning and end of being" (*Questions to Thalassius, question 60).*

Deeply rooted in the patristic tradition, Maximus understood salvation through Christ primarily as deification. His teachings on the mystery of deification appears in all his writings. The Mystagogy *shows how deification comes to us through participation in the liturgy and is demonstrated in our love for neighbor. In this text from his more speculative* Questions to Thalassius *(comments on difficult passages in the scriptures) he lays out the ontological status of deification on the basis of his pan-Christic view of reality.*

Question: If in the coming ages God will show his riches (Eph. 2:7), how is it that the end of the ages has come upon us (1 Cor 10:11)?

Response: He who, by the sheer inclination of his will, established the beginning of all creation, seen and unseen, before all the ages and before that beginning of created beings, had an ineffably good plan for those creatures. The plan was for him to mingle, without change on his part, with human nature by true hypostatic union, to unite human nature to himself while remaining immutable, so that he might become a man, as he alone knew how, and so that he might deify humanity in union with himself. Also, according to this plan, it is clear that God wisely divided "the ages" between those intended for God to become human, and those intended for humanity to become divine.

Thus *the end* of those ages predetermined for God to become human has already *come upon us,* since God's purpose was fulfilled in the very events of his incarnation. The divine Apostle, having fully examined this fact [. . . : a lacuna here in the text], and observing that the end of the ages intended for God's becoming human had already arrived through the very incarnation of the divine Logos, said that *the end of the ages has come upon us* (1 Cor 10:11). Yet by "ages" he meant not ages as we normally conceive them, but clearly the ages intended to bring about the mystery of his embodiment, which have already come to term according to God's purpose.

Since, therefore, the ages predetermined in God's purpose for the realization of his becoming human have reached their end for us, and God has undertaken and in fact achieved his own perfect incarnation, the other "ages"—those which are to come about for the realization of the mystical and ineffable deification of humanity—must follow henceforth. In these new ages God *will show the immeasurable riches of his goodness to us* (Eph 2:7), having completely realized this deification in those who are worthy. For if he has brought to completion his mystical work of becoming human having become like us in every way save without sin (Heb 4:15), and even descended into the lower regions of the earth where the tyranny of sin compelled humanity, then God will also completely fulfill the goal of his mystical work of deifying humanity in every respect, of course, short of an identity of essence with

God; and he will assimilate humanity to himself and elevate us to a position above all the heavens. It is to this exalted position that the natural magnitude of God's grace summons lowly humanity, out of a goodness that is infinite. The great Apostle is mystically teaching us about this when he says that *in the ages to come the immeasurable riches of his goodness will be shown to us* (Eph 2:7).

We too should therefore divide the "ages" conceptually, and distinguish between those intended for the mystery of the divine incarnation and those intended for the grace of human deification, and we shall discover that the former have already reached their proper end while the latter have not yet arrived. In short, the former have to do with God's descent to human beings, while the latter have to do with humanity's ascent to God. By interpreting the texts thus, we do not falter in the obscurity of the divine words of scripture, nor assume that the divine Apostle had lapsed into this same mistake. Or rather, since our Lord Jesus Christ is the beginning, middle, and end of all the ages, past and future, [it would be fair to say that] the *end of the ages*—specifically that end which will actually come about by grace for the deification of those who are worthy—*has come upon us* in potency through faith.

Or again, since there is one principle of activity and another of passivity, [we could say that] the divine Apostle has mystically and wisely distinguished the active principle from the passive principle respectively in the past and future "ages." Accordingly, the ages of the flesh, in which we now live (for scripture also knows the ages of time, as when it says that man *toiled in this age and shall live until its end* [Ps 48:10]), are characterized by activity, while the future ages in the Spirit, which are to follow the present life, are characterized by the transformation of humanity in passivity. Existing here and now, we arrive at the *end of the ages* as active agents and reach the end of the exertion of our power and activity. But in the ages to come we shall undergo by grace the transformation unto deification and no longer be active but passive; and for this reason we shall not cease from being deified. At that point our passion will be supernatural, and there will be no principle restrictive of the divine activity in infinitely deifying those who are passive to it. For we are active agents insofar as we have operative, by nature, a rational faculty for performing the virtues, and also a spiritual faculty, unlimited in its potential, capable of receiving all knowledge, capable of transcending the nature of all created beings and known things and even of leaving the "ages" of time behind it. But when in the future we are rendered passive (in deification), and have fully transcended the principles of beings created out of nothing, we will unwittingly enter into the true Cause of existent beings and terminate our proper faculties along with everything in our nature that has reached completion. We shall become that which in no way results from our natural ability, since our human nature has no faculty for grasping what transcends nature. For nothing created is by its nature capable of inducing deification, since it is incapable of comprehending God. Intrinsically it is only by the grace of God that deification is bestowed proportionately on created beings. Grace alone illuminates human nature with supernatural light, and, by the superiority of its glory, elevates our nature above its proper limits in excess of glory.

So it does not seem, then, that *the end of the ages has come upon us* (1 Cor 10:11), since we have not yet received, by the grace that is in Christ, the gift of benefits that transcend time and nature. Meanwhile, the modes of the virtues and the principles of those things that can be known by nature have been established as types and foreshadowings of those future benefits. It is through these modes and principles that God, who is ever willing to become human, does so in those who are worthy. And therefore whoever, by the exercise of wisdom, enables God to become incarnate within him or her and, in fulfillment of this mystery, undergoes deification by grace is truly blessed, because that deification has no end. For he who bestows his grace on those who are worthy of it is himself infinite in essence, and has the infinite and utterly limitless power to deify humanity. Indeed, this divine power is not yet finished with those beings created by it; rather, it is forever sustaining those—like us human beings—who have received their existence from it. Without it they could not exist. This is why the text speaks of the *riches of goodness* (Eph 2:7), since God's resplendent plan for our transformation unto deification never ceases in its goodness toward us.

Translated by Paul M. Blowers, from Paul M. Blowers and Robert Louis Wilken, *On the Cosmic Mystery of Christ. Selected Writings from St. Maximus the Confessor,* 115–18. Copyright 2003. By permission of Saint Vladimir's Press, 575 Scarsdale Road, Crestwood, New York 10757.

MEISTER ECKHART
SERMON 101

This homily opens a four-sermon cycle on the birth of the Word in the soul, a group of sermons fittingly preached during the Christmas season, possibly in the first years of the fourteenth century when Meister Eckhart was provincial at his home convent in Erfurt in Saxony. The question-and-answer format suggests that it was delivered to his Dominican brethren. This cycle contains some of Eckhart's most penetrating statements on the way in which the Divine Word is born in the Eternal Father and in the soul united with God (see section 1.5).

The first of the homilies takes as its text the Introit, or opening chant, of the Sunday within the Octave of Christmas. Eckhart creates his own German version of this passage from Wisdom 18:14 to introduce the three themes of the cycle (my emphasis): "When all things lay in the midst *[i.e., medium] of silence, then there descended down into me from on high, from the royal throne, a secret Word." The three issues introduced here are developed at length in the first sermon and the remaining three:* where *in the soul the Word is born;* how *we are to conduct ourselves with regard to the birth; and* what *we gain from it.*

"Dum medium silentium tenerent omnia et nox in suo cursu medium iter haberet, omnipotens sermo tuus, Domine, de caelis a regalibus sedibus venit" (Wis 18:14). Here, in time, we are celebrating the eternal birth which God the Father bore and bears unceasingly in eternity, because this same birth is now born in time, in human nature. St. Augustine says: "What does it avail me that this birth is always happening, if it does not happen in me? That it should happen in me is what matters" [actually Origen, *Homily 9 on Jeremiah*]. We shall therefore speak of this birth, of how it may take place in us and be consummated in the virtuous soul, whenever God the Father speaks his Eternal Word in the perfect soul. For what I say here is to be understood of the good and perfected man who has walked and is still walking in the ways of God; not of the natural, undisciplined man, for he is entirely remote from, and totally ignorant of this birth. There is a saying of the wise man: "When all things lay in the midst of silence, then there descended down into me from on high, from the royal throne, a secret word." This sermon is about that Word.

Three things are to be noted here. The first is, where in the soul God the Father speaks his Word, where this birth takes place and where she is receptive of this act, for that can only be in the very purest, loftiest, subtlest part that the soul is capable of. In very truth, if God the Father in his omnipotence could endow the soul with anything more noble, and if the soul could have received from him anything nobler, then the Father would have had to delay the birth for the coming of this greater excellence. Therefore the soul in which this birth is to take place must keep absolutely pure and must live in noble fashion, quite collected and turned entirely inward; not running out through the five senses into the multiplicity of creatures, but all inturned and collected and in the purest part: there is his place, he disdains anything less.

The second part of this sermon has to do with man's conduct in relation to this act, to God's speaking of this Word within, to this birth: whether it is more profitable for man to co-operate with it, so that it may come to pass in him through his own exertion and merit—by a man's creating in himself a mental image in his thoughts and disciplining himself that way by reflecting that God is wise, omnipotent, eternal, or whatever else he can imagine about God—whether this is more profitable and conducive to this birth from the Father; or whether one should shun and free oneself from all thoughts, words and deeds and from all images created by the understanding, maintaining a wholly God-receptive attitude, such that one's own self is idle, letting God work within one. Which conduct conduces best to this birth? The third point is the profit, and how great it is, which accrues from this birth.

Note in the first place that in what I am about to say I shall make use of natural proofs, so that you yourselves can grasp that it is so, for though I put more faith in the scriptures than in myself, yet it is easier and better for you to learn by means of arguments that can be verified.

First we will take the words: "In the midst of silence there was spoken within me a secret word." "But sir, where is the silence and where is the place where the word is spoken?" As I said just now, it is in the purest thing that the soul is capable of, in the noblest, the ground—indeed, in the essence of the soul which is the soul's most secret part. There is the silent "middle," for no creature ever entered there and no image, nor has the soul there either activity or understanding. Therefore, she is not aware there of any image, whether of herself or of any other creature.

Whatever the soul effects, she effects with her powers. What she understands, she understands with the intellect. What she remembers, she does with memory; if she would love, she does that with the will, and thus she works with her powers and not with her essence. Every external act is linked with some "middle," or means. The power of sight works only through the eyes; otherwise it can neither employ nor bestow vision, and so it is with all the other senses. The soul's every external act is effected by some means. But in the soul's essence there is no activity, for the powers she works with emanate from the ground of being. Yet in that ground is the silent "middle": here is nothing but rest and celebration for this birth, this act, that God the Father may speak his word there, for this is by nature receptive to nothing save the divine essence, without mediation. Here God enters the soul with his all, not merely with a part. God enters here the ground of the soul. None can touch the ground of the soul but God alone. No creature can enter the soul's ground, but must stop outside, in the powers. Within, the soul sees clearly the image whereby the creature has been drawn in and taken lodging. For whenever the powers of the soul make contact with a creature, they set to work and make an image and likeness of the creature, which they absorb. That is how they know the creature. No creature can come closer to the soul than this, and the soul never approaches a creature without having first voluntarily taken an image of it into herself. . . .

For a person to receive an image in this way, it must of necessity enter from without through the senses. In consequence, there is nothing so unknown to the soul as herself. Accordingly, one master says that the soul can neither create nor obtain an image of herself [Cicero, *Tusculan Disputations* I.27.67]. Therefore, she has no way of knowing herself, for images all enter through the senses, and hence she can have no image of herself. And so she knows all other things, but not herself. Of nothing does she know so little as of herself, for want of mediation.

And you must know too that inwardly the soul is free and void of all means and all images, which is why God can freely unite with her without form or likeness. Whatever power you ascribe to any master, you cannot but ascribe that power to God without limit. The more skilled and powerful the master, the more immediately is his work effected, and the simpler it is. Man requires many means for his external works; much preparation of the material is needed before he can produce them as he has imagined them. But the sun in its sovereign mastery performs its task (which is to give light) very swiftly: the instant its radiance is poured forth, the ends of the earth are full of light. More exalted is the angel, who needs still less means for his work and has fewer images. The highest Seraph has but a single image: he seizes as a unity all that his inferiors regard as manifold. But God needs no image and has no image: without any means, likeness, or image God operates in the soul—right in the ground where no image ever got in, but only he himself with his own being. This no creature can do.

"How does God the Father give birth to his Son in the soul—like creatures, in images and likenesses?" No, by my faith, but rather just as he gives birth to him in eternity: no more, no less. "Well, but how does He give birth to him then?"

Now see: God the Father has a perfect insight into himself, profound and thorough knowledge of himself by himself, and not through any image. And thus God the Father gives birth to his Son in the true unity of the divine nature. See, it is like this and in no other way that God the Father gives birth to the Son in the ground and essence of the soul, and thus unites himself with her. For if any image were present there would be no real union, and in that real union lies the soul's whole beatitude.

Now, you might say, there is by nature nothing in the soul but images. Not at all! If that were so, the soul could never become blessed, for God cannot make any creature from which you can receive perfect blessedness. Otherwise, God would not be the highest blessing and the final goal, whereas it is his nature to be this, and it is his will to be the beginning and end of all things. No creature can constitute your blessedness, nor can it be your perfection here on earth, for the perfection of this life, which is the sum of all the virtues, is followed by the perfection of the life to come. Therefore you have to be and dwell in the essence and in the ground, and there God will touch you with his simple essence without the intervention of any image. No image represents and signifies itself: it always aims and points to that of which it is the image. And, since you have no image but of what is outside yourself (which is drawn in through the senses and continually points to that of which it is the image), therefore it is impossible for you to be made blessed by any image whatsoever. And therefore there must be a silence and a stillness, and the Father must speak in that, and give birth to His Son, and perform his works free from all images.

The second point is, what must a man contribute by his own actions, in order to procure and deserve the occurrence and the consummation of this birth in himself? Is it better to do something towards this, to imagine and think about God?—or should he keep still and silent in peace and quiet and let God speak and work in him, merely waiting for God to act? Now I say, as I said before, that these words and this truth are only for the good and perfected people, who have so absorbed and assimilated the essence of all virtues that these virtues emanate from them naturally, without their seeking; and above all there must dwell in them the worthy life and lofty teachings of our Lord Jesus Christ. They must know that the very best and noblest attainment in this life is to be silent and and let God work and speak within. When the powers have been completely withdrawn from all their works and images, then the Word is spoken. And so it says, "In the midst of the silence the secret word was spoken unto me." And so, the more completely you are able to draw in your powers to a unity and forget all those things and their images which you have absorbed, and the further you can get from creatures and their images, the nearer you are to this and the readier to receive it. If only you could suddenly be unaware of all things, then you could pass into an oblivion of your own body as St. Paul did, when he said: "Whether in the body I cannot tell, or out of the body I cannot tell; God knows it" (2 Cor 12:2). In this case the spirit had so entirely absorbed the powers that it had forgotten the body: memory no longer functioned, nor understanding, nor the senses, nor the powers that should function so as to govern and grace the body, vital warmth and body-heat were suspended, so that the body did not waste during the three days when he neither ate nor drank. Thus too Moses fared when he fasted for forty days on the mountain and was none the worse for it (Ex 24:18), for on the last day he was as strong as on the first. In this way a man should flee his senses, turn his powers inward, and sink into a forgetting of all things and himself. Concerning this a master addressed the soul thus: "Withdraw from the unrest of external activities, then flee away and hide from the turmoil of inward thoughts, for they but create discord" [Anselm, *Proslogion* 1]. And so, if God is to speak his Word in the soul, she must be at rest and at peace, and then he will speak his Word and himself in the soul—no image, but himself!

Dionysius says: "God has no image or likeness of himself, for he is intrinsically all goodness, truth and being" [*Divine Names* 9.6]. God performs all his works, whether within himself or outside himself, in a flash. Do not imagine that God, when he made heaven and earth and all things, made one thing one day and another the next. Moses describes it like that, but he really knew better: he did so for the sake of people who could not conceive or grasp it any other way. All God did was this: he willed, he spoke, and they were! God works without means and without images, and the freer you are from images, the more receptive you are for his inward working, and the more introverted and self-forgetful, the nearer you are to this.

Dionysius exhorted his pupil Timothy in this sense saying: "Dear son Timothy, do you with untroubled mind soar above yourself and all your powers, above ratiocination and reasoning, above works, above all modes and existence, into the secret still darkness, that you may come to the knowledge of the unknown super-divine God" [*Mystical Theology* 1.1]. There must be a withdrawal from all things. God scorns to work through images.

Now you might say, "What does God do without images in the ground and essence?" That I cannot know, because the soul-powers receive only in images; they have to know and lay hold of each thing in its appropriate image. They cannot recognize a horse when presented with the image of a man; and since all things enter from without, that knowledge is hidden from my soul, which is to her great advantage. This not-knowing draws her into amazement and leads her to eager pursuit, for she perceives clearly "that it is," but does not know "how or what it is." When someone knows the causes of things, then he at once tires of them and seeks to know something different, complaining and always protesting, because knowing has no resting point. And so this unknown-knowing keeps the soul constant and yet spurs her on to pursuit.

About this, the wise man said: "In the middle of the night when all things were in a quiet silence, there was spoken to me a hidden word. It came like a thief by stealth" (Wis 18:14–15). Why does he call it a word, when it was hidden? The nature of a word is to reveal what is hidden. It revealed itself to me and shone forth before me, declaring something to me and making God known to me, and therefore it is called a Word. Yet what it was remained hidden from me. That was its stealthy coming in a whispering stillness to reveal itself. See, just because it is hidden one must and should always pursue it. It shone forth and yet was hidden: we are meant to yearn and sigh for it. St. Paul exhorts us to pursue this until we espy it, and not to stop until we grasp it. After he had been caught up into the third heaven where God was made known to him and he beheld all things (2 Cor 12:2–4), when he returned he had forgotten nothing, but it was so deep down in his ground that his intellect could not reach it; it was veiled from him. He therefore had to pursue it and search for it in himself and not outside. It is all within, not outside, but wholly within. And knowing this full well, he said: "For I am persuaded that neither death nor any affliction can separate me from what I find within me" (Rom 8:38–39).

There is a fine saying of one pagan master to another about this. He said: "I am aware of something in me which shines in my understanding; I can clearly perceive that it is something, but what it may be I cannot grasp. Yet I think if I could only seize it I should know all truth" [quotation unidentified]. To which the other master replied: "Follow it boldly! for if you could seize it you would possess the sum-total of all good and have eternal life!" St. Augustine spoke in the same sense: "I am aware of something within me that gleams and flashes before my soul; were this perfected and fully established in me, that would surely be eternal life!" [*Confessions* 10.40]. It hides, yet shows itself; it comes, but like a thief with intent to take and steal all things from the soul. But by emerging and showing itself a little it aims to lure the soul and draw her towards itself, to rob her and deprive her of herself. About this, the prophet says: "Lord, take from them their spirit and give them instead thy spirit" (Ps 103:29–30). This too was meant by the loving soul when she said: "My soul dissolved and melted away when Love spoke his word" (Song 5:6). When he entered, I had to fall away. And Christ meant this by his words: "Whoever abandons anything for my sake shall be repaid a hundredfold, and whoever would possess me must deny himself and all things, and whoever will serve me must follow me and not go any more after his own" (Mt 16:24, etc.).

But now you might say, "But, good sir, you want to change the natural course of the soul and go against her nature! It is her nature to take things in through the senses in images. Would you upset this ordering?" No! But how do you know what nobility God has bestowed on human nature, not yet fully described, and still unrevealed? For those who have written of the soul's nobility have gone no further than their natural intelligence could carry them; they had never entered her ground, so that much remained obscure and unknown to them. So the prophet said: "I will sit in silence and hearken to what God speaks within me" (Ps 84:9). Because it is so secret, this Word came in the night and in darkness. St. John says: "The light shone in the darkness; it came into its own, and as many as received it became in authority sons of God; to them was given power to become God's sons" (Jn 1:5, 11–12).

Now observe the use and the fruit of this secret Word and this darkness. The Son of the heavenly Father is not born alone in this darkness, which is his own: you too can be born a child of the same heavenly Father and of none other, and to you too he will give power. Now observe how great the use is! For all the truth learnt by all the masters by their own intellect and understanding, or ever to be learnt till Doomsday, they never had the slightest inkling of this knowledge and this ground. Though it may be called a nescience, an unknowing, yet there is in it more than in all knowing and understanding without it, for this unknowing lures and attracts you from all understood things, and from yourself as well. This is what Christ meant when he said: "Whoever will not deny himself and will not leave his father and mother, and is not estranged from all these, is not worthy of me" (Mt 10:37), as though he were to say: he who does not abandon creaturely externals can be neither conceived nor born in this divine birth. But divesting yourself of yourself and of everything external does truly give it to you. And in very truth I believe, nay I am sure, that the person who is established in this cannot in any way ever be separated from God. I say he can in no way lapse into mortal sin. He would rather suffer the most shameful death, as the saints have done before him, than commit the least of mortal sins. I say such people cannot willingly commit or consent to even a venial sin in themselves or in others if they can stop it. So strongly are they lured and drawn and accustomed to that, that they can never turn to any other way; to this way are directed all their senses, all their powers. May the God who has been born again as man assist us to this birth, eternally helping us, weak men, to be born in him again as God. Amen.

From *Meister Eckhart. Sermons and Treatises. Vol. I,* 1–12, translated by M. O'C. Walshe. Copyright 1979. Reprinted by permission of The English Sangha Trust, Amaravati Buddist Monastery. Walshe, following the edition of Pfeiffer, numbers this Sermon 1, but in the critical edition it is Sermon 101. I have adapted the Walshe translation in several places to reflect the critical edition.

5.

THEOLOGIA DEUTSCH

CHAPTER 53

The Theologia Deutsch, *or* Theologia Germanica, *is the title that Martin Luther gave to a treatise he discovered and edited to show that his own view of the Gospel was not an innovation, but had been found both among the Fathers of the church, as well as among more recent German theologians. Luther's two editions of the work not only cemented the connection between Reformation theology and some elements in late-medieval mysticism but also gave the book a considerable role in later Protestant piety. It was translated into many languages, and about two hundred editions were published between the sixteenth and the twentieth centuries. A manuscript prologue attributes it to "a wise, judicious, truthful, just man, God's friend, who in earlier times was a member of the Teutonic Order [a military religious order], a priest and warden in the house of the Teutonic Order in Frankfurt." The anonymous priest lived toward the end of the fourteenth century. The fifty-three chapters of the best surviving version seem to be based upon spiritual conferences, but some parts may be later additions to the lost core version.*

The Theologia Deutsch *sets forth a distinctive view of the Christological path to divinizing union. The work presents a strong, almost dualistic, contrast between the fundamental virtue of obedience to God and the archetypal sin of disobedience. Although the tract was influenced by the speculations of Eckhart and his followers, the* Theologia Deutsch *is fundamentally practical, even experiential, in its teaching. Like Luther, the author had a negative view of nature since Adam's Fall, in one place saying, "Therefore, the devil and nature are one."*

The tract is deeply Christocentric: Taking up the cross and following Christ in loving obedience is the only way back to God. All these themes show why Luther was so attracted to the Theologia. *According to the treatise, obedient imitation of Christ's suffering is aimed at deifying union, both here and hereafter. Few medieval mystical texts put more emphasis on the soul's ability to attain the status of "a divinized or godlike person" in this life. (In a number of chapters deification and the birth of the Son in the soul are used interchangeably.) Chapter 53 is a summation of the key teachings of the* Theologia.

CHAPTER 53.THE SECOND SAYING: "NO ONE COMES TO ME UNLESS THE FATHER DRAWS HIM"

Christ also says, "No one comes to me unless the Father draws him" (Jn 6:44). Here "the Father" is to be understood as the perfect, single good that is all and above all and without which and outside of which there is no true being or true good, and without which no true, good work ever took or will take place. Because it is now all, it must also be for all and above all. It cannot be any of those things that a creature, as creature, can comprehend or understand. For what the creature can comprehend or understand as a creature, that is, in its creatureliness, is all something, this or that, and it is all creature. If the perfect and single were something, this or that, that a creature understands, it would not be all nor for all, and it would not be perfect either. This is why it is also called "nothing." People think it is not one of the things that from its creatureliness a creature can comprehend, understand, think about, or name. And so when this nameless perfect being flows into a fruitful person in whom it gives birth to his only begotten Son and itself in it, then this perfect being is called "Father."

This, then, is how the Father draws to Christ. When something is uncovered to the soul or the person and revealed by this perfect good as in a vision or a rapture, there is born in the person a desire to approach the perfect good and unite with it. As this desire grows greater, more is revealed to him, and as more is revealed to him, so he desires more and is drawn on. In this way the person is drawn and attracted to union with the eternal good, and this is the Father's drawing. The person is therefore taught by the one who draws him that he cannot attain the oneness, unless he comes through Christ's life. It is now that he adopts the life previously mentioned. Two sayings of Christ are important here. In one he says, "No one comes to the Father except through me," that is, through my life, as previously said. In the other saying he says, "No one comes to me"—that is, no one should lay claim to the life and follow me—"unless he is touched and drawn by the Father," that is, by the single good and perfect, about which St. Paul says: "When the perfect comes, then the partial will be destroyed" (1 Cor 13:10). This means that in whatever person that same perfect is recognized, found and savored, as far as is possible in this world, to this person all created things seem as nothing in comparison with this perfect, as it is in the truth, for outside the perfect and without it there is no true good or true being. Whoever possesses, recognizes or loves the perfect possesses and recognizes all and all good. As the parts are all united in the perfect in one being, what significance does anything more or anything other have for him, or what significance do the parts have for him?

What is said here all pertains to the outward life and is a path and point of access to a true, inward life; and the inward begins after the outward. When, as is possible, the person savors the perfect, all created things and even the person himself become as nothing to him. As one understands in the truth that the perfect is all and above all, it follows necessarily that one must attribute all good to that same perfect, and not to any creature such as being, life, understanding, knowledge, ability and so on. It follows that the person lays claim to nothing, neither life, being, ability, knowledge, doing or not doing, or anything that one can call good. In this way the person becomes poor and as nothing in himself, and everything that is created in and along with him. And so, first of all, there arises a true, inward life, and then increasingly God himself becomes the person; consequently there is nothing more that is not God or of God, and there is nothing that can lay claim to anything for itself. God, then, as the eternal, only perfect One, is, lives, understands, is able, loves, wills, acts and does not act. That is how it should be in truth, and where things are different, it could be better and more right for them. A good path and point of access to all of this is that one should realize that the best is the most loved and that one should choose the best, stick to it and unite oneself with it. First, in creatures—but what is the best in creatures? It is where the eternal, perfect good and what belongs to it most shines, is effective, understood and loved. But what is it that is God's and pertains to him? It is everything that one rightly and truly can call good. If one can stick to the best that one can understand in creatures, remain with it and not backslide, one comes again to something better and to something better again, as long as the person understands and savors the fact that the eternal, one perfect is immeasurably and innumerably above all created good.

If the best has to be the most loved and one follows it, then the eternal, only good should be loved above all and alone. The person should cling to it alone and unite himself with it, as far as possible. If one is to attribute all good to the eternal, only good, as one rightly and in truth ought to, then one must also rightly and in truth attribute to him the beginning, continuation and completion, so that nothing should remain for the person or creature. That is how it should be in truth, whatever people say or sing. In this way, one would come again to a true, inward life. But how it would then proceed or what would then be revealed, or how it would be lived out, nobody speaks or sings about. At least, it was never spoken with the lips or considered or understood by the heart as it is in the truth.

What has been said here at some length summarizes, as it rightly and in the truth ought to, the fact that there is absolutely nothing in a person that might lay claim to anything, want, desire, love or strive after anything except God and the Godhead alone, that is, the eternal, only, perfect good. If there is something in the person that does lay claim to or wants, strives after or desires anything other or more than the eternal good, that is too much and is wickedness.

Furthermore, if the person can reach the point at which he is, in relation to God, as the hand is to a human being, that should be sufficient for him, and should really be so. Every creature rightly and in the truth owes that to God, and especially every rational creature, and most particularly humankind. This is in addition to the one thing previously written for you. If, of course, the person gets so far as to imagine and consider that he has reached this stage that the devil then sows no ashes there, with the result that nature seeks and finds its ease and rest, its peace and happiness in this and enters into a foolish, disordered freedom and carelessness, this is completely alien to a true, godly life and far removed from it. This happens to the person who has not walked and will not walk the right path and enter by the right door, that is, through Christ, as previously said. He imagines he will or can do otherwise or come by another path to the highest truth, or he imagines he has perhaps arrived there. He certainly has not. That is shown by Christ, who says: "If anyone wants to enter otherwise than through me, he will never rightly enter or come to the highest truth, but is a thief and a murderer" (Jn 10:1). May he help us to get rid of self, die to our own will and live only for God and his will, who yielded his will to his heavenly Father, who lives and rules eternally with God the Father, in the unity of the Holy Spirit in perfect Trinity. Amen.

Translated by David Blamires, *The Book of the Perfect Life. Theologia Deutsch—Theologia Germanica,* © AltaMira Press, 95–98. Used with permission.

UNION WITH GOD

Becoming one with God has often been seen as the defining characteristic of mysticism, although the ways that mystics have described their sense of God's direct presence have been quite varied. The term *mystical union* occurs as early as the late fourth century, but was employed sparingly by Christian mystics. It is only in the modern study of mysticism that mystical union (*unio mystica*) attained a central place.

The Bible's use of the language of union is sparse, which is why a few texts took on great importance in the later tradition. Perhaps the most frequently cited biblical passage in the history of Christian mysticism is Paul's claim in 1 Corinthians 6:17 that "He who adheres to God becomes one spirit with him." In John's Gospel, Jesus' prayer for his disciples that "all may be one as you Father are in me and I in you" (Jn 17:21) was also much cited by later mystics. These texts, however, suggest rather different views of union—oneness of spirit, and a oneness that shares in the essential unity of the three persons in the one God.

Pagan Neoplatonic mystics, especially Plotinus (204–70), left profound analyses of the metaphysical and existential meaning of mystical union (*henôsis*). This concern with mystical union appears to be the reason why some Fathers, such as Augustine, avoided the language of union, except when speaking about how believers are united in the Body of Christ. Nevertheless, other Christian mystics were willing to speak about being united to God, even in an essential way. Among the earliest uses of *mystical union* or *mystical fellowship* (*koinônia mystikê*) are those found in the Macarian *Homilies,* one of which is the first selection given here. Other Eastern Christian texts speak more clearly of a union that involves identity or merging. Evagrius Ponticus (see section 2.2) used an analogy often repeated in later mystical literature. Speaking of the eventual union of fallen minds with God, he said: "When minds flow back into him like torrents into the sea, he changes them all completely into his own nature, color, and taste. . . . And as in the fusion of rivers with the sea no addition in its nature or variation in its color or taste is to be found, so also in the fusion of minds with the Father no duality of natures or quaternity of persons comes about" (*Letter to Melania* 6). At the beginning of *The Mystical Theology* (see section 9.1) Dionysius also spoke of union with God. A passage from *The Divine Names* 2.9 provided a classic account of a uniting with God. In this text (often commented upon) Dionysius describes his teacher Hierotheus as "not only learning but experiencing [i.e., passively receiving] divine things," and because of his sympathy with them, being "perfected in a mystical union [*henôsis mystikê*] and an untaught faith in them." Maximus the Confessor (see section 12.3) was the first to use three comparisons for union with God repeated by many authors— a drop of water in wine, molten iron in fire, and air in sunshine. These images suggest a fusion of being, but were actually used by most mystics to illustrate loving union of wills.

Extensive analyses of the forms of union began in the twelfth century in the West. Although these presentations are varied, they fall into two broad traditions. The first takes its cue from the Pauline text cited above, insisting that union with God is a "union of spirits" (*unitas spiritus*), that is, a uniting of willing and loving in which the infinite Divine Spirit and the finite created spirit nonetheless always maintain their ontological distinction. The selection from Bernard of Clairvaux given below is a good example of this perspective. In the thirteenth century, however, there was a surge of accounts that speak of union of identity or indistinction with God (*unitas identitatis/unitas indistinctionis*). Although this form of union often used philosophical categories drawn from Neoplatonic philosophy, it was not an academic revival, but was part of the lived experience of the exponents of the New Mysticism. The foremost spokesman of the union of identity in which the soul becomes annihilated in order to be totally merged with God is Meister Eckhart. Selection 3 is one of Eckhart's best-known sermons on mystical unity, here presented as the true poverty of spirit.

Union of identity remains controversial. Does such a view elide the distinction between Creator and creature that is essential to Christian faith? Perhaps so, but two points should be borne in mind in evaluating claims to such strong forms of union. First, Eckhart, as well as the other proponents of mystical identity such as Marguerite Porete (see section 5.4), insisted that while identity is reached on one level, on another level there always remains a distinction between God and creature. Second, many mystics continued to employ both kinds of union language, perhaps reflecting a similar commitment to both identity and distinction.

After the condemnations of Marguerite Porete and Eckhart, later mystics wrestled with how best to correlate their understanding of union and the church's teaching. The selection from the Dutch mystic John Ruusbroec is one of the most subtle attempts to incorporate an Eckhartian sense of mystical identity into a more complete analysis of the interpenetrating forms of union realized both in this life and the next. Teresa of Avila and John of the Cross both attempted to clarify mystical union understood as spiritual marriage. The proper view of union remained an important issue in the Golden Age of French Mysticism during the seventeenth century. The selection from Francis de Sales is a summation of traditional teaching on mystical union, while the passage from Marie of the Incarnation represents a personal account of becoming one with God.

1.

MACARIUS
HOMILY 10

The homilies ascribed to the Desert Father Macarius of Egypt (circa 300–circa 390) were not written by him, because the context of these writings is clearly the early monasticism of Syria, not of Egypt. The homilies appear to come from the 380s, and were probably composed in Mesopotamia by an as-yet-unidentified author. The ascription of these fifty sermons, as well as the "Great Letter" that accompanied them, to the noted Egyptian ascetic gave them great authority in the Christian East, and also in the West after their translation into Latin and subsequently into several vernaculars. The "Pseudo-Macarian" homilies are among the most ecumenical of all Christian mystical texts, treasured by Orthodox, Catholics, and many Protestants.

There has been a good deal of discussion concerning the relation of these sermons to the Messalian heresy, a Syrian monastic movement condemned for various errors from the late fourth century on (see section 14.1). Places in the Macarian homilies reflect some of the accusations made against the Messalians, but it is hard to think that such a valuable spiritual document is heretical. What is clear is that the deeply embodied spirituality of these texts expresses a rather different style of early Christian mysticism from that found in contemporary Greek authors. The following homily gives some sense of this difference. The text contains one of the earliest uses of the language of mystical union (here "mystical fellowship": koinônia mystikê) in the Christian tradition.

BY LOWLINESS OF MIND AND EARNESTNESS THE GIFTS OF THE DIVINE GRACE ARE PRESERVED, BUT BY PRIDE AND SLOTH THEY ARE DESTROYED

Souls that love truth and God, that long with much hope and faith to put on Christ completely, do not need so much to be put in remembrance by others, nor do they endure, even for a while, to be deprived of the heavenly desire and of passionate affection to the Lord; but being wholly and entirely nailed to the cross of Christ, they perceive in themselves day by day a sense of spiritual advance towards the spiritual Bridegroom. Being smitten with heavenly longing, and hungering for the righteousness of the virtues, they have a great and insatiable desire for the shining forth of the Spirit. Even if they are privileged through their faith to receive the knowledge of divine mysteries, or are made partakers of the gladness of heavenly grace, they put no trust in themselves, thinking themselves to be somebody, but the more they are permitted to receive spiritual gifts, the more insatiable they are of the heavenly longing and the more they seek on with diligence. The more they perceive in themselves a spiritual advance, the more hungry and thirsty they are for the participation and increase of grace; and the richer they are spiritually, the more do they esteem themselves to be poor, being insatiable in the spiritual longing for the heavenly Bridegroom, as the scripture says, "They that eat me will still be hungry, and they that drink me will still be thirsty" (Ecclus 24:29).

Such souls, which have the love of the Lord ardently and insatiably, are ready for eternal life, because they have been granted deliverance from the passions, and they obtain perfectly the shining forth and participation of the unspeakable and mystic fellowship of the Holy Spirit in the fullness of grace. But there are many souls that are feeble and slack, not seeking to receive here on earth, while they are still in the flesh, through patience and longsuffering, sanctification of heart, not partial but perfect, and they have never hoped to partake in the Paraclete Spirit in perfection with all conscious satisfaction and assurance, and have never expected to be delivered through the Spirit from the passions of evil. Having at one time received the grace of God, they have been deceived by sin and have given themselves over to some form of carelessness and remissness.

Such as these, having received the grace of the Spirit and possessing some comfort of grace in rest and aspiration and spiritual sweetness, presume upon this, and are lifted up, and grow careless, without contrition of heart and without humility of mind, neither reaching the perfect measure of freedom from passion, nor waiting to be perfectly filled with grace in all diligence and faith. They felt assured and took their repose and remained satisfied with their scanty comfort of grace, the result of which advance to such souls was pride rather than humility, and they are at length stripped of whatever grace was given to them, because of their careless contempt, and because of the vain arrogance of their self-conceit.

The soul that really loves God and Christ, though it may do ten thousand righteous deeds, esteems itself as having done nothing, by reason of its insatiable aspiration after God. Though it should exhaust the body with fastings and with watchings, its attitude towards the virtues is as if it had not yet even begun to labor for them. Though diverse gifts of the Spirit, or revelations and heavenly mysteries, should be given to it, it feels in itself to have acquired nothing at all, by reason of its unlimited and insatiable love to the Lord. All day long, hungering and thirsting through faith and love, in persevering prayer, it continues to be insatiable for the mysteries of grace and for the accomplishment of every virtue. It is smitten with passionate love of the heavenly Spirit, continually stirring up within itself through grace an ardent aspiration for the heavenly Bridegroom, desiring to be perfectly admitted to the mystical, ineffable fellowship with him in the sanctification of the Spirit. The face of the soul is unveiled, and it gazes upon the heavenly Bridegroom face to face in a spiritual light that cannot be described, mingling with him in all fullness of assurance, being conformed to his death, ever looking with great desire to die for Christ, and trusting with assurance to receive by the Spirit a perfect deliverance from sin and from the darkness of the passions; so that having been cleansed by the Spirit, sanctified in soul and body, it may be permitted to become a clean vessel to receive the heavenly unction and to entertain the true King, Christ himself; and then it is made ready for eternal life, being henceforward a clean dwelling-place of the Holy Spirit.

For a soul to reach these measures, however, does not come all at once, or without trial. Through many labors and struggles, and long time, and earnestness, with trial and manifold temptations, it gains the spiritual increase and advance, even to the perfect measure of freedom from passion, in order that willingly and bravely enduring every temptation with which it is plied by evil, it may then be privileged to obtain the great honors, spiritual gifts, and heavenly riches, and thus become an inheritor of the heavenly kingdom in Christ Jesus our Lord, to whom be glory and might for ever. Amen.

Translated by A. J. Mason in *Fifty Spiritual Homilies of St. Macarius the Egyptian* (London: SPCK, 1921), 76–78.

2.

BERNARD OF CLAIRVAUX

ON LOVING GOD

CHAPTER 10.27–29

The treatise On Loving God, *addressed to Cardinal Haimeric, the papal chancellor, and written about 1130, is one of Bernard's most attractive works. It sets out the main lines of his teaching about how the soul returns to God through the activation of the power of love. The work begins with a discussion of why and how we should love God: "You want me to tell you why and how God should be loved? I say that God himself is the reason for loving God; and the way to love him is without a way." Throughout the work the abbot insists that love for God must be pure—"God is not loved without a reward, although he should be loved without regard for one." Bernard's presentation is structured around four degrees of loving: (1) the carnal love by which a person loves himself for his own sake; (2) the progressive love in which a person loves God but for his own benefit; (3) the free love by which a person loves God for God's sake; and finally (4) the perfect love in which a person loves himself only for God's sake. This fourth degree—and at this point Bernard wonders if it can ever be attained in this life—involves union with God. This is not a union of substances, but a loving union of wills according to 1 Corinthians 6:17.*

THE FOURTH DEGREE OF LOVE: MAN LOVES HIMSELF FOR THE SAKE OF GOD

Happy the man who has attained the fourth degree of love; he no longer even loves himself except for God. "O God, your justice is like the mountains of God" (Ps 35:7). This love is a mountain, God's towering peak. Truly indeed, it is the fat, fertile mountain (Ps 67:16). "Who will climb the mountain of the Lord?" (Ps 23:3). "Who will give me the wings of a dove, that I may fly away to find rest?" (Ps 54:7). "This place is made peaceful, a dwelling-place in Sion" (Ps 75:3). "Alas for me, my exile has been lengthened" (Ps 119:5). When will flesh and blood (Mt 16:17), this vessel of clay (2 Cor 4:7), this earthly dwelling (Wis 9:15) understand the fact? When will this sort of affection be felt that, inebriated with divine love, the mind may forget itself and become in its own eyes like a broken dish (Ps 30:13), hastening towards God and clinging to him, becoming one with him in spirit (1 Cor 6:17), saying: "My flesh and my heart have wasted away; O God of my heart, O God, my share for eternity" (Ps 72:26)? I would say that man is blessed and holy to whom it is given to experience something of this sort, so rare in life, even if it be but once and for the space of a moment. To lose yourself, as if you no longer existed, to cease completely to experience yourself, to reduce yourself to nothing is not a human sentiment but a divine experience (Phil 2:7). If any mortal, suddenly rapt, as has been said, and for a moment is admitted to this, immediately the world of sin (Gal 1:4) envies him, the evil of the day disturbs him (Mt 6:34), the mortal body weighs him down, the needs of the flesh bother him, the weakness of corruption offers no support, and sometimes with greater violence than these, brotherly love calls him back. Alas, he has to come back to himself, to descend again into his being, and wretchedly cry out: "Lord, I suffer violence" (Is 38:14), adding: "Unhappy man that I am, who will free me from this body doomed to death?" (Rom 7:24).

All the same, since scripture says God made everything for his own purpose (Prov 16:4), the day must come when the work will conform to and agree with its Maker. It is therefore necessary for our souls to reach a similar state in which, just as God willed everything to exist for himself, so we wish that neither ourselves nor other beings to have been nor to be except for his will alone, not for our pleasure. The satisfaction of our wants, chance happiness, delights us less than to see his will done in us and for us, which we implore every day in prayer saying: "Your will be done on earth as it is in heaven ..." (Mt 6:10). O pure and sacred love! O sweet and pleasant affection! O pure and sinless intention of the will, all the more sinless and pure since it frees us from the taint of selfish vanity, all the more sweet and pleasant, for all that is found in it is divine. It is deifying to go through such an experience. As a drop of water seems to disappear completely in a big quantity of wine, even assuming the wine's taste and color; just as red, molten iron becomes so much like fire it seems to lose its primary state; just as the air on a sunny day seems transformed into sunshine instead of being lit up; so it is necessary for the saints that all human feelings melt in a mysterious way and flow into the will of God. Otherwise, how will God be all in all (1 Cor 15:28) if something human survives in man? No doubt, the substance remains though under another form, another glory, another power. When will this happen? Who will see it? Who will possess it? "When shall I come and when shall I appear in God's presence?" (Ps 41:3). O my Lord, my God, "My heart said to you: my face has sought you; Lord, I will seek your face" (Ps 26:8). Do you think I shall see your holy temple? (Ps 26:4).

I do not think that can take place for sure until the word is fulfilled: "You will love the Lord your God with all your heart, all your soul, and all your strength" (Mk 12:30), until the heart does not have to think of the body and the soul no longer has to give it life and feeling as in this life. Freed from this bother, its strength is established in the power of God. For it is impossible to assemble all these and turn them toward God's face as long as the care of this weak and wretched body keeps one busy to the point of distraction. Hence it is in a spiritual and immortal body, calm and pleasant, subject to the spirit in everything, that the soul hopes to attain the fourth degree of love, or rather to be possessed by it; for it is in God's hands to give it to whom he wishes; it is not obtained by human efforts. I mean he will easily reach the highest degree of love when he will no longer be held back by any desire of the flesh or upset by troubles as he hastens with the greatest speed and desire toward the joy of the Lord (Mt 25:21, 23). All the same, do we not think the holy martyrs received this grace, at least partially, while they were still in their victorious bodies? The strength of this love seized their souls so entirely that, despising the pain, they were able to expose their bodies to exterior torments. No doubt, the feeling of intense pain could only upset their calm; it could not overcome them.

3.

MEISTER ECKHART
SERMON 52

Sometimes called the "Poverty Sermon," this homily is one of Eckhart's most famous. It was translated into Latin and used by a number of later mystics, including John Ruusbroec. The Poverty Sermon represents Eckhart at his most challenging. The sermon's organization, with its triple analysis of true poverty as wanting nothing, knowing nothing, and having nothing, has a clarity unusual in the Meister's homilies. It appears to be among the last of Eckhart's sermons, possibly preached in Cologne in 1327 for the Feast of All Saints. The nature of poverty was one of the most controversial religious issues of the thirteenth and fourteenth centuries. Eckhart's answer to what constitutes true poverty characteristically moves quickly past external poverty to explore the inner poverty of the annihilation of the will that leads back to our pre-creational state and even beyond, breaking through to identical union with the God beyond God. Recent scholarship has shown that some phrases in the sermon echo Marguerite Porete's condemned work, The Mirror of Simple Annihilated Souls *(see section 5.4).*

Beati pauperes spiritu, quoniam ipsorum est regnum caelorum. Beatitude itself opened its mouth of wisdom and said: "Blessed are the poor in spirit, for theirs is the kingdom of heaven" (Mt 5:3). All angels, all saints, and everything that was ever born must keep silent when the Wisdom of the Father speaks: for all the wisdom of angels and all creatures is pure folly before the unfathomable wisdom of God. This Wisdom has declared that the poor are blessed.

Now there are two kinds of poverty. The one is external poverty, and this is good and much to be commended in the person who practices it voluntarily for the love of our Lord Jesus Christ, for he himself possessed this on earth. About this poverty I shall say no more now. But there is another poverty, an interior poverty, to which this word of our Lord applies when he says: "Blessed are the poor in spirit." Now I beg you to be like this in order that you may understand this sermon: for by the eternal truth I tell you that unless you are like this truth we are about to speak of, it is not possible for you to follow me.

Some people have asked me what poverty is in itself, and what a poor person is. This is how we shall answer. Bishop Albert [Albert the Great] says a poor person is one who finds no satisfaction in all things God ever created, and this is well said. But we shall speak better, taking poverty in a higher sense: a poor person is one who wants nothing, knows nothing and has nothing. We shall now speak of these three points, and I beg you for the love of God to understand this wisdom if you can; but if you can't understand it, don't worry, because I am going to speak of such truth that few good people can understand.

Firstly, we say that a poor person is one who wants nothing. There are some who do not properly understand the meaning of this: these are the people who cling with attachment to penances and outward practices, making much of these. May God have mercy on such folk for understanding so little of divine truth! These people are called holy from their outward appearances, but inwardly they are asses, for they are ignorant of the actual nature of divine truth. These people say that a poor person is one who wants nothing and they explain it this way: A person should so live that he never does his own will in anything, but should strive to do the dearest will of God. It is well with these people because their intention is right, and we commend them for it. May God in his mercy grant them the kingdom of heaven! But by God's wisdom I declare that these folk are not poor men or similar to poor men. They are much admired by those who know no better, but I say that they are asses with no understanding of God's truth. Perhaps they will gain heaven for their good intentions, but of the poverty we shall now speak of they have no idea.

If, then, I were asked what is a poor person who wants nothing, I should reply as follows. As long as a person is so disposed that it is his will with which he would do the most beloved will of God, that person has not the poverty we are speaking about: for that person has a will to serve God's will—and that is not true poverty! For a person to possess true poverty he must be as free of his created will as he was when he was not. For I declare by the eternal truth, as long as you have the will to do the will of God, and longing for eternity and God, you are not poor: for a poor person is one who wills nothing and desires nothing.

While I yet stood in my first cause, I had no God and was my own cause: then I wanted nothing and desired nothing, for I was bare being and the knower of myself in the enjoyment of truth. Then I wanted myself and wanted no other thing: what I wanted I was and what I was I wanted, and thus I was free of God and all things. But when I went out from my free will and received my created being, then I had a God. For before there were creatures, God was not God: He was that which he was. But when creatures came into existence and received their being, then God was not God in himself—He was God in creatures.

Now we say that God, inasmuch as he is God, is not the supreme goal of creatures, for the same lofty status is possessed by the least of creatures in God. And if it were the case that a fly had reason and could intellectually plumb the eternal abyss of God's being out of which it came, we would have to say that God with all that makes him God would be unable to fulfill and satisfy that fly! Therefore let us pray to God that we may be free of God that we may gain the truth and enjoy it eternally, there where the highest angel, the fly and the soul are equal, there where I stood and wanted what I was, and was what I wanted. We conclude, then: if a person is to be poor of will, he must will and desire as little as he willed and desired when he was not. And this is the way for a person to be poor by not wanting.

Secondly, a person is poor who knows nothing. We have sometimes said that a person should live as if he did not live either for himself, or for truth, or for God. But now we will speak differently and go further, and say: For a person to possess this poverty he must live so that he is unaware that he does not live for himself, or for truth, or for God. He must be so lacking in all knowledge that he neither knows nor recognizes nor feels that God lives in him; more still, he must be free of all the understanding that lives in him. For when that person stood in the eternal being of God, nothing else lived in him: what lived there was himself. Therefore we declare that a person should be as free from his own knowledge as he was when he was not. That person should let God work as he will, and himself stand idle.

Everything that ever came out of God is directed toward pure activity. The proper work of man is to love and to know. Now the question is: Wherein does blessedness lie most of all? Some masters have said it lies in knowing, some say that it lies in loving: others say it lies in knowing and loving, and they say better. But we say it lies neither in knowing nor in loving: for there is something in the soul from which both knowledge and love flow: but it does not itself know or love in the way the powers of the soul do. Whoever knows this, knows the seat of blessedness. This has neither before nor after, nor is it expecting anything to come, for it can neither gain nor lose. And so it is deprived of the knowledge that God is at work in it: rather, it just is itself, enjoying itself God-fashion. It is in this manner, I declare, that a person should be so finished and free that he neither knows nor realizes that God is at work in him: in that way can a person possess poverty.

The masters say God is a being, an intellectual being that knows all things. But we say God is not a being and not intellectual and does not know this or that. Thus God is free of all things, and so he is all things. To be poor in spirit, a person must be poor of all his own knowledge: not knowing any thing—not God, nor creature, nor himself. For this it is necessary that a person should desire to know and understand nothing of the works of God. In this way a person can be poor of his own knowledge.

Thirdly, he is a poor person who has nothing. Many people have said that perfection is attained when one has none of the material things of the earth, and this is true in one sense—when it is voluntary. But this is not the sense in which I mean it. I have said before, the poor person is not he who wants to fulfill the will of God, but he who lives in such a way as to be free of his own will and of God's will, as he was when he was not. Of this poverty we declare that it is the highest poverty. Secondly, we have said he is a poor person who does not know of the working of God within him. He who stands as free of knowledge and understanding as God stands of all things, has the purest poverty. But the third is the strictest poverty, of which we shall now speak: that is when a person has nothing.

Now pay earnest attention to this! I have often said, and eminent authorities say it too, that a person should be so free of all things and all works, both inward and outward, that he may be a proper abode for God where God can work. Now we shall say something else. If it is the case that a person is free of all creatures, of God and of self, and if it is still the case that God finds a place in him to work, then we declare that as long as this is in that person, he is not poor with the strictest poverty. For it is not God's intention in his works that a person should have a place within himself for God to work in: for poverty of spirit means being so free of God and all his works, that God, if he wishes to work in the soul, is himself the place where he works—and this he gladly does. For, if he finds a person so poor as this, then God performs his own work, and the person is passive to God within him, and God is his own place of work, being a worker in himself. It is just here, in this poverty, that man enters into that eternal essence that once he was, that he is now and evermore shall remain.

This is the word of St. Paul. He says: "All that I am, I am by the grace of God" (1 Cor 15:10). Now this sermon seems to rise above grace and being and understanding and will and all desire—so how can St. Paul's words be true? The answer is that St. Paul's words are true: it was necessary for the grace of God to be in him, for the grace of God effected in him that the accidental in him was perfected as essence. When grace had ended and finished its work, Paul remained that which he was.

So we say that a person should be so poor that he neither is nor has any place for God to work in. To preserve a place is to preserve distinction. Therefore I pray to God to make me free of God, for my essential being is above God, taking God as the origin of creatures. For in that essence of God in which God is above being and distinction, there I was myself and knew myself so as to make this man. Therefore I am my own cause according to my essence, which is eternal, and not according to my becoming, which is temporal. Therefore I am unborn, and according to my unborn mode I can never die. According to my unborn mode I have eternally been, am now, and shall eternally remain. That which I am by virtue of birth must die and perish, for it is mortal, and so must perish with time. In my birth all things were born, and I was the cause of myself and all things: and if I had so willed it, I would not have been, and all things would not have been. If I were not, God would not be either. I am the cause of God's being God. If I were not, then God would not be God. But you do not need to understand this.

A great master says that his breaking-through is nobler than his flowing out, and this is true. When I flowed forth from God all creatures declared: "There is a God"; but this cannot make me blessed, for with this I acknowledge myself as a creature. But in my breaking-through, where I stand free of my own will, of God's will, of all his works, and of God himself, then I am above all creatures and am neither God nor creature, but I am that which I was and shall remain for evermore. There I shall receive an imprint that will raise me above all the angels. By this imprint I shall gain such wealth that I shall not be content with God inasmuch as he is God, or with all his divine works: for this breaking-through guarantees to me that I and God are one. Then I am what I was, then I neither wax nor wane, for then I am an unmoved cause that moves all things. Here, God finds no place in man, for man by his poverty wins for himself what he has eternally been and shall eternally remain. Here, God is one with the spirit, and that is the strictest poverty one can find.

If anyone cannot understand this sermon, he need not worry. For so long as someone is not equal to this truth, he cannot understand my words, for this is a naked truth that has come direct from the heart of God. That we may so live as to experience it eternally, may God help us. Amen.

From *Meister Eckhart. Sermons and Treatises. Vol. II*, 269–76, translated by M. O'C. Walshe. Copyright 1981. Reprinted by permission of The English Sangha Trust, Amaravati Buddhist Monastery. Walshe, following Pfeiffer, numbers this Sermon 87, but in the critical edition it is Sermon 52.

4.

JOHN RUUSBROEC

THE LITTLE BOOK OF ENLIGHTENMENT

CHAPTERS 9–13

John Ruusbroec is the most famous of Dutch mystics. His long life (1293–1381) spanned one of the most troubled centuries of the Middle Ages, but he does not dwell on the contemporary problems of church and society. Rather, Ruusbroec concentrates on the soul's progress toward the "common life," that is, our sharing in the interaction of the divine persons in the Trinity. Ruusbroec's mysticism was set forth during an era in which there were many debates about mysticism and mystical union. He was aware of at least some of Eckhart's writings, and he was careful to qualify, and even to criticize, what he thought were some of Eckhart's excesses.

*Ruusbroec was particularly concerned about the proper understanding of union with God. The traditional Latin view of union was that of the "union of spirits" (*unitas spiritus*) in which God and the human person become united in perfect willing through the action, or mediation, of grace. Some of the women mystics of the thirteenth century, as well as Meister Eckhart, advanced a view of indistinct union. Beginning in the early fourteenth century, the Free Spirit heretics were accused of claiming that they had achieved such deep indistinction with God that they were no longer bound by the laws of morality or the commandments of the church (see section 14.2). Ruusbroec was a strenuous opponent of these errors, and he used the debate to work out an original theology of three interpenetrating and coexisting levels of union with God. The first is "union through an intermediary," that is, through the action of grace conveyed in the sacraments. The second is "union without an intermediary," our being rapt into* *the life of the three Persons in the Trinity. Ruusbroec's third form of union, "union without difference," sounds much like Eckhart's "union of indistinction." For the Dutch mystic, however, such union, though it involves becoming lost in a state of unknowing that finds no distinction in God, not even that of the Trinity, always coexists with and implies union with intermediary and union without intermediary.*

CHAPTER 9

. . . This experience [of motionless beatitude] is our superessential beatitude which is an enjoyment of God and of all his beloved. This beatitude is the dark silence that is always inactive. It is essential to God and superessential to all creatures.

CHAPTER 10

And there you must accept that the Persons yield and lose themselves whirling in essential love, that is, in enjoyable unity; nevertheless, they always remain according to their personal properties in the working of the Trinity. You may thus understand that the divine nature is eternally active according to the mode of the Persons and eternally at rest and without mode according to the simplicity of its essence. It is why all that God has chosen and enfolded with eternal personal love, he has possessed essentially, enjoyably in unity, with essential love. For the divine Persons embrace mutually in eternal complacency with an infinite and active love in unity. This activity is constantly renewed in the living life of the Trinity. There is continuously new birthgiving in new knowledge, new complacency and new breathing forth of the Spirit in a new embrace with a new torrent of eternal love. All the elect, angels and men from the last to the first, are embraced in this complacency. It is in this complacency that heaven and earth are suspended, existence, life, activity and maintenance of all creatures, save only the aversion from God through sin which comes from the creatures' own blind perversity. And out of the complacency of God flow grace and glory and all the gifts in heaven and on earth and in each individually according to his need and to his receptivity. For the grace of God is prepared for all men and awaits the return of every sinner. When he, by means of the touch of grace, decides to take pity on himself and trustfully call on God, he always finds pardon. So whosoever, by means of grace with loving complacency, is brought back to the eternal complacency of God will be caught and embraced in the fathomless love which is God himself, and he is forever renewed in love and virtue. For while we please God and God pleases us, then love is practiced and eternal life. But God has loved us eternally and has cherished us in his complacency and we should consider that rightly; and thus our love and complacency should be renewed, for through the relations between the Persons in the divinity there is always new complacency with new out-flowing of love in a new embrace in unity. And this is without time, that is to say, without before or after in an eternal present, for in the embrace in unity all things have been consummated. And in the out-flowing of love all things are being achieved. And in the living fruitful nature all things have the potentiality to occur, for in the living fruitful nature the Son is in the Father and the Father in the Son, and the Holy Spirit in them both. For it is a living and fruitful unity which is the source and the fount of all life and all genesis. And for this reason all creatures are there without themselves as in their eternal origin, one essence and one life with God. But in the bursting-out of the Persons with distinction, so the Son is from the Father and the Holy Spirit from them both. There God has created and ordered all creatures in their own essence. And he has remade man by his grace and by his death, so far as it lies in his power. He has adorned his own with love and with virtues and brought them back with him to their beginning. There, the Father with the Son and all the beloved are enfolded and embraced in the bond of love, that is to say, in the unity of the Holy Spirit. It is this same unity which is fruitful according to the bursting-out of the Persons and in the return, an eternal bond of love which can nevermore be untied. And all those who know themselves to be bound therein must remain eternally blissful. They are all rich in virtues and enlightened in contemplation and simple where they rest enjoyably, for in their turning-in, the love of God reveals itself as flowing out with all good and drawing in into unity and [as] superessential and without mode in an eternal repose. And so they are united to God, by intermediary, without intermediary, and also without difference.

CHAPTER 11

They have the love of God before them in their inward vision as a common good that flows out in heaven and earth, and they feel the Holy Trinity inclined towards them and within them with plenitude of grace, and for this reason they are adorned with all virtues, with holy exercises and with good works without and within. Thus they are united with God by means of the intermediary of divine grace and of their holy life. And because they have given themselves to God, whether in action or in abstention or in endurance, they always have peace and inner gladness, solace and savor, which the world cannot receive nor any hypocritical creature, nor any man who seeks himself and has himself in mind more than the honor of God.

Secondly, these same interior, enlightened persons have the love of God before them in their inward vision whenever they want, as drawing or calling in towards unity. For they see and feel that the Father with the Son by means of the Holy Spirit stand embraced with all the elect and are brought back with eternal love into the unity of their nature. This unity is constantly drawing or calling in all that has been born out of it naturally or by grace. And therefore these enlightened people are lifted up with free mind above reason to a bare vision devoid of images. There lives the eternal invitation of God's unity, and with imageless naked understanding they go beyond all works and all practices and all things to the summit of their spirit. There their naked understanding is penetrated with eternal clarity as the air is penetrated by the light of the sun. The bare elevated will is transformed and penetrated with fathomless love just as iron is penetrated by the fire. And the bare elevated memory finds itself caught and established in a fathomless absence of images. Thus the created image is united threefoldwise above reason to its eternal image, which is the source of its being and of its life. This source is essentially conserved and possessed in unity with a simple contemplation in imageless emptiness. Thus one is raised above reason, threefold in unity and one in trinity. Nevertheless, the creature does not become God, for the union occurs by means of grace and love returned to God. And for this reason the creature experiences distinction and alterity between itself and God in its inward vision. And though the union is without intermediary, the manifold works that God does in heaven and earth are, however, hidden from the spirit. For though God gives himself as he is with a clear distinction, he gives himself in the soul's essence, where the soul's powers are unified above reason and undergo God's transformation in simplicity. There all is full and overflowing, for the spirit feels itself as one truth and one richness and one unity with God. Nevertheless there is still an essential forward inclination and that is an essential distinction between the essence of the soul and the essence of God; and that is the highest distinction that can be felt.

CHAPTER 12

Hereafter follows the unity without difference, for the love of God is not only to be considered as flowing out with all good and drawing in into unity, but it is also above all distinction in essential enjoyment according to the bare essence of the divinity. And for this reason enlightened people have found within themselves an essential inward gazing above reason and without reason, and an enjoyable inclination surpassing all modes and all essence, sinking away from themselves into a modeless abyss of fathomless beatitude, where the Trinity of the divine Persons possess their nature in essential unity. See, here the beatitude is so simple and so without mode that therein all essential gazing, inclination and distinction of creatures pass away. For all spirits thus raised up melt away and are annihilated by reason of enjoyment in God's essence which is the superessence of all essence. There they fall away from themselves and are lost in a bottomless unknowing. There all clarity is turned back to darkness, there where the three Persons give way to the essential unity and without distinction enjoy essential beatitude. This beatitude is essential to God alone and to all spirits it is superessential. For no created essence can be one with God's essence and perish of itself, for then the creature would become God, which is impossible. For the essence of God can neither diminish nor increase; nothing can be taken from him, neither can it be added to him. Nevertheless, all loving spirits are one enjoyment and one beatitude with God without difference. For the blessed essence which is the enjoyment of God himself and all his beloved, is so plain and simple that there is neither Father, nor Son, nor Holy Spirit, according to personal distinction, nor any creature. But there all the enlightened spirits are raised out of themselves into an enjoyment without mode that is overflowing above all fullness that any creature has ever received or ever may receive; for there all the elevated spirits, in their superessence are one enjoyment and one beatitude with God without difference. There the beatitude is so simple that no distinction can enter into it evermore. Christ desired this when he prayed his heavenly Father that all his beloved should be brought to perfect union, just as he is one with the Father in enjoyment, by means of the Holy Spirit (Jn 17:21–23). Thus he prayed and desired that he in us and we in him and in his heavenly Father should become one in enjoyment, by means of the Holy Spirit. And that, I think, is the most loving prayer that Christ ever made for our beatitude.

CHAPTER 13

But you should also note that his prayer was threefold, as St. John has shown us in the same Gospel. For he prayed that we might be with him, that we might behold the glory which his Father has given him (Jn 17:24). Because of this, I said in the beginning that all good people are united with God by means of the grace of God and their virtuous life. For the love of God is always flowing into us with new gifts. And those who take heed of this are filled with new virtues and holy practices and with all good things, as I have said to you before. This union, with fullness of grace and glory in body and soul, begins here and lasts eternally.

Next, Christ prayed that he should be in us, and we in him. This we find in many passages in the Gospel. And this is the union that is without intermediary, for the love of God is not only out-flowing but it is also drawing-in into unity. And those who feel and experience this become interior, enlightened men. Their higher faculties are raised above all practices to the bareness of their essence. There the faculties become simplified above reason in their essence and because of this they are filled and overflowing. For in this simplicity the spirit finds itself united with God without intermediary. And this union, together with the exercise which is proper to it, will endure eternally, as I have already said.

Then Christ further prayed the highest prayer: that all his beloved should be brought to perfect unity, even as he is one with the Father; not as one as he is one single substance of divinity with the Father, which is impossible for us, but as one and in the same unity where he is, without distinction, one enjoyment and one beatitude with the Father in essential love.

Christ's prayer is fulfilled in those united to God in this threefold manner. With God they will ebb and flow, and [will] always be in repose, in possessing and enjoying. They will work and endure and rest in the superessence without fear. They will go out and in and find nourishment both within and without. They are drunk with love and have passed away into God in a dark luminosity.

Jan van Ruusbroec, *Beocsken der Verclaringhe,* edited by G. de Baere, introduced by P. Mommaers, translated by Ph. Crowley and H. Rolfson (Corpus Christianorum, Continuatio Mediaevalis 101), Turnhout, Brepols Publishers, 1989, 136–52, lines 284–481. Used with permission.

TERESA OF AVILA
THE INTERIOR CASTLE 7.1-2

Teresa of Avila's Interior Castle, *or* Mansions, *composed in 1577, is her most finished work. Although not written in the first person, it is obvious that the "certain person" she refers to is herself. The* Interior Castle *is noted for its careful structure and apt use of symbols, as well as its subtle analysis of the different states of the progress of the soul. The treatise is an ordered account of the seven mansions, or series of rooms, that exist in the palace of the King (the Divine Bridegroom). The first three mansions are primarily active, dealing with the soul's cooperation with God's grace in attaining what has been called acquired contemplation. The final four mansions deal with the passive, or infused, contemplation in which God draws the soul into ever-deepening stages of union by his action alone. Mansion Four is called the "prayer of quiet," a term that Teresa used rather differently in different writings. Mansion Five is the "prayer of union," where the stilling of the soul's faculties begins. Mansion Six is the stage of the "spiritual espousals, or bethrothals"—the place of extraordinary states of mystical consciousness, such as ecstasy, rapture, locutions from God, and the like. It is also the stage where the soul is wounded by love. In her earlier writings these experiences represented the height of the mystical path, but now Teresa sees them as the last preparation for Mansion Seven, the "spiritual marriage," a union with the Trinity in the center of the soul. This selection gives the first two sections of Teresa's analysis of spiritual marriage.*

THE SEVENTH MANSION

Chapter 1. Treats of the sublime favors God bestows on souls that have entered the seventh mansion. The author shows the difference she believes to exist between soul and spirit, although they are both one. This chapter contains some noteworthy things.

1. You may think, sisters, that so much has been said of this spiritual journey that nothing remains to be added. That would be a great mistake: God's immensity has no limits, neither have his works; therefore, who can recount his mercies and his greatness? It is impossible, so do not be amazed at what I write about them, which is but a cipher of what remains untold concerning God. He has shown great mercy in communicating these mysteries to one who could recount them to us, for as we learn more of his intercourse with creatures, we ought to praise him more fervently and to esteem more highly the soul in which he so delights. Each of us possesses a soul but we do not realize its value as made in the image of God, therefore we fail to understand the important secrets it contains. May his Majesty be pleased to guide my pen and to teach me to say somewhat of the much there is to tell of his revelations to the souls he leads into this mansion. I have begged him earnestly to help me, since he sees that my object is to reveal his mercies for the praise and glory of his name. I hope he will grant this favor, if not for my own sake, at least for yours, sisters—so that you may discover how vital it is for you to put no obstacle in the way of the Spiritual Marriage of the Bridegroom with your soul, which brings, as you will learn, such signal blessings with it. . . .

3. When our Lord is pleased to take pity on the sufferings, both past and present, endured through her longing for him by this soul which he has spiritually taken for his bride, he, before consummating the celestial marriage, brings her into this his mansion or presence chamber. This is the seventh Mansion, for as he has a dwelling place in heaven, so has he in the soul, where none but he may abide and which may be termed a second heaven.

4. It is important, sisters, that we should not fancy the soul to be in darkness. As we are accustomed to believe there is no light but that which is exterior, we imagine that the soul is wrapped in obscurity. This is indeed the case with a soul out of the state of grace, not, how-

ever, through any defect in the Sun of Justice, which remains within it and gives it being, but the soul itself is incapable of receiving the light, as I think I said in speaking of the First Mansion. A certain person was given to understand that such unfortunate souls are, as it were, imprisoned in a gloomy dungeon, chained hand and foot and unable to perform any meritorious action: they are also both blind and dumb. Well may we pity them when we reflect that we ourselves were once in the same state and that God may show them mercy also.

5. Let us, then, sisters, be most zealous in interceding for them and never neglect it. To pray for a soul in mortal sin is a far more profitable form of almsgiving than it would be to help a Christian whom we saw with hands strongly fettered behind his back, tied to a post and dying of hunger—not for want of food, because plenty of the choicest delicacies lay near him, but because he was unable to put them into his mouth, although he was extremely exhausted and on the point of dying, and that not a temporal death, but an eternal one. Would it not be extremely cruel of us to stand looking at him, and give him nothing to eat? What if by your prayers you could loose his bonds? Now you understand.

6. For the love of God I implore you constantly to remember in your prayers souls in a like case. We are not speaking now of them but of others who, by the mercy of God, have done penance for their sins and are in a state of grace. You must not think of the soul as insignificant and petty but as an interior world containing the number of beautiful mansions you have seen; as indeed it should, since in the center of the soul there is a mansion reserved for God himself.

7. When his Majesty deigns to bestow on the soul the grace of these divine nuptials, he brings it into his presence chamber and does not treat it as before, when he put it into a trance [in the Sixth Mansion]. I believe he then united it to himself, as also during the prayer of union; but then only the superior part was affected and the soul did not feel called to enter its own center as it does in this mansion. Here it matters little whether it is in the one way or the other.

8. In the former favors our Lord unites the spirit to himself and makes it both blind and dumb like St. Paul after his conversion (Acts 9:8), thus preventing its knowing whence or how it enjoys this grace, for the supreme delight of the spirit is to realize its nearness to God. During the actual moment of divine union the soul feels nothing, all

its powers being entirely lost. But now he acts differently: our pitiful God removes the scales from its eyes (Acts 9:18), letting it see and
understand somewhat of the grace received in a strange and wonderful manner in this mansion by means of intellectual vision.

9. By some mysterious manifestation of the truth, the three persons
of the most Blessed Trinity reveal themselves, preceded by an illumination that shines on the spirit like a most dazzling cloud of light. The
three persons are distinct from one another; a sublime knowledge is
infused into the soul, imbuing it with a certainty of the truth that the
three are of one substance, power, and knowledge and are one God.
Thus that which we hold as a doctrine of faith, the soul now, so to
speak, understands by sight, though it beholds the Blessed Trinity neither by the eyes of the body nor of the soul, this being no imaginary vision. All the three persons here communicate themselves to the soul,
speak to it, and make it understand the words of our Lord in the
Gospel that he and the Father and the Holy Spirit will come and make
their abode with the soul that loves him and keeps his commandments
(Jn 14:23).

10. O my God, how different from merely hearing and believing
these words is it to realize their truth in this way! Day by day a growing astonishment takes possession of this soul, for the three persons of
the Blessed Trinity seem never to depart; it sees with certainty, in the
way I have described, that they dwell far within its own center and
depths; though for want of learning it cannot describe how, it is conscious of the indwelling of these divine companions.

11. You may fancy that such a person is beside herself and that her
mind is too inebriated to care for anything else. On the contrary, she is
far more active than before in all that concerns God's service, and
when at leisure she enjoys this blessed companionship. Unless she first
deserts God, I believe he will never cease to make her clearly sensible
of his presence: she feels confident, as indeed she may, that he will
never so fail her as to allow her to lose this favor after once bestowing
it; at the same time, she is more careful than before to avoid offending
him in any way.

12. This presence is not always so entirely realized, that is, so distinctly manifest, as at first, or as it is at times when God renews this
favor, otherwise the recipient could not possibly attend to anything
else nor live in society. Although not always seen by so clear a light, yet

whenever she reflects on it she feels the companionship of the Blessed Trinity. This is as if, when we were with other people in a very well-lighted room, someone were to darken it by closing the shutters; we should feel certain that the others were still there, though we were unable to see them.

13. You may ask: "Could she not bring back the light and see them again?" This is not in her power; when our Lord chooses, he will open the shutters of the understanding: He shows her great mercy in never quitting her and in making her realize it so clearly. His divine Majesty seems to be preparing his bride for greater things by this divine companionship, which clearly helps perfection in every way and makes her lose the fear she sometimes felt when other graces were granted her.

14. A certain person so favored found she had improved in all virtues: whatever were her trials or labors, the center of her soul seemed never moved from its resting place. Thus in a manner her soul appeared divided: a short time after God had done her this favor, while undergoing great sufferings, she complained of her soul as Martha did of Mary (Lk 10:40), reproaching it with enjoying solitary peace while leaving her so full of troubles and occupations that she could not keep it company. . . .

Chapter 2. Treats the same subject: explains, by some delicately drawn comparisons, the difference between spiritual union and spiritual marriage.

1. We now come to speak of divine and spiritual nuptials, although this sublime favor cannot be received in all its perfection during our present life, for by forsaking God this great good would be lost. The first time God bestows this grace, he, by an imaginary vision of his most sacred humanity, reveals himself to the soul so that it may understand and realize the sovereign gift it is receiving. He may manifest himself in a different way to other people; the person I mentioned, after having received Holy Communion, beheld our Lord, full of splendor, beauty, and majesty, as he was after his resurrection. He told her that henceforth she was to care for his affairs as though they were her own and he would care for hers: He spoke other words that she understood better than she can repeat them. This may seem nothing new, for our Lord had thus revealed himself to her at other times; yet this was so different that it left her bewildered and amazed, both on account of the vividness of what she saw and of the words heard at the time, also

because it took place in the interior of the soul where, with the exception of the one last mentioned, no other vision had been seen.

2. You must understand that between the visions seen in this and in the former mansions there is a vast difference; there is the same distinction between spiritual espousals and spiritual marriage as between people who are only betrothed and others who are united forever in holy matrimony. I have told you that though I make this comparison because there is none more suitable, yet this betrothal is no more related to our corporeal condition than if the soul were a disembodied spirit. This is even more true of the spiritual marriage, for this secret union takes place in the innermost center of the soul where God himself must dwell: I believe that no door is required to enter it. I say, "no door is required," for all I have hitherto described seems to come through the senses and faculties as must the representation of our Lord's humanity, but what passes in the union of the spiritual nuptials is very different. Here God appears in the soul's center, not by an imaginary but by an intellectual vision far more delicate than those seen before, just as he appeared to the Apostles without having entered through the door when he said: "Peace be with you" (Jn 20:19).

3. So mysterious is the secret and so sublime the favor that God thus bestows instantaneously on the soul, that it feels a supreme delight, only to be described by saying that our Lord vouchsafes for the moment to reveal to it his own heavenly glory in a far more subtle way than by any vision or spiritual delight. As far as can be understood, the soul, I mean the spirit of this soul, is made one with God who is himself a spirit, and who has been pleased to show certain persons how far his love for us extends in order that we may praise his greatness. He has thus deigned to unite himself to his creature: He has bound himself to her as firmly as two human beings are joined in wedlock and will never separate himself from her.

4. Spiritual betrothal is different and like the grace of union is often dissolved; for though two things are made one by union, separation is still possible and each part then remains a thing by itself. This favor generally passes quickly, and afterward the soul, as far as it is aware, remains without his company.

5. This is not so in the spiritual marriage with our Lord, where the soul always remains in its center with its God. Union may be symbolized by two wax candles, the tips of which touch each other so closely

that there is but one light; or again, the wick, the wax, and the light become one, but the one candle can again be separated from the other and the two candles remain distinct; or the wick may be withdrawn from the wax. But spiritual marriage is like rain falling from heaven into a river or stream, becoming one and the same liquid, so that the river and rain water cannot be divided; or it resembles a streamlet flowing into the ocean, which cannot afterward be disunited from it. This marriage may also be likened to a room into which a bright light enters through two windows—though divided when it enters, the light becomes one and the same.

6. Perhaps when St. Paul said, "He who is joined to the Lord is one spirit" (1 Cor 6:17), he meant this sovereign marriage, which presupposes his Majesty's having been joined to the soul by union. The same Apostle says: "To me, to live is Christ and to die is gain" (Phil 1:21). This, I think, might here be uttered by the soul, for now the little butterfly of which I spoke dies with supreme joy, for Christ is her life [see Mansion Five].

7. This becomes more manifest by its effects as time goes on, for the soul learns that it is God who gives it life, by certain secret intuitions too strong to be misunderstood, and keenly felt, although impossible to describe. These produce such overmastering feelings that the person experiencing them cannot refrain from amorous exclamations, such as: "O Life of my life, and Power that upholds me!," with other aspirations of the same kind. For from the bosom of the Divinity, where God seems ever to hold this soul fast clasped, issue streams of milk, which solace the servants of the castle. I think he wishes them to share, in some way, the riches the soul enjoys; therefore from the flowing river in which the little streamlet is swallowed up, some drops of water flow every now and then to sustain those who in bodily things must serve the bride and Bridegroom.

8. A person who was unexpectedly plunged into water could not fail to be aware of it; here the case is the same, but even more evident. A quantity of water could not fall on us unless it came from some source—so the soul feels certain there must be some one within it who lances forth these darts and vivifies its own life, and that there is a sun whence this brilliant light streams forth from the interior of the spirit to its faculties.

9. The soul itself, as I said, never moves from this center, nor loses

the peace he can give who gave it to the Apostles when they were assembled together (Jn 20:19). I think this salutation of our Lord contains far deeper meaning than the words convey, as also his bidding the glorious Magdalene to "go in peace" (Lk 7:50). Our Lord's words act within us, and in these cases they must have wrought their effect in the souls already disposed to banish from within themselves all that is corporeal and to retain only what is spiritual, in order to be joined in this celestial union with the uncreated Spirit. Without doubt, if we empty ourselves of all that belongs to the creature, depriving ourselves of it for the love of God, that same Lord will fill us with himself.

10. Our Lord Jesus Christ, praying for his Apostles (I cannot remember the reference), asked that they might be made one with the Father and with himself, as Jesus Christ our Lord is in the Father and the Father in him (Jn 17:21). I do not know how love could be greater than this! Let none draw back from entering here, for his Majesty also said: "Not only for them do I pray, but for them also who through their word shall believe in Me" (Jn 17:20); and he declared: "I am in them" (Jn 17:23).

11. God help me! how true these words are, and how clearly are they understood by the soul that in this state of prayer finds them fulfilled in itself! So should we all but for our own fault, for the words of Jesus Christ, our King and our Lord, cannot fail. It is we who fail by not disposing ourselves fitly, nor removing all that can obstruct this light, so that we do not behold ourselves in this mirror wherein our image is engraved.

12. To return to what I was saying. God places the soul in his own mansion which is in the very center of the soul itself. They say the empyreal heavens, in which our Lord dwells, do not revolve with the rest: so the accustomed movements of the faculties and imagination do not appear to take place in any way that can injure the soul or disturb its peace.

13. Do I seem to imply that after God has brought the soul thus far it is certain to be saved and cannot fall into sin again? I do not mean this: whenever I say that the soul seems in security, I must be understood to imply for as long as his Majesty thus holds it in his care and it does not offend him. At any rate, I know for certain that though such a person realizes the high state she is in and has remained in it for several years, she does not consider herself safe, but is more careful than

ever to avoid committing the least offense against God. As I shall explain later on, she is most anxious to serve him and feels a constant pain and confusion at seeing how little she can do for him compared with all she ought. This is no light cross but a severe mortification, for the harder the penances she can perform, the better is she pleased. Her greatest penance is to be deprived by God of health and strength to perform any. I told you elsewhere what keen pain this caused her, but now it grieves her far more. This must be because she is like a tree grafted on a stock growing near a stream that makes it greener and more fruitful (Ps 1:3). Why marvel at the longings of this soul whose spirit has truly become one with the celestial water I described? [Mansion Six].

14. To return to what I wrote about. It is not intended that the powers, senses, and passions should continually enjoy this peace. The soul does so, indeed, but in the other mansions there are still times of struggle, suffering, and fatigue, though as a general rule, peace is not lost by them. This center of the soul or spirit is so hard to describe or even to believe in, that I think, sisters, my inability to explain my meaning saves your being tempted to disbelieve me; it is difficult to understand how there can be crosses and sufferings and yet peace in the soul.

15. Let me give you one or two comparisons—God grant they may be of use; if not, I know that what I say is true. A king resides in his palace; many wars and disasters take place in his kingdom but he remains on his throne. In the same way, though tumults and wild beasts rage with great uproar in the other mansions, yet nothing of this enters the Seventh Mansion, nor drives the soul from it. Although the mind regrets these troubles, they do not disturb it nor rob it of its peace, for the passions are too subdued to dare to enter here where they would only suffer still further defeat. Though the whole body is in pain, yet the head, if it be sound, does not suffer with it. I smile at these comparisons—they do not please me—but I can find no others. Think what you will about it—I have told you the truth.

From *The Interior Castle or the Mansions Translated from the Autograph of Saint Teresa of Jesus by the Benedictines of Stanbrook,* revised and annotated with an introduction by the Very Rev. Prior Zimmerman, OCD (London: Thomas Baker, 1921), 261–77. I have revised the language of the text and made several corrections.

JOHN OF THE CROSS
THE SPIRITUAL CANTICLE

STANZA XXII

John of the Cross wrote the first thirty-one stanzas of the poem titled "Songs Between the Soul and the Bridegroom" while he was in prison in 1578. He later reworked this recasting of the Song of Songs in two versions, the Sanlucar text finished circa 1582 in thirty-nine stanzas, and the Jaen text of forty stanzas completed circa 1585. At the request of Mother Ana de Jesus he composed prose commentaries on both versions in 1584 and 1585. In his prologue John cautions the reader about the limits of any commentary, saying, "Since these stanzas were composed in a love flowing freely from abundant mystical understanding [abundante intelligencia mística], I cannot explain them adequately and I do not intend to do so." Nevertheless, The Spiritual Canticle, *especially the longer version, part of which is given here, is John's most complete presentation of the three stages of the mystical life, the purgative, illuminative, and unitive (see section 5.1). It is also the saint's fullest exploration of the erotic model of loving union, involving both temporary spiritual betrothal and the higher and permanent spiritual marriage. The first twelve stanzas describe the bride's anxious search for the Divine Bridegroom through the purgative and illuminative ways. Stanzas XIII–XXI deal with the transition between illumination and the movement into the preliminary union of the betrothal. Stanzas XXII–XXXV deal with the spiritual marriage, while the final stanzas (XXXVI–XL) discuss the soul's desire for the glory of heaven.*

STANZA XXII

The bride has entered Into the pleasant garden of her desire
And at her pleasure rests, Her neck reclining
On the gentle arms of the Beloved.

COMMENTARY:
"THE BRIDE HAS ENTERED"

... 3. For the better understanding of the arrangement of these stanzas and of the way by which the soul advances until it reaches the state of spiritual marriage, which is the very highest (and which by the grace of God I am now about to treat), we must keep in mind that before the soul enters this state she must be first tried in tribulations, in sharp mortifications, and in meditation on spiritual things. This is the subject of this canticle until we come to the fifth stanza, beginning with the words: "A thousand graces diffusing." Then the soul enters on the contemplative life, passing through the ways and straits of love that are described in the course of the canticle until we come to the thirteenth, beginning with "Turn them away, O my Beloved!" This is the moment of the spiritual betrothal. Then the soul advances by the unitive way, as the recipient of many and very great communications, jewels, and gifts from the Bridegroom as to one betrothed, and grows into perfect love. All this is described in the stanzas from where the betrothal is made with "Turn them away, O my Beloved," down to the present stanza that begins with "The bride has entered."

The spiritual marriage of the soul and the Son of God now remains to be accomplished. This is, beyond all comparison, a far higher state than that of betrothal, because it is a complete transformation into the Beloved; whereby they surrender each to the other the entire possession of themselves in the perfect union of love, wherein the soul becomes divine, and, by participation, God, so far as it is possible in this life. I believe that no soul ever attains to this state without being confirmed in grace, for the faithfulness of both is confirmed; that of God being confirmed in the soul. Hence it follows, that this is the very highest state possible in this life. As in the consummation of carnal marriage there are "two in one flesh" (Gen 2:24), as sacred scripture says, so also in the consummation of spiritual marriage between God and the soul there are two natures in one spirit and love, as we learn from St. Paul, who made use of the same comparison, saying: "He who adheres to our Lord is one spirit with him" (1 Cor 6:17). So, when the light of a star or of a candle is united to that of the sun, the light is not that of the star, nor of the candle, but of the sun itself, which absorbs all other light in its own.

4. It is of this state that the Bridegroom is now speaking, saying: "The bride has entered," that is, has gone out of all temporal and natural things, out of all spiritual affections, ways, and methods, having left on one side and forgotten all temptations, trials, sorrows, anxieties, and cares, and is transformed in this embrace. Therefore, the following line says, "Into the pleasant garden of her desire."

5. This is like saying that she has been transformed in God, who is here called the pleasant garden because of the delicious and sweet repose that the soul finds in him. But the soul does not enter the garden of perfect transformation, the glory and the joy of the spiritual marriage, without passing first through the spiritual betrothal, the mutual faithful love of the betrothed. When the soul has lived for some time as the betrothed of the Son of God, in perfect and sweet love, God calls her and leads her into his flowering garden for the consummation of the spiritual marriage. Then the two natures are so united, what is divine is so communicated to what is human, that, without undergoing any essential change, each seems to be God. Yet in this life the union cannot be perfect, though it can neither be described nor conceived.

6. We learn this truth very clearly from the Bridegroom himself in the Song of Songs, where he invites the soul, now his bride, to enter this state, saying: "Come into my garden, O my sister, my bride: I have gathered my myrrh with my aromatic spices" (Song 5:1). He calls the soul his sister, his bride, for she was such in the love and surrender that she made of herself to him before he had called her to the state of spiritual marriage, where, as he says, he gathered his myrrh with his aromatic spices, that is, the fruits of flowers now ripe and ready for the soul. These are the delights and grandeurs communicated to her by himself in this state, that is, he communicates them to her in himself, because he is to her the pleasant and desirable garden.

The whole aim and desire of the soul and of God in all her works is the accomplishment and perfection of this state, and the soul is therefore never weary until she reaches it. In this state she finds a much greater abundance and fullness of God, a more secure and lasting peace, and a sweetness incomparably more perfect than in the spiritual betrothal, seeing that she reposes between the arms of such a Bridegroom, whose spiritual embraces are so real that through them she lives the life of God. Now is fulfilled what St. Paul referred to when he said: "I live, now not I, but Christ lives in me" (Gal 2:20). And now that the soul lives a life so happy and so glorious, as it is the life of God, consider what a sweet life it must be—a life where God sees nothing displeasing, and where the soul finds nothing irksome, but rather the glory and delight of God in the very substance of itself, now transformed in him. Hence the next line reads, "And at her pleasure rests, her neck reclining. . . ."

7. The neck is the soul's strength, by means of which its union with the Beloved is accomplished; for the soul could not endure so close an embrace had she not been very strong. And as the soul has labored in this strength, practiced virtue, overcome vice, it is fitting that she should rest there from her labors, "her neck reclining on the gentle arms of the Beloved."

8. This reclining of the neck on the arms of God is the union of the soul's strength, or, rather, of the soul's weakness, with the strength of God, in whom our weakness, resting and transformed, puts on the strength of God himself. The state of spiritual matrimony is therefore most fitly designated by the reclining of the neck on the gentle arms of the Beloved; seeing that God is the strength and sweetness of the soul, who guards and defends it from all evil, and gives it to taste of all good.

Hence the bride in the Song of Songs, longing for this state, says to the Bridegroom: "Who shall give you to me, my brother, nursed at the breasts of my mother, that I may find you alone outside and kiss you, and no one despise me" (Song 8:1). By addressing him as her brother she shows the equality between them in the betrothal of love, before she entered the state of spiritual marriage. By saying, "Nursed at the breasts of my mother" she means: You dried up the passions and desires, which are the breasts and milk of our mother Eve in our flesh, which are a hindrance to this state. The "finding him outside" is to find him in detachment from all things and from self when the bride is in solitude, spiritually detached, which takes place when all the desires are quenched.

There I, being alone, "kiss you," who are alone. This is to say that my nature, now that it is alone and stripped from all impurity, natural, temporal, and spiritual, may be united with you alone, with your nature alone without any intermediary. This only happens in the spiritual marriage, in which the soul, as it were, kisses God when none despises her nor makes her afraid. For in this state the soul is no longer molested, either by the devil, or the flesh, or the world, or the desires. Here is fulfilled what is written in the Song of Songs: "Winter is now past, the rain is over and gone. The flowers have appeared in our land" (Song 2:11–12).

Adapted and corrected from the translation of David Lewis, *The Dark Night of the Soul, A Spiritual Canticle, and The Living Flame of Love of Saint John of the Cross* (London: Thomas Baker, 2nd ed., 1891), 296–300.

FRANCIS DE SALES
THE TREATISE ON THE LOVE OF GOD
BOOK 7, CHAPTERS 1 AND 3

Francis de Sales (1567–1622) was the most noted exponent of the "Devout Humanism" that characterized French spirituality and mysticism in the seventeenth century. As he once said, "I am as human as anyone can possibly be." As a young student in Paris, grace had rescued him from the temptation to despair. Francis devoted his life as bishop, preacher, spiritual guide, and writer to win others to the love of God by his gentle manner and irenic approach in an age of religious hatred and conflict. He was closely associated with the aristocratic circles that initiated the great age of French mysticism; in later years he worked with his friend St. Jane Frances de Chantal in establishing a new form of religious life for women (see section 4.4).

Francis's main contributions to Catholic spirituality were two very influential books. The Introduction to the Devout Life, first published in 1608, was a landmark in the history of Christian life and thought, because of how it proposed a spirituality for people in all walks of life. Published in 1616, The Treatise on the Love of God was a summary of Catholic mystical teaching centered on, as the preface puts it, "the birth, the progress, and the decay of the operations, characteristics, benefits, and excellence of divine love." Addressed to a fictional "advanced soul" (Theotimus), the twelve books of the treatise begin with a general section devoted to the preparation for and birth of divine love (books 1 and 2), the progress and perfection of love (book 3), its decay and ruin (book 4), and its two main exercises: complacency and benevolence (book 5). The remaining books are directly mystical. Book 6 deals with love as exercised in prayer, while book 7 concerns the union of the soul with God in prayer. Books 8 and 9 consider how the love of conformity and the love of submission relate to forms of ecstasy. Finally, the last books deal with further aspects of unitive love: the commandment to love God above all things (book 10); how love directs and organizes all the virtues (book 11); and advice concerning how to progress in love (book 12).

CHAPTER 1.
OF THE MANNER IN WHICH LOVE
UNITES THE SOUL WITH GOD IN PRAYER

We are not speaking here about the general union of the heart with God, but to certain particular acts and movements that the soul that is recollected in God makes by way of prayer, inclining to a still more intimate union with his sovereign Goodness. There is a difference between uniting or joining one thing to another, and clasping or pressing one thing against or upon another. To join two objects, nothing more is necessary than a simple application that unites without leaving any interval between them. In this manner the vine is united to the elm tree, and the jasmine to the arbors that may be seen in gardens. But to clasp or press together a strong application is needed, which increases the power of the union, as we see when ivy is joined to trees. It is not only united, but so closely bound that it penetrates their bark.

The comparison furnished by the love of infants for their mothers should not be forgotten, because of its innocence and purity. Look at a sweet little child to which a mother presents her breast. It throws itself into her arms, gathering and folding its little body into the bosom and this beloved breast. And see how the mother in reciprocal fashion, as she receives it clasps it tight to her breast and kisses its mouth with hers. See then how the little baby, drawn by its mother's hugs, for its part agrees with the union between itself and the mother. It too squeezes and presses itself as much as it can to the mother's breast and face. It seems as if the baby wants to submerge and hide itself in that beloved bosom from which it came. At this stage, Theotimus, the union is perfect. It is one, but it proceeds from both the mother and the baby. And yet it depends totally on the mother, for she drew the baby to her; she first took it up in her arms and pressed it to her bosom. The baby's strength was not sufficient to clasp and hold itself so tight to its mother. But the poor little baby does all that it can for its part. It joins itself to the maternal breast with all its strength, and not only consents to the sweet union which its mother makes, but contributes to it with all the feeble efforts of its heart. . . .

Thus, Theotimus, Our Lord, showing the most admirable breast of his divine love to the devout soul, draws her wholly to him, gathers her up, and in a manner of speaking enfolds all her powers in the bosom of his sweetness that is more than maternal. Then with burning love, he clasps the soul, joins with it, presses and glues her on his sweet lips and on his delicious breasts, kissing her with the sacred "kiss of his mouth" and making her savor "his breasts sweeter than wine" (Song 1:1). The soul, allured by the heavenly sweetness of these caresses, not only consents and gives herself to the union that God makes, but cooperates with all her power, forcing herself to join and press more and more to the divine Goodness. But she does this in such a way that she fully acknowledges that her union and connection to the sovereign sweetness depends wholly on the divine operation, without which she could not make the least effort in the world to be united to him. . . .

Happy the soul that, enflamed with love, lovingly preserves in the tranquility of her heart the sacred feeling of the presence of God! By this means her union with the divine Goodness will always increase, though by imperceptible degrees, and she will in the end find herself penetrated and imbued with the infinite sweetness of God. Now when I speak about the sacred feeling of the presence of God, I do not mean to speak about a sensible feeling; but I speak about that which resides in the summit and supreme point of the spirit where divine love reigns and performs its main exercises.

CHAPTER 3.
OF THE SOVEREIGN DEGREE OF UNION, PRODUCED BY RAPTURE AND SUSPENSION

Whether the union of the soul with God be formed imperceptibly or sensibly, the Almighty is always its author; because we cannot be united without going to him, and as Jesus Christ himself assures us,

"No one can come to me except the Father draw him" (Jn 6:44), which words are perfectly conformable to those of the bride, "Draw me; we will run after you to the odor of your ointments" (Song 1:3). The perfection of this union consists in the two qualities of purity and strength.

With regard to the former, we may be influenced by different motives in approaching a person; for example, we may wish to speak to him, to see him more plainly, to obtain some favor from him, to lean upon him, to be in a better position to receive the fragrance of the perfumes with which his clothes are sprinkled. Then we approach and are united; though this is not precisely our motive; we have some other object in view, which can only be attained by these means. But if, in approaching any person, we have no other intention than that of being united to him, it is termed pure and simple union.

Thus many persons approached our divine Lord; some to hear him speak, as Mary Magdalene; others to obtain the cure of their maladies, as the infirm woman mentioned in the Gospel; others to adore him, as the wise men; others to minister to him, as Martha; others to convince themselves of his divinity, as St. Thomas; others to embalm him with perfumes, as Magdalene, Joseph, and Nicodemus; but his dear Sulamite [i.e., the bride] seeks only to find him, and having found him, she thinks only of retaining possession of him forever: "I have found him whom my soul loves; I held him, and I will not let him go" (Song 3:4). Jacob, as St. Bernard observes [*Sermons on the Song of Songs* 79.4], held the Almighty and pressed him strongly, yet he consented to let him go, on condition of receiving his benediction. But the Sulamite will not relinquish her beloved Spouse, notwithstanding the superabundant blessings he showers on her, because she seeks only the God of benediction, and not the benedictions of God, saying with David, "What have I in heaven, and besides you what do I desire upon earth? You are the God of my heart, and the God that is my portion forever" (Ps 62:25–26). We have also an example of this in the Mother standing at the foot of the Son's cross. O Mother of life! what do you seek on the mount of Calvary in this region of death? I seek, she might have replied, the life of my existence, my only son, without whom I cannot live. And why do you seek him? I seek to be close by him. But now he is in the midst of "the sorrows of death" (Ps 17:5). Ah!, I want not the joy, the delights he can impart; I seek only himself, my beloved Son, and all the affections of my heart make me seek to be united to that lovable Child, my tenderly Beloved! In the state of union of which we speak the soul aims at nothing more than to be in the company of him whom alone she loves.

When to the purity of union is joined a strength that renders it very close and intimate, theologians call this "inhesion or adhesion," because by it the soul is so caught up, attached, glued, and affixed to the Divine Majesty, that she finds it difficult to disunite herself. Consider a person who listens with profound attention to the sweetness of a fine piece of music; or, more extravagantly, look at a man deeply engaged in playing cards. Speak to him of important occupations that require his presence elsewhere, you will see him forgo even his meals, without being able to relinquish these frivolous pursuits. Ah, Theotimus, how much more closely attached to God should be the soul that is inflamed with love for this infinitely perfect object and actually united to him by the bonds of his infinite sweetness! Such a man was the vessel of election [St. Paul], when he said, "That I may live to God, with Christ I am nailed to the cross" (Gal 2:19). He also says that nothing, not even death, shall ever be able to separate him from his beloved Master. Love often produces a similar effect between two friends; thus, "the soul of Jonathan was knotted with the soul of David" (1 Kgs 18:1). I have elsewhere cited a celebrated maxim of the ancient Fathers that friendship capable of terminating is not real friendship.

Consider, Theotimus, an infant attached to its mother's breast and neck; it is necessary to tear it from there by violence to convey it to its cradle; it resists the efforts made to take it from the place of its repose and source of its happiness. While one hand is detached from her, it clings more closely to her with the other, and by its tears proves its regret at being forced from the place where it felt so happy. When its body has been removed from her, its heart and eyes remain with her, and it does not cease to implore by its tears that it may be replaced on its mother's bosom, until the incessant rocking of its cradle has lulled it to sleep. Thus, a soul that has carried the practice of union so far as to be closely and intimately attached to the divine Goodness, cannot easily detach herself, nor be removed by others, without a kind of violence that occasions her much suffering. If her imagination is diverted from it, her understanding keeps its ground more firmly; if her understanding becomes detached, she redoubles her efforts through the will.

In fine, if the will is compelled by repeated distractions to relinquish its hold, she turns back every moment toward her Dear, from whom she cannot be entirely separated. Striving as much as she can to rejoin the sweet bonds of her union with him by the frequent returns she makes, as if by stealth she feels the pain of St. Paul who was caught between two desires (Phil 1:23)—while she ardently desires to be freed from all exterior occupations to remain interiorly united to Jesus Christ, the very union she seeks teaches her that she must proceed to the work of obedience.

The blessed Mother Teresa [*Life*, chapters 18 and 20] observes that when union becomes so perfect as to attach the soul to God in this manner, it does not differ from what is termed rapture, suspension, or cessation of the spirit; it is called union, or suspension, or cessation when it lasts but a short time, and rapture or ecstasy when it continues for a considerable period. This is so because when the soul is so strongly united to God that she cannot detach herself from him, she lives in God rather than in herself; as a crucified body belongs to the cross to which it is nailed and ivy to the wall whereon it is fastened.

To avoid all ambiguity, Theotimus, you should know that charity is the bond of perfection (Col 3:14), and in proportion as our charity increases our union with God becomes more intimate. But we are not speaking of that permanent and habitual union that subsists, whether we wake or sleep. We speak of the union formed by the act, which is in itself nothing more than an exercise of charity and love. Imagine that St. Paul, St. Denis, St. Augustine, St. Bernard, St. Francis, St. Catherine of Genoa, and St. Catherine of Siena still live on earth, and that after having supported great labors for the love of God, they have yielded to sleep. Represent to yourself on the other hand, a soul inferior in sanctity to the saints we have just cited, but actually occupied in the prayer of union, during the repose of these great saints. I ask you, Theotimus, which of them is more closely attached and more intimately united to God? Is it the devout soul who prays, or the saints who sleep? Will you have any hesitation in giving the preference to these ardent lovers of the Almighty? Is it not clear that having a greater degree of charity, their affections, though asleep in some way, are still engaged and tied to their Master with whom they are inseparable? But you will say, how can it be that a soul that is actually engaged in the prayer of union and in a state of ecstasy should be less closely united to God than those who sleep, however great may be their sanctity? Listen to what I say, Theotimus: that soul is more advanced in the work of union; the souls of the saints are more advanced in union itself. The saints are united; they are not being united, because they are asleep. The former soul is being united, that is, she is in the actual practice and exercise of union.

This exercise of union with God may also be practiced by means of short but frequent aspirations, which may be called transports of the heart in God, in the manner of ejaculatory prayers for this intention. O divine Jesus! who will grant me the happiness of forming but one spirit with you (1 Cor 6:17)! At last, Lord, rejecting the multiplicity of creatures, I want nothing less but unity with you! You, O Lord, are sufficient for me; in you I find the one thing that is necessary for my soul (Lk 10:42). O the true friend of my heart, unite my poor and single soul to your one singular Goodness. You are all mine, Lord; when shall I be able to say that I am entirely yours! The magnet attracts iron and unites it closely to itself; O Lord Jesus, my Beloved, be the magnet of my heart; clasp, press, and unite my heart forever upon your paternal breast! Why do I not live in you, my God, since I have been created for you alone? The small portion of spiritual substance I have received from you longs to be engulfed in its great source, which is the abyss of your Goodness. Since your heart loves me, O Lord, why not force me to it, as I really want? Draw me, and I shall run after your attractions so that I can cast myself into your paternal arms and remain there closely united to you for eternity. Amen.

Adapted and corrected from the translation in *A Treatise on the Love of God by St. Francis de Sales* (London: Keating and Brown, 1835), 293–97.

8.

MARIE OF THE INCARNATION
THE RELATION OF 1654

Marie of the Incarnation (1599–1672), an Ursuline nun and missionary to Canada, was one of the major female mystics of the seventeenth century. Born into a middle-class family, Marie Guyart was married to Claude Martin, to whom she bore one child before Claude died in 1618. In 1631 she abandoned her son to the care of relatives to join the Ursuline order, wishing to devote herself to teaching others and not to a life of pure contemplation. Even before her entry into religion, the young widow had embarked on a mystical journey that she was eventually to describe in two Relations, *or sketches of her life, composed under orders from her confessors: the first of 1633 (fragmentary), and the second of 1654. In 1639 Marie and several companions sailed to Quebec, then a small outpost of some three hundred people. Here she spent the rest of her life.*

Marie was influenced by the classics of French mysticism, particularly Francis de Sales's Introduction to the Devout Life. *She also read Teresa of Avila and John of the Cross in translation. Her account of her growth in mystical prayer, however, has many original elements, especially its unusual long and complex itinerary of thirteen stages. Like Teresa's, Marie's notion of union is fundamentally an erotic one, making use of the Song of Songs. Also like Teresa, she has a remarkable ability to analyze the interior states of the soul's progress. The twelfth of her stages, which lasted from 1639 to 1647, features descriptions of mystical dereliction (see section 11), while the thirteenth is an account of final union with Christ involving spiritual death, a state of victimhood, and the attainment of true spiritual poverty and purity of spirit.*

THE THIRTEENTH STATE OF PRAYER
(PARAGRAPH LXVI.1–5)

Let me say, then, that God has created the rational soul free, endowing it with the power to effect its salvation through grace, and with those other helps implanted in the church founded by the Precious Blood of Jesus Christ. As the soul becomes aware of its dignity through the working of grace which reveals its vocation and its capacity, if it is faithful, it wishes to try to correspond by constantly reaching toward its highest and unique good. If this longing is pure, the Divine Goodness, who alone knows his creature and can see into the most secret parts of the spirit, bestows on this soul streams of light and fire; and, in short, gives it the key of knowledge and love and puts it in possession of his treasures.

The soul, finding itself overwhelmed in this way, wants to wander in those rich and fertile pastures, in these gardens and rooms made accessible to it. There its powers delight in a taste of wisdom impossible to describe. The divine pleasures, the nourishment and rest it receives, the holy intoxication it enjoys move it to sing a loving wedding hymn. This continues until through rapture Love itself puts an end to it in the streams of divine delights. Then he causes it to swoon in him, bringing it to participate in these holy raptures.

Awakening from this ecstasy, it begins its song again, speaking to and by the one who moves it so powerfully: "Let us exult and rejoice, remembering your breasts as better than wine. Thus the just and the right of heart love you" (Song 1:4). All this occurs spontaneously, effected by the fullness of the Spirit, bearing a meaning that makes the soul, as it were, dissolve with love. From this is born that exultation leading to torrents of tears which form a paradise in the soul because it delights in God in inexpressible intimacy. This condition spreads to the senses. The sensitive part of the soul is completely penetrated so that it can say, "My spirit and my flesh rejoice in the living God" (Ps 84:3).

So far there is no limit in this interior life. It seems to the soul that there is nothing beyond the joy it possesses in this life, and that it has been permanently established in this state where it is overwhelmed by the immense riches of its Spouse. Concerning the holy mysteries of faith, it possesses them through an infused knowledge from the Spirit who directs it with such certitude and so little obscurity that it cries, "O my God, I no longer have faith; it is as though you had drawn back the curtain." In this experience it is "leaning on her beloved, surfeited with delights" (Song 8:5). It neither sees nor tastes nor desires anything but him. Thus engulfed and lost in delights, it does not see what is going to happen or where the Spirit will lead it.

This divine Spirit who is infinitely jealous and pitiless where interior purity is concerned, wanting sole possession of its domain, begins to assault the sensitive and lower part of the soul, causing it to suffer various privations which are excruciating. Nature, however, which has its own ruses and skills, wishes to have its own say; it does not want to surrender its citadel or its portion of spiritual goods which it has found more completely to its taste than all the other satisfactions it had formerly enjoyed with creatures. These now seem like nothing but subjects of mortification and distaste. Thus, unable to draw close to the joys of the spirit and finding nothing in those other joys, it does not know what to latch on to. It takes the offensive. It does its best to hold onto those good things of the spirit to which it had grown accustomed, and from which it draws its life and its sustenance in order to bear cheerfully all the difficulties and weariness to which the Spirit has reduced it in order to make it flexible and obedient. It feels everything is denied it, that all its efforts are useless, and that its lot is the captivity where it finds itself.

I have said that this sensitive part was without support and that it had a strong distaste for creatures because it had been allured by the sweetness of spiritual things. Nevertheless, it would very quickly have returned to these had it not been restrained by a hidden virtue, "by the laws of the Spirit which carnal man does not understand" (1 Cor 2:14). This virtue places the soul, as it were, among the dead, although it does not completely die. It is very deeply wounded, however, so as to let the highest part of the soul enjoy in peace all those blessings which it possesses exclusively. In this state which I call death with regard to spiritual goods, there are several degrees because in corrupt human nature there are numerous nooks and crannies and a store of deviousness and shrewdness always ready to spring into action. The spirit of grace, however, cuts this short and acts so that this rabble is deprived of eating the food from this table which has not been laid out for it. It is on this point that the true distinction between the lower and higher parts can be discerned. But this is not all. We are only at the first step in the state of victim and the acquisition of poverty of spirit.

Nature being thus brought to naught, first by penance and second by the deprivation of what sustained it, and thus made amenable to the Spirit's guidance—nature is now humbled beyond telling. Meanwhile, the higher part of the soul experiences true satisfaction in seeing itself freed from what harmed it the most and in enjoying in true purity its sovereign and unique good. The understanding and the will now possess light and love in a way far beyond anything I have so inadequately tried to describe.

The Spirit of God, however, who wants everything for himself, seeing that the understanding, no matter how pure it may be, always mingles an element of its own with the divine actions—something which in this spiritual state is a grave impurity—suddenly puts an end to this through his divine power. Thus the understanding is suspended and rendered utterly incapable of the most ordinary acts which it does not even recognize as being acts, because in their simplicity they are almost imperceptible. The will, having been ravished by God and enjoying his embraces, has no further need for the understanding to provide it with material to stir up its fire. On the contrary, the understanding would only injure the will because it is so active. The will is like a queen who enjoys her divine Spouse in an intimacy of which the seraphim (with their fiery language) could speak better than a creature who has at her disposal only a language of flesh, incapable of expressing such high and exalted things.

Years pass in this way; but this divine Spirit, who is the inexhaustible source of all purity, still wants to conquer the will. Even though it was the Spirit who stirred these divine movements and made it sing a constant wedding hymn, nevertheless the will remained enmeshed in its own action. This the Spirit could not endure since it wished, like a jealous person, to be absolute master. In this sense, as it is he who is love, it is true to say that "love is strong as death and jealousy hard as hell" and that no one is exempt. "Its lamps are fire and flame" so that they must consume everything without exception (Song 7:6).

Then this loving activity, although very delicate, sweeter than all sweetness in the embrace of the divine Spouse, like an endless chain binding and centering the will in its sovereign and unique God, comes to a halt and is suspended as are also the memory and the understanding. These two powers are so connected in what concerns the spiritual life that on this point I am going to treat them in a single article. Behold, then, the victim, in that state to which the Spirit of God, loving infinitely the purity of souls espoused to the Son of God, reduces them in order to bring them to that condition where he wishes to take his pleasure in them. This bed is narrow and one must make room for him so that he will be its only Master and Spouse and its free and peaceful possessor.

After this action—so painful for these ennobled powers—what will happen? Could one think that they might remain thus, fixed and immovable, like the dead? It is unbelievable how painful this deprivation is for them, above all during the solemn feasts of the church in which are represented the mysteries of our redemption. Formerly, these had been their delightful nourishment—a pleasing nourishment, rich in faith through the lights the Holy Spirit communicated on each of the holy mysteries. Now it is impossible for them to reflect on them. Sometimes the person who is led in this way is in fear, unable to understand that she is in the true way since she cannot rest quietly in what is most holy and most solemn in the church. She does violence to herself, wanting to draw her understanding from the laziness into which she thinks it has fallen. But in vain! All this effort is due to lack of understanding of the divine action and to the natural urge to act.

After repeated and rigorous efforts, she realizes that [with] the power of the soul having lost its natural function through a supernatural way there is nothing to be gained by so much effort. However, this natural appetite of the soul to act by means of its own highest powers does not die until the Spirit of God who guides it interiorly makes it die once again, being merciless in the matter of purity. This is done, as I have said, in order to prepare a dwelling, free of all noise, for the divine Spirit who delights in peace and silence.

Now that the will has been deprived of its loving activity, the soul in its unity and in its center remains in the embrace of its spouse, the adorable Word Incarnate. This state is a sweet and loving breath which never ends. It is an exchange of spirit to Spirit and from spirit into Spirit. I cannot express it in any other way, except by the words of St. Paul which verify it when he says: "Jesus Christ is my life and my life is Jesus Christ. It is not I who live but Jesus Christ who lives in me" (Gal 2:19).

It seems that one should be silent in this simple communication. But, no! Divine love, that spiritual monitor, "has lamps of fire and flame" (Song 7:6). He wishes to purify even further. Even in this breath there is still something imperfect in the loving power of the will. He consumes this—and here at last is the sacrifice of the victim and here, finally, that true, pure, and essential purity of spirit.

It must be noted that in proportion to what occurs in the spirit in order to bring to an end anything impure along this spiritual way, God permits several external crosses in order that his will be accomplished in everything, as St. Paul says, "that they may be conformed to the image of his Son" (Rom 8:29). I repeat, one must endure great interior and exterior trials which would have terrified the soul had it seen them ahead of time, and which would even have made it abandon everything rather than endure more than it had already experienced had not a secret strength sustained it. For it seems that the waters of tribulation through which the soul has passed by so many spiritual deprivations have extinguished the fire which gently consumed its noblest part so that, deprived of all its powers, God alone was its only enjoyment. In fact, the poor soul does not itself recognize where it is. A cloud has formed, a kind of spiritual obscurity which has clouded its vision, and it seems that what it had possessed in its sovereign and unique good, the adorable Word Incarnate, has been taken from it. Finally, in his compassion he dispels the cloud, and the soul experiences, though very late, the sense of this passage: "Behold, my ditch has become a flowing stream and my river a sea" (Eccles 24:43). It possesses more abundantly than ever the blessings of the adorable Word Incarnate who inundates and engulfs it in himself in a manner worthy of his largesse. I have had to make this little discourse of my own experiences in order to explain in some fashion what I mean concerning that essential poverty of spirit and the state of victim.

From *Marie of the Incarnation. Selected Writings,* edited by Irene Mahoney, OSU (New York: Paulist Press, 1989), 171–75. Used with permission.

PART THREE

IMPLICATIONS OF THE MYSTICAL LIFE

MYSTICISM AND HERESY

Christianity has always insisted on the need for correct belief (orthodoxy). This is clear from the New Testament where, in the Gospel of Matthew, Jesus is described as giving authority to the apostles to bind and to loose (Mt 18:15–20). The Greek word *hairesis* originally meant "choice" and referred to particular schools of thought among philosophers. Paul uses it in a negative sense when he writes to the Corinthians, "there have to be factions [*haireseis*] among you, for only so will it become clear who among you are genuine" (1 Cor 11:19). In the early second century Ignatius of Antioch, writing to the Trallians, says: "I exhort you then—not I, but the love of Jesus Christ—make use only of Christian food; keep away from any strange plant, which is heresy" (Trall 6.1). Toward the middle of the century, 2 Peter 2:1 denounces the false prophets and teachers who have introduced "destructive heresies" into the community. Given that mysticism is a part of Christian teaching, there is always a possiblity that some mystical teachings, like other doctrines, could be judged erroneous and heretical. But what does the actual history tell us?

Some students of mysticism have argued that the emphasis on inner experience fostered by the mystics means that conflict between mysticism and institutional religion is inevitable, although this conflict has often been muted and disguised. But a consideration of the history of mysticism, both in Christianity and in other religions, argues for a form of dialectical relationship between the mystical and the institutional elements of religion such as that put forth by Gersom Scholem, the great scholar of Jewish mysticism. Scholem held that mystics attempt to make new and direct contact with the divine reality at the source of the tradition. When they try to communicate their sense of the divine presence to their contemporaries, mystics must make use of the language and symbols of the tradition in order to be understood. Hence mysticism in Judaism and in Christianity has been for the most part a force that has upheld and enriched tradition. But, argued Scholem, the ineffable nature of the mystical sense of God also means that the inherited complex of symbols and language is never completely adequate to convey the message, and so mystics often attempt to stretch, transform, and deepen their tradition. This can lead to tension with established authority, especially if a mystic claims a new and higher perspective than that found in the representatives of institutional religion. The history of Christianity suggests that such tensions, conflicts, and denunciations for heretical error are not purely accidents, but that they reflect certain explosive tendencies in the interaction between mysticism and religious authority. The selections given in this section present some of these explosions and their results.

1.

MYSTICAL HERESY IN EARLY CHRISTIANITY

During the course of the second and third centuries conflicts over the nature of correct belief gradually differentiated the emerging "orthodox," or "Great Church," tradition from alternative readings of Christianity that came to be labeled as heresies, at least by their opponents. What role did mystical elements play in the emergence of orthodoxy and its continuing efforts at clarification during the patristic period (circa 100–600 CE)?

I.
GNOSTICISM

Gnosticism is the broad term used to cover a variety of groups, mostly expressing adherence to Christ, that emerged in the second century. Despite considerable differences among these groups, Gnostics generally held to some form of metaphysical dualism (i.e., the idea that the material world was evil, the product of a malign deity), as well as the belief that the soul, or its higher part at least, was innately divine. Christ was seen as a redeeming spirit (not a true corporeal human) who came down into this world to redeem some spirits through his gift of "saving knowledge" (*gnôsis*). The term *gnôsis* had been used by Paul (e.g., 1 Cor 13:2) and other scriptural writers (Wis 2:14). Part of the struggle over "Gnosticism" was to define what was proper *gnôsis* and to determine how it related to faith and love.

The discovery of Gnostic texts among the fourth-century manuscript hoard buried at Nag Hammadi in Egypt demonstrated the presence of a strong mystical element in many Gnostic treatises and writers, especially the greatest Gnostic teacher, Valentinus (circa 100–175). Many of these elements seem to have originated in Hellenistic philosophical mysticism, such as the divinity of the soul, its descent and ascent, the contemplation and vision of God as the soul's goal, and the possibility of attaining union with God. The rejection of Gnosticism by the orthodox majority helped shape the boundaries and limits of later expressions of mysticism. Three of the most critical areas will be touched on here: (1) the issue of whether the soul is innately divine; (2) the relation between mystical teaching and the "rule of faith" (*regula fidei*); and (3) esotericism, that is, the concept that higher truth and contact with God are restricted to an elite few.

(1) The Soul Is Not Innately Divine

Gnostics, like many Platonists, held that the soul was divine, a spark fallen into the material universe. Christian writers beginning as early as Justin Martyr about 150 CE argued that the soul as created by God was not innately divine, but only capable of divinization through the action of grace.

TEXT I. JUSTIN MARTYR, *DIALOGUE WITH TRYPHO THE JEW* 6

"It makes no matter to me," he said [Justin's instructor in Christianity is speaking], "whether Plato or Pythagoras, or, in short, any other man held such opinions. For the truth is so, and you would perceive it from this: the soul assuredly is or has life. If, then, it is life, it would cause something else, and not itself, to live, even as motion would move something else than itself. Now, that the soul lives no one would deny. But if it lives, it does not live as being life, but as partaking life. But that which partakes of anything is different from that which it partakes. Now, the soul partakes of life, since God wills it to live. Thus, then, it will not even partake of life when God does not will it to live, for to live is not its attribute, as it is God's. . . ."

Adapted from the translation in ANF 1:198.

(2) *Mystical Teaching Is Governed by the Rule of Faith*

Many Gnostics claimed to have received new revelations that superseded what was found in the body of texts gradually emerging as the New Testament. The orthodox opponents of the Gnostics appealed to what had been publicly "handed over" by the apostles, that is, the tradition of belief found in the churches believed to have been founded by the apostles and enshrined in the accepted "apostolic" writings. Canonical texts interpreted by the bishops, the successors to the apostles, came to constitute what was called the rule of faith, or norm of Christian belief. Visions, revelations, or claims to contact with God were to be judged by their conformity to this standard. This passage from Irenaeus of Lyons expresses the centrality of the rule of faith found in tradition as the criterion for judging claims to special contact with God.

Text II. Irenaeus of Lyons, *Against Heresies,* Book 3.2–3

Again, when we refer them [the Gnostics] to the tradition that originates from the apostles and which is preserved by means of the successions of presbyters in the churches, they object to tradition, saying that they themselves are wiser not merely than the presbyters, but even than the apostles, because they have discovered the unadulterated truth. . . . It comes to this, therefore, that these men do not consent to either scripture or to tradition. . . .

Therefore, it is within the power of all, in every church, who may wish to see the truth, to contemplate clearly the tradition of the apostles manifested throughout the whole world. And we are in a position to reckon up those who were appointed by the apostles as bishops in the churches, and we can demonstrate the succession of these men down to our own times—those who neither taught nor knew anything like what these people rave about. For if the apostles had known hidden mysteries, which they were in the habit of imparting to the perfect apart and privily from the rest, they would have delivered them especially to those to whom they were also committing the churches themselves. For they were desirous that those they were leaving behind as their successors, delivering up their own position of teaching, should be very perfect and blameless in all things (1 Tim 3:2). . . .

Adapted from the translation in ANF 1:415.

(3) The Rejection of Esotericism

Many Gnostic groups were esoteric and elitist in the sense that they restricted salvation to those persons whose souls contained the divine spark that had fallen from heaven. One of the major turning points in the evolution of Christian mysticism was its confrontation with the question of whether or not more direct and secret (i.e., mystical) contact with God was something that was open to all believers, at least potentially. The orthodox consensus was that it was—a decision that created a distinction between Christian mysticism and the contemporary evolving early stages of Jewish mysticism, as well as the later mysticism of the Islamic tradition. Although Augustine lived after the Gnostic crisis, the following text is an apt summary of this aspect of the orthodox reaction against Gnostic error. Augustine's point is that all hear the same message, but they receive it in different ways, according to their level of spiritual progress.

TEXT III. AUGUSTINE OF HIPPO, *HOMILY ON JOHN* 98.3 (JN 16:12: "I HAVE MUCH MORE TO TELL YOU, BUT YOU CANNOT BEAR IT NOW")

Having ascertained this, therefore, at the outset, that the very things that are equally heard by the spiritual and the carnal are received by each according to the slender measure of his own capacity (by some as babes, by others as those of riper years; by one as milk, by another as solid food [1 Cor 3:2–3]), there seems to be no necessity for any matters of doctrine being retained in silence as secrets and concealed from infant believers as things to be spoken of apart to those who are older, or possessed of riper understanding. And let us regard it as needful to act thus, because of the words of the Apostle, "I could not speak to you as spiritual, but as carnal" (1 Cor 3:1). For even his statement that he knew nothing among them but Jesus Christ and him crucified (1 Cor 2:2), he could not speak to them as to spiritual folk, but as carnal folk, because even that statement they were not able to receive as spiritual. But all who were spiritual among them received with spiritual understanding the very same truths that the others only heard as carnal. . . .

Adapted from the translation of James Innes in *St. Augustine. Lectures or Tractates on the Gospel according to St. John* (Edinburgh: T. & T. Clark, 1874), 380.

II. Messalianism

Messalianism is the archetypal mystical heresy in orthodox Christianity. The terms *Messalians* and *Euchites* (both names mean "those who pray," one in Syriac, the other in Greek) appear in the late fourth century. These names indicate groups of Syrian ascetics who were seen as holding suspect positions by the Greek-speaking bishops of the East. Several late-fourth-century texts, notably the *Homilies* attributed to Macarius (see section 13.1) and the Syriac *Book of Ascents*, reflect some of the views attributed to the Messalians, but it is not easy to say if these are actually Messalian texts, or works that were trying to correct the excesses of those who had taken traditional themes of ancient Christian Syrian asceticism and mysticism too far. Whether or not Messalianism actually ever existed as a concrete movement, "Messalianism" as a constructed heresy was of significance both in the East and the West, because it was an early version of charges against such errors as over-reliance on personal prayer, neglect of the sacraments and church order, and claims to have experienced bodily visions of God. These accusations were to feature in many later attacks on mystical heresy.

TEXT IV. THEODORET OF CYRRHUS
CHURCH HISTORY, BOOK 4, CHAPTER 11

About the same time the heresy of the Messalians sprang up. Those who have rendered them into Greek call them Euchites.... They are sometimes called Enthusiasts, because they regard the agitating influences of a demon by whom they are possessed as indications of the presence of the Holy Spirit. Those who have thoroughly imbibed this heresy shun all manual labor as a vice; they abandon themselves to sleep and declare their dreams to be prophecies.... Their great desire of concealing their error leads them to shamelessly deny it, even when convicted of it, and induces them to condemn in others the very sentiments which they hold themselves.

[The text continues with the account of how Flavian, later bishop of Antioch, deceived an aged adherent of the heresy named Adelphius to reveal his views.] The old man said that the rite of baptism was of no benefit to those who received it, and that perseverance in prayer alone could expel the demon which dwells within us, "because," said he, "everyone who is born is, by nature, as much a slave of the demons as he is the descendant of the first man. When the demons are driven away by the fervency of prayer, the most Holy Spirit visits us and gives us sensible and visible signs of his own presence, by freeing the body from the perturbation of passion and the soul from evil propensities, so that henceforth there is no more need of fasting for the subjugation of the body, nor of instruction for the restraint and direction of the soul. Whoever has enjoyed this visitation is delivered from all inward struggles; he clearly foresees the future and gazes with his own eyes upon the Holy Trinity."

Theodoret, *Church History* 4.11, as translated in *History of the Church by Theodoret and Evagrius* (London: Henry G. Bohn, 1854), 165–67.

2.

THE HERESY OF THE FREE SPIRIT

Forms of heresy attracting numbers of people were rare in the early Middle Ages in the Latin West. From the eleventh century on, however, there was a significant growth of popular movements condemned as heretical. Heresies of a mystical nature first appeared in the second half of the thirteenth century, but grew rapidly in the late Middle Ages. These heretics were accused of many of the same errors as the Gnostics and Messalians, such as neglect of the sacraments and of ecclesiastical authority, pretensions to higher knowledge of God, esotericism, and also the licentiousness that such clandestine groups were often thought to indulge in. Some new themes also emerged, especially claims of mystical annihilation leading to identity with God. The desire to achieve annihilation of the created will, at least on some level, was a central feature of much mystical thinking in the late Middle Ages. So too was the hope of attaining a state of quietude or indifference to all save God. Although these mystical themes were capable of explanations that stayed within the boundaries of the rule of faith, they were ideas that could (and doubtless did at times) lead to dangerous practices.

*The late-medieval manifestations of these tensions in the relation between mysticism and the teaching authority of the church have been grouped under the heading "The Heresy of the Free Spirit." The importance of the "freedom of spirit" (*libertas spiritus*) given to the Christian through acceptance of Jesus as Lord is found in scripture; as Paul put it, "Where the Spirit of the Lord is, there is freedom" (2 Cor 3:17). Many orthodox mystics had made use of this* *theme. At the Council of Vienne (1311–12), however, a commission set up to investigate dangerous forms of mysticism produced a decree titled "Ad Nostrum," listing eight errors ascribed to "beghards and beguines," men and women who led unregulated religious lives. The list centered on the teaching of those who believed that they had attained such "a degree of perfection and spirit of freedom" that they were no longer capable of sinning and were not subject to the church or to any human authority. After this, the term* Free Spirits *became widely used to single out those who made such dangerous claims. (One of the people the council Fathers had in mind was Marguerite Porete, since some of the articles drawn from her* Mirror of Simple Annihilated Souls *are reflected in the Vienne condemnation—see section 5.4.) Historians today doubt that the Free Spirits ever constituted a distinct movement or large group. What is clear is that there were growing fears of dangerous mysticism in the late Middle Ages and that these fears set many of the criteria used in subsequent centuries for the investigation and condemnation of what was seen as mystical heresy.*

TEXT I.
THE COMPILATION CONCERNING THE NEW SPIRIT (CIRCA 1270)

The earliest appearance of many of the errors ascribed to the Free Spirit comes from an investigation held in Germany in the 1260s. Two wandering preachers were said to have spread errors to an undetermined number of men and women. A list of ninety-seven erroneous articles was collected from the suspects (later more articles were added). The list was sent to the Dominican theologian Albert the Great, who made comments on the heretical nature of the articles by linking them to well-known ancient heresies. The list is heterogeneous and even contradictory, featuring claims to identity with God, attacks on the church, and the customary esotericism and antinomianism (i.e., freedom from the moral law).

THE COMPILATION CONCERNING THE NEW SPIRIT.
THIS CONTAINS NINETY-SEVEN ERRORS.

1. To make small assemblies and to teach in secret is not contrary to faith but is contrary to the evangelical way of life where it says: "I have always taught openly in the Temple where all the Jews meet together; I have said nothing in secret" (Jn 18:20). And in Matthew 10:27: "What you hear in the ear, preach from the housetops."

2. To say that the soul is taken from the substance of God is the Manichaean heresy, as Augustine says. Mani said that the God of light made immortal beings from himself. Some philosophers who lived before Mani also held this heresy.

11. To say that someone can come to the state where he has no need of God is a blasphemy against God whom all creatures need lest they fall into nothingness, as Pope Gregory says. Hence it says in Hebrews 1:3: "He bears all things in the power of his Word"; and Acts 17:28: "In him we live, and move, and have our being."

14. It is the same to say that a person can become God.

15. It comes down to the same thing to say that a person can arrive at such a state that God works all things in him. . . .

19. Where it says that a person is not good unless he leaves God for God's sake is likewise Pelagian foolishness.

21. To say that someone can come to the point where he cannot sin is likewise Pelagian obstinacy.

25. That a soul united to God is made divine is also Pelagian, because Pelagius thought that he could be transformed into God by prayer and fasting in day and night service to God.

44. Where it says that the person united to God ought not to fast or pray is the Pelagian error, because Elias, Moses, and Christ, who were all greatly united to God, fasted and prayed.

58. To say that a person may become equal to the Father and surpass the Son is not only heretical but even diabolical. Lucifer said: "I shall be like the Most High" (Is 14:14).

61. To say that nothing is a sin except what is thought to be a sin is Pelagian heresy.

63. To say that nothing that is done below the belt by good people is a sin is the heresy of Elioristus, who was a disciple of Julian and a Pelagian.

72. To say that a person can be admitted to the embrace of divinity and then receive the power to do what he wants is Pelagian.

94. To say that a person in this life can attain a state where he is not able to sin is a lie against the true teaching.

FROM THE APPENDED ARTICLES

106. A person united to God ought to fulfill the body's pleasure boldly in any way whatsoever, even with a religious of either sex.

113. Such a person can licitly and without fear keep another person's property even if the owner is unwilling.

116. They say they ought not reveal the grace they possess to learned clerics because they would not know what it is. The learned only know what is on the page, but these folk know through the experience by means of which they say they drink from the divine sweetness.

Translated by Bernard McGinn from Wilhelm Preger, *Geschichte der deutschen Mystik im Mittelalter* (Leipzig: Dörffling, 1874), 461–70.

TEXT II. LETTER OF POPE CLEMENT V (APRIL 1, 1311)

This letter, written to the bishop of Cremona commanding him to take action against heresy in his diocese, is the earliest official use of the term *Free Spirit*.

To our Venerable Brother Rainer, Bishop of Cremona. The beloved of the Lord and peacemaker Solomon, after the different works he composed under the inspiration of the Holy Spirit, spoke out at last in his Song of Songs as one already made perfect and well prepared, having trodden the world under his feet and now bound by the embraces of the Spouse. He handed down a place worthy of study in that book in which he introduced the love of heavenly things and the desire of divine things under the image and mystical names of Bridegroom and bride, teaching how by charity's fervor one can arrive at a share in God's life. . . . Therefore, the bride is the "vineyard of the Lord Sabaoth" (Is 5:7), which the true Father of the household hedged about with virtues; he pulled up the stones of heresy and the thorns and weeds of vice, and he planted his elected bride in its midst, building a tower of virtues and graces to protect her and a winepress in it seething with the discernment that gives grace and protection against vices and sins (Mt 21:33). . . . [The image of the church as bride-vineyard leads Clement to a treatment of Song of Songs 2:15: "Catch us the little foxes that destroy the vines, for our vineyard has flourished," traditionally interpreted as the heretics who seek to destroy the church.]

Recently, indeed, as we have heard with sorrow and report with a great mental pang, in some parts of Italy, especially the province of Spoleto and also in the surrounding regions, some ecclesiastics and layfolk, religious and seculars of both sexes, accursed folk alienated from the bosom of Mother Church, . . . have taken up a new sect and a new rite completely untrue to the way of salvation, hateful even to pagans and those living like animals, and far removed from the teaching of the apostles and prophets and the truth of the Gospel. They call it the spirit of liberty, that is, it allows them to do whatever they want. . . . [The remainder of the letter is a treatment of the difference between true and false freedom, which became a major theme in fourteenth-century mystical literature.]

Translated by Bernard McGinn from *Regestrum Clementis Papae V* (Rome: Tipographia Vaticana, 1887), Vol. VI:423–24.

TEXT III. THE DECREE "AD NOSTRUM" OF THE COUNCIL OF VIENNE

The decree was drawn up in the autumn of 1311, issued in May 1312, and incorporated into canon law in 1317. In the following translation I have italicized those articles that seem to be related to errors for which Marguerite Porete was executed.

Here is what has come to our attention, not without great displeasure, we who are passionately bound by vow to help the Catholic faith prosper in our times and to root out heretical depravity from the lands of believers. An abominable sect of certain evil men known as beghards and some faithless women called beguines in the vernacular has arisen in accursed fashion in the Kingdom of Germany through the activity of the Sower of evil deeds. In their sacrilegious and perverted teaching they hold and assert the following errors:

First, that someone in the present life can acquire so great and such a degree of perfection that he is rendered totally without sin and is not able to advance farther in grace, for, as they say, if someone were always able to advance, he could become more perfect than Christ.

Second, that when one has attained this degree of perfection one does not have to fast or pray, because then sensuality is so perfectly subject to spirit and reason that a person can freely give the body whatever pleases it.

Third, that those who are in the state mentioned above and in the spirit of freedom are not subject to human obedience nor obliged to any precepts of the church, because, as they claim, "Where the Spirit of the Lord is, there is freedom" (2 Cor 3:17).

Fourth, that a person in the present life can attain final beatitude in every degree of perfection, just as it is gained in the blessed life.

Fifth, that any kind of intellectual nature in itself is naturally beatified, and that the soul does not need the light of glory to elevate it to seeing and enjoying God in a beatific way.

Sixth, that it is the mark of the imperfect person to exercise himself in acts of virtue, and the perfect soul frees itself from the virtues.

Seventh, that the kiss of a woman, since nature does not incline to it, is a mortal sin; but the act of intercourse, since nature does incline to it, is not a sin, especially when strongly tempted.

Eighth, that at the elevation of the Body of Jesus Christ there is no need to rise or to pay it reverence. They claim that it would be a mark of imperfection for them if they were to come down from the purity and height of their contemplation to the point of having some thoughts about the mystery or sacrament of the Eucharist or about the passion of the Christ's humanity.

. . . On the basis of the office committed to us, we must of necessity extirpate this hateful sect and its abominable errors from the Catholic Church, lest they spread any farther and corrupt the hearts of the faithful in an accursed way. With the approval of the Holy Council, we condemn and totally reject this sect and its aforementioned errors, and we most strenuously forbid that anyone from here on hold, approve, or defend these errors.

Translated by Bernard McGinn from Henry Denzinger, *Enchiridion Symbolorum Definitionum et Declarationum de Rebus Fidei et Morum* (Freiburg: Herder, 1911, 11th edition), 207–8.

Meister Eckhart's Condemnation

Fear of Free Spirit heretics was strong in the Rhineland cities, such as Cologne, Strasbourg, and Basel. In 1317, while Meister Eckhart lived in Strasbourg, its bishop conducted an investigation that produced lists of the errors of people he referred to as "those whom the crowd calls beghards and 'bread-for-God' sisters, and who call themselves children, or brothers and sisters, of the sect of the Free Spirit and of voluntary poverty." Several of Eckhart's sermons reflect his criticism of suspect forms of mysticism, albeit the Dominican was more inclined to try to persuade than to persecute.

Eckhart's own preaching, however, also came under suspicion, especially after he moved to Cologne, whose archbishop, Henry II, was a noted heresy hunter. In mid-1326 Henry prepared at least two lists of suspect articles taken from Eckhart's preaching and writing. With the support of the local Dominicans, Eckhart defended himself at a hearing on September 26, 1326, and appealed to the pope at Avignon. On February 13, 1327, he preached a public sermon regarding his innocence and willingness to retract any possible errors. At his trial he correctly pointed out, "I am able to be in error, but I cannot be a heretic, for the first belongs to the intellect, the second to the will." Eckhart went to the papal court where two commissions were appointed to investigate the articles against him. He defended himself once again at a hearing probably held in late 1327. On January 28, 1328, the aged theologian died.

Archbishop Henry and Pope John XXII, however, were convinced that Eck-

hart's views (if not his person) were not only dangerous but also heretical. On March 27, 1329, the pope issued the bull "In agro dominico," absolving Eckhart of personal heresy but damning his memory and condemning twenty-eight propositions from his works. The pope was particularly exercised by Eckhart's public preaching of these dangerous teachings. As he put it in the prologue to the bull: "Hence this man, thinking to sow thorns and obstacles against the very clear truth of faith in the field of the church, as well as harmful thistles and poison thorn bushes, made many dogmatic pronouncements that clouded the true faith in the hearts of many, and he taught them in his preaching before the uneducated crowd, and even introduced them into his writings."

What follows is the list of the condemned articles, as well as Eckhart's defense of one of the articles from the trial documents. It should be noted that the conclusion of the bull says that Eckhart rejected these articles "insofar as they might generate" a heretical meaning in the minds of the faithful. The pillar of Eckhart's defense had been that the articles need to be interpreted "insofar as" they were intended to support faith and morals and therefore continued to be capable of an orthodox explanation.

TEXT I.
THE BULL "IN AGRO DOMINICO"

The first article. When he was once asked why God did not make the world sooner, he responded, then as now, that God could not make the world sooner, because a thing cannot act before it exists. Hence, as soon as God existed, he also created the world.

The second article. In the same way, it can be granted that the world has always existed.

The third article. In the same way, once and for all, when God came into existence, when he begot his Son, co-eternal and coexistent with himself in all things, he also created the world.

The fourth article. In the same way, in every form of operation, even an evil one (evil as much in punishment as in fault), God's glory is manifested and shines out in equal fashion.

The fifth article. In the same way, someone who finds fault with another, even in the very sin of faultfinding praises God, and the more he finds fault and the more he sins, the more he praises God.

The sixth article. In the same way, anyone who blasphemes God himself praises God.

The seventh article. In the same way, a person who prays for some particular created thing prays badly and prays for something bad, because he is asking for the negation of the good and of God, and he prays that God be denied to him.

The eighth article. Those people honor God who do not look for possessions, nor honors, nor usefulness, nor internal devotion, nor sanctity, nor reward, nor the kingdom of heaven, but who renounce all these, and even what is their own.

The ninth article. I recently thought whether there was anything that I would ask or desire from God. I want to give careful thought to this, because were I to receive something from God, there I would be under or beneath him like a servant or slave, and he would be the lord in his giving. But this will not be our way in eternal life.

The tenth article. We are being totally transformed into God and converted into him. Just as in the sacrament the bread is converted into Christ's body, so in a similar way I am converted into him, because he makes me his one being and not just similar to him. By the living God it is true that there is no distinction.

The eleventh article. Whatever God the Father gave his Only-Begotten Son in human nature he gave all the same to me. I do not make exception for anything, neither union nor holiness, but he gave me the whole just as he did him.

The twelfth article. Whatever sacred scripture says about Christ, the same is also true about every good and divine person.

The thirteenth article. Whatever is proper to the divine nature, the whole is proper to the just and divine person. This the reason why such a person does whatever God does, and he has created heaven and earth with God, and he is the generator of the Eternal Word, and without such a person God would not know how to make anything.

The fourteenth article. A good person ought to so conform his will to God's will that he wills whatever God wills. Because God wills me to have committed sin in some way, I should not will that I had not committed sin. This is true penance.

The fifteenth article. If a person were to commit a thousand mortal sins, if he were in the correct frame of mind, he ought not to wish that he had not committed them.

The sixteenth article. God does not command an exterior act in the proper sense.

The seventeenth article. In the proper sense an exterior act is not good or divine, nor does God perform it or give birth to it in the proper sense.

The eighteenth article. Let us bring forth not the fruit of the exterior acts that do not make us good, but of the interior acts that the Father who remains in us does and produces.

The nineteenth article. God loves souls, not the exterior work.

The twentieth article. The good person is the Only-Begotten Son of God.

The twenty-first article. The nobleman is that Only-Begotten Son of God whom the Father has given birth to eternally.

The twenty-second article. The Father gives me birth as his Son and the same Son. Whatever God does is one; therefore, he gives birth to me as his Son without any distinction.

The twenty-third article. God is one in every way and according to every respect, so that no multiplicity can be found in him either in the intellect or outside it. Whoever sees two or distinction does not see God. God is one, and outside and above number, nor is he counted with anything. There follows: Therefore, no distinction exists or can be understood in God himself.

The twenty-fourth article. All distinction is foreign to God, both in nature and in the persons [of the Trinity]. The proof is that the nature is one and this one thing, and each of the persons is one and the one thing that is the nature.

The twenty-fifth article. When it says, "Simon, do you love me more than these others?" (Jn 21:15), the meaning is yes, more than these others, and indeed well, but not perfectly. In the first and second cases [i.e., of love and better love] there is more and less and degree and order, but in the one [highest love] there is neither degree nor order. He who loves God more than his neighbor loves well, but not yet perfectly.

The twenty-sixth article. All creatures are one pure nothing. I do not say that they are a little bit, or a something, but that they are pure nothing.

Furthermore, an objection was made against Eckhart that he preached two more articles in these words:

The first article. There is something in the soul that is uncreated and uncreatable. If the entire soul were such, it would be uncreated and uncreatable. And this thing is the intellect.

The second article. God is neither good, nor better, nor best. Hence, I speak as wrongly when I call God good as if I were to call white black.

... Finally, both from the report of the theologians and from our own examination, we find the first fifteen articles, as well as the two final ones, to contain the error and stain of heresy, as much as from the sound of the words as from the sequence of thoughts. We find the other eleven (beginning with "God does not command") very bad-sounding, extremely reckless, and suspect of heresy, though with many explanations and additions they might be able to take on or have a Catholic meaning. . . .

Translated by Bernard McGinn from *Enchiridion Symbolorum,* edited by Henry Denzinger (Freiberg: Herder, 1911), 214–16.

TEXT II.
ECKHART'S DEFENSE OF ARTICLE 22

Eckhart once preached: "The Father gives birth to me without cease, and I say more: he gives birth to me his Son and the same Son. . . . Everything that God does is one; therefore, he gives birth to me as his Son without any distinction" (sermon 6). This passage appears in the lists of suspect articles that the Dominican was presented in mid-1326. Eventually the text made it into the bull "In agro dominico" as article twenty-two. Eckhart explained the passage as follows in his two defenses.

(A) Cologne Defense of September 26, 1326

That it says in the same article that "God gives birth to me as his Son . . . without any distinction," sounds bad at first look. Nevertheless, it is true, because the Son born in me is that very Son who is of the Father's nature without any distinction. He is one indistinct person without any division, not one person in me and another in someone else. And so he is indistinct from me and undivided, or not separate, as if he were not in me. He is in all things and everywhere insofar as he is God. I think that this is the true and sane Christian faith, and it gives honor to God and his Only Son through whom the Father has given us rebirth and adopted us as children by his ineffable love. What I've said agrees with what St. Thomas says in the *Summa theologiae* IaIIae, q. 108, a. 1.

Translated by Bernard McGinn from *Meister Eckhart. Die deutschen und lateinischen Werke* (Stuttgart and Berlin, 1936–), Processus Coloniensis I, n. 131, in *Die lateinischen Werke,* Vol. 5:296.

(B) Avignon Defense of 1327

In the *Votum* or record of Eckhart's Avignon trial, this article is number nineteen. The document has a scholastic character with four parts:

(1) the article; (2) the reason why it is deemed heretical; (3) a summary of Eckhart's defense; and (4) a rebuttal of this.

(1) The nineteenth article [i.e., bull 22] is thus: He says that the Father gives birth to me as his Son and the same Son. Whatever God does is one; therefore he gives birth to me as his Son without any distinction.

(2) As it sounds, this article, like the preceding, we judge heretical, because it holds that God gave birth to the person speaking . . . , as his Son and the same Son in unity, without any distinction. The reason that he gives for it is also heretical. . . .

(3) He defends this article as he did its predecessors, [by saying] that the Son is without any distinction the one whom the Father gave birth to by nature in the Trinity and whom he gives birth to in us through grace, in the way that one seal is imprinted on many pieces of parchment and one face produces many images in different mirrors.

(4) In itself the argument is true that the same Son of God born by nature in the Father is he through whom we are adopted as children of God. Nonetheless, this has no relevance, because although the Only-Begotten Son of God is the same in himself and is also indistinct in all things in himself and from himself, nevertheless, he is not the same person with all the children of adoption, nor are all the children of adoption the same person with the Only-Begotten Son of God without any distinction, as the article states. Nor do the examples help. . . .

Translated by Bernard McGinn from Franz Pelster, "Ein Gutachten aus dem Eckehart-Prozess in Avignon," *Aus der Geisteswelt des Mittelalter* (Münster: Aschendorff, 1935), 1117–18.

4.

THE CONDEMNATIONS OF QUIETISM

The fourteenth-century attacks on mystical error established a template upon which later forms of suspicious mysticism were judged. The problematic points often echoed those found in patristic attacks on the Gnostics and the Messalians, such as the accusations of sexual antinomianism in the name of "freedom of spirit," as well as of indifference to the sacraments and external practices of the faith. The Free Spirit debates brought to the fore a new issue concerning mystical annihilation and identity with God. A second issue that emerged in the late Middle Ages concerned interior illumination. How was the enlightenment claimed by some mystics related to the truth found in scripture and to the public teachings and practices of Christianity? Could enlightenment ever trump external forms of religion? In the sixteenth and seventeenth centuries a third problem emerged relating to interior prayer. What was the supreme form of contemplation and how did it relate to lower types of prayer and to external observances? Could interior surrender to God ever become so perfect that it consisted of one continuous act of adoration? If such a state were possible, did its maintenance cancel out other religious obligations? A fourth, and final, cause for concern was the status of pure, or disinterested, love, another ancient theme in Christian mysticism, but one that became troubling as mystics worried about the nature and limits of such love. Was it ever legitimate to love God in such a way that one no longer cared even about one's own salvation, but was happy to accept damnation, if that were God's will?

Some of these issues surfaced in the reaction against the Radical Protestant

Reformers of the sixteenth and seventeenth centuries, such as George Fox (see section 10.11), but it was in Catholicism that the quarrels were especially drawn out and resulted in official condemnations of mystical errors. In sixteenth- and seventeenth-century Spain some groups were accused of being "alumbrados," that is, "enlightened ones." The first of these, the "alumbrados of Toledo," seem to have been a movement of Catholic reform that arose in the second decade of the sixteenth century under Franciscan auspices. They were accused of a Lutheran doctrine of faith and of practicing a mystical abandonment (dejamiento) that led to neglect of the sacraments. In 1525 the Spanish Inquisition condemned forty-eight errors associated with the group. (In the wake of this condemnation many mystics, such as Ignatius of Loyola and even Teresa of Avila, came under suspicion.) Later other dangerous mystics were detected in southern Spain, the "alumbrados of Llerena" in the late sixteenth century, and the "alumbrados of Seville" in the early seventeenth century. These groups, condemned in 1574 and 1623, seem to have been more like the Free Spirit heretics of the fourteenth century, at least in the eyes of their opponents.

I.
QUIETISM IN ITALY

Quietism was the most significant early modern mystical heresy. Quietism takes its name from "the prayer of quiet," a term used by many Orthodox mystics, such as Teresa of Avila (see section 3.7). *Quietism* came into use in the 1680s to describe the teaching of Miguel de Molinos (see section 4.5). In the broad sense Quietism is any form of mystical piety that stresses interior passivity to the neglect of exterior practice. More narrowly Quietism signifies the errors of Molinos, Madame Guyon, François Fénelon, and their followers.

The impact of the writings of Teresa, John of the Cross, and other mystics led to considerable discussion in the seventeenth century of the relation between meditation and contemplation, the different forms of contemplation, and the transition from "acquired contemplation" (in which the soul cooperates with God) to "infused contemplation" (a pure gift of God). The passivity of infused contemplation was often seen as involving total abandonment and annihilation of the self. These issues were discussed by mystical writers such as Juan

Falconi Bustamente (1596–1638), who appears to have been the first to speak of the "one act," a single continuous state of infused prayer. Molinos and his associates developed and (in the eyes of their opponents) perverted these teachings. In the controversies between 1675, the date of the publication of Molinos's *Spiritual Guide,* and 1685, the year of his arrest, he and his followers were accused of falling into the errors of beguines and the alumbrados. After Molinos's confession in 1687, on November 20 of that year Innocent XI issued a document called "Coelestis Pater," condemning sixty-eight heretical errors in the Spaniard's writings and spiritual direction. What follows is a selection of the condemned articles arranged under the major issues in dispute.

I. Text. Bull "Coelestis Pater"

(1) Mystical Annihilation

1. It is necessary for a person to annihilate his powers, and this is the interior way.
5. By doing nothing the soul annihilates itself and returns to its principle and its source, which is the essence of God. When it is transformed into this it remains divinized and then God remains in himself, because then there are no longer two things that are united, but one thing only; and the reason that God lives and reigns in us is that the soul annihilates itself in its power of acting.
61. When the soul has come to mystical death, she can no longer will anything other than what God wills, because she no longer has a will; God has taken the will from her.

(2) The Interior Way. About twenty of the objectionable articles deal with the interior way and how it releases a person from external practices. Only article 62 mentions the "one act."

34. To give thanks to God by word and tongue does not belong to interior souls who ought to remain in silence and not place any obstacle to God who works in them. The more they resign themselves to God, the more they are unable to say the Our Father.
35. It is not fitting for souls on this interior way to perform operations, even virtuous ones, by their own choice and activity. Otherwise these souls

would not be dead. They should not make acts of love toward the Blessed Virgin, the saints, or Christ's humanity, because given that these are sensible objects, love for them will also be sensible.

62. Through the interior way one arrives at a continuous immobile state in imperturbable peace.

(3) INDIFFERENCE

7. The soul should not think about reward or punishment, nor paradise or hell, nor death or eternity.

12. A person who gives his free will to God should not be concerned about anything, neither hell nor paradise. He should not desire his own perfection, or virtues, or his own holiness, or his own salvation, hope of which he should expel from himself.

(4) IMAGELESS PRAYER AND INFUSED CONTEMPLATION

21. In prayer it is necessary to remain in dark and universal faith with quiet and forgetting of every particular and distinct thought of the attributes of God and the Trinity, and thus to remain in God's presence, adoring, loving, and serving him, without the production of any acts because God is not pleased with them.

57. Through acquired contemplation one comes to the state [i.e., infused contemplation] where one no longer commits sin, either mortal or venial.

(5) TEMPTATION AND SIN IN THE STATE OF INFUSED CONTEMPLATION. This libertine doctrine, condemned in fifteen articles, is not found in Molinos's writings, but may reflect his spiritual direction.

17. When the free will has been handed over to God, and the care and consideration of our soul left to him, there is no more reason to have any concern for temptations, nor should any resistance be made to them, save a negative one that uses no effort. And if nature is aroused, it is important to allow it to be aroused, because that is nature.

41. God permits and wishes us to be humiliated in leading us to true transformation, because in some perfect souls, even when not possessed, the demon inflicts violence on their bodies and makes them commit carnal acts, even while awake and without a clouding of their minds, by physically moving their hands and other members against their will. The same

can be said about other acts that are sinful in themselves, but not sinful in this case because there is no consent to them.

These articles are condemned as heretical, suspect, erroneous, scandalous, blasphemous, offensive to pious ears, reckless, and particularly weakening, subversive and seditious of Christian discipline.

Translated by Bernard McGinn from Henry Denzinger, *Enchiridion Symbolorum* (Freiburg: Herder, 11th ed., 1911), 356–63.

II.
QUIETISM IN FRANCE

The Quietist debates in France lasted from about 1685 to 1700 and saw a shift of theological focus. In France there was still discussion over how to relate inner states of higher prayer to the continuing requirements of external practices of religion, but the meaning of pure love and its relation to the holy indifference that allowed a soul to surrender concern even for its own salvation emerged with greater force in the French stage of the quarrel. Madame Guyon and her teaching was the focus of the debate (see section 1.6). After her husband's death in 1679, Guyon devoted herself to a life of mystical prayer and extensive writing under the direction of Fr. François La Combe, who appears to have been influenced by the writings of Molinos. They were both arrested in 1687 on charges of heresy. Guyon was soon freed through the influence of Madame de Maintenon, the king's secret wife. The support of de Maintenon and Guyon's growing friendship with the royal tutor, François Fénelon, gave her freedom for a few years, but by 1693 de Maintenon and others turned against her. Guyon requested an investigation to clear her name, and a commission was set up at Issy, consisting of the powerful bishop of Meaux, Jacques Bénigne Bossuet (1627–1704), and two others, to look into her views. In March 1695 the Commission of Issy issued thirty-four articles expressing Catholic truth in the matters under dispute. Both Guyon and Fénelon signed the articles.

The situation soon grew more complicated. Guyon was arrested for bad faith in signing the articles and yet continuing to propagate her views. Fénelon came to her defense, especially in his *Maxims of the Saints* of 1697 (see section 5), where he defended pure love as orthodox and in conformity with the teaching of the approved mystics. For two years Fénelon and Bossuet engaged in a war of pamphlets over the nature of pure love, contemplative prayer, and holy indifference. The real struggle, however, was being fought out in Rome, where French political pressure on Pope Innocent XII eventually led him to issue a letter on March 12, 1699 ("Cum alias"), in which he declared a relatively mild condemnation of twenty-three articles drawn from Fénelon's *Maxims*. Fénelon immediately submitted, and even Guyon was released from prison in 1702 after she reaffirmed her submission to the Issy articles and the papal letter. Nevertheless, serious damage had been done to Catholic mysticism, which remained under suspicion for the next two centuries. The following passages from the Issy Articles and the papal letter "Cum alias" highlight the issues under dispute.

(A) The Issy Articles

When Fénelon was nominated to the see of Cambrai, he joined the Issy commission and insisted on adding four articles to the thirty already agreed upon. Hence, there is some conflict among various articles (e.g., articles 9 and 33), a fact that allowed Fénelon and Bossuet to interpret the Issy document in different ways. The Issy Articles are meant to express not errors but the opposite—declarations of correct belief on mystical matters.

5. Every Christian in every state, although not at every moment, is obliged to will, desire, and explicitly ask for his eternal salvation as something that God desires and which he wants us to desire for his glory.
9. A Christian is not allowed to be indifferent with regard to his salvation, nor to the things related to it. Holy indifference pertains to the things of this life (not including sin), and to the giving of spiritual consolation or of aridity.
13. In the most perfect life and prayer all acts are united solely in charity insofar as it animates all the virtues and commands their exercise, according to what St. Paul says: "Charity bears all, believes all, supports all" (1 Cor 13:7). Thus one can say of charity all one can say of the other Christian acts that it rules and for which it prescribes distinct exercises, although they are not always sensibly and distinctly perceived [Fénelon's addition].
19. Perpetual prayer does not consist in a perpetual and unique act that

one supposes to be without interruption and which should never be repeated, but rather in a habitual and perpetual disposition and preparation to do nothing that displeases God and to do everything in order to please God. The contrary position, which would exclude in a certain state, however perfect, all plurality and succession of acts, would be erroneous and opposed to the tradition of all the saints.

33. Pious and truly humble souls can be inspired to a submission and consent to God's will even when, by an impossible supposition, God, instead of rewarding them with the eternal goods that he has promised to just souls, were to hold these souls by his will in eternal torments without depriving them of his grace and love. This is an act of perfect abandonment and pure love, practiced by the saints, and which can be usefully employed by truly perfect souls with a very special grace without shrinking from the other acts indicated above, which are essential to Christianity [Fénelon's addition].

Translated by Bernard McGinn from *Oeuvres complètes de Bossuet* (Nancy: Thomas et Pierron, 1863), Vol. 9:464–66.

(B) Papal Brief "Cum Alias" of March 12, 1699

As in other papal documents, these articles express errors ascribed to Fénelon.

1. There is a habitual state of the love of God which is pure charity without any admixture of a motive of one's self-interest. Neither fear of punishment nor desire for reward have any more part in it. God is no longer loved for the sake of merit, or for the sake of perfection, or for the sake of finding happiness in him through love.

2. In the state of the contemplative or unitive life every motive of interested fear or hope is lost.

6. In this state of holy indifference we no longer wish for salvation as our own salvation, as eternal liberation, as reward of our merits, and as our greatest interest of all; but we wish for it with a complete will as God's glory and pleasure, as the thing that he wills, and which he wishes us to will for his own sake.

16. There is a state of contemplation so sublime and perfect that it becomes habitual in such a way that as often as the soul actually prays its prayer is contemplative, not discursive. At that state it is no longer necessary to return to meditation and its methodical acts.

19. In this sense it can be said that the passive and distinterested soul no

longer wishes even love itself insofar as this is its perfection and its happiness, but it only wishes it insofar as it is what God wants from us.

23. Pure love alone constitutes the whole interior life; and from it arises the one principle and the one motive of all the acts that are deliberate and meritorious.

These articles are condemned and rejected, both in the obvious sense of the words and in the implied connection of the positions, as reckless, scandalous, evil-sounding, offensive to pious ears, pernicious in practice, and even particularly erroneous.

Translated by Bernard McGinn from Henry Denzinger, *Enchiridion Symbolorum* (Freiburg: Herder, 11th ed., 1911), 368–70.

5.

FRANÇOIS FÉNELON

EXPLICATION OF THE MAXIMS OF THE SAINTS REGARDING THE INTERIOR LIFE

Explication of the Maxims of the Saints, *published in 1697, was an unlucky book. Its author, François de Fénelon (1651–1715), archbishop of Cambrai, intended it as a careful scientific analysis of the differences between true and false mysticism in the midst of the Quietist controversy. But the work itself was to be condemned, although mildly, by Innocent XII, as noted above. How had such a contretemps happened? In the 1690s Fénelon had become close to Madame Guyon (see section 1.6), seeing her as a living example of the "pure love" that he believed was the essence of mysticism. As Guyon's works came under suspicion for Quietism, Fénelon sought to assist her. Shortly after both Fénelon and Guyon subscribed to the thirty-four articles issued at Issy, Bishop Bossuet had Guyon imprisoned. Fénelon then broke with his former friend and rushed into print with a series of tracts attacking Bossuet, defending Guyon, and providing his own interpretation of the Issy Articles. The most important of these works was* Maxims, *in which Fénelon marshaled his extensive knowledge of the mystical tradition to support his view of pure love. Bossuet was infuriated and responded in kind with his own series of attacks. In this "Battle of the Olympians," as it has been called, Bossuet and his patron Louis XIV had the ultimate political weapons. The pressure they put on the pope eventually led to a condemnation of Fénelon, though not as a heretic, as they had wished. Fénelon accepted the mitigated condemnation and his own exile from court.*

I.

FOREWORD

I have always believed it necessary to speak and write about interior paths as soberly as one can. Although they involve nothing that is not manifestly conformed to the unchangeable rule of faith and to gospel morality, nonetheless it seems to me this matter demands some measure of reticence. The average reader is in no way fruitfully prepared to undertake such difficult reading. It is to expose the purest and most sublime aspects of religion to the derision of profane minds, in whose very eyes the mystery of Jesus crucified is already a scandal and a folly. It is to place in the hands of the least meditative and least experienced the ineffable secret of God dwelling within human hearts, and such people are not capable, either of instructing themselves in it, or of being edified by it. Furthermore, it is like setting a trap for all credulous and indiscreet souls by which they might fall into illusion—they might easily imagine that they are already in all the states detailed in the books: thus they become visionaries and discontents. Rather, if one keeps them in ignorance of all the states that are above them, they will not be able to enter into the ways of disinterested love and contemplation except by the attraction of grace, without their imagination being enflamed by these readings in any way whatsoever. This is what has persuaded me that it was necessary to keep as silent as possible about this matter for fear of overly exciting the curiosity of the public that has neither the experience nor the light of grace necessary to examine the works of the saints. . . . But since this curiosity has of late become widespread, I think that it is now just as necessary to speak about it as it had formerly been desirable to keep quiet about it.

I propose in this work to explain the experiences and expressions of the saints in order to prevent them from being exposed to the derision of the impious. At the same time, I wish to clear up the true sense of these holy authors for the mystics of our day, in order that they may know the true value of these expressions. When I speak of "holy authors," I am limiting myself to those who are canonized, or whose memory lingers sweetly throughout the whole of the church and whose writings have been solemnly approved after much contention. I speak only of saints who have been canonized or admired throughout all of the church for having practiced and handed on to posterity the practice of that type of spirituality that appears throughout their writings. Doubtless, it is not possible to reject such authors, nor accuse them of having innovated against the tradition.

I wish to show how far these authors are from having harmed the dogma of the faith and from favoring illusion. I wish to show the mystics that I do not at all weaken that which is authorized by the experiences and the maxims of these authors who are our models. I wish thereby to engage them to believe me when I make them see the precise limits that these same saints have marked out for us, beyond which it is never permitted to proceed. The mystics to whom I speak are neither fanatics nor hypocrites who hide the mystery of iniquity under a feigned perfection. It would not please God if I were to address the word of truth to those people who do not carry the mystery of faith in pure conscience: they deserve nothing other than indignation and horror. I speak to the simple mystics, naïve and docile. They must understand that illusion has always followed closely behind the most perfect paths. Since the origin of Christianity, false Gnostics, detestable people, wished to merge with the true Gnostics who were the contemplative and the most perfect among the Christians. The beghards falsely imitated the contemplatives of the previous century, such as St. Bernard, Richard, and Hugh of St. Victor. Bellarmine remarks that the expressions of mystical authors are often criticized for their ambiguities. "It ordinarily happens to those who write mystical theology," he says, "that their expressions are blamed by some and praised by others, because they are not taken by everyone in the same sense" [*On Ecclesiastical Writers* (Paris, 1658), 382]. Further, Cardinal Bona says that "those who are in passive contemplation are the least skilled in expression but they are most excellent in practice and in experience" [*The Short Way to God*, chapter 10]. In effect, there is nothing so difficult as clarifying those states that consist in operations so simple, so delicate, so abstract from the senses, or in always making in each instance all the correctives that prevent illusion and that explain them in the rigor of theological dogma.

This, then, is what has scandalized some of those readers who have read the books of the mystics, and what has thrown others into illusion. In the last century, when Spain was filled with so many saints of marvelous grace, the alumbrados were discovered in Andalusia and cast the greatest saints into suspicion. Thus St. Teresa, Balthazar Alvarez, and

Blessed John of the Cross needed to justify themselves. Ruusbroec, whom Bellarmine calls a great contemplative, and Tauler, that apostolic man so famous throughout all of Germany, had been defended, the one by Denis the Carthusian, the other by Blosius. St. Francis de Sales was not exempt from contradiction, and his critics were not able to grasp to what degree he had joined an exact and precise theology with a light of grace that was very profound. He had to make an apology to Cardinal de Bérulle. Thus the chaff obscured the good grain, and the purest authors on the interior life needed explanation in order that some expressions taken in the wrong sense not alter pure doctrine.

These examples should make our mystics sober and restrained. If they are humble and docile, they should leave to the church's pastors not only final decision regarding doctrine, but even the choice of all the terms that are appropriate to employ. St. Paul never wished to eat meat and in so doing scandalize the least of his brethren for whom Christ had died (Rom 14:21). So how could we be so attached to a particular expression if it were to scandalize some weak soul? The mystics should remove all ambiguity when they learn that their terms have been abused, corrupting what is holiest. Those who have spoken without forethought in an improper and exaggerated manner should explain themselves and leave nothing to be desired for the edification of the church. May those who were mistaken on the basis of doctrine not be content just to condemn the error, but admit to having believed it. May they give glory to God; may they have no shame for having erred, which is the natural lot of human beings. And may they confess their errors humbly, since these will no longer be their own errors when they have been humbly confessed. It is to disentangle the true from the false in a matter so delicate and so important that two great prelates have presented to the public thirty-four propositions that contain substantially the whole of the doctrine concerning interior paths [the Articles of Issy were issued by Bishops Bossuet and Noailles]. In this work I claim only to explain their principles at greater length.

All interior paths lead toward pure or disinterested love. This pure love is the highest degree of Christian perfection; it is the end of all the ways that the saints have known. Whoever admits nothing beyond this is within the limits of tradition; whoever transgresses this limit has already gone astray. If someone should doubt the truth and perfection of this love, I offer to show him a universal and evident tradition from the Apostles down to St. Francis de Sales without a single interruption. When desired, I shall present publicly a collection of all the passages of the Fathers, the schoolmen, and the holy mystics, who speak unanimously. In this collection it will be seen that the Fathers have spoken as strongly as St. Francis de Sales, and that regarding disinterested love they have made the same suppositions about salvation that scornful critics mock so much when they encounter them in the saints of the last few centuries. St. Augustine himself, whom several people believed to be against this doctrine, teaches it no less than the others. It is true that it is crucial to explain this pure love thoroughly, and to mark precisely the limits beyond which its disinterest can never go. Its disinterest cannot exclude the will to love God without limit, neither in the degree nor the duration of the love. It cannot exclude conformity with the will of God, who desires our salvation and wishes that we desire it with God for God's glory. This disinterested love, always inviolably attached to the written law, makes all the same acts and practices all the same distinct virtues as interested love with this unique difference: It practices them in a manner that is simple, peaceful, and fully disengaged from any motive of its own interest.

Holy indifference, so praised by St. Francis de Sales, is nothing but the disinterest of this love, which is always indifferent, and which has no desire for its own interest, but is always determined and desiring in a positive way what God makes us wish by his written law and by the attraction of his grace.

To reach this state it is necessary that love be purified; all interior trials are nothing other than love's purification. Even the most passive contemplation is nothing but the peaceful and uniform exercise of this pure love. One only passes insensibly from meditation (the state in which one undertakes methodical and discursive actions) into contemplation, the acts of which are simple and direct, just as one passes similarly from interested to disinterested love. The passive state and transformation in spiritual marriage and the essential or immediate union are nothing but the full purity of this love, the state of which is habitual in very few souls, though it is never invariable nor exempt from venial sin. When I speak of all the different degrees, the names of which are little known among the majority of the faithful, I do it only because these names have been consecrated by the usage of a great number of the saints approved by the church, who have explained their own experience in these terms. Moreover, I relate them only to explain them with more rigorous precaution. Finally, all interior paths lead to pure love as their end, and the highest of all degrees in the pilgrimage of this life is the habitual state of this love. It is the foundation and capstone to the whole building. Nothing would be rasher than to attack the purity of this love, so fitting to the perfection of our God—to whom everything is owed—and to God's jealousy, which is a consuming fire. But likewise nothing would be so rash as to wish, by fanciful refinement, to rid this love of the reality of its acts in practicing distinct virtues. Finally, it would be neither less rash, nor less dangerous, to place the perfection of the interior paths in some mysterious state beyond the established one of a habitual state of pure love.

It is in order to guard against all these dangers that I propose to treat the whole of this matter in this work in articles arranged according to the different degrees that the mystics have shown us in the spiritual life. Each article will have two parts. The first will be the truth that I shall approve, which will contain all that is authorized by the experience of the saints and which amounts to the sound doctrine of pure love. The second part will treat falsity in this matter; there I shall explain the precise point at which the danger of illusion begins. In thus relating what is excessive in each article, I shall describe it and condemn it with all theological rigor.

Thus my articles will be, in the first part of each, a collection of exact definitions concerning the expressions of the saints, boiling them down to one incontestable sense that can no longer permit any ambiguity whatsoever, nor alarm the most timorous souls. This will constitute a sort of dictionary by its definitions, the goal being knowledge of the precise meaning of each term. These collected definitions will form a simple and complete system of all the interior paths, which will have a perfect unity, since all will fundamentally treat the exercise of pure love, taught as boldly by the Fathers of the church as by the most recent saints. On the other hand, the second part of each of my articles will display all that the false principles involve—they enable the most dangerous illusion against faith and against morals under the appearance of perfection. In each article I shall try to mark where the ambiguity begins, and to censure all that is harmful, without ever weakening at all what the experience of the saints authorizes. . . .

II.

ARTICLE VIII

[The italicized text was condemned as Article 7 of "Cum alias."]

TRUE. Holy indifference, which is never anything other than the disinterest of love, becomes in the most extreme trials what the holy mystics have called abandonment, viz., that the disinterested soul abandons itself to God totally and without reserve in everything which concerns its self-interest. But it never renounces either love or any of the things that concern the glory and will of the Beloved. *This abandonment is nothing other than the abnegation or renunciation of oneself that Jesus demands of us in the Gospels after we have left all things behind. This abnegation of ourselves concerns only our self-interest,* and must never hinder the disinterested love we owe to ourselves and to our neighbor on account of the love of God. *The extreme trials in which this abandonment must be exercised are the temptations by which the jealous God desires to purify love by making it see no resource or hope for its self-interest, even with regard to eternal matters.* These trials are described by a great number of saints as a terrible purgatory that can exempt those souls that endure it with full fidelity from the Purgatory of the next life. As Cardinal Bona puts it, it belongs "only to the insane and the impious to refuse to believe these hidden and sublime things and to despise them as false, as if they were not clear, though they are attested to by people of very venerable virtue, who speak from their own experience about what God works in their hearts" [*The Short Way to God,* chapter 5]. These trials are only temporary. The more the souls in this state are faithful to the grace that allows them to purify themselves from all self-interest by a jealous love, the shorter these trials are. Souls' hidden resistance to grace under specious pretexts is common: It is their eager and interested effort to retain the sensible supports of which God wishes to deprive them that makes their trials so long and painful, for God does not make his creature suffer in order to suffer fruitlessly. It is only to purify it and to overcome its resistance.

The temptations that purify love of all self-interest do not at all resemble other common temptations. Experienced directors can discern them by certain marks. But nothing is as dangerous as mistaking the common temptations of beginners for the trials that serve as the full purification of love in the most elevated souls. This is the source of all illusion: It is this that makes one fall into the horrid vices of misguided souls. We should only assume these extreme trials in a minuscule number of very pure and mortified souls whose flesh has long been submitted to the spirit and who have solidly practiced all the Gospel virtues. This is the lot of lowly and innocent souls until they are fully ready to make a public confession of their miseries. These souls must be docile to the point of never voluntarily faltering in any of the difficult and humiliating things one can ask of them. They must not be attached to any consolation or any freedom. They must be detached from everything, even from the path that teaches them this detachment. They must be willing to take on all the practices that one will want to impose on them. They must not hold fast to their own type of prayer, or experiences, or readings, or people they have at other times consulted with confidence. It is necessary to prove that their temptations are of a different nature than common temptations insofar as the true means of calming these temptations is to desire that they do not find any apparent support for self-interest in them.

To speak in this way is to repeat word for word the experiences that the saints have themselves described. At the same time, it is to anticipate the dangerous drawbacks into which one might fall through credulity if one hastily admitted these rarest trials in practice. There are very few souls who have arrived at this perfection in which there is no more to be purified save the residue of self-interest mixed with divine love.

FALSE. Interior trials remove, once and for all, sensible and visible graces. They likewise suppress distinct acts of love and of the virtues. They place the soul in a real and absolute inability to open up to his superiors, or to obey them in the essential practice of the Gospel. They cannot be distinguished from common temptations. In this state one can hide from one's superiors, escape from the yoke of obedience, and find needed relief and illumination in books or unauthorized persons, however much one's superiors forbid it. The director can suppose that one is undergoing these trials without having thoroughly tested the state of the soul's sincerity, docility, mortification, and humility. The director can right away have this soul purify its love of all self-interest during temptation, without having the person perform any act in his own self-interest to resist the temptation that presses on him.

To speak in this way is to poison souls. It is to remove from them the weapons of faith necessary to resist the Enemy of our salvation. It is to confuse all the paths of God. It is to teach rebellion and hypocrisy to the church's children.

Translated for this volume by Geoff Chaplin from *Oeuvres de Fénelon*, 3 vols. (Paris: Firmin Didot, 1861), Vol. 2:2–4, 14–15.

CONTEMPLATION AND ACTION

Mysticism involves not just intense forms of contact with God, of whatever duration, but also a transformed life. It is part of a process that begins, as we have seen, with acts of asceticism, reading the scripture, spiritual direction, and preparatory forms of prayer, but it is meant to spill out and over into a new mode of living. Many of the texts already found in this collection have spoken about the new life that the mystic is to live, but in Christianity the relation between forms of direct contact with God and everyday life has often been discussed under the rubric of the relation between the contemplative life and the active life. This way of framing the effect of meeting God on how we live was part of the classical heritage of Greece and Rome that Christians adopted and transformed. Greek philosophers had discussed the difference between the *bios praktikos,* the life of the citizen with its political duties, and the *bios theôretikos,* the life of the philosopher given over to speculative pursuit of truth. These notions were adopted by Christians when they took over the term *theôria contemplatio* to describe the vision of God promised in scripture (see section 10.1).

But Christians altered the meaning of the terms. Action and contemplation were no longer understood as alternative lifestyles, as they had been among classical authors; rather, they were seen as related modalities of the life of every believer. The active life (*vita activa*) was that part of existence in which the Christian is called upon to serve his neighbor in love, while the contemplative life (*vita contemplativa*) is that aspect devoted to love of God and desire for the vision of God. All Christians are called upon to make use of both modalities, though in differing degrees depending on their station in the church.

Although Christians considered both forms of life necessary, there were many ways of understanding how they were to be related. The standard model, worked out in the patristic period, saw the contemplative life as higher and more desirable, but the active life often as more pressing due to the obligations of Christian love. This perspective, represented here by selections from Gregory the Great, Bernard of Clairvaux, and *The Cloud of Unknowing*, held to some kind of oscillation between the two lives as the best that could be hoped for in this fallen world. In the late Middle Ages, however, some mystics questioned this paradigm and argued that the supreme form of Christian life was not pure contemplation, but a fusion of contemplation and action on a higher level, where one could be (in words once used of Ignatius of Loyola) "active while in contemplation" (*in contemplatione activus*). This approach to the mystical life is illustrated here by selections from two fourteenth-century mystics, Eckhart and Catherine of Siena, but many other texts could have been used from such mystics as Ignatius and Teresa of Avila. The issue remains, if under different names, so the section closes with a passage from Thomas Merton (the most recent author included in this anthology), reflecting on the nature of contemplation and how it calls for communication with others, whatever the difficulty.

1.

GREGORY THE GREAT
PASTORAL CARE 2.5

Origen and other Greek Fathers had already taken up the issue of the relation between the contemplative and the active lives. The Alexandrian was the first to see in some paired figures of the Old and New Testaments biblical proof for the superiority of contemplation over action. The most important of these twinned figures were the sisters Mary and Martha visited by Jesus in Luke 10:38–42. Origen identified Mary with contemplation and Martha, who was "busy about many things," with action, so Jesus' statement that Mary "has chosen the best part which shall not be taken from her" proved the superiority of contemplation. Many later mystics followed Origen's view, but by no means all. Augustine took up the question and laid down three principles that governed the discussion of the relation of the active and contemplative lives during much of Western history: (1) Both forms of life are good; (2) the contemplative life is higher; and (3) contemplation should yield to action when the neighbor's need requires it. Augustine's view was taken up and developed by Gregory the Great in a number of places in his writings. Gregory was a contemplative monk who become an active pope. He insisted that all Christians, even the active laity, were called to some measure of contemplation. The Augustinian-Gregorian position calls for a necessary oscillation between action and contemplation for all Christians, but especially for the rulers of the church (rectores/pastores), that is, the bishops who are called upon to be the models of a life that is the highest form of both action and contemplation. The following text is a passage from Gregory's handbook for bishops (and by extension all priests), known as the Pastoral Care *(Regula Pas-*

toralis), composed about 590. In it he holds up Paul, Moses, and Christ himself as the model for bishops to combine contemplative love of God with active charity toward their flock.

CHAPTER 5.
THE RULER SHOULD BE A NEIGHBOR
IN COMPASSION TO EVERYONE AND
EXALTED ABOVE ALL IN THOUGHT

Let the ruler be neighbor in compassion to everyone and exalted above all in thought, so that by the love of his heart he may transfer to himself the infirmities of others, and by the loftiness of his contemplation transcend even himself in his aspirations for the invisible things. Otherwise, while he has lofty aspirations, he will be disregarding the infirmities of his neighbors, or in accommodating himself to the weak, will cease to seek that which is above. Thus it was that Paul was led into paradise and searched into the secrets of the third heaven (2 Cor 12:2–4), and yet, though raised aloft in that contemplation of invisible things, he recalled his mind's vision to the bed of carnal men, and set up norms for their secret relations, saying: "For fear of fornication, let every man have his own wife and let every woman have her own husband. Let the husband render the debt to his wife and the wife also in like manner to her husband" (1 Cor 7:2–3). And a little farther on: "Defraud not one another, except perhaps by consent for a time that you may give yourselves to prayer, and return together again, lest Satan tempt you" (1 Cor 7:5).

Note that he is already introduced to the secrets of heaven, yet by condescending love he gives thought to the bed of carnal persons; and though he raises the vision of his heart to invisible things, being himself elevated, yet he turns in compassion to the secrets of those who are weak. He reaches the heavens in contemplation, yet in his solicitude he does not ignore the couch of the carnal, for being united by the bond of charity to the highest and the lowest alike, though in person mightily caught up to the high places by the power of the Spirit, he is content in his loving-kindness to be weak with others in their weakness. Therefore, he said: "Who is weak, and I am not weak? Who is scandalized, and I am not on fire?" (2 Cor 11:29).

Hence, too, he says: "And I became to the Jews, a Jew" (1 Cor 9:20). He did this, not by abandoning his faith, but by extending his loving-kindness. Thus, by transfiguring the person of the unbeliever into himself, he purposed to learn personally how he ought to compassionate others, how he should bestow on them what he would rightly wish them to bestow on himself, if their places were interchanged. Therefore, he says again: "Whether we be transported in mind, it is to God, or whether we be sober, it is for you" (2 Cor 5:13). For he knew how to transcend himself by contemplation and how to employ restraint by his condescension for his hearers.

Thus Jacob, as the Lord leaned on the ladder above and the anointed stone was below, saw angels ascending and descending (Gen 28:11–18), which was a sign that true preachers do not only aspire by contemplation to the Holy Head of the Church above, namely, the Lord, but also descend to its members in pity for them. Thus Moses frequently goes in and out of the Tabernacle; and while within he is caught up in contemplation, outside he devotes himself to the affairs of the weak. Inwardly he considers the hidden things of God, outwardly he bears the burdens of carnal men. In doubtful matters, too, he always returns to the Tabernacle to consult the Lord in front of the Ark of the Covenant. He thus, no doubt, sets an example to rulers, that when they are uncertain what dispositions to make in secular matters, they should always return to reflection, as though to the Tabernacle, and there, as it were, standing before the Ark of the Covenant, should consult the Lord, whether they should seek a solution of their problems in the pages of the Sacred Word.

Thus the Truth itself, manifested to us by assuming our human nature, engaged in prayer on the mountain and worked miracles in the towns (Lk 6:12). He thus showed the way to be followed by good rulers, who, though they strive after the highest things by contemplation, should nevertheless by their compassion share in the needs of the weak. Then, indeed, charity rises to sublime heights, when in pity it is drawn by the lowly things of the neighbor, and the more kindly it stoops to infirmity, the mightier is its reach to the highest.

But those who rule others should show themselves such that their subjects are unafraid to reveal their hidden secrets to them. Thus, when these little ones are enduring the waves of temptation, they will have recourse to the pastor's understanding as to a mother's bosom; and in the solace of his comforting words and in their prayerful tears they will cleanse themselves when they see themselves defiled by the sin that buffets them. Hence also it is that in front of the doors of the Temple there is a sea of brass for washing the hands of those who enter the Temple, that is to say, a laver, supported by twelve oxen, whose faces are plainly visible, but whose hinder parts are not visible (3 Kgs 7:23–24). What else is symbolized by the twelve oxen but the whole order of pastors? Of these the Law says, as Paul reports: "You shall not muzzle the mouth of the ox that treads out the corn" (1 Cor 9:9). We see the work they do openly, but do not see the rest that later awaits them in the secret requital of the strict Judge. Those, however, who make ready in their patient condescension to cleanse the confessed sins of the neighbor, support the laver, as it were, in front of the door of the Temple. Whosoever, then, is striving to enter the gate of eternity, may reveal his temptations to the mind of the pastor, and cleanse the hands of thought or deed, as it were, in the laver of the oxen.

Now, it happens frequently that, while the ruler's mind in his condescension learns of the trials of others, he also is assailed by the temptations which he gives ear to; for in the case of the laver, too, that was mentioned as serving the cleansing of the multitude, it is certainly defiled. In receiving the filth of those who wash in it, it loses its limpid clearness. But the pastor need not fear these things at all, for when God weighs all things exactly, the pastor is the more easily delivered from temptation, as he is the more compassionately afflicted by the temptations of others.

From *St. Gregory the Great. Pastoral Care*, translated and annotated by Henry Davis, SJ (New York: Paulist Press, 1950. Ancient Christian Writers), 56–59. Used with permission.

BERNARD OF CLAIRVAUX
SERMONS ON THE SONG OF SONGS 50

In commenting on the Song of Songs, Bernard took up the famous verse in Song 2:5 where the bride says, "He set charity in order in me." The "order of charity" (ordo caritatis) was a major theme in Christian mysticism for many centuries—how are we to arrange the various forms of love to which we are called so that all can be observed in their proper relationship? Among the issues involved in the correct ordering of charity, not least was that of the relation of active love of neighbor and contemplative love of God. As might be expected, Bernard adheres to the traditional view set down by Augustine and Gregory the Great: Contemplative love of God is always higher, but contemplation must yield to action, as the Gospel teaches, when our neighbor's need calls out for active assistance. Where Bernard advances beyond his sources is in rooting this teaching in his theology of charity, with its two forms of love of action and love of feeling based upon the Song of love, as the following part of sermon 50 shows.

Love exists in action [*actus*] and in feeling [*affectus*]. And with regard to love in action, I believe that a law, an explicit commandment, has been given to men (Dt 5:6); yet how can one's feelings correspond to the commandment? The former therefore is commanded in view of merit, the latter is given as a reward. We do not deny that the present life, by divine grace, can also experience the beginning and progress of love of feeling, but we unreservedly maintain that its consummation is in the happiness of the life to come. How then should that be ordered which can in no way be fulfilled? Or if you prefer to hold that affective love has been commanded, I do not dispute it, provided you agree with me that in this life it can never and will never be able to be fulfilled by any man. . . .

This is what I should say if we were agreed that affective love were a law commanded. But that seems especially to apply to love in action, because when the Lord said: "Love your enemies," he referred right afterwards to actions: "Do good to those who hate you" (Lk 6:27). Scripture also says: "If your enemy is hungry, feed him; if he is thirsty, give him drink" (Rom 12:20). Here you have a question of actions, not of feeling. But listen also to the Lord's command about love of himself: "If you love me, keep my words" (Jn 14:15). And here too, by enjoining the observance of the commandments, he assigns us to action. It would have been superfluous for him to warn us to act if love were but a matter of feeling. Hence it is necessary that you accept as well that commandment to love your neighbor as yourself (Mt 22:39), even if it is not expressed as clearly as this. Do you then consider that you do enough to fulfill the command to love of neighbor if you observe perfectly what the natural law prescribes for every man: "What you would not wish done to yourself, avoid doing to another" (Tob 4:16); and also: "Always treat others as you like them to treat you" (Mt 7:12)?

There is an affection which the flesh begets, and one which reason controls, and one which wisdom seasons. The first is that which the apostle says is not subject to the law of God, nor can be (Rom 8:7); the second, on the contrary, he shows to be in agreement with the law of God because it is good (Rom 7:16)—one cannot doubt that the insubordinate and the agreeable differ from each other. The third, however, is far from either of them, because it tastes and experiences that the Lord is sweet (Ps 33:9); it banishes the first and rewards the second. The first is pleasant, of course, but shameful; the second is emotionless but strong; the last is rich and delightful. Therefore, by the second good deeds are done, and in it love reigns: not that of the feelings, which, growing richer with the seasoning of wisdom's salt (Col 4:6), fills the mind with a mighty abundance of the sweetness of the Lord (Ps 30:20), but that rather which is practical, not yet indeed imparting the delightful refreshment of sweet love, but still vehemently aflame with the love of love itself. "Do not love in word or speech," he said, "but in deed and in truth" (1 Jn 3:18).

Do you see how cautiously he takes a middle path between vitiated and affective love, while distinguishing from both the love that is active and salutary? He neither finds room in this love for the figment of a lying tongue, nor does he yet demand the flavor of loving wisdom. "Let us love in deed and in truth" (1 Jn 3:18), he says, because we are moved to do good more by the vigorous urging of truth than by the feeling of relished love. "He set love in order in me" (Song 2:4). Which of these loves do you think? Both of them, but in reverse order. Now the active prefers what is lowly, the affective what is lofty. For example, there is no doubt that in a mind that loves rightly, the love of God is valued more than love of men, and among men themselves the more perfect is esteemed more than the weaker, heaven more than earth, eternity more than the flesh. In well-regulated action, on the other hand, the opposite order frequently or even always prevails. For we are more strongly impelled toward and more often occupied with the welfare of our neighbor; we attend our weaker brothers with more exacting care; by human right and very necessity we concentrate more on peace on earth than on the glory of heaven (Lk 2:14); by worrying about temporal cares we are not permitted to think of eternal things; in attending almost continually to the ills of our body we lay aside the care of our soul; and finally, in accord with the saying of the Apostle, we invest our weaker members with greater honor (1 Cor 12:23), so fulfilling in a sense the word of the Lord: "The last shall be first and the first last" (Mt 20:16). Who will doubt that in prayer a man is speaking with God? But how often, at the call of charity, we are drawn away, torn away, for the sake of those who need to speak to us or be helped! How often does dutiful repose yield dutifully to the uproar of business! How often is a book laid aside in good conscience that we may sweat at manual work! How often for the sake of administering worldly affairs we very rightly omit even the solemn celebration of Masses! A preposterous order; but necessity knows no law. Love in action devises its own order, in accord with the command of the householder, beginning with the most recent (Mt 20:8), it is certainly dutiful and correct, without favoritism (Acts 10:34), swayed not by worldly values but by human needs.

But not so affective love, since it always leads the ordering from the first. It is the wisdom by which all things are experienced as they are; as for example, the higher the nature the more perfect the love it evokes; the lower evokes less, the lowest nothing. The truth of love determines the previous order, but this order the love of truth lays claim to itself. Now true love is found in this, that those whose need is greater receive first (1 Jn 4:10). And again, loving truth is evident if we maintain in our feelings the order it maintains in the reason.

But you, if you love the Lord your God with your whole heart, whole mind, whole strength (Mk 12:30), and leaping with ardent feeling beyond that love of love with which active love is satisfied and having received the Spirit in fullness, are wholly aflame with that divine love to which the former is a step, then God is indeed experienced, although not as he truly is (a thing impossible for any creature), but rather in relation to your power to enjoy. Then you will experience as well your own true self, since you perceive that you possess nothing at all for which you love yourself, except insofar as you belong to God: you pour out upon him your whole power of loving. I repeat: you experience yourself as you are, when by that experience of love of yourself and of the feeling that you feel toward him, you discover that you are an altogether unworthy object even of your own love, except for the sake of him without whom you are nothing.

As for your neighbor whom you are obliged to love as yourself (Mt 19:19): if you are to experience him as he is, you will actually experience him only as you do yourself: he is what you are. Then you who do not love yourself, except because you love God, consequently love as yourself all those who similarly love him. But you who love God cannot love as yourself a human enemy, for he is nothing in that as he does not love God (1 Jn 4:20). Yet you will love him so that he may love God.

From *Bernard of Clairvaux. On the Song of Songs III*, translated by Kilian Walsh, OCSO, and Irene M. Edmonds. Copyright 1979 by Cistercian Publications, Inc., Kalamazoo, Michigan. All rights reserved.

3.

MEISTER ECKHART
SELECTIONS FROM SERMON 86

This sermon is one of the most difficult and fascinating of those ascribed to Meister Eckhart. Although some of its vocabulary is unusual for the Dominican, its teaching conforms to his thought, and there seems to be no good reason to doubt his authorship. Since the time of Origen, the account in the tenth chapter of Luke's Gospel about Jesus' visit to the home of Mary and Martha had been given a spiritual interpretation in which Martha represented the active life, while Mary, whom Jesus praised as "having chosen the best part" (Lk 10:42), signified the contemplative life. Eckhart boldly reverses the paradigm, praising Martha above Mary, and thereby creating a new understanding of the relation between the active life and the contemplative life. Eckhart alters the teaching found in Gregory, Bernard, and others, by arguing that a new kind of action, performed out of "a well-exercised ground," is superior to contemplation, at least as ordinarily conceived. This fusion of action and contemplation has been described as a form of "inner-worldly" mysticism that represents one of the Dominican's most important contributions to the history of mysticism. Since the sermon is long and contains a number of digressions, the form given here skips the asides and concentrates on the essential teaching about the relation of Mary and Martha.

"INTRAVIT IESUS IN QUODDAM CASTELLUM, ET MULIER QUAEDAM MARTHA NOMINE EXCEPIT ILLUM" (LK 10:38)

St. Luke says in his gospel that our Lord Jesus Christ went into a little town, where he was received by a woman named Martha, and she had a sister named Mary who sat at the feet of our Lord and listened to his words, but Martha moved about, waiting on our Lord. Three things made Mary sit at our Lord's feet. One was that the goodness of God possessed her soul. The second was unspeakable longing: she desired she knew not what, and wanted she knew not what. The third was the sweet solace and joy she gained from the eternal words that flowed from the mouth of Christ.

With Martha too there were three things that made her move about and wait on the beloved Christ. One was her mature age and the ground of her being that was so fully trained that she thought none could do the work as well as she. The second was wise understanding, which knew how to do outward works perfectly as love ordains. The third was the great dignity of her beloved guest. . . .

Now Martha says, "Lord, tell her to help me" (Lk 10:40). This was said not in anger, but it was rather affection that constrained her. We can call it affection or teasing. How so? Observe. She saw how Mary was possessed with a longing for her soul's satisfaction. Martha knew Mary better than Mary knew Martha, for she had lived long and well and life gives the finest understanding. Life understands better than delight and light what one, under God, can attain to in this body, and in some ways life shows it more clearly than the eternal light can. For the eternal light makes known oneself and God, not oneself apart from God; but life makes one known to oneself, apart from God. When one sees oneself alone, it is easier to tell what is like and unlike. St. Paul makes this plain, and so do the pagan masters. St. Paul in his ecstasy saw God and himself in spiritual fashion in God, and yet each virtue did not present itself clearly to his vision (2 Cor 12:2–3), and that was because he had not practiced them in deeds. By practicing the virtues, the masters came to such profound discernment that they recognized the nature of each virtue more clearly than Paul or any saint in his first rapture.

Thus it was with Martha. Hence her words, "Lord, tell her to help me," as if to say, "my sister thinks she is able to do what she wishes to do, as long as she sits and receives solace from you. Let her see if it is so: bid her get up and go from you." The latter part was kindly meant, though she spoke her mind. Mary was filled with longing, longing she knew not why and wanting she knew not what. We suspect that she, dear Mary, sat there a little more for her own happiness than for spiritual profit. That is why Martha said, "Bid her rise, Lord," fearing that by dallying in this joy she might progress no further. Christ answered her, "Martha, Martha, you are fretting and fussing about many things. One thing is needful. Mary has chosen the best part, which shall never be taken away from her" (Lk 10:41). Christ said this to Martha not by way of rebuke, but answering and reassuring her that Mary would become as she desired. Why did Christ say "Martha, Martha," naming her twice? Isidore says there is no doubt that prior to the time when God became man he never called any person by name who was lost; but about those whom he did not call by name it is doubtful [reference not identified]. By Christ's calling I mean his eternal knowing: being infallibly inscribed, before the creation of creatures, in the living book of Father, Son, and Holy Spirit. Of those named therein and whose name Christ uttered in words, none was ever lost. This is attested by Moses, who was told by God himself, "I know you by name" (Ex 33:12), and by Nathaniel, to whom our beloved Christ said, "I knew you when you lay under the fig-tree" (Jn 1:48). The fig-tree denotes a spirit that rejects not God and whose name is eternally inscribed in God. Thus it is demonstrated that no one ever was or will be lost, whom Christ ever named by human mouth out of the eternal Word.

Why did he name Martha twice? He meant that every good thing, temporal and eternal, that a creature could possess was fully possessed by Martha. The first mention of Martha showed her perfection in temporal works. When he said "Martha" again, that showed that she lacked nothing pertaining to eternal bliss. So he said, "You are careful," meaning: "You are among things, but they are not in you," for those who are careful are unhindered in their activity. They are unhindered who organize all their works guided by the eternal light. Such people are with things and not in them. They are very close, and yet have no less than if they were up yonder on the circle of eternity. "Very close," I say, for all creatures are "means." There are two kinds of means. One means, without which I cannot get to God, is work or activity in time, which does not interfere with eternal salvation. "Works" are performed from without, but "activity" is when one practices with care and understanding from within. The other means is to be free of all that. For we are set down in time so that our sensible worldly activity may make us closer and more like to God. St. Paul meant this when he said, "Redeem the time, for the days are evil" (Eph 5:16). "Redeeming the time" means the continual intellectual ascent to God, not in the diversity of images but in living intellectual truth. And "the days are evil" should be understood thus: Day presupposes night, for if there were no night, it would not be or be called day—it would all be one light. That was Paul's meaning, for a life of light is too little, being subject to spells of darkness that oppress a noble spirit and obscure eternal bliss. Hence too Christ's exhortation: "Go on while you have the light" (Jn 12:35). For he who works in the light rises straight up to God free of all means: his light is his activity and his activity is his light.

Thus it was with dear Martha, and so he said to her: "One thing is needful," not two. When I and you are once embraced by the eternal light, that is one. Two-in-one is a fiery spirit, standing over all things, yet under God, on the circle of eternity. This is two, for it sees God but not immediately. Its knowing and being, or its knowing and the object of knowledge will never be one. God is not seen except where he is seen spiritually, free of all images. Then one becomes two, two is one: light and spirit, these two are one in the embrace of the eternal light. . . .

But to return to our argument, how Martha and all the friends of God are "with care" but not "in care"; there temporal work is as noble as any communing with God, for it joins us to him as closely as the highest that can happen to us except the vision of God in his naked nature. And so he said, "You are with things and with care," meaning that she was troubled and encumbered by her lower powers, for she was not given to indulge in spiritual sweetness: she was with things and not in things . . . [There is a lacuna here.]

Three things especially are needful in our works: to be orderly, understanding, and mindful. "Orderly" I call that which corresponds in all points to the highest. "Understanding" I call knowing nothing temporal that is better. "Mindful" I call feeling living truth joyously present in good works. When these three points are one, they bring us just as near and are just as helpful as all Mary Magdalene's joy in the wilderness.

Now Christ says, "You are troubled about many things" (Lk 10:41)—not just one thing. That means: when, perfectly simple, wholly unoccupied, she is transported to the circle of eternity, she is troubled if any "means" intervene to spoil her joy up there. Such a person is troubled by this thing, and is anxious and distressed. But Martha stood maturely and well grounded in virtue, with untroubled mind, not hindered by things, and so she wished her sister to be equally established, for she saw that she was not grounded in her being. Her desire came from a mature ground, wishing her all that pertains to eternal bliss. That is why Christ said, "One thing is needful." What is that? It is the One that is God. That is what all creatures need, for if God took back what is his, all creatures would perish. If God were to withdraw his own from the soul of Christ, where their spirit is united with the eternal Person, Christ would be left merely a creature. Therefore that One is truly necessary. Martha feared that her sister would stay dallying with joy and sweetness, and wished her to be like herself. Therefore Christ spoke as if to say: "Never fear, Martha, she has chosen the best part: this will pass. The best thing that can befall a creature shall be hers: she shall be blessed like you." ...

Now Christ says, "You are troubled with many things." Martha was so well grounded in her essence that her activity was no hindrance to her: work and activity she turned to her eternal profit. This was somewhat mediated, but nobility of nature, industry and virtue in the above sense help greatly. Mary was a "Martha" before she was a "Mary," for when she sat at the feet of our Lord, she was not "Mary": she was so in name, but not in her being, for she was filled with joy and bliss and had only just entered school, to learn to live. But Martha stood there in her essence, and hence she said, "Lord, bid her get up," as if to say "Lord, I do not like her sitting there just for joy. I want her to learn life and possess it in essence: bid her arise that she may be perfect." She was not called Mary when she sat at Christ's feet. Mary I call a well-disciplined body, obedient to a wise soul.

Now our good people imagine they can reach a point where sensible things do not affect the senses. That cannot be: that a disagreeable noise should be as pleasant to my ear as the sweet tones of a lyre is something I shall never attain to. But this much can be attained: that when it is observed with insight, a rational God-conformed will submits to the insight and bids the will stand back from it, and the will answers, "I will, gladly." Lo and behold, then strife changes to joy. For what a person has gained by heavy toil brings him heart's delight, and then it bears fruit.

Again, some people hope to reach a point where they are free of works. I say this cannot be. After the disciples had received the Holy Spirit they began to do good works. And so, when Mary sat at the feet of our Lord, she was learning, for she had just gone to school to learn how to live. But later on, when Christ had gone to heaven and she received the Holy Spirit, she began to serve: she traveled overseas and preached and taught, acting as a servant and washerwoman to the disciples. Only when the saints become saints do they do good works, for then they gather the treasure of eternal life. Whatever is done before, repays old debts and averts punishment. For this we find evidence in Christ. From the very beginning when God became man and man became God, he began to work for our salvation, right to the end, when he died on the cross. Not a member of his body but practiced particular virtues. That we may follow him faithfully in the practice of true virtue, may God help us. Amen.

From *Meister Eckhart. Sermons and Treatises. Vol. I,* 79–89, translated by M. O'C. Walshe. Copyright 1979. Reprinted by permission of The English Sangha Trust, Amaravati Buddhist Monastery. Walshe, following Pfeiffer, numbers this as sermon 9, but in the critical edition it is sermon 86.

4.

THE CLOUD OF UNKNOWING

CHAPTERS 17–18 AND 21

The Cloud of Unknowing, *as mentioned previously (see section 8.3), is the best-known summary of what has been called affective Dionysianism, that is, a reading of the Dionysian corpus that finds impulses of love beyond any form of knowing as the instrument that brings the soul to union with God. The Cloud contains in chapters 68–73 an important discussion of the spiritual experience of finding God in nothingness. Here, the author distinguishes between contemplation accompanied by rapture, after the pattern of Moses (Ex 24:5ff), and the contemplation represented by Aaron, who as priest could see God in the Temple as often as he entered. Of these latter contemplatives, chapter 71 says, "There are some who are so refined by grace and in spirit, and are so familiar with God in this grace of contemplation that they may have the perfection of it whenever they will, in their ordinary state of soul, whether they are sitting, walking, standing, or kneeling." The Cloud, however, was written for ordinary contemplatives, and the chapters given below, with their distinction of three stages in the two lives of action and contemplation, show that the author, unlike Meister Eckhart, John Tauler, and others, held that the most desirable state of life was the perfection of contemplation, not the union of action and contemplation in a higher synthesis. In this he was a traditionalist among the new currents of the fourteenth century.*

I. CHAPTERS 17–18

17. That a true contemplative will not meddle in the active life nor with what goes on about him, not even to defend himself against those who criticize him.

In the Gospel of St. Luke we read that our Lord came to Martha's house and while she set about at once to prepare his meal, her sister Mary did nothing but sit at his feet. She was so intent upon listening to him that she paid no attention to what Martha was doing. Now certainly Martha's chores were holy and important. (Indeed, they are the works of the first degree of the active life.) But Mary was unconcerned about them. Neither did she notice our Lord's human bearing, the beauty of his mortal body, or the sweetness of his human voice and conversation, although this would have been a holier and better work. (It represents the second degree of the active life and the first degree of the contemplative life.) But she forgot all of this and was totally absorbed in the highest wisdom of God concealed in the obscurity of his humanity.

Mary turned to Jesus with all the love of her heart, unmoved by what she saw or heard spoken and done about her. She sat there in perfect stillness with her heart's secret, joyous love intent upon that *cloud of unknowing* between her and her God. For as I have said before, there never has been and there never will be a creature so pure or so deeply immersed in the loving contemplation of God who does not approach him in this life through that lofty and marvelous *cloud of unknowing*. And it was to this very cloud that Mary directed the hidden yearning of her loving heart. Why? Because it is the best and holiest part of the contemplative life possible to man and she would not relinquish it for anything on earth. Even when Martha complained to Jesus about her, scolding him for not bidding her to get up and help with the work, Mary remained there quite still and untroubled, showing not the least resentment against Martha for her grumbling. But this is not surprising really, for she was utterly absorbed in another work, all unknown to Martha, and she did not have time to notice her sister or defend herself.

My friend, do you see that this whole incident concerning Jesus and the two sisters was intended as a lesson for active and contemplative persons of the Church in every age? Mary represents the contemplative life and all contemplative persons ought to model their lives on hers. Martha represents the active life and all active persons should take her as their guide.

18. How to this day active people will criticize contemplatives through ignorance, even as Martha criticized Mary.

Just as Martha complained about Mary so in every age active persons have complained about contemplatives. How often it happens that the grace of contemplation will awaken in people of every walk and station of life, both religious and lay alike. But when after searching their own conscience and seeking reliable counsel they decide to devote themselves entirely to contemplation, their family and friends descend upon them in a storm of fury and criticism severely reproving them for idleness. These people will unearth every kind of dire tale both true and false about others who have taken up this way of life and ended up in terrible evils. Assuredly, they have nothing good to tell. . . .

II. CHAPTER 21

21. A true explanation of the Gospel passage: Mary has chosen the best part.

"Mary has chosen the best part." What does this mean? Whenever we speak of the best, we imply a good and a better. The best is the superlative degree. What then are the options from which Mary chose the best? They are not three ways of life since Holy Church only speaks of two, the active and the contemplative. No, the deeper meaning of the Gospel Story from St. Luke which we have just considered is that Martha represents the active life and Mary the contemplative life, and without one of these lives no one may be saved. So when a choice narrows down to two, one of them may not be called best.

Nevertheless, although the active and the contemplative are the two ways of life in Holy Church, yet within them, taken as a whole, there are three parts, three ascending stages. These we have already discussed [chapter 8], but I will briefly summarize them here. The first stage is the good and upright Christian life in which love is predominantly active in the corporal works of mercy. In the second, a person begins to meditate on spiritual truths regarding his own sinfulness, the Passion of Christ, and the joys of eternity. The first way is good but the second is better, for here the active and contemplative life begin to converge. They merge in a sort of spiritual kinship, becoming sisters like Martha and Mary. This is as far as an active person may advance in contemplation except for the occasional intervention of special grace. And to this middle ground a contemplative may return—but no farther—to take up some activity. He should not do so, however, except on rare occasions and at the demand of great need.

In the third stage a person enters the dark *cloud of unknowing* where in secret and alone he centers all his love on God. The first stage is good, the second is better, but the third is best of all. This is the best part belonging to Mary. It is surely obvious now why our Lord did not say to Martha, "Mary has chosen the best life." There are only two ways of life and, as I said, when a choice is only between two one may not be called best. But our Lord says, "Mary has chosen the best *part* and it shall not be taken from her."

The first and second parts are good and holy but they will cease with the passing of this mortal life. For in eternity there will be no need for the works of mercy as there is now. People will not hunger or thirst or die of cold or be sick, homeless, and captive. No one will need Christian burial for no one will die. In heaven it will no longer be fitting to mourn for our sins or for Christ's Passion. So then, if grace is calling you to choose the third part, choose it with Mary. Or rather let me put it this way. If God is calling you to the third part, reach out for it; work for it with all your heart. It shall never be taken from you, for it will never end. Though it begins on earth, it is eternal.

Let the words of the Lord be our reply to active persons who complain about us. Let him speak for us as he did for Mary when he said, "Martha, Martha." He is saying, "Listen, all you who live the active life. Be diligent in the works of the first and second parts, working now in one, now in another. Or if you are so inclined, courageously undertake both together. But do not interfere with my contemplative friends, for you do not understand what afflicts them. Leave them in peace. Do not begrudge them the leisure of the third and best part which is Mary's."

CATHERINE OF SIENA

THE DIALOGUE

CHAPTERS 64 AND 76

Catherine of Siena (1347–80) is one of the most remarkable women in Christian history. Born into a middle-class family, she was known for her piety and visions from childhood. About 1365 she received the habit of a Dominican tertiary. Her mystical gifts, including marriage to Christ, an exchange of hearts with him, and a mystical death in 1370, are typical of many ecstatic women. But Catherine broke with this pattern in the 1370s as she gathered around her a group of clerical and lay admirers and felt increasingly called by God to take an active role in the troubled age in which she lived. Especially in the last five years of her life Catherine emerged as an apostola, *a woman called by God to spread his message of love and peace. As her biographer, the Dominican Raymond of Capua, put it: "From that time on the Lord began to show himself familiarly and openly to his spouse [Catherine] not only in secret, as he had formerly done, but also in public, both while she was on the road and staying in some place"* (Large Life 2.6). *Catherine's political role in helping bring the Avignon papacy back to Rome, in trying to bring peace to the Italian city-states, and in preaching the need for church reform is a clear example of the combination of contemplation and action, but she went further by making this message integral to her teaching.*

The saint's main work, her Dialogue *composed 1377–78, is an extended series of conversations between her and God in ten sections following a pattern of petition to God, his response, and Catherine's thanksgiving. The work is not constructed in a linear fashion, but presents a theology of redemption structured according to a network of interlocking symbols and images. The central symbol is the blood of Christ, the fluid that redeems, bathes, nourishes, and binds us to the Savior. Christ himself is presented as the three-stage bridge or ladder that leads us to God (chapters 26–87): (1) Christ's feet are the affections that enable us to move upward; (2) Christ's heart represents the stage of loving union; and (3) Christ's mouth is the stage that combines inner peace and the call to apostolic action. In the following two selections Catherine dwells on the reciprocity of love of God and love of neighbor found in this third stage of the mystical life. God is speaking in these excerpts.*

I.
CHAPTER 64

I want you to know that everything, imperfect and perfect, is manifested and acquired in me, and so it is manifested and acquired also by means of your neighbor. Simple folk know this well, because in many cases they love creatures with spiritual love. If you have received my love honestly without any self-interest, you will drink your neighbor's love in an honest way. It is like filling a jug at a fountain, because if you draw it forth from the fountain and drink from it, the jug will be empty, but if you drink from it in me, it will not be empty but will always be full. In this manner love of neighbor, spiritual and temporal, ought to be drunk in me without any self-interest.

I charge you to love me in the same love that I have loved you. You cannot do this for me, because I have loved you without being loved. Every love that you have for me is a love that comes from duty and not from graciousness, because you ought to do it. I love you from graciousness and not from duty. This is why you cannot give me the love that I am requesting of you. And therefore I have put you in the midst of your neighbor, so that you can do for him what you cannot do for me, that is, to love him without any self-interest from graciousness and without looking for any benefit. And what you do for him I consider as done for me.

My Truth showed this when he said to Paul who had been persecuting me, "Saul, Saul, why do you persecute me?" (Acts 9:4). He considered that Paul was persecuting me when he persecuted my faithful. Thus, your love should be honest—you should love them with the love with which you love me.

II.
CHAPTER 76

Now I say that you know that everything I have told you was what was given you in the response of my Truth. In his person I have told you what was said from the beginning, so that you recognize the excellence of the place where the soul is who has climbed up to the second stage, where the soul recognizes and gains such a great fire of love that she quickly runs up to the third stage, that is, to the mouth where she has manifestly come to the state of perfection.

By what means did she come? By means of his heart, that is, the memory of the blood where she is baptized again, leaving behind imperfect love through the recognition that she drew from heartfelt love by seeing, tasting, and experiencing the fire of my charity. She has come to the stage of the mouth and therefore she will demonstrate this by performing the tasks of the mouth. A mouth speaks with the tongue that is in it; it tastes with its taste. The mouth takes in what is offered and presents it to the stomach, and the teeth chew it up because food cannot be absorbed in any other way.

It is the same with the soul. First she speaks to me with the tongue that stands in the mouth of her holy desire, that is, the tongue of holy and continual prayer. This tongue speaks both exteriorly and mentally: mentally offering me sweet and loving desires for the salvation of souls; and exteriorly it speaks by proclaiming the teaching of my Truth, warning, giving counsel, and confessing without any fear of the punishment that the world may desire to cause her, but ardently confessing before every creature in different ways and to each according to its station.

I say that she eats by taking the food of souls in my honor at the dinner table of the most holy cross (see Jn 4:34). This food cannot be eaten in true perfection in any other way or on any other table. Because the food cannot be absorbed in any other way, I say that she chews it with the teeth (that is, of love and hate), two rows of teeth in the mouth of holy desire. She takes this food chewing it with hatred of herself and with love of virtue, both in herself and in her neighbor. She chews up every injury: mockery, rudeness, tortures, and reproaches with great persecution; she bears hunger and thirst, cold and heat, as well as painful longings and sweatings for the salvation of souls. She chews up all these things in my honor, bearing and sustaining her neighbor. After she has chewed up this food, she enjoys its taste, savoring the fruit of her effort and the delight of the food of souls, tasting it in the fire of charity for me and for her neighbor. And so this food comes down into the stomach, because out of desire and hunger for souls she is disposed to wish to receive it in the heart's stomach with heartfelt love, loving and lovingly in love of neighbor. She takes delight in it and chews it over in such a way that she loses her affection for corporeal life through the power of eating this food upon the dinner table of the cross, that is, of the teaching of Christ crucified.

Then the soul grows fat in true and real virtue and becomes so expanded through the abundance of this food that in the case of her sense appetite she bursts the clothing of her own sensuality, that is, the body that covers over the soul. A person who bursts dies, and so the sensual will is left dead. This is why the well-ordered will of the soul lives in me, clothed with my eternal will, and why the sensual will is dead.

This is what the soul does who has in truth attained the third stage of the mouth. The sign that she is there is this: Her own will dies when she tastes the attraction of my charity, and therefore she found peace and quiet in her soul in [Christ's] mouth. You know that the mouth gives the peace [i.e., kiss of peace at Mass]. Hence the soul finds peace in this third state in such a way that nothing is able to disturb her because she has lost and drowned her own will. When this will is dead it gives peace and rest. She gives birth to virtues for her neighbors without any pain. It is not that pains are not pains in her, but for the dead will they are not pains because she voluntarily bears pain for my name.

Such souls traverse with care the whole teaching of Christ crucified. They do not slow down in their advance for any injury that may be done to them, nor for any persecution, nor for any pleasure that they discover (that is, the pleasure that the world wants to give them). But they step over these things with true strength and perseverance, clothed with the love of my charity, tasting the food of the soul's salvation with true and perfect patience. Such patience is the demonstrable proof that the soul loves perfectly and without any self-interest, for if she loved me and her neighbor for her own benefit she would be impatient and would slow down in her progress. Because they love me through myself since I am the highest Good and worthy to be loved, and because they love themselves and their neighbor through me, to give glory and praise to my name, therefore they are patient and strong in suffering and in perseverance.

Translated by Bernard McGinn from *S. Caterina da Siena. Il Dialogo,* edited by Giuliana Cavallini (Rome: Edizioni Cateriniane, 1968), 139–40, 168–71.

THOMAS MERTON
NEW SEEDS OF CONTEMPLATION

The Cistercian monk Thomas Merton (1915–68) has been called the most significant figure in twentieth-century American Catholicism. Merton's quest reflected the searching of his generation, and his ability to communicate the importance of spiritual questions to the modern world was second to none. He was not a plaster saint, or a figure from another age, but a contemporary whose fundamental honesty about the problems of church and society, as well as his own failures, continues to guarantee him a wide audience.

Merton was more than just an apologist for the monastic life. Although he never abandoned monasticism, he realized how challenging it was to be a real monk. He summarized the monk's special role in the Asian Journal *that he kept during the trip to the East to meet with Buddhist monks, the journey on which he died. The monk, he said, "is a marginal person who withdraws deliberately to the margin of society with a view to deepening fundamental human experience." Although a marginal man during his life, especially in its last decade, Merton became passionately involved in many public debates, such as racial and social justice, peace and war, and the relations of East and West. He wrote extensively throughout his lifetime, not only on religious concerns, but also on literary and political issues.*

A good deal of his output deals with spirituality and mysticism, both in its historical dimensions and in current applications. One of the books that he himself valued most highly was the work he called New Seeds of Contemplation, *a 1962 revision of* Seeds of Contemplation *first published in 1949, not long after his groundbreaking spiritual autobiography* The Seven Storey Mountain. *It contains some of Merton's most penetrating comments on how contemplative experience demands communication with others.*

WHAT IS CONTEMPLATION?

Contemplation is the highest expression of man's intellectual and spiritual life. It is that life itself, fully awake, fully active, fully aware that it is alive. It is spiritual wonder. It is spontaneous awe at the sacredness of life, of being. It is gratitude for life, for awareness and for being. It is a vivid realization of the fact that life and being in us proceed from an invisible, transcendent and infinitely abundant Source. Contemplation is, above all, awareness of the reality of that Source. It *knows* the Source, obscurely, inexplicably, but with a certitude that goes both beyond reason and beyond simple faith. For contemplation is a kind of spiritual vision to which both reason and faith aspire, by their very nature, because without it they must always remain incomplete. Yet contemplation is not vision because it sees "without seeing" and knows "without knowing." It is a more profound depth of faith, a knowledge too deep to be grasped in images, in words or even in clear concepts. It can be suggested by words, by symbols, but in the very moment of trying to indicate what it knows the contemplative mind takes back what it has said, and denies what it has affirmed. For in contemplation we know by "unknowing." Or, better, we know *beyond* all knowing or "unknowing."

Poetry, music and art have something in common with the contemplative experience. But contemplation is beyond aesthetic intuition, beyond art, beyond poetry. Indeed, it is also beyond philosophy, beyond speculative theology. It resumes, transcends and fulfills them all, and yet at the same time it seems, in a certain way, to supersede and to deny them all. Contemplation is always beyond our own knowledge, beyond our own light, beyond systems, beyond explanations, beyond discourse, beyond dialogue, beyond our own self. To enter into the realm of contemplation one must in a certain sense die: but this death is in fact the entrance into a higher life. It is a death for the sake of life, which leaves behind all that we can know or treasure as life, as thought, as experience, as joy, as being.

And so contemplation seems to supersede and to discard every other form of intuition and experience—whether in art, in philosophy, in theology, in liturgy or in ordinary levels of love and of belief. This rejection is of course only apparent. Contemplation is and must be compatible with all these things, for it is their highest fulfillment. But in the actual experience of contemplation all other experiences are momentarily lost. They "die" to be born again on a higher level of life.

In other words, then, contemplation reaches out to the knowledge and even to the experience of the transcendent and inexpressible God. It knows God by seeming to touch Him. Or rather it knows Him as if it had been invisibly touched by Him.... Touched by Him who has no hands, but who is pure Reality and the source of all that is real! Hence contemplation is a sudden gift of awareness, an awakening to the Real within all that is real. A vivid awareness of infinite Being at the roots of our own limited being. An awareness of our contingent reality as received, as a present from God, as a free gift of love. This is the existential contact of which we speak when we use the metaphor of being "touched by God."

Contemplation is also the response to a call: a call from Him who has no voice, and yet who speaks in everything that is, and who, most of all, speaks in the depths of our own being: for we ourselves are words of his. But we are words that are meant to respond to him, to answer to him, to echo him, and even in some way to contain him and signify him. Contemplation is this echo. It is a deep resonance in the inmost center of our spirit in which our very life loses its separate voice and re-sounds with the majesty and the mercy of the Hidden and Living One. He answers himself in us and this answer is divine life, divine creativity, making all things new. We ourselves become his echo and his answer. It is as if in creating us God asked a question, and in awakening us to contemplation he answered the question, so that the contemplative is at the same time, question and answer.

The life of contemplation implies two levels of awareness: first, awareness of the question, and second, awareness of the answer. Though these are two distinct and enormously different levels, yet they are in fact an awareness of the same thing. The question is, itself, the answer. And we ourselves are both. But we cannot know this until we have moved into the second kind of awareness. We awaken, not to find an answer absolutely distinct from the question, but to realize that the question is its own answer. And all is summed up in one awareness—not a proposition, but an experience: "I AM."

The contemplation of which I speak here is not philosophical. It is not the static awareness of metaphysical essences apprehended as spiritual objects, unchanging and eternal. It is not the contemplation of abstract ideas. It is the religious apprehension of God, through my life in God, or through "sonship" as the New Testament says. "For whoever are led by the Spirit of God, they are the sons of God. . . . The Spirit Himself gives testimony to our own spirit that we are the sons of God." "To as many as received him he gave the power to become the sons of God. . . ." And so the contemplation of which I speak is a religious and transcendent gift. It is not something to which we can attain alone, by intellectual effort, by perfecting our natural powers. It is not a kind of self-hypnosis, resulting from concentration on our own inner spiritual being. It is not the fruit of our own efforts. It is the gift of God who, in his mercy, completes the hidden and mysterious work of creation in us by enlightening our minds and hearts, by awakening in us the awareness that we are words spoken in his One Word, and that Creating Spirit (*Creator Spiritus*) dwells in us, and we in Him. That we are "in Christ" and that Christ lives in us. That the natural life in us has been completed, elevated, transformed and fulfilled in Christ by the Holy Spirit. Contemplation is the awareness and realization, even in some sense *experience*, of what each Christian obscurely believes: "It is now no longer I that live but Christ lives in me."

Hence contemplation is more than a consideration of abstract truths about God, more even than affective meditation on the things we believe. It is awakening, enlightenment and the amazing intuitive grasp by which love gains certitude of God's creative and dynamic intervention in our daily life. Hence contemplation does not simply "find" a clear idea of God and confine him within the limits of that idea, and hold him there as a prisoner to whom it can always return. On the contrary, contemplation is carried away by him into his own realm, his own mystery and his own freedom. It is a pure and a virginal knowledge, poor in concepts, poorer still in reasoning, but able, by its very poverty and purity, to follow the Word "wherever he may go."

SHARING THE FRUITS
OF CONTEMPLATION

We do not see God in contemplation—we *know* Him by love: for he is pure love and when we taste the experience of loving God for his own sake alone, we know by experience who and what he is.

True mystical experience of God and supreme renunciation of everything outside of God coincide. They are two aspects of the same thing. For when our minds and wills are perfectly free from every created attachment, they are immediately filled with the gift of God's love: not because things necessarily have to happen that way, but because this is his will, the gift of his love to us. "Everyone who has left his home or his father, or his mother, or his wife for my sake shall receive a hundredfold and shall possess eternal life."

We experience God in proportion as we are stripped and emptied of attachment to his creatures. And when we have been delivered from every other desire we shall taste the perfection of an incorruptible joy.

God does not give his joy to us for ourselves alone, and if we could possess him for ourselves alone we would not possess him at all. Any joy that does not overflow from our souls and help other men to rejoice in God does not come to us from God. (But do not think that you have to see how it overflows into the souls of others. In the economy of his grace, you may be sharing his gifts with someone you will never know until you get to heaven.)

If we experience God in contemplation, we experience Him not for ourselves alone but also for others.

Yet if your experience of God comes from God, one of the signs may be a great diffidence in telling others about it. To speak about the gift he has given us would seem to dissipate it and leave a stain on the pure emptiness where God's light shone. No one is more shy than a contemplative about his contemplation. Sometimes it gives him almost physical pain to speak to anyone of what he has seen of God. Or at least it is intolerable for him to speak about it as his own experience.

At the same time he most earnestly wants everybody else to share his peace and his joy. His contemplation gives him a new outlook on the world of men. He looks about him with a secret and tranquil surmise which he perhaps admits to no one, hoping to find in the faces of other men or to hear in their voices some sign of vocation and potentiality for the same deep happiness and wisdom. He finds himself speaking of God to the men in whom he hopes he has recognized the light of his own peace, the awakening of his own secret: or if he cannot speak to them, he writes for them, and his contemplative life is still imperfect without sharing, without companionship, without communion.

At no time in the spiritual life is it more necessary to be completely docile and subject to the most delicate movements of God's will and his grace than when you try to share the knowledge of his love with other men. It is much better to be so diffident that you risk not sharing it with them at all, than to throw it all away by trying to give it to other people before you have received it yourself. The contemplative who tries to preach contemplation before he himself really knows what it is, will prevent both himself and others from finding the true path to God's peace.

In the first place he will substitute his own natural enthusiasm and imagination and poetry for the reality of the light that is in him, and he will become absorbed in the business of communicating something that is practically incommunicable: and although there is some benefit in this even for his own soul (for it is a kind of meditation on the interior life and on God) still he runs the risk of being drawn away from the simple light and silence in which God is known without words and concepts, and losing himself in reasoning and language and metaphor.

The highest vocation in the Kingdom of God is that of sharing one's contemplation with others and bringing other men to the experimental knowledge of God that is given to those who love him perfectly. But the possibility of mistake and error is just as great as the vocation itself.

In the first place the mere fact that you have discovered something of contemplation does not yet mean that you are supposed to pass it on to somebody else. The sharing of contemplation with others implies two vocations: one to be a contemplative, and another still to teach contemplation. Both of them have to be verified.

But then, as soon as you think of yourself as teaching contemplation to others, you make another mistake. No one teaches contemplation except God, who gives it. The best you can do is write something or say something that will serve as an occasion for someone else to realize what God wants of him.

A BRIEF CRITICAL BIBLIOGRAPHY ON CHRISTIAN MYSTICISM

I. TRANSLATIONS

Classics of Western Spirituality (New York: Paulist Press, 1978–). The series now includes more than a hundred volumes on Jewish, Christian, and Islamic spirituality.

Cistercian Publications (Spencer-Washington-Kalamazoo, 1969–). More than three hundred volumes in two series:

1. *Cistercian Fathers Series.* Translations of the works of the major Cistercian authors.
2. *Cistercian Studies Series.* Original monographs on the history of monasticism along with translations of classic monastic texts from East and West.

Many other mystical texts are available in individual translations, as well as in some of the series cited in this book.

II. WORKS ON MYSTICISM

1. HISTORIES AND HANDBOOKS IN CHRONOLOGICAL ORDER

A History of Christian Spirituality, edited by Louis Bouyer et al. (New York: Seabury, 1982). Three volumes of the four-volume French original (1960–66) were translated.

Christian Spirituality I, II, and III. These three volumes are part of the ongoing *World Spirituality. An Encyclopedic History of the Religious Quest* (New York: Crossroad, 1985–), under the general editorship of Ewert Cousins. These volumes, the most recent general history of Christian spirituality, comprise:

1. *Christian Spirituality. Origins to the Twelfth Century,* edited by Bernard McGinn, John Meyendorff, and Jean Leclercq (1985).
2. *Christian Spirituality. High Middle Ages and Reformation,* edited by Jill Raitt in collaboration with Bernard McGinn and John Meyendorff (1987).
3. *Christian Spirituality. Post-Reformation and Modern,* edited by Louis Dupré and Don E. Saliers in collaboration with John Meyendorff (1989).

Bernard McGinn, *The Presence of God. A History of Western Christian Mysticism* (New York: Crossroad-Herder, 1991–   ). Four volumes thus far (of six projected). The most detailed history of mysticism in English.

1. *Foundations of Mysticism. Origins to the Fifth Century* (1991).
2. *Growth of Mysticism. Gregory the Great Through the Twelfth Century* (1994).
3. *The Flowering of Mysticism. Men and Women in the New Mysticism: 1200–1350* (1999).
4. *The Harvest of Mysticism in Medieval Germany (1300–1500)* (2005).

The New Westminster Dictionary of Christian Spirituality, edited by Philip Sheldrake (Louisville: John Knox, 2005). The best current one-volume encyclopedic survey.

Minding the Spirit. The Study of Christian Spirituality, edited by Elizabeth Dreyer and Mark Burrows (Baltimore: Johns Hopkins, 2005). Twenty-five essays from the *Journal of the Society for the Study of Christian Spirituality.* A valuable resource for contemporary approaches to spirituality and mysticism.

2. RECENT STUDIES (1980–2005)

Bouyer, Louis. *The Christian Mystery. From Pagan Myth to Christian Mysticism* (Edinburgh: Clark, 1989). A general account of the development of Christian mysticism.

Carlson, Thomas A. *Indiscretion. Finitude and the Naming of God* (Chicago: University of Chicago, 1999). The role of Dionysian apophaticism in the post-Heideggerian discussion.

Davies, Oliver, and Denys Turner, editors. *Silence and the Word. Negative Theology and Incarnation* (Cambridge: Cambridge University Press, 2002). Ten essays on negative theology and mysticism.

De Certeau, Michel. *The Mystic Fable. Volume One. The Sixteenth and Seventeenth Centuries* (Chicago: University of Chicago, 1992. French original 1982). This difficult study is one of the most important new approaches to mysticism of the past quarter century. See also de Certeau's *Heterologies. Discourse on the Other* (Minneapolis: University of Minnesota, 1986), which contains several important essays on mysticism.

Dupré, Louis. *The Deeper Self. An Introduction to Christian Mysticism* (New York: Crossroad, 1981). A brief introduction.

Fanning, Steven. *Mystics of the Christian Tradition* (London and New York: Routledge, 2001). A historical overview.

Forman, Robert K. C. *Mysticism, Mind, Consciousness* (Albany: SUNY Press, 1999). A representative of the "pure consciousness" theory of mysticism. See also two books edited by Forman:

1. *The Problem of Pure Consciousness. Mysticism and Philosophy* (Oxford: Oxford University Press, 1990).

2. *The Innate Capacity. Mysticism, Psychology, and Philosophy* (Oxford: Oxford University Press, 1998).

Hollywood, Amy. *Sensible Ecstasy. Mysticism, Sexual Difference, and the Demands of History* (Chicago: University of Chicago, 2002). An analysis of the role of mysticism in contemporary French thought.

Idel, Moshe, and Bernard McGinn, editors. *Mystical Union in Judaism, Christianity, and Islam. An Ecumenical Dialogue* (New York: Continuum, 1996). Six essays on the meaning of mystical union in the three traditions.

Katz, Steven T. Four volumes edited by Katz and published by Oxford University Press have been important to contemporary debates about the "constructed" nature of mysticism:

1. *Mysticism and Philosophical Analysis* (1978).

2. *Mysticism and Religious Traditions* (1983).

3. *Mysticism and Language* (1992).

4. *Mysticism and Sacred Scripture* (2000).

Kessler, Michael, and Christian Sheppard, editors. *Mystics. Presence and Aporia* (Chicago: University of Chicago, 2003). New perspectives on mysticism presented through a dozen essays.

Louth, Andrew. *The Origins of the Christian Mystical Tradition. From Plato to Denys* (Oxford: Clarendon, 1981). A useful study of the beginnings of Christian mysticism.

Marion, Jean-Luc. *God Without Being* (Chicago: University of Chicago, 1991). An important philosophical work on the retrieval of Dionysian apophatic thought.

McGinn, Bernard, and Patricia Ferris McGinn. *Early Christian Mystics* (New York: Crossroad, 2003). Brief presentations of twelve mystics from the second to the twelfth centuries.

McIntosh, Mark A. *Mystical Theology. The Integrity of Spirituality and Theology* (Oxford: Blackwell, 1998). A fine introduction to current discussions of mystical theology.

Parsons, William B. *The Enigma of the Oceanic Feeling. Revisioning the Psycho-*

analytic Theory of Mysticism (New York: Oxford University Press, 1999). Analyzes Freud's attitude toward mysticism.

Roy, Louis. *Mystical Consciousness. Western Perspectives and Dialogue with Japanese Thinkers* (Albany: SUNY Press, 2003). A philosophical and comparativist study.

Ruffing, Janet K., editor. *Mysticism and Social Transformation* (Syracuse: Syracuse University, 2001). Ten essays on the social role of mysticism from various perspectives, historical and theoretical.

Sells, Michael A. *Mystical Languages of Unsaying* (Chicago: University of Chicago, 1994). A major study of apophatic mysticism (Plotinus, Eriugena, Ibn Arabi, Eckhart, and Marguerite Porete).

Szarmach, Paul, editor. *An Introduction to the Medieval Mystics of Europe* (Albany: SUNY Press, 1984). A selection of essays on fourteen medieval figures.

Tamburello, Dennis. *Ordinary Mysticism* (New York: Paulist Press, 1996). A good short introduction to the nature of Christian mysticism.

Turner, Denys. *The Darkness of God. Negativity in Christian Mysticism* (Cambridge: Cambridge University Press, 1995). Important study of apophaticism, both historical and theoretical.

Vergote, Antoine. *Guilt and Desire. Religious Attitudes and Their Pathological Derivatives* (New Haven, Connecticut: Yale, 1988). A psychological approach to mystical experience.

Wainwright, William J. *Mysticism. A Study of Its Nature, Cognitive Value and Moral Implications* (Madison: University of Wisconsin, 1981). An example of the American philosophical approach to mysticism.

Woods, Richard, editor. *Understanding Mysticism* (Garden City, New York: Image Books, 1980). A selection of noted essays.

3. CLASSIC INTERPRETATIONS OF MYSTICISM (1880–1980)

Balthasar, Hans Urs von (1905–88). *The Glory of the Lord. A Theological Aesthetics,* 7 volumes (San Francisco: Ignatius Press, 1982–89. German original 1961–69). Balthasar's theological views on mysticism are scattered throughout this series (his masterpiece), as well as in his other writings.

Bataille, Georges (1897–1962). *Eroticism* (London: Calder & Boyars, 1962). A provocative examination of the relation between mysticism and eroticism.

Bergson, Henri (1859–1941). *The Two Sources of Morality and Religion* (Notre Dame: University of Notre Dame, 1977). First published in 1932, this book by the noted French philosopher views mysticism as the dynamic element in religion.

Bremond, Henri (1863–1933). *A Literary History of Religious Thought in France from the Wars of Religion Down to Our Own Times,* 3 volumes (London: SPCK, 1928–36). A partial translation of *Histoire littéraire du sentiment religieux en France depuis la fin des guerres de religion jusqu'à nos jours,* 11 volumes (1915–33). The still-unrivaled account of the Golden Age of French spirituality and mysticism.

Butler, Cuthbert, OSB (1858–1934). *Western Mysticism* (New York: E. P. Dutton, 1923). A study of monastic mysticism, concentrating on Augustine, Gregory, and Bernard. Butler's book helped correct the Neoscholastic view of mysticism that considered Teresa of Avila and John of the Cross as the ultimate authorities.

Hügel, Friedrich von (1852–1925). *The Mystical Element of Religion as Studied in Saint Catherine of Genoa and Her Friends,* 2 volumes (London: James Clarke & Co., 1908; 2nd ed. 1923). A difficult but indispensable book. Hügel's work is both an exposition of mysticism and a theory of religion, comparable to that of his friend William James.

Inge, W. R. (1860–1954). *Christian Mysticism* (London: Methuen, 1899). Dean of St. Paul's in London, Inge's historical study was one of the first significant works in English. He also wrote:

1. *Studies of English Mystics* (1906).
2. *Personal Idealism and Mysticism* (1907).
3. *The Philosophy of Plotinus,* 2 volumes (Gifford Lecture, 1918).
4. *Mysticism in Religion* (1948).

James, William (1842–1910). *The Varieties of Religious Experience* (New York: Modern Library, 1994). Lectures 16 and 17 of James's Gifford Lectures of 1901–2 remain among the most discussed presentations of mysticism. On James, see G. William Barnard, *Exploring Unseen Worlds. William James and the Philosophy of Mysticism* (Albany: SUNY Press, 1997), and the introductions in *The Varieties of Religious Experience. Centenary Edition* (London and New York: Routledge, 2002).

Jones, Rufus M. (1863–1948). *Studies in Mystical Religion* (London: Macmillan, 1909). This Quaker scholar of religion was interested in mysticism from his student days. See also:

1. *Spiritual Reformers in the 16th and 17th Centuries* (1914).
2. *Some Exponents of Mystical Religion* (1930).
3. *The Flowering of Mysticism* (1939).

Leclercq, Jean, OSB (1910–93). *The Love of Learning and the Desire for God* (New York: Fordham University Press, 1961. French original 1957). A noted exploration of Latin monastic culture and its mysticism.

Lossky, Vladimir (1903–58). *The Mystical Theology of the Eastern Church* (London: James Clarke, 1957. French original 1944). A study of the centrality of mystical theology in Eastern Christianity.

Maréchal, Joseph, SJ (1878–1944). *Studies in the Psychology of the Mystics* (London: Burnes, Oates and Washbourne, 1927). A partial translation of *Études sur la psychologie des mystiques,* 2 volumes (1926–37). Maréchal was a major Neothomist philosopher. These volumes, collecting essays dating back to 1908, remain among the best studies of comparative mysticism from a philosophical perspective.

Maritain, Jacques (1882–1973). *Distinguish to Unite, or The Degrees of Knowledge* (New York: Scribner, 1959. French original 1932). The noted Catholic philosopher sought to find the inner harmony between the epistemologies of Thomas Aquinas and John of the Cross.

Otto, Rudolph (1869–1937). *Mysticism East and West* (New York: Macmillan, 1932). A series of lectures on the comparative study of mysticism concentrating on Meister Eckhart and Shankara.

Rahner, Karl, SJ (1904–84). A Catholic theologian who wrote extensively on mysticism, beginning with essays on the spiritual senses published in the 1930s and continuing on in the many volumes of his *Theological Investigations.* Rahner summarized his views on spirituality and mysticism in *The Practice of Faith: A Handbook of Contemporary Spirituality* (New York: Crossroad, 1983. German original 1982).

Schweitzer, Albert (1865–1975). *The Mysticism of Paul the Apostle* (London: A. & C. Black, 1931. German original 1929). Schweitzer, one of the most influential twentieth-century Protestant voices in favor of mysticism, distinguished between Hellenistic God-mysticism and Pauline Christ-mysticism.

Stolz, Anselm, OSB (1900–42). *The Doctrine of Spiritual Perfection* (New York: Crossroad, 2001. German original 1936). One of the first books to argue that biblical and patristic sources form the essential core of Christian mysticism.

Thurston, Herbert, SJ (1856–1939). *The Physical Phenomena of Mysticism* (Chicago: Regnery, 1952). An English Jesuit's investigation of the paranormal states of some mystics.

Underhill, Evelyn (1875–1941). *Mysticism. A Study in the Nature and Development of Man's Spiritual Consciousness* (Cleveland: Meridian Books, 1955). First published in 1911, Underhill's long introduction is probably the most read English work on mysticism. Underhill did much to introduce mysticism to the English-speaking audience. Among her other works on the subject:
1. *The Mystic Way* (1913).
2. *Practical Mysticism* (1914).
3. *The Essentials of Mysticism* (1920).
4. *The Mystics of the Church* (1964).

Zaehner, R. C. (1913–74). *Mysticism Sacred and Profane. An Inquiry into Some Va-*

rieties of Preternatural Experience (Oxford: Oxford University Press, 1957). Zaehner, a student of comparative religion, attacked the drug-induced account of mystical experience popularized by Aldous Huxley in *The Doors of Perception* (1954). His study of Christian, Hindu, and Muslim mysticism was based on a Christian theological perspective.

ABOUT THE EDITOR

BERNARD MCGINN received a License in Sacred Theology from the Pontifical Gregorian University in Rome and a Ph.D. in History of Ideas from Brandeis University. He taught at the Divinity School of the University of Chicago for thirty-four years and is now the Naomi Shenstone Donnelley Professor Emeritus. The author of seventeen books and the editor of eleven, McGinn's research has centered on the history of apocalypticism and the role of mysticism in the Christian tradition. His most noted publications on mysticism are the four volumes of his projected six-volume history of Western Christian mysticism under the title *The Presence of God*. He also serves as the editor-in-chief of *The Classics of Western Spirituality*, published by Paulist Press. Professor McGinn is a fellow of the Medieval Academy of America and a fellow of the American Academy of Arts and Sciences. He has served as president of the American Society of Church History and of the American Catholic Historical Association.

A NOTE ON THE TYPE

The principal text of this Modern Library edition
was set in a digitized version of Janson, a typeface that
dates from about 1690 and was cut by Nicholas Kis,
a Hungarian working in Amsterdam. The original matrices have
survived and are held by the Stempel foundry in Germany.
Hermann Zapf redesigned some of the weights and sizes for
Stempel, basing his revisions on the original design.

Modern Library is online at
www.modernlibrary.com

MODERN LIBRARY ONLINE IS YOUR GUIDE TO CLASSIC LITERATURE ON THE WEB

THE MODERN LIBRARY E-NEWSLETTER

Our free e-mail newsletter is sent to subscribers, and features sample chapters, interviews with and essays by our authors, upcoming books, special promotions, announcements, and news. To subscribe to the Modern Library e-newsletter, visit **www.modernlibrary.com**

THE MODERN LIBRARY WEBSITE

Check out the Modern Library website at
www.modernlibrary.com for:

- The Modern Library e-newsletter
- A list of our current and upcoming titles and series
- Reading Group Guides and exclusive author spotlights
- Special features with information on the classics and other paperback series
- Excerpts from new releases and other titles
- A list of our e-books and information on where to buy them
- The Modern Library Editorial Board's 100 Best Novels and 100 Best Nonfiction Books of the Twentieth Century written in the English language
- News and announcements

Questions? E-mail us at **modernlibrary@randomhouse.com**.
For questions about examination or desk copies, please visit
the Random House Academic Resources site at
www.randomhouse.com/academic.